The Proviso

BOOK I IN THE TALES OF DUNHAM

Moriah Jovan

B10 MEDIAWORX
KANSAS CITY MISSOURI

PUBLISHED BY:

B10 MEDIAWORX

PO Box 1233
Liberty, MO 64069-1233
b10mediaworx.com

The Proviso
Copyright © 2008 by Moriah Jovan
Cover reissue May 2013

ISBN-13: 978-0-9817696-1-5
ISBN-10: 0-9817696-1-6

Editor: Lorna M. Lynch

Proofreader: M. Elizabeth Palmer

"Legend of a Cowgirl" lyrics used with permission from Imani Coppola.

Rand, Ayn. *Atlas Shrugged: 35th Anniversary Edition.* New York: Dutton, 1992. Excerpted under Fair Use.

Publisher's Cataloging-In-Publication Data
(Prepared by The Donohue Group, Inc.)

Jovan, Moriah.
    The proviso / Moriah Jovan.

    p. ; cm.

    ISBN-13: 978-0-9817696-1-5
    ISBN-10: 0-9817696-1-6

1. Shakespeare, William, 1564-1616. Hamlet--Adaptations. 2. Inheritance and succession--Fiction. 3. Mormons--Missouri--Fiction. 4. Cousins--Fiction. I. Title.

PS3615.O93 P76 2008
813/.6   2008929008

20130511.07.eab

126

erotic *wall street*

paganism **politics** atheism

libertarianism latter-day saints

money **caution** *objectivism*

capitalism rush **kansas city**

cursing *nude art*

mormon

A lot of people contributed to the creation of this story
whether they know it or not,
but only one pulled me through it by my hair.

I love you, Dude.

Acknowledgments

Dude and our Tax Deductions #1 and #2

Monica Tachibana, Elizabeth Palmer, Julianne Weight, Jan Leonard, Sheila Reams, Jeanne Johnston, Deb Lefler, Jennifer Cavanaugh, Janice Feldman, Teresa Alexander, and Dawn Triplett

Lorna Lynch for her critique and Elizabeth Palmer for her proof

Nick and Katherine Senzee, and Andy and Chad Livingston

James McKinley (sorry 'bout that "romance novel ending," Prof) and Lois Spatz, Professors Emeriti, UMKC Department of English Language and Literature

My critique group in '94 who, I'm pretty sure, would not appreciate being named here. They suffered through a Knox who was far, far more cruel, knew a Bryce and Giselle who were vastly different, and only started to get to know Ford.

The rest of my family (most of whom won't read this because they'll know that since I wrote it, it'll be filthy), who love me no matter what

Vince Melamed, Gary Barnhill, Trisha Yearwood, and Don Henley, for the song "Walkaway Joe," which, in 1994, made me start wondering about how much a mother might sacrifice to save her child . . .

OKH ENTERPRISES
SUCCESSION PROVISO

April 3, 1985

Upon owner and president Oliver Lake Hilliard's death, OKH Enterprises (hereinafter referred to as the Company) shall be managed by a chief executive officer appointed by the Board of Directors at will and whenever the need arises. The Company shall then revert to the full control and ownership of F. Knox Oliver Hilliard on December 27, 2008, his fortieth birthday, provided he has married and produced an heir.

Oliver Lake Delano Hilliard

Kansas City, Missouri
4/3/85

CHECK OUT THE WAY HE WALKS. I WONDER IF HE FUCKS AS GOOD AS HE looks?"

Miss Justice McKinley looked down at the textbooks on the desktop in front of her and felt violated by the predatory tone coming from the woman in the row behind her. Really, she'd thought she'd left all this junior high queen bee business when she graduated from college, but apparently, some girls just never grew up.

She was very beautiful, Sherry was, glossy black hair, very thin, very well dressed—and she knew it. She stood out in the lecture hall full of students who watched and listened to Chouteau County prosecutor Knox Hilliard's *bon mots* in between student introductions.

Sherry's worker bees laughed and slid comments back and forth about Sherry's tastes, most of which, in Justice's opinion, were unprintable. Justice even flinched at one particularly nasty remark that she couldn't avoid hearing, then the back of her chair was kicked and she tossed a glance over her shoulder in irritation.

"Sherry," Worker Bee Number One whispered, "stop it. She's gonna get mad."

"What's she going to do, read me Bible stories? Look at her! She's drooling all over her pretty little dress. She wouldn't know what to do with him if she had him."

Justice swallowed at the cruelty in the girl's voice, the nanny-nanny-boo-boo singsong close in her ear, and she cringed at the whisper. "I bet she wants to fuck Knox Hilliard as much as I do. Pay attention, little girl."

It was a good thing Justice was in front of Sherry and her courtiers because her face flooded with color. She averted her gaze from Professor Hilliard and tried to cool the hot rage and mortification that welled up inside her. It wouldn't have bothered her so much if Sherry hadn't cut so close to the truth.

Then it was the Queen Bee's turn to introduce herself. She kicked Justice's chair again and Justice blinked away stinging tears before looking up at the handsome attorney.

"Miss Quails," Professor Hilliard said, his deep voice resonating from the front row of the lecture hall all the way to the most remote corners of the back. "Your turn. What kind of law do you want to practice?"

"Corporate," she said shortly, "but what I really want to talk about is what you're doing this weekend? *All* weekend?"

The room held its collective breath at her brazenness and the professor stared at her as if she'd lost her mind. Then a smile, quick and blinding, flashed across his face. Justice stared at him in awe, as she had for the entire two hours she'd been in this class. If Justice had ever needed to see an example of male beauty and masculine grace, Knox Hilliard was it. Too bad he was only subbing for the real professor.

He began to chuckle as he came closer to Sherry and therefore, closer to Justice. "See me after class and I'll see what I can arrange," he murmured, his predatory tone matching Sherry's perfectly.

"Certainly . . . Knox."

He still chuckled as he continued with the next person down the row. Justice averted her eyes. Soon she heard, "And what about you, Miss McKinley?"

Justice started, and looked up at him; he watched her expectantly. She could feel her face burn and she cleared her throat. Her nerve endings tingled and she felt slightly nauseated. "I—I want to be a prosecutor," she said and then, to her horror, she added, "like you."

Sherry and her clique snickered openly.

Surprise flickered in the man's ice blue eyes and he smiled in kind bemusement. "Why?"

Justice swallowed again. She felt as if she were on trial, as if her answer would determine her whole future. In three years, half the people in that classroom would be competing for the coveted coup of being hired and trained by Knox Hilliard. Yes, her answer today *would* determine her whole future.

"I—I want to help people," she began, caught up in the suddenly changing colors of his eyes and for a brief moment, she forgot all about Sherry. "I think that criminals . . . that they have too many rights. It's too easy to hurt others for fun and profit." She went on, gaining confidence in her opinion and strength in her voice as she always did when she spoke on something she believed in.

"There's no sense of right and wrong anymore. Um, personal property rights—meaning oneself and one's belongings—were meant to be held sacred. That's what the Founding Fathers wanted. Life and valuables are cheap now, partly, um, because of the eroding family base and partly because the legal system doesn't punish criminals well enough. I want to help make the law a deterrent again—to, oh, legally avenge those whose lives are violated by someone else."

Silence reigned throughout the lecture hall, and Justice could not quite meet the probing gaze of the professor. She stared at her books and tried to hold back tears of frustration and embarrassment.

Then Sherry laughed. Her friends laughed. The room exploded in laughter—raucous, jeering guffaws aimed at Justice, who was only now aware that she had displayed an appalling naïveté for her entire class to see.

This was going to be a long three years.

"ENOUGH!"

The roar was violent, livid, and thoroughly effective as it echoed off the walls of the abruptly silent room. Justice's head snapped up to see Professor Hilliard leisurely stroll across the dais away from her, his hands in the pockets of his fine gray suit. His face was hard as he glared up at the rows and rows of open-mouthed students.

"How dare you," he murmured, his tone dangerous. His lazy syntax and country twang were gone. He spoke with precision, his diction flawless. His easygoing manner had disintegrated to hard cynicism in the blink of an eye and Justice stared at him, confused—his outrage had been so immediate, so effortless.

"How dare you denigrate the career goals of a fellow student. I daresay none of you have thought that deeply about what you want and why you want it. None of you have displayed that kind of passion or expressed yourselves so eloquently that the room was enthralled with what you said. None of you were courageous enough to say what you really thought. How dare you sit on your pretentiously cynical asses and laugh at idealism. Idealism is what created this country; it's what drives it; it's what allows you to be here on daddy's money."

He pointed to different sections of the room in turn. "You. You. You." He began the trek back across the platform toward Justice. She caught the faintest whiff of an elegant cologne as he leaned alongside her toward Sherry. "And you, Miss Quails," he purred, and it was not a nice purr.

Justice gulped, glad she was not on the receiving end of the latent violence in his voice. "*You* can go fuck yourself, because I certainly won't."

The collective gasp was palpable. Sherry stammered in confused outrage, even as Professor Hilliard's regard softened and settled upon Justice who, with tears of mixed gratitude and mortification in her eyes, looked away from his large harshness

3

and golden darkness.

Fingertips under her chin gently forced her face around and up. She blinked to get rid of her tears before his clever ice—no, now dark—blue eyes saw them.

"Do you believe in vigilante justice, Justice?"

She gulped. "No," she whispered.

"What about theft versus crimes against the body?"

"Property is to be held as sacred as the body and vice versa," she responded in a voice made stronger after clearing her throat.

"Revenge?"

"No excuse."

"Biblical and all that."

"Yes."

"Black and white?"

"No. Right and wrong."

Justice followed his line of reasoning without effort because she knew these things, believed these things, believed in the brilliance and genius of the Founding Fathers.

They had touched, somehow, this experienced attorney somewhere in his mid-thirties and Justice, a twenty-two-year-old (today) law student who'd been in classes for a whole five days.

His thumb drifted across her cheekbone as he stood looking down at her; Justice was only minimally aware of the lecture hall full of spellbound students. His mind connected with hers even as his fingertips connected with her skin.

"Very good, Justice," he murmured.

She stared up into Knox Hilliard's sapphire eyes and fell in love.

Giselle Cox reached out and brushed the girl's shoulder. She started, turned, nearly cowering in fear of whatever cutting remark she assumed Giselle would make, her hazel, almost amber, eyes wide.

"You were very good in there," Giselle said quietly, aware of the wary glances cast their way because she got attention wherever she went whether she wanted it or not. Today, she wanted it; no one who knew any better would bother this girl now that Giselle had marked her just by talking to her.

Giselle inspected Justice closely. Her appearance needed some serious help. She was taller than Giselle by at least three or four inches. An early '80s-type shirtwaist dress made of printed chintz with a wide white collar hid a body type Giselle could only guess at, but if the legs were anything to go by, she had a lot of potential.

Her hair was a mess. It was a dull dark red mahogany color, frizzy, in a French braid that went to her waist and did nothing to contain the out-of-control frizz.

Her face was odd. That was the only way Giselle could describe it. She had a strange color of foundation on as if she were trying to hide acne, but the skim coat of makeup was smooth, so she must be hiding freckles. That'd go with the hair. Too bad, too, because the girl had exquisite bone structure. Giselle was tempted to take the girl for a makeover just because she'd been so fabulous in class, but cracking open her chrysalis and letting *that* butterfly loose would have some serious and long-lasting complications.

Heaven only knew, *Professor Hilliard* didn't need any more complications at the moment, *especially* considering what had happened in class. For a variety of reasons, no one would believe for a moment his initial response to Sherry's proposition had been anything other than an attempt to let her save face, but he'd be lucky not to get fired or sued—or both—over how he had spoken to her after that and then actually *touched* a student. The F-bomb in class, even.

Giselle snorted. *Professor Shit-for-Brains.*

No, better Justice look like this for as long as possible in case he was tempted to do something even more stupid.

Justice continued to look down and she mumbled something Giselle couldn't hear, then her eye was caught just over Justice's shoulder. Knox stared at her from a staircase across the hall. He slid a cold glance over to Sherry and her brood who huddled together, their outrage palpable. Giselle looked at them, looked back at him and raised an eyebrow. He nodded once and left.

Still mumbling. Dammit, she wished she didn't have to talk to the top of the girl's frizzy red head.

"Justice," Giselle murmured, dipping her body down so she looked up into the girl's face. She smiled gently as Justice raised her head. "You just go about your business. Believe in yourself and your opinions. Have faith. I don't know you, but I'm very proud of you."

Another encouraging smile, then she left the building.

To lie in wait.

"Sherry!" Giselle said brightly as the bitch came around a corner. "Can I, uh, *talk* to you a minute?"

"Sure, Giselle!"

Giselle's lip almost curled at the girl's delight at having *finally* caught her attention. There were only two reasons Sherry would know her name after only one week in class.

Ten years older than most of the other students, Giselle was a third year on the five-year plan. It wasn't the most prestigious position to be in, that was for sure, but given her age, the fact that she already had a PhD, and, oh, the fact that she and *Professor Hilliard* clashed loudly, publicly, and often, she garnered a certain deference—even from other professors.

It also made her a target for crushes of both genders.

Leaving her giggling friends under a tree, Sherry followed Giselle eagerly to an out-of-the-way spot in a thick stand of trees. Giselle turned only to find the girl backed up to a big tree, preening for her. She smiled seductively and approached her slowly with a swing in her hips.

"I know what you want," Giselle murmured.

Sherry sucked in an anticipatory breath. "Really?"

"You've made it clear enough all week."

Giselle reached out a hand when she was close enough to touch, and Sherry closed her eyes, waiting for Giselle's kiss.

Sherry couldn't even screech when her head was snapped back against the tree, Giselle's hand clamped around Sherry's throat and squeezing just enough.

"I'm going to tell you this once and I want you to make sure it gets spread around," she whispered in Sherry's ear. "Leave. Justice. McKinley. Alone. If I hear even a suggestion of a rumor that you, your skank patrol, or anyone else not even associated with you are giving her a hard time, you'll regret it. I think the *last* place you want to be for the next three years is on my shit list. You're *so* not his type," she muttered, and with one last look of sheer disgust, she let Sherry go.

She turned to run, but Giselle grabbed a handful of her hair and jerked her back, whispering in her ear. "You make sure now, to remind people that they are to be nice to her. How'd you like to be on *his* shit list, too?"

"No, no. I'm sorry. Please let me go," she whimpered. "Please."

And Giselle did. She ran crying back to her friends, but no one approached Giselle with accusations of what had happened in the glade.

Sherry left two weeks later, but Giselle continued to watch over Justice long after her impassioned speech was forgotten by all but three people.

1: The First Wife

THE KANSAS CITY CRIME SCENE UNIT HAD HAD TO DREDGE LEAH WINCOTT'S body from a pond, so the casket remained closed. There was only one reason any bride of Knox Hilliard—especially one who had a child already—would turn up dead.

Bryce knew he should probably stop sneaking glances at one particular mourner while his friend and client lay at the front of the chapel garnering her due respects. Leah's death had too many implications to allow distraction, but he'd taken one look across the room and he could think of nothing but the woman who'd caught his attention.

She sat in a darkened back corner alone, her arms folded across her delectable chest. In one hand, she held a Dixie cup filched from one of the funeral home's restrooms. She took a sip, then stared down into it. She looked good in black. No, she looked like a queen in black.

Anger, not sorrow. He didn't know what kind of a relationship she had had with Leah, but he could feel the rage radiating from her in waves. By the time a funeral rolled around, most people had passed the anger stage of grief, or at least they hid it for the rest of the mourners. Not this woman; she seethed and her modest dress didn't do a thing to mitigate her mood.

He studied her from where he stood in the midst of a cluster of people who had shown up at Leah's visitation to witness the last event in the debacle of the most awaited and debated wedding on Wall Street.

Two weeks earlier, the OKH Bride, the woman who, with two tiny words would enable one man to inherit the majority shares of a Fortune 100 company, had been snatched from her dressing room and murdered just before she could say "I do."

Still the woman he watched sat slumped in her chair, her expensively shod feet resting on the folding chair in front of her. Dull blonde corkscrews cascaded just beyond her shoulders. She had already plowed her fingers through them several times in a futile effort to keep them out of her eyes. Finally, she huffed, set her Dixie cup down on the chair next to her, reached up, and began to braid her hair back.

Bryce sighed. He wished she hadn't done that. On the other hand . . .

The black velvet of her short bodice shimmered subtle gold and stretched over her breasts. His nostrils flared, just a bit, at the thought of stroking gently over one of them, pausing to flick at her nipple with a thumb.

Her knee-length silk-and-chiffon skirt had risen until the hem caught on something indiscernible about her thigh that was distinctly out of place. It took him out of the moment of sexual fantasy and into the realm of sheer curiosity at what would require one to wear a heavy black strap around one's thigh. He couldn't think of a reason at the moment, but it didn't matter. She'd finished braiding and she returned to her previous attitude: slouched, her arms folded, scowling at the floor.

An older woman in black passed behind her, pulled her fingertips lightly across her back in what seemed to Bryce a loving caress, and said something to her when she looked up.

Now he could see her face in its entirety and he sucked in a breath. He'd seen her before, in a Pre-Raphaelite painting he remembered studying in freshman humanities more than twenty years before. Lilith, Adam's first wife, who demanded equality with Adam and left Eden in a snit when he refused.

Bryce had never forgotten that tale, nor the painting. The idea that Adam had had a wife before Eve had shocked him to his core at the time. Further, the particular point of Lilith's complaint against Adam had aroused Bryce painfully. As he watched the warm, breathing Lilith across the room from him, he didn't have to wonder if she'd demand to be on top.

He wondered how she'd go about demanding it.

The older woman had stopped speaking and waited for Lilith's response. Her mouth tightened and she looked away, off into nothing, thinking. Finally, she glanced back up at the woman, nodded once, and spoke. He could read her lips.

Okay, Mom.

The mother walked away with a pat on Lilith's shoulder. As she arose, her full skirt caught again, on the chair this time, and he sucked in a sharp breath. More to the point, what would require a woman to wear a nine-millimeter semi-automatic pistol strapped to her thigh at a visitation, under a cocktail dress, with no other trappings of law enforcement? The black lace of the top of her stocking only added to the arousing effect of the odd juxtaposition of delicate lace and lethal steel.

This Lilith had him harder than Collier's painting.

Dammit, she mouthed as she swept her hand down her body to straighten her dress and cover the gun. The black-and-gold fabrics flared and shimmered when she turned from him. Her ridiculously high heels forced the muscles of her legs into sharp relief and his eyes widened at the latent power he saw there when she strutted away into the dark recesses of the funeral home until she disappeared.

He hung back, loath to follow her. He raised his left hand to feel his face, the burn scars that disfigured him, mocked him, kept him from approaching women because he hated the flinching, the fake politeness.

Monster.

He'd overheard that frightened whisper long ago when the scars were still relatively fresh, and though it didn't make him angry anymore, it did serve to remind him of his sin, the punishment for his sin.

The image of that woman, Lilith, dangerous, muscular, on her knees in front of him, his hand clutched in her hair, her mouth around him, flared in his mind. He thought he'd never catch his breath.

His feet took it upon themselves to trace her path, following a hint of a perfume he knew would belong to a Lilith: spice and flowers with a hint of sex. Far away from the chapel, toward a small, dimly lit room at the other end of the building, he rounded a corner and heard a delicate female voice, filled with anger.

He stopped, ducked back a bit, listened.

"Say it, Knox."

A sudden whoosh of air. "Okay, okay," came a man's voice. Knox Hilliard's—the fiancé of the woman in the casket. "You were right. I'm sorry," he murmured. "Giselle, you don't know how sorry I am."

Giselle.

Not Lilith. His disappointment was deep and sharp, but she made it disappear with the unexpected sorrow in her whisper. "Oh, I'm sorry, too, Knox. I shouldn't have said that."

There was a pause, then the sound of rustling fabric. Bryce risked a peek around the corner and saw her engulfed in Hilliard's arms, his face in the crook of her neck, her arms wound around his shoulders and her fingers curled into his hair.

"Come home with me tonight," he murmured, one hand undoing her braid and the other splayed across her buttocks, crushing her to him. "Please. I need you."

Bryce's heart thundering in his chest, he pulled himself away from the tableau in front of him and dropped back against the wall. His mind churned through the implications of that even as the silence lengthened, only to be pierced with the soft sounds of kissing.

He didn't wait to hear her response. Nauseated, he pushed away from the wall and stalked out of the funeral home.

That Leah Wincott, Bryce's friend and client, had died for the sake of a man who had a mistress—it angered him.

That Bryce wanted a woman he didn't know, who wouldn't be interested in him anyway, the mistress of Leah's groom—it enraged him. *Lilith*, succubus.

That the man between Lilith and Leah was Knox Hilliard, well . . . Bryce felt thoroughly, inexplicably, betrayed.

Again.

2: Romeo & Juliet

ONE NIGHT," KNOX WHISPERED INTO HER MOUTH AS THEIR KISS SOFTENED. In the aftermath of Leah's death, with all the attendant guilt and grief, Giselle understood that he needed her. She couldn't say she didn't need him that way, too, but . . .

"You know what I'm going to say," she murmured, pulling away from him. She placed her palms on either side of his tanned, ruggedly handsome face and looked into his ice blue eyes. She studied him and for the first time noticed how he had aged under the weight of constant stress. Thirty-five going on forty-five. "If we *ever* have sex, it can't happen because of something like this. We're not teenagers anymore and it's about fifteen years too late for us. All you want right now is comfort sex and I won't do that. I deserve more, *especially* from you."

He sighed.

"Besides, what about last month?"

He pulled away from her and stared at her warily. "What about last month?"

Her mouth pursed. "You know what about last month. I was there, remember? You took one look at that girl and you were a goner. I don't know how you planned to work that out with marrying Leah, considering your excruciating monogamy, but you weren't subtle about it."

"I am not going to discuss that with you right now. Maybe not ever."

Giselle watched Knox pace in utter turmoil, but she had her own guilt to deal with; she could have prevented Leah's death if she'd followed her gut.

Honey, thank you, but I don't need a bodyguard. I'm the most high-profile woman in the country right now and Fen wouldn't dare have me killed. Once I'm married to Knox, Fen won't have any reason to try to kill you again.

Leah, I don't have a good feeling about this.

Giselle! Put that gun away and stop pacing. If you can't do that, leave. I'm about to get married in front of five hundred people. I don't need your fidgets on top of mine.

But—

Out!

Okay, you know what? I'm going to go get Knox.

You do that.

Leah's rich south Texas drawl still echoed in her head, even after two weeks. Giselle had no doubt that Knox loved the woman in the casket. She also didn't doubt that his guilt over her death was now exponentially worse: not only had he taken Leah's side of the argument *but* . . .

"Now you're stuck with the added guilt of falling in love with a woman you weren't getting married to and can't have anyway."

He flinched.

"And you want *me* to kiss your wittow owwie and make it all better."

"Yes, I do," he shot back. She found herself pulled into his arms again, his big hand wrapping around the back of her thigh, pressing her into his arousal, her skirt gathering over his wrist as he stroked upward. They kissed with the confidence and familiarity of thirty years of history.

Knox didn't do much for her, but she had her doubts as to the existence of what she really wanted. Thirty-four and at the breaking point of her quest for celibacy, finally giving in and making love with the man who'd spent half his life being her boyfriend would be . . . convenient, an incredibly elegant solution to every issue that surrounded them.

Temptation rose within her, though only on an intellectual level. At this point in their lives, their circumstance, it didn't much matter that his arousal for her was conditioned reflex. Why should she expect him to give her what she couldn't give him?

"Now, see, that's the answer to the problem right there."

The kiss ended abruptly with that smug pronouncement from the doorway and Giselle groaned as she turned and walked away from Knox and the man who had sought them out.

"Fuck you, Sebastian," Knox snapped.

"No, fuck *her*," Sebastian drawled. "Marry her. Knock her up. I don't care in which order that happens. Start adoption proceedings. Something."

Knox sighed. "Dude, I don't need this right now. I'm burying my fiancée."

"Yeah, and we're going to be burying *you* next since Giselle won't actually die when she's torched and shot."

That prediction held quite a bit of truth, so Giselle said nothing. Knox, too, remained silent.

She looked at her cousin out of the corner of her eye as he stared between her and Knox. Sebastian, at thirty-eight, was six-foot-two of classic black Irish, his trademark scowl exuding darkness and danger. His handsome face did nothing to mitigate his sinister air.

"We'd kill each other before a year was out," Knox muttered after a long moment.

Giselle nodded. "That's true."

"You two have been together on and off since before you knew what tongues were for. Lots of people get married with less than what you have. Fen's never going to believe you won't end up together, so the only way to keep Giselle safe is for you to marry her. If she's married to you, he won't be able to go after her again without getting the entire KCPD up his ass. You hide behind the FBI, so let her hide behind you. Everybody's safe and happy until the turnover of OKH to you."

Giselle's throat clogged and she wrapped her arms around herself, suddenly chilled to her soul. "Sebastian," she murmured over her shoulder, "just for one moment, think about the child we'd have to have to fulfill the proviso, will you? Leah came with a daughter, so that was the perfect solution. Marriage I could live with just to win the game because nothing would keep us from getting divorced as soon as possible. But a child? No. Whether we had one or adopted one would make no difference. It would bind us together for the rest of our lives. I love Knox dearly, but not that much and not that way."

"That about sums it up for me, too," Knox added.

"Oh, that explains the groping."

"Let me put it this way," Giselle said, her patience strained. "I *refuse* to have or adopt a child on such mercenary terms. It's immoral and it would make both of us whores, so there really is no point to getting married at all."

Sebastian said nothing for a moment, then, "Well. Now that you put it that way."

"You know what?" Knox said. "Forget OKH. I don't want it."

"What do you mean, you don't want it?" Sebastian asked slowly.

"I have no interest in it and it's not worth the price."

Giselle turned to gape at Knox.

"Uh, Knox," Sebastian said after a moment of stunned silence, "you've spent your entire life preparing to take over that company when you turn forty. When, exactly, did you have this change of heart?"

"The minute I became the Chouteau County prosecutor," he snapped. "I can't manage shit. I put people in jail and I teach. That's all I'm good at."

"That was eight years ago. Could you not have told us this sooner?"

He groaned. "I didn't know how much I dreaded it until I was waiting for the wedding to start. I never got cold feet about getting married. I had cold feet about having to take a job I'm not suited for and don't know how to do. Now I have to take it because Fen's killed two people to get it and keep it."

Giselle raised her hand. "Uh, hello?"

"Suck it up, princess. You're still alive."

Sebastian's mouth tightened. "There are exactly two immediate solutions to the problem, neither of which you—or Giselle—are willing to carry out. So, of course it's up to me to bail your ass out."

"Nobody asked you to, so don't act like you're the martyr of the piece."

"Well, I'll be damned if I sit back and let him continue to walk all over you two like he did Oliver and Leah without consequence."

"Sebastian," Giselle said, impatient. "None of this is Knox's fault. I don't understand why you're taking it out on *him*. And he *did* try."

Sebastian grunted. "Well, that's true. Knox, I'm sorry this is happening to you. However, since it is happening to you, you now have two options: Cut and run or stay and fight. Staying and doing nothing isn't an option because he will not trust that you don't want OKH anymore. How you fight is up to you, but what you're doing hasn't worked, so think of something else." Giselle leaned against the wall and closed her eyes. "Either kill the bastard or let Giselle do it. She's earned the right to it at this point."

She'd certainly fantasized about it often enough.

"Whatever gets done to him, I have to do it," Knox muttered.

"But you're not doing anything," Sebastian returned. "That's my point."

Neither Knox nor Sebastian said anything for the longest time, which was uncharacteristic. Giselle opened her eyes and looked from one stubbornly set face to the other. Knox finally opened his mouth but when nothing came out, he closed it with a snap. Giselle watched him speculatively, wondering if he would tell Sebastian he'd fallen in love with another woman just a month before.

Knox caught her look and glared at her in warning. Sebastian witnessed the exchange and awaited an explanation, but neither she nor Knox felt like enlightening him. Yet.

Giselle huffed. "You," she said, pointing at Knox, "go back to your crooked little outfit up there in Chouteau County and act like the corrupt bastard that you are. Whether you want your inheritance or not, the only way you're going to get out of it is by being dead. You," she said, pointing at Sebastian, "business as usual. Any which way this turns out, you win, so I don't understand why you're bitching and moaning over a smattering of extra paperwork that Jack's taking care of anyway. You would've done this a long time ago if Knox had come to his epiphany earlier."

"Congress."

"Don't use that as an excuse. There's not enough brawn back there to string you up, much less brains. I daresay if you do get called up, you'll find the whole thing a lark." She pushed herself off the wall. "I'm going home. I'm tired." Giselle strode toward the door, expecting that Sebastian would move out of her way. He did, but he raised an eyebrow in a futile attempt to intimidate her.

"And what are you going to do, my lovely?"

"You don't need to know."

"Don't move."

The distinguished silver-haired gentleman halted at the cold round pressure at the back of his head. He stiffened when Giselle wrapped her delicate hand around his throat, thumb and middle finger pressed just deeply enough into his carotids to keep him still.

She leaned forward so that her mouth brushed his ear.

"You are alive by the grace of Knox Hilliard, who has requested in good faith that I not kill you," she whispered conversationally. "If you try to have me killed again, if you attempt to kill Knox at all, if you pull any more stunts like killing any future brides, I'll consider that a breach of good faith on your part. I should blow your head off for murdering Leah.

"Consider: I didn't die in the fire your goons set. I didn't die when your goons shot me. I'm alive and both of your goons are dead and barbecued—and the prosecutor was happy I did him the favor of cleaning up after him. So instead of being in the ground, I'm here. With you. Your security hasn't a clue and the only thing keeping me from putting a bullet in your head right now is Knox. Have you learned nothing about me over the last thirty years? Do you really think you can take me on and win?"

She felt his gulp against her fingertips.

"I didn't think so. Good day to you, Fen. Oh, I almost forgot. Mom said to tell you Thanksgiving dinner'll be at her house this year, two o'clock sharp, as usual."

3: Ready-Mixed Concrete Company, 1935

BRYCE, ARE YOU OKAY?"

Bryce sat in his leather chair looking out over the city. High up in One KC Place, corner office, all glass, he could see for miles—so very apropos for a pit bull of a trial lawyer.

He pursed his lips as he held his fingers steepled under his chin, feeling more like a teenaged boy with his first crush than a thirty-eight-year-old mover and shaker.

"I'm fine," he muttered, answering his assistant's question without turning. He didn't mind Arlene's nosiness. It was nice to have a woman care about him, fuss over him, even if he did pay her to do it. His housekeeper did that, too. Her daily harangues about his need for a wife always made him smile and shake his head. This morning, however, he found no amusement in it whatsoever.

Lilith.

He'd spent the last two nights googling that damned painting, studying it, re-reading its history and provenance and myth, comparing it to the woman who'd made him fantasize about things he hadn't bothered to fantasize about in five years. It was part of the permanent collection in a gallery in England; he knew he had no hope of buying it, but he'd sent an email of inquiry anyway. Just in case. No one had responded.

Giselle.

Arlene snorted. "Fine, my ass." Normally that would've pulled a grin out of him. Today . . . no.

Knox Hilliard's lover.

"Here's your *Wall Street Journal*. Leah's all over it."

Bryce spun around and snatched it out of her hand, then snapped it open.

OKHE bride murdered, groom suspected

He skimmed the first couple of paragraphs until his attention caught:

> Fen Hilliard, current CEO of OKH Enterprises, was questioned in the matter of Wincott's death, but released after several hours. No evidence has been found to connect either Fen Hilliard or Knox Hilliard to her murder, but investigations of both continue in light of Knox Hilliard's questionable reputation in his community and Fen Hilliard's apparent motive.

"I think Knox did it," Arlene offered.

Bryce grunted. "He had no reason to," he murmured, "but Fen sure as hell did."

"Fen Hilliard would *never* do something like that," Arlene said, low, her voice so full of anger it shocked Bryce. He looked up at her, puzzled. She went on. "Fen Hilliard signs the paychecks of half my family. He rescued OKH when we thought it was going to go under and he saved us. He's a good man, a generous man."

Ah, yes. Kansas City's knight in shining armor. Fen had taken the rattletrap die cut and metal machining company his brother Oliver, Knox's father, had built, saved it from failure, and turned it into a billion-dollar success. He'd also married Knox's mother after a not-so-respectable mourning period, which always made Bryce's eyebrow rise. The entire metro saw Fen Hilliard as a kind and caring man, and adored him for his generosity to his employees and the community—

—a modern version of Boss Tom Pendergast, straight out of 1930s Kansas City. Unlike Pendergast, however, Fen didn't have a monopoly on government concrete contracts, nor could he use the Kansas City police department as his personal errand boys, nor did he have enough political power to put a man in the Senate.

Bryce *did* tend to forget that his opinion of the CEO of OKH Enterprises differed greatly from everyone else's. Bryce shouldn't have been surprised at Arlene's vehemence. She idolized Boss Tom, too.

"And," she added, "I would think *you* of all people would know better than to assume someone's guilty just because everything points in his direction."

His eyebrow rose at that, just enough to let her know she'd gone too far. Her mouth tightened and she turned to walk out of his office. He would've fired anyone else for saying that, true or not.

He went back to his paper.

> According to the terms of the proviso Knox Hilliard's father had secretly approved and slipped into the corporate charter just days before his death, Knox Hilliard's inheritance of OKH Enterprises is guaranteed so long as he is married and has a child by his 40th birthday.
>
> When WSJ asked Fen Hilliard what these terms meant for his leadership, he said, "It's my great pleasure to safeguard my nephew's inheritance for him. I'm looking forward to the handoff so I can pursue other opportunities and maybe go fishing."
>
> There is some concern that Fen Hilliard's decision to take the company public some years ago has actually made an end run around the proviso, but legal experts who have studied the clause have come to the consensus that Knox Hilliard will be entitled to the majority shares the company holds for itself and will be its de facto CEO at that point, and that his claim would hold up in court if challenged.
>
> However, if Knox Hilliard does not fulfill the terms of the proviso, Fen Hilliard will remain at its helm indefinitely.
>
> To complicate matters, Knox Hilliard's cousin, financier Sebastian Taight, suddenly began to acquire OKHE stock at a steady pace two years ago. Taight is known across the country for his "Fix-or-Raid" protocol with regard to troubled companies that hire his consulting services. What he plans to do with OKH Enterprises, whether Knox Hilliard inherits or not, is unknown and Taight has refused to comment.
>
> To date, Knox Hilliard's wedding and announcement of a birth are the most anticipated social events on Wall Street and financial quarters across the country, especially as the deadline, Knox Hilliard's 40th birthday, looms. If he fulfills the terms of the proviso, his net worth could increase by as much as a half billion dollars.

Bryce didn't think Fen should've been released so easily from questioning since he had so much to gain from Leah's death. *Lucky bastard.* No, not lucky. Scheming, thorough, untouchable.

Just like Knox.

Bryce's lip curled with cynical resentment. Bryce had spent *days* in interrogation for the murders of his wife and four children because he'd had so much to gain from his wife's death. He'd been charged and his criminal trial docketed before the fire investigator had come back with the evidence that cleared him.

No, Knox hadn't killed Leah; he had everything to lose, but it wouldn't matter. Every lawyer in town joked that the FBI had been back and forth to the Chouteau County prosecutor's office so many times, the Missouri Department of Transportation had to repave that section of highway every six months.

The successor to an already corrupt prosecutor's office and blatantly continuing the tradition, Knox lived under the FBI's microscope. Despite that, he had a reputation as the best prosecutor in the ten major counties that made up the Kansas City metro area. His true talent, though, lay in turning baby lawyers into courtroom lions; his name on an attorney's CV guaranteed a stellar career path. Under Knox's leadership, the Chouteau County prosecutor's office had evolved into a residency program for litigators whose tales of corruption and dirty money had yet to be substantiated by the feds.

Knox Hilliard: Suspect Number One for his bride's death on the basis of his reputation alone, which preceded him all the way to Washington.

In a sidebar:

> Yesterday, OKHE stock price plummeted in the wake of another of Sebastian Taight's mass buys. The SEC is expected to disallow any more buys by Taight if he does not account for his voting record as a majority shareholder. In addition, there are some murmurings on Capitol Hill about the legitimacy and legality of Taight's raids.
>
> Senator Roger Oth (R-Penn.), Taight's most vocal opponent, said today, "He and businessmen like him need to be brought to heel by someone with some power. As far as I can see, Congress is the only entity with that kind of power." Before being elected to office, Senator Oth was the CEO of Jep Industries, a company Taight dismantled after having been hired to restructure and streamline its operations. Taight would give no reason for his decision to break Jep Industries.

And Sebastian Taight was the monkey wrench in the power play between OKH's current CEO and its heir. Venture capitalist Taight had his fingers in so many pies, nobody could keep track of them all; he even speculated heavily in art. Wall Street had given up trying to figure him out years ago. Though scrupulously honest, he had a reputation for taking any leverage where he could get it, being completely ruthless about it, and remaining silent to the press. The drumbeats on Capitol Hill calling for Taight's head got a little louder every time he thumbed his nose at the SEC, every time he refused to explain his Fix-or-Raid policy. His aggressive takeover of OKH had sharply increased the Senate's interest in hauling him before a panel hearing.

Taight had the power to crush both Fen and Knox Hilliard and to all appearances, he had begun the process. Until the night of Leah's visitation, Bryce, along with the rest of the financial industry, had assumed Taight to be on the warpath with both

Hilliards, but now . . .

Before Lilith—*Giselle*—had caught his eye, Bryce had observed Taight shouldering up with Knox, giving him support, not leaving him to face the cream of society (Bryce couldn't really call them *mourners*) alone. The men were cousins, but they acted more like brothers. No, Taight wasn't at war with Knox, which only left the question of why he wanted OKH so badly he was willing to destroy it to get it away from both Fen and Knox—and why Knox treated him like a brother anyway.

Fen Hilliard, Sebastian Taight, and Knox Hilliard, three of the most brilliant men in the Midwest, were a family very publicly at war. Whatever else had gone wrong in that family, their collective genius couldn't be dismissed.

Bryce's email dinged and he glanced at it to see if it required immediate attention. The art gallery that had *Lilith*. His eyes widened and he clicked on the subject line.

Subject: Lilith

Dear Mr. Kenard,

Thank you for your inquiry regarding *Lilith* by the Hon. John Collier. We regret to inform you that the painting is not for sale. Please let us know if there is anything else we may be able to help you with.

M. Stevens,
Curator

Though Bryce knew he wouldn't have been able to have it at any price, disappointment still struck him behind his breastbone. He went to a website he'd bookmarked and pulled up *Lilith*. As he stared at it, he wondered what it would take to possess the real one, the one in the little black dress who answered to the name of Giselle.

4: No Static At All

J USTICE BOUNCED ALONG THE RUTTED DRIVEWAY TOWARD THE FARMHOUSE, her old car's struts unable to absorb the shocks. Truly, she didn't know how much longer it could take the eighty-four-mile round-trip commute from River Glen to the University of Missouri at Kansas City three days a week. If she believed in a God at all, she'd be on her knees the other four days begging for its longevity, at least for the six semesters until she graduated from law school. With any luck, she'd continue to be able to arrange her schedule as well as she had this semester—

—even if that meant she wouldn't have Professor Hilliard, who, she had learned, taught Tuesday and Thursday classes almost exclusively if he taught at all. She needed those two days during the week to work, to the point that it might be non-negotiable.

Once she had parked in her usual spot, she sat for a moment, taking in her lifelong home as if she had never seen it before, compared and contrasted it to the fine old neighborhoods surrounding UMKC. Then there were the relatively new subdivisions south of KCI airport along I-29 at the northern edges of Kansas City . . . fine new houses of the type she would never live in.

She sighed.

The dilapidated farmhouse, indistinguishable from any other plain white-clapboard-clad gothic farmhouse across the Midwest, listed on one corner. That could never be repaired without shoring up the foundation and she couldn't possibly hope to raise that kind of money. The yard was barren, packed dirt bisected by a poorly maintained gravel drive; her father used it to park worn out and rusting farm machinery.

The corrugated steel barn to the east of the house displayed a lace of rust, the animals it occasionally housed their only real income.

The wheat fields would give a poor crop; Justice had wanted to plant corn, as she suspected a good yield could be sold to an oil company for ethanol, but her father had dismissed her idea. Those fields were worn out—and the wheat proved it—but her father also wouldn't hear of letting her turn the cattle out into them. Certainly, it would be more economical to let them eat the wheat than pay for harvesting.

Very good, Justice.

She bit her lip, looked at the ragged wheat, then to the south where the cattle grazed, then back to the wheat and made an executive decision. She flipped open her cell phone and called a neighbor, explained what she wanted to do, and arranged to swap chores. She would mow his fields if he would combine and bale hers. Her father would have to live with it, though she knew she'd have to tread lightly and present him with a *fait accompli*.

That done, she mentally went over the list of other things she had to do this afternoon and evening, then sighed, seeing her future in the past that lay before her in all its pathetic glory. Hopefully, she could bring it back a little once she graduated from law school and had a regular income.

Justice got out of her car and walked into the house, hearing the familiar squeaks in the bare floorboards beneath her feet on the way to the kitchen. Despite what her father thought, it had not been foolish to spend so much money on the appliances that took up most of the otherwise primitive kitchen: a used Viking with six star burners, two ovens, and a warming drawer; an older Sub-Zero double refrigerator; and two fairly new freezers.

Her father's anger had more to do with what she hadn't bought than what she had, even though his complaints subsided when she demonstrated how fast they had paid for themselves. Still, he didn't really know how much she made because she spent it as fast as she got it: tuition, books, cell phone, aircard, gas, car insurance and repairs. The beef sales funded the farm, but her meal delivery business funded her education.

She had very little left over and she couldn't afford debt she wouldn't be able to repay on a junior assistant prosecutor's salary, much less as a defense attorney if she were forced to it. If she could get through law school without having to take out student loans, she would be very proud of herself.

No one else would be.

She filled a large pot with water and set it to boil, then turned on her mother's old tape deck; the silence got to her and she battled it with the music she'd found in the attic, cassette tapes her mother had stashed away before she died. It was in those boxes Justice had found the music of her heart: Rush. Nugent. U2.

And the music of her memories of her mother: Earth Wind & Fire, Carole King, Doobie Brothers.

She pressed play and heard Bette Midler's voice.

"Some say love . . . "

Justice hid in the endless shadows of the barn listening to her mother sing a cappella while she milked cow number two. Justice would have helped her, but she would stop singing if she knew anyone listened and oh, Justice did so love to hear her mother sing.

She had never heard this song before, which she deduced from the lyrics must be called "The Rose." She bit her lip at the words, suddenly feeling a sadness emanating from her mother in a thick wave. Where had it come from? Her mother was never sad; always light, always smiling, Justice's mother was the prettiest woman Justice had ever seen.

Suddenly she stopped singing and murmured, "Where is that girl? It's gone five."

"Here, Mama," Justice said, stepping into the barn proper, as though she had just come from the house. "I'm sorry I'm late."

A smile, quick and warm, lit her face. "Good morning, Iustitia. Will you turn on the radio, please?"

She didn't want the radio. She wanted whatever was in the tape player, which happened to be Hall & Oates.

"Thank you, baby. Cows three and four need to be milked yet."

Libby McKinley didn't see any reason to name any animal that provided food, money, or clothes. The dogs had names because Justice's father had insisted, but the barn cats didn't. The only animal Justice had been allowed to name was her own cat, Pontificate. She hadn't known what that word meant at the time, but thought it a neat word when she'd heard her mother say it to her father.

He hadn't known what it meant, either, so he'd stormed out of the house.

A week after Justice had heard her mother singing sad songs in the barn, she had almost tumbled over into sleep when she felt the familiar depression of the bed. Her mother snuggled up to her and it only vaguely occurred to Justice that she had been sleeping with her a lot more lately.

"Iustitia," whispered her mother in the dark of her room, her body warm and soft against her, "you have no idea how badly I want you off this farm."

Justice didn't understand that. She loved the farm, the work, the chores, even the animals, though her mother didn't know she thought of some of them as pets. "Why, Mama?"

"Because this is not the place for you. You have a keen mind and I want you to use it for something besides mindless, endless chores. You'll be old before your time."

"I don't understand."

"Of course you don't and you won't until you're stuck where I am. I want you to remember this, Iustitia. I want you to remember that I wanted you educated, off this farm, doing something grand and making a mark in the world. That I wanted you to have a philosophy and stick with it, believe in it, even if it's not mine."

That struck Justice as a funny phrasing. "What do you mean, 'wanted'?"

"Do you know how old I am?"

Of course she did. Everyone knows that about their parents. "Twenty-three."

"Yes. Do you know how old your father is?"

"Forty-one."

"Do the math, Iustitia. How old was I when you were born?"

Justice gulped. She would be fourteen in five years. Did that mean . . . ?

"That's right. I don't want that for you. I want you to understand that having children when you're young is a trap—not that I regret having you because I love you dearly and I wouldn't trade you for a seat in the Senate—but I want you to make a name for yourself, something grand and wonderful. The earlier the better. Promise me this."

Justice didn't understand her sense of urgency, her insistence. Thinking back, everything her mother ever did or said had paved the path to this moment.

Something bad was going on.

"What is it, Mama? What's happening?"

"I don't know, Iustitia. I just— I don't feel well. I need you to remember this and remember that I wanted you to get an education, to leave here. Whatever you do, do not be stupid like I was and let a man sucker you. You don't belong here. I don't belong here. If I had listened to my father, well . . . "

Upon looking at her mother in her casket two years later, it occurred to Justice that she had never looked prettier or younger: twenty-five and not a day older than that. Justice had never seen her like that. The doctors said she had a heart attack, but Justice didn't believe that. Twenty-five-year-old mothers didn't have heart attacks.

They do if they were born with a heart problem, one doctor told her bluntly when she had challenged him with an eleven-year-old's certainty of medicine.

"Come, child," said an old man she had never met, his hand heavy on her shoulder to steer her away from the rest of the mourners. "I want to talk to you."

She wrested away from him. "Who are you?" she whispered.

"Your grandfather. Libertas's—er, your mother's father."

"I don't know you."

"No, but you will. Perhaps I won't fail you like I failed your mother."

They sat together in a corner, talking. Well, not conversing: Her grandfather speaking, Justice listening. Absorbing the things he said, understanding more of what her mother had tried to teach her, but had not fully understood herself because she hadn't had time to before Justice's father had seduced her, gotten her pregnant, and been forced to marry her or go to jail.

Justice had known none of this until that moment.

And at that moment, her father chose to make a scene, yelling and screaming about what her grandfather had done to him, and how dare he attempt to glom onto Justice for his own evil purposes.

But Justice found comfort in her grandfather's teachings and so she did chores in the barn and waited until after her father had gone to bed. Her grandfather would come to her in the dead of night with books of histories and documents and theories and fables. The hayloft became Justice's classroom and her grandfather her professor.

Then he, too, died and left her with no one but her father, who didn't know what she did when he wasn't looking and didn't care—as long as she wasn't "messing around with books, because books don't do nothin' but put ideas in your head. This is your home and I'd just as soon you stay here and take care of it with me."

"Okay, Papa," she whispered, seeing all her mother's and grandfather's hopes burn off like an early-morning fog in ten o'clock sunshine. "I will." He was all she had in the world now.

"That's enough of you," Justice muttered as she killed the sad music before her mood tanked. But she had to push the eject button on the tape deck several times before it would obey, and her humor gradually worsened each time it refused. She had very little patience with the thing, preferring instead to play the mp3 files on her laptop, but the tape player was one of few precious links to her mother.

Her plan was simple: Fulfill her mother's and grandfather's aspirations for her and still keep her promise to her father. She juggled so much now that having only one regular job to work around would be a respite.

She'd wanted to be a prosecutor because her grandfather thought it a noble profession, but in order to help with the farm after she got a job, she only had two counties to choose from: Chouteau and Buchanan. The Clay and Jackson County seats were too far to drive every day. She had always figured this reality into her plans and had known nothing about the Chouteau County prosecutor until that day two months ago, when he had defended her, validated her, touched her.

Even had she been inclined to think about breaking her promise to her father, leave the farm, go somewhere else, that was out of the question now. If the Chouteau County prosecutor wouldn't hire her, she'd work in legal aid just to work in *that* courthouse.

I daresay none of you have thought that deeply about what you want and why you want it.

She swept her fingertips across her chin where Professor Hilliard had touched her so gently and smiled dreamily.

She turned on talk radio and knew by the voice coming out of the speakers that it was four o'clock. If she timed it right, she could cook all evening to get her week's orders filled and write while chili and stroganoff simmered.

Her spirit lightened considerably when she sifted through the mail and found the latest *National Review*. She flipped through the pages quickly to find the article she had written and submitted on a lark, bolstered by one man's faith in her opinions.

She had never expected it to be published.

She had also never expected to be asked to write more.

The water boiled and Justice got to cooking in earnest. She assembled a plate for her father, who picked it up, fished a can of beer out of the refrigerator, and walked right back out of the kitchen without a word.

How long Martin McKinley would pout about her schooling this time, Justice couldn't guess. It had taken him three months into her undergrad for him to speak to her. She shrugged. Sometimes it bothered her that his silence, intended to punish her, didn't bother her.

Two hours later she had enough of a break from cooking to crack open her laptop, make the rounds of her favorite political blogs, and post a few comments. Her email chimed.

> **Subject: Come aboard!**
> **Reply-to: hhew@townsquared.org**
>
> Justice,
>
> We've been following your comments for a while and we just read your piece in the National Review. We think you have a lot of potential as a columnist and we'd like to invite you to become a permanent contributor at TownSquared.
>
> Let us know!
>
> Cheers,
> The TownSquared Crew

She gasped. Giggled. Squealed, even. TownSquared was the biggest conservative blog on the 'net and they wanted *her* to write for *them*?

Very good, Justice.

5: Hot, Loose & Clean

APRIL 2005

GISELLE PUT HER BACKPACK ON A REMOTE CORNER OF HER DESK, CAREFUL not to dislodge the piles of papers and microcassette tapes that littered it. She sighed. It just couldn't happen that folks would respect her space and the clearly marked IN box she had set up to reduce just such clutter.

She hated clutter.

After collecting a bottle of water from the fridge, she set herself to putting her night's work in order. Not as much as it looked, once it was in a nice, tidy pile, but it didn't take into account the digital dictation on the server. If she finished early, she could go home to study or, more likely, sleep.

The clock read 4 P.M. when Giselle put the buds in her ears and began to type. Briefs, pleadings, letters, contracts—she could do them all by heart. One day, very soon, she would be the one dictating and not the one transcribing. She couldn't wait to get the hell out of this cubicle, which she resented all the more after having built a business and nurtured it for so many years—

—only to watch it burn to the ground. Starting over again at her age and with her background really sucked.

"Thanks a bunch, Uncle Fen," she grumbled.

Since it was still a half hour before the end of the workday, the office bustled with secretaries, paralegals, and lawyers going this way and that. Giselle sat off the beaten path, but that didn't stop many attorneys from making pointed detours to her desk to drop off work, to chat, and every so often, in the case of the more persistent, to ask her out.

She'd typed for some time before she caught the sight of an approaching attorney out of the corner of her eye and sighed. That particular puppy had been hot to trot for a while now. She had politely declined numerous invitations, but that didn't stop him from pursuing her anyway and making himself a general pain in her ass.

Ralph (who insisted everyone pronounce it "Rafe") propped his hip on her desk and waited for her to finish typing a phrase. Though she would like to ignore him and work, she couldn't. If the attorneys wanted to monopolize her time with chitchat, they could, though it threw her off her self-imposed schedule. It was now six o'clock. She wanted to leave by midnight.

"What can I do for you, Rafe?" she asked once she clicked the Dictaphone off, remaining polite but aloof, hoping he would get the hint.

"Go to the Ford exhibit at the Kemper Gallery with me on Saturday?"

Ever so thankful her weekends consisted of study groups, she shook her head. "I have plans this weekend."

"Ford's an artist. Have you ever *seen* his art?" he asked, sly.

She sighed. "Rafe, I really *do* have plans, but I've explained this to you before. I don't date outside my faith." That wasn't exactly true, but it did provide her a convenient out.

"Right. How could I forget all about you nice little Mormon girls?" It was nothing she hadn't heard before, with the same contempt, and from more interesting men than Ralph. "I think that's just a bullshit excuse."

Her eyebrow rose. "Oh? So are you saying that I'm using it as an excuse not to go out with *you?*"

His face hardened just a bit. She knew men's moods, so she didn't miss the change in demeanor. Ralph had always seemed relatively harmless, but now her annoyance turned to wariness. She kept her face carefully blank until—

He leaned into her personal space and murmured, "I could make things very difficult for you here."

She stared at him a minute before she burst out laughing. "Is that the best you can do?"

Ralph drew back at that, his surprise evident. His lips thinned and the rusty cogs in his head ground to come up with a reply. Giselle chuckled. "I thought so. If you have work for me, please drop it in my box and I'll have it done by the time you come in in the morning."

His nostrils flared at having been dismissed. "I don't think you want to cross me, Miss Cox."

"Ralph," she said slowly, pronouncing the "lph" sound with great precision. Rising from her chair, she closed the gap between them until her nose nearly touched his. "I am not going to *fuck* you." Her husky whisper made his breath shorten. "Not today. Not tomorrow. Not in a thousand lifetimes." Adrenaline pulsed through her arteries even as Ralph's humiliation visibly warred with his arousal. "You go on with your threats and intimidation. Go to Hale. Tell him whatever you like. I *dare* you." She smirked. "I guarantee you won't like the consequences."

She rocked back on her heel and crossed her arms over her chest, one eyebrow raised. He gulped, but attempted to save face: "You're going to be very sorry about this, Miss Cox."

"Ralph." Giselle and Ralph both started at the deep, hoarse male voice behind them and turned to see who had spoken with such ice. She felt Ralph tremble as she gaped, up up up, at the most beautiful man she had ever seen. She felt a jolt of desire as she stared at him, her body tingling for a real man the way it had only once before, long ago and far away.

He continued, "When you're feeling froggy, you just go ahead and jump."

"Hey, buddy!" Ralph said, his bright tone manufactured and patently false.

The stranger's bright green eyes flashed fire and his lips pressed together in a thin line. His big body radiated tension and a hint of his divine cologne wafted her way. Intimidating under any circumstances, the burn scars that matted the left half of his face and disappeared down into his collar made him fascinatingly ferocious.

Black hair. Fair skin that would tan easily and probably very dark in the summer sun. Chiseled features on the unscarred side of his face. She couldn't place his ethnicity, but he was extraordinarily exotic to her.

Those eyes, that face: Perfect weapon.

Giselle felt the heat between her legs, the wetness, as she examined him head to toe, shameless in her inspection, wondering what lay beneath all that finely tailored silk, wool, and cotton . . .

. . . wondering how long she'd remain a "good little Mormon girl" if *that* man had the good sense to ask her out.

She reluctantly drew her gaze away from him to look over her shoulder at Ralph, who had lost all color. He stood to his full height, though it gave him no advantage against this beautiful stranger's height and mass.

"Pack up your desk, Ralph," the man rumbled.

"You don't work here."

"I'll inform your boss I've invited you to hand in your resignation. I don't think he'll mind."

"Aw, man," he whined, but forced a laugh. "It's just a little running gag Miss Cox and I have some fun with, right, Giselle?"

"Pffftt. Nice try."

"Your office better be cleaned out when I leave here tonight." His order, so final, so threatening, made Giselle want to take another quick glance. Her breath caught at his power.

"You can't prove anything."

The man crossed his massive arms over his broad chest and drawled, "Can't I."

Ralph's lip curled and he glared at Giselle before stalking off, as if it were her fault. She supposed that in his mind, it was.

"Thank you," she said with her most flirtatious smile. She looked at him wide-eyed, wanting—*begging*—him to invite her to . . . something. Dinner, maybe. Ballet-theater-symphony-opera, preferably. She would love to dress up for this man. "I was afraid I'd have to take him out back and give him a good spanking."

He didn't laugh at her dumb joke. "You're welcome," he said tersely, turning to go.

Damn!

"Well, wait," she said and offered her hand for him to shake. Her flirting lacked finesse because she was too direct, too open, too . . . unpracticed. It had never mattered to her before this moment when she needed to stall him long enough to figure out how to keep his attention. "I'm Giselle Cox."

His eyebrow rose and he stared right back at her, ignoring her hand. "Miss Cox," he murmured with a slight sneer and a curt nod. His disparaging glance swept her from head to toe, then he turned again to walk away.

Her breath caught and her chest hurt right behind her sternum the way it had the only other time a man had left her breathless. She could only stare after him, stunned, speechless, moisture stinging her eyes.

She recovered herself in time to snap, "So I guess I did something to deserve that."

He stopped short and she studied him further while awaiting his apology.

A custom-tailored olive silk/linen blend suit accentuated the perfect musculature of his torso. The hems of his pants cuffs gathered artfully upon the leather of his Italian loafers. His sleek hair just brushed the collar of the white shirt peeping up from his lapel. Precisely half an inch of snowy cuff appeared from the sleeve of his coat. His left hand—as scarred as his face—bore no ring and contrasted sharply with his cuff. Diamond cufflinks sparked tiny rainbows in a random stream of last-gasp sunset.

Turning halfway, he pinned her with that weapon he had. She felt dizzy under that stare, his disfigured beauty radiating raw sex and power. His expression remained stony. "I'm sure," he replied, his tone measured and precise, "that you think you're entirely blameless."

Her eyes widened and her nostrils flared. Oh, no. No. Men did not talk to her like that. She drew up every bit of her five feet, four and five-eighths inches, done with her starry-eyed infatuation. "'Scuse you. You don't know me from Eve."

His eyebrow rose at that. "Lilith, maybe?"

With that, he continued on his way, leaving her dumbfounded, breathless, and thoroughly aroused.

What the *hell* had made him say that?

Shock.

Shock at seeing her, of actually meeting her. Here. In his own lawyer's office. Working as a second-shift transcriptionist.

It hadn't occurred to him that Knox's lover might work for a living. Knox always took care of his women well; he could afford to with all the untraceable money that ran through his office. Certainly, Leah had had the best of everything.

He fought the urge to turn around and walk backward just so he could inspect her more closely: faded Levi's, white tee shirt, and flamboyant vest that looked like a refugee from a Mardi Gras rag bag; rich golden-red hair—*why* had he thought it dull blonde?—in a ponytail, bound with a pert yellow ribbon and dripping those large, loose corkscrews down to her nape.

If only he didn't know that she wore a gun under cocktail dresses at funerals.

If only he hadn't heard her say *I am not going to fuck you* with the bored amusement of a woman who knew what to do with a man who couldn't understand the word no.

If only she hadn't turned on the charm once Ralph had been disposed of and looked at Bryce like *that*.

He sucked in a sharp breath and it caught.

Women just didn't look at him like that anymore and hadn't since the fire. More than one who'd found his wallet intriguing had spoken to his necktie in an effort to avoid looking at his face. Most children scrambled to stay away from him, the combination of his big body and scarred features overwhelming.

Monster.

He almost laughed. He could afford to now that he knew that the woman who'd tormented him for the last six months, a woman he'd assumed would react the same way the rest of the female population did, had found him attractive enough to let him know exactly what she wanted from him and how she wanted it, Knox be damned.

He *must* have imagined it.

Deep breath. He held it, then puffed it out again in a whoosh. She'd completely blown his mind.

Again.

All the way through the meeting with his attorney he felt distracted, scattered.

"Bryce? You with me?"

He shook his head to clear it. "That typist you have out there—the redhead—"

"Giselle? What about her?"

"Your idiot attorney Ralph 'Call Me Rafe' hit on her as I was walking in. He's a walking sexual harassment suit. He threatened to get her fired if she didn't sleep with him."

Geoff Hale's eyes narrowed. "I'm going to get rid of that son of a bitch."

"I suggested he have his office cleaned out by the time I left here tonight. I hope you don't mind me stepping into your business like that, but he was a little too pushy for my comfort."

Hale's eyebrows rose. "Oh. Well thank you, then. I'll send a quick email to HR." He turned to his computer for a moment and as he typed, he continued, "You know, he's been nothing but trouble from day one. Giselle's more valuable to me than three of him."

"Oh?" Bryce kept his voice casual to invite more comment, the perfect way to glean more information about her without arousing suspicion.

"Brilliant woman. Going to law school on the five-year program and she's interning for me this summer." Bryce hid his surprise. "She'll be a good trial attorney. Enough ego and charm to pull anything off and the brains and wit to back it up. I'm just hoping not to lose her to Hilliard's office, since that's where everyone wants to go. Not that I've asked her, come to think of it," he added absently while finishing his email with a flourish.

Bryce's heart quickened, but he controlled his expression. "Ah. Does she, uh, have any connections to any local attorneys?"

"Not that I know of. Why?"

"Curious is all."

For some reason, Bryce kept what he knew to himself. Mentioning her intimate involvement with Knox Hilliard would definitely get her fired, but he didn't know why he felt compelled to protect her.

"Is she married?"

Hale glanced at him then and his mouth twitched. "I forgot to mention that she's pretty," he said, "but I see you noticed that."

Bryce kept his expression carefully blank. "I'll take that as a no."

"I can, uh, put a bug in her ear as to your interest."

"I'm not," Bryce murmured, his tone carefully masking his frustration with himself for going too far. Hale was no fool, but he said no more about Giselle Cox, and for that, Bryce was grateful.

"Oh, by the way," Hale said as he shook Bryce's hand at the office door once their annual meeting had come to a close, "my condolences on your client. Leah Wincott, was it?"

The mention of Leah's name was enough to bring back some of the anger that had dissipated with the discussion of other matters. "Yeah," he muttered. "Very nice lady."

"I wish I could believe Knox killed her," Hale said, "but he's got too much to lose."

"That's kind of the way I figured it," Bryce said, then continued, "I don't know why Leah finally agreed to marry him, but she must have had her reasons. For what it's worth, she was very happy; he treated her well."

Hale looked thoughtful. "Fen's the most likely suspect, but nobody'd believe it."

"Agreed," Bryce said, then started. "Hey, isn't Fen your client?"

"Oh, no," Hale returned. "I haven't met a Hilliard yet that I liked and that includes the old man. Fen and I had a couple of meetings before I decided I didn't want to do business with him."

"Why?"

"Don't know. He's honest. Smart. He's good to the community, good to his employees. There's just . . . something. I'd trust Knox before I'd trust Fen. At least with Knox, you know exactly what you're getting. And that proviso? Taight? That whole situation's a nasty tangle."

And your "valuable" typist is intimately mixed up in it.

"I'm going home," Hale said on a yawn. "What time is it anyway?"

Bryce looked at his watch. "Twelve-thirty in the morning. Geez, Geoff, I'm sorry."

He waved a hand. "No need to apologize. It'll be in your statement at the end of the month."

"I'm sure," Bryce returned.

As Bryce walked to the elevator, he couldn't help but cast a look toward Giselle Cox's desk. Her empty chair, blank computer, and tidy desktop all bespoke the end of her shift. He felt a great disappointment settle in the region of his solar plexus, but he only sighed and continued on his way.

He stopped cold when he got to the parking garage and stared at the occupant of the only other car in the lot besides his.

She couldn't see him from the angle at which her car, an older model generic Chevy, sat. From what he could tell, she might be asleep or she might be hurt, for her head tilted back against the seat rest.

Refusing to think about the consequences of his actions, he walked across the lot and noted her open car windows. The April breezes that wafted through stirred her ponytail and the ends of the ribbon just a bit.

Once he got within speaking distance, he could see her dozing, a thick textbook open and lying face down on her chest. Even as he watched, her head lolled to the right so that he caught sight of the underside of her jaw and throat.

He imagined all the things he wanted to do to that throat; remembered her as she had been that night six months ago with her skirt pulled up enough for him to see the top of her black stocking; *needed* to see the rest of her body stripped bare for his pleasure.

Bryce squatted down beside the car and just watched her for a moment. "Miss Cox," he murmured, then found himself nose to nose with a very lethal woman— and she had the barrel of *that* gun bored right in the middle of his forehead.

She flipped it up and away from him once recognition dawned, but her face still held that tense, wild look of someone startled out of her wits.

"I'm so sorry," she murmured, her voice husky with sleep. His cock strained at his fly and he gulped. She rubbed her eyes, shoved her gun in the waistband of her jeans, and put the textbook in the backpack next to her, then stretched as far as she could within the confines of her car.

He said nothing as he watched her. She had taken off her vest and the thin white tee shirt did nothing to hide the lacy nearly-nothing bra she wore underneath it. Her nipples had hardened in the cool night air, begging for a nip, a lick, a tug.

A bite. Bryce released a strangled breath.

She came down from her stretch with a hard glint in her eyes, an ice blue that could probably sear a man in half. He had the oddest feeling that he had seen those eyes somewhere before.

"What do you want." Clipped, hostile. Not a question.

"I wanted to tell you how foolish it is to sleep in an empty Plaza parking garage in the middle of the night with your windows rolled down, but I see it's occurred to you."

"Indeed," she said, tight-lipped. "Anything else?"

Neither her expression nor her tone held any hint of desire or anything remotely complimentary—just anger with a great deal of contempt thrown in for good measure. He shouldn't be surprised. He'd burned that particular bridge behind him.

And rightly so! Another man's lover, even. Although . . . from looking at the car, it didn't seem as though Knox took care of her very well and certainly not as well as he'd taken care of Leah.

"I wanted to know if you'd like a late dinner," he said, shocking himself.

She blinked. "'Scuse me?"

He'd boxed himself in well. "Dinner. Or breakfast. Whatever."

"Oh, I don't think so," she sneered. She shoved her car key into the ignition and turned the engine over.

"I saved your job." Lame. True, but lame.

"Lame," she snapped. "Whatever you assumed about me? Dead wrong, so keep your derision to yourself. I don't know who you are or who you think you are, but I assure you: You have never met a woman like me, and you never will again."

So saying, she reached over and grabbed the knot of his necktie to pull him to her. Surprised, he didn't fight, but when her lips touched his and her tongue swept his mouth, he returned it with the same fire.

Then he wrapped his hand around the back of her head, crushed her to him, and took the kiss away from her.

Directed it.

Deepened it.

Lengthened it.

He opened his eyes to watch her. Her face was a study in desire, her eyes closed, her breath ragged, her tongue matching his stroke for stroke, shift for shift. She sighed into his mouth and released his tie to caress his neck, the scars there, her thumb stroking his jaw line while their tongues mated.

Suddenly she sucked in a deep breath and her eyes popped open, staring at him as if she'd lost herself somewhere inside him. She had. He'd surprised her, taken the power position away from her and she didn't know how to take it back.

He knew this as surely as he knew his own name.

She jerked away from him, her breathing heavy and her eyes wide. "You—" She stopped. Swallowed. "I—" Bit her lip. Fumbled for the gear shift.

Bryce stood, then wrapped his hand tightly around her chin. He tilted her head up until she looked up at him, an odd mixture of panic and passion in her expression.

"Be careful what you wish for, Miss Cox," he purred. "You might get it." Then he turned and strode toward his own car without looking back, wondering what she'd make of *that*.

6: Energizer Rabbit

August 2005

"AH, SUNDAY AGAIN," SEBASTIAN INTONED FROM THE SOFA WHERE HE watched a movie and drank a bottle of wine. "I don't even know why you bother going to church. You're not the most sterling example of Mormon womanhood ever."

Giselle went into the kitchen to mix up her sugar-free pink lemonade electrolyte booster, then cut ham and cheese into cubes to snack on before going to church. "*Technically,* I am."

"With your mouth? And your penchant for killing hitmen?"

She went into the living room to eat and Sebastian put the movie on pause. So. He wanted to actually . . . talk? And he'd downed nearly a whole bottle of wine; he must have as much on his mind as she had on hers.

"You know as well as I do that cursing and killing in self-defense wouldn't keep me from being able to go to the temple if I wanted to."

"I'm pretty sure threatening to kill a man in cold blood would get you that excommunication you've been bucking for for the last couple of years."

"Threatening and doing—two different things."

"That's rich, coming from a woman who's never made a threat she hasn't carried out."

"Okay, look. Say I go to the bishop and say, 'Ready to go to the temple now' and he whips out the list of questions. I can answer every single one honestly. I pay my tithing. I don't drink, don't smoke, don't do drugs. I'm honest, I believe in Christ, I don't batter my spouse—"

Sebastian laughed.

"—I support the prophet. I'm still a virgin and I'm thirty-five. I'd say that's a pretty decent track record and oh, guess what? Instant temple recommend. And there I go, off to St. Louis or Nauvoo or wherever and make my covenants with the Lord. My mom would be so proud."

"You forgot that general and all-encompassing unresolved issues question."

"I have no unresolved issues. Just because I'm not exactly, you know, leadership material doesn't mean I don't qualify as a Good Girl. And what do you mean, bucking for an excommunication?"

"You know exactly what I mean. Your opinions'll get you in trouble faster than murdering Fen will."

True. Giselle had always been different; she knew it, everybody at church knew it. She garnered respect and friendships across various social strata in the ward, but everyone knew she'd eventually say or do something scandalous because she managed to do it with amazing regularity—usually without meaning to.

"I don't spout false doctrine."

Sebastian grunted. "No, I know you don't. Your problem is you're as attracted to the profane as you are the sacred. You can't bring yourself to pick one and stick with it, so you straddle the fence between them." She fidgeted at his usual perception. "As far as I can see, there's no reward in sticking with the sacred. So tell me something: Would you tell your bishop why all the double-A batteries in this house disappear so fast?"

Heat rose in her cheeks. "Digital camera, asshole."

Sebastian smirked. "So *technically*, you aren't. He'd laugh you out of his office with a 'Stop doing that and come back to see me again in six months.' Speaking of that, buy your own batteries or do it the old fashioned way 'cause I'm not supporting your habit anymore. And oh, let's not forget your *pièce de résistance*. Would you tell him about *that?*"

Something had changed inside Giselle once she'd turned that corner into territory that few people would understand. She had killed—and she felt absolutely no remorse.

"No," she admitted. "'Specially after what happened to Knox."

"Well. That's apples and oranges, but I see your point. And do you actually plan on going to the temple?"

"I would never go alone," she murmured, looking down into her glass at the pink concoction she drank by the quart. "If I happened to find a dude I liked who could marry me in the temple, I'd go then."

Sebastian snorted. "You aren't going to find Hank Rearden at church." Hank

Rearden, the fictional narrator of a political fable by a fringe political philosopher. Patheticpatheticpathetic.

"I'm not holding out any hope, no. But I'm not cluttering up my life with a string of almosts and maybes and potentials, and I'm not interested in random fucking. If I can't have exactly what I want, I'll go without." She paused when she caught his upraised eyebrow and slid down into the upholstery. "Mostly," she grumbled.

"If your collection of erotica is anything to go by, you don't know what the hell you want. Some of that shit's not so fun when you try it and the rest of it's just not worth the trouble. Ask me how I know."

She was too old and too honest with herself to say that she was still *technically* a virgin because it was what she'd been taught all her life: No sex before marriage. Don't put oneself in temptation's way. Avoid the appearance of evil. Marriage to a worthy member of the priesthood—

—in the temple, where the words "'til death do you part" were not part of the ceremony; marriage was for *eternity*.

Giselle had always wanted that, a good LDS man with a sexually adventurous streak.

Yeah, but how would you know? People lie.

She'd prepared, been obedient, but her childbearing years were fading fast, even as her libido ramped up on her way from thirty-five to forty, and all the while, the pool of desirable Mormon men dwindled to nothing. She personally knew ten other never-married women in the same boat and unless she ran into some smart, educated divorced man or widower (probably looking for a mother for his kids) who might not be thoroughly disgusted by what she'd ask for in bed, she was shit out of luck.

"Quite frankly, Giz, you're not going to find Rearden *outside* the church, either. Quit waiting for—" He waved a hand. "—fantasy man and let me fix you up with somebody. I know half a dozen CEOs who'd fall in love with you, respect you, treat you well. So they aren't members of the church, but they're good men. If you want to get married and have kids before your eggs dry up, you're going to have to figure out what you'll give up for it. Forget the temple marriage and settle for walking down the aisle like normal people." He chuckled. "Or marry Knox. That'd solve his problem, my problem, *and* yours."

Giselle's lip curled, but she had begun to consider it lately as she got another year older—and a lot more tired.

Tired of going to church and hearing about how to be a better wife and mother, being asked to take on extra tasks because she didn't have a family to take up her time, feeling the outsider *not* because she had unorthodox opinions, but because she was a single woman in a church that was all about family.

"Celibacy's not natural at our age, Giz. We've had this conversation before."

Tired of not having a warm, breathing, naked man in bed with her every night, a man who would understand her and love her in spite of the sharp edges she didn't want dulled, a man who would make all these years of celibacy worth the wait.

Giselle closed her eyes and took a deep, soft breath now that she had a face and a body to go with her yearning—that beautiful man with the burn scars and the magnificent green eyes who exuded sex and power, who had disapproved of her for reasons she didn't know. She remembered his face and wondered how she could be so stupid as to allow herself—*again*—to fantasize about a man who was unavailable to her.

"Okay, out with it. Who is he?"

Damn Sebastian, his eye for detail, his unerring gut instincts. "I— I don't know," she admitted.

"What did he do to you?"

He took my breath away.

She looked down at her scarlet linen skirt and picked at a piece of nonexistent lint. "He was contemptuous of me," she murmured. "I don't know why. It made me mad and then we had an argument and then I— We . . . kissed."

"That's—uh, different," he said finally, surprise heavy in his voice. "You let a strange man in your personal space long enough for him to kiss you?"

She could feel the flush creep back up her face and deepen at the memory of that kiss. She cleared her throat. "Um, well, I— I, uh . . . Actually, I kissed him." Sebastian stared at her as she haltingly told him what happened, his astonishment growing with each word.

"When did this happen?"

"In April. At work. Hale's client."

"So that's why you've been moping around for the past four months like a kicked puppy." She said nothing. "He was contemptuous of you but he wants to fuck you."

"I think so, yes. I don't understand."

"So find out who he is from your boss and ask him."

Her head snapped up, her eyes wide in horror. "Oh, I don't think so. The man dresses more expensively than you do."

Sebastian said nothing to that. She knew he would empathize with any man of wealth beset by women whose interest in him was driven solely by his net worth.

"I can't— There's just no way I could work that out without looking like a whore." *Especially* with that face, which must make it exponentially more difficult for him. "Besides, he made it clear what he thought of me."

"What makes you think he's a Rearden?" Sebastian asked slowly.

"He's a warrior. You can tell. He's bigger than you. He's— The way he looked at me?" She sucked in another deep breath and released it slowly.

Sebastian pursed his lips. "You better be careful with that, Giz. Not many men could throw a woman on the bed, fuck her until she can't walk, make her do exactly what he wants her to do—and then *not* carry that outside the bedroom. Bigger than me, huh? I can pick you up and toss you over my shoulder."

"Yeah, a lot of guys could do that. No one's ever had the balls to try. That's my point."

"No, no *LDS* man has ever had the balls to try. You haven't given anyone else half a chance."

She said nothing else for a moment. There was that other thing—

"He, um . . . he called me Lilith."

"So he knows his art well enough to catch the resemblance."

"That's not the way he meant it, Sebastian. It wasn't a compliment."

He gave a Gallic shrug. "That only means he *definitely* wants to fuck you."

"And that he's pissed about it," she said, trying to be matter-of-fact, to recover her nerves. "It doesn't make any difference. I'm not going to throw myself at a rich man, much less one who doesn't like me."

"Would you fuck him if you got the chance?"

She looked at Sebastian without seeing him, her tongue running over her teeth in thought. Finally, she drew in a deep breath and whispered, "In a heartbeat."

Sebastian's eyes widened and he pulled away from her, blinking. "Giz," he murmured, "that's— Uh— Wow. You're about at the end of your rope, aren't you?"

"Yeah. I am." She glanced at the clock and saw that she should have left fifteen minutes ago.

Sebastian relaxed again, took a sip of his wine, savored it, then lapsed into brooding. Giselle said nothing for a long while, too engrossed in her own thoughts to care much about his, but the lengthening silence finally caught her attention.

"Okay, I spilled my guts to you, but you're the one swilling expensive wine like it's orange juice. What's your problem?"

Sebastian's mouth twitched in thought and he still wouldn't look at her. He took another sip. "Same as yours. I want a family. A wife, kids."

That startled her. "Where's this coming from? You've been a libertine since you decided proselytizing was for the birds halfway through your mission."

"I haven't fucked a woman since Vanessa left. Three years ago."

She knew that; it was downright noteworthy. Possibly worrisome.

"I'm almost forty. I'd like to have someone at my funeral besides you and Knox— provided Fen hasn't managed to kill either of you by then. I don't know. Maybe I'm just getting too old to be that profligate, plus I think I maxed out my condom budget."

Giselle chuckled.

"Ah, I don't even know why I think I could have a relationship that lasts longer than a week and doesn't crumble the minute I get out of bed."

"You were with Vanessa for three months. That's a record for you."

He shrugged. "You notice I didn't beg her to stay or chase after her when it was time for her to go back to school. And I sure as hell wasn't interested in playing house with a twenty-year-old who was in love with someone else anyway."

"Did that bother you?"

"Of course not. I'm an opportunist."

"Was. Talk about *my* celibacy being unnatural."

"Okay, so that makes me *more* pathetic than you are. What am I missing, Giz? I'm not hideous. I'm semi-literate. I have a fairly decent job and I can pay my bills."

She pursed her lips. "For you, it's all about the clothes. You go around in your cutoff jeans seven-eighths nekkid, strutting around like a Parisian peacock without a dime to your name, you're relaxed, funny, having a good time. It *rains* women. I've seen you break out that freight train mojo, French accent optional, and damn, it works like a charm—and it would get any other man thrown in jail for assault. So you pick one or two, fuck 'em, send 'em home, and everybody had a good time.

"But then you put on a suit or a tux, you turn into cool King Midas and everything is Serious. Business. You don't smile or laugh. You rarely speak. You're totally unapproachable. The minute you put on that black suit—you need to find another color, by the way—women become the enemy and Versace is your suit of armor."

"Giz, that's not fair. I never wear Versace."

"You need to find some way to mix the King Midas with the Freight Train, some workable concoction of your multiple personalities. Oh, I know. Buy some khakis."

"Money and sex don't coexist in my brain, Giz. You know that. It's either one or the other and society—society functions—all about money. And I'm sure as hell not thinking about money when I'm up to my eyeballs in burnt umber and beautiful women."

Giselle thought about that a minute. "Well, what about one of your clients? Don't tell me you've not run across one tall, curvy blonde CEO somewhere out there?"

"I'm Satan, remember? The minute a CEO figures out she has to call me to come bail her out, my chances are reduced to less than nil."

She sighed. "If that reputation bothers you so much, stop being so subtle. Stop coddling people, letting them think they're doing all the work and all you're there to do is milk their bank accounts. Every time you go into a company, they see what they want to see—and you let them. You lead them gently to their enlightenment, you don't force them to face their weaknesses head-on, then they think they did it all themselves. You'd never let me get away with that. All *I* ever hear is 'Suck it up, princess.'"

"Well, of course. I don't have time to be your invisible hand. Besides, people who can't face their weaknesses are boring and I refuse to live with a boring woman." He paused. "So are you going to church today or not?"

She sighed. "Not, I guess. I wasn't sure I wanted to go today anyway, so I got Sister Evans to substitute teach for me."

"Why? You like to teach."

Giselle pursed her lips. "This week's topic is the law of chastity." Sebastian gaped at her for a split-second before he burst out laughing. "Me teaching a bunch of married women what does and does not constitute chastity is about as fun as going to church on Mother's Day and being asked to babysit since, you know, I *must* not have anything better to do." She scowled at him. "Shut up. It's not funny."

"Yes it is." He rubbed his eyes with the heels of his palms, still laughing. "Okay, well. Since you're not going to church, come play tennis with me. That ought to make you feel better."

"All right, but put a shirt on. I get tired of wading through the drool you leave in your wake."

"Heh. Cheesecake after?"

"Absolutely not."

"They have the low-carb version now."

"Oh? Well, okay. You're buying."

"I always do."

7: Whosoever Looketh on a Woman

WHEN IS THIS GOING TO END?

Bryce looked at his watch. Ten more minutes of home and family. *Why* had he come to church today?

To purge Giselle Cox.

He closed his eyes and swallowed. He could only hope that the subject of chastity wouldn't rear its ugly head, but the second it crossed his mind, the speaker referenced cleaving unto one's wife. He hadn't cleaved unto any woman in years.

An ache grew like a cancer behind Bryce's breastbone.

Chastity was relatively easy, self-stimulation notwithstanding, when a man had a burnt-to-a-crisp face that made women flinch.

Until *her*, the Chouteau County prosecutor's lover. No flinching there—just raw lust.

Brains. Muscle. Weaponry.

That kiss, the one she'd initiated, the one he'd taken away from her, the one she couldn't control or take back.

Bryce knew what he wanted from a woman. He'd come to terms with it halfway through his marriage, but went mostly without because he wouldn't beg for bad sex. Good thing, too, since Michelle had had a habit of indiscriminately fucking anyone else who appealed to her.

He looked around at the chapel, which was not that different from the one he and his family had attended when they lived just a couple of miles away, across the Missouri-Kansas state line in Mission Hills. Fundamentally identical to any Mormon church building, it was comfortable and spartan in its bland décor with no crosses or crucifixes. No distractions.

Bryce hadn't set foot in one but a few times since the fire. Had he expected anything to change in the past five years?

He bowed his head for the closing prayer, feeling nothing but bitterness and anger at the abandonment of a God he'd served so faithfully for over three decades.

He'd subverted his nature and quelled his base desires.

He'd followed church teachings to the best of his ability, all the while ignoring philosophies that called to his intellect.

He'd fulfilled his father's expectations as a good and righteous priesthood holder in the Church of Jesus Christ of Latter-day Saints—

—and spent every day of it in absolute misery.

He should have listened to his best friend, his college roommate, the only person who had ever told him the truth.

"You don't want Michelle! You're marrying her because your father bought her act and you're going along with his program—as usual. She's lying to you."

"I think I'd have been able to figure that out by now."

"You're too invested in being pure and righteous to give a shit. What you are is pressured. The minute you got off the plane from your mission, your dad started in on you, hammering you to find a nice girl to take to the temple. Well, I'm here to tell you, pal—Michelle. Ain't. It."

"There's nothing wrong with her."

"Oh, other than that she's a promiscuous, manipulative, deceitful cunt?"

"She's not a c— That's not true."

"Cunt, Bryce. Say it. For once in your life, call it what it is. Cunt."

Bryce said nothing, but he felt sick to his stomach for even hearing it, much less that his best friend had said it—about his fiancée.

"Don't you walk away from me. Someone has to give you the facts of life and I'm designating myself the official bad guy. Your father is too damned myopic to see her for what she is. Great guy, your dad, but unbelievably naïve."

Bryce's mind had tied itself in a knot by this time and his soul hurt. *"You have never been able to back up what you say about her."*

"You know what? You're exactly right. So let's talk about you instead. I notice the women you like to talk to: Smart. Edgy. I notice the type of women who catch your eye: Muscular. Solid. A woman you can throw at a bed and fuck. Hard."

Bryce stared at him, shocked. *"I can't believe you said that."*

"Oh, what? That I actually noticed it or that I called you on it? You're not exactly the mild-mannered and slow'n'easy type of guy. Peter Priesthood? Not you. You play football like a savage. No one on campus will play racquetball with you anymore. You've publicly humiliated more than

one of your professors and then forced them to defend the grades they gave you in retaliation."

Bryce didn't see himself that way. The man his best friend had described was . . . horrible. Not a nice guy. Totally not worthy of holding the priesthood.

"But get you to church or with your dad and your spine melts. You just can't admit that the women you like are the ones who'll go toe to toe with you intellectually and make you work to get them backed in a corner—and then you go in for the kill every single time. Funny thing? They like it. They come back for more, stronger, better, to throw it right back at you and the harder you have to work, the more you like it. They probably like sex that way, too. I'll bet you've wondered more than once what it'd be like to slam one of those women up against a wall and fuck her."

Bryce couldn't breathe. How had he known? He fought those images constantly, the ones that came to him unbidden when in the company of women he found smart and . . . a little dangerous. He wrestled with those temptations and had gone so far as to stop talking to women he'd thought about in that way. He knew he couldn't resist them if he spent any time with them, especially the brunette starlet who'd propositioned him with an explicit description she must have pulled straight out of his fantasies.

He gulped at that memory, at his desires, at his shame—because he'd had to stop and think about whether he wanted to say no or not.

"That's who you are. Accept it, grab it, enjoy the hell out of it, go on with your life. There is no reason for you to deny who you are. You can still go to church and be a good person. The church doesn't care how you like sex as long as you're faithful to your wife. Face up to who you are and what you want, find a woman who wants the same things you want, who can match you in brains and in bed and you'll be just fine. There is no sin in that."

"No, I— That's not me. That's not who I want to be."

"You're never going to be your dad and there's nothing wrong with that. Fuck him if he can't appreciate you for who you are."

Bryce's jaw ground and his hands clenched as he fought the urge to plow his fist in his roommate's face.

"Gah. Fine. Whatever. Go ahead and marry Michelle. I'll support you, I'll be your best man, and I'll never speak of it again once the vows are said. But I'm telling you now, you're lying to yourself. Even if Michelle isn't what I think she is and you have a nice, quiet little life together, it'll still be the worst mistake you ever make—and you'll live with it every single miserable day, wondering what else you could've had if you'd had an ounce of common sense and half that much courage."

Bryce bent over and buried his head in his hands, shuddering from the agony of that conversation ringing through his head even after twenty years. Recalling it was a fairly frequent ritual by now.

Now, on top of everything else, he lived with the anger and bitterness of a disillusioned zealot: the irreconcilable differences between what he wanted and what his father had expected of him; Michelle's infidelity and public piety; Michelle's war of manipulation and deceit against which he had no defenses—

—and most especially the deaths of his four children and in such a catastrophic manner.

Bryce had no place in these pews.

Yet . . .

This was his cultural identity, a good portion of his own identity and what made him him. This church, this lifestyle, was all he'd ever known, all he'd ever wanted to know. He'd done everything asked of him, but now he felt empty, abandoned, unloved—and had since the week after he'd walked out of the San Diego temple at twenty-four a married man.

Bryce went home after sacrament meeting unable to stomach any more.

Nobody had approached him to say hello. He'd attracted some glances, but mostly of the preoccupied type, as if they had so much on their minds that they didn't see him. He understood that. He remembered those days, his years as a lay clergyman on the fast track to bishop, when Sunday meant meetings from dawn until dusk, when he had had too much to think about to welcome new people. He didn't want to have to introduce himself and then explain where he came from and his presence there.

The few people he recognized hadn't recognized him. He didn't mind. He didn't want to have to talk about where his family went, what happened to his face.

As for the people who had noticed him and shied away, he couldn't judge them any more harshly than anybody else, since he had that effect on everybody—

—but one.

Miss Giselle Cox.

Knox Hilliard's lover.

Who had made herself very clear about what she wanted from him, what she knew he could give her.

He'd never known temptation like her, not even as a young man. He *lusted* after her and his breath shortened at the thought of her body, naked under his, what he wanted to do to her, what he wanted her to do to him.

He wondered if could bury his pride enough to pursue her, to seduce her away from her lover. Bryce didn't care that she obviously had a great deal of experience; he minded that her experience included Knox Hilliard.

No, he decided, he did *not* want to go where Hilliard had been.

8: Greedy Enemy of the State

G ISELLE AND SEBASTIAN SAT AT THE CONFERENCE TABLE, GISELLE STUDYING and Sebastian tapping away on his laptop. Fox News blared in the background. Knox came through the front door and up the four steps to the conference room, dumping his briefcase and computer on the table. He, too, sat down to work without a word.

"Feds finally decide you didn't kill Leah?" Sebastian muttered after a while.

Knox grunted. "Don't even know why they bother investigating me anymore for anything. Over a year. Waste of taxpayer money."

"Breaking news this afternoon from Kansas City, Missouri. OKH Enterprises CEO Fen Hilliard has announced the formation of an exploratory committee for a possible run for the Senate seat that will be vacated at the end of this term—"

All three of them turned toward the TV and gaped. Giselle's breath caught in her throat and she felt the blood drain from her face. Knox dropped his head in his hands.

"You have got to be kidding me," Sebastian whispered, eyes wide. "FUCK!" he roared, slamming his hands on the table as he got up and started to pace, his hand rubbing his mouth. "I gotta go make some calls," he muttered finally, his long legs eating up the distance from the dining room to his office. Giselle winced when the door slammed.

She and Knox traded sober glances. Fen had put Sebastian in check brilliantly, thus setting Knox and Giselle back in play if he decided to call Giselle's bluff. Giselle never bluffed. Though she dreaded the consequences of taking Fen's life, she would see it done.

"Murder doesn't wash clean, Giselle," Knox offered softly, reading her expression with the ease of a lifetime spent together.

She looked away, biting her bottom lip, nauseated.

> *"Should Democrat Fen Hilliard win the seat, he will tip the balance of power in the Senate. Some on Wall Street speculate that he would bring the necessary leverage to pass legislation that would force his nephew, financier Sebastian Taight, to cease his takeover of OKH Enterprises. How such legislation might impact the financial landscape is unknown at this time.*
>
> *"Taight, infamous for his Fix-or-Raid policy, has been accused by various corporate executives and members of Congress of deliberately sabotaging companies that have hired his services. Though no fault has been found in various audits across the spectrum of companies Taight has taken over, a Hilliard win in the Senate could trigger long-anticipated hearings on Capitol Hill to call Taight to answer these allegations and account for his business practices.*
>
> *"On a related note, another of Hilliard's nephews, Knox Hilliard, Chouteau County, Missouri prosecutor and heir to OKH Enterprises, was only recently cleared of last year's murder of his bride. No other suspects are in custody at this time, but investigations into the allegations of corruption in his office are ongoing."*

Knox snorted. "They make us sound like a couple of thugs."

The office door flew open and Sebastian was even more angry. "Gets worse," he snapped, leaning over the table toward Knox. "Kenard's on the guest list for the fundraiser next month."

Knox paled underneath his perpetual tan and he wiped his hand down his face.

"This is what's going to happen," Sebastian said. He took up pacing again, his hands on his hips and the expression he got when he had to churn through thousands of possibilities to deal with a problem. "You— Giselle—" She started, but he went on. "You are going to go to that fundraiser with me next month and if Kenard shows up, you are going to keep him away from Fen. I'll attempt to keep Fen away from Kenard."

"Are you out of your fucking mind?" Knox demanded.

Sebastian stopped and stared at him, an eyebrow cocked wickedly. "Are you concerned for Fen's life or that—Bonus!—Kenard will *love* her?"

Knox looked at him stonily.

Sebastian smirked. "That's what I thought."

"Okay," Giselle said, "I missed the boat. Who is this person and what am I supposed to do with him and why am I doing it and why doesn't Knox want me to?"

"Bryce Kenard," Sebastian explained, "is the most powerful tort lawyer in Kansas City. Possibly in the Midwest. He's filthy rich—like, maybe he has a couple bucks more or less than I do—and he has influence. He keeps his politics to himself, and for Fen to court him means that he can't come up with enough campaign money from amongst his cronies. Kenard's support could be the difference between his running for Senate and not. Giselle," he continued, his tone urgent, "it is *imperative* that you keep him away from Fen. If Fen doesn't get Kenard's support that night, he'll have to work that much harder to drum up the kind of cash Kenard could give him."

"That makes no sense. Why couldn't he get it any other time?"

"Kenard gives people one chance to pitch ideas at him. If they don't get him in the first thirty seconds, they don't get him at all. You know Fen likes to put on a show and he'll think that'll impress the hell out of him without having to say a word."

"Okay. What am I supposed to do with him?"

"All you have to do is be yourself," Knox mumbled. "He's brilliant and he likes nothing more than erudite conversation."

"Your job is to lead him away from Fen—preferably out of sight and as far away from the party as possible—and fuck his mind. He'll forget everything else but you and Fen will know that he was singularly unimpressed."

"I don't like this idea," Knox pronounced.

"Of course you don't," Sebastian snapped. "Pee on her leg before she leaves for the party, whydontcha?"

Giselle looked at Sebastian. "Why is Knox being pissy?"

Sebastian looked at Knox and smirked. "Ask him. If he tells you the truth, I'll give you three months' rent free."

She looked at Knox, who sat stone-faced. "Well?"

At which point, Knox whipped out his checkbook and wrote a check to Sebastian for three months of her rent. Sebastian howled and Giselle decided she didn't care why Knox was upset; she'd take the money and keep her curiosity to herself.

Once Sebastian had calmed down enough to get back to business, he leaned across the table and got right in her face. "This is very important. You must have scared Fen enough to get him to back off you two, but now he's coming after me. There's just too much anti-Taight sentiment on Capitol Hill. He could easily get me shut down—and he'd most definitely be able to haul my ass in front of the Senate. Wouldn't Fen love to have me and Knox sitting at a table in front of him and the nation, grilling us like we were teenagers again." He dug a credit card out of his wallet and flipped it at her. "Go get a dress. Make sure you have cleavage."

9: Margaretha Zelle

"VERY NICE," SEBASTIAN DRAWLED WITH APPRECIATION WHEN GISELLE emerged from her bedroom on the evening of Fen's exploratory fundraiser. The strapless dress, reminiscent of 1950s Hollywood glamor, had two layers. The pencil underskirt of white brocade was beaded and sequined along the edges of its floral motif and the hem just kissed the toes of her black sling-back heels. A long slit up the right side allowed Giselle her full stride and relatively quick access to the gun strapped around her thigh without marring the skirt's narrow lines.

The full black silk taffeta overskirt had a slight train. The front of it parted in an A shape from waist to floor and flared out like a cape when she walked. It framed the white underskirt with stark elegance. A small decorative pouch hung from an inconspicuous strap on the inside of the skirt to function as a pocket or, should she care to wear it on her wrist, a reticule.

Above her skirts, a lightly silver-embroidered and jet-beaded black velvet corset hugged her torso well enough to guarantee that just the right amount of bosom blossomed over its top so as to tease without being vulgar.

She'd dressed her hair in a modified, messy chic Gibson girl style. A diamond and ruby bracelet, borrowed from Sebastian's mother, sparkled loosely on her wrist and Giselle's own diamond earrings dangled from her earlobes.

"Rubies," Sebastian said once he'd carefully assessed the details of her presentation. "Wear your ruby drops. Are you sure about going strapless?"

Giselle glanced down at the puckered indentation in the soft hollow just under her left shoulder. "Fen needs to see it so he can commence kissing my ass."

"Make sure you don't let Kenard wheedle the story out of you."

"Pffftt."

"I've heard he's clever like that."

Once she'd changed her earrings, Sebastian held out a white mink bolero jacket for her, also borrowed from his mother.

"This is what you need to know," Sebastian told her in the limo on their way to the Nelson-Atkins Museum of Art. "Kenard's a widower. He's an honorable man and a consummate gentleman. He's also a member of the church—"

"Really?" Giselle perked up, suddenly a lot more interested in this project.

"Don't. He's apparently one of those super-strict letter-of-the-law Pharisee types. You know, the kind you don't like, *and* he was on the fast track to bishop before his wife died. He won't appreciate any seriously heavy flirting—not that you know how to do that anyway. Talk about philosophy, art, literature, music. If you end up talking about the church, keep your heresies and sacrilege to yourself. No profanity. Whatever you do, do *not* talk about politics. Don't give him any reason to ditch you and go back to the party. If he shows up, it's because he thinks Fen is an honorable man and he's seen no evidence to the contrary. Don't begrudge him that."

"What's Knox's problem with him?"

Sebastian slid her a look. "He paid your rent, so he must not want you to know."

"Yeah, that was *his* transaction. This is *yours*. Two completely different obligations."

Sebastian laughed. "I really am a bad influence on you. Knox and Kenard have history that involves Kenard's late wife and they haven't spoken in ten, twelve years. Something like that. Either Kenard didn't want to face reality or he didn't get the memo about Knox's taste in women."

"Which does not include married ones."

"Better. Young married anorexic blonde ones."

"Ooh. Four strikes, he's out."

"I don't know anything other than what I've told you, but there's probably a lot more to the story. Knox is pretty tight-lipped about him."

No wonder he had reacted so vehemently to this little scheme. There were few things Knox wouldn't share with her, but if he didn't, it had hurt badly enough that he'd buried it. Once Knox buried his pain, he didn't dig it up if he could help it.

"I haven't felt inclined to socialize or do any business with him because of that. I've seen him around here and there, but I've never met him."

She looked out the window, her fist clenched between her mouth and the cold glass.

"Hey, Giz." Sebastian snapped his fingers in front of her face. "Do what I told you to do and don't let your outrage on Knox's behalf get in the way. Shit, I shouldn't have said anything at all, 'cause now you'll wear it on your sleeve and fuck it all up."

She sighed, unable to deny the probability of that. "I'll try."

The limousine came to a halt in front of the art gallery's great wrought iron doors festooned with enormous lit Christmas wreaths, their windows aglow with the lights of a grand party. Sebastian swept her into the building and checked her jacket.

Kirkwood Hall, the heart of the gallery, was marble-clad, four stories high, and punctuated by twelve enormous marble columns. In the center of the hall stood a twenty-foot Christmas tree decorated with white lights, enormous silver and gold glass balls, and red velveteen ribbon. To their right lay the Rozzelle Court restaurant, a faithful replica of a fifteenth century Italian villa courtyard. Inside, a catering service had prepared a feast of hors d'oeuvres. In the open gallery above the courtyard, a chamber orchestra played Christmas carols.

Many important people milled about, all dressed in high fashion, all vying for attention. Giselle wasn't particularly impressed, considering she had arrived with King Midas. The place echoed with the sounds of titters and guffaws, murmurs and bluster, and the click-clack of women's heels.

"So, where is he?"

"I don't see him. It's possible he won't show. Let's go find Fen." She trembled.

"Make nice, now, Giz," Sebastian murmured. "You hurt his feelings at Thanksgiving this year, ignoring him like you did. You were downright rude about it, too."

"Oh, fuck him. I haven't heard any apologies coming my way, and until I do, he's not funny." After wandering a bit, they found him almost where they came in, going from one cluster of chatting people to the next, shaking hands, laughing, introducing Trudy. Giselle had to admit that Fen was a handsome man, as tall as Knox, his near-white hair coiffed with refined elegance, his face pleasingly carved, his nose perfectly straight and patrician. Incredibly fit, he wore his tuxedo with aplomb. Charismatic, generous, and blessed with a silver tongue, he was the perfect picture of a senatorial candidate and cameras adored him. He turned the heads of women a fraction his age.

Knox would look exactly like Fen in twenty years, a true Hilliard but for the blond hair and blue eyes Trudy had given him. Not for the first time, Giselle wondered if Fen was Knox's father, but she said nothing. The three of them had worn that topic out years ago.

Knox's mother was exquisite as usual, her blonde hair swept up in a chic knot and her slim figure wrapped in a mint silk ruched gown that had a few too many ruffles for Giselle's taste. She resisted the urge to rip one or two of them off to streamline the damn thing, but as she and Sebastian drew closer to Fen and Trudy, she contented herself with one disparaging glance down her aunt's body.

Giselle curled her lip slightly, just enough for Trudy to see her contempt, and Trudy clenched one fist at her side, as if she wanted to hit Giselle. It wasn't as if she hadn't before, but now Giselle wasn't an awkward thirteen-year-old slavishly devoted to earning the approval of her beautiful aunt, and Giselle raised an eyebrow, daring her to say a word. Trudy looked away.

"Ah, Sebastian, Giselle." Fen greeted them expansively, as if he hadn't tried to kill Giselle twice and threatened Sebastian with a seat in front of a Senate panel. "So glad to see you here. I didn't realize you would be interested or I would have invited you myself."

"I'm always intrigued when the CEO of a company I have a controlling interest in decides to run for Congress."

"Come, come, Sebastian. I'm sure nothing will change for you when I win a Senate seat." His voice held the slightest hint of a threat, detectable only to people who knew him very well. "Giselle," he murmured, taking her hand and kissing it. "How are you?"

"I'm just fine, thanks; haven't seen any goons lurking around corners lately." She smiled sweetly.

Fen leaned toward her. "You just can't help getting your digs in, can you?" he gritted, his mouth locked into a grin. "One of these days, I'm going to slap the teeth right out of your smart mouth, little girl."

She turned her head so that she could whisper in his ear. "Aw, I *did* hurt your wittow feewings."

He drew away from her slowly, still in candidate mode, all four of them still smiling. His gaze caught on her shoulder then and he sucked in a breath. When he swallowed, Giselle chuckled and a faint flush rose in his cheeks.

"Is that remorse I see, Unk?" Sebastian drawled. "And you didn't even send her a get-well card."

Fen's jaw clenched behind his smile. "Move along, you two. I don't want to babysit you all night, particularly since you insist on acting like children. I'd prefer you leave altogether."

"No can do, Fen," Sebastian replied with an entirely fake chuckle. "We're just here to eat your food, drink your booze, and be a general pain in your ass."

"As usual."

They left him there fuming. Giselle still chuckled, but Sebastian's body radiated tension and his muscular arm felt like wool-and-silk-covered cast iron under her hand. He picked up a glass of champagne from a passing waiter's tray and downed it in one swallow.

"I gotta figure out how to get out from under Fen's thumb," he muttered. "Remember when he caught you, me, and Knox blowing up frogs with the bike pump when we were kids? And threatened to tell my dad? I feel like that right now."

"I've been thinking about this since he announced last month," Giselle murmured, disengaging from him to snag a waiter to request ice water. Sebastian looked down at her, his eyebrow cocked, waiting. "It's a threefer. First, you need to block as much of Fen's fundraising as possible, like tonight. I'm sure all your friends feel just as threatened by whatever Fen plans to do to you."

"Already done. Next?"

"You need a Truman."

He stuck his tongue in his cheek. "Raise up a rival candidate. Wouldn't that be hilarious? Senator from Taight—but I'd rather not back a Democrat if I can avoid it."

"Kevin Oakley."

Sebastian started, his eyes widening. "Isn't he the prosecutor who decided you'd done him a favor by taking out the assholes who shot you?"

"Yes, he is and there are rumors around school he's itching to get on with the next step in his career. He and Knox are friends, so there's your in with him."

Sebastian rocked back on his heels, his hands behind his back, and stared off into the distance.

"And did you read the *National Review* article I left on the conference table?" At his absent nod, she said, "The one on intellectual property rights? Byline Justice McKinley?"

"Yes, and it gave me some ideas on a few tech pies I could put my fingers in. I googled her, read some of the stuff she's been writing on some of the smaller conservative blogs. She's like a baby Thomas Sowell."

"Baby's about right. She's twenty-three."

"How do you know?"

"I go to school with her, that's how I know." Giselle kept the other little piece of information concerning Justice McKinley to herself for now, since Knox still refused to talk about that. "She's a regular little political prodigy, all strict constructionist pro-life *atheist*. People are starting to listen to her and talk about her and—" Giselle couldn't help a wicked chuckle. "—she's tying the religious right up in knots."

"Shit. I could barely spell my name when I was twenty-three, but now that you mention it, she is a bit irrationally exuberant."

Giselle chuckled, then continued, "My thinking is if Kevin could speak with her, they may be able to help each other further their own careers. He's not quite her brand of politician, but she won't be happy until Thomas Jefferson rises from the dead."

Sebastian pursed his lips. "Even if he wins, he'll be powerless to help me. Fen has no such problems because he wants my head more than the rest of the looters and he's the only one who can actually deliver it via the SEC. He'll have instant clout."

"All Oakley needs to do is give Fen a good fight. The Senate's not going to want to yank your chain too soon and show its hand if there's a good chance Fen'll lose the election. It'll buy you enough time to get through the transfer or takeover of OKH.

"After that, if you do end up sitting in front of Fen and his newfound senatorial friends, it'll be a whole different fight that you can win on your terms without the distraction of OKH or the threat of the SEC, especially considering your attorney— you know, that *poor* young man who was cheated of his rightful inheritance on his wedding day when his bride-equipped-with-child was tragically and mysteriously murdered. That evil Fen Hilliard, just like OJ Simpson. Ya know he did it, but the glove doesn't fit."

Sebastian actually smiled in public, which made Giselle blink. "Go on, Giz," he muttered over another glass of champagne. "I've always admired your deadpan delivery."

"The trick is when Kevin should announce his intentions. Fen needs to get comfy and spend a bunch of whatever cash he manages to scrounge up. Once Kevin announces and it becomes known that you're backing him, Fen's going to have a hard time replenishing whatever he spends because nobody's going to want to throw good money after bad.

"Third. When reporters start calling you for comments on Senator Oth's anti-Taight bitterness, refer them to Knox. He can hem and haw like the good ol' boy redneck he pretends to be—now, y'all know this is off the record, mind—mumble a few things about how he doan know nuttin' 'bout nuttin', but seems to him maybe Oth either wasn't a very good businessman—and what does that say about his leadership in the Senate?—or Taight caught him with his hand in his employees' cookie jar. Oopsie. Maybe compare Jep Industries to Enron, Tyco in passing. Jep employees lost their jobs, yeah, but that Taight, you know, he made sure they got to take their 401(k)s with 'em. That should make that rabid skunk back off and Knox could make you look like a martyr once he gets through working that shucks-n-p'shaw mojo he uses on his juries.

"You can*not* get into a full-on war with Oth while Fen's in the picture, but you do need to get him to quit riding you. The publicity is what's going to kill you if you don't answer it. Kevin can make Fen retreat and Knox can make Oth shut up. Once Oth is questioned, the deal you made with Hollander Steelworks will come out. You'll end up being the sainted hero and savior of the pensions and jobs of twelve hundred people—not to mention what it'll do for Hollander. Between Kevin and Knox, you should be able to stay out of Washington for the next three years until after OKH is no longer an issue. If it doesn't work all the way through Knox's fortieth, hire a Washington-savvy publicist to take you the rest of the way."

Sebastian stared at her without speaking for a while. "Bless your little politico heart, Giz," he said slowly. "You *do* come in handy occasionally."

Giselle took the opportunity to preen a bit. She very rarely impressed Sebastian because he expected her to function on his level all the time. She continued,

"The only downside of that is if it makes Fen feel totally irrelevant—which it very well could—he may go off his rocker and three years is long enough for him to devolve back to primordial ooze. I wouldn't put it past him to do something devastating to me, Knox, you—or all three of us—if he thinks he's going to lose everything any which way he looks at it. He's already gotten somewhat unpredictable and that makes me nervous. He has a taste for killing when he can't get his way and the fact that we can't prove anything only feeds his arrogance."

Sebastian grunted. "I trust the next time he tries to kill you, you'll find him up in Chouteau County somewhere and put him out of our misery."

"I plan to, but that might wreck my newfound ambitions if it comes to light."

"What newfound ambitions?"

She didn't bother to suppress a nasty snicker. "One of the Jackson County APs, Craig Wells, the one who wanted to throw me under a bus to cut his teeth on Knox? He's been sniffing around Oakley's job."

"Knox says he's been sniffing around your leathers."

"Oh, good heavens, yes. A codpiece would be less obvious than his hard-on. He just magically happens to show up places I hang out, like the law library and the grocery store. He never talks to me, pretends he doesn't see me, but really. How stupid do you have to be to stalk a woman who you know for a fact carries a nine-mil and uses it? I've considered kicking his ass just for daring to think about me nekkid, but I'm not sure Kevin would forgive me for that. So my little revenge fantasies have morphed into a run for Jackson County prosecutor as a possible career move some time in the distant future once I've got some serious time in a courtroom under my belt."

"Yesterday I would've mocked you for that. Today, not so much. You going to have Knox train you?"

"Please. Which one of us do you think would end up dead first? I've had quite enough of Professor Shit-for-Brains, thankyouverymuch. I don't know what curve he grades me on but it isn't the one he uses for the rest of the class."

"You got him back for it on his student evaluations last year. He was pissed."

"Did he think I'd sit still for that?"

"Apparently so."

She huffed.

"Well, thank you, Giz. Sometimes I forget just how damned smart you are."

"I noticed," she muttered.

He paused to think, but his attention caught elsewhere. "Oh, damn. I almost forgot why we're here. There's Kenard," he said, turning toward the south end of the hall where there were more clusters of people chatting. "He's the man with the burn scars on the left side of his face."

10: Mine

BRYCE HADN'T WANTED TO COME TO THIS THING, ESPECIALLY CONSIDERING how he felt about Fen Hilliard and what he suspected about the man's involvement in Leah's murder, but curiosity won out. He'd spent every other weekend the past two months playing golf with Fen and various other business leaders about town just to see how Fen played chess.

Fen had treated Bryce like an old friend without once mentioning his campaign. He was likable, suave, and not in the least bit slick or smarmy. No hint of good ol' boy politics. Not a whiff of courtship. He had his act down cold and Bryce could appreciate Fen's patience, shrewd strategy, and forethought.

In all that time, however, Bryce hadn't said much, preferring to listen instead, to observe Fen's modus operandi, to wait for the thirty-second pitch that never came. Even the invitation to this little get-together had no hint of political purpose in it, but Bryce laughed when the courier delivered it. So. This was the thirty-second pitch.

At least now he knew Fen intended to carry his personal philosophy of philanthropy right on into Congress with him and Bryce had no intention of backing that with either his checkbook or his influence. Giving away money as a private citizen or a corporation was Bryce's idea of generosity of spirit and community service. Using taxpayer money to do it was bullshit.

In addition, though Bryce didn't know Sebastian Taight personally, he definitely didn't like the witch hunt Fen's announcement had triggered. It would've happened eventually, but if Taight went down, half the extraordinarily successful entrepreneurs in the country would go down with him. That didn't bode well for anyone, not to mention what it would do to the economy.

Fen's campaign had less to do with political ambition and a need to protect the public from rampaging capitalist pigs, but more to do with Taight's takeover of OKH. Bryce wouldn't trust Fen Hilliard to hold his nine-iron for him.

Bryce sighed as he returned to nursing his Perrier, disengaged from the people who had clumped around him. The company he kept at these inane functions was the most amusing he could find, but some evenings, like tonight, that didn't say much. Bored out of his mind, he wondered if this was preferable to knocking around a dark, silent, empty house at Christmas time.

Absorbed in watching the play of light on the surface of his sparkling water, Bryce thought he saw a head of honey-colored hair in his periphery and his gut clenched.

Only one person he had ever met had hair that color, subtle in its blondeness and its redness at the same time. No hairdresser, no matter how talented or expensive, could duplicate the complicated highlights of commingling blonde and red strands.

He turned and looked for her, unable to credit that *she* might be here. His breath caught in his throat when he saw her. When she turned a bit, he realized that she went about on Sebastian Taight's arm and a pain struck him behind his sternum as she chatted amiably—almost familiarly—with Fen and Trudy Hilliard.

First Knox, then Taight and the rest of the Hilliards. It stood to reason that if she was fucking Knox, she would know Taight and definitely Knox's mother—but what kind of typist and law student had these kinds of connections? He knew no one in society by the name of Cox or who had ties to a Cox family.

Bryce drank in her appearance more fully, able to take his time and notice small details that pleased but did not surprise him. She had such an air of understated elegance, he had to wonder if she had a gun strapped to her thigh.

Her black and white dress showed off her pale shoulders to exquisite advantage and gave her hair a subtle brilliance. He liked the red earrings.

The slight plump of her breasts above the black corset caught his attention. His mind filled with images of them bare, flushed with passion, her nipples begging him to lick and suck them. He drew in a sharp breath and his erection strained against his fly. She turned away from him then and he studied the delineation of well-developed muscles in her arms and upper back. He remembered her legs the night of Leah's visitation.

Collier's *Lilith* was soft, round, lush.

Giselle Cox was most definitely not.

I notice the type of women who catch your eye: Muscular. Solid. A woman you can throw at a bed and fuck. Hard.

Brilliant woman . . . She'll be a good trial attorney. Enough ego and charm to pull anything off and the brains and wit to back it up.

I notice the women you like to talk to: Smart. Edgy.

I assure you: You have never met a woman like me, and you never will again.

Taight led Miss Cox away from the Hilliards and she strolled about on his arm for a moment before they came to an abrupt halt. She began to talk and gesture, a highball glass of something clear over ice in one hand, while Taight listened intently. He sipped at his champagne, never taking his eyes off her, then he grinned at her. She returned it, but began to speak again and did so at some length. Taight's expression gradually transformed from amusement to— Respect?

He wondered what Giselle Cox could possibly have to say that would have a notorious and semi-reclusive billionaire's rapt attention. Taight very rarely attended society events and if he did deign to grace an affair with his presence, he mingled very little. He rarely spoke and he never showed any emotion.

Taight's presence at a party for a man he had declared war upon, a woman on his arm, and his uncharacteristic public display of humor—incredible. Quite a few of the gathered shot intermittent glances at the pair, no less intrigued than Bryce.

And her! No anger tonight, no rage. Just amusement. He remembered her clumsy attempt at flirting, her straightforward charm, her obvious hope for him to ask her out—possibly more. He'd insulted her and her anger had resurfaced. He'd kissed her and she'd sunk into desire. He'd called her out and flustered her. Her moods swung wildly and she made no effort to hide them.

He could only see Miss Cox in profile, but he could read her amazingly expressive face from where he stood. She smirked once at something Taight muttered, and though she didn't show any other overt signs of humor, Bryce could feel her amusement in palpable waves across the distance between them and pulse through his body. Whatever she said had been funny enough to make Taight nearly laugh and Bryce heard one woman actually gasp.

Jealousy, hot and vicious, seized his gut and his lip curled. Knox Hilliard knew her intimately. Sebastian Taight treated her as an equal, though not as a lover—at least, not as Bryce would have treated a lover—or would have treated *her* if she were *his* lover.

What did a second-shift transcriptionist and over-age student have to offer that she could capture two brilliant men's attention? All his adult life, he'd known women who craved attention and did anything they could to get it. He knew when a woman faked obliviousness to attract more attention. Giselle Cox, absorbed in her conversation with Taight, either hadn't noticed the attention they garnered or didn't care.

She had Bryce tied in knots, a room full of men watching her with speculation, and a room full of women studying her as if to learn something.

A lovely peal of laughter rang out from her vicinity and Bryce looked up from her breasts to find himself staring into those ice blue eyes that seemed so familiar as to be eerie.

She blinked, and held his gaze. She blinked again, but had turned her attention back to Taight with a smile of genuine warmth. As if she hadn't recognized Bryce. No, more than that—as if he didn't exist.

Regret, deep and sharp, joined his jealousy and rode him hard. His jaw ground and he looked back down into his glass. He had blown any chance he might have had with her and he flinched at the way he had dismissed her with such finality. All he'd had to do was ask her out for dinner when she'd begged him to—*before* he'd pissed her off.

One hand stuffed in his pocket, he looked down at the floor and tried for all the world not to let her get to him the way she did.

That kiss. It tormented him, now months after it had happened, but she must have forgotten it. Such a fool. Between Hilliard and Taight, why would she remember Bryce at all?

Bryce looked up again just as Taight bent to murmur something in her ear, then left her standing there, striding away from her and toward the owner of a foundering company. Once alone, her palpable humor vanished. The people who observed this grew puzzled, Bryce no less so.

After a couple of seconds of looking down into her glass, she closed her eyes and breathed deeply, slowly in her nose, then out through the O of her lips. She did that several times, her breasts swelling with each inhalation. His own breath caught in response.

Suddenly he found her looking straight at him again. Deliberately, this time, and she held his gaze. Her mouth—that cherry-kissed mouth with full lips that could probably work miracles on a man's anatomy—twitched. A corner of it turned up; not quite a smile, not quite a smirk.

Oh, no. She hadn't forgotten at all.

Adrenaline surged through him as he returned her stare. The fantasies of his youth, the ones that had tortured him with their wickedness, the ones he'd tried so hard to quell at such great cost, curled around him. The predator in him surged and howled, all traces of regret and jealousy gone. Bryce cocked an eyebrow at her and she acknowledged him with a miniscule shift of her shoulders and lowered eyelids.

Miss Giselle Cox, whoever she was, promised the fulfillment of every one of his long-denied yearnings. She was dangerous—and he knew he'd give up everything he had to have her:

His pride.

His net worth.

His salvation.

She put her glass on a passing waiter's tray, then turned without warning and sashayed, not toward him, but across Kirkwood Hall to Sculpture Hall. She disappeared behind the Christmas tree, then reappeared, her steps slow and studied, her back straight and head high, as if she had all the time in the world and nowhere in particular to go. He watched her progress across the marble floor, deftly and graciously weaving through clumps of chatters without fanfare.

He followed her at some distance through the grand hall, then through the sculpture room that was littered with clusters of chatting people who stilled slightly as she glided by. A couple of men started to follow her but happened to glance up at Bryce; he merely had to raise an eyebrow at their impudence to send them scurrying back to their cliques.

A corner of his mouth turned up, grateful for his scarred face for the first time ever.

Then his eyes narrowed as he tracked her with a hunter's skill. Sebastian Taight had just become mistressless. He'd deal with Knox Hilliard later—and Knox would lose.

Finally she reached the staircase that led down to the Bloch building, the hideous modern addition that marred the landscape and lines of the original gallery. She smoothly descended to the wide landing, but instead of going down the next set of stairs to the new building, she turned right to go up the dimly lit stairs to the European exhibits. Those collections were not on display at this time of day and technically, people were not allowed to go wandering the gallery at will, although they often did.

She unhooked the velvet rope that blocked off that section of the museum, which didn't surprise him. A woman who was so sure of herself that she'd kiss a man she didn't know and then be surprised when it got turned back on her would do exactly what she pleased, regardless of the obstacles.

She stopped then and looked over her shoulder at him, that same not-smile-not-smirk on her face. She raised one eyebrow and deliberately dropped the rope on the floor. He ached in ways he hadn't since before the fire and his breath caught.

Bryce stood transfixed as she ascended the staircase step by deliberate step, her white skirt held in her right hand. Her hips swayed. The short train of her black skirt slithered behind her. Her delicate hand slid up the copper banister and though half the room watched, as riveted as he, no one tried to stop her.

His feet moved of their own accord. He absently excused himself through the crowd, irresistibly drawn after her as if she were Calypso, ensnaring him with his own lust—

—then found himself detained by some policy wonk who not only didn't notice that Bryce had other plans, but felt entitled to the contents of his brain.

Left or right? A few more of the terminally clueless gathered around him. Which way would she go and would he see her with all the people suddenly demanding his attention? How would he find her? His jaw ground at the thought of losing her to the labyrinthine hallways and myriad exhibits because people he didn't know wanted a piece of him.

"Excuse me," he barked, interrupting someone who purposely stood in his way to spout drivel, then plowed his way out of the committee of vultures around him to find her and catch her.

She had turned left.

11: Check

OVER A FIFTH GLASS OF CHAMPAGNE, SEBASTIAN WATCHED GISELLE WALK across the room. Kenard had a hunger, a raw lust, in his face that was unexpected, given what little he knew. Sebastian studied the room's male occupants as a full half of them turned to watch her cross the floor.

Perhaps he'd underestimated Giselle's appeal. On any day Sebastian thought about it and felt generous, he would classify Giselle as passably cute.

He saw two men start out after her, tongues dragging the floor. Kenard's snarl quelled them instantly and it hadn't gone unnoticed by the milling partygoers. Sebastian pursed his lips. The man had marked Giselle as his territory like the alpha wolf he was reputed to be, though his reputation with women could most kindly be described as . . . nonexistent.

Better than Sebastian's, anyway.

He followed the two of them into Sculpture Hall to see what would transpire next and he leaned against a wall somewhat out of the way, his arms crossed over his chest.

Kenard got caught in a web of moochers who gathered around him, clamoring at him for his time, his attention, his money. It took a great deal of rudeness and strength for the man to break through that to follow her. He clipped down the first staircase, bounded up the next one three steps at a time, then disappeared in a flash around a corner, his tux coat flaring out after him.

Sebastian was very pleased. Not only had Giselle neatly mapped out the next phase in their war with Fen, she'd caught Kenard's attention as he'd asked her to and with wild success. For the rest of the night tonight, Kenard wouldn't be thinking about campaigns, money, or politics and from the look of things, Kenard's mind was the last thing he wanted fucked.

He wondered if perhaps he'd gotten Giselle into a wee bit more trouble than she could handle herself, but she had her Glock and she loved a challenge. On the other hand, considering her desperation to hold onto her oh-so-precious virginity (however inefficiently), her behavior surprised Sebastian. Giselle had never had talents toward seduction, so where that femme fatale had come from tonight, he didn't know. Further, considering he'd specifically told her not to use it as a diversionary tactic and why, it completely confused him.

Unless . . .

. . . she wanted whatever Kenard would give her.

Would you fuck him if you got the chance?

In a heartbeat.

Sebastian's jaw dropped and his eyes widened.

The man dresses more expensively than you do . . . He's a warrior. You can tell. He's bigger than you.

Kenard?!

Now, *that* man would give Giselle exactly what she thought she wanted and a whole host of other things that would blow her little virgin mind. Stunned for a moment, Sebastian could only look at the now-empty staircase and turn that over in his head.

He was contemptuous of me . . . It made me mad and then we had an argument and then I— I . . . kissed him.

Giselle had unintentionally made her thirty-second pitch in a fit of anger and Kenard had bought the store.

He called me Lilith . . . It wasn't a compliment.

Then Sebastian began to smile. Whatever else he could say about Giselle's half-baked philosophies and inability to choose between the sacred and the profane, she did her best work by instinct—and her instincts had led her straight to Kenard.

He turned to see if Fen had observed this vignette and as he expected, Fen hadn't missed a second of anything. His jaw worked in his cheek. Though he mingled and smiled and shook hands with everyone who grabbed his attention, he watched Giselle lure Kenard, his biggest chance at campaign funding and support, away from the party that he'd intended as a four-hour thirty-second pitch. He had no way to salvage that without making a complete fool of himself and ruining his credibility by begging. Trudy Hilliard murmured something to Fen and he nodded, his lips tight.

Fen caught Sebastian watching him. The subtle anger in Fen's face made Sebastian grin and salute. Then he burst out laughing, startling most of the people there who knew him only as a dour and self-contained corporate raider.

12: Grimm Reality

WHERE WOULD SHE GO? ON A HUNCH, BRYCE FOLLOWED HIS NOSE, HER perfume as distinctive as she. He turned to take another set of stairs, hitting two landings in quick succession. The gallery, immense and only very dimly lit, had innumerable nooks and crannies in which to lose oneself by choice or by accident.

As he gained the top step, he turned immediately right to go into the Asian collection, then left, but stopped. He knew she'd passed by here; her scent lingered and drove him mad. He would not leave this museum tonight without a piece of her, if not all of her.

The trail stopped at the immense Chinese Temple room, two stories high, and, as always, even during exhibition hours, dimly lit. A section at the farthest end of the room was nearly closed off by a richly carved mahogany wall that looked Moorish in design. He could see the bodhisattva prominently displayed on the back wall, framed by the threshold of the wooden partition. As his eyes adjusted, he saw her silhouette where she sat on a Barcelona ottoman the size of a twin bed in front of the statue, very still, her back to him.

Then she turned her head and spoke over her shoulder. "Gorgeous, isn't he?"

He started at the sound of her voice, so smooth, so calm, so . . . fragile. How could a woman who brimmed with such decadent sexuality have such a fragile voice?

"Not sure I'd use that term, no," he murmured vaguely as he began his trek toward her.

She chuckled, then looked up at him once he reached the bench. "This is my secret place, where I come to get away from the world and meditate."

Her humor pulsed through her voice and radiated from her like a shimmering silvery heat wave off hot asphalt.

He sat next to her, throwing one leg over the ottoman, then turning so he, too, faced the bodhisattva and knew he would never reach that state of enlightenment. He searched for words and felt her steady gaze on him as he did so. He didn't know what to say to a woman he resented for her sexual relationship with Hilliard and possibly Taight, but still wanted for himself. He couldn't rid himself of the sudden visual of actually stripping her naked and laying her down on the ottoman right then and there.

Behold, I say unto you, wickedness never was happiness.

Whatever. Righteousness sure as hell hadn't been a picnic. Wickedness couldn't be any worse.

He hooked one heel on the edge of the upholstery and laid his arm over his flexed knee. He leaned into her just enough so that his lapel touched her bare shoulder. Watching her, daring her to say a word or make a move, he planted his left hand on the leather behind her, sliding his fingers underneath her, his thumb caressing her backside. She sucked a sharp breath in through her nose and her eyes widened slightly, but she held his gaze and stayed right where she was even though he continued to caress her fabric-covered buttock and made it clear he had no intention to remove his hand.

She reached out. The pad of her right thumb just brushed his forehead between his eyebrows, a gesture that startled him. He wasn't used to a woman's touch. "I apologize for nearly killing you," she murmured.

She laid her warm palm flat on the scarred half of his face, nearly covering his eye, and her fingers furrowed into his hair. She continued to stroke the spot where she had bored the barrel of her gun the night she'd kissed him. He had never received a touch so intimate—an intimacy far beyond sex—from any woman, not even his wife.

"I was very tired that night and you startled me."

"I doubt I was in any imminent danger," he murmured as she took her hand away. He wished she would continue to touch him. He wished she hadn't touched him at all. "You seem to be a woman who's almost always in control."

Miss Cox smiled then, a wide smile that made her amusement more than clear. The corners of her eyes crinkled merrily. "Oh, *always*. And some people think that's a bad thing."

"I suppose it depends on context."

That comment hung in the air as he began to inspect her face, her straight nose and full mouth, her throat, her breasts, her—

"What's this?" he breathed and touched a quarter-sized round indentation puckering the skin below her left shoulder. On her back, just over her shoulder, was another puckered scar, much larger and jagged around the edges. He looked into eyes that had darkened from ice blue to gunmetal gray. "Someone shot you."

She flashed him a wicked grin. "Two someones, actually."

He opened his mouth to ask the next logical question, but—

"Why did you follow me up here?" she asked in a rush, her gambit clear.

"Why did you want me to?"

She laughed then, a laugh that sparkled with delight. He reached for and gripped her chin in his palm, bringing her to him. His mouth captured hers, startling her into opening for him. Her eyes were wide for a moment, then he felt her sigh into his mouth and fall into his kiss. Her eyes closed, her mouth followed his lead; he felt her hand on his face again.

His thigh brushed a metal-hard bulge along hers, through a layer of fabric, and at that moment, he knew exactly what he wanted to do to her and how.

Kenard's strong hand, huge, rough, heavily calloused, held her jaw with just enough force to keep her where he wanted her. His hand lay perilously close to her throat; she didn't know whether that terrified her or excited her. But his kiss . . .

Ohhh.

Giselle had never been kissed so thoroughly, so expertly, so without inhibition.

Harshly exquisite, his mouth took hers with a confidence and experience that intimidated and exhilarated her beyond all reason. She touched his face again, felt the burn scars. Her arousal increased. Nearly painful sensation rolled through her when his tongue found hers, and the feel of his hand almost right *there* bordered on sensory overload.

She wanted more.

She opened her eyes to find him watching her while he kissed her. With a little shake of her head, she easily dislodged his hand to wrap her arms around his neck. Her fingers in his silky hair, drawing him close, she kissed him heatedly, but she couldn't direct it. He overpowered her too easily.

Giselle sighed when his mouth left hers to explore her cheek, his now-free hand cupping her breast, that thumb caressing the skin at the top of her corset.

Just then, the hand that teased her buttocks swept up her back and curled around the curve of her waist. His mouth kissing, licking, nipping the column of her neck, he pressed her downdowndown slowly, carefully, until she half lay on the bench. He rose then and caught her behind her knees to pull her legs up onto the bench.

He had kissed her again before she realized he knelt over her, his hands bracing himself on the upholstery on either side of her face, his knees similarly situated on either side of her hips.

Bryce Kenard, conquering lord. Conquering Giselle.

An odd and unexpected pleasure at being at this great man's mercy shuddered through her. He could do any number of wicked things to her right here, right now—and she'd let him.

She closed her eyes again, needing to just—*feel*—everything he did to her. She wound her arms up and around his forearms to clutch his arms, large and tight, covered by the fine wool-silk blend of his tux coat. He returned his attention to her neck to tease and nip. Her breath came hard and fast, short and ragged when he slowly worked his way over her collarbone, laved the indentation that marked her, then down over the skin of her chest.

She gasped and arched her back when he tucked his mouth in her cleavage, licking, kissing. She couldn't think, couldn't breathe when he began to undo the buttons of her corset with his teeth.

Suddenly embarrassed that she had lost control with a stranger so completely and voluntarily—so much so that she would allow him to undress her—she made a weak move to dislodge him. He ignored her. Four, six, eight buttons down, her corset fell open, baring her to the waist.

He rose up a bit to study her torso, his breathing strained to its limit, and she swallowed. Overwhelmed, saturated with adrenaline and desire, she whispered,

"Let me go."

Kenard's gaze met hers then, his emerald eyes hard, an eyebrow cocked. "No."

Her eyes widened and her mouth dropped open and she suddenly didn't know what to do. No man had ever dared cross her, to completely disregard her wishes.

He took advantage of her confusion and kissed her again, his mouth and tongue hard, pressing her into the upholstery. His hand swept up her ribs to cup her breast, his thumb stroking her nipple until she could only think of what he was doing to her, what else she wanted him to do to her.

"Giselle," he whispered harshly in her ear, "come home with me. Now. Tonight."

If this man was a member of the church, he was most definitely *not* on the "fast track to bishop." And if she did what she wanted to do, she'd be on the fast track to a broken heart with nothing to show for it.

Would you fuck him if you got the chance?

In a heartbeat.

Or . . . not.

Pressing her hands against his chest, she shoved at him, surprising him with her strength and nearly knocking him off the wide ottoman. He struggled for balance long enough for her to roll out from under him, desperately clutching her corset, and bolt across the room to one of the glass cases. Her chest, damp from his tongue and brushed by the cool air of the vents overhead, heaved as she looked at him warily, trying to button up her corset, wondering what the hell had just happened.

Her fingers didn't work because she trembled too badly, and she couldn't suck in her breath long enough to close it all the way. She watched him rise from the bench and walk toward her slowly, carefully. She was vaguely gratified to note that his breath came as hard and fast as hers, and sweat dotted his brow. He wiped his hand down his face as he approached her.

"This is insane," she murmured, her back pressed into a corner of the pillar behind her, her hands still struggling with her buttons as she watched him warily. He stopped when he was within an arm's length and gently brushed her hands aside to button her corset up himself.

"Isn't this what you wanted?" he asked, gruff though not unkind. "Suck in a breath."

She somehow managed to do that. "I—" But what could she say? That it was the only thing she wanted at the moment, and she knew she must not have it? That she felt embarrassed at having this sort of intimacy with a stranger, and, moreover, liking it? That she liked the way his knuckles caressed her as he re-dressed her? That she wanted to take him home and keep him forever?

That she felt more powerful at this moment than she had in her life, like a goddess with the world at her feet?

That her purpose was to distract him enough to keep him away from Fen, and therefore, nothing between them could ever come to fruition because it was all a lie?

She cleared her throat. "I, um, I— It was more than I expected, I think."

"Frankly, it wasn't nearly enough for me."

"I don't know you," she whispered.

"Ah, but I wasn't the one who issued the invitation, was I?"

Her breathing had calmed little by the time he had almost finished buttoning her up and her mind still whirled. "I think— Um— I think I need to go home."

"Let me take you there."

That was out of the question. Her nerves couldn't take much more of this without giving him everything he wanted. Now. Tonight. As he'd demanded.

He was a stranger.

She'd lied to him.

She did *not* want him to know where she lived.

In twenty-five years of on-and-off with Knox, she had only once felt so out of control and so eager to give herself over to a man—on one glance, fifteen years before—and the wedding ring on *that* man's finger had curtailed that in two seconds flat.

Knox didn't do this to her; he never had. This was something she had never truly believed existed and, at the same time, always wanted.

"I don't think that would be a good idea."

He said nothing for a moment; then, having finished his task with her only vaguely noticing, he pursed his lips. "Not in control now, are you?" he drawled, smug.

She gasped in outrage, but he shut her up with a harsh kiss, taking whatever she had to give and a whole lot of what she hadn't intended to give him at all. It took a few seconds for her to decide whether to break the kiss or not.

Finally, Giselle pulled away from him with some difficulty and only succeeded because he'd once again underestimated her strength. "I don't—" She hesitated and flinched at how it would sound. She cleared her throat again and said it anyway. "I've never done this sort of thing before."

His eyebrow rose and he smirked. She flushed, mortified at what he must have already assumed about her. With that, she turned on her heel. She strode through the room and away from him without another word. Embarrassed, aroused, confused, and completely disoriented, she headed out the door and ran to the right.

"Giselle, wait!"

She heard his commanding roar, but she did not heed it. If she could make it out of the gallery without his catching her, she'd be lucky. However much of the rest of the evening was left, Sebastian was going to have to do his own distraction. She couldn't take another second of this.

She clicked down the stairs, but stopped to hop and take off her shoes. She hiked her skirts over her knees, her Glock and stocking top clearly visible. Fen would have a heart attack that she'd come to his party armed and he'd make sure to inform her of his displeasure.

Away. She had to get away from that man, away from that room where she could never go back without memories of being half undressed and so almost *taken* on a Barcelona ottoman in an art museum by a stranger—a stranger who could've forced her.

No, no force necessary. She had a nine-millimeter strapped to her thigh that she'd completely forgotten. She could've wrapped her legs around his hips with it on and she still wouldn't have remembered she had it.

That was a man who'd fuck her the way she wanted, until she begged for more. He'd taken her on—twice now—and completely overwhelmed her both times.

Feeling very vulnerable and very afraid of her own lust, of what was happening to her, of what he did to her, she ran through the European exhibits, down the second staircase and up the third, sprinted straight through Sculpture Hall, then Kirkwood Hall. Her stockinged feet slid on the polished stone floor when she took the ninety-degree turn to the north exit, and she had to touch the floor with her fingertips to keep both her speed and her balance. She looked over her shoulder to see him closing in on her. She burst out of the art gallery winded and ran halfway down the drive to the limousine. The driver recognized her and her distress, and quickly caught up with her. She didn't give him enough time to get out to open her door; she threw it open and scrambled in. She thought she may have shut the door on her skirt. "Go, go. Go, please."

The limousine had pulled around the horseshoe and down the drive when Kenard burst out of the gallery. She looked at him through the back window. Bent over, his hands on his knees, his chest heaving and his breath white in the frigid December air, he watched her leave.

13: Contrived Ignorance

CHANGED MY FOCUS AND DIDN'T GET A CHANCE TO COPY THE NEW TEXT list . . ."

Unlike the rest of the class, Justice didn't have any reason to groan at this news. She never bought textbooks until she knew what was absolutely necessary to her success in a class, so she had no books to exchange.

Her constitutional law professor droned on and she glanced down at the sheet of paper, scanning it to calculate an approximate cost. Her eyes widened in shock at one particular author's name and she swallowed heavily, blinked, looked again. No, that couldn't be. He would have told her . . .

Wouldn't he?

Juell Pope, JD, LLM, PhD, author of half the textbooks on the list in her hand.

" . . . Dr. Pope's constitutional theories more in-depth this semester . . ."

The lecture went on, but Justice barely heard it for the buzzing in her ears and the blurring of the titles in front of her.

" . . . country lawyer up in River Glen, just north of Chouteau City, but died about six years ago. One of the greatest legal minds of the twentieth century. Ms. McKinley, something wrong?"

She looked up slowly at her professor as if in a daze. "No," she croaked, cleared her throat. "No, I'm fine."

But she wasn't. Deep betrayal cut through her soul. Why had she had to go to law school to find out her grandfather had been such a well-respected scholar?

Snatches of her grandfather's teachings flitted through her mind. When her professor asked her a question meant to stump her, she answered it by rote, only vaguely aware of the semi-tense silence her answer had garnered.

Then, "Ms. McKinley, how did you know that?"

I know this material better than you ever will.

"Um, I— I don't know. I, uh—" Justice panicked, trying to think of an answer that didn't include *because Juell Pope is my grandfather and he drilled this into me in my hayloft.* She cleared her throat. "I happened to have read that for an assignment last semester, is all."

"Really! Stay after class, please. I'd love to talk to you about it."

I wouldn't.

"Sure. Okay. Uh, no problem."

Her after-class interview with her professor went more smoothly than she had expected, given her state of total shock and her instinct to keep her identity and accomplishments separate from her grandfather's. The professor seemed impressed with Justice's answers and requested that she email that particular assignment to her as soon as possible. With a lump in her throat, Justice agreed, though the assignment didn't exist and it was just another fire to put out, albeit more emergent than the rest: Around campus, where everyone had laptops and every square inch was hot, ASAP meant, "by the time I get back to my office."

She did have one paper, though, that she had written long ago under her grandfather's direction; he'd decreed it adequate but certainly not up to her capabilities.

It would have to do.

Justice trudged out into the bitter January air in the direction of the student union to eat and get the books on her list. She drew wary glances and whispers as she passed clusters of law students here and there, but no one spoke to her. Mindful of the attention, she clutched her backpack straps more closely in front of her and pretended not to see.

At least no one mocked her to her face as Sherry had and the whispers she'd caught here and there contained no ridicule of her.

It was almost as if people were . . . afraid . . . to speak to her, but she had no idea why. Justice wasn't particularly shy; she spoke in class, but took care not to dominate the discussions. She didn't sit on the front row and she made sure to make herself as inconspicuously conspicuous as possible. She thought she successfully projected the image of ambitious law student without being completely obnoxious about it.

But the fact was that she had no friends here. She couldn't even count Giselle Cox, who flew from classes to study groups to the cafeteria and back again before she left campus around three. Justice was completely alone and except for the occasional murmured comment or question in class, almost no one had spoken to her in three semesters. She didn't figure this semester would be any different and if anyone had connected her physical presence on campus with Justice McKinley, political commentator, she didn't know it.

She bowed her head, as much to shelter herself from others' observation and lack of camaraderie as from the sharp wind. Not for the first time, she wished she could do this law school thing online, where she felt safe, comfortable, confident, where no one could watch her and point at her and whisper about her.

Once in the warmth of the cafeteria, she fumbled with her burdens in front of the microwave, found a secluded spot after she'd sufficiently nuked her food, opened her laptop, and sent the paper her professor had requested. She dug into her lunch then and began to cruise her blogs.

It had only taken six months as a regular blogger at TownSquared for her to come to some national attention, augmented by the two articles she'd published in *National Review*; because of that exposure, other blog owners had reached out to her, requesting columns here and there, then more regularly. The blogging position at TownSquared overflowed her schedule, but with each new request came an offer of payment and *that* she wouldn't refuse.

Conversation swirled around her as she began to write a new article. Her sudden brush with her grandfather's greatness not an hour ago still rattled her, but as she thought about it, ideas for future blog posts inundated her. Her fingers burned through the keys as she typed, vaguely aware that the din and crush of lunchtime diners swelled.

"... Hilliard's not teaching in the fall."

Justice stopped typing immediately, but attempted to disguise the fact that she'd begun to eavesdrop on the conversation behind her.

"I heard he's taking a sabbatical for the next three, four semesters."

"Shit."

No kidding. Well, now at least Justice wouldn't have to agonize over how to take one of his classes *and* pay for the extra gas, ever hoping her car didn't simply expire on the highway somewhere. It didn't matter anyway; Justice had a plan. She had no doubt that her CV would get his attention and earn her a coveted position in the Chouteau County prosecutor's office.

"I wouldn't take a class from him. I don't like him, don't like his opinions, don't like his politics or the way he runs that county up there."

"You believe all that bullshit?"

"Look, where there's smoke there's fire. There're plenty of lawyers coming out of that office talking about the mysterious cash that gets passed around. If one person calls you an ass, you figure they're having a bad day. If three people do it, buy a saddle."

Justice's breath caught in her throat.

She'd heard the rumors, of course. Of that and other things, but she actively avoided such nonsense because, in her opinion, if he were guilty, he would have been arrested and put in prison. That was the way the system worked.

"Fucking Republicans. The only reason he keeps getting elected is because he killed that guy."

Justice choked.

"Bullshit *again*. He wasn't even charged for that, much less convicted."

"It's a racket. He's a racket. One big fucking conspiracy and all the rednecks up there love him for it."

"So do the women."

"It's that fucking bad-boy bullshit they like. Leaves us nice guys out in the cold."

Justice shoved her earbuds in her ears and cranked up the tunes—she didn't care what—unable to listen to such gossip one minute longer.

So do the women.

And how well did she know that! Half the women who walked around the law school halls bemoaned the fact that they hadn't been quick enough during registration to get in his class that semester. Justice couldn't stand to hear that many smart grown women squee like prepubescent girls over a boy band and she refused to play the adolescent games, even in private. No googling, no listening to gossip, and, since no one talked to her, no contributing to gossip, either.

Justice's grandfather had taught her the value of dignity and in her opinion, that extended to the collecting of information about the object of one's affections. It should happen organically, over time, with exposure.

Not with Google.

There was nothing anyone could say that would diminish the impact Knox Hilliard had made on her that day almost a year and a half before, but she didn't want to take the chance. Plenty enough time to get to know him after she'd acquired the job that would give her daily access to him.

Her email chimed. The professor who had requested the paper her grandfather had thought merely average:

> Justice, please come to my office at your earliest convenience. I would like you to submit this to the law review.
>
> Dr. Smythe

Justice gulped, again unable to believe the words in front of her, but her attention caught when the diners around her stirred a bit. She looked to the door to see Giselle Cox walk in—well, *strut*, really—with Neal, an older (rather unattractive, in Justice's opinion) law student with whom she ate lunch every day.

Justice wasn't the best judge of appearance, but it seemed to her that Giselle was . . . average. If that. Curly dark blonde hair usually in a ponytail, light eyes, pale skin, and orthodontic-perfect teeth. Short, compact body dressed in the same sorts of things everyone else wore: faded jeans, a heavy yellow sweater, hiking boots. Really the woman was wholly unremarkable to Justice's eye, except for a mysterious . . . something . . . that made people notice her and defer to her. It wasn't just her age, although Justice figured that contributed to it; no, it was something more nebulous, some sort of intense energy.

Half the people Giselle and Neal passed stared at them openly, but neither noticed as they continued to talk and laugh on their way to get food.

Justice sighed, pulled the earbuds out of her ears, and began to shut down her laptop. She'd eaten well, written well, and generally done *well* today, not to mention the fact that she had learned she carried the DNA of "one of the greatest legal minds of the twentieth century." It might take her a while to get used to the idea, to get over being angry with her grandfather for keeping that from her, but it did bolster her confidence.

"I wouldn't touch Giselle Cox with my ten-inch pole and I don't care that she's cute," came the voice of one of the men behind her. "She'd kick my ass."

Believe in yourself and your opinions. Have faith. I don't know you, but I'm very proud of you.

"You know," replied his companion, "it's not like she's hot or anything, because she's not, but there's just something to be said for a woman with power."

"And a gun stuck in her jeans."

"Fuck, yeah."

Justice gulped.

Power.

How Giselle got it, who gave it to her, why she deserved to have it, Justice didn't understand, but she wanted to.

She just had to figure out how to go about getting some of it.

14: Friends in Low Places

MARCH 2006

MEET ME AT TASSO'S TONIGHT AT 9:30

THE TERSE EMAIL FROM HIS BEST FRIEND—THE ONE WHO'D PEGGED HIM SO neatly so long ago, the one he hadn't considered any kind of a friend for over a decade now—danced in front of his mind's eye like the snowflakes under the street light in front of him. As he sat in his car in the restaurant's parking lot, his vision blurred by the March late-season sleet collecting on his windshield, he didn't have to wonder why he'd actually shown up.

Giselle.

Naturally, she would have shared what had happened in December with Knox, and Knox wanted to stake his claim.

The clock read 9:39 P.M. and still he debated whether to go in or not. The pain of betrayal had lessened with time, distance, and doubt, but had sharply resurfaced almost a year and a half ago at Leah's visitation.

He braved the cold and ice to get to the door of the restaurant, his collar up and his scarf around his face. He didn't really want to be seen with the Chouteau County prosecutor, but this was a good place to meet: dark and neutral. Plus, he loved Greek food, which was probably why Knox had picked it in the first place. Knox would have remembered that. Knox remembered everything.

Small lanterns on the tables in their private cubbyholes punctuated the dim interior. A floor show of belly dancers was in full swing and the waitstaff yelled enthusiastically back and forth at each other. Bryce knew no patrons would notice or identify him, but the staff here knew him all too well.

"Hi, Bryce," said the hostess. "Come with me." It vaguely disturbed him that she knew who awaited him. She led him to a dark corner. He didn't sit.

"You're late."

"I'm always late."

"I hate late. So. You want to make love to her and I've wanted to make love to her since before I knew what that was, and she chose you. Are we even now?"

Bryce didn't pretend ignorance or misunderstanding, though that was not quite what he'd expected Knox to say, heavy sarcasm notwithstanding.

"I don't want to make love to her," he found himself replying.

Knox looked up at him, surprised.

He leaned down, his fists on the table, and got right in Knox's face, his voice hard. "I want to *fuck* her."

Knox stared at him and Bryce took a second to thoroughly enjoy his shock—then he noticed that Knox's eyes were the same ice blue as Giselle's. And Taight's. *Shit.* Bryce sighed with an odd combination of confusion, relief, and guilt, then shook his head at himself.

Resignedly, he cast a glance askance at the carafe of orange juice and signaled a waitress. "Sandra, please take this back," he muttered, swiping it off the table and ignoring what Knox would want. "A steak and a salad for him, the usual for me and a big bowl of tzatziki. Water. Lots of it. Please."

"Thank you, Mother," Knox sneered once she'd left. Bryce slid into the seat across from Knox. "I see you're on a first-name basis here."

Bryce ignored that and grabbed a sugar packet to have something to occupy his hands. "You have a lot of explaining to do and I don't need you passing out before you answer all my questions."

"Screw you. I don't owe you *anything.*"

Bryce's jaw worked in thought and he stared down at the table. He said nothing because he couldn't dispute that. Strike two. How else had he willfully misjudged the only man who'd ever told him the truth, no matter how nasty or painful?

"Michelle lied to you," Knox groused. "I never touched that crazy fucking bitch you married. You know that and you always have. It was just easier for you to blame me than your own shitty judgment in women—especially considering the fact that I hated her and I specifically told you not to marry her. And on top of all that, she was a blonde and skinny as a rail."

"You're right," Bryce admitted with a heavy sigh. "I knew. I didn't want to *dis*believe her and . . . I'm sorry."

Knox grunted. "That's a helluva way to split that hair. I'm the one who should be holding the grudge. Do you actually know how many other men she was sleeping with?"

"No. What I do know is that the men she liked were a lot smaller than me."

Knox looked at him for a moment and then murmured, "Tell me something. If I could've proven it to you, would you've listened to me?"

Bryce looked off toward the belly dancers without seeing anything at all. "No. I was too invested in avoiding the kind of women I like."

They sat in companionable silence for a long while, their friendship having begun in college and never really waning except for Bryce's determination to be angry with Knox for something he hadn't done. And, as he always had, Knox promptly forgave and forgot.

"You and Taight are related to Giselle," Bryce finally said.

Knox barked a laugh. "Don't tell me. It's the eyes, right?"

Come home with me tonight . . . Please. I need you.

"I'm going to assume, for the sake of my own sanity, that neither of you is her brother."

"Cousin," he confirmed with alacrity. "Close enough to be creepy, not close enough to contaminate the DNA, and legal to breed in twenty-three states."

"So Fen—"

"Fen's her and Sebastian's uncle by marriage. Our mothers are sisters."

Their food came then and conversation ceased as they ate. Knox's grumpy mood changed markedly once he got some real food in him and the orange juice wore off. It'd always been that way, Bryce remembered absently, thinking that they'd taken up where they'd left off. Nobody would have guessed that they hadn't spoken in a dozen years.

"I want to know about Leah Wincott," Bryce finally said, when it was clear that Knox had given all he intended to give him concerning Giselle. At least for now—and at this point, he wasn't sure he wanted to know anyway.

"Well, I didn't kill her, if that's what you're thinking."

"I never thought you did."

Knox's fork stopped halfway to his mouth as he stared at Bryce. "You didn't?"

Bryce had never seen Knox so shocked so many times in the course of an hour. "No," he replied warily, wondering where Knox's mind had gone. "Fen's the only likely candidate."

"What do you know?" he demanded.

"I don't *know* anything," Bryce returned, irritated. "You've got no reason to kill her; he's got every reason in the world and I don't know anyone who really thinks you killed her. Your problem is your reputation versus his reputation. It's not like you don't have a track record." After a minute, he gestured at Knox with his fork. "I'm listening. Start talking."

"Fen killed my father. Insulin overdose. Obviously looks like natural causes for an old diabetic with heart disease."

Bryce's eyebrow rose.

"Remember I told you my mom kicked me out of the house when I was fifteen because I accused her of having an affair with Fen? And I went to live with my aunt and cousin?" Bryce nodded, recalling his shock over finding out that his roommate was the heir to a fortune and how that had come about—

"Giselle was the cousin?"

"Yes. Well, the proviso is dated just about a week after Trudy kicked me out, and then my dad died the week after that. I tell you what. That proviso's been the bane of my existence, stuck in professional limbo, never feeling like I had a place in life until I turned forty. And hell, when I was fifteen, forty-year-olds were damn near on their deathbeds."

—and all the sleepless nights when the nineteen-year-old heir had paced their dorm room trying to figure out how to pass the next twenty years or how to weasel out of the course his uncle had set for him. "What was your father *thinking?*"

Knox sighed. "I don't know."

"So . . . how do you know Fen murdered your father and why haven't you had him investigated?"

"After you and I parted company, Giselle and I were over at the estate clearing out my old bedroom. We went to Fen's office to ask him something and overheard him confessing to his bishop. I've had him under investigation ever since. Short of exhuming my father—and insulin is damn near the perfect weapon, so I haven't bothered—I can't find anything."

"Did you confront him?"

"Yes. He didn't deny it."

"So he's had it in for you since."

Knox waved a hand. "He likes me and he'd rather not kill me. First, I'm the heir. That just looks bad. I'm the most conspicuous person in ten counties and the FBI camps on my doorstep. I disappear, Fen's suspect number one. Second, I have a reputation that he doesn't dare breach since, you know, the entire city thinks I'm capable of murder." Bryce smirked and Knox rolled his eyes. "Fen doesn't have the balls to come after me, vicariously or otherwise. Third, he's squeamish and he has an unfortunate tendency toward half-assed contrition: He won't dirty his own hands; he'll confess to the bishop and get excommunicated—but he won't give any of it up.

Fourth, after Giselle and I confronted him about killing my dad, he got scared we'd just get married to fulfill the proviso and that'd be that."

"Would you?"

"No. I don't give a fat rat's ass about OKH and Sebastian's welcome to it."

"You found your place in life."

"Sure did. You know Fen had me chasing my tail all those years, telling me to go here, get this degree. Go there, get that degree. 'Prepare for the handoff, son. I'm just holding OKH for you to take over.' And he meant it. He flat-out told me he wasn't going to let me be a trust fund frat boy who couldn't be trusted to drive a car, much less run a company, and he was going to make sure I knew how to do that job."

"And got pissed off at you for wanting to be a prosecutor instead of learning how to take care of OKH," Bryce muttered.

Knox nodded. "Or at least get a job making some real money. I had another offer in the Clay County prosecutor's office, but Nocek found out, came courting. Fen blew his top when I told him, said Nocek was bad news and I'd get stuck in that cesspool. It was the last place Fen wanted me to go, so naturally, that's where I went."

Bryce cast back in his memory, years before when they had just graduated from law school and settled into their new jobs, how tense Knox had grown, how closed-mouthed he had been about his boss and the rumors of corruption in the Chouteau County prosecutor's office. Knox had walked out of Bryce's life not long after that, so Bryce had never known what happened. "You were miserable."

Knox nodded. "I was young and dumb. Flattered. See, Nocek thought I had a trust and unlimited access to OKH funds that he could squeeze out of me, but I didn't, which pissed him off—and then I realized I couldn't get out of that office any way but in a pine box."

"You're kidding."

Knox shook his head. "Bad things happened to people who left or talked. Nocek used the sheriff's department as his personal thug patrol. So I bided my time, cut my teeth on the hardest cases they could foist off on me, and found out I really liked the job.

"Nocek made his money fixing cases, which I didn't know for a couple of months. Then he informed me he expected me to contribute to the widow'n'orphan fund like the rest of the crew. There were three attorneys in that office who didn't, but they were so subtle, Nocek didn't know they weren't on the take. I latched on to them, but I wasn't very successful at hiding my winning streak. Nocek rode my ass constantly because I wasn't bringing any money into the office. Then after I ki—"

Knox stopped abruptly. Took a deep breath. Gulped down his water.

Bryce began to laugh and Knox glared at him. "Shut up. Anyway, after—well, after *that* was all over with, he left me alone for another couple of months, but it was too late. I'd had enough of his bullshit, so I forced him to resign and name me as his successor."

"And the untouchable Knox Hilliard was born, all with the tacit approval of the federal prosecutor."

"Well, you know. You turn vigilante—"

"Twice."

"—and you get the undying loyalty of every cop in the state. So now I'm happy with what I do. I know as well as I know the penal code that I'm not cut out to be a CEO of anything. I'm not a manager. I don't even manage my own staff; my executive AP does that and I don't know how I got anything accomplished before he came to work for me. I'm just a redneck lawyer in a backwater of a county that's *still* a cesspool. And I like it that way."

"Doesn't hurt that you have your pick of the brightest legal minds coming out of every law school in the Midwest, either, corruption be damned. How'd that happen?"

Knox grunted. "Lucked into it. About five years ago, a friend called me, said she needed a sub for her class for a week and then my name got passed around when somebody needed a fill-in. One semester, one of the emeritus professors died the day before class started and I got called. I guess a few of the students were impressed enough to drop their CVs at my office after they graduated. Kinda bloomed from there."

"You're faculty now, though?"

"Part time. One class a semester is the most I can squeeze in, if that. I don't even bother to keep office hours. Obviously the county takes precedence and if someone needs a face-to-face conference, they have to come up to Chouteau City to do it."

"So you and Taight are working together to take OKH?"

"I wouldn't call it working together so much as trying to get the other one to do all the heavy lifting. The irony is neither one of us wants it. We just want Fen not to get it because he killed one person to have it and one person to keep it. And it all started when he tried to kill Giselle to keep her from marrying me."

Bryce's gut clenched. "He what?"

"Mmmm, that's right," Knox said around his bite. "The first time, he burned her bookstore. She lived in the apartment above it and she would've died in it except she couldn't sleep that night and just *knew* something was wrong. Girl has the instincts of a she-wolf. The alarms had been disabled and she barely got out with her purse and her laptop and that was it. Fortunately, she was the only one who actually lived in the building."

Bryce thought his heart had stopped at the word "burned." Knox looked up then and breathed, "Oh, dude, I'm sorry. I didn't think."

He shook his head to clear it. "I—" He gulped. "It's an excruciating way to die," he whispered, hoarse.

Knox sighed, but didn't speak again until Bryce had recovered himself, cleared his throat again, and said, "Go on."

"Well, anyway, when that didn't work, Fen sent a couple of hit men after her." He stopped and ate some more.

"That explains the bullet holes," Bryce muttered.

Knox speared him with a glance. "Holes? Plural?"

"The ones in her shoulder?"

He snickered. "Hole. That was a through-and-through. They had to dig the other one out of her hip."

It was just so . . . *wrong* . . . that Bryce found that arousing.

"So they're still out looking for her?"

"Naw. She killed 'em, one gun in each hand. No hesitation. No remorse. It was a regular little shoot-out, but it put her in the hospital for a few days. Then he went after Leah instead. Giselle put a gun to his head, told him that if he did it again, she'd take him out. Of course, Giselle can get a little out of control now and again, and she never makes threats she won't carry out. Fen knows she was serious and he won't play chicken with her, but if he pushes her to it, I hope she has the good sense to do it in my county."

Bryce's eyes widened and he didn't know what to do, what to think. What he did know was that he was very, very hard.

"Obviously, Fen doesn't want me to fulfill the proviso. He hasn't decided yet if he wants to test the limits of Giselle's patience, but I wouldn't put it past him to try if he manages to cozy up to her again."

Bryce's brow wrinkled.

"Fen and Giselle have a very strange relationship."

"Strange how?"

"They amuse the hell out of each other. Always have. If it weren't for the whole killing thing, they'd be best buds. Every so often, Fen gets comfortable with her again and forgets that she doesn't play games. He'll drop his guard, do something that pisses her off, and then he'll spend the next little while kissing her ass until she cools down. She hasn't cooled off since he had her shot and that's the longest she's ever been mad at him. I think she hurt his feelings."

Bryce stopped chewing and stared at Knox. "Hurt *his* feelings?"

"Because she doesn't find him amusing at the moment. Don't feel bad; Sebastian and I don't understand it, either. Anyway, after Leah was killed, I finally decided that I don't need OKH so badly I'm willing to put another woman in front of him, especially the woman I want."

Bryce looked at him carefully. "The woman you want," he said slowly, "which is *not* Giselle?"

"Hell no."

That tore it. "Oh, so she's just a booty call for you."

Knox's jaw and fork dropped at the same time. "What the *fuck?*"

"I overheard you at Leah's visitation. You took her home."

Knox stared at him, the tic in his cheek working. "You know," he said, "you've always been stupid about women. First of all, if you were eavesdropping, you deserve what you hear. Second of all, if you're going to eavesdrop, you could have the courtesy to stick around for the whole conversation. Third, didn't you learn your lesson about assuming the worst about my sexual habits the *first* time I was accused of banging a woman you thought belonged to you?"

Uh oh.

He threw his napkin on the table and started to rise. "You know what, Bryce? Fuck you. I'm tired of being the one getting the shaft when a woman's got you in knots."

"Siddown," Bryce growled and wasn't surprised when Knox looked at him expectantly, waiting. It was a familiar exchange. "I'm sorry," he muttered when he looked down at his plate, thoroughly abashed. "Again."

It took a moment before he heard Knox settle back into his seat. "Yeah, I asked her to go home with me," Knox said low, his voice unusually raspy. "Don't tell me you've never needed to hold on to somebody when your life's been ripped out from under your feet."

Oh. Bryce swallowed.

"But wait. I forgot. *You* don't have anybody you can beg comfort sex from who'll still love you the day after whether she gives it to you or not."

He flinched.

"She said no. Happy now? Again?"

Yes, but . . . He decided to keep his curiosity in check for the moment.

Knox drew in a deep breath before continuing a moment later. "So here I am, four serious girlfriends and a dead fiancée later, barely thirty-seven, still not married and with no child on the way, the clock ticking—and it's because of all this that Leah's dead. And make no mistake. Whatever you think about me or my relationship with Leah—oh, look, more assumptions—I loved her."

Bryce's eyes narrowed. "I didn't assume anything about Leah. She told me what you did to her."

Knox rolled his eyes.

"You blackmailed her and manipulated everything around her so she'd have no choice. I can think of at least three felonies you committed to get her into bed."

He speared Bryce with a glance. "Did she *tell* you she had no choice? In those words?"

Bryce pursed his lips.

"Yeah, I didn't think so. She had a choice. She was just more willing to bail her daughter out of a homicide charge than she was to keep her virtue intact. Not my problem. The deal was she had to sleep with me a week and—Surprise!—she *loved* it. Rachel found out, threw it back in her face, and disappeared. After that, Leah figured she had no reason to go back to Houston at all except to pack up her shit and put her house on the market. She was back in bed with me in two weeks flat and she was there for five years, saying no every time I broached the subject of marriage."

"Well," Bryce conceded, "she *did* tell me she didn't want Rachel to have squatter's rights to OKH."

"I didn't either, so I didn't push very hard."

"So that was why Leah wasn't as threatening to Fen as Giselle."

"Exactly. He saw Giselle as a way-too-convenient solution to the problem that I could leverage at any moment, Leah or no Leah. Giselle's loyal to me and she's low profile, so no one would connect her death to me or OKH if he hid it well enough. Leah finally decided that she'd best marry me to keep Fen off Giselle's back, so fuck you very much. *Again.*"

Well, he did have a point.

"Giselle was so nervous before the wedding she was radioactive, so Leah told me to make Giselle stay away from her. Stupid shit that I am, I decided that Leah should have her way on her wedding day."

"Is that why she was so mad at Leah's funeral?"

"That and a shitload of guilt for not following her gut regardless of what Leah wanted. I should have trusted her instincts, but I didn't want to upset Leah. If Giselle had been with her . . . " His voice, heavy with regret, trailed off and Bryce said nothing. Another moment of silence passed before Knox collected himself enough to continue. "So now here I am, a year and a half later wanting to be free to pursue this other woman without having to fulfill anything, without putting her in Fen's line of fire. She's too young to have to deal with that and I'm not that selfish."

That jolted Bryce. "Young? Except for Giselle, you've never liked young. You were dating postgrads when you were a freshman."

Knox didn't say anything for a while. Then, low, "She's twenty-three."

Bryce pulled back a bit. "Whoa," he breathed. "That's a serious change for you. Don't tell me she's blonde, too."

"Oh, no. She's a redhead. I haven't gone completely nuts."

"What's so special about her that you'd go from Mrs. Robinson to Lolita?"

"You ever heard the name Justice McKinley?"

Bryce choked on his water. "You're kidding me."

"Nope."

"Does she even know you exist?"

"She has a crush on me."

"Oh, shit. You were her professor."

"Substitute professor. For one week. And don't think that doesn't give me the willies."

"You haven't had her in any of your classes since?"

"Once this semester ends, I won't teach any more classes until she graduates. After I turn forty, I'll go find her and hope like hell she's not attached by then."

"She's an atheist, isn't she?"

"Why would that make a difference to me? I'm not allowed to step foot in the only church I have any interest in."

A companionable silence descended as they ate. After a bit of the edge had been knocked off Bryce's appetite, he said,

"So . . . the takeover."

Knox pursed his lips and thought for a long moment. "Sebastian hates Fen," he said finally, "always has, and the feeling's mutual. But he kept his mitts off OKH in deference to me until Fen went after Giselle."

"Really. Why?"

"Sebastian thinks his sole purpose in life is to be Giselle's mother. A few days after her fire, he told Fen if I didn't have OKH on my fortieth birthday for any reason, he'd take it. If I were dead, he'd take it. If he did anything more at all to Giselle, he wouldn't wait until I was forty to take it. Fen loses the company to Sebastian, no question. If I fulfilled the terms of the proviso, he'd lose it to me, no question. Giselle was fine with that."

"Fen thought he was bluffing."

"Well, you know. Sebastian does bluff a lot, so it wasn't unreasonable of Fen to assume that. So after Giselle got shot, Jack Blackwood summoned Fen to New York—"

"Jack *Blackwood*? Jack the Ripper?"

"Yeah, him. Blackwood Securities. He and Sebastian go way back."

"Shit. Even I would think twice about crossing that bastard."

"Exactly. Fen wasn't sufficiently cowed by Sebastian's threat, but he wasn't going to ignore an invitation from one of the biggest power brokers in the country. When he got there, Jack plunked down solid numbers for him. He told him Sebastian was not only prepared to take it, but he was prepared to burn it down to the ground, to boot. Every last employee, every last nut, bolt, and washer. Sebastian had OKH's parted-out resale value calculated to within ten bucks."

Bryce's eyes widened. "He wouldn't," he breathed. "Thousands of people?"

"No, he wouldn't," Knox drawled. "Another bluff, but enough of one that Fen wasn't going to chance it. Having everything you've built and love taken away from you by someone who would take care of it is one thing; seeing it completely destroyed for no reason other than revenge is another. And having Blackwood as your enemy just isn't good business. It didn't occur to Sebastian—nor would it have occurred to me—to threaten him if he touched any other woman I wanted to marry."

"And then Leah suddenly stepped in front of Giselle, too, so she became the priority threat."

"Right. The day after the funeral, Giselle told him she'd kill him regardless of what I wanted."

"What do you want?"

"I want Fen on death row. I'm not interested in having him dead before the world knows what he did. I'm not going to hide behind Giselle's skirts and I'm not going to let her have her head. Whatever happens to Fen, I'm the one who needs to do it.

"After Giselle got shot, Sebastian doubled his stake in OKH and began going to the shareholder and board meetings just to make sure Fen knew he was on the warpath. Sebastian's blocked a couple of major business decisions just by having such a large voting share."

"Causing the stock price to fall."

"And Sebastian picked up more shares. The SEC got very upset with him when he refused to explain and stopped approving his buys. Everybody in the country's selling OKH short now."

"So Fen decided to run for office and put Taight's head on the block since Roger Oth is already running his mouth about the way he shut down Jep Industries."

"Right."

"That's what I figured. After Leah was murdered, Wall Street pretty much gave up on you fulfilling the proviso. How much does Blackwood know?"

"Not sure. Sebastian usually doesn't explain anything to anyone ever, but Jack's the one steering the takeover because it's just so complex. He's taken out long odds in Vegas on me actually fulfilling the proviso, so I suspect Sebastian hasn't told him anything. He has a reputation for being crazy like a fox. Nobody'd bet on me at all if Jack hadn't." Knox harrumphed. "Not that it'd do *me* any good."

"So what was Taight's next move or has he made it yet?"

Knox paused for a moment as if trying to decide how to articulate it. "This has thrown Sebastian for a loop. He doesn't think politically because he's never had to. He thinks in terms of the principles of capitalism and he's always had the money, power, and leverage to do what he wants without really coloring inside any line he doesn't like. Too, he has people to clean up after him when he goes a little too far. He doesn't know what to do when he runs into someone with more authority and power than he does, because there just isn't anyone like that. The only idea he could come up with was to block Fen's fundraising efforts as much as possible."

"That's weak."

"Yep."

"So he has no plan."

"Oh, he has one now. Blocking Fen's access to money is the first part. Second part: Kevin Oakley's going to run against Fen on Sebastian's dime."

Bryce chuckled. "Sebastian Pendergast. Okay, next?"

Knox smirked. "Have you been watching the news? Oth has been forced to start answering questions about why he called Sebastian to fix Jep Industries in the first place. Sebastian's people refer the reporters to me and I very subtly imply that once Sebastian got to Jep, he found that the employees' pensions were at risk. He rode to the employees' rescue and, being the longsuffering and altruistic citizen that he is, decided to take the publicity hit instead of embarrassing or otherwise demanding Oth account for himself. And, oh, damn, I said too much and this is off the record, right? Oth's going to have to shut his fat mouth about Sebastian's villainy if he wants to save himself, but by then, the bell will have been rung.

"Add me to the mix as the attorney representing the man who's trying to rip my inheritance out from under me, and the whole thing becomes this tantalizing mystery. Either way, it'll start to make Fen stink to high heaven, not to mention Oth and any of the other five senators who have it in personally for Sebastian. By the time the handoff rolls around, I'll look like the underpaid little public servant and college professor who was almost cheated of his inheritance by his evil uncle-slash-stepfather."

"And Taight will look like the genius saint who decided that if you couldn't have it, neither would Fen—and spent millions of his own money to take it down."

"Yes. It won't keep Sebastian out of the hot seat forever, but it only needs to work until after OKH is settled for good. Once that's out of the way, Sebastian can recruit his similarly disenfranchised pals to help him fight any future anti-Taight legislation on their terms instead of letting Sebastian try to do it alone under the Senate's terms—and with one hand tied behind his back, to boot. Obviously, none of them can step in while OKH is smack in the middle of it because they're as in the dark as everyone else is, but that won't keep them from contributing to Oakley's campaign."

That made Bryce burst out laughing. "What do you mean he doesn't think politically? That's brilliant."

Knox looked up at him sharply. "Sebastian didn't come up with this. This is Giselle's brain child."

Bryce stared at Knox for a moment, his mouth open, before he closed his eyes and sat back, taking a deep breath. He could feel every last drop of blood in his body rush to fill his cock. He didn't even care enough to keep his reaction from Knox's not-so-observant eye and he figured he deserved it when Knox started to laugh at him.

"Heh. She just gave your IQ a blow job and she's not even here. *Priceless!*"

Bryce couldn't deny that. On the other hand, he wasn't sure why that surprised him once he'd finally figured out she'd dropped from that particular family tree. Bryce took another deep breath. "Okay, so you can cross me off your list of people you need to convince to stay away from Fen."

Knox grimaced. "Yeah. About that. You got crossed off the list at Fen's fundraising party. That's why you're here wanting to know if Giselle and I are lovers—besides the fact that you stuck your ears where they didn't belong."

It took him a couple of seconds before he understood, before anger exploded in his gut. His jaw clenched. His nostrils flared.

"Oh, simmer down," Knox drawled. "It was the only idea Sebastian could come up with on short notice. All he knew was he had to keep your money and Fen separated. I didn't think you'd take a call from me and you'd be suspicious of Sebastian calling out of the blue. Given that you were the only serious money possibility he couldn't talk to personally beforehand, he sent Giselle in to get you the hell away from Fen and fuck your mind. She didn't know your name and we didn't know she'd met you before. How was I supposed to know you'd evolved from Peter Priesthood into alpha male? You haven't talked to me in, what, twelve years?" He shrugged. "You were my best friend and you know my history. Sebastian respects your reputation. We didn't know you'd figure out Fen killed Leah and that I *didn't*."

"There are a lot of things you two don't know," Bryce said, his eyes narrow.

"Yeah," Knox snapped, now obviously impatient. "Like, we don't know what happened that night between you and Giselle because she hasn't said a word about it. Sebastian said you followed her like a wolf in heat and made sure every male in that room knew she was your territory. Then a half hour later, she came flying through the gallery looking like she'd been thoroughly fucked. You ran after her, missed her, and went back in so pissed that you punched Sebastian when he wouldn't tell you where she went. Since she didn't shoot you, we figured there was something else going on.

"What we *do* know is that something happened between you, what—a year ago?—you kissed her or something? And she was fidgety for months. We've never seen her like that before. When she came home alone from the Nelson that night, she was a hot mess, and she's been a hot mess ever since."

Bryce thought about that, thought about how fidgety he'd been after that kiss in the parking lot, the mess he'd been when he'd gotten home from the gallery. Thought about the fact that she wanted him as badly as he wanted her and had from the moment they'd met at Hale's.

He *needed* to know.

"So *have* you fucked her?"

Knox looked at him speculatively and waved his fork, not answering Bryce's question. "What happened to you? You're dropping the F-bomb like it's the Word of the Day and you took Giselle on and won, which is—amazing—especially for the Bryce Kenard I knew way back when."

Bryce grunted. "I don't know why you have to ask. Michelle. Then it was the fire and my kids dying."

"I can understand that, but I think there's something else. What?"

Bryce paused for a long time, then said, "I don't know. I lost some memories after the fire; don't know if it was the fire or the coma. I think something happened early in my marriage and I think it was significant." He shrugged. "Then I read *Atlas Shrugged*."

Knox burst out laughing and he laughed until he was coughing and wiping tears from his eyes. "Oh, damn. That's our family manifesto. If I'd known you were going to go that nuts, I'd have shoved it in your hands in college. You were a downright prude."

"I would've been horrified. Attracted, but horrified. It took what little sex I got—all of it bad—and no outlet for my anger with Michelle to make me accept that you were right."

Knox, still chuckling, said, "The sweetest sentence in the English language: 'You were right.' Congratulations on getting in touch with your dark side and for picking the right woman."

"I didn't pick her," Bryce admitted after a long silence. "She picked me and she made sure I knew it. Well?"

"No, I haven't. Neither has anyone else, might I add."

"Don't split hairs with me. You're a prude of a different color and I know how you differentiate."

Knox snorted. "Okay, no. No making love, no having sex, no fucking, no whatever you want to call it. Not even close. Bryce, she's my cousin. We grew up together. We're all members of the church or used to be. What, you figured out we were related, but it didn't occur to you she might actually be sitting in church on Sundays?"

"Neither you nor Taight are in there with the program and she hangs with you both. Why should I believe she's any different?"

"Well. I see your point, but Sebastian just up and left."

Bryce raised an eyebrow. "And you were excommunicated."

"Yeah, so I didn't feel obliged to sleep alone anymore for the temple marriage I wasn't ever going to get. Giselle does what she wants and what she wants is to save it for marriage like she's supposed to."

"And she's how old?"

"Thirty-six."

"I call bullshit."

Knox paused, his tongue in his cheek. "Well. She's not pure as the wind-driven snow, no. She owns stock in Duracell and has a shelf full of erotica—and her taste runs to kinky." He shuddered. "But for a woman her age with raging hormones, she's holding out as well as can be expected. Whatever happened at the gallery with you was completely out of character for her. Sebastian was shocked. Now he's just seriously annoyed."

Bryce had ceased to think. It was too— Too much. Too good, too bad, all at the same time.

I've never done this sort of thing before.

So she hadn't—and not only had he not believed her, he'd thrown it back in her face for daring to say it. No wonder she'd looked so horrified. He sure as hell hoped he'd made no other dead-wrong assumptions he'd be obliged to account for.

"So are you done with the church?"

"Maybe," Bryce answered slowly, low, "I don't know. I think so. I don't fit. I never did." Knox sighed, but said nothing. He didn't have to; Bryce knew his opinion and it wouldn't have changed in twenty years. "Do you really expect me to believe Giselle's a virgin?"

"Yes, I do. If she'd have given it up for anybody, it'd been for me—" Bryce flinched. "But no. She's been . . . how do I put this? . . . waiting for someone to sweep her off her feet." He waved a hand. "Congratulations."

"She ran away from me."

"You scared the shit out of her, and not your face, either. She's always been too invested in her fantasy man to know what to do with a real one. She's had the law of chastity beaten into her for the last thirty years, same as we all did, but she also has a turbocharged libido *and* she's heading to forty. It's not like there are a lot of single LDS dudes her age who know the drill and would keep their hands off, right? So she doesn't date outside the church much at all in case she falls off the deep end with the first guy who strokes her just right who would then treat her like shit in the morning. She has almost no control and she knows that."

So do I.

"She doesn't know I'm a member," Bryce muttered.

"Yeah, she does. She went in thinking she'd get a nice evening of philosophical discourse with an unthreatening male about her age she could relate to on a cultural level."

Bryce couldn't help his wry chuckle. "Now, if you and she are that close, why haven't I ever met her?"

Knox abruptly stopped chewing and stared at him for a moment with an expression Bryce couldn't decipher, which was rare enough that it made him uncomfortable. "Huh," he said after another few seconds. "Well, you were married by the time we got to BYU, so what difference would it have made? She's exactly what you've always liked in women, and I wasn't about to put *her* between you and Michelle, since *I* wasn't having a picnic being between you. Not to mention what that would've done for the state of your soul. You're welcome."

"I hate it that you know me that well."

"And I hate it that you didn't know me well enough when it counted."

That found its mark and Bryce's mouth tightened with guilt. He looked at the tablecloth and fiddled with a fork. "I'm sorry," he said for the umpteenth time tonight, not knowing how he could really make it right.

"Look," Know finally said. "It's done, gone, kaput. Ding dong the bitch is dead. I'm just glad you're talking to me again. I wasn't sure you'd show up at all."

"And you're not with Giselle."

"No. So are we square now? I'm in love with a twenty-three-year-old rising star conservative pundit-cum-kingmaker and I'm pretty sure Giselle's in love with you."

Bryce's gaze snapped up to Knox's, feeling as if his heart had stopped. "What did you say?"

"Dammit, I feel like I'm in junior high again. Do I stutter? You want her. She wants you. Figure it out."

15: Litanie des Saints

IT WAS EARLY MORNING BEFORE BRYCE GOT HOME AND STEPPED INTO A VERY hot shower. He leaned on the wall, took his hard phallus in his hand, and thought about Giselle, that night in front of the bodhisattva, what he'd wanted to do to her then, what he still wanted to do to her.

This is Giselle's brain child.

What he wanted to do to her mind.

His head back, hot water streamed down his face as he thought about her, her brain, her body—

One gun in each hand. No hesitation. No remorse . . . They had to dig the other one out of her hip.

His breath came harder, faster.

She just gave your IQ a blow job and she's not even here.

He wanted that woman, her mind, her expressive face, her gestures and the humor that radiated from her body like her sweet perfume—hell, the entire gamut of her mood swings—across a dinner table from him, sitting beside him.

Talking to him.

Making him laugh.

Fucking his mind.

She put a gun to his head . . .

He wanted that woman, her warrior's soul, her fearlessness, her ferocity—in his bed and underneath him.

In front of him.

On her knees.

Sucking his cock.

The way he'd fantasized the first time he'd seen her.

He sagged against the shower wall, his head low and his chest heaving, his orgasm having left him drained.

This just wasn't going to work for him anymore. It wasn't enough. It had never been enough and masturbation definitely didn't qualify as a component of a chaste lifestyle—

—not that he had any reason to care anymore.

In that entire conversation, Bryce had learned only four things that actually meant anything to him: Giselle had very little experience with men; she had a brilliant mind; she had a dark soul like his, which she displayed like a trophy; and

I'm pretty sure she's in love with you.

Bryce couldn't think, could barely move, and only did so enough to slide down the wall and sit on the floor of the shower, knees bent, legs spread, arms crossed over them, head back against the wall. He stayed in the shower until the hot water ran out, then let the cool water sluice over him.

She owns stock in Duracell and has a shelf full of erotica . . .

He took a deep, shuddering breath and released it on a groan.

. . . her taste runs to kinky . . .

He didn't care about Fen Hilliard. Didn't care about Knox's predicament—tragic, but oh well. Didn't care about Taight's war or that Bryce had nearly broken the man's jaw. The only thing about Taight's political problems he cared about was that Giselle had laid out an ingenious strategy for him. He didn't care about anything in that whole saga except Giselle—and he didn't even know why.

One overheard proposition and the glimpse of a nine-millimeter strapped around Lilith's thigh; one kiss in a parking lot; one rendezvous on an ottoman at an art gallery: Why? Why had those few moments been so profound and why did he keep churning them over in his mind now eighteen months later?

She's been . . . waiting for someone to sweep her off her feet . . . Congratulations.

Bryce snorted.

Giselle had grown up in the church and, according to Knox, still attended regularly. She also knew Bryce was a member of the church, although since he'd undressed her and propositioned her (*assaulted her, you mean—no wonder she ran*), she'd probably deduced a few truths about his state of mind.

At least he wouldn't have to explain anything to her, nor she him. The goal of any dating relationship in the church was marriage; one didn't waste time dating for any other reason, especially not at their ages. Chaste, thus *rapid*, courtship, then marriage in the temple for eternity. They could both recite the drill by rote, and in that context, her inexperience didn't surprise him in the least.

Too bad for her, then, if she'd held out for a temple marriage all these years. It didn't matter how badly Bryce wanted her; if he pursued her and she made that a condition of any kind of relationship, he'd walk away.

Bryce had mentally broken his covenants time and time again since he'd come home from the hospital alone, without his children, without his face. But without his face, he'd had no chance of finding a woman fascinating enough to break them in deed. He didn't know how to charm, how to seduce, how to do what ordinary looking men knew how to do. He'd never had to learn.

Shit, Bryce, have you ever had to work to get a girl you wanted to go out with you?

No. His face had done all the work for him; he couldn't remember ever having asked a girl or a woman out in his life. After he'd come home from his mission and gone north to UCLA, he'd had his pick of the most beautiful women in southern California. There was no shortage of beautiful women in Kansas City, either, so the invitations hadn't stopped just because he wore a wedding band.

Monster.

He could let his wallet do the work for him now, he supposed, but that was no better than paying for sex and *that* he wouldn't do.

Eventually, Bryce arose, turned off the water and stepped out of the shower. He roamed naked through his bedroom, nearly oblivious to the cold, and rummaged around for his wallet. Then, with it in hand, he went downstairs to the kitchen. Over the sink, he unfolded the leather and retrieved a small piece of paper that proclaimed him a church member in good standing: His temple recommend, his pass to the Holy of Holies, the House of the Lord, the Temple of God. It had expired, but no matter.

He searched for and found an ancient box of matches. He lit one corner of the paper and held it while he watched the flame catch and flare.

16: The Island of the Day Before

May 2006

GISELLE WALKED OUT OF THE LAW BUILDING INTO THE GORGEOUS MAY Friday after she'd finished her last final, headed for her car. Her arms wrapped around the books clutched to her chest, she breathed a sigh of relief. She didn't know how she'd survived the semester, really. It was bad enough that she had to listen to people wax poetic about *Professor Hilliard's* brilliance and marvel in scandalized whispers about his reputation up in Chouteau County for murder and corruption. That only made her roll her eyes and snort a lot, and amongst Giselle's study buddies, the inexplicable hostilities between her and Professor Hilliard had turned into a running joke. But . . .

Like a new word that she'd learned and kept hearing in conversation, Bryce Kenard's name had haunted her all semester. Snatches of overheard conversation here. Classroom examples of exquisite courtroom strategy there. Her malpractice professor had even made him the subject of an assignment, which had required an unbelievable amount of research.

Before it had come out of Sebastian's mouth in November, Giselle didn't remember hearing his name at all. Now she knew almost every professional thing there was to know about the man.

Bryce Kenard: A god at the UMKC School of Law—

—a god she'd experienced intimately, a god who wanted her. With every mention of his name, with every telling of the tales of his genius, his cunning, his ruthlessness—pain, sharp and hot, sliced her deep in her soul.

Giselle . . . Come home with me. Now. Tonight.

She wished she had; at least she'd have something more of him to keep in her heart than she had now.

Giselle wanted to lie on her bed curled up into a ball and stay that way all weekend.

By the time she'd finished her Bryce Kenard malpractice assignment in late March and had almost grown used to hearing his name wherever she went, her mind started playing tricks on her. She saw him everywhere, usually at the courthouse. Just glimpses, nothing solid. One day she could swear he was trying to catch up with her to speak with her, only to be waylaid by people needing his attention. The next day she would chastise herself for thinking such thirteen-year-old-girl things. Why did she think he would come to her? Why did she hope? She had run away from him; no man with an IQ point to call his own would pursue a woman after that.

She swallowed the gob of ick that collected in her throat.

It had occurred to her (mostly only every other day) to go to his office and explain that she hadn't wanted to run away from him, to explain why she had shown up at the gallery, apologize, then let him decide what to think. But a con was a con, and she knew what she would think and do if someone had deceived her that way, destroyed her trust, made a fool of her.

The bottom of her world had dropped out and she didn't even know why. What was it about him that made her do crazy, risky things she'd never considered doing before? And with a *stranger*?

At church, she had learned not to put herself in temptation's way, so she hadn't.

At karate, she had learned not to put herself in danger's way, so she hadn't.

Then a man she didn't know had hurt her feelings, so she'd kissed him in retaliation and then she'd put herself at the mercy of the same man, with little more information than she'd had before—

—except that he knew the rules of engagement for faithful members of the church as well as she did. Clearly he had left the church behind, and she couldn't say she didn't want to follow him right out the door and into bed.

That scared her to death.

"First rule of karate," she whispered to herself. "Don't be stupid."

She reached her car and sagged against it, her eyes closed, to relive that night: his tongue in her mouth, his mouth on her breasts, his lips surrounding the hole in her shoulder, his voice in her ear—hot, insistent, demanding.

Not in control now, are you?

His sardonic challenges of her power. She could feel her body's arousal at the thought of how brazen it had been to take him up the stairs and lie under him half naked in a public place: how wonderfully, deliciously wicked.

"Giselle."

She gasped and whirled, embarrassed that whoever had said her name might read her mind, see her arousal. The wind whipped her hair across her face so that she couldn't see, and when she pulled it aside, her eyes widened.

She gulped and backed up, closer to her car, even though he kept a respectful distance between them and she didn't fear him.

Shame. The only emotion she knew at that moment was shame for her deceit.

The true crime? She'd gone ahead with the plan even though deceiving him would mean the end of any hope of a relationship with him.

"Giselle, I—"

Giselle couldn't read the expression on his face. A hodgepodge of things flitted across his carved-and-scarred features that she didn't understand.

"I— I, um— Please go away," she blurted. "It was a mistake; I'm sorry."

Don't cry. Don't cry don'tcry dontcrydontcry

He looked at her with that same unreadable expression and spoke carefully. "Sorry for what?"

Frustrated, she let out a whoosh. "Just— Everything, okay? I'm sorry I yelled at you, sorry I put a gun to your head, sorry I led you up the stairs and gave you the wrong idea about me."

"What idea do I have?"

You think I'm a slut.

She gritted her teeth to keep the tears at bay and snapped, "Didn't anybody ever tell you it was rude to answer a question with a question?" She turned and opened the door, threw her books and her purse across to the passenger seat, and dropped behind the steering wheel.

"Giselle, please wait."

"I can't," she answered as she started her car and put it in reverse, though she didn't lift her foot off the clutch enough to actually move. What was she waiting for?

"Please have lunch with me. Talk with me. That's *all.* Please."

And have him excoriate her for lying to him in the middle of a restaurant? No thanks.

"I can't," she said again, too ashamed now to even look at him. "I— I have plans."

After that, he caught her when he saw her; not often, usually at the courthouse and apparently only when he had a free moment.

"Giselle, please," he said every time. "One meal, please. I just want to talk. That's *all.*" He didn't bother to hide the pleading in his voice and it broke her heart, made her breathless at what she had done to a god.

In late June, he found her at the library, standing in the fiction stacks, perusing

Christopher Moore. Incredibly intimidated, achingly aroused, still ashamed and embarrassed, frightened and hurting more than she thought possible, she snapped, "Stalking me?"

His nostrils flared and his eyes blazed. Without saying a word, he turned on a heel and left.

She stepped out into the aisle to watch him walk away, anger in every long step, in his back, in the shake of his head, in the violent punch of the elevator button. He looked back at her then and stared at her until the elevator arrived, his mouth tight, his jaw clenched, his gaze hard.

Ducking back into the stacks, she put her forehead down on the bookshelf to cry.

17: Recovering Bitch

GOOD LUCK," SAID MISS LOGAN'S ATTORNEY AS HE SQUEEZED HER UPPER arm lightly, then disappeared through a set of courtroom doors to give her a moment to prepare.

She glanced in a mirror that added to the décor of the quaint mid-nineteenth century American county courthouse, and sighed at her reflection. Taken as a whole, she was entirely underwhelming. Taken in parts, she was even less interesting than that.

Her hair: Dirty-dishwater blonde, slicked back into a tight French twist at the back.

Her eyes: Brown.

Her face: Plain, though perhaps sporting a little too much makeup.

Her body: Tall, big boned, nearly five feet eleven inches barefoot. She classified herself as less than svelte on days she felt generous. Though she had to admit that her breasts had a nice shape, the DD cup dismayed her. Her belly protruded enough to make her look about six weeks pregnant, but all her attempts at flattening it failed. Her hips—a particular point of David's ridicule—matched her breasts.

Her outfit: Ridiculous. No Audrey Hepburn or Jackie O., she didn't carry the classic Chanel look well. The color, Pepto Pink, would have washed her out but for her makeup. Sensible low black pumps did nothing for her feet or calves.

She had crafted every detail of what she saw in the mirror, so her sudden melancholy over it irked her. What she looked like at home, in private, shopping, attending the occasional society soiree—well. She did the best she could with what she had. She used to think herself passably pretty for an Amazon, but then she'd married a man who disagreed.

As she intended, the world took her as she presented herself without question as to what lay underneath. She relied on her talent and her ladylike mien to carry her through her workday and to garner the respect she required to do business. Once she got into character each morning, she fooled the world and relied on her persona to lessen her insecurity and sharpen her advantage—

—and she had done this for twelve years. She had the act down cold.

So now here she loitered in the foyer of the Chouteau County courthouse waiting to hear her fate. Her persona gave her no advantage today; she dreaded whatever the prosecutor had decided to do with her.

She turned and gracefully sat on a bench by the courtroom doors, as ladylike as ever. She stared across the foyer to the grand walnut staircase, lost in her thoughts.

"Miss Logan?"

She turned, startled. The time had come; they would wait for her no longer. She cleared her throat, calmed her heart, and arose from the bench. Slow. Easy. As if she were the most gracious hostess of the most magnificent mansion on Ward Parkway.

The almost ridiculously young underling sent to fetch her smiled.

"Thank you," she murmured, her tone perfectly modulated. She stepped through the door he held open for her. *Thank God*, no trembles and no squeaks, though her life's work hung in the balance.

She couldn't help the pace of her heart, the dryness of her throat, the fear that ran through her as she took measured steps down the aisle of the courtroom toward the prosecutor and the judge who awaited her.

She *could* help how she reacted to it all.

Calm, poised, gracious as always, she stood at the defense table by the chair meant for her, but she did not sit. It finally occurred to her attorney to arise and pull it out for her. She nodded her thanks as she sat.

It never failed to surprise men when she refused to pull out her own chair. Most had forgotten what a real lady was, if they ever knew in the first place, the etiquette lost to history. She used that to her advantage, without fail and without mercy.

"Thank you for joining us, Miss Logan," Judge Wilson began. "Let's recap for the court reporter, shall we?"

No, let's not.

He looked down at the papers in front of him.

"You are the founder and CEO of HR Prerogatives, a human resources outsourcing company.

"In May of 1999, you hired David Webster to be the chief financial officer. You and he never had any relationship other than work until you were in New York on a business trip on September 11, 2001. You witnessed the planes crashing into the World Trade Center, and under the stress of that, you married him. During your marriage, you were raped and beaten, but his behavior at home was so at odds with his behavior at work you became suspicious of him."

He should have won an Oscar.

"Then you realized he had been embezzling from you his entire tenure at your company. You felt the only way you could prove it was to stay in the marriage."

Keep your friends close and your enemies closer.

Judge Wilson looked over his spectacles at her. "You should've called the police."

When have the police ever helped me?

She kept her face expressionless with the ease of twelve years of practice.

"He had access to your cash reserves and offshore accounts set up to receive the transfer of your employees' 401(k) funds, which you found out only an hour before all the transactions went through. You hacked into your own computer system from a remote location and killed the pension transactions, but he did manage to take your reserves and left your company deeply in debt."

He paused and still she remained silent, impassive.

"You realize, of course, any other prosecutor in the metro would've charged you as well."

"Your Honor," Knox Hilliard said with a bit of impatience, "she doesn't need to be sent to her room to think about what she did."

The judge glared at the prosecutor. "One more crack like that and I'll send *you* to your room to think about a contempt citation."

Hilliard's cough didn't quite disguise his laugh.

"Miss Logan, Mr. Hilliard has a proposition I hope you'll be agreeable to."

She had no choice and the implication that she did was insulting. The man she dreaded most in the world right now—for more than a few reasons—rose from the prosecution's table.

To his credit, Hilliard seemed to take no pleasure from this, despite his reputation toward the corrupt and sadistic. During the three years of investigation into David's embezzlement schemes, hours of testimony prep, and a year-long trial, he had never treated her with anything but excruciating politeness, if not downright compassion.

"Eilis," he addressed her then, respectfully and, as always, pronouncing her name precisely: EYE-lish. He had used it from the very first, never asking her her preference. Such behavior by any other man would have warranted a cold, ladylike set-down, but not for a man significant to her in ways he would never know. And after the stress of her four-year journey with him, her name on his tongue had become a comfort to her.

Until today.

"I would like to propose putting HR Prerogatives in receivership."

She started and looked at him sharply. Receivership! The man whose judgment on this issue she'd dreaded so much might have just saved her, depending on whom he appointed as her trustee.

That was a double-edged sword.

He went on. "I'm not here to destroy you or your company, or to put all your employees out of their jobs. Should you agree to receivership, your appointed trustee will be Sebastian Taight."

She swallowed a gasp, kept her composure—but she fought for it. Her attorney nodded sagely. That certainly tarnished her favorable opinion of Mr. Hilliard. *How* had he suddenly turned into her enemy?

Nauseated, she wondered if he'd uncovered her connection to OKH Enterprises and Fen Hilliard, and decided to take his vengeance upon her now. Of all the consultants available, he had chosen the only one who could put her out of business completely or hand her over to Fen on a silver platter:

King Midas.

Sebastian Taight in charge of her company frightened her. His close family ties to both Knox and Fen Hilliard terrified her. She quelled her instinct to shudder.

She spoke finally. "Is that the best offer I can expect?"

The prosecutor nodded solemnly. "Yes."

The judge broke into her silence and said, not unkindly, "Mr. Taight has never before agreed to be the trustee for a receivership and I'd take it if I were you. You couldn't be in better hands."

Still silent, Eilis studied the ogee edge of the table. Yeah, she could just bet why he'd agreed to take her receivership as his first ever. She finally nodded because she had no choice.

"That would be acceptable. Thank you."

18: Brass in Pocket

KING MIDAS WALKED IN LIKE A MEDIEVAL MARAUDER, HIS STRIDE LONG and arrogant. He carried nothing in his hands or over his shoulders: no legal pad, no briefcase, no laptop, no manpurse. With every step he seemed to take inventory of *her* company as if it were about to become his.

She hated him for that.

Eilis had never met him, never seen him. No one, woman or man, had ever told her how tall, lean, and achingly, heart-*stoppingly* handsome he was. Because she'd only heard the horror stories, she had conjured him up in her mind as an aged Quasimodo with a God complex.

His slightly salted raven hair gleamed and his ice blue eyes shimmered so light against his hair and his suit, she could see them from a distance. Sebastian Taight, classic black Irish, who had made her immediately, unexpectedly, shockingly breathless and aroused on first sight.

She hated herself for that.

She knew what he'd do first and she dreaded it. He made a fortune speculating in art and he would have been apprised of her assets. Boxed in as she was amongst the Chouteau County prosecutor, the Midwest's most notorious financial guru as her babysitter, and the CEO of OKH Enterprises, she didn't have a chance.

The news reports of the OKH Proviso Instrument were vague enough that no one knew quite how the three players were allied, if at all, though everyone had their hypotheses and theories. Before yesterday, she could have drawn no conclusions other than the obvious one everyone drew: Taight had positioned himself to take OKH Enterprises away from both Fen and Knox in a hostile takeover on or just after Knox's fortieth birthday, despite what the proviso stated explicitly.

Eilis sucked in a deep breath, her lungs expanding almost beyond capacity. With one bad decision, albeit made under extreme circumstances, she had gone from frying pan to fire to ash fertilizer. No one but Eilis knew that she had become wrapped up in that OKH proviso mess the minute Knox had appointed Taight her trustee. She could only have faith that if infamously thorough Knox Hilliard hadn't stumbled upon her secret by now, he wouldn't. No one would.

If either Knox or Sebastian Taight found out, she would lose everything—Fen Hilliard had promised her that.

Truthfully, Eilis didn't want to hate King Midas, in the abstract or otherwise. She had observed the OKH debacle from afar and without comment to her CEO colleagues ever since the man had begun purchasing its shares. She had cheered quietly, hoping he would win it in the end. When Knox announced his engagement to Mrs. Leah Wincott, a widow with a daughter, Eilis breathed a sigh of relief.

Leah Wincott's murder—on her *wedding day*, yet!—shocked the financial community to its core. The Street rumbled and cracked with the not-so-hushed rumors of Fen's involvement. No one wanted to believe it (least of all Eilis), but there could be no other explanation and suddenly, Taight's war became *important* to Eilis. She, along with the rest of the country, *needed* him to take OKH away from Fen.

Unfortunately, Knox was a complication. Collateral damage.

Now, though, she found herself at the mercy of the man the financial community feared for his eccentricities, obscure reasoning, and unpredictability. She swallowed a sharp pang of regret that she'd not met this brilliant—and most definitely beautiful—man before Knox had made him her enemy.

Scylla, meet Charybdis.

Eilis took a deep breath. *Where* had her Inner Bitch gone now that she needed her so very badly?

From where she stood behind the all-glass walls of her office suite, she could look down onto the labyrinth of cubicles filled with people whose livelihoods depended on her. For now. They knew nothing of the details and they were jittery. Many had left for other, more stable, positions. If the deal with Midas worked out, those who remained would survive this storm and their lives would go on, their nerves calmed when stability reigned again.

He walked down the main aisle alone, unnoticed it seemed, though how such a man could go unnoticed was beyond her. If he looked up, he would see her there, but he didn't. His initial inspection over with, he stared straight ahead, his long-legged gait eating up the yards between them as if he knew exactly where he was going—which he probably did.

He disappeared underneath the glassed mezzanine that was her office and she knew it wouldn't be long before he was there, with her. Sure enough, his steps echoed on the stairs. She kept her back turned when he reached the reception area of her office and then her door, being deliberately rude to him. Watching him in the reflection of the glass, her breathlessness increased as he entered her office and came closer and closer to her without speaking.

He stood beside her and looked down at the patchwork of cubicles without speaking. She was very aware of his presence, his fragrance, his height.

This would be so much easier if she weren't so unexpectedly attracted to him.

"You're not a good gambler," he said finally. Eilis hid her reaction. Whatever she'd expected, his mild manner was not it.

"I built this company. How do you think I did that?" she asked, her voice, as always, perfectly modulated.

"And you lost it. How do you think you did *that?* It's not the making of a company, Mrs. Webster. It's the keeping of it and the growing of it that counts."

She did not flinch, though she wanted to. *Becoming Mrs. Webster,* that which had been her biggest—gamble? Was that what he thought it was?—and one she would pay for for the rest of her life.

No, Eilis was an *excellent* gambler.

When backed into an emotional corner, however, she invariably zigged when she should have zagged. Not that she would tell *him* that.

"Believe it or not, Knox did you a favor," he added, as if for good measure.

She resisted the urge to snort, instead calling up her persona from years of practice. She said calmly, "I'm quite sure you both think you've counted quite a coup."

He slid a glance at her and she was unaccountably pleased that she didn't have to look down at him. "I don't have to do this, Mrs. Webster. I can find someone else to do it if you'd like."

"Would it make any difference?" she asked, still calm.

That was the way she always was. Calm, quiet, unassuming. She'd begun her career hard, ruthless, but as her reputation for such grew, her enemies used it to sabotage her business deals. Forced to abandon that approach, she had concocted Miss Logan, splendidly, flawlessly ladylike.

She hated it, but it worked exponentially better than she could have ever dreamed. The intimidation and discomfort men felt when she forced them to pay her homage as a lady never went away and its element of surprise was ever present.

Oh, yes, it was a power play of immense proportions, but it had taken a heavy toll on her over the years.

He turned back to the window and said, "You know better than that."

As raiders went, he was better than most. She couldn't lie to herself—if he had no ulterior motive, he would do a good job with fairness and honesty. If his track record held, she would have her company back in less than the three years the receivership was slated to run, unless he chose to buy her out. He could do anything he wanted with her as long as the bills got paid.

She resented him just for being called in to do what she could have done herself had she had time and briefly resented the prosecutor for not asking her her opinion.

"Mrs. Webster—"

"I no longer use that name," she murmured, struggling to keep her composure, to keep her tears at bay at the tone of sympathy she had heard in his voice. "Miss Logan, if you please."

"Miss Logan." He complied so easily. Why did that irritate her? "Shall we get started?"

Miss Logan's obvious distrust of him annoyed the hell out of him, but he couldn't say why because this was the way it *always* was.

Sebastian was sympathetic to her situation; he was sympathetic to all situations. He too would be resentful if he were the one staring a court-ordered receivership in the face.

The barely veiled venom of the beginning of his relationship with this woman was mild compared to most, and she had more reason than anyone else in the world to hate him. It wasn't as if *she* had called him to come rescue her, and anyone could've made the mistake of hiring a thief as one's CFO. Senator Oth's entire executive staff had been a den of thieves.

Of course, Oth hadn't married his CFO, either.

Damn Knox for badgering him into being this woman's trustee, and damn that judge for being such a good friend to Knox that he'd ordered it. In Sebastian's opinion, his relationship to Knox made this whole thing one big fat conflict of interest.

"If it makes you feel any better," he heard himself saying as, together, they moved away from the glass toward her private office, her inner sanctum, windowless and clad in maple, "I don't want to do this any more than you want it done. I do have better things to do with my time than rescue a company that doesn't interest me."

He felt her surprise and relief, but she only said, "I see," without emotion.

Stifling a sigh, he went through her office to *her* desk, sat in *her* chair, in front of *her* computer, to gain access to *her* company's records. Being considered a villain on first sight was so common in his life as to be a cliché.

He was surprised when she spoke again, her voice still measured and perfect. "I'm curious, Mr. Taight. If this is such a burden to you, why did you accept?"

He grunted. "Family. Loyalty. Trust."

She showed no emotion at that and, unsatisfied that she hadn't cracked, he turned back to the computer.

He clicked through her computer files. He made note of spreadsheets and databases, mentally mapping out matrices and indices to begin his work, all too aware she stood only a few feet from him, watching. Silent, impassive. He'd never before been a trustee for a company in receivership, but he had hauled enough companies out of bankruptcy by a breath to know what he needed to do and what to look for without preparation.

That could be the only reason why Knox had asked him to do this. Of course, Knox probably had other, more sinister ulterior motives, but he didn't know what they were and he didn't care. He'd find out eventually because Knox *never* did things the easy way.

Eilis Logan's company was very well positioned for salvation and Sebastian was curious as to why she hadn't taken the obvious steps to do so herself. She was certainly capable of it.

He happened across a file of digitized documents that hadn't been in the paperwork he'd been given and saw why Knox had asked him to do this. He sent an email: **FOUND THE FORDS. THX.**

"Mr. Taight—"

"Sebastian, please."

"Mr. Taight," she went on in that same ladylike moderation, not a shred of passion in it. "Are you going to need me for anything here? If not, I would like to take a vacation."

Sebastian stilled and looked up at her and allowed himself to see her as a man saw a woman. It wasn't that he didn't notice beautiful women, because he did. On a detailed, aesthetic level, he very much noticed and appreciated every woman's beauty, but he had learned through the years that he couldn't seduce any woman when he was thinking very left-brain things. Unless a woman was thoroughly entranced by a discussion of the inflation-proof bond, nothing would happen while he was in a suit.

He'd tried that. It had gone very badly—several times.

It wasn't even as if he hadn't already carefully cataloged this woman in his mind, head to toe and she was beautiful—but she hid it very well and very deliberately.

No matter what she did, she wouldn't have been able to hide her very aristocratically sculpted face, with the exception of the nose that had obviously been badly broken and never set straight. She had high cheekbones, a fine forehead, and strong-but-not-masculine jaw. Her mouth was full, though she wore a color of lipstick designed to hide that fact. She wore brown contact lenses—why?—and there was something under all that foundation that looked like a thin scar running from eyebrow to jaw.

And her body—Sebastian shocked himself with his very right-brained thinking about the perfection that was Miss Eilis Logan. Tall and lush, she was a Viking queen. The Chanel made it perfectly clear that this woman was built like a fertility goddess. In Sebastian's estimation, she was flawless, and Sebastian knew he had good taste in women.

"I would prefer you stay involved in the process, Miss Logan," he said slowly, not really sure how to deal with her request, because no one he'd worked with had ever made such an outrageous one before. "Your employees will need you here to give them confidence and you might learn something you could use in the future. I'll also need your input and assistance with things I can't know, such as employee issues."

"I have a cell phone," she said levelly.

That was a bluff. He knew he'd won the battle with his deliberate mention of her employees. If for nothing else, she had a reputation for how much she cared about the people who worked for her.

"Okay, if that's how you want to play it," he said flatly, unaccountably angry with her now. "The answer's no. I'm not going to let you walk off the field just because I'm the one quarterbacking now. If this is going to be a problem for you, you can take it up with Knox."

That got a reaction. Her nostrils flared a tad and her jaw clenched only the slightest bit. Well, in for a penny, in for a pound. If that got a reaction from her, he'd go for broke.

"One of the things I'm going to do," he continued, with that same flat, heartless tone that should tell her his patience had run out, "is sell off every Ford painting this corporation owns. I'm requesting, nicely, that you hand them over so that I can start building your cash reserves. Together, they're worth tens of millions of dollars, which will be a good head start."

Her silent stoicism told him everything he needed to know. She had expected this; she had probably even thought of doing that herself and hadn't been able to bring herself to.

"If you had done that six months ago, I wouldn't be here," he said, now thoroughly pissed off that she hadn't blinked an eye. Taunting a client was uncharacteristic for him and he didn't like the fact that he wanted to get a reaction from her so badly that he was willing to grind it in.

He stopped and took a deep breath before he really let loose and mentioned the second, third, and fourth things she should've done. That would be downright mean.

Sebastian had a speech he had perfected over the years that he used without fail. He didn't want to break people's spirits; he didn't ridicule their choices and he was always careful to maintain respect for them and sympathy with their situations. Once these people in distress got to know him it seemed, oddly, that his presence was of comfort to them in their time of greatest stress and grief.

Not that anyone ever actually noticed that. They never saw what *he* had done to salvage their companies the minute he left for good, check in hand, and only knew what *they* had done. He always pulled his punches, handled everyone with kid gloves, hoping they would learn from their mistakes and from changing their business strategies. Today, though, he hadn't used his normal speech on her, and he didn't know why other than that she was so damned uncrackable.

"I love those paintings," she finally admitted with great dignity.

"Sentiment has no place here, although I will admit that if you had sold them off one at a time for a quick fix, you'd be worse off now than you are."

He saw a split-second flash of heartbreak in her face that must have been extreme to be seen through her mask of makeup. She turned away. Finally, she said, "May I keep one? It's not on the books."

"Does the corporation own it?"

"Yes," she said, her voice tinged with a nearly imperceptible despair.

For reasons he didn't understand, instead of the same flat "no" he would've normally given anyone in her position, the same one he'd given her about a vacation, he asked, "Which one is it?"

"*Morning in Bed.*"

He sucked in a breath and his eyes widened. "You own *Morning in Bed?*"

"Yes."

That painting was worth tens of millions by itself. If she sold that along with the rest of them, she'd be more than half salvaged. Still, he hesitated. "Let me think about it. In the meantime," he continued briskly, "I would like you to go to the Ford exhibit with me Saturday evening so that you can see for yourself the value of letting them all go."

"I can't," she said smoothly. "I have other plans."

Sebastian was immediately suspicious. A woman who owned nine Fords, including the most notorious one, hadn't planned to attend the Ford exhibit where a new painting would be unveiled? Did she hate his presence so much that she would give that up rather than go with him? It wouldn't be the first time that had happened, though, so it was entirely possible. He figured if he couldn't get a date with her under cover of business, he may not be able to get a date with her at all.

He inclined his head. "As you wish, Miss Logan."

Then he walked out of her office and out of her building, now even more pissed off that Knox had badgered him to do this for one entirely different reason. He wanted Eilis Logan in his bed. Badly—

—but he didn't know how the hell he was going to get her there.

19: Clinical, Intellectual, Cynical

GISELLE SAT ON A PICNIC TABLE BY BRUSH CREEK JUST OFF CAMPUS, FEEDING bread to the ducks and geese. She couldn't take this much longer. Sebastian, irritated, had accused her of "moping around the house like a love-struck sixteen-year-old girl for the last seven months." Knox was angry because she had assiduously avoided him. She hadn't returned her mother's phone calls or emails in two weeks and Lilly had resorted to hounding both Sebastian and Knox as to Giselle's state of mind. She hadn't shown up at any of her extended family's frequent functions because she just couldn't take Fen on any level after he'd called her in the middle of class to yell at her for going to his party armed.

She just wanted to be alone for a while with no one jabbering in her ears, making demands, lecturing her on propriety, threatening her life and livelihood and grades, or shaming her for a heinous breach of trust.

She knew Bryce's office address: downtown, in a prestigious skyscraper convenient to the Jackson County Courthouse. She still had no idea what to do with that information or if she'd do anything at all.

"Boy, you just don't know a good thing when it steps right in front of you, do you?"

"Go away," she muttered. "Don't you have fathers and fiancées to avenge, women to marry, and children to sire?"

"You're a hot mess. Move over."

She did and he climbed up onto the table beside her.

He leaned in to kiss her and she leaned away from him. "No more. I'm done with this."

"Done with what?"

"Done with you."

Knox said nothing and she dared not look at him. He could tease her out of her funk now, but it would come back the next day anyway. She was worn out and overwhelmed and very unhappy.

"I'm done with this semi-incestuous relationship. Done with the Shakespearean tragedy that is your life. Knox, I have no stake in OKH, but because of it, everything I had has been taken away from me except my life and that's only because I got lucky. Twice. I'm tired. I want— No, I *need* a resolution."

He handed her a bottle of cold water, which she took. "I'm sorry," he said.

"I know," she replied with a sigh. "Me too."

He caught her mouth then and coaxed her tongue to play, twenty-five years of familiar, so very comfortable. She sighed into his mouth, fell into the kiss, closed her eyes—

—and found herself comparing him unfavorably to Bryce Kenard. She opened her eyes then and pulled away from him. "That wasn't fair. What if somebody saw us?"

"Oh, it'd just give your reputation another layer of mystique."

"Pffftt. *Professor Hilliard* is pissing me off."

"*Miss Cox* yanks my chain plenty, too, so don't act like you're all lily white."

She sighed. "I'm guessing you're here because Sebastian bitched at you to bitch at me?"

"Yeah. You're not home enough for him to kick your ass and when you are, you're sleeping. He thinks I know all your little hiding places."

"Well, you don't."

"You're right about that. I've been to every shoe store in town."

She cracked a reluctant smile.

"Lemme guess. Bryce Kenard."

She swallowed.

"Talk to me, Giselle."

"He, um— At the gallery, he—" She stopped. Took a deep breath. "He wanted— He asked me to go home with him and— Um, and I wanted to, but I was there to trick him. I mean, I couldn't— Not on a lie."

"Oh, is *that* what this is about?"

"That and the fact that he thinks I'm a slut," she said in a rush. "I'm *mortified*."

He said nothing for a moment. Then, "So tell him the truth. Throw yourself on his mercy. You've got nothing to lose."

"Like I want to invite someone else to read back my pedigree for me? I think not.

Sebastian takes care of that quite nicely, thank you."

"That's a dodge. He intimidates you and you don't like it."

"Fuck you."

Knox took some of her bread to throw to the ducks. Neither of them spoke for a long time, then he said, "I've been wanting to ask you something. Was I that obvious?"

"When?"

"That day in class last year, that week I subbed for Grady."

Giselle had to cast back in her memory a bit before she remembered. "I thought you didn't want to discuss it?"

"I do now. Talk."

"Hmm. Well. It was obvious to me. I think the rest of the class was just too shellshocked to notice."

"Shellshocked?"

"Knox, you were . . . enraged. I haven't seen you that angry since you tried Tom Parley and you've never shown that side of you in class. You turned from hottie heartthrob law professor into badass Chouteau County prosecutor. And how you looked at her— I have never seen you look at any woman that way, not Leah, not me, not any other woman you've ever loved." She paused. "By the way, did you get in trouble for that?"

His eyebrow rose. "Giselle," he drawled.

"Of course not! Untouchable Knox Hilliard strikes again." Giselle huffed. "So if Leah hadn't been in the picture, would you have nabbed her after class and taken her to the Den of Iniquity? 'Cause that's what it looked like you wanted to do."

His silence told her everything she needed to know.

"Oh, Knox," she sighed. "More guilt?"

"I went home that day feeling like the worst bastard who ever lived. I could barely look at Leah. Then she died—" His mouth tightened. "I know you haven't told Sebastian any of this because he hasn't cracked my head open."

She waved a hand. "I'm torn. I see your point and I agree with it, but this really is your fight and Sebastian has a right to resent that you want to abandon ship now that he's steering it. Why don't you seek her out and tell her how you feel, lay it all out for her, and let her decide whether she wants to be with you or not? She's in love with you."

"She wouldn't understand it even if I recited it line and verse. And even if she did, no woman in her right mind would step into my mess voluntarily. You know I don't like women not in their right minds and, aside from her crush on me, Justice McKinley *is* in her right mind."

"I don't think that's fair. I mean, if I were her, I'd want to know that the man I wanted actually wanted me, too. I wouldn't want to live my life wondering and dreaming and wishing."

"Giselle, she's *fourteen years* younger than me. She's not old enough to know what she wants. I've never been one of *those* professors and I don't like younger women. Forty-year-old women are hot to trot. You have no idea."

Giselle's mouth dropped open.

He caught her look. "Oh. Right. I guess you do know. The point is, this is killing me. She's young enough to be my daughter; hell, I've raised a girl her age. What am I supposed to do with her? By the time she turns forty, I'd have to pop Viagra like they're aspirin just to barely keep up. And then there's the perv factor. As in, 'Oh, gee, I was fourteen when she was born.'"

"And Leah was fifteen when you were born." She paused. "All you'd have to do is have your executive give her a little ringy-ding, ask her to come in for an interview. Everybody would assume that you're courting her name just as much as every other office and every other think tank in the country. Her name would skyrocket if Knox Hilliard, Trainer of Baby Litigators, sought her out and nobody would ever have to know that all you want is a little redheaded teddy bear. Keep her as an AP, train her, wait until after your birthday and then explain it.

"Or, in the alternative, hire her, train her, and let her go none the wiser. She needs a backbone and it would take her six years to get where you could get her in six weeks."

"My world would crush her," he murmured so low she could barely hear him. "I would crush her."

"Knox, you gave her name to her. Do you not get that? She's well respected across the country and powerful people have begun to court her opinions. Every time you hear her quoted on talk radio, every time you read her blog posts, every time you open a magazine or a newspaper and see her byline—you did that. You validated her, gave her some confidence." Giselle paused. "Online and in print, anyway.

"She hides behind her computer. She still walks around school like she deserves nothing, like she's only there by the grace of God and Knox Hilliard—and that might get taken away any day. She should be walking around like the genius that she is, but— In two, three years, you could turn her into a real power player in politics or law or both. At the very least, finish the job you started."

Knox said nothing for a long while, then, "Her CV is on my desk. I was going to have Eric interview her and then send her on her way."

Giselle gasped and her eyes widened. "She came to you?" He nodded morosely. It took her a bit of thought and silence to work that through; she had never expected that the girl would have the guts to seek Knox out herself.

"Oh, I get it. You think that once she sees you in your world—not as knight-in-shining-armor Professor Hilliard—she won't look at you the same way she did that day and you don't want to watch her get disillusioned with you."

"I find it inconvenient that you can read my mind."

That made Giselle laugh. "Master of the overstated understatement."

He flashed her a grin. "Did you like that?"

"You dumbshit," she said and pushed him off the table.

That made him laugh in turn and he hopped back up on the table. He sobered then. "Me, my name, my office—it would taint her, not make her. Her career would be over before it really began and could kill Oakley's chances, to boot."

Giselle couldn't deny that. Kevin Oakley would have enough to answer for if his long friendship with Knox came to light. Now that Justice had agreed to endorse Kevin as a senatorial candidate, her employment in a corrupt prosecutor's office would cast doubt on her character and, by extension, diminish Kevin's credibility.

"I just want to see her again, let her go, and then find her when this is all over with. Maybe she needs the world to knock her around a little bit—and I refuse to put her where Fen'll feel obliged to kill her. If it weren't for his unpredictability, I'd do it, but I can't take that chance."

Giselle sat and thought about that for a while. "You do have a point," she said slowly, looking off into the distance. "Well," she finally said, "I can appreciate that you want to take the high ground, so I'll not argue with you about it."

"Giselle, do you know why I'm so good at what I do?"

"Not really, no. I don't think of you that way."

"Huh. Well, I'll tell you why. It's my memory. So this is what I have to say to you: 'If it were me, I'd want to know that the man I wanted actually wanted me, too. I wouldn't want to live my life wondering and dreaming and wishing.'"

Her breath caught in her throat. "Bastard," she grumbled.

"Coward."

20: *Fenemies*

G ISELLE LAY AWAKE ALL NIGHT WITH KNOX'S PARTING SHOT RINGING IN her ears.

Coward.

Her situation and his weren't perfectly analogous, but he'd used her own words against her. Did they apply any less to her and this man, this Bryce Kenard (whose very name screamed testosterone) with whom she'd spent so little time, and every second of it in intensely erotic foreplay?

That's a dodge. He intimidates you and you don't like it.

Knox was right and she hated when that happened, especially when Sebastian agreed, since they so very rarely did. Knox had wasted no time in tattling on her to Sebastian, who said, "So? It's not like you pulled off some elaborate scam and made a fool of him. But," he added, "you need to get the monkey off your back first so you can have a fresh start. Kenard doesn't need to be mixed up in this. He's done nothing to deserve it."

Knox agreed with that assessment, too. She had no chance when both of them ganged up on her.

She made up her mind and she wouldn't wait until the family's Labor Day barbecue to have her say, so she went to Fen immediately. Once having made the decision to seek Bryce Kenard out, she wouldn't let it lie one more second.

Giselle didn't dare go unarmed. She also didn't bother to stop at the guard's desk or pause when the metal detector shrieked at her, or in any way acknowledge the men who hollered behind her and scrambled to keep her from going any farther into the building.

"Stand down, gentlemen," boomed a deep voice from the mezzanine above the massively expansive terrazzo-and-marble front lobby of OKH Enterprises. "Everything's fine. My wayward niece just wants to throw a little tantrum at me."

Protests followed her as she took the stairs of the grand staircase two at a time, her strong legs eating up the distance between him and her. She ignored everyone but the man she had come to see.

She had a strange balance of power with him that she'd had since she was a child. She didn't always understand it, but occasionally it proved useful.

Yes, he'd tried to kill her twice, which had bankrupted her and obliged her to undergo emergency surgery, respectively.

Yes, she'd calmly and deliberately threatened to kill him, a hand on his throat and a gun to his head.

Yes, he felt as free to dress her down as any of her other aunts and uncles.

Yes, they usually had a good time together once he made her laugh again.

"Come in, Giselle, come in," Fen Hilliard said graciously. He held the door to his office suite open and guided her through the floor of assistants' desks arranged as if it were a bank lobby. They all looked at her warily, this sacrilegious woman appearing at the CEO's office wearing tight leathers and boots, with a Glock stuck in the back of her waistband. She smiled slightly at one young male assistant who couldn't take his eyes off of her. She winked at him and he blushed.

"Stop flirting with my people," Fen hissed once he had ushered her into his private office and closed the doors behind them. "You dare come to me armed?"

"Pfffft. I'd be a fool not to."

"I wouldn't be stupid enough to kill you here, Giselle."

"There is that. You don't have the stomach to do it yourself."

He ignored that and rocked back on a heel to rake her with a glance and gesture at her clothes. "And—and this," he sneered. "You couldn't have dressed properly? You disrespect me in my own house?"

"Oh, do you mean the house that Uncle Oliver built?"

His jaw clenched. "Oliver built a shack. I razed it and plowed the fields and built a plantation."

"Wasn't the only field of his you plowed, was it?"

He slapped her then and she retaliated immediately with the back of her closed fist, striking him with double his strength. It forced him to stumble backward, and he held his nose as blood gushed from it. Though as big as Knox, he was weaker than she and she had made sure to remind him of that fact, in case he'd forgotten.

"Well," she said, breathing heavily and watching him warily in case he decided to finally show a little courage, but the flow of blood from his nose kept him occupied.

"Now that the niceties are out of the way, I'll state my business."

"Make it snappy. I don't have time for your little-girl shenanigans."

"That's rich, coming from a guy who murdered his brother to fuck his wife—and killed an innocent woman who never did anything to him. And by the way, I'm still mad about that second hit you put out on me."

"Yes, and you've been sulking about it for the last three years, so stop it. It annoys me when you sulk." He stared at her stonily, waiting, holding a handkerchief to his nose.

"I want to go about my merry business without having to look over my shoulder. You leave me be. Today. Forever."

Fen looked at her speculatively. "Kenard."

She started. "How did you know that?"

"Please. After you pulled a Cinderella and he rearranged Sebastian's face? Half of Kansas City's moneyed thinks Bryce Kenard is fucking Sebastian Taight's mistress, and isn't that deliciously scandalous. I actually wasn't sure you wouldn't go down that road with him, since *you* don't seem terribly invested in a temple marriage anymore and *he* is completely disillusioned with the church. So since you're here, I'm going to assume you're not sleeping with him. Yet."

"No and I don't know if I'll ever get to, considering why I was at your party that night."

He waved a hand. "Oh, I don't think you have anything to worry about," he murmured, still dabbing at his nose. "Deceit's not your style."

"Huh. He doesn't know me, so that's not the way he's going to see it."

Suddenly, Fen laughed. "Believe me, he'll forgive you for it. Seduction's not your style, either, though you did display amazing potential. I knew the minute you led him around that corner you weren't playing any game at all, much less the one Sebastian wanted you to play."

Giselle huffed. "Look, Fen, I don't want you wrapped up in any relationship I might have with him. You and I are not a package deal and I want your word."

"If I honor your request and if he doesn't work out the way you hope, then you end up with Knox again— All bets are off. I'll go back to seeing if you can be killed. Color me curious."

She looked at him for a bit, more than willing to let him think she'd marry Knox in a heartbeat when it came down to the wire. She nodded. "I'd agree to those terms. But. What I told you after you killed Leah still stands. Any more of Knox's women die, you die. And oh, in case you are elected—not likely—and the ATF or whoever pulls a Waco on Knox and he dies ever so conveniently? Being a senator won't protect you from me."

He pursed his lips and held his nose and stared at her, not speaking for a long time. She waited for him to close the deal, but he didn't.

"Why," he finally said, slowly, "couldn't you have been my daughter?"

Giselle's breath caught in her throat and her eyes widened. "What?"

Fen gestured to one of the wing-back chairs in front of his desk. He sat in the other once she took the seat he offered.

"Didn't you ever wonder why I took such an interest in your life?"

"I thought you just wanted to boss me around the way you bossed Knox around."

Fen grunted. "No. I wanted to be the father of a girl who took life by the throat and throttled the hell out of it."

"I had a father."

"Who died too young. I will admit, though, that Sebastian did a very good job of raising you. If he ever has children, it'll be interesting to watch him raise them as an adult and not as a child himself."

"Sebastian was never a child. He was a man by the time he was ten."

He nodded. "That's true."

"You wanted to send me to a girl's school and turn me into a debutante. If you like me for who I am, if you like how Sebastian trained me, why would you want to change me?"

He thought about that for a moment, staring off into the distance. "Sebastian went on his mission when you were fifteen. You'd learned all you could from him and I thought you could use a little balance. I just assumed you'd hit your sweet spot on your own, which you did. I didn't know Knox was already teaching you those things."

Neither said anything for a moment, then Giselle asked, "Fen, I'm curious. How long have you and Trudy been lovers?"

"Since 1964. Oliver was gone to 'Nam. She was lonely. I was available and all too willing to climb in bed with a beautiful woman who wanted me there. Then I went in '67 and that was about the time Oliver came home."

"So, Knox...?"

"Not my son. Wasn't possible because I was in Vietnam then."

She sat quiet a moment, trying to digest that. Then,

"Why'd you have to kill Oliver? That was dirty pool."

He looked straight at her and said, very deliberately, "Giselle, there comes a time in a man's life when he has to protect the people he loves. You of all people should know how that feels. And if you ever repeat what I'm about to tell you, I'll put you in the ground myself."

Giselle smirked. "I'm listening."

"Oliver was a bastard. He had fists like hams and he used them."

Giselle gaped at him, her mind suddenly whirling. She had never seen evidence that Knox's father had been abusive and Knox's only complaint had been Oliver's distance and unavailability while he was busy building OKH.

"Did you *see* this for yourself?" she asked carefully.

"No, Giselle," he drawled as if she were slow. "A man doesn't beat his wife in front of witnesses if he can help it. Trudy was terrified."

Giselle's confusion cleared immediately. Trudy. That explained *everything*, but she didn't dare cast aspersions on her aunt. Trudy was Fen's line in the sand and Giselle didn't want to give him a *personal* reason to kill her.

"I see," she finally said. "I didn't know."

"I'm not sure anyone does; if they do, nobody's talking. Killing Oliver wasn't about my affair with Trudy and it wasn't about OKH. It was about keeping Trudy safe and I didn't feel Knox needed to know what his father was doing to his mother. When she kicked him out of the house, it was to protect him in case Oliver got it into his head that Knox was my son. There were no DNA tests at that time, remember."

Oh, that was just too much.

"Fen, you know that's bullshit. She's always thought of Knox as a nuisance. You didn't want Oliver to come down on you if he caught wind of your affair."

He shrugged. "Okay, point taken. But," he added, spearing her with a glance, "if you'd kept your mouth shut, it would've ended with just Oliver dead, no one the wiser, and no proviso to fight over."

Giselle ground her jaw, but didn't say anything, because that was absolutely true. She'd spent the last two decades carrying the guilt of a fourteen-year-old girl's mistake.

Walking in on Aunt Trudy making love with Uncle Oliver's brother, "Uncle" Fen.

Throwing up on the carpet.

Covering her ears while Aunt Trudy yelled at "Uncle" Fen to get out.

Getting slapped halfway across the room by an enraged Aunt Trudy, cowering in front of her, crying, "I'm sorry, Aunt Trudy, I'm sorry" over and over again.

Telling Knox when he found her hiding, crying at the back of the estate because she was too shocked he'd tracked her down to think up a good lie.

Reluctantly stumbling along behind Knox as he stormed into the mansion to confront his mother.

Walking off of the Hilliards' Ward Parkway estate with Knox, frightened by Aunt Trudy's violence and ashamed that she had caused Knox to be cast out of his home and lose everything he owned and loved.

Riding the bus all the way home to the east side, silent, clinging to him and he her.

Lying to her mother about how she'd gotten a bruise over half her face, afraid her mother would say she got what she deserved, only to get wept over and hugged and rocked like a little baby when Knox made her tell the truth.

And then years later, finding out that Fen had killed Uncle Oliver because she had opened her mouth . . .

"Ah," Fen murmured, suddenly smug, "I see you've been flagellating yourself for this entire fiasco. Good. Keep at it."

She sighed. "Why didn't you tell the bishop all this when you laid it out for him? Why didn't you tell us this when we confronted you? It's not like we wouldn't have understood, all things considered."

"By then it was irrelevant. I didn't feel guilty for killing Oliver. I felt guilty for taking his company and liking it and resenting a fifteen-year-old kid for that damned proviso Oliver slipped in when I wasn't looking. Why do you think I paid for Knox's education? It wasn't his fault and I daresay it's as burdensome to him as it is to me."

"But you didn't feel guilty enough to give it up, and now you've sunk to the level of murder to keep it. There's no honor in that."

"True." He rose then, which cued her to do the same. "It's a deal, Giselle," he said, offering his hand for her to shake and she did, firmly. "As long as you and Knox don't get back together."

"You understand this doesn't nullify my warning."

"Yes. And you understand you keep your mouth shut about Oliver. I think you've learned your lesson about speaking out of school."

Her mouth tightened. "Done." She turned to go.

"Giselle?" She looked over her shoulder at him and he had that hard gleam in his eye again. The wannabe father had vanished. "Don't ever come back here armed. And next time? Wear a damned dress."

She flashed him a wicked smile, winked, and walked out, unwilling to let him see how his chastisement had shaken her. Fen was right; she'd definitely learned her lesson about keeping her mouth shut.

21: Misfit So Alone

ONCE GISELLE TOLD BRYCE'S FRIGID ASSISTANT HER NAME, SHE WARMED instantly, eager to tell her where he could be found. Giselle found that encouraging and very . . . amusing.

Half of Kansas City's moneyed thinks Bryce Kenard is fucking Sebastian Taight's mistress. She chuckled.

Giselle patiently subjected herself to the search at the courthouse, surrendered her weapon, and resentfully dug out her permit when demanded. Frisked, wanded, and all but tossed on the x-ray conveyor belt, she was finally allowed in the courthouse.

All the way through the building, up stairs, through doors, she garnered stares. Some of these people knew her from law school and gaped at her leathers, her intensity. Kevin Oakley saw her, tried to catch her attention, but she ignored him. Though she hadn't spoken with him since the day he'd declined to charge her with homicide, he could wait. Politics could wait.

She got to the right division before she slowed at all. Her heart pounding and her mouth dry, she ducked into the restroom to calm herself a bit before getting on with her business here. Leaning back against the wall, she bent over and took some deep breaths, not thinking about what she intended to do. If she thought about it at all, she knew she'd change her mind and then she'd regret it for the rest of her life.

She looked in a mirror once her breathing had slowed and she felt more capable of acting like a civilized human being. Her face was red, as she had expected, thus hid any marks Fen's hand might have made. She bent down to splash cold water on her face and gargle some of it to ease the dryness of her mouth.

The restroom door opened suddenly and though Giselle took no real notice, a flash of dull, frizzy, indeterminate red did catch in her periphery and she looked up into the mirror.

"I'll be damned," she breathed when she caught Justice McKinley staring at her, frightened determination written all over her face.

Giselle locked glances with her in the mirror, wondering if she knew or suspected what Giselle had done for her or if she knew about her connection with Knox. She couldn't think of any other reason the girl would detain her, now of all times and here of all places.

Couldn't she have done this at school, when she had unlimited access and time?

"Can I help you, Justice?" she asked gently.

Justice, looking very young and naïve, swallowed a bit. "I— I want—" She pursed her lips and looked away, shaking her head. "Never mind. It's stupid."

Giselle turned, leaned back against the sink, and crossed her arms over her chest. "Say whatever you have to say to me, Justice," she demanded not-so-gently this time, impatient to get on with her goal. She wouldn't suffer being waylaid too long, even by this girl, especially when she could talk to her any day of the week.

Justice started and opened her mouth. "I want to be like you," she blurted finally.

Giselle blinked. "Why?"

"You— You're powerful and—" She looked at the floor and whispered, "I want to learn that."

Let Knox teach you; he'll show you the power you don't know you have yet.

Giselle watched her for several long seconds before Justice raised her eyes to find out why Giselle hadn't answered.

"I can't teach you how to be that," she said once Justice had fully concentrated on her face. "You have to come to it on your own, through hardship and fear. You have to know who you are and what you believe and you have to take stock of that every day. You have to walk barefoot through fire on broken glass. You have to stand up to people who frighten you under conditions that terrify you. You have to be honest with yourself about what you really want. You have to be willing to fail.

"Power is acquired, earned. You'll have many opportunities in your life to earn bits and pieces of it. You'll make bad choices; learn from them and do the best you can with them. Do not, under any circumstances, dither over what the right choice might be every single time you're presented with one. It won't teach you anything and you'll be a bore at cocktail parties."

Justice's hazel eyes had widened and Giselle smiled, reaching out to rub her shoulder, surprising both of them. Giselle almost *never* touched people she didn't know, or allowed them to touch her. On the other hand, she'd touched this girl once and at that moment had become vested in keeping her safe, in smoothing her road for her, in helping her travel the path that led to Knox.

"You'll do fine. Now," she said briskly, turning away from Justice and back to the mirror to do some last-minute primping, "I need to go take some of my own advice." She caught Justice's look of confusion when she turned to walk toward the door. She opened it a crack and then looked back over her shoulder. "Acquiring power is a never-ending process, Justice. Every day you have to wake up and prove to the world all over again that you deserve it. There should never come a day when you wake up and say, 'Okay, I'm powerful now; I'm done.' *Never.*"

With that, she left the restroom and found the correct set of courtroom doors. She opened one quietly, tiptoed in and stood silently against the back wall to watch Bryce Kenard do what he did that made him the god of the UMKC School of Law.

Bryce had used the architecture of this closing argument so often he could recite it in his sleep. It wasn't that he didn't believe it—no, he believed every word of what he said and because of that, he could sell it to the jury. Every time. Sadly, he had too many cases that required this closing argument; thus, he had to deliver his closing by rote. Otherwise, he could make himself insane with the grief of his own loss.

"This trial is not and never was an issue of suing a poor, hapless doctor who tried his best yet lost the struggle between life and death. It's about a little girl who had a bad doctor and *died* as a direct result of his incompetence." His client had bowed her head and her tears fell slowly and silently. That wasn't an act on her part, and he felt her pain acutely for a moment before forcing himself to shake it off.

"Ladies and gentlemen," he said as he placed his hands on the jury box and leaned into them, making sure they could all see his scars up close and personal. "The medical community saved my life; I'm grateful every day that I have my life because of a team of brilliant surgeons, specialists, nurses, and therapists. I'm immensely grateful that my caretakers are so competent and dedicated to their art and their patients.

"I'm not here to ask you for money for my client. I'm not asking you to pass judgment on the medical community. I'm not even asking you to send a message to it that it should police its own so that people like us, you and me, don't have to. I'm just asking you to help me clean it up one bad doctor at a time, and maybe, just maybe, let Melissa Hawthorne's mother sleep a little better at night."

He nodded his thanks to the jury and walked to his chair. There weren't that many people in the gallery, so the woman who stood against the back wall was hard to miss. His eyes widened as he stared at her for the split-second before he turned to sit. Soon, the jury left to begin deliberations and he rose, clutching his sobbing client to his chest.

He knew only too well how it felt to be suddenly childless.

Bryce released her after a while so she could leave and turned back to the table to gather his papers and laptop and Blackberry, to put his briefcase back together before he confronted Giselle. He talked to his interns, piled his things into the box one of them carried, and gave them instructions.

He took his time, sorting through the remnants of his closing argument, feeling his client's grief and his own wrapped up in it, but now . . .

She was at the back of the room and he didn't seem to hurt quite as much. "Stalker," he muttered, still feeling the sting of her parting shot at the library. He'd be damned if he appeared too eager to talk to her after that.

She awaited him patiently as he dawdled, then strolled up the aisle toward her, the very last person out of the courtroom. He never imagined she could look like that in a million years and the thought crossed his mind that he could certainly stand to look at her for the rest of his life.

Tight oxblood leather pants clung to her legs like a second skin. She had heavy Doc Martens on her feet. Though a voluminous white cotton blouse floated around her torso, he could see the curve of her breasts through the laces that held the front together. Her honey corkscrews fell to her shoulders, a wide fringed-and-beaded black scarf from her forehead to her crown holding her hair away from her face. A small dog could've jumped through the golden hoops that hung from her ears. Her face was slightly flushed and whatever way she'd made up her eyes—he didn't remember the name of that stuff—only enhanced her exotic look.

She might intimidate him a little if he didn't know how she responded to him.

He stopped in front of her, glaring at her. He smelled her perfume and felt the amusement that rippled his way. "Stalking me?" he snapped

She pursed her lips and thought about that for a few seconds. "You tell me. Your secretary all but drew me a map once I told her my name."

His jaw clenched. Of course she'd have noticed that.

"I want to talk to you," she continued, somewhat breathily. "I've needed to say something to you since December and I— I just haven't been able to."

"So say it."

"Mmmm, that's going to take a while. Tell you what," she said, pushing herself off the wall. "How about you meet me at Kauffman Garden at six?"

He considered. Finally, he figured that if this was all he would ever get from her, he'd take it and tuck it away in his memory.

"Fine." Unwilling to leave her, her scent, her humor, but needing to make his point, he walked away and didn't look back.

22: No One Brighter Than You

GISELLE STOOD IN THE V BETWEEN HER OPEN CAR DOOR AND HER CAR, facing west and watching the sun on its course toward the horizon. Waiting.

She had dressed carefully in a sundress of navy linen with white polka dots. The modest bustline fit closely and didn't show a hint of cleavage between the triple spaghetti straps. Over that, she wore a light white short-sleeved shrug. The full bias-cut skirt fell from the empire waistline to her knees. Navy sandals gave her another four inches of advantage.

She'd replaced her black hair scarf with a white one. She'd removed the kohl and kept the makeup to a minimum. She'd changed out her gold hoops for pearl studs.

This was her Sunday best.

Though she had invited Bryce to wring her out and hang her up to dry on her own sins, she refused to look and feel like a ragamuffin during the ordeal or give him any more reasons to think she would use her body to get something from him.

Six o'clock came and went. Her pinging nerves settled into acute disappointment. So, he had decided to show his contempt for her by standing her up. Well, she supposed she deserved it. Twenty minutes later, she still waited because she didn't know what else to do. Her nose stung. She blinked back tears. She chewed on the inside of her bottom lip. Several cars turned in the lot, but she couldn't see them, wouldn't look, and didn't know when he drove in and parked, or if he drove in at all.

She only knew when he appeared next to her and settled himself back against her car. She couldn't see his face because she didn't turn toward him, embarrassed and deeply regretful that she had ruined her chance to be with this man. He would not look kindly on her deceit, but at this moment, she only cared that he'd shown up after all.

"You rang?" he said after a moment. Ooh, still angry.

She pursed her lips, screwing up her courage to say what she had to say.

"I lied to you."

She felt his body shift against the car as if she had startled him. He said nothing for a long time. "Is that why you've been brushing me off?" he asked, his voice grainy and hoarse.

"Mostly, yes."

Another few seconds ticked by in silence. Silence was good, she guessed. At least he hadn't raged at her, run her character into the ground. Yet. And he hadn't asked her what she'd lied about. Interesting.

She glanced over her shoulder at him. He wore the same clothes he'd had on in court today, with the exception of his suit coat. The sleeves of his white dress shirt were folded and bunched at his elbows, he had no tie, and the two top buttons at his neck were undone.

"Has anybody ever told you that you're too hard on yourself?"

Where did that come from? "No."

"They should've."

She didn't know what to say. He seemed to want to talk about something completely different from what she had meant for them to talk about.

"I'm not as honorable as I should be. Why should anyone cut me any slack for that?"

"Is that what you want to be?"

"Honorable? Of course."

"Define it."

She turned then and looked up at him sharply. "Define it?"

"Define honor. What it means to you."

Huh. "What do you want me to say? It's whatever that's noble and virtuous that I'm not."

"Surely you have your own definition."

She barked a humorless laugh. "There are no words to describe what true honor is. I only know I don't see it in my mirror."

He fell silent. A good span of time passed before he spoke again. "What happened between June and today that made you finally willing to talk to me?"

Though determined not to lie to him again, she still needed to keep some things to herself for now. "I had to tie up some loose ends before I sought you out."

"I see," he said, though clearly he didn't. "I don't really recall that we've had enough conversation for you to have had the opportunity to lie to me."

"It wasn't what I said. It's what I did."

"Okay. So—talk."

And there it was. Her gut clenched and she felt as if she had jumped out of a plane without a parachute. "I went to the Nelson that night specifically to keep you engaged and distracted, away from Fen Hilliard and the party. The goal was to occupy you so Fen wouldn't be able to find you. I—" She stopped and took a deep breath. "I didn't know who you were when I went there. Bryce Kenard was just a name to me—a favor for people who respect you enough to want to protect you."

"But then you knew."

"Yes. And I did it anyway."

"What actually happened, on the bench—was that part of your master plan with this Bryce Kenard whom you didn't know?"

"Ah, no. Most definitely not. I'd been told you enjoy good conversation."

"Would you have done that if you hadn't been on orders to distract me?"

She pondered that, because it hadn't occurred to her to ask herself that. Finally, she shrugged. "I'm sure something would've happened between us somehow."

"Okay. So what's the problem?"

She turned her head and looked at him carefully, cautiously. His tone was too casual, but he still didn't look at her. "What do you mean, 'what's the problem?'"

"I mean, a year and a half ago, you and I met at Hale's, I insulted you, you put a gun to my head and told me I was six kinds of a bastard, then I kissed *you*. And you ran away."

She sucked in a long breath.

"Eight months after that," he continued blithely, "not only were you not mad at me, you lured me to a dark and quiet place where I had my way with you. And you ran away. I've tried to talk to you several times since March. And you've run away. Was there more that happened any of those times that I didn't notice or don't remember?"

He knew. He knew what he did to her, taking her power away from her, overwhelming her, keeping the upper hand with her. Taking her on and making her back down. He wanted her to acknowledge it, give it words, make it real.

She declined to answer since she would let him take only so much.

"I just wanted to talk to you, Giselle," he said after a moment, weary now. "I thought I made that perfectly clear."

"I was ashamed because I'd deceived you," she said, low.

He looked at her sharply. "You should've just told me that up front. Then I would've told you that *I* didn't do anything to you that *I* wouldn't have done anyway." Her eyes widened a bit and she swallowed; she could feel the heat rising in her as he held her stare, one eyebrow cocked at her as if to dare her to comment. Then, casually, "Does your boss know you're Knox's cousin?"

Giselle's mind went blank. "Excuse me?"

He grinned suddenly, wickedly, his teeth flashing white, pretty against his dark face. Giselle's heart picked up its pace. "I'll take that as a no."

"It's the eyes, right?"

He barked a genuinely amused laugh and wiped a hand over his mouth, then his amusement seeped away. After a very long silence, he murmured, "I . . . have my own confession to make." He took a deep breath, stuffed his hands in his pockets, and bowed his head. "I saw you at Leah's visitation. I overheard Knox ask you to go home with him."

Her eyes widened and she swallowed. "Oh," she breathed, her gut churning, "so that's why you were angry with me at work."

"Yes."

"I haven't— I didn't—"

He held up a hand. "You don't owe me an explanation for anything, Giselle. I was wrong and I was wrong to take it out on you."

"Did you think—" She almost didn't want to know. "At the Nelson, did you think I was sleeping with Sebastian, too?"

His hesitation was all the answer she needed and her nose started to sting again.

"I see." She paused. "I suppose I can't blame you. Apparently, the rest of society thought that, too."

"Well, I wasn't sure, really. You didn't act like lovers and he's not known for his prowess with women, so it was actually quite shocking that he showed up with any woman at all, spoke, and then laughed. The Junior League nearly had an orgasm."

That did pull a tiny smile out of her, but . . . "I knew that's what you thought of me, but I thought it was because of what I did with you, on the bench."

"That's really why you were avoiding me, isn't it?" he asked quietly.

She shrugged and looked away. "Mixed bag."

"The look on your face was— When you ran out on me, I knew I was off base somewhere. I didn't care who you were sleeping with, Taight or whoever or how many—it was that it was *Knox*."

Her brow wrinkled and she looked back at him. "I don't understand. Why Knox but not any other man?"

He sucked up a deep breath. "Knox is my best friend from UCLA. My wife told me she'd been having an affair with him and I— I didn't know what to believe."

Giselle's mind spun at those not insignificant pieces of information. "I guess I can understand that," she muttered finally and lowered her head to stare at the ground and think. "Caught between your best friend and your wife. Loyalty's dicey sometimes."

"Knox made the choice for me. He walked away."

"I don't blame him."

"So after Fen's party, he and I had dinner, at his request. Well, to be more precise, he summoned me. He told me the whole shebang. Fen, the proviso, Taight."

"When did this happen?"

"In March."

"Knox doesn't usually meddle," she mused, almost to herself, "so Sebastian must have been hammering him to do something. Why did you bother going?"

"You. I needed to know for sure. He knows my taste in women and he knows me well enough to figure out I'd be stewing about it. He gave me the answers but he refused to give me your phone number, tell me where you live, set up a date. Nothing. He said he wasn't going to make it easy for me and I needed to pay penance for being a bastard to you both. That I needed to work for it so I'd value it." He paused. "Hence, stalking. I knew where you worked and I knew you were in law school, so . . ."

She wrapped her arms around herself, even though she had no reason to be cold. "I'm assuming he *did* tell you what he and I *haven't* done?"

"Yes. He was very clear on that point."

"So now I don't know if you pursued me because Knox redeemed your low opinion of me or if you want me in spite of your low opinion of me," she muttered. Dammit. She was going to cry. "That's just so . . . *flattering*. I should've got a clue when you called me Lilith."

He sighed. "When I first saw you, before I overheard your conversation— You look like a painting."

"But you didn't mean it that way and you weren't subtle about it."

"Giselle, I'm sorry," he breathed. "Is there anything I can do or say so you'll give me a chance?"

She laughed without humor. "I came here thinking you were going to truss me up like a Christmas goose for conning you and send me packing. Now I'm offended and you're the one repenting. I'm a little discombobulated right now, so forgive me if I don't know what to say."

He remained silent for a bit. Then, "Why did you haul me into your car that night?"

She looked up at him sharply. "Because you hurt my feelings. Would you rather I have slugged you? I have a hell of a right cross."

His mouth quirked then and she suddenly saw the humor in what she'd said. "Do you do that to every strange man who hurts your feelings?"

That pulled a puff of laughter out of her and she couldn't help the beginnings of a smile. "Well." She cleared her throat. "Men—strange or otherwise—don't dismiss me out of hand. You got my point, didn't you?"

"Oh, I most assuredly did," he said with a smirk, "and you got mine."

She studied him, his face. Intellectually, aesthetically, she understood that his burn scars made him ugly, but to her, he was beautiful. Powerful. He'd attained godlike status in the courtroom despite scars that should frighten juries. Most people would have taken their money and hidden away from the world, but not him. Oh, no. He'd set out to conquer it and he'd succeeded.

He pushed himself away from the car and strode around the back to the passenger side. "I'm hungry. Find us a place to eat."

It occurred to her to protest his abrupt, imperious command, but it had unexpectedly made her breathless and somewhat tingly between her legs. She figured this was a battle best left un-picked and dropped into her seat, though she didn't bother to start the car. She watched him get in and, once he'd settled and looked straight back at her, she said, "Apologize."

He opened his mouth to speak, but then he did a double take. "Who hit you?" he demanded, instantly ferocious, lethal. A panther.

She had forgotten that the evidence of Fen's slap would be visible on her fair skin. A chuckle escaped her, then it turned into a rolling laugh. "Doesn't matter, but if it makes you feel any better, the other guy looks worse."

With the back of his hand, he reached up and gently caressed that cheek. Her breath caught. "I'm sorry, Giselle," he whispered. "For my assumptions, for my anger. All of it, everything. And I'm sorry for being late; I had an appointment I forgot about and I didn't know how to get in touch with you. I was *so* glad to see you—" He took a deep breath. "Can we start over? Where we should've started a year and a half ago if I hadn't been an ass? Please?"

His dark tan made him seem much more dangerous than at Christmas and made his vivid eyes gleam with a magical green fire. Giselle found herself entranced.

"I'd like that," she breathed.

He flashed that pretty smile for her again and said, "So are you going to drive or are you going to let me starve?"

She laughed then. "Now, you know I'm going to pick the most expensive restaurant in town, right?"

"I was counting on it. Plaza III, I'm guessing?"

"Absolutely."

Still chuckling, she started the car, then drove them to the steakhouse on the southwestern corner of the Country Club Plaza. They said nothing on the way.

Although only a mile away from Kauffman Garden, the silence during the drive had made her a nervous wreck by the time she found a spot on Ward Parkway.

She turned off the engine and bolted out of the car as fast as she could, needing to be on her feet and away from him and his largeness, his power, his raw sexuality. Her back to him, she heard and then felt him come up behind her and splay his large hand across her back, and that—oh, that was electrifying.

His momentum took him around her and she looked up just in time to close her eyes as he kissed her. Softly at first, and then a little deeper. Her hands—she didn't know what to do with her hands and her arms, and she oh, so wanted to touch him. Hesitantly, lightly, she furrowed her left hand in his hair and laid her right hand on his chest, her thumb on the little nub of nipple through the fabric of his dress shirt and undershirt. He sucked in a breath and she stopped thinking, stopped caring about everything as his tongue found hers.

They kissed. Long, slow, lazy. Giselle heard herself hum her desire into his mouth.

He pulled away from her finally and she opened her eyes to again find his green gaze studying her. "I'm hungry," he repeated softly, though this time the words held so much, much more. "Come eat with me. Talk with me. Laugh with me."

23: Cocked & Locked

WHILE AWAITING A TABLE, THE CONVERSATION STARTED HESITANTLY, Giselle unsure what this evening would bring. Having dinner with him—being kissed by him—had not been on her short list of possible endings to her confessional. Hearing his confession . . .

He set her at ease by keeping his distance, asking her questions that made her think, listening to her answers, and making it clear that whatever evil she thought she had done him, he thought it nonexistent at best and irrelevant at worst. He made her *feel* honorable—

—and he obviously wished to redeem himself in her eyes.

"How did you come to work for Hale?" he asked suddenly.

She shrugged. "Answered an ad. It's a good job while I'm in law school and I needed the money and the benefits. Transcribing has always turned out to be my fallback position. I don't like the work itself, but it's a good position and I like my boss. And no, he doesn't know about Knox, so I'd appreciate it if you kept it to yourself."

"I could've busted you out on that that night if I felt like getting you fired."

She inclined her head. "Then thank you."

Once seated, they warmed to an easy repartee, talking and laughing without touching. It didn't occur to her that that might be odd, considering the months and the hours, the information and the foreplay that had led up to this.

It didn't matter that she'd drawn him into her zealously guarded personal space, wanted him to be there. At this moment, it was enough to look in his eyes, see them focus on her face; to look at his mouth, see the liberally flashing grin; to look at his brow, see it wrinkle intensely as he listened to what she said and prepared his own argument.

"Sebastian told me you're a member of the church," she said.

"I figured you were, considering your family."

"So in the context of what's passed between us thus far, does this mean we're both a tidge left of expectations?"

"Way more than a tidge. Do you care?"

She hesitated. "Um, yeah. A little. Not as much as I should, I think."

As the evening deepened, she relaxed completely. They ate together easily, as if they had eaten together their whole lives and nothing was a surprise anymore, and she ate as she always had without shame.

He seemed not to care that she put away a tartare appetizer, a pound of fine rare prime rib, a pitcher of water, and a dinner salad at one sitting. She blithely told him about her lifelong struggle with her weight and that Leah, a registered dietitian, had taught her how to eat. He remarked that he couldn't argue with the results and eagerly complied with her request that he take her dinner rolls as well as his. He, like her, preferred his salad last.

"So, where'd you get your salad-last habit?" she asked with a smile.

"Scotland. You?"

"Your mission?" He nodded as he chewed. "I picked mine up all over the rest of Europe."

"Your mission?" he returned once he'd swallowed his bite.

"Absolutely not. That's not my gig. Sebastian lived in Paris for years and I went to visit him the summer between my sophomore and junior years at BYU. He took me all over."

They explored each other intellectually, philosophically, spiritually, and aesthetically, bouncing back and forth from the sacred to the profane, the profound to the absurd, and touching all points in between.

"I keep hearing Senator Oth and his cronies backpedal their anti-Taight rhetoric," Bryce said coolly, trying to stifle a smile.

Giselle laughed. "Oh, you know about that."

"That was brilliant. I'm very impressed."

"Don't be too impressed. I wasn't sure any of the parties would react the way I hoped and too much depended on decisions other people had to make."

"When's Kevin going to announce?"

"Not sure. September, possibly October. I'd rather he wait until he finds out whether Justice McKinley will endorse him or not. I'd also like to know how Fen's fundraising's been going. I know he's spent quite a bit of money, but not as much as I wanted him to by now."

"Justice McKinley—she's the girl Knox is keeping on ice?"

"Oh, yes," Giselle said with a smirk. "She shook him up but good and she has no idea."

All four elbows shamelessly on the table, they leaned over their plates toward each other, hungry for more of each other's minds. She had never been so engaged and entertained in all her life. She couldn't stop smiling and laughing, and she could feel the heat rise in her face. She imagined that her eyes must be what they called "sparkling" in books, although she wasn't sure how eyes could sparkle, really. She certainly *felt* sparkly.

"What's your middle name?"

"Giselle."

He chuckled. "Okay. What's your first name?"

"Celia. My mother insisted I be named after my four-greats grandmother—but so were six of my cousins, which is why my father insisted I go by my middle name. What's yours?"

"Duncan."

"You're a Scot through and through, aren't you?"

"Not quite. There's some Apache floating around in there somewhere, but I'll be damned if I know where."

"Ah, that explains the tan," she said and he laughed.

Gradually, the conversation turned silly. "I," she said between bites, pointing her fork at him imperiously, "saw Mötley Crüe in concert on their Dr. Feelgood tour. That's how much of an eighties hair band relic I am."

He laughed yet again, another in a long series of laughs, chuckles, and grins. "Yes, but I," he said, mimicking her fork gesture, "caught Metallica when nobody had heard of them yet."

"Impressive!"

"But I felt guilty about it," he muttered wryly and she laughed.

"I lift weights to Rob Zombie, but I run to Beethoven and Tchaikovsky." And they went on with their game of one-upmanship of esoteric and closeted musical tastes.

"Are you from here?"

"No," he said. "I'm from San Diego and met Knox at UCLA after my mission; we were roommates in the freshman dorm."

"Did you room with him the whole four years?"

"Yeah, he and I got along fairly well—wasn't hard since he spent most of his free time surfing and I spent mine dating—so no point in changing anything. I got married right after I graduated, then we both went to BYU for law school. I got a good job offer here straight out of law school, liked it, and stayed. I've lived here since ninety-three and I have no plans to go back to California."

"Surely you had job offers elsewhere?"

"None where I had friends who could introduce me to the city."

"Ah. What was your major?"

"Finance. When were you at BYU?"

"Eighty-eight. Knox and I overlapped two years and I practically lived at his house. I'm surprised I didn't meet you then."

He looked at her strangely for a moment, then blinked and shook his head. "I was married then." Ah, yes. That might have been awkward, all things considered. He paused for a long time, studying his plate, then, "I'm glad I didn't. I was a different person then and you'd have scared the shit out of me."

Giselle laughed. "And now you're not quite as scared of me as I'd like."

"Ah, you noticed."

"Anyway," she said in a rush, redirecting the conversation and he chuckled at her. "I graduated and came home for my master's."

That quelled his laughter and his brow wrinkled. "Master's?"

With a sardonic grin, she said, "I'm way too old not to have been around the graduate school block a time or two. I have a PhD in English lit."

"Really! So . . . law school—?"

"I owned a bookstore for seven years," she said matter-of-factly. "I shared space with a patisserie on one side of me and a confectionary on the other. Maisy and Coco weren't my business partners, exactly; we just figured if we knocked down our walls and unified our décor, we'd all make more money and it worked.

"But it burned—Knox probably told you some of that. It bankrupted all of us because we'd taken on new debt to expand and our insurance policies didn't cover that. We all had to start over again because we couldn't rebuild. There's not much else out there for an English degree that I actually wanted to do—and certainly nothing that makes any money. I don't want to get caught up in university politics, either; I'd rather teach than publish and that's a no-no. After I'd spent about six months curled up in bed, Knox and Sebastian kicked my ass to do something and I decided to be a bit more practical in my education than I had before."

"An indie bookstore's risky, with the discounters and big boys; I'm impressed you kept it open that long."

Her brow wrinkled a bit. "Bryce, Decadence wasn't a bookstore with food. It was a *destination*. I stocked romance novels of all kinds. Couple that with Maisy's gourmet chocolates and wine, and Coco's pastries, the events we put on every weekend . . . I was doing very well; we all were. I was never going to be independently wealthy, but I made a lot of money doing something I loved."

"Decadence?" he murmured.

She could feel herself flush a bit, but ignored his invitation to banter; she wanted, no, *needed* to explain. "We were going to open locations down in Olathe and up in Chouteau County, and we gambled everything we had to get the loans we needed."

His expression changed from sensuous to pitying in a heartbeat, which she felt deep in her soul. Sometimes it was nice to be pitied as long as it didn't last too long; her family would not be so indulgent of her. "So . . . do you *want* to be a lawyer?"

Her mouth tightened a bit as she looked down. "It wasn't my first career choice, no, but Knox had always thought I'd be good at it, and I was intrigued enough that it was a distant second. I didn't have the luxury of doing what I *wanted* to do after we were burned out." When he opened his mouth to ask the next of about a dozen logical questions, she stiffened and he stopped, understanding that that topic of conversation was closed for now. She'd explained. The loss of her bookstore was not something she wanted to revisit any further.

He had his own off-limit topics of conversation, which happened to be his wife, his children, and his own fire. Other than telling her that his wife and children had died in that fire and trading the odd fact that their respective fires had happened the same night, he closed himself off about that.

"What about your family?"

He waved a fork. "I'm the youngest child of three in a family with not too many people in it to begin with. My sister, the sibling right before me, is fifteen years older than I am. My brother is almost twenty years older than I am. Most of my nieces and nephews are older than I am. My mother had cancer and died about four years ago and my father died soon after that. I was in the hospital then and didn't know for a while."

"Oh, that's horrible."

He shrugged. "My mother was forty-five, my dad fifty-five, when I was born—and I wasn't a welcome surprise. They thought they were finished. My dad had climbed pretty high up in the church hierarchy and he was not prepared for another child. I didn't see him much because he was always at church meetings, so I didn't get to know him as well as I'd have liked. And I always knew they wouldn't be around as long as other people's parents."

After an interval during which their plates were cleared, coffee and dessert declined, Bryce relaxed back in his chair and studied her. While somewhat uncomfortable with that, Giselle was all too willing to have the excuse to study him right back.

Finally, he said, low and way too casually for her comfort, "Wasn't your bookstore fire meant to kill you?"

Giselle blinked and her gut began to churn. "Yes," she said, wary. "How much has Knox told you, exactly?"

His emerald gaze bored into her, his face inscrutable. "One gun in each hand," he murmured, his jaw clenched. Her eyes widened and she sucked in a long breath of air. One of his eyebrows rose. "Two bullet wounds. Threatened Fen at gunpoint. You were armed at Leah's funeral and at the gallery."

Giselle didn't understand where this had come from or what it meant to him. Well. She supposed she'd rather they'd parted company at the garden than have to account for herself to him here, now, after a nice dinner and several hours into intellectually orgasmic conversation. She didn't want him to know how much she craved his regard, his approval, but she'd be damned if she'd apologize or feel shame for who she was or how she lived her life.

She took a deep breath and notched her chin up a bit. "How did you know I was armed at Christmas?"

But she caught her breath when a slow, predatory smile began to spread across his face. She could smell his sensual cologne and his eyes were unblinking.

"Did you think I wouldn't be able to feel it?" he purred. "Are you armed? Right now?"

Biting on the inside of her lower lip, she watched him carefully. "Do you want me to be?"

"Yes."

Giselle's heart began to race at his tone and she felt the lava between her legs. The focus had turned; he was seducing her now and she wanted to be seduced. She sat up and leaned as far across the table as she could without actually standing. "I'm *always* armed," she said on a husky whisper, startled when she found him immediately nose to nose with her.

"I like that," he whispered back, never dropping her gaze. "I like it a lot."

Bryce reached a hand up to her face and softly cupped her chin in his hand, his thumb drawing lightly across her bottom lip. Her body responded to the caress, as light as a feather, as devastating as his kiss that night in the parking lot. Without thinking, she touched her tongue to his thumb and it was his turn to draw a sharp breath.

"Who slapped you?" he asked in that same whisper, still touching her mouth.

"Fen," she breathed, unable to do anything but follow wherever he led.

"You said he looked worse."

"I broke his nose."

Bryce burst out laughing then and all the people at the tables around them looked up to see what was so funny. He sat back and gave her a lopsided grin.

Bemused for a moment, her mind cleared and she smiled as she relaxed back into her chair. He *liked* that, and her heart lifted.

Want me. Need me. Love me. Beg me.

A Cheap Trick song suddenly played in her head, and she knew she'd fallen in love—but not tonight. Long ago, that night in the parking lot, when he took her kiss away from her and turned it on her.

"You went to see Fen today?"

"Yes."

"What was with the leathers?"

Giselle laughed then, startled out of the intensity of her thoughts. "That's my kickin'-ass-and-takin'-names outfit. Fen hates it, so I wore it to annoy him."

"I thought you were mad at him?"

"Oh, yes. He accused me of sulking for the past three years."

"Not that you have no reason to," he muttered sarcastically, but switched gears before she could reply. "Where *do* you live, by the way?" he asked conversationally, as if he hadn't just shattered her world, as if he hadn't just snatched her soul and wrung it out. Made her like it.

But she kept her cool and her mouth twitched. "Seven blocks from here. With Sebastian." She couldn't help but laugh at the look of shock on his face.

"How did that happen?"

"I moved in with him after my fire. He came and got me that night and pretty much took care of me and I just never moved out."

"What about your parents? They seem absent in all this."

"My father died when I was three. My mother's had a hard life, being a young widow with nothing, and now she's enjoying retirement with my Aunt Dianne— Sebastian's mother. Sebastian and Knox, my mom, Aunt Dianne, they're my *immediate* family. My Uncle Charlie, Sebastian's father, was my father figure, but he died about ten years ago."

"And what does your mother think?"

"My mom keeps her opinions and speculations to herself, but I wouldn't be surprised if she's figured some of it out. My Aunt Dianne's a genius with money and she would've been following Sebastian's takeover of OKH. We told them my bookstore fire was ruled an accident and that I got caught in a drive-by shooting. I'm not sure they believed us and between them, they probably have a couple of close theories."

"Why don't you just tell them?"

"I have a very large tribe and we all get together constantly. They're smart; I'm sure a few of them suspect Fen murdered Leah, but most wouldn't believe it and they certainly wouldn't believe what else he's done. Fen's charming and generous; he spreads the love and money around—and he's not insincere about it. Most of my family don't see him any differently than the rest of the city does. If they do, they aren't about to say so. It's one thing for people to have their private suspicions, but another to split the tribe down the middle."

Bryce's face cleared in understanding. "Fen Hilliard to the rescue," he muttered.

"Exactly."

"I watched Knox dance to his tune when we were in college. I never trusted him, even though I'd never met him. Knox said you find him amusing."

She shrugged. "I have a twisted sense of humor, but for us, it's not personal. It's business. I get that."

"Why do you live with Sebastian and not your mom?"

"It's convenient to all the places I really need to be. I can walk to school and work if I want or need to, not to mention the Nelson. She lives north of the river pretty close to Knox, and my car can't take the punishment of that commute. She'd rather I live with her because she thinks Sebastian's a bad influence on me and that I'm just way too brazen to be allowed out in public."

"Is he? A bad influence on you?"

"He'd corrupted me by the time I was six." She grinned at the confused look on his face. "We grew up together, in the ghetto. My mom and I lived across the alley and up three doors from Sebastian and his parents. There were a lot of . . . older single white men that lived along our route to school." His face cleared in understanding.

"And Sebastian was a pretty boy."

"Very. It only took him one *very* close call to figure out he was going to have to find some way to deal with it himself, so he had a gun by the time he was eleven. He's lucky he didn't kill himself—or me—trying to learn how to use it."

"Did he ever have to?"

She tried not to smirk and her eyebrow rose a little, then he laughed. "I've been Sebastian's sidekick since before I could walk. Once he started making serious money, he needed someone at his back he could trust. Knox was too busy squiring debutantes on Trudy's command and being her perfect country club trophy son to be available when Sebastian needed him to be. That left . . . me."

"He was a loan shark," Bryce breathed. Giselle could feel the awe in his voice and she smiled. "So that's how he made his money."

"He'll tell you it's because he's never *borrowed* money in his life."

"Good point."

"So my mother thinks that Sebastian taking me in hand so early has left me completely unmarriageable. Add in his blatant promiscuity and all she really expects of me is to stop sleeping with Knox."

He laughed. "Well, I know you're not unmarriageable nor sleeping with Knox, so why haven't you married?"

"I have a philosophy: If I can't have exactly what I want, I go without. I didn't have anything left after my fire. No clothes, no money, no furniture, no credit, no—" She caught the flash of pain on his face and stopped. "Well," she murmured, "you know more about that than I do. So I decided to go with that and stay as uncluttered as possible. I still don't have much. I choose my jewelry, my perfume, my clothes, based on my opinion of its worthiness to be in my bedroom and I have very stringent criteria. I choose my men the same way."

He raised an eyebrow. "Men?"

"That's my point. There aren't any, haven't been any and it's not just because I've been a good Mormon woman saving myself for a temple marriage."

"So what are you looking for?"

"Hank Rearden," she said, clipped, hopinghopinghoping he'd get that.

He gaped at her for a moment, aghast, then his eyes half closed and he purred, "Really."

She breathed a sigh of relief then, because he did get it, and she wouldn't have to get into details. "I see that name rings a bell."

"Indeed it does." His mouth pursed, and Giselle waited for him to continue. After a moment, he speared her with those eyes. Oh! Those eyes! "Do you have *any* idea what that really means?" he asked slowly, making it very clear to her that he did know what it meant.

"I think," she said, her words measured, "I may have a clue now. What does it mean to you?"

He studied her, then murmured, "It's everything I need to know about who you are and what you want—and no, you don't know the first thing about it. But you'll learn."

And I'm the man who's going to teach you. Tonight.

It hung in the air as heavy as if it'd been said and Giselle felt drugged, shot up with adrenaline and passion. Her heart thundered. "Would you really have taken me home that night, even thinking—?" she whispered.

"Yes," he said, immediate, sure, his eyebrow raised. "To stake my claim."

Giselle remained silent for a moment because she didn't want him to know what that had done to her. "What about your temple covenants?" she asked carefully.

He shrugged. "I spent my entire life doing what I was supposed to do, what I was told would make me blessed and happy. Not only was I miserable in my marriage, I wasn't even blessed enough to keep my children. I hated everything about my life, hated myself for trying to be exactly what I wasn't. I have nothing to lose and everything to gain."

Giselle swallowed and looked down, fiddling with the napkin she still held, because that was a terrible, terrible conundrum.

Bryce said nothing for a long, long while and when finally she raised her gaze, she found him staring at her speculatively. He sat relaxed, his elbow on the arm of his chair, his cheek resting on his fingertips.

Finally he opened his mouth and rasped, "I followed you up the stairs and down into the tunnel."

Giselle pulled in a soft, deep breath, her eyes widening at the second reference pulled from *Atlas Shrugged*, when the heroine lured her would-be lover down into a train tunnel, where they consummated their relationship.

She could feel the heat gathering within her, that same heat she'd had when she had lain on the ottoman with him, under him, at his mercy. She bit her lip and continued to stare at him, and he her.

"Galt," she whispered, and then he smiled again: slow, easy, wicked.

"That's right. Do you remember when Francisco tried to explain to Rearden the parallel between money and sex?"

"Yes."

"He said, 'The man who is proudly certain of his own value will want the highest type of woman he can find, the woman he admires, the strongest, the hardest to conquer—because only the possession of a heroine will give him the sense of an achievement.'"

His face was inscrutable and Giselle couldn't give name to what went on inside her body. She never, ever wanted it to stop.

He stared her down with those brilliant green eyes, and Giselle swallowed, unable to do anything but breathe in long, soft strokes and bite her bottom lip. She could feel his mouth on her neck, her shoulder, down her arms. She could feel him inside her, stroking her, but he was sitting across a table from her and she'd never known a man inside her. He effortlessly seduced her with mere words.

Bigger than me, huh? I can pick you up and toss you over my shoulder.

Yeah, a lot of guys could do that. No one's ever had the balls to try.

Bryce Kenard did—and he'd succeeded.

To stake my claim.

She was his. She knew it.

He knew it.

Bryce went on quoting Rand, his voice growing more hoarse with each word until he couldn't vocalize some syllables. "'Tell me what a man finds sexually attractive and I will tell you his entire philosophy of life. Show me the woman he sleeps with and I will tell you his valuation of himself.'"

Giselle swallowed and said the only thing she could think of. It came out in a whisper. "Why Galt?"

"Galt was superior to Rearden. In. Every. Way." Bryce didn't smile, didn't drop his gaze, didn't do anything else while he watched her struggle with what he'd done to her, continued to do to her with each word that dropped from his tongue.

Suddenly, he threw his napkin down on the table and stood in one rapid sweep of movement, growling, "Let's go." Once he'd dropped a pile of cash on the table, he held his hand out to her.

Giselle looked at his hand, then up at him, his face serious and intense. If she allowed him to pull her out of her chair, the last shred of whatever speck of virtue she had left would slip away from her. She hesitated for a moment, but then placed her hand in his and let him draw her up on her feet.

They emerged from the cool air into oppressive heat and humidity. Here, there was no cooling off once the sun went down, such as she'd come to appreciate when living in the heart of the Rocky Mountains. The air here didn't wash clean and crisp as it did in Provo Canyon, in Utah Valley; instead, it was moist, heavy, ripe, fecund.

Like Giselle.

He let go her hand and said nothing. She chose the direction they went on purpose, toward her home, the one she shared with Sebastian.

It was a little past midnight on a Saturday morning and she worked the situation over in her head. She looked up at him, but he didn't return her look. He simply strolled along, looking ahead. She knew his reasoning: He wanted to give her the opportunity to think and say no without any more coercion or seduction.

She halted him once so she could balance herself on his arm to slip off her heels and loop them in her fingers, to walk barefoot. It was a convenient excuse to touch him, to feel his strength under her hand.

Giselle shouldn't have hesitated to say no thanks. It'd been drilled into her from puberty that one didn't put oneself in situations where temptation could take hold. He knew that as well as she did. Yet she found herself curiously without conflict about saying yes.

Everything she'd ever wanted had come true for her: The shared faith, culture, language of Mormonism, regardless that neither of them exemplified its teachings; that could be rectified. The shared philosophies of Rand, of excellence, money, sex. The shared political ideas and common goals and higher education.

But they were *strangers* and Giselle had a problem with that. He wanted her. He wanted to conquer her, to take her. She wanted him to. The thought both thrilled and terrified her, because no man had ever had been able to keep her off balance until this one, and she couldn't decide if she wanted to get back on track.

On the other hand, Knox had vouched for him. He would know what kind of man Bryce Kenard was and wouldn't send her with a man who didn't live up to his standards.

It took a long two blocks of silence before Bryce's patience ran out. He stopped abruptly, gripped her arm, and yanked her around tight to his big body, his mouth in her ear, hot, raspy, pounding:

"I want to fuck you, Giselle. Hard and fast. Once, twice, a thousand times. I wanted to fuck you at Leah's funeral. I wanted to fuck you the night we met. I wanted to fuck you at the museum. I've wanted to fuck you all night tonight. For two years I haven't thought of anything *but* fucking you. Do you understand me?"

24: Hammer of the Gods

HE RELEASED HER AS SUDDENLY AS HE HAD CAPTURED HER, ARMS WIDE, stepping back. She trembled and drew a shaky breath as she stared at him, sober, wary. She'd known the evening would boil down to this decision, but not like *that*.

She throbbed from the intensity of her arousal.

This was audacious and strong, the first salvo in his declaration of war on her strength, her will. She respected it, responded to it. Her shoulders stiffened and her chin rose in the air, ready for the challenge.

"We've spent a whole, what? maybe half a day total with each other, if that?" she finally said.

"Yes."

"This would be very stupid."

"Yes."

"If we do this, it's done and there's no going back. I lose my virginity, you break your covenants. That's possible excommunication for me, but an absolute certainty for you."

"Yes."

For a few minutes more she stared at him and then finally made up her mind. She spoke, her voice hard and her eyes narrow.

"You don't get the luxury of fucking me and leaving me in the morning. You know the protocol as well as I do, so you don't get a pass. You stay with me until we're mutually sick of each other or we decide we can't live without each other."

It was his turn to stare at her while he thought. After what seemed forever, he nodded. "Done."

After one moment more of staring at him, attempting to suss out any deceit or ulterior motives, she turned and continued toward home, he beside her. A few feet later, she snatched his hand to pull him into a run toward her house.

By the time they had reached the front door, they were out of breath and he crushed her between his body and the front door for a scorching kiss, his fingers wrapped in hers against the door over their heads.

She needed this—brash and bold, powerful and brilliant, exotic and hot-blooded—and oh! how he wanted her.

Giselle broke his kiss, turned and punched her code into the keypad by the door, then opened it when it clicked. Thundering percussion and operatic voices hit them when they entered the house; the music shook the walls and the floor.

"What *is* that?"

"*Carmina Burana,*" Giselle breathed. "Let it wrap around you and fill you."

"Where's it coming from?"

"Downstairs. Sebastian's working."

Leading the way to her bedroom, she closed the door behind him. Then, suddenly unsure, she dropped her shoes and just stood there, wondering what was next.

Not for long. Bryce knew exactly what to do.

There was no mindless fumbling for buttons and such. In one smooth move, he slipped her jacket off, ripped the dress zipper down her ribs, slid the straps off her shoulders, and let the dress fall to the floor.

His gaze swept down her almost-nude body to see the holster and weapon he surely must have felt when he'd grabbed her and propositioned her. She bent to it and he growled, "Leave it on."

Giselle couldn't breathe, couldn't move, couldn't believe she would get exactly what she'd always wanted from a man who would not hesitate to give it to her. And then some.

Leave it on.

She'd never imagined such a thing in her whole life.

Bryce deftly unhooked the front of her strapless bra and let it fall to the floor while lifting her so that he could suck on her nipple. Giselle went limp. Her back arched and her head dropped back.

"Wrap your legs around me," he said, rough, demanding, and she did that. He pressed his cock up into the V of her legs, stopped only by two or three layers of fabric. "Feel that?"

"Yes," she whispered, barely able to think, much less talk.

"You want it?"

"Yes."

He lowered her just until her mouth was level with his, her arms wrapped around his neck. One big hand cupping her ass, he pressed her tight to him so she couldn't forget how hard he was. The other big hand cupping the back of her head, he pulled her to him for a kiss.

It was nothing like any kiss she'd ever had, even from him: hungry, hot, wet, nasty. He demanded her submission. His tongue teased her lips and tongue mercilessly. He sucked her soul right out of her. He *devoured* her and she ached in ways she didn't know she could ache.

Bryce carried her the two steps to her bed and abruptly dropped her. She caught herself on her elbows, her legs spread wide. She looked up, up, up at him, this enormous man who wanted to fuck her and had told her so outright.

Giselle gasped when he bared his chest for her and couldn't help but bite her lip, then watch as his hands undid his trousers. She stopped breathing when he revealed his long, hard cock and he let his pants slide down his legs.

"Back up," he muttered, and she did, then he knelt on the bed, crawling on all fours toward her, dark, lithe, like a panther. Her chest heaved from how much he intimidated her and how that aroused her. He rose tall and proud on his knees between her legs and she was so dizzy with desire and pleasure that she thought she'd pass out.

"Lift your hips."

She did and he pulled her panties—her last guard—down her legs and tossed them over his shoulder.

"Open your legs."

She did. He drew his finger down her belly to her vulva.

"You shave," he murmured as he ran his finger over all the little creases before he slipped two fingers up inside her. Giselle had never felt anything like that before. She arched her back and moaned, her eyes closed.

"And you're dripping. Open your eyes. Look at me."

Giselle opened her eyes and looked up at him, watched him take his fingers out of her and lick them. Her breath caught yet again and he gave her a wicked smile.

"You wanted Hank Rearden."

"Yes," she whispered.

"He's a girl's fantasy. Galt is a woman's. Choose. Now."

"Kenard."

Bryce started in surprise and stared at her for a moment as if dumbstruck. Then he smiled, slow, soft, perhaps even happy, just before that pretty smile turned predatory. He gripped her ankles then released them to run his hands up her legs, caressing gently. Finally, he hooked his hands behind her knees, flexed them, then yanked her across the bed toward him, spreading her legs wider, wider. He nestled the tip of his cock just inside her, teasing her.

"This," he whispered, his voice nearly gone. He balanced himself over her, his hands on either side of her head. "Is fucking." And he drove his hard cock right into her, smothering her surprised shriek of pain with his mouth.

And oh, it hurt. He was so big, so powerful. So hard, so solid. He stretched her beyond what she thought possible.

She liked it.

He didn't move while he kissed her, pinning her hard into the bed with his hips. He was inside her, filling her, until the pain ebbed. Her arms wrapped around him and she felt every bump and ridge of his naked back under her fingertips. Her body adapted and her muscles began to work. She clenched around him when his mouth left hers to suck and bite her nipples until she couldn't do anything but release a hard, shuddering sigh and lift her hips, inviting him to take her.

"Fuck me," she whispered finally when she needed to feel him move inside her. She wrapped her legs around his thighs, wondering if there would be anything in her life more wonderful than being filled by this man.

"Say, 'Please fuck me, Bryce,'" he commanded against her breasts, his breath brushing across her wet skin.

"Oh, *please* fuck me, Bryce."

And he did. Over and over again. Hard and fast, as he'd promised. She lost count of how many times she died, how many times she arched her back, meeting him thrust for thrust, clutching at the platform behind her, her arms stretched overhead, crying out with the intensity of the sensations gathering in her and bursting.

Bryce pulled her up sharply, his hand wrapped around the back of her neck, and kissed her cruelly. Giselle could taste herself on his tongue and she wanted more of that. It was then she realized that she couldn't take his kisses away from him, because she tried. She did what he had done to her in the parking lot and succeeded for about half a second before she felt him smile against her mouth.

And take it away from her again.

She wrapped her arms around his neck and sighed when she felt his hands on her hips, rough, sliding down, down between her legs, spreading her apart farther and farther. Again he gripped her hips, pulled her up a bit, then brought her back down hard on his cock, impaling her. She cried out yet again and collapsed against his chest, holding on because she didn't have the stamina or strength for much more.

They were so close she didn't know where she ended and he began. All she knew was how incredible she felt pressed against and connected to Bryce Kenard: two souls, one body.

"Ride me," he said in her ear. "Use your knees."

So she did, finding strength she didn't know she had. He wrapped his hands around her hips, helped her for several strokes until she thought her legs would give out. Then he brought her down hard, kept her there as he began to come, holding her still, thrusting up into her once, twice, three times.

And when Bryce came—oh, that was spectacular, his hoarse, tortured roar, the arch of his body away from her, the tension in his face and his arms, his pleasurably painful grip on her hips. She felt him so deep within her she wanted to weep with joy, even while she watched him take his pleasure from her—the sight left her breathless: He was *majestic*.

Her thighs trembling, with no more strength left, she wrapped herself around him, out of breath and very sore, very tired, his body still buried inside hers.

Then he ripped the Velcro of her holster, slipped it out from between them, and set it carefully on the floor. He rolled her down into the duvet and covered them both up to sleep.

"Sebastian told me you were a consummate gentleman," Giselle whispered much later after they had dozed entwined, she curled on top of him. The music had stopped long ago, leaving the house silent. Her lips brushed his scarred left ear, kissing, speaking, her left hand stroking his smooth right cheek and her fingers running through his thick, silky black hair.

"Not in bed," he murmured, his arm around her and his hand caressing her arm, holding her tight to his chest. "I have no interest in being a gentleman in bed. This is what I like, what I want. It's what I want with you."

"I thought it was wonderful. Thank you."

"What you wanted? Expected?"

"Oh," she sighed, "much, much better."

He said nothing for a moment, his chest rising and falling slow and easy under her body. He startled her when he finally spoke. Soft. Reverent. "Thank you, Giselle. I knew it'd be good with you, but if I'd known it was going to be *that* good, I'd've been more insistent."

Giselle chuckled. "I let you in my bed because you had the balls to try."

He looked up at her sharply then, his eyebrow raised. "You didn't *let* me do anything. If it hadn't been your bed tonight, it'd have been mine. You're in bed with me because I'm more powerful than you are and I'm not going to let you forget it."

"That was an arrogant thing to say!" she gasped, rising a bit on her elbow and not really knowing if she was more offended or aroused.

"It ain't bragging if you can do it," he said, smug amusement dripping from every word. "If I'd pressed the point, I could've fucked you on that bench and then I could've taken you home and fucked you again." She sucked in a sharp breath because she knew that was true. But still! "I'm the alpha, Giselle. Your bed *is* my bed. Any bed you and I are in together is my bed. You know it. I know it. Deal with it."

"Bullshit," she snapped. "I'm the alpha in this house and wherever I go. I don't even have to think about it. Men stay out of my way and the CEO of a *Fortune 100 company* is afraid of me."

"Ooh, I think I hit a nerve," he mused, looking up at her and caressing her jaw with a finger. She shivered. "You were looking for someone who could take you. Congratulations. You found him."

Giselle huffed and sat up. She rolled to bounce out of bed, but as fast as she was, he was faster. Mid-roll, he grabbed her around the waist and roughly planted her on all fours. She gasped when he plunged himself inside her, digging his fingers into her hips and yanking her back onto him. Half appalled, completely aroused, she closed her eyes and moaned, arching her back in utter ecstasy.

"You were saying?" he murmured in her ear. She sighed when she felt his lips pressing softly against her shoulder once, twice, three times, making her cant her head to give him better access. His calloused fingers caressed her damp hair away from the skin of her neck—

—and his teeth sank into her nape. Giselle's eyes popped open. She drew in a long, tortured breath and released it on a shattered whisper. "*Bryce!*" She felt him smile against her skin before he released her and rose up straight behind her. He withdrew a bit before he thrust again. And again. Hard.

Oh, she liked this. It was nasty, savage. A battle. Suddenly, he sucked in a rough breath. "A tattoo," he breathed reverently as he traced the skin over her sacrum with a finger and she sighed. She groaned and dropped her head when he buried himself in her yet again, caressing the two Chinese characters with his fingers while taking lazy strokes in and out of her. "What does it mean?"

Eyes closed, she could feel him stretching her even more than before. She could feel her juices flow free with the sensation of the tender flesh of the inside of her thighs sliding along the outside of his muscled legs. She wanted—no, she needed—him to move, to take her again.

"What does it mean, Giselle?" he demanded, pulling away from her, then plunging into her again, twice, three times.

One bite.

She was his.

"Warrior Queen," she whispered.

He fucked her again. She felt every brutal stroke, coming before Bryce drove himself in her for the last time. "Ah, *Giselle!*"

Out of breath, her limbs trembling from holding up so much weight in such an unfamiliar position, she dropped to her stomach and he shamelessly fell on top of her. It was a welcome weight, one she'd longed for her entire adult life, one she'd almost given up on getting. She felt him entwine his fingers with hers and kiss her shoulder, nip her earlobe, lick that spot on her neck where he'd bitten her.

Since they had already slept, they talked. She was finally sated enough to have an actual conversation and too tired and weak to do anything but. His mouth wandered over her skin and her soul reveled in that.

"You're nasty," she whispered.

"Yes, I am," he agreed with alacrity. "And you knew that the first time I kissed you."

"And ruthless."

"That's what they tell me."

"And vicious."

"Check."

"And I'm in love with you."

"Were you in love with me before or after I told you I wanted to fuck you?" he whispered in her ear as he nuzzled her.

"I fell in love with you when you took my kiss away from me. Did you think I'd give you my virginity just to check and make sure?"

"Are you sorry?"

She opened her eyes and turned her head to look across the dark of her room, thinking. "Um, I don't know yet. I guess I'm supposed to be, huh?"

"That's usually the way it works, yes."

"Are you?"

"No," he muttered swiftly, decisively between kisses, licks, nips. "This is who I am, what I've wanted my whole life and fought against. Even if I had acknowledged this part of me, it would've horrified me. When I was twenty-four, I would've taken one look at you and been forced to accept who I was, what I wanted— And I was already fighting it with everything I had. You would've chewed me up and spit me out, which would've validated who I was *trying* to be."

"Oh, that's probably true."

"It's not like you can hide that everything you do, everything you say, everything you think makes you conspicuous in a roomful of Mormon women, but at the same time, you're just a nice Mormon girl and I like that."

"Let me tell you something," Giselle sighed, her eyes closing because what he was doing to her was so . . . comforting. His weight on hers, pressing her into the mattress, their legs entwined, his cock lying languid in the valley between her buttocks. She didn't have the strength for another round and she hurt. On the other hand, she might not have a choice—and that thrilled her. "It's not easy being me, walking this fine line between the letter of the law and the spirit of cultural expectations."

"I empathize."

"No, you don't. You can't. You're a man and it's different for women. A woman doesn't have the luxury of being able to be a hard ass when she needs to be, so if she's inclined that way, she stifles it or channels it in a different direction. You can be a hard ass when you need to be and then you're praised for being that and a kind and loving father and husband."

Bryce huffed and murmured, "About that loving father and husband routine— it's expected to extend all the way into the bedroom. There is no such thing as being a hard ass in bed. It's supposed to be a giving, a nurturing process, unselfish, soft, sweet. Sharing. Making love. *Always.* This," he told her, sweeping her arms lightly with his palms. She sucked in a breath, closing her eyes when he continued to do so as he spoke. "What I've done to you tonight, fucking, taking, greed, lust—that's the opposite of what we're taught about how it should be between a man and a woman. It's prideful and selfish."

"Mmmm," she whispered. "I need to turn over. I want to look at your face."

He lifted himself away from her and she turned, welcoming him back to her with a smile and outstretched arms. She wrapped her legs around his thighs and felt the smoothness of his chest on one side where the hair had burnt off and the other where she could feel the ridges and bumps of his scars.

"For like-minded people, in the taking," Giselle breathed, "the giving is inherent. Yin and yang. There can't be one without the other. I give you pleasure when I take what I want from you. In the selfish pursuit of my own pleasure, you benefit. Enlightened self-interest. Works with money. Works with sex."

"I never thought of it that way."

"You were too afraid of being labeled selfish." She snickered. "Just like Rearden. Galt had no such issues."

"Ouch and touché," he murmured as he kissed her.

She grinned wickedly against his lips. "Seems to me somebody got his themes and characters messed up. Good thing I picked you, huh?"

He chuckled. "That surprised me." They kissed for long moments, their tongues playing, not expecting it to lead anywhere. "And it meant a lot to me. Thank you," he whispered.

"There was no other choice. I posit," she murmured between kisses. She could kiss this man forever and not get enough. "That it's much better to be open about who you are and not get what you really want than settle for something not quite what you wanted in the first place."

"Tell that to a zealous twenty-one-year-old freshly returned missionary who's one big raging hormone and being exhorted at every turn to do his duty, get married, and procreate."

Giselle said nothing for a moment for their kissing, then, "I see your point. What happened to you between then and now?"

"I got tired of doing the right things for the wrong reasons with the wrong woman and getting my ass kicked by life. Tonight, I've done the wrong thing for the right reason with the right woman. And I don't intend to get my ass kicked again."

Giselle smiled and ran her fingers through his hair. He kissed her again and she tried—again—to take it away from him. He chuckled and upped the ante, refusing to let her, which left her breathless and thoroughly aroused. Again.

"If I'm asked,'" she whispered, placing her palms on either side of his face, stroking his skin with her thumbs and watching him as she quoted, "'to name my proudest attainment, I will say: I have slept with Hank Rearden. I had earned it.'"

He laughed wryly. "You really do like Rearden better than Galt, don't you?"

"He had real depth. He was the most noble character in the book."

25: Control Issues

"HOW THE HELL SHOULD I KNOW WHEN SHE CAME IN LAST NIGHT AND why is it my business?"

"You live with her!"

"So what? She's got a mother and it's not me. She pays me rent. That's how the roommate relationship works."

"What do you mean, you're not her mother? You act like her mother and mine, too, come to think of it."

The low rumble of two men arguing in another room brought Bryce slowly to consciousness, though he never forgot where he was or why he was there or the woman he was with or every single thing he'd done to her. And oh, the things she'd done to him. His head dropped back on the pillow and he smiled.

In the taking, the giving is inherent.

Why had he not read it that way to begin with? *You were too afraid of being labeled selfish . . . Just like Rearden. Galt had no such issues.*

He had to admit she'd nailed his ass to the wall on that, but she'd said "Kenard" without hesitation when asked to choose.

I'm in love with you.

He sighed with a sudden feeling of deep, deep contentment—something he had never felt with Michelle, not even on their wedding day.

Sunlight seeped through the cracks of drawn blackout drapes. The two of them were uncovered, the duvet long since abandoned on the floor. Giselle apparently still slept, her back spooned tight against his ribs as she sought warmth, her head on his outstretched arm, her breast filling his palm, his thumb absently caressing her nipple.

Her hair spread across his chest and tickled his skin. He lay spread-eagled, his other hand fondling her silky curls, bringing them to his nose for sniffing (vanilla), turning their conversation and their sex over in his head, reliving it, waiting for her to awaken. To start all over again.

"Look, if you're so worried, go look in her room and see if she's there."

Bryce didn't know exactly what was going on, but it sounded like it could get ugly when determined footsteps on the hard wood got closer and closer. The door swung open and the two people he least wanted to see at that moment burst in and stopped cold.

"Gi— Holy shit."

Knox looked like he had been hit in the head with a two-by-four, staring at Bryce, his mouth hanging open. Taight, on the other hand, looked very pleased.

"Get out," Bryce snarled, and Taight hauled Knox back and closed the door with a salute.

"Oops," Giselle muttered against his arm.

"Did you bring me back here specifically to make a point to Knox?"

"I have no points to make to Knox and Knox has a woman. Sort of. Maybe. Which you know very good and well. I brought you back here because it was the closest available bed."

Bryce started to laugh, but that gradually declined when Giselle turned over. He immediately felt he needed to further explore her breasts and other body parts that he had neglected last night.

And the hole in her right hip.

"Before we do this again," she sat up and announced, "I need to pee and brush my teeth. That is the first thing I do every single morning, without fail, and in that order."

"Fair warning: I'll follow you and fuck you in the shower."

Her eyes opened wide and she looked down at him, grinning like a child at the possibility that she would get exactly what she wanted on Christmas morning. "That would be sublime, thank you."

"Oh, now you're just making fun of me."

She arose with great care and groaned at every slow step she made toward the bathroom. "You have got to be kidding me," she breathed as she stopped, bent over, and massaged the muscles on the insides of her thighs. He grinned, totally satisfied with his night's work. She looked back at him then and smirked. "I would never make fun of a man whose idea of sweet nothings is 'I want to fuck you, Giselle.'"

"I wouldn't be with a woman who wouldn't find that romantic."

Finally she disappeared into the bathroom. Once he heard the sound of a faucet and then the brushing of teeth, he decided that it would be a good idea to do the same.

With no embarrassment on either of their parts, they went about their business in the bathroom, glancing at each other in the mirror. She broke out a new tooth-brush from her dentist-office stash and said, "Now mine won't be lonely anymore."

He turned her toward the mirror and wrapped his arms around her to look at their nude reflection. She smiled, her eyes soft and dreamy as she leaned back into him and watched him inspect her.

"I like that you shave," he murmured, dragging his fingertip along her bare mons.

"I don't," she whispered. "It's lasered." She laughed again when his mouth dropped open. "Shaving's a bitch and waxing hurts."

Her body was perfect. She was much shorter than his wife had been; in fact, she could fit under his chin. She was muscular yet curvy, unlike Michelle, who had been neither muscular nor curvy. Giselle's breasts were bigger than he'd expect on a weightlifter and he was oh, so grateful for that. Her ass was reasonably tight but nicely rounded. She had nice hips, though the right one sported a larger bullet hole than the one in her shoulder.

He caressed it with his thumb, studied it in the mirror, along with others, he saw now. Old scars, slashes here and there. "What's this?" he murmured as he traced a long, thin gash on the outside of her right thigh with a finger.

She smiled. "A knife wound." His eyes widened a bit and his cock stirred as he met her gaze in the mirror. She continued, "You don't make black belt without a few injuries. I think that one took sixteen stitches."

"Black belt," he breathed. "That explains the bodhisattva, the meditation. Most people pray."

"Meditation is silent, a quest for emptiness. Praying is a conversation. They each serve their purpose."

He said nothing for a long while as he traced her body, her scars, with his finger-tips. "This one?" he asked when he found a very old, very odd-shaped scar under her left breast that he would have missed had he not been looking so closely.

She pursed her lips and remained silent for a few beats and then, "Glass bottle. Sebastian and I were out collecting one night and the debtor had arranged an ambush."

He smirked. "What happened?"

She hesitated again. "Let's just say he paid us what he owed us. Eventually. We didn't know where he got the money and we didn't care."

With a finger, he made a sweeping motion around it, then around again. Visions of his own all-American boyhood flashed through his mind: football, surfing, church, Boy Scouts, suburban school. He compared it to the vision of her girlhood of guns, ghettos, and back alley collections and—

"That's *fuckable*," he finally breathed and she laughed.

"I wouldn't be with a man who didn't find a few war wounds attractive."

No, nothing fragile or breakable about this woman.

"You're perfect."

"Mmmm, so are you."

"No. We're Beauty and the Beast, is what we are."

She scowled. "I don't see you that way. Whatever you think about the way you look? Ditch it. Only my opinion counts and I think you're perfect."

"You didn't see me before the fire and I have no pictures."

"Before the fire, you were married."

"And about a week away from being divorced."

"Because you were miserable."

"And because she wasn't you."

"You didn't know me then."

"I feel like I've known you forever," he murmured, dipping his head to nibble and taste the crook of her neck, licking the mark he had given her. "You are so familiar to me, it's like we met long ago. Giselle, I've spent two years thinking of you, what it would be like to be in bed with you, what you must have in that warrior's soul of yours."

"You had a six-month head start on me, then."

They watched each other carefully for a long moment, then Bryce kissed and nibbled at her ear. "I don't know when I fell in love with you, Giselle, but I don't remember a time when I wasn't."

She turned her head then and caught his mouth in a kiss he didn't care about taking away from her.

"You bit me," she breathed into his mouth.

"I did," he whispered back. "You're mine. I want every male in the world to know that."

"Mmmm, I like that. But don't think I won't give back as good as I get."

"Counting on it."

26: O Fortuna

SEBASTIAN HAD GONE HOME AFTER SPENDING THE DAY WITH THE DELECTABLE Miss Logan and painted like a man possessed, following the heavy percussion and extravagant voices of *Carmina Burana* that resounded throughout his massive studio.

He scowled in irritation when Giselle came clattering in the door overhead until he realized by the sound of the footsteps that she had someone with her—a man. There was only one man she'd bring into this house and for only one reason, so his irritation died as fast as it had flared.

Sebastian continued to paint, the erotic music loud and heightening what was happening above his head, thereby informing what happened on his canvas. It wasn't long until her cries could be heard over the pounding music every time she came. Snapped out his funk by his thorough delight at her sudden and unexpected debauchery, Sebastian laughed out loud.

It did occur to him he should probably have the place soundproofed, especially if Kenard became a regular overnight guest. Yeah, it was funny tonight, but by tomorrow, Sebastian would be seriously annoyed. On the other hand, it would shock him speechless if she *didn't* move out of Sebastian's house and into Kenard's soon. Within the week.

That might suck a bit. He liked having her around, kinda like a cat without the litter box.

He continued to paint long into the night and after all the noises above him had ceased, until he was distracted by the sound of Knox letting himself into the house and then coming down the stairs to his studio.

"What the hell is wrong with you?" Sebastian barked, angry at the interruption.

"It's eight o'clock in the morning and you look like shit," Knox shot back. "I came to talk to you about Eilis Logan. And where's Giselle? Her car's not out there."

Sebastian grinned. "Giselle is just fine, I do believe. What do you want to know about Logan?"

"Can she be rescued?"

He pursed his lips while he cleaned his brushes and knives. He'd had no idea he'd painted the night away, although he did admit that what he'd painted was particularly exquisite, once he stepped back and looked.

He didn't answer, but led the way upstairs to the kitchen to fix himself some breakfast. Knox rooted around in the refrigerator, then sat down at the conference room table and ate part of a leftover steak to temper the orange juice.

"You're a shithead, you know that?" Sebastian said. "You could've just told me she had all that art to begin with, and I would've taken the receivership without you having to hammer away at me. Why do you have to do everything the hard way?"

"You don't seem to mind that when you dig yourself into a hole and you need me to pull you back out."

"Okay, fine. I'll be sure to tell Congress you're the biggest weapon in my Fix-or-Raid arsenal. Happy now?"

"Ah, recognition for my genius at last."

"Madness, not genius."

"And always with a method. Eccentric hermit money brokers have no room to talk. Are you going to sell her art?"

"Absolutely. With the sale of the eight Fords alone, she'll be almost halfway out of the red. I'm still in shock that she'd keep them while her company went deeper and deeper—and who knows what other treasures she's got stored away somewhere. I'm shocked she didn't clean house. She's so top-heavy that building should be leaning like Pisa. And why hasn't she taken her company public? She's got two great products that she hasn't put on the general market . . . why? Her marketing sucks. Nothing makes sense."

"I wondered about that, especially the part about clearing out her executive ranks," Knox muttered absently, "but that's not my area of expertise so I wanted you to figure it out." He stopped for a minute to think. "I like her. I don't know why. I just wanted to give her someone who could make her do what she needed to do. Did you read Webster's trial transcripts?"

Sebastian shook his head.

"When I was trying to decide whether I wanted to prosecute her or not," Knox said, "I started looking at the dates of the thefts. It looked to me like if she hadn't married Webster, he'd have been able to take everything: pensions, art, other assets. So I asked her how she found out and blammo. Stray piece of paper on the bedroom floor about a week after he moved into her house. She was only able to catch him before he got everything *because* she married him and she *stayed* married to him to rescue her company. He hid it so well it took her six months to figure out where it was all going and prove it."

Sebastian stared at him for a long moment and then said, "Maybe she's a better gambler than I thought." He hoisted himself up on the kitchen counter and brooded. He did that a lot and his family had long ago accepted that they just had to wait until he was finished and then said whatever it was he needed to say. Knox continued to eat.

"She also owns *Morning in Bed*," he finally said.

Knox choked.

"It's not on the books. She 'fessed up—why, I don't know because I would've never found out. I can only conclude she really does value her company more than she values her standing in the art community."

"Nobody knows who owns that painting, so she has no standing."

Sebastian grunted. "True. I'm thinking about letting her keep it with no one the wiser."

Knox got up and cleaned up his breakfast mess. "That's very out of character for you."

"She didn't have to tell me at all."

Knox started laughing at once. "Oh, I see. You want to fuck her."

"Shut up," Sebastian snarled.

He held up his hands, still grinning. "Hey, I make no judgments. I told you I like her and I do respect her. She's one of the most unique women I've ever met, certainly, and she's got brains. But the Jackie O. schtick leaves me cold."

Sebastian waved a hand. "Camouflage."

"Say, where'd King Midas go while you were trying to figure out how to run your freight train over her track?"

"No idea. I was too surprised it was happening at all."

Knox continued to chuckle as they left the conference room and went down the four stairs to the corridor, shaking him down about Giselle's whereabouts, which made Sebastian pissy. It made him so pissy, in fact, that he suggested Knox open her bedroom door and see if she was there.

He did.

"Gi— Holy shit."

Sebastian did smile then. The bed was trashed, the room reeked of sex, and the guilty parties were naked. Giselle slept curled up against Kenard, her back against his ribs, his arm her pillow. Knox nearly swallowed his tongue.

"Get out." That nasty snarl came from the man in the bed, who had propped himself up on one elbow. With the burn scars that matted half his face and apparently, the entire left side of his body, he looked as deadly as he sounded. Sebastian curled his hand around Knox's collar and dragged him of the doorway, then closed the door.

"Well, *that* was refreshing and unexpected!" Sebastian crowed, poking at Knox, wanting to see him lather up.

Knox punched him in the sternum—hard—and stalked off to the living room, where he flopped on the couch and turned on the TV. "If you're hooking for any more reaction from me, you're wasting your time. I've got my own problems and nowhere on that very long list is a notation to be jealous of Bryce when—Remember!—I went out of my way to make sure he knew she was ripe for his picking. And *then* I had to go kick Giselle's ass into gear. You'd'a thought they were a couple of damned eighth graders."

That was true and Sebastian growled, unsatisfied with the reaction he'd gotten. That was two people in two days Sebastian had been unable to bait successfully. No matter. He knew he could get Giselle and how. He scrounged around for the envelopes he knew he had somewhere.

"Knox," he said blithely, "you wanna go to the Ford exhibit tonight?"

"And be treated like a leper? You know I'm *persona non grata* all over town."

"Oh, good, because I only have two invitations and I wanted to make sure you didn't want one before I gave them to Giselle and Kenard."

Knox turned around and stared at him, then started laughing. "Oh, you're a bastard."

Sebastian chuckled. "Yes, I am. Couldn't crack that damn façade Eilis has and your reaction to our newly deflowered Giselle in there was highly unsatisfactory. I'm scraping the bottom of the barrel for cheap entertainment this morning."

"Cheap entertainment? Open her damn door and watch. Any woman who'd bring a man home and *not* lock her door wants to be watched." And so saying, Knox turned up the volume on the TV. "I'd love to be at that exhibit just to see his face. You should've seen him when I told him she'd threatened Fen at gunpoint."

"I'm guessing, since he's in there with her, that he finds her fuckable *because* of her proclivities, not in spite of. I mean, any man who can bed Giselle is not a man to be fucked with. He's so beyond bitter and angry, he could chew concrete." Knox made no reply. "Oh, here they are. Hey, are you still serious about not wanting OKH?"

"Dead serious."

Sebastian went into the living room and as he passed Knox, he walloped him in the back of the head. He dropped into the club chair across from him and put his feet up on the coffee table. "Out with it. What does Giselle know that I don't?"

Sebastian watched as Knox flipped through the channels until he settled on *Animaniacs*. Naturally. "There's a woman I want. That's what Giselle knows. All I need is to get through my birthday alive and go get her."

Sebastian couldn't fault that logic. "But does she want you?"

"Yes. And I have no interest in running a company."

"You have a degree in accounting."

"And so I'm a prosecutor who understands white-collar crimes better than most and I'm a whiz with paper trails. I can't imagine being chained to a desk poring over the tax code." Knox shuddered. "I should've stayed in California."

Sebastian made no reply to that. It would be futile to point out that Knox wouldn't give up his job for anything, even to be a professional surfer.

"I might have a solution for your issues with being a CEO," Sebastian said slowly, staring at the coffee table, thinking out loud. "I'd make Eilis Logan CEO."

Knox grunted. "Good luck with that. She can't even manage what she built herself." With that, he hauled himself out of the couch and started toward the front door. "I'm out of here. I can't take any more of the second-hand fuckfest."

"You should've heard her last night."

"Make her go downstairs."

Sebastian's mouth thinned. "I think not. That's *my* bedroom."

"When was the last time you used it?"

That hit its mark and Sebastian's teeth ground. Knox laughed. "Yeah, that's what I thought. You better figure out a way to get Logan in bed and quick. Now that you've got a woman in your cross hairs that you'll actually have to spend time to seduce, you'll be insufferable. Oh wait," Knox said blithely as he opened the front door, "you can't. You're her trustee. That would be . . . immoral. And I think it'd be funnier'n'hell to figure out how it might be illegal and throw your ass in jail for it. Check and mate." He smiled benignly at Sebastian, then slammed the door behind him.

Sebastian shook his head and went back to work. He knew *how* he was going to haul Eilis out of bankruptcy; it was a matter of how fast he could make it happen and how hard she'd fight him. He wanted her and he'd made up his mind he *would* have her. Somehow.

What Sebastian wanted, Sebastian got.

Always.

27: Standing on Higher Ground

A soft knock sounded on Giselle's bedroom door. "Hey, Giz," Sebastian called politely, "when you come up for air, I want to talk to you. Bring Kenard."

Giselle sighed and looked over at her clock. "It's three o'clock and I'm hungry."

"You always do what he says?" Bryce muttered from beside her, his face buried in the pillow and his arm in the curve of her waist.

"Absolutely not. Sebastian's all about wine, women, and song and thinks everybody else should be, too. He wouldn't interrupt if it weren't important to him. Plus, it's Saturday. He'll have Bryant's."

"Oh, that's all you really needed to say."

An hour later, wrapped up in terry cloth from head to toe, she waddled, still groaning, out to the conference room holding hands with Bryce, who wore only a low-slung towel around his hips. A solid twelve, thirteen hours of fucking, and she could feel every minute of it in her muscles that hurt oh, so badly she could barely walk.

She liked it. She didn't know if any other event in her life could ever compete.

"I know you've met already. Sorta. Bryce, Sebastian. Sebastian, Bryce."

"Sorry about punching you at Fen's party."

"Eh, don't worry about it. It was worth it." Sebastian shot a glance at Giselle. "Having a little trouble walking this afternoon, Giz?"

"Oh, I'm sorry. *Who* hasn't gotten laid in the last four years?"

Sebastian curled his lip at her and she chuckled.

As soon as they'd settled themselves in with the barbecue, Sebastian's irritation with her gave way to a calculating smirk and she caught her breath, wondering how he would retaliate. First Knox, then her. Sebastian was on a roll today.

He slid two white envelopes across the table at her and said, "Giz, I would like you and Kenard here to come to the Ford opening tonight."

She sucked in a deep breath. No. Not that. Anything but that. Sebastian grinned when she slouched down in her chair and glared at him, folding her arms over her chest.

"Something wrong, Giz? Is there some *reason* you don't want to go to an exclusive Ford showing tonight?"

"You're an asshole, you know that?"

She could sense Bryce's confusion, but she didn't care to explain and finally Sebastian got down to business.

"I'm actually glad—" He shook his head and let loose a chuckle, his eyebrows raised. "—although *extremely* surprised—that you're here. I was going to contact you next week."

That startled Bryce, distracted him. Yay.

"I need a secret trust," Sebastian explained. "I had heard you were especially good at those. And I'm curious. Why *are* you so good at this? You're a trial attorney."

Bryce shrugged. "I was getting divorced and wrapping up my assets so she couldn't get to them."

"Ah. That's a bitch."

"Yes, she was," Bryce muttered emphatically, and Giselle hurt for him all of a sudden, without knowing why.

Sebastian cleared his throat to dislodge his foot. He pulled out a thick file and slid it across the table. He began to eat while Bryce looked them over. "Knox asked me to be the trustee for this receivership and I'm starting to lay some groundwork."

Giselle leaned over Bryce's arm to read and her eyes widened at the very high eight-figure numbers—all in red. Giselle's bankruptcy didn't even begin to approach that. HR Prerogatives. Eilis Logan.

"That's a *beautiful* name," Giselle whispered reverently.

"It's Gaelic," Bryce murmured and Giselle smiled. "Irish for Elizabeth." While Bryce and Sebastian discussed this woman's situation, she relived the most magical hours of her life. She could afford to be a little cavalier about it because she had a man who'd be in a lot more trouble with the church than she would be when they chose to repent later—and he knew it.

She was unreasonably glad she had something to give back to this man who had given her what she thought she would never have.

"Giz? Earth to Giselle." Sebastian snapped his fingers in her face to get her attention. "Keep your mind off his cock for more than three seconds, would you?"

Bryce slid her a glance and chuckled, but Giselle sighed. "Did you hear me say this woman owns *Morning in Bed?*"

Giselle sputtered and she sat up to take a long drink, unable to speak for a moment. "Are you serious?"

Sebastian shrugged. "I haven't seen it and it's off the books, so I can only assume she was telling me the truth. Nobody in her situation would just spin that out of thin air because it's a waste of time."

"Okay, stop." Bryce leaned over the documents, one elbow on the table, his hand rubbing his forehead. "I'm lost. Start at the beginning. Who's Ford and why are these paintings that valuable?"

Giselle touched his arm and he looked at her with lust in his expression, his thoughts clearly split between business and sex—with her. She smiled softly, but explained anyway. "Ford is an artist. This lady," she said, tapping the papers, "owns nine extremely valuable paintings and selling them would cure over half of her ills."

Bryce looked suitably impressed, but Sebastian said, "The one she doesn't have on the books is worth about four of the others put together."

"Why?"

"Ford is a recluse," said Giselle. "No one knows who he is or anything about him. The people who do know aren't talking. Part of the value of his paintings is exactly that—that no one knows who he is. The work itself is just sublime. People don't just like his work, they have orgasms over it. People who *don't* like his work still like his work. It's a fascinating phenomenon."

"*Morning in Bed* is rumored to be a self-portrait," Sebastian continued. "It supposedly has clues painted into it that would help someone figure out Ford's identity. It was bought anonymously immediately upon its release by a private broker-age, it's never hung anywhere but at its premiere, and nobody knows who owns it—except us, now."

He got up and pulled a coffee table book out from a stack on the buffet. He looked through it until he found the right page and swung it around to show Bryce. "That's it," he said, pointing to it.

Giselle knew every nuance of that painting.

Morning sunlight streamed through an unseen window on a bed clothed only in white sheets, and occupied by a man. A nude man, whose body was the essence of masculine perfection and beauty. He lay on his stomach on the edge of the bed, his head propped on his right arm and turned toward a pillow beside him. His left arm, possessed of a hamlike fist, stretched out across the bed to crumple nearly half of the pillow in his grasp. One leg was crooked, thrown wide and tangling in the rumpled sheets, the other a straight line from his muscular buttocks to his toes. His scrotum lay nestled between his legs. And while the abused pillow and most of the man's body were bathed in the new sun, his face lay in shadow—no features, no hair, no anything that would make him recognizable to anyone.

Bryce studied it for a moment before saying, slowly, "I don't know how this can be called a self portrait."

"Its only real value," Giselle said, "is that Ford has never exhibited a man and as far as anybody knows, he's never painted one other than this. Because of that, everyone assumes that it's him."

"That makes this the closest thing to proving who Ford is?"

"Exactly," Sebastian agreed. "Whoever owns this painting is arguably the most powerful person in the contemporary art world, other than the people who actually do know who he is."

"Taight, you speculate in art. What do you think?"

"I think it's a gag to see how many self-important people will swallow the rumors and drive its price through the roof. Is it Ford or isn't it? Does it have clues painted in it or doesn't it? Can Ford be found or can't he? The painting itself has no more value than any other Ford painting except that it's a rare subject for him. You could reasonably expect to pay twice as much as any other Ford painting. It's the rumors that give it four times that value."

"Would you buy it?"

"If I were strictly speculating, absolutely not and certainly not at that price. I don't think Ford can keep his identity a secret much longer and the value of that painting will either skyrocket or plummet depending on who he turns out to be. If he's somebody famous for something else, up it goes. If he's a nobody, it falls to about twice the level of the other Fords, where it really should be. But it doesn't matter. Any way you cut it, the return on investment is too low for me to bother with it. His other work won't change in value much one way or another because the art is what it is."

"Also," Giselle added, "people are getting a little blasé about his anonymity and restless with his work. Yes, it's divine, but he's been a one-trick pony for too long. Tonight's the opening of something new."

"So that's where we're going tonight? To see this artist's work?"

She swallowed and shifted. "Yes." She shot Sebastian a hateful glare and he smirked anew. That bastard was enjoying this, especially the fact that he'd successfully piqued Bryce's curiosity.

Bryce closed the book and set it aside, looking down at the documents again, flipping through the pages until he stopped at the inventory. "And this—woman— has the most valuable one."

"She says she does."

"Or she has a forgery."

Sebastian shrugged. "It's very possible. I'd have to see it first and have it appraised."

"I can't imagine she'd give it up," Giselle pointed out.

"She doesn't want to, which is why it isn't on her books. I told her I'd think about it."

Giselle stared at him hard and long, confused by that. "That's not your style," she said slowly. "There's something else going on here you're not saying."

Bryce's head snapped up then to stare at Sebastian. "I know why," he said with a smirk. "Got your face between her legs?" Giselle laughed at Sebastian's immediate scowl. "What's the trust for? What's going in it?"

"I'm going to fund it. I want at least a few of those paintings, but I don't want her to know. The trust will buy the paintings once they go on the block."

Giselle shot him a look. "You *can't* be speculating on Fords."

"No, I'm not."

"Really," Giselle said, tilting her head and watching him carefully. For once, Sebastian squirmed. Giselle's mouth dropped open and she gasped. "You're in love with her. You wouldn't do that for a woman you just want to fuck."

"Okay, so what? Mind your own business, Giselle."

"Hey, you're the one who told Knox to open my door and you knew very good and well Bryce was here, so you have no room to talk."

"You didn't lock it."

"I forgot."

"Bullshit. You'd've been ecstatic if I'd thrown you a deflowering party this morning."

"All right, children," Bryce interrupted, amusement heavy in his voice. "When I get in the office on Monday, I'll start the process."

"Thank you," Sebastian said, and leaned back in his chair, locking his fingers behind his head. "So, Kenard. What made you chuck a lifetime of being the perfect example of Latter-day Saint priesthood to fuck a virgin renegade intellectual with a taste for rough sex the first chance you got?"

Giselle rolled her eyes, but Bryce only smirked and looked straight at her. "A virgin renegade intellectual with a taste for rough sex."

Sebastian laughed. "I knew I'd like you, Kenard. Welcome to the pack."

28: Dirty White Boy

THEY WALKED INTO THE KEMPER MUSEUM OF CONTEMPORARY ART & Design fashionably late after having gone to Bryce's home so he could change into semiformal wear.

They had watched each other as they dressed, Bryce in a black suit and Giselle in a pale yellow silk evening gown, the sleeveless top randomly studded with pearls. He chose a pale yellow tie, which made her smile. "Where's the Glock?" he murmured low. She had begun to appreciate that his voice deepened and hoarsened when he was aroused.

"Here," she said, putting the gun, in its holster, in his big hand. She propped her foot on his bed, her skirt pulled up to show him that she wore nothing underneath it but white lace garters and stockings. He grinned as he wrapped the wide band around her thigh and tightened it. "Harder," she whispered, watching him, waiting.

"How hard do you want it?" he muttered as he ripped open his fly and backed her up against the wall. He bunched her skirt up around her waist, lifted her, and plunged into her. She smiled and sighed as she wrapped her legs around him.

They mingled a bit before making the rounds of the exhibit. The new painting to be unveiled hung from long cables attached to the ceiling. A jazz band played standards, the smoky alto reminiscent of Diana Krall.

"Well, we're attracting a lot of attention tonight," Giselle murmured.

"I guess it's now been confirmed I'm fucking Sebastian Taight's lover," he returned wryly and she laughed. The corners of her eyes wrinkled in merriment and her ice blue eyes, now having darkened to steel gray, twinkled. He'd received a welcome boost to his ego on the information that everyone in the city found it amazing and scandalous that he'd seduced a beautiful woman away from Sebastian Taight—two equally rich men and she'd chosen the ugly one. Oh, yes, that was shocking.

"Kevin!" Giselle called and waved at the Jackson County prosecutor and his wife. Oblivious to the fact that the people around them vied for an introduction to Giselle, she pulled Bryce through the crowd as the other couple battled to meet them in the middle.

"Well, hello, Miss Cox," he murmured once they'd shaken hands. Introductions of Bryce and Jill Oakley were made, though Kevin and Bryce did know each other in passing. "Nice to see you again when you haven't been cleaning up after me or running through the courthouse. Knox tells me you're the one to blame for my sudden career change."

"No good deed goes unpunished and I'm always willing to take out your trash— but don't act like you hadn't already thought about it. Your boredom can be heard loud and clear all the way from Twelfth Street to Rockhill Road and back. Have you spoken with Justice McKinley yet?"

"Oh, yes. She's, uh, interesting."

"Mmmm, but more importantly, she's getting very influential."

Bryce remained silent while they chatted for another few minutes, listening to her, what she had to say, how she said it.

She just gave your IQ a blow job and she's not even here.

That feeling of deep contentment pulsed through his chest.

One gun in each hand. No hesitation. No remorse.

The sex was as incredible as he'd ever hoped, wanted, craved for so many years with a smart, dangerous woman he could throw at a bed and fuck.

The prosecutor and his wife broke away a little sooner than Bryce would have liked. He found the whole process fascinating—and that Giselle had gotten the political ball rolling made him unaccountably proud of her. Then he started. Did he have any *right* to be proud of her?

I'm in love with you.

She'd demanded he not leave her once they'd crossed over into sin, but now he wanted more than that from her. And given their shared cultural identity, he didn't have to wonder if she'd want the same.

Bryce and Giselle were approached in an ever-increasing stream of people eager to learn the identity of the woman who'd made the society grapevines as Cinderella, Sebastian Taight's lover—until she'd very conspicuously abandoned him and invited Bryce Kenard deep into the bowels of the gallery with a look. Her sprint'n'slide back through the gallery in a serious state of deshabille, Kenard hot on her heels, had only set the gossip mill running overtime.

Everyone wanted to know her name and provenance, but no one had dared ask Bryce once he'd put his fist in Taight's face and Taight was unapproachable under any circumstances. Likely no one had known to ask Fen and Fen Hilliard wasn't one to volunteer information.

"Giselle Cox," Bryce said over and over again to people he knew, and tonight, it seemed he knew everybody. "Taight and Hilliard's cousin. Trudy's niece."

While that came out of left field for everyone, it was no less jaw-dropping. Bryce had no idea how his credibility would stand up under the scrutiny of his association with Knox either as best friend or relative, but he refused to dodge it. After all these years, Knox deserved whatever support Bryce could offer him.

The only other jaw-dropping part about it—to which Giselle was oblivious and of which Bryce was most acutely aware—was the unvoiced question of *why* Giselle had chosen the ugly one. On the other hand . . .

" . . . seen the way she looks at Kenard? She's head over heels."

"I noticed that. Nothing mercenary about her. Very sweet, especially after what he's been through."

That tidbit he'd heard on his way to the restroom. It made him smile, made warmth spread through him. He still didn't know exactly what she saw in him either, but here, tonight, with her, he felt normal again, like the man he'd been before the fire.

Fen and Trudy made their appearance to a cacophony of society clamoring for information. Bryce exchanged amused glances with Giselle when the Hilliards were good-naturedly called to account for hiding their relationship to Cinderella. When Trudy shot her a hateful look across the room, Giselle chuckled and blew her a kiss.

"I hate that bitch," Giselle murmured. "It doesn't matter what Fen does to me, I'll give him a mulligan almost every time. Trudy . . . no."

Puzzled, Bryce said, "Why?"

Giselle's mouth tightened. "Trudy," she said finally, "is not a nice person. I was an adult before I realized how much Fen protected me and Knox from her, how much Fen went behind her back to support Knox."

"Then why is he with her?"

"I think he's possessed."

Bryce laughed at her wry tone. "Apparently that works both ways, since he slapped you for calling her a whore."

"Yeah, and look how that turned out."

Fen sported the bandage over his nose with the pride of a warrior freshly off the battlefield. "Giselle, Kenard," he said expansively as he shook Bryce's hand and hugged Giselle. Trudy made it a point to ignore Giselle and thus Bryce; she would have wandered off, but Fen kept her at his side. "Well, Giselle, I must give you credit for being a fast worker. You only came to see me *yesterday*." Trudy started and shot a look at her husband, but Bryce just chuckled. "I told you he wouldn't hold your little, ah, masquerade-that-wasn't against you."

"So you did and no, he didn't. But for all you know, this could be our first date."

"Not with that bright neon glow of the newly fucked you've got."

Giselle laughed. "I daresay you'd have been disappointed in me had I come alone."

"True, true. Are you armed?" Giselle tilted her head and pursed her lips. "Of *course* you are! Does that mean you're still sulking?"

Bryce bit back a laugh.

"Do I act like I'm sulking?"

"Now that you mention it, no. Glad to see you've returned to your usual humor, my girl." He gestured to Bryce with his champagne glass. "So who's plowing whose field now?"

"My field was virgin *yesterday*."

"And then it was plowed last night. By a *squatter*. Hypocrite much? How are you going to explain this to your mother?"

"Oh, she'll be thrilled I finally stopped sleeping with Knox," Giselle returned dryly and Fen released a genuine belly laugh.

Bryce thought it best not to get in the middle of this conversation, no matter how bizarre. Giselle had had years of practice at handling him and while Bryce definitely didn't like being referred to as a squatter, it *was* true.

He would rectify that as soon as possible.

"So what happened to your nose?" she asked innocently.

Fen waved a hand. "I happened to be behind a door my assistant came slamming through."

"That's terrible. Is it broken?"

"Yes. But I'm not going to have it reset. I decided that a broken nose lends character to a face. I was simply too perfect as a senatorial candidate before. So in retrospect, I believe it'll be a good thing. I should thank my assistant and give her a raise."

Both Bryce and Giselle burst out laughing.

"So, Kenard, I'm guessing you're not on board with my campaign?"

"Yeah, you're not going to get any money from me," Bryce murmured with a sigh of false regret. "If you'd asked me in December, I could have told you then."

"Ah, but then you wouldn't have met my charming niece, would you?"

Bryce inclined his head. "That's true, but now I have even fewer reasons to donate. Fire. Bullets. Ponds. Insulin. You know how it is."

His eyebrows rose. "I see the children haven't wasted any time brainwashing you. And you believe their cockamamie story?"

"Didn't Knox tell you? He and I were roommates in college. I have a long history of being able to see your hands pulling the strings."

"Ah," he said, betraying no shock except for the sudden, though infinitesimal, tension in his body. "You'll believe what you want, I suppose."

"In any case, I'm flattered to be considered worthy of inclusion into such august company."

"Well, knowing my nephews, I'm sure you'll take the alpha position in no time." They moved on after that, leaving Bryce still chuckling.

"He cracks me up," Giselle said.

"That was the most fucked-up conversation I ever heard," Bryce muttered, "all things considered."

"I'm easily entertained."

"Apparently. Does he always just casually discuss what he's done?"

"He'll allude to it. He knows we can't prove it and calling him out publicly would get us a lot of bad publicity we don't want and wouldn't be able to overcome."

"And an easily won libel suit to boot."

"Exactly. It would defeat our purpose and he knows that. And really, we're the only ones he *can* talk about it with. Now that I'm with you and someone else has Knox's britches in a twist, there's only one immediate solution to the problem. Neither Knox nor I want to do that for obvious reasons and Sebastian prefers financial warfare."

"Indeed. You want something to eat?" Bryce asked after he'd snagged an hors d'oeuvre off a passing tray.

"No," she mumbled absently, standing on tiptoes to look over the crowd. "I don't trust what's in some of that stuff." He thought that a little extreme and said so. That caught her attention. "Do you like what I look like naked?"

"Very much. Sometimes I even like what you look like not naked."

"Do you want my nakedness to look the same always until I'm an old lady?"

"That would be nice."

"Then trust me when I tell you I don't want food because, as you should know by now, I like to eat. A lot."

He laughed and picked her up, wrapping her tight in his arms. He twirled her around and around, kissing and nipping her neck. "You're beautiful," he said as he let her slide down his body. He chuckled when that firearm bulge brushed against his thigh. "You really don't trust Fen, do you?"

"Goodness, no. He's never gone back on a deal, but now he's just curious to see how many more lives I have. Two down, seven to go."

"What makes you think that?"

"Oh, he said so yesterday."

For some sick and twisted reason buried down deep in his dark soul, Bryce found that hilarious. "Let's see this exhibit."

Except for his sudden obsession with *Lilith*, Bryce didn't get art. He had none save the books that lined his walls. That wasn't to say he didn't like a few pieces here and there. He simply didn't care enough to study it, purchase it, and find a place to put it. He certainly wouldn't dislodge any of his books for it. For *Lilith*, he would've dislodged his books, but now he wouldn't have to.

Once they reached the entrance of the actual exhibit and he saw what "a Ford" actually was, he looked in wonder. He knew Giselle watched and waited for his reaction, but this—this he had not expected.

"See? I told you."

Nudes. On canvases five feet square, each hung at a different angle. Women in all stages of life, in all shapes and sizes, of every race imaginable. The artist had captured them in such a way as to make them all beautiful regardless of one's personal taste.

"This is—" he murmured, taking it all in. "Magnificent."

Giselle smiled and squeezed his hand, leading him into the labyrinth. Each woman leaped off the canvas at him and Bryce wanted to touch to see if they were real. He didn't know much, but he did know it must have taken amazing skill and talent to pull this off.

Neither of them said anything as they roamed through the partitions slowly with the rest of the attendees. Finally, Bryce asked, "What do these do for you?"

"They make me want to *be* them. See, that one? That's what I wish I looked like. Taller. Curvier. Like—well, like *Lilith*."

"Yeah, I'm not agreeing with you there, Giselle." She looked up at him, puzzled, and he bent down to speak in her ear, "*Lilith*—these women—they're for making love. I'm not interested in making love. You're solid, built to fuck. That's what I like."

Giselle blushed, ducked her head, tried to hide her smile. He loved that he could fluster her. "Don't you ever want to make love?" she asked softly. Her sudden shyness warmed his soul.

"Yes," he returned, "but that takes time to do right and I haven't felt like taking that kind of time yet." He cocked an eyebrow at her. "Have you?"

She snickered, but looked away to hide her growing redness. "No."

Bryce chuckled, then said, "There are a lot of pregnant women in this collection."

"Mmmm, that's his hallmark. He adores pregnant women."

They had almost reached the end of the exhibit when the announcement of the unveiling of the new Ford painting echoed over the hum of the partygoers. The crowd began to move toward the front of the gallery where it hung tarped. Giselle stayed back a bit to study another painting.

"C'mon, Giselle. Let's go find a good spot. Now I'm really curious."

"Mmmm, in a minute. I don't like to be too close."

She fidgeted when he finally pulled her away from the painting and ended up toward the back of the gathering. The gallery director had asked for a brush-stick drum roll as he hushed the crowd and introduced the work.

"This latest Ford painting," he began, "marks a sharp turn in the artist's direction, as you will see. It is called," he said with a pause for dramatic effect, then grabbed the cable that held the tarp and pulled, "*Rape of a Virgin.*"

The crowd gasped and stepped back as one. Bryce's jaw dropped, stepped back as if shoved.

No air, no breath.

Damn near dizzy.

The crowd buzzed, turned, stared. Somewhere in the back of his mind, he noticed this, but he was too shocked to care.

As of not even twenty-four hours ago, he knew that body and bed intimately—and they were on display on a five-foot-wide by eight-foot-tall canvas for the entire world to see. His cock swelled as he closed his eyes and let his head fall back with a sigh.

Bryce thought he should feel guilty for enjoying his slide right down into the featherbed of hedonism, but he didn't. He was achingly aroused by the fact that other men looked between her nude portrait and her clothed presence, their lust for her plain in their faces, the same lust that had always tortured Bryce—and they could not have her.

Right here, right now, she stood at Bryce's side, unabashedly bearing the mark he'd given her that proclaimed her his lover.

He opened his eyes again to stare at that painting, at her—

Mine.

Giselle trembled against him and crushed his hand between both of hers. He returned her squeeze, but he was uneager to break the spell. Finally her discomfort registered somewhere in the depths of his consciousness and it did vaguely occur to him that the silence in the room was not normal.

He was enchanted.

"I— I have no words," he finally whispered.

Painted from directly above in the manner of *Morning in Bed*, laid out on a rumpled white sheet over a mattress supported by a broad black platform, she lay on her stomach on the bed at a diagonal, nude. Her right knee crooked across the bed. Her right hand stretched out to the edge of the bed and over it, desperately reaching, her fingers wide. Her left arm was slung high and up over her head, bound to an iron ring in the wall with a white strap secured by a highly stylized and detailed padlock. Her left leg stretched far out under her, her foot dropping off the mattress. A red strap and a padlock of a different design, though equally stylized and detailed, bound the left ankle to the leg of the bed.

Her honey curls, their length greatly exaggerated, fanned out over the bed and glowed like the most vivid of flames. The skin of her back, arms, and legs betrayed the cuts of a weightlifter's musculature. Her tattoo was detailed precisely, the two Chinese characters—Warrior Queen—vertical over her spine, the tail of the last character nearly disappearing into her cleft. Her vulva peeked out tantalizingly from between her legs.

An open dog-eared Bible lay on the bed by her pillow as if she had just put it down, and nearly touching her left hip was a well-worn copy of *Intercourse*, also open but turned over, spine up and broken. She stared at what rested beside the bed with a desperate yearning. There, on a simple chair just an inch or two out of reach, were two gold keys: One graphically carved in the shape of a phallus that was clearly meant to open the lock of the white strap that held her arm; the other in the shape of a baby's pacifier, which opened the padlock of the red strap at her ankle.

Definitely not Lilith. Not in any way.

The agony of a woman who couldn't get what other women got, what she should expect to get, what she very clearly craved, had been captured with exquisite precision. Bryce swallowed heavily when his gaze settled fully on the pacifier.

Giselle's sniffling through the deafening silence caught his attention then and he looked down at her. He finally understood the depth of her anxiety when she whispered, "Talk to me, please. Please don't hate me."

His eyes widened. "How could you think—"

Bryce clutched the back of her head and pulled her fiercely to him, kissing her as wickedly as he had the night before, taking everything she would give him and hoping she would find value in what little he could give her.

Thunderous applause broke out when she wrapped an arm around his neck, and Bryce smiled against her lips. He could feel her relieved, delighted laugh and her tears that moistened both their cheeks. "I don't know what to say," he murmured against her mouth. "It's— It's breathtaking. You're breathtaking."

"It'll be hung all over the world. You don't mind other men seeing it?"

"No," he whispered harshly. "I *want* them to look and know that woman is *mine*." His thumb caressed the bite mark on her nape. That she hadn't bothered to try to hide it made him hard. "And everyone in this room knows that." She sucked in a sharp breath, closed her eyes, closed her mouth on his so that he would kiss her again. He obliged, then murmured, "You're *not* a virgin anymore and *I* am the one who took it from you."

She smiled. Blushed. "Maybe we should go home. We're going to get attacked by the vultures any minute and there's press here."

"Oh, no," he replied. "We're not going anywhere. I want to enjoy this."

That made her laugh but soon she was surrounded for autographs and to field questions about Ford's identity. Flashes popped as cameras got her image to compare and contrast to the one on the portrait.

Kevin and Jill Oakley stared at her in stunned amusement.

Trudy, and to some extent, Fen, struggled with the onslaught of people who, because they couldn't get to Giselle, hounded them instead.

Bryce chuckled to himself and shook his head as he watched Giselle graciously speak with people and politely refuse to give up The Name. With his arm draped possessively over her shoulders, he answered the many questions that came his way. The crush around them eventually lessened, then thinned completely as the band reassembled and began its next set. Bryce took her hand then and kissed the back of it. Giselle blushed again and smiled shyly when he murmured, "Dance with me?"

They slow danced for an hour, Giselle staring up at him with a love-drugged expression that soothed his soul and gave him hope. They kissed intermittently, softly, slowly, closely observed but uninterrupted except for Fen, who caught her arm as he and Trudy made their exit.

"Your mother's going to swat your behind until you can't sit down," he murmured, and Giselle laughed.

"What, are you going to tattle on me?"

"I will if you don't tell me who Ford is."

"Pffftt. Fen," she drawled, "that keeping my mouth shut thing works two ways. It's a bitch, ain't it?"

"Then you asked for it. You'll get sent out to cut a switch."

Giselle was still snickering when Bryce swept her around and under his arm for another dance. He looked over the crowd absently until something caught his eye. Far across the immense room a man leaned against a wall, away from everyone else and in the shadows, his arms crossed, a glass of champagne in his hand. He stared straight at Bryce with a smirk on his face, then tipped the glass at him.

It only took a microsecond before Bryce burst out laughing. When Giselle looked up at him, he gestured vaguely toward the man; once she saw who he meant, she chuckled.

"Ford."

She looked back up at Bryce and murmured, "I knew there was a reason I let you fuck me. Let's go home so you can do it again."

"You didn't *let* me do anything, Warrior Queen."

She snorted, and he grinned.

He took her back to her bed, the one on which Giselle's torment, her hunger and agony, was on display for the entire world to see. That bed—the one where she'd lain under him, her head, heart, arms, and legs wrapped around him, matching him wit for wit, kiss for kiss, word for word, thrust for thrust.

Bryce couldn't imagine a future without her in it, without her in his bed, in his heart—

—but his gut clenched at the thought of what he'd have to tell her, what he hadn't thought to tell her before he'd staked his claim.

29: The Arrival of the Queen of Sheba

SEBASTIAN ATTEMPTED TO MINGLE, BUT, AS USUAL, SOCIETY VIEWED HIM with utmost suspicion—which was why he didn't get out to these soirees much. Women he might have liked to approach watched him warily, ready to bolt. He'd let it be known very publicly and very cruelly some years ago that gold diggers were not welcome in his personal space. That had made him completely radioactive around the world.

Men he might have liked to cultivate for places on future high-level management teams hid their suspicion of him little better. Of course, he had a tendency to burn people's bridges for them if they said the wrong thing, but only Sebastian knew what that was. That had happened in Prague. And Amsterdam. Possibly Berlin. He didn't quite know how all the things he did in Europe followed him back to Kansas City.

Very few people outside of his family weren't afraid of him at first blush, and lately that had been the sum total of two people: Oakley and Kenard—

—who was about to find out what his lover of less than a day looked like on a five-by-eight-foot canvas. Nude.

He was pleased when the only real emotion he could see in the man's face was awe. Then he kissed Giselle obscenely in the midst of two hundred and fifty silent people who awaited his reaction with bated breath. Sebastian was slightly surprised the man didn't back her up against the wall and fuck her right then and there, and he almost smiled. That boded well for Kenard's staying power with her, and, much as Giselle was a pain in Sebastian's ass sometimes and he enjoyed the hell out of picking on her, he loved her and wanted to see her happy.

He wandered around, watching people post-new-painting-unveiling, observing

Giselle's newfound notoriety, quietly chatting with not-yet-declared senatorial candidate Kevin Oakley, studying the rest of the exhibit, drinking a punch that was slightly less offensive than the cheap bubbly, and generally milling about brooding over why Miss Logan hadn't wanted to be with him tonight.

Bored and only happening to catch a glimpse of a very tall blonde entering the gallery long after the unveiling, he ambled along behind her to see what he could see. When she turned, his breath caught in his throat and he nearly dropped his glass.

She had one green eye and one blue eye, and they sparkled merrily as she looked around her. Her mouth was full and curving in a generous yet sensual smile. She had soft, straight butter-blonde hair to the middle of her biceps where it curled at the ends and lacked the harshness of any chemical coloring.

Her body was lush, shown to perfection in a shimmering iridescent dark copper gown cut like a double-breasted tuxedo jacket that flared out into a long bell skirt to her ankles. Her lapels were iridescent black. Her sleeves stopped just below her elbows and were turned up in French cuffs that matched her lapels. She had high heels on, which made her stand head and shoulders above everyone else.

She was stunning, a Viking goddess, and he smiled, looking down into his glass and shaking his head. Whatever he'd expected Eilis Logan to look like under all that badly fitting Chanel, pancake makeup, brown contact lenses, and hair-darkening gel, this was *not* it.

His sharp eye caught details no one else ever did, though, and he thought it odd she'd hide the scar on her face for business but not for pleasure. However, once he got a good look at it and saw that it made her look as if she were perpetually crying, he understood. And those eyes! No wonder she wore colored contacts. He was *fascinated* by the fact that her eyes were two different colors.

He walked over to her, hooking her elbow in his right hand and gently pulling her away from the paintings. She gasped in protest and then stilled when she saw who he was, suddenly angry that she'd been caught.

"I have an eye for detail, Miss Logan," he whispered in her ear, not having let go of her and, in fact, pulling her even closer to him. Any excuse—he'd take it. "I will admit you have a very good act."

She looked straight at him, no shorter than he in heels. Her two different-colored eyes blazed. He wondered how long he could keep from backing *her* up against a wall, although right now, it didn't look like his usual freight train seduction strategy would actually work. She was already fit to be tied.

"Let me go," she whispered hotly, and he was very pleased to know there was passion and fire under that luscious skin—and that he really could get to her. "I didn't come here to be 'on.' I came here to enjoy myself without being reminded of my humiliation by every mogul in the room."

He could see how that would be distressing to her, now that she mentioned it. "I'm sorry," he said and released her, stepping back and into cool King Midas once again. "I didn't think."

"No, you didn't," she shot back, though still quiet. "I would like for you to figure out when it would be most convenient to let me have a vacation. I need one. Badly. If I must take it up with the prosecutor myself, then I will do so. Now, if you'll excuse me, I'd like to go look at this man's work in peace."

"Wait," he said, unsure what he was going to say. She had barely turned and she stopped, looking over her shoulder at him. "I— May I accompany you through the exhibit?"

"Why?"

His mouth tightened. "Because I would like to, if you would allow me the pleasure."

Her eyes widened at his sudden formality, but he was rather impressed with himself for not making himself look like a complete buffoon. He'd said what he meant to say.

"Pleasure? You don't even like me."

He looked at her, confused. "Why would you assume that?"

She stared at him for what seemed like hours, then finally said, "Well." Her mouth twitched indecisively for a moment. "All right. I suppose I can't stop you."

It wasn't much, but it was a start. Time to try the next step.

"Eilis, may I get you something to eat? Drink?"

She hesitated for a moment, put a hand to her belly, bit her lip, then shook her head. "No, thank you," she murmured.

Sebastian's eyebrow rose. He'd seen that gesture too many times in his life not to know what it meant. Too bad, too, because she fulfilled Sebastian's fantasies to the last detail.

He didn't dare tell her that.

"All right. Would you like to see the new painting first?"

"No," she murmured dismissively. "I like to do things in their proper order."

Well, *that* was interesting. He filed that away for future reference.

He'd already seen the exhibit, so he watched her—watched her unutterably expressive face express so much awe and reverence that he wondered how she kept her façade intact for twelve hours a day when she was "on." He wanted to ask her, but figured that he couldn't get in any more trouble by keeping his mouth shut. Only, he wasn't good at that.

"Where are you going?" he blurted as they went from one painting to the next.

She shot him an annoyed glance, but didn't answer. She just went back to her study of Ford's work. He could tell she wanted to touch. She shied away from the nudes whose body types were similar to hers as if it pained her to see them. She was drawn to the nudes who were smaller and more muscular, less voluptuous than she. He wanted to call her on it just to see what she'd say, but he dared not.

Her reaction didn't surprise him in the least. He had found that, by and large, straight women who liked Ford's nudes invariably compared themselves, figuring out what they wanted to look like and attempting to visualize themselves as anything other than what they were. He knew for a fact that Giselle became wistful over the women who didn't look a thing like her because she knew she'd never attain what she saw as perfection. Giselle's favorite Ford painting looked like Eilis—

—and every Ford nude Eilis owned had a body type similar to Giselle's.

Finally they came to the new piece that hung high up from the gallery's ceiling. Sebastian thought it might be Ford's finest work ever.

She gasped. "Oh," she breathed as she stepped back and took it in. The scar that looked like a tear began to sparkle as an actual tear tracked down it faithfully. "That's *shattering*," Eilis murmured.

"How so?" he asked quietly, not wanting to ruin the mood, but oh, so curious.

"He—" She stopped. "She— I'm—" She stopped again. "I'm *her*." Giselle looked nothing like Eilis, so of *course* Eilis wished to be what she couldn't. Just like the rest of womankind. The breath on which she'd expelled her admission was barely audible. "I want that."

Of *course* she did.

Sebastian kept his mouth carefully closed, hoping she wouldn't have to be reminded that not only could she not buy any more of these, she had to sell the ones she had. Finally, he couldn't stand it and said the most diplomatic thing he could think of, hoping to distract her enough that he wouldn't have to be the bad guy.

As usual.

"Eilis, I've decided to let you keep *Morning in Bed*."

She turned to him then, wide-eyed. "You— You're going to let me keep it?"

"Yes. I'll have it verified as original and appraised, have the insurance updated, make sure it's properly secured, but I'll let you keep it."

The tears welled in her eyes then and they spilled over. She threw her arms around him and hugged him, and he could feel her crying. "Thank you, Mr. Taight," she whispered. "Thank you so much."

Sebastian's eyes closed and he was ever so glad for all the crisp fabric in between them or she would have surely felt his arousal. He hesitantly put his arms around her and lightly patted her back once, twice. He certainly didn't mind this particular flavor of a beautiful woman's attentions but he had *never* gotten a random grateful bear hug from a woman not related to him.

She was oblivious to the stares they garnered, but he wasn't. A beautiful woman. With Sebastian Taight. Who was not Cinderella. Who was not only not afraid of him, but hugging him.

It had been preposterous enough when Kansas City's moneyed thought King Midas had a lover at all, much less one who had been swept off her feet and out from under his nose by the city's hideously scarred and notoriously ruthless tort lawyer—until, just tonight, Kenard had most accommodatingly clarified Sebastian's relationship to Giselle.

Of *course* Miss Cox wasn't his lover! Of *course* Miss Cox was his cousin! With that totally logical explanation, society had gone back to its usual humor about Sebastian's social toxicity.

Until Eilis hugged him.

She drew back a few seconds later, obviously embarrassed by her outburst. "I'm sorry," she laughed, sniffled, then wiped her tears with a finger. He actually thought to offer her his handkerchief, and she took it with a watery smile.

"Where are you going?" he blurted yet again.

Her brow wrinkled in confusion. "I'm sorry?"

"Your vacation. Where do you plan to go?"

She looked in his eyes for a long time, as if searching for some ulterior motive for asking. Oh, he had one, but in his opinion, wanting to be around her every day and enforcing her presence there so he could have a chance at seducing her didn't really tip the evil scale too much.

"I'm going to find Ford," she finally murmured. "I want him to mak—paint me."

Well.

He was pretty sure he wasn't going to be able to find a convenient time for her to go anywhere.

She couldn't believe she'd told him that—Sebastian Taight of all people. And what had almost escaped her mouth! She could only chalk it up to her shock that he had just *known* she was the same Miss Logan who dressed in sensible shoes and the classic Coco Chanel suit at work.

Nobody had ever figured that out on first glance before and usually, not even second, third, or fourth. She liked it that way; it allowed her a great deal of freedom she would not otherwise have. Not even Fen Hilliard recognized her out of costume.

Sebastian pursed his lips and looked down at the floor, his hands behind his back. He rocked back on his heels. "How are you going to find Ford?" he asked her. "No one else has ever been able to."

"I have *Morning in Bed*," she replied, her confidence gathering steam as she realized that he might point out all the ways she would fail, but he wouldn't make fun of her. "I've found the clues that are embedded in it." *What clues?* She'd never found any clues, but saying she had might make her case stronger.

"Ah." He didn't speak for a moment. Then, "Care to share?"

"Certainly not. You're obviously as much a Ford aficionado as I am and I would never give you that kind of leverage."

"Is that what you think of me?"

"You have a reputation, Mr. Taight. You play by the rules, but you interpret them liberally. You like having leverage and you don't cut anybody any slack. I would presume that this would be one of those times that you'd take finding him first as your due."

He stared at her with that intense, incredibly handsome face and again she felt shivers run up and down her spine. He was taller than she by only a smidge, but a smidge was enough at her height. He was well built and muscular, his body broad and much bigger than hers, a man she wouldn't smash to pieces if—

She swallowed and turned away from him then, disturbed by the sudden visual of herself naked, straddling Sebastian Taight's naked hips, his huge hands wrapped around her waist. He was King Midas, her enemy: Related to both Knox and Fen Hilliard, having complete control of her company, taking away her paintings—she shouldn't dare think of King Midas that way. Certainly, no one else did, so what was *her* problem?

Eilis felt his hand on her elbow, guiding her deeper into the rest of the gallery and away from the Ford exhibit. They walked in silence past many modern pieces, most of which she didn't like.

"I have trouble communicating with women," he said suddenly, startling her. "I— A while back— Uh, hmm. I'm not good with—" He stopped. Swallowed. "Women are afraid of me." He stopped again, took a deep breath. "Ah, well, uh— So in trying not to scare anybody, I don't say the right things and then they're not only scared, they're mad, too."

He hadn't had any trouble communicating with her Thursday. Was she afraid? Yes, because of what he could do to her company. Was she angry? Yes, because he'd picked her out so easily. Neither had had anything to do with his communication skills.

"Why are you telling me this?"

"Because I want to ask you something and I don't know if it'll come out right. I'll probably upset you and then you'll—"

Leave. He bit it off, but it hung heavy in the air.

"What do you want to ask me?"

He hesitated. She could sense his discomfort and felt sorry for him. "May I kiss you?"

She blinked. Interesting. He'd asked permission. And oh, how she was tempted! "I don't think that's a good idea, Mr. Taight. You're my trustee and I'm being punished for having made a very bad decision in my personal life. I'm not sure my judgment in men is all that good."

"I see. You're right, of course," he said graciously as they continued their stroll through the gallery.

30: Jasmine in my Mind

THE AIR WAS COOL FOR AN AUGUST SUNDAY IN THE MIDDLE OF THE afternoon and the breeze blew Giselle's hair all around her. Bryce sat on a picnic table in Cancer Survivor's Park, his legs hanging off the edge. She sat on the table facing him.

Despite her soreness, she'd draped her left knee over his thigh and stretched her right leg out behind him. The inside of her thigh caressed his tight denim-clad ass and she was about as close to him as she could get without being naked and on top of him.

Neither spoke as they shared a dish of gourmet cheeses until—

"I feel weird because I'm not at church right now," she murmured, "and why."

"You go to church often enough that not going is an event?"

She nodded. "Every Sunday. It's a respite for me, like meditating in front of the bodhisattva."

He said nothing for a moment. Then, "I've only been a few times since the fire. The last time I went was after I met you at Hale's." She started. "I wanted to find some answers as to how to deal with you."

"Because you thought Knox and I were lovers."

He nodded.

"So how'd that work out for you?"

He grimaced. "It didn't."

"I'm sorry."

"I'm not. I'm here with you."

She smiled, delight curling through her, but it faltered.

"What?"

She sighed. "It's— I don't— We still don't know each other very well."

"Yes, we do." He tapped her sternum with a finger. "We just don't know details and time provides those."

"You haven't talked about your children or your wife much. I know you loved your kids and didn't like your wife and . . . that's about it."

He grunted and pulled away a bit; he picked out another piece of cheese. He stared blankly in front of him, his mouth pursed. "Where to begin? My wife's name was Michelle. She was the most faithless, evil woman I've ever met."

"How'd you end up married to her then?"

He took a deep breath. "I was trying to avoid women like you," he murmured without a shred of humor, and Giselle shifted, surprised. "I've always loved women like you, dangerous, strong. Educated women with edgy personalities. Women who like to fuck. Hard. Nasty. I thought I was sinful just for wanting that and Michelle was not that. She was sweet and demure, a little light in the IQ department but not enough to be annoying. She talked exactly the right Good-LDS-Girl talk and walked exactly the right Good-LDS-Girl walk. In public. I envisioned our life together as quiet and calm, which didn't really excite me, but I thought she would cure me of my nastiness."

Bryce glanced at Giselle slyly and she smiled.

"She fooled me. Fooled my parents, my siblings. Knox was the only person who told me I was making a mistake, but he was the lone voice in the wilderness and his opinion was competing with everyone else's and my goal of—" He gestured in the air, searching for words.

"Purification."

He pointed at her and nodded. "That's it. My father hated Knox, thought he was a bad influence on me. They went head-to-head on doctrine a couple of times and—"

"Knox knows doctrine like the back of his hand."

"And he's not shy about shining a bright light on the church's less-than-stellar history. My dad wouldn't talk to Knox after the second time he got trounced."

Giselle said nothing for a bit. Then, "So . . . you got married in the temple."

"Yes, in San Diego. Michelle lied through her teeth to get her temple recommend. It took maybe a week? two weeks? for her to show her true colors. She . . . " He took a deep breath. "She *hated* me."

Giselle's mouth dropped open. "Why?" she breathed. "Why did *she* marry *you?*"

He shrugged. "Her parents liked me and pressured her into it. She went along with it because I was arm candy with money potential. I was really naïve and she knew she'd be able to keep partying because I wouldn't suspect anything. Perfect trophy husband, perfect cover, potentially unlimited funds."

"Was she pretty?"

"She was a model. Blonde. Tall and thin, fragile. Exactly what I wasn't that attracted to. I figured that between not really being attracted to her and her fragility, I wouldn't be tempted to indulge my, ah, kinks. Somewhere in the first six months or so she must have figured out I *had* kinks because that's when she started to hate me. I was too big for her tastes."

Giselle smirked. "Which part?"

He burst out laughing, then touched his nose to hers. "Every. Inch. Of. Me," he purred, but caught Giselle's grin in a kiss, brief but hot. They were still chuckling when he continued. "Michelle needed physical control and she chose her partners based on their size and willingness to submit and take punishment."

"So . . . what *did* you get from her?"

"Very little. I didn't understand what she wanted, why she didn't like sex with me—well, hell, why *I* didn't like sex with her."

"You're lying there trying not to think about your kink, because you thought even thinking about it's sinful, and she's out indulging hers."

He nodded. "I didn't know any of this. I found her fetish stash right after she got pregnant with my youngest and I'd already started divorce proceedings. I didn't know what it was, told my divorce lawyer, and he sat me down and gave me the facts of life."

"Did that shock you?"

He grinned suddenly. "What shocked me was that the things I'd been trying so hard *not* to fantasize about since I hit puberty had a name and a lifestyle that went with it—and that what I wanted was at the *vanilla* end of the spectrum."

Giselle began to laugh. "She didn't know you had a little taste for that then?"

"I think she did," Bryce returned. "I think she didn't want me to get any more of a taste for it than I already had and that's when my size became an issue for her."

"Because she was afraid you'd top her."

"Yes. And I would've. So she went elsewhere. Lots of elsewheres."

"Oh," Giselle breathed, her eyes wide. "Um— Maybe this is closing the barn door after the horse gets out, but—"

"No, Giselle," he said wryly, "I don't have any diseases. I wouldn't be here if I did."

"It never even occurred to me to ask," she said, rolling her eyes. "Oh, so savvy."

"By the time I started the divorce, I'd moved out of the bedroom. I couldn't live with her pathology anymore. Constant manipulation. My oldest daughter didn't know which end was up most days after Michelle got through with her head. If she'd been a good mother and it was just the adultery, I would have stayed with her for the kids. I wouldn't have liked that, either, but the sex wasn't enough to get mad about and I wasn't missing anything."

"So you were caught between enduring to the end or saving your kids."

"Yes. If I'd seen it earlier, I'd have done it a lot sooner, but I was busy working and trying to make sure their basic needs were met."

"Basic needs?" Giselle asked warily. "What does that mean? You weren't poor."

"It means," he said, his face starting to harden as he looked back off into the distance, "that Michelle wouldn't take care of them. I had to hire a live-in nanny to make sure they got fed and clothed and to school on time. I gave the *nanny* a credit card to buy them clothes and school supplies and whatever else they needed. Gas for the car to take them where they needed to go. I didn't dare give one to my wife. How screwed up is that?"

"I'm not following. This had to have evolved over time."

"Michelle," he said slowly, "controlled me by being completely dependent. I had to leave her a to-do list every morning or the kids wouldn't get fed. That's when I hired the nanny. Money. I had to go shopping with her because she'd gotten me deep in debt more than once when I trusted her with any—that was her game. When I took money away from her, she wouldn't do anything autonomously. She'd call me for any decision, no matter how small, sometimes four, five times a day. Before I got the nanny, she would occasionally even refuse to pick up the kids for school because I wasn't there to drive her. That infuriated me and it was exhausting."

Giselle stared at him. "So she was topping from the bottom. You didn't understand that, either, I bet."

"I thought it was your run-of-the-mill manipulation; my lawyer had to explain that to me, too. But it wouldn't have made any difference because I had to protect my kids. So I decided to start my own practice, you know, be at home, watch my kids. It was a good decision, as it turned out. I'd already made a bit of a reputation so I was ready to go out on my own, but basically, it was so I could muzzle her and keep an eye on them. I decided she had to go when I saw and heard what she was saying to them on a sustained basis—messing with their heads—"

"Like?"

He pursed his lips and stared off into the distance. "She'd tell my girls they were fat, dress them in clothes that were too small, starve them and tell them they were on a diet. I didn't know about that until Andrea refused a cookie because she was on a diet. She was five when that happened. Emme was nine at the time and it might have been too late for her without some serious therapy, I don't know."

Lilly, you let that girl eat whatever she wants; no wonder she's so damned fat. I don't know how Knox can stand to touch her, much less kiss her.

Trudy, you shut your mouth before I slap it shut.

Giselle gulped.

"She'd have Luke, my eight-year-old, go get, say, an expensive vase, take it to the front hall. The floor was marble and she'd tell him to drop it and see what happened. He'd do it, it'd shatter, and she'd scream at him for doing such a stupid thing, make him clean it up. I don't know how many times she did that before I saw it for myself. And he was barefoot."

Giselle didn't know if she'd ever catch another breath.

He raised an eyebrow at her. "More?"

"Not right now," she whispered.

"Anyway, it took me a year to lay the groundwork, then another year for everything else to come together. The divorce was about to be finalized when the fire happened. I was relieved she was dead, but I'd rather have had the divorce if I could've kept my kids. I got a life insurance payout, so that made me suspect number one for murder and I didn't care. I was too heartbroken over my kids." He stared up at the sky. "Emme was ten. Luke was eight. Andrea was six and Randy was three."

Giselle put her hand to the burn scars on his face and caressed them. "I'm sorry," she whispered. "But you know your children are just fine now, don't you?"

"Intellectually, yes, but . . ." He took a deep breath. "Giselle, I *really* don't want to talk about this anymore."

She supposed she could understand that and though she wanted him to trust her enough to tell her about his fire, she wouldn't push. "Okay." They fell silent to listen to the familiar goings-on around them. Children squealed, cars whizzed past. Sirens blared somewhere, fountains gurgled, and horns honked. Birds sang and a small bee buzzed around Giselle's hair because it smelled like watermelon. She cleared her throat.

"Bryce," she murmured, "about this alpha thing."

"Yes?"

"I won't play those games outside the context of sex. And sometimes not even then."

"Are you asking me or telling me?"

"Telling you," she said sharply, looking him straight in the eye. "I won't obey. I won't ask permission to live my life the way I want to and I won't be controlled."

He nodded. "Agreed. I want it in bed. I don't want to live it." He paused and took a deep breath. "Um, Giselle, I—" he began, stopped, looked away. She watched him and her spine tingled as if she were in trouble. He finally looked back at her and after another long moment, he said, "I can't have any more children."

Her breath caught in her throat. Her eyes widened and she swallowed. Hard.

"*Oh.*" It was a whisper, a breath.

"I should have told you that sooner, I know, but the conversation never came around to it and it never occurred to me. You're thirty-six. I guess I just assumed you wouldn't be interested. Then, when I saw that painting last night— It hit me in the gut. I didn't want to tell you after that; I wanted to enjoy what was left of the weekend. I figured it might be a deal breaker. I— I'm sorry I didn't say anything at dinner."

"*I* didn't do anything that *I* wouldn't have done anyway," she murmured, though without humor. It was her turn to be silent, her mind in complete turmoil. She cleared her throat. "That would be a new concept for me," she finally said. "I mean, you know. You grow up in the church, children are by default part of your future. Being with a man and deliberately *not* having any isn't part of the plan."

"I do *not* want any more," he said emphatically. "If I hadn't had a vasectomy after Randy was born, I'd do it now and I will *not* get it reversed." He said that with such finality she didn't dare argue. "Children are the most precious, noisy, wonderful, obnoxious little creatures on the planet, especially if you made them. But when they die before you do, even one of them—" His mouth tightened. "I don't want to have more with you and go through my life wondering when and how the Lord's going to take them away from me because I broke my covenants."

She stared at him, shocked to her core. "Do you really believe he would do that?" she whispered.

"He's already done it and for a helluva lot less than fornication."

"The Lord doesn't work that way!"

"Oh, really? When was the last time you read your scriptures? He's all about punishment."

Her nostrils flared. "*Bryce*—"

"No, Giselle," he snapped. "No— *Hell* no. Don't ask me for children, don't ask me to go back to church, don't spend any time fantasizing about me repenting so we can get married in the temple. I'm telling you right now, it won't happen. If you want to be with me, those are the terms and I *never* gave you any reason to think otherwise."

Her nose stung and her eyes watered. She disentangled her body from his and stood, took a deep breath and released it, hoping she wouldn't break down right there. "Um, I— I'm going to have to percolate on that a while."

He said nothing for a long moment as he studied the ground. Then he nodded. "That's fair."

"It's three-thirty," she said, her throat tight. "I have to be at work at four."

31: Crazy Faith

"MISS LOGAN," SEBASTIAN SAID BRISKLY AS HE STRODE INTO HER OFFICE early Monday morning. Eilis turned from the window where she'd watched him come into the building. She figured if she could think of him as a piece of art, then it would be okay to admire his beauty.

"Mr. Taight," she said calmly, levelly, as he plopped a backpack on the table that sat in the middle of the massive office, then pulled out a pad of green engineer's paper and a mechanical pencil. She watched as he sat in one of the armless designer chairs that surrounded the conference table and began to write on his tablet. Curious, she wandered over to him and saw that he was creating mathematical formulas and plugging in values, working them all without benefit of a calculator.

"Do you always do that by hand?" she asked softly.

"Yes," he grunted. "Helps me think." He continued to scratch out numbers in a bold hand and Eilis saw that his handwriting was very . . . him. He spoke again as he whipped over his formulas with lightning speed. No wonder he didn't use a calculator. It would slow him down.

"I need you to bring me your employee list sorted as to pay scale and management level. Please."

"Why?"

She almost gulped when Sebastian stopped writing immediately, his body still, then he looked up at her slowly. "Why?" Tension radiated from his body and Eilis wanted to look away from him. She didn't dare.

"Miss Logan," he said as he threw his pencil down and leaned back in his chair, one arm on the table, the other along the back of the chair, his fingers steepled at his temple. He put his leg up on the chair next to him. "Do you understand that what I'm going to do is what you should've done long ago? Tell me something: You're a brilliant woman, I'm assuming well educated, and very, very savvy. You have a good reputation for making all the right moves, David Webster aside. In fact, I hear that early in your career, you were quite the ruthless *bitch*. How in the *hell* did you miss doing the most obvious things you needed to do to save this company? It's not like you were without resources."

Eilis wasn't going to answer that. She had her reasons and they weren't any of his business. And as for "ruthless bitch" . . . well, that was true, and Eilis had traded on it as long as she could before being forced to become Miss Manners. Her Inner Bitch had abandoned her, betrayed by Chanel.

He went on. "You know exactly what I'm going to do with that list. I'll give you the option of presenting the other three points of my reorganization plan and letting your employees think that the good stuff is all your idea and I'm just your court-appointed supervisor who was the big bad meanie who cleaned your house for you. You've thought about doing everything I'm going to do to this company. You just haven't had the balls to do it."

"You have no way of knowing that," she murmured, stung, and aching to correct his assumption. Not daring to.

"Sure I do. I never miss details, Miss Logan. I should think you'd have figured that out."

Eilis fought the urge to suck in a sharp breath at his reference to how easily and how fast he'd picked her out at the Ford exhibit.

"I usually never let a CEO know what I'm going to do before I do it. It hurts too much and they wouldn't have thought of it themselves anyway. But you already knew what I was going to do and you got your back up. Well, Miss Logan, if it's a fight you want, I'll give it to you and without question— You. Will. Lose. Do I make myself clear?"

Heaven help her, she liked King Midas much better than Sebastian Taight, who'd been so solicitous of her Saturday night, who tried too hard, was too nice, because he didn't want to scare women any more than he already did.

She spoke again, evenly, holding her hand up in a fist. She counted off three points of his four-point plan on her fingers as if she'd actually read it. She hadn't; it was in his head.

And hers.

"One: Clean house.

"Two: Sell the art.

"Three: Mass market the personality screening tests instead of keeping it a proprietary tool for our clients. Create a small business version of the HRP Full Management System software and distribute it widely."

She watched him as his eyes widened just a little bit and she thought she saw approval there. Then he slowly began to clap as he stood, unfolding his lithe body to his full height. She had to look up at him a little bit; she liked that.

Eilis was barely able to stand still, not jump, when he slammed his hands on the table and got in her face.

"So why the *hell* didn't you do that before you got this far in the hole?" he barked.

She would not flinch, would not look away, would not step back. Would not would not wouldnot wouldnotwouldnot. But *why* was he so angry with her? No one had *ever* told her anything about Sebastian Taight ever getting angry about anything. Ruthless, cold, heartless, yes. Passionately angry, no.

"I have my reasons," she said evenly.

"I guarantee you could have no reason that would be good enough to excuse this mess."

She hated to let him continue to think that, but she had no choice.

"Why don't you tell me which ones give you the worst taste in your mouth? No, wait. Let me guess. It's the one you *deliberately* left off the list, which is to take your company public."

His mouth compressed in a thin line when she didn't answer that charge.

"You have two choices," he said low, with none of the patience he'd displayed last week. "You can do this and I'll stand in the background and hold your hand or I'll rip this company right out from under you because you don't seem to be fit to run it at this point."

That was when she knew he'd gone beyond his breaking point, but she had no idea why or how. She'd left him amicably at the Ford exhibit very soon after he'd requested a kiss and he'd walked into her office not ten minutes ago.

She gathered herself up, dignified, calm, gracious. "What have I done or said to deserve this?"

He blinked. It was a half a minute before his mouth tightened and he withdrew and sat in his chair. He wiped his mouth and he looked away. "Nothing," he said, low. "I apologize."

It was Eilis's turn to be surprised.

Sebastian took a deep breath and sat up to stare at his pad, his right hand clenching around his pencil. "Tell me which one of those bothers you most. Please."

She didn't want to trust him. He was the enemy.

"Taking the company public," she said, never wavering or trembling.

He put his hands over his face. "Why?"

"I have a reason and you'll have to trust me that it's a very good one."

He sighed and sat back in his chair again. "All right, Eilis," he muttered and she liked her name on his tongue, so she didn't protest his familiarity. He must not have realized he'd called her by her first name. "I'm not going to argue with you about it right now. If you could get me that list, please?"

What the hell was wrong with him? He'd never treated a client like this before and he didn't consider her any less of a client just because she was under court order.

He knew why.

He kept remembering how she'd looked at the Ford exhibit, all that gorgeous blonde hair, that perfect fertility goddess body, the luscious skin, the divine perfume, the broken nose, the scar, and those eyes! Two different colors. He caught his breath yet again at the memory.

And he'd come in here this morning to find . . . that. That woman who hid from something he didn't understand. That getup killed his hard-on now that he knew what she really looked like. Coco Chanel should rot in hell for that monstrosity she had on.

Eilis had made him mad the minute he'd walked into this office and looked at her, because she *knew* how to dress and this was purposely disgusting. She was not a woman who needed a makeover.

Then she'd stood up to him, calm, ladylike, and asked what she'd done. He had no defense for that. What was he supposed to say? *I hate that rag you're wearing* would probably not win him any brownie points. Nor would *Go home and get something decent on* or, his personal favorite, *Take that off and go lie on the couch. Wait for me while I lock the door.*

"Eilis," he said when she brought him the list he'd asked for. He noticed she hadn't taken exception to his calling her by her first name. He loved her name; it melted on his tongue like mint chocolate chip ice cream. "I apologize again. I'm just impatient this morning. I really need to get you through this receivership as fast as possible."

So I can take you home to the bed that I haven't used in years.

"Do you have a timetable?" she asked quietly and sat down beside him.

Interesting. She didn't wear perfume to work; all he could smell was a cheap generic soap. *Dammit.*

"Yes, I do." He began to write it out for her and he felt her start beside her. He looked at her, because it was out of character for her to show any emotion, even such a small thing as a twitch.

"You're writing with your left hand," she murmured.

"I'm ambidextrous," he muttered, inordinately pleased that she'd noticed that.

"Does your hand get tired?"

If I haven't had a woman in a while, it sure does. Then he laughed at himself for his Beavis-and-Butthead sense of humor. "Just depends on which hand's closer to the pencil." *Heh heh.*

"Ah."

He figured that was about all she had to say about that.

"For the rest of the week, you and I are going to go over this employee list with a fine-toothed comb. Next Monday and Tuesday, I'm going to clean house. You're welcome to be here, but you don't have to be. I'll take the heat for that; it's part of my job. Thursday and Friday, we'll rearrange everyone according to skills and interests.

"Christie's and Sotheby's are booked a year out, but Christie's has agreed to tentatively schedule us for February. In the meantime, you can set the timetables for the screening tests and the software betas, but I would like them working and possibly in limited distribution by the time we go to auction.

"My underwriter is Blackwood Securities. Jack Blackwood is very particular and very hard to get. He's a friend of mine and has agreed to do this for you at my request. He has a list of specific things he'll require you to have accomplished before he starts drawing up your IPO. I have it on my laptop, so I'll print it for you later. I'm hoping that the auction of your Fords will be the *last* thing we actually do to move you into his territory."

"Mr. Taight—"

"Sebastian, please."

"Mr. Taight—" He sighed. "—I don't want to take my company public."

Sebastian kept writing, feeling her watch him. He betrayed everything about himself with every word he wrote, if she only knew enough to make the right connections. He'd make sure that by the time this receivership was over, she'd have all the clues she needed to figure it out.

One year. It was all he could take. He'd give her one year.

"When it comes right down to it, Eilis, whether you want to or not is immaterial. We're doing things *my* way now because *my* way always works."

Yeah, that was a good way to get her in bed. Brilliant.

Eilis watched as he wrote faster than she could type, listing everything. His handwriting on the left hand was completely different from the right hand. The left hand flowed; it wasn't nearly as angular as the right hand.

In fact, everything he wrote with his right hand looked like an American had written it; vertical, tall, bold. Everything he wrote with his left hand looked European, like a European copperplate.

She looked at his face as his wrote; it betrayed nothing. This was effortless for him, just something he did.

He *fascinated* her.

Eilis certainly did not want to take her company public, but if she protested too much, he'd get suspicious and start Knox to digging deeper into her life than he already had, and that was the last thing she needed.

None of this made sense. King Midas was really trying to put her back on her feet. This wasn't the evil Sebastian Taight she'd heard rumors about all these years, but of course, no one had told her he was drop-dead gorgeous, either.

She asked before she thought. "What makes you decide whether to fix or raid?"

He stopped writing again and stayed still, looking at his pad. She wondered if he didn't even know his own pattern and thus, no one else could. Then he turned his head and looked her straight in the eye and said, "I take companies whose ownership and/or management can't be salvaged."

She managed to quell any reaction to that. So, he'd been serious when he'd threatened to rip her company right out from under her. He continued,

"In the end, it all comes down to the people, the leaders. I despise bad management. If the owners can't be trained, if they fight me—and remember, I only go to companies when they call me for help—if they can't be persuaded that their way doesn't work and thus, needs to be changed, I take it." He stopped for a moment and she knew he was letting that sink in a minute. It was a threat, a promise, a fact. "I'm always willing to look at options if they're presented to me logically, but I've been doing this too long to mess around with bullshit. And no, Wall Street can't figure out why I do what I do because they don't know the players' personalities like I do. And no, I'm not going to let the Senate pound it out of me, either, so I'd suggest you keep that to yourself."

Eilis couldn't help it. Her eyes widened and she pulled away from him a bit at the distinct threat in his voice.

The corner of his mouth twitched up and his eyes darkened to lavender. "Ah, she does have a soul underneath all that Chanel."

The only thing that saved her from his seeing her blush was the heavy makeup. And then, because she couldn't seem to keep her curiosity in check, she said,

"What really happened at Jep Industries, with Senator Oth?"

His cocked at eyebrow at her. "What do *you* think happened?"

Eilis studied him in return a moment, wondering if this was a test or if he was fishing for her impressions. "I think," she finally said, carefully, "that his executive staff was diverting cash flow and he either didn't know or he couldn't figure out how to stop it and fix it on his own."

His mouth twitched a bit. "Very good," he murmured. "So why didn't I have them prosecuted?"

"I'm assuming because you couldn't prove it without getting Roger indicted."

"Precisely. And why did I lay off twelve hundred people?"

Eilis had to think about that for a moment, to think about what she knew of Roger Oth and his company, to follow the flow chart she'd built in her head from rumor, speculation, and absolutely no facts. It took a minute, but then the entire plan blossomed in her mind. "The 401(k) accounts were about to be cleaned out. The only way you could stop the pending transactions was if Jep Industries didn't exist anymore." He inclined his head in what she realized was approval. "Then you dismantled Jep enough that Hollander Steelworks could absorb it piecemeal without arousing anyone's curiosity."

There was a light of great respect in his eyes that warmed Eilis to her soul. "Yes."

"Was that your idea?"

He shook his head. "Knox's."

Eilis started. "He's a lawyer."

"With a degree in accounting and a penchant for taking the scenic route around a problem. Mitch Hollander needed Jep's products to stay in business and he begged me not to shut it down, but we couldn't find anyone qualified enough to run it. Don't think we didn't try; too many businesses would've gone under without Roger's goods."

"How long did it take you to figure out they were stealing?"

"Three days. It took three of us two weeks to follow the paper trail to its source."

"And then another two weeks to shut it all down." Eilis fought the urge to betray any emotion. Jep's circumstances too closely mirrored her own, only Eilis hadn't been able to call for help.

"Yes."

"You said you only go where people call you."

"Typically, yes."

"What about OKH Enterprises?"

He pursed his lips as he stared at her and it seemed like he was wondering if or how much to tell her. "I don't know why you'd ask about that," he said softly, and she knew she'd given away far more than she'd meant to, just by asking. "The Journal's all over it."

"The alliances are fuzzy," she finally said, not looking away from him.

His eyebrow rose. "Really? What do you think the alliances are?"

"Before or after you were assigned as my trustee?"

He sat back and folded his arms over his chest. "Both."

"Everybody I know thinks you're at war with both Knox and Fen. That's the assumption I made until he assigned you to me. Now, I don't know what to think."

"Really!" He seemed surprised by that and tapped his fingers on his mouth. "Interesting. I didn't know that was how it was being read." Then he went back to his work, not having answered her original question and only leaving her with more.

32: R.O.I.

EILIS WATCHED HIM COME IN THE DOOR, AS TALL AND ELEGANT AS HE HAD Thursday and the day before. She'd have said arrogant if he were any other man, but Sebastian hadn't come off as arrogant once she'd met him, talked to him.

No, not arrogant. Preoccupied. Thinking, always thinking. Living in his head.

The backpack he carried was an interesting choice for a man who wore immaculate black (she wondered if he wore any other color) custom tailored suits, crisp white dress shirts, black silk ties, and never, ever looked rumpled. It didn't take anything away from his sinister air.

Sinister

Sin

Eilis thought Sebastian Taight looked like six feet, two inches and two hundred twenty pounds of pure *sin*.

He stopped at a cubicle and introduced himself to its occupant. Eilis tilted her head. That was . . . odd. Even more odd—he went to several cubicles and introduced himself, shaking hands. The cubicles' occupants smiled and laughed. Sebastian didn't, but none of the employees who'd spoken with him seemed to notice or care.

Why would he do that?

Eilis's insides turned over at the thought that it might be possible for him to take her company away from her through her employees. Sneaky bastard!

But . . . nowhere in her dictionary of evils that defined Sebastian Taight was an entry for sneaky. Oh, no. Sebastian Taight was the most cunning of devils: He did it to one's face, in the open, where everyone could see. He was thoroughly transparent.

Not that anyone noticed that.

Eilis had watched more than one CEO go down because they didn't believe his brazenness, his honesty. They'd been so busy looking for schemes and machinations they never found that they hadn't seen what Sebastian Taight wanted them to see.

That still didn't explain why he was chumming up with her employees.

He worked his way toward her office without looking up, without acknowledging her presence, by going to this cubicle or that cubicle, talking to people. Eilis suddenly realized that she didn't know quite how King Midas actually worked. There were lots of tales, lots of bitterness, lots of buyer's remorse once owners and CEOs had convinced themselves that Sebastian hadn't done anything for them but collect a fee. But nobody had described the *process* to her.

Perhaps she should just be grateful for the knowledge that he wasn't interested in raiding her company.

Finally he disappeared under her mezzanine floor and she could hear his footsteps coming up the stairs. Soon, he had dropped his backpack on the table and joined her at the window again, as he had his first day at HRP. He was silent for a long time, his hands behind his back. When he decided to speak, it took every ounce of control Eilis had built up over the years not to show how startled she was.

"May I make a suggestion?" he asked politely and she somehow knew that if she said no, he would respect that, but he would remember it.

I take companies whose ownership and/or management can't be salvaged.

"Please."

"I suggest you not stand here watching your employees work. It's nerve-wracking and I don't think nervous employees are very productive."

"I'm not *watching* them," she said calmly, hurt that he had found fault with her management style instead of just her books and bad decisions.

"They don't know that. All they know is they don't feel free to check email, instant message, surf the 'net on their breaks or lunch. Whether they do those things on your time is a delicate balance, but they need to know you trust them to do what you hired them to do. By and large, if they're surfing on your time, they don't have enough to do and they're bored, or they don't like their jobs."

Eilis said nothing. This was who she was, how she validated her existence. Watching over what she'd built was part of her morning routine.

"Obviously," he said when she remained silent, "it's up to you."

He turned away from the window and strode to the table. Eilis watched him in the reflection in the glass as he took out a laptop, pens, pencils, and a pad of his green engineering paper—

"We do have office supplies, Mr. Taight," she said, turning.

"Sebastian, please. And yes, I'm quite sure you do, thank you." He sat then and opened his laptop. She watched the screen as he promptly began to check emails, instant message, and surf the 'net—and none of those things were related to business. She waited for him to finish whatever personal business he was taking care of.

And waited.

And waited. Half an hour.

She was outraged.

"Why are you doing that? You're supposed to be working!"

She knew she'd stepped into his trap before she'd finished the question, but couldn't stop the words from coming out. "Object lesson number one," he murmured, his stare boring into hers. She kept her face carefully controlled and the rush of blood to her face was hidden, thankfully, by the heavy foundation. She fought to keep her composure.

"One thing you need to learn," he continued softly. "There is a breed of intelligent people out there you don't seem to understand because it's not your breed. They need constant stimulation. They think so fast that it only takes them fifteen minutes to do something another person would need an hour to do. You gain productivity when you understand, find, and exploit those people to the hilt—and they will *thank* you for it."

Eilis stared at him, not really understanding what he was telling her. She had built an outsourcing human resources company. Did he think he knew more than she?

"Let me put it another way," Sebastian continued when she didn't speak. "I'll bet a good half of your employees have some sort of personality or mood disorder, and they're either on medication for it or they've developed a bunch of coping mechanisms to deal with it."

Horrified, she said, "*What?*"

"Attention-deficit disorder. You could throw hyperactive, hypomanic, and possibly mildly bipolar somewhere in there and call it good."

"Oh, no, you would *not* find those kinds of people here," she declared. "My screening test filters them out."

His eyebrow rose. "Really."

"Yes."

"I want to take one of those tests."

Only too glad to comply, she went to her office and got one out of her own files and brought it back to him. He looked it over, then began filling in the bubbles. He did it faster than anyone she'd ever seen. Once he was finished, he gave it back to her. "Score that, if you would, please."

She called to her assistant Louise and asked her to take it down to the scoring room, then wait for the results and bring them back. Sebastian turned back to his laptop and tapped into her server, as her CIO had granted him access to the wireless network. He said nothing as he perused digitized employee files. Every so often, he said, "Huh."

Louise came back and gave the results to Eilis. When she looked down, she gasped—actually gasped.

She looked at him and he smirked.

"You flunked this on purpose," she stated matter-of-factly and laid the test and results on the table.

"You'd really like to think that, wouldn't you?"

"No, I know it."

"Eilis, if I did it on purpose, it means your test can be beaten and is therefore worthless. If I didn't, it means you wouldn't have hired me. Now, which one would you prefer to think?"

Eilis didn't know what to think. She calmly sat and looked her test over, looked at his answers and could verify that they were consistent with the little bit of Sebastian Taight she knew. She swallowed.

"I wouldn't have hired you," she said softly.

"Object lesson number two. You and your clients are missing out on a lot of good, productive people. Even if you can't get your clients on board, you would be well served to give people like me a second glance. Give them challenging work they enjoy and *lots* of it." He stopped to peruse the employee database again, then, suddenly, "How does your CIO hire programmers?"

"I don't know."

"Does he use the screening test?"

"No. He refuses to, but he does an excellent job, so I let him do what he wants."

"Do you know why he refuses to use it?"

Eilis looked back at Sebastian's test then and thought about the collective strangeness of the programmers who worked for HRP. Then she understood what he was saying, now on an even deeper level. "Yes," she said quietly. "I know why."

"Object lesson number three. Now," he said, picking up the employee list, "I need to have the hard copy contracts of your officers and executives."

Eilis Logan had no business in human resources, that was clear to Sebastian. She didn't know what kind of talent she had working for her. She didn't know how to delegate effectively. She didn't know how to match weaknesses and strengths to the workload.

She couldn't fire anyone. And because of that, she'd been suckered by a thief.

On the other hand, she had built a very successful business in spite of her deficiencies. She was doing something right and Sebastian knew where the disconnect was: HRP grew. It just did it very slowly and very inefficiently.

Well. Sebastian would fix that pronto, with some very well-placed dynamite.

He sent the digitized officer and executive contracts to his employment lawyer for dissection, along with a detailed list of accomplishments for each, provided by Eilis, her computer files, and by listening to the employees. What they *didn't* say was more telling than what they did, and their body language screamed paranoia.

HR Prerogatives was not a fun place to work and Sebastian was all about having fun with one's work.

33: Opportunity Loss

SEBASTIAN AND KNOX WERE CLEARLY STARTLED WHEN GISELLE CAME IN THE front door from work at one in the morning, hauling the forty-pound bag of textbooks she'd bought that day. They watched her as she dumped them on the table across from Sebastian, then pulled her gun from her waistband and put it on top of her books. Knox sat at the foot of the enormous conference table, the files spread out in front of him covering more than half the length of the table. Banker's boxes full of papers sat in the two chairs that flanked him, his laptop was open, and his Glock served as a paperweight.

She went to the fridge. She was *not* happy and while Knox would mind his own business, it wouldn't be long before Sebastian started with the third deg—

"Uh, Giz, it's Tuesday. Shouldn't you be going to Kenard's every night and fucking his brains out? I thought you'd be practically moved out by now."

"I'm re-thinking," she said shortly. Knox raised an eyebrow.

Sebastian sat back in his chair. "Oh, don't get all squeamish now that you're out of bed and back to real life."

"I'm not. He's fixed."

Silence. Then, "Well, Giz, there are worse things in the world than not having kids. Like, oh, spending the rest of your life alone with your vibrator."

She snarled at him, then dropped into the chair across from him with a package of pepperoni. "Coming from you, that's rich."

"She's got a point," Knox muttered. "You want sixteen kids, but you'd settle for eleven."

Sebastian grunted.

Knox sat back then and folded his arms over his chest. "So, uh, this weekend—?"

"Better than I ever dreamed possible. It's like the evening couldn't have turned out any other way. Went to dinner and talked for hours and hours and hours. Man's brilliant."

Sebastian snorted. "So he fucked your mind first."

"Oh, yes," she sighed.

"What did he have to say to get you in bed?"

She looked at the wall behind Sebastian, a smile twitching at the edges of her mouth. "'I want to fuck you, Giselle.'" Both of them stared at her, their mouths open, before they burst out laughing. Sebastian laughed until tears rolled down his cheeks. She went on. "I mean, what's any girl in her right mind gonna say to that? No? Hardly."

"Giz, that's not exactly a normal seduction technique. And coming from a man *that* big with *that* face? Trust me. I know from seduction."

"Oh, please. You don't seduce. You overwhelm. How's Ms. Eilis Logan, by the way? Let me guess. Tall, blonde, rubenesque. You met her a whole week ago and you haven't railroaded her into bed yet? Or did you decide not to bother getting her to the Den of Iniquity?"

"Shut up."

"I told him I'd find a way to throw him in jail if he fucked her before her receivership was over," Knox offered.

"Oh, nice job," Giselle said and bumped fists with Knox.

"We are not talking about me!" Sebastian roared. "We're talking about Giz."

Knox laughed. "I'm stuck on 'I want to fuck you, Giselle.'" He wiped his mouth, contemplating Giselle, still looking a bit stunned. "This would never have happened when we were at college. Look at you," he said, pointing to her arms. "Those are just the bruises I can *see*. What's that on the back of your neck? He *bit* you?" Sebastian looked terribly smug then. "Does he look any better?"

She popped a piece of pepperoni in her mouth. "No. And I have fingernails."

"Freak. I knew there was a reason I didn't want to marry you."

"Yeah, the same reason I didn't want to marry *you.*" She sighed. "I honestly don't know how *any* woman could pass him up."

Sebastian said, "You're the only woman in the world a man like that could've said 'I want to fuck you' to and expected it to work. And you think *I'm* a freight train." He paused. "Remember Francisco's speech to Rearden."

She sat up suddenly, her eyes wide. "Oh! He quoted that at me! Before that, I'd told him I was looking for Rearden and it was like, he went from gentleman to predator in a microsecond." She smiled wistfully. "He made me choose between Rearden and Galt."

"Crafty bastard. What'd you say?"

"Kenard."

Sebastian's face softened a bit and Knox sucked in a breath. "Giselle," he said. "That's— That was profound."

"I didn't even have to think about it." She sobered and slid down in her chair again, unhappy. "Then he saw that painting."

"Uh, Giz. I was there. He *loved* it."

"Yes. Except for the pacifier part and he realized kids were going to be an issue."

Sebastian stared at her for a long time, making her squirm. "What?" she snapped. Then his jaw dropped.

"You're scared," he said in wonderment.

"Pffftt. Not." Not of Bryce, anyway. Exactly.

He began to laugh again. "He is precisely what you thought you wanted and now you don't know what the hell to do. He's a whole 'nother animal than what you thought he was going to be, isn't he? Somewhere deep down inside, you thought you could keep the upper hand with a Rearden. But Kenard doesn't let you. He doesn't need your protection. He can't be terrified or intimidated. He'll win any game you play with him."

Giselle sat quiet for a while, eating, thinking, ignoring Sebastian's pointing and mocking, though he soon subsided when she didn't respond.

"That's not it," Knox murmured, still staring at her, studying her. "Or at least not all of it. Obviously she likes the Tarzan thing as well as she thought she would or she wouldn't have spent the entire weekend being his rag doll and using him for a scratching post."

"Well, that's true," Sebastian murmured after a bit. "All right, Giz, out with it. Remorse? Guilt? What?"

She swallowed, unwilling to confide in her family, her best friends in the world, but needing guidance. "All I wanted to do was tell him I lied to him and let him rant at me, then leave so I could come home and cry. I expected to never see him again."

"But you ended up in bed with him instead."

"At the gallery," she said, nodding toward Sebastian, "you told me he was on the fast track to bishop and it didn't take long to figure out that wasn't true. But I guess I thought he would know— I thought he'd want— I mean, he grew up the same way we did and he knows the routine: date, temple marriage, sex, kids. Okay, so we had sex first, but I assumed he'd eventually want to get back on the straight and narrow."

"And he doesn't," Sebastian said flatly.

She shook her head. "No kids, no church, no repentance, no temple. Take it or leave it."

"Don't confuse remorse with betrayal, Giselle," Knox said. "You're not sorry you fucked him before he married you. You're sorry you got two-thirds of your dreams blown away."

"For nothing," Sebastian said.

"No," Knox snapped. "Not nothing. Bryce wouldn't fuck her and dump her. I'll bet *she* walked away from *him*."

"That's not fair!" she protested. "I just need some time to sort all this out."

"Do you *want* to be with him?"

She looked at Knox. "Yes, but he— He's so wounded."

Sebastian started. "I thought you liked that."

"Not on the outside. The inside. What if all he wants is someone to heal him so he can move on? Nobody can heal anybody else. I don't know what I'd do if he left me now that I've given him everything I have."

Neither had anything to say to that. Sebastian wouldn't; he'd never been in love until this woman whose receivership Knox had given him. He didn't have a clue.

Finally, Knox spoke. "Bryce isn't like that, Giselle. When he made snap decisions, they were excellent ones. It was when he started listening to what other people wanted him to do and second-guessing himself that he got into trouble. Somewhere along the line, he's learned to trust his own judgment. Okay, so he's a freak in bed, but he's an honorable man. Honorable men don't expect their women to heal them; they either deal with it or their women heal them with their presence and their love. Don't assume that's what he wants from you and don't try to do it for him. All you have to do is be there and love him. He's *never* had that."

"Just because he's never had it doesn't mean I'm obliged to give it to him."

"True, but do you want to ditch him just because you *think* he *might* suck you dry and leave you? Don't you want to find out for sure? Ride the ride and see where it goes. For you, not for him."

Coming from Knox, that was significant and she looked at him. "How do you deal with that, people sucking you dry and leaving you?"

He shrugged and looked away. "I teach. Comes with the territory." He cleared his throat and looked down at the table. Suddenly she realized she had never known how deeply that affected him. No wonder he had always clung to her when everything else in his life went south. No matter they had never been lovers and weren't in love and wouldn't have been able to live together, she was his only constant.

"Why didn't you tell me you'd talked to Bryce in March? In fact, why didn't you tell me about him and what I needed to know when I came home from the Nelson that night? You saw what a wreck I was." Tears gathered in her eyes. "You could've made it so easy for me."

He flinched.

"Giselle," Sebastian rumbled. *Giselle.* Not *Giz.* She gulped at the edge in his voice. "Don't you start in on Knox. He didn't have to go to Kenard at all, but he did. For you. Then Kenard did what he was supposed to do and pursued you. *You* are the one who threw it back in his face. So Knox stepped in again to make this work. For you." He stood and leaned across the table, got in her face, stabbed his index finger into the tabletop right in front of her. She reared back, her eyes wide.

"You're an adult," he snarled. "You knew what you had to do to get all this squared away and you weren't willing to do it because he turned your tidy little hypocritical and self-righteous Molly Mormon world upside down. So now you're pissed he won't give you everything you *assumed* he'd give you and you're scared he'll break your heart. Well, what about *his* heart? He's not a manwhore. What about what *he* gave *you*? That was no less valuable than your virginity. You're using this as an excuse not to follow through because being with a man you can't emasculate scares the shit out of you and you'd never marry a man you could emasculate or you would've by now."

Sebastian slowly sat and Giselle closed her eyes and swallowed, uncaring that tears rolled down her cheeks and dampened her tee shirt. She sniffled and looked away, feeling the implications of every word Sebastian spoke deep in her soul— His disappointment in her, his anger on Bryce's and Knox's behalf. "I'm sorry," she whispered, but she didn't know for what, really, or to whom she said it.

Knox remained silent for a long while. When he spoke, his voice was hoarse. "It would be a mistake for you to let him go, Giselle. He's a good man and he's been in love with you for a long time."

Another minute of silence passed before she wiped her eyes.

"And," he added, "he wouldn't be so pissed off if he really didn't believe anymore. Think about that a while."

Give him time. Love him.

She heard it as clearly as if he had said it.

She nodded and slowly stood to pick up her Glock. "Night."

After closing her door, she turned her lights up only enough to see what she was doing and put her gun in its spot on her night stand. She took off her clothes, slow, easy, the way Bryce had done it when they'd returned from the Ford exhibit.

Soft seduction, slow and easy, languid, long-lasting. Candles. Soft music. Oils. Massage. Quiet conversation. Hushed laughter. Cherries and strawberries and warm, melted chocolate, for which they had found a variety of uses. They'd slept nearly twelve hours after that, both completely worn out, too sore and raw for any more.

She couldn't look at her bed without remembering what she'd done to him there, what he'd done to her, that he'd taken her wherever he wanted to go. Just because he could.

Once she stepped into the hot shower, she was beset by the memory of what Bryce had done to her here, too.

He doesn't need your protection.

Sebastian was right. Bryce Kenard didn't need protection. He could protect *her*. Much bigger, much stronger than most men, he could lift all one-sixty of her with ease. She nearly melted when she thought of that magnificent body of his, burnt, shredded, sliced, wounded, with that incredible musculature underlying his skin. He had those eyes, that face . . .

He did intimidate her, that was true. The way he could lift and manipulate her body. And it would do whatever he wanted it to, like a rag doll.

That didn't frighten her; it aroused her. Being intimidated aroused her. Being taken aroused her. Being weaker aroused her.

Leave it on.

Being stripped down to her skin, understood for herself and wanted *because* of it, not *in spite* of it—it was better than she'd ever hoped for.

. . . he turned your tidy little hypocritical and self-righteous Molly Mormon world upside down.

Don't confuse remorse with betrayal, Giselle . . . You're not sorry you fucked him before he married you.

She sighed. Of course the two of them would distill her issues to their essence and stake her in the heart with them.

Be careful what you wish for, Miss Cox . . . you might get it.

Ares. The god of war, of violence and bloodlust.

He was angry, bitter, and deeply hurt, his soul as scarred as his body—a soul that had started out dark and savage anyway.

. . . being with a man you can't emasculate scares the shit out of you . . .

Yes, Giselle feared him. She feared his eventual disappointment or resentment if she couldn't deliver what he really needed. She feared he would someday go back to the church, regret having lain with her, having broken his covenants with her and for her, having given up that part of himself that had always striven to be faithful, righteous, and pure.

Perhaps it was for the best that he couldn't have children. She didn't think a child's fragile soul could handle all that underlying rage. Knox said Bryce had been a wonderful father and she believed that. She had no doubts he would continue in that vein, but children could sense things and then they assumed and extrapolated other things from those sensations that usually bore no resemblance to the truth.

Giselle got out of the shower and dried herself off, looking at her naked body in the mirror. Bruises everywhere, bites. She hummed to herself as she tried to figure out how he'd given her each one and relived the entire weekend.

I want them to look and know that woman is mine.

She was his. He'd marked her. She liked that he'd marked her.

He had fared no better. She'd marked him similarly, once high on the inside of his thigh and once just over his shoulder blade. She'd grabbed the upper hand with him once by virtue of a surprise attack—

—and a couple of very strong scarves.

She smiled when she remembered his surprised, hearty laughter at awakening to find himself bound, blindfolded, and at her mercy. "Oh, it's like that for you, is it?" he'd asked wryly.

"So . . . who's the alpha again?"

"I don't need rope."

Then she sobered. At thirty-six, it would only be a matter of time before age betrayed her and then what would he think? Giselle was no great beauty and never had been. The Dunham women didn't age as well as they'd have liked, but what woman did, really? Once Bryce met Giselle's mother and the rest of her aunts, he would know everything he needed to know about how Giselle would look in fifteen years.

Giselle would probably start packing the weight back on again. Her hips would spread out again—and not in that sexy fertility goddess way. Her breasts would sag, though probably not as quickly since she wouldn't have children. She'd go gray. She had started to find streaks of gray in her hair a couple of years ago. They had since multiplied, but as long as people continued to mistake them for the cleverest of blonde highlights, she could delay her surrender to Miss Clairol.

She turned all the lights out and rolled into her bed, covering up with the duvet that still had traces of chocolate. She couldn't bring herself to launder it because it smelled like Bryce. She buried her nose in it and breathed deeply, then used it to mop up the tears that began to fall.

Yes, she feared him. On looking into a future with Bryce Kenard, whose soul had shattered long ago, she felt real fear: The fear of proving inadequate to the task of being *that* wolf's mate. What had she told Justice McKinley not five days ago?

You have to be willing to fail.

Giselle didn't know if she could live with that depth of failure.

34: Pink Slip

SEBASTIAN HAD COMPLETELY EXPOSED WEAKNESSES EILIS DIDN'T KNOW SHE had. Thus, she was very careful not to be at her window over Cubicleville the next morning, even though she wanted to watch him come in the door, watch how he talked to people.

The lunch room was underneath her mezzanine office suite. She had made it her business to take her breakfast of a bagel and fat-free cream cheese to work and eat there so she could watch him without being seen.

A little after eight, he walked in, and the people he talked to yesterday greeted him by his first name; he remembered every one of theirs. He very deliberately stopped and talked to different people today, even going so far as to enter the cubicle paths. He passed out of her sight when he did that.

He emerged a while later and she heard snatches of conversation as he drew closer.

"Hi. I'm Sebastian Taight. Who are you and what do you do?" Oh so direct, which was par for his course, but then, no one seemed to take offense. Firm handshake, warm smile on the employee's part.

That person, whose name and job description were a mystery to Eilis, told Sebastian everything about himself except his social security number and his job description.

"Yes, but what do you do?" Sebastian asked after this recitation.

"Well, a whole bunch of stuff."

"Like what?"

"I run reports and stuff."

"What kind of reports?"

"Customer databases and other stuff."

"Do you like your job?"

The man's face dimmed, but only for a split second. If Eilis noticed it, Sebastian definitely would. "Sure. HRP's a great place to work."

Eilis felt a sharp pain behind her sternum. He was lying through his teeth. He stayed because he had bills to pay and probably a family to provide health insurance for.

"Glad to hear it," Sebastian said, shook the man's hand and called him by name.

He only stopped in two more cubicles with the same routine. The last was Karen Cheng's, the ad executive who had some questionable ideas about marketing, but did what Eilis asked and did it well.

Karen wasn't an inexperienced executive straight out of college; Eilis would put her in her late thirties with an impressive portfolio. She was short and rather roundish, like an apple. Her bad perm did nothing to improve her nondescript brownish hair. Her glasses did her no favors, but didn't do anything against her, because her face was pretty in an exotic way.

Sebastian ran through the same routine, but unlike the others, Karen stood to speak to him, shook his hand firmly and with complete detachment. "What do you do?" he asked her.

"I am supposedly in charge of marketing," she said coolly and Eilis could see the surprise in Sebastian's face. Eilis began to get a bad feeling.

"Supposedly?"

"Yes. I have ideas. I have good ideas. They don't meet the approval of my supervisor."

Eilis's gut clenched and her throat stopped up. *She* was Karen's supervisor.

"I see," Sebastian said after a slight pause. "Do you like it here?"

"No. I'm creative. I want to create. I'm not allowed to do that."

Eilis swallowed. Hard.

"Then why do you stay?"

"Because I have a child with leukemia and I need the benefits. When she dies, I'm leaving."

Eilis put a hand to her mouth and barely fought back tears. *When.* Not *if.*

Sebastian tilted his head and looked at Karen for a moment and then said, "Please come upstairs with me." Those who had gathered around gasped and scattered immediately. Karen gulped, but she didn't hesitate. Proudly, she went up the stairs with Sebastian, who was careful to climb at her pace and level. Eilis knew Karen thought she'd be fired, and truthfully, Eilis didn't have a clue if she would or wouldn't be. Sebastian could do exactly what he wanted to do.

But she was obviously at her tipping point and when asked directly, she couldn't lie, couldn't keep the bitterness out of her voice.

It was another hour before Eilis had the nerve to go upstairs. Sebastian and Karen were nowhere to be found. "Louise, where's Mr. Taight?"

"In the conference room with Karen. I hope he doesn't fire her. That poor daughter of hers . . ."

Louise knew. Eilis didn't.

They were in there all day long, and except for the moment a pizza delivery man showed up with a veritable feast, the doors didn't open. The restrooms on this floor had an entrance directly from the conference room, so neither came out for potty breaks, either.

"I don't think he'd order pizza for someone he's going to fire, do you?"

"Louise," Eilis said, "I honestly don't know what to think about that man."

To her shame, at that moment, the only thing she could really think about was the smell of that pizza wafting throughout the suite. Her stomach gurgled and she went to her office for a rice cake. Well, two.

At 4:15, the doors opened and Karen walked out. She didn't seem to notice Eilis and Eilis could only see Karen wipe her face.

Eilis went into the conference room to find Sebastian cleaning up the pizza and pop. She looked longingly at the leftovers he'd thrown away, but then snapped herself out of it with some difficulty because her stomach grumbled. He didn't acknowledge her presence.

She spoke hesitantly. "Did you—?" She couldn't bring herself to say the F-word.

"No," he said shortly. "I didn't fire her."

"She was crying."

Sebastian turned on her then, his face stone cold. Her stomach roiled and she thought she might puke. He reached behind him and picked up two of those engineer's pads he liked. Every page was written on and the writing fluffed up the pads until the two of them together were about three inches thick.

"I picked her brain, Eilis. I picked her brain, which is something her *supervisor*—" Eilis flinched. "—should've done the minute she was hired. She was crying because she was so grateful that someone *finally* listened to her.

"And I want to tell you something else. Karen faked your test. She beat it. She knew what it would say about her if she did it honestly and she needed this job. I don't even know why you bothered hiring a marketing executive if you weren't going to use her or listen to her. I'm leaving," he muttered as he dropped the pads of paper into his backpack. "I'll see you tomorrow."

With that, he brushed past her and walked out. Eilis barely made it home before she broke down and cried.

Eilis was tempted to stay home the next day without calling in. She was the CEO. She could do that. Sebastian Taight's opinion of her couldn't get any lower.

She hadn't slept. She'd spent the night at her kitchen table with a pencil and a pad of paper it'd taken her a half hour to find. What she wanted to write there, she didn't know. The only thing she'd written for the longest time was "Karen Cheng."

Then she wrote down what she knew about Karen, which was everything she'd learned that day and nothing more.

Then she wrote her assistant's name, Louise Brummel, and everything she knew about her, which wasn't much.

Then she wrote her CIO's name, Michael Pritchard, and what she knew about him, which was that he went to MIT and wouldn't use the screening tests and was all of twenty-six years old. End of list for Michael.

She went through every executive and every employee whose names she could remember and after Michael's very short list, none of them had any entries. Eilis knew nothing about her employees.

Each and every one of her employees and everything about them couldn't be known; she understood that. What she needed to know was that the rank and file were being managed well enough that they were productive and she couldn't know that without knowing their supervisors.

HR Prerogatives had always had a good name as a caring employer. It paid well, it provided good benefits. All Eilis asked in return was a good day's work, but how could she get that from people who hated their jobs? Management style flowed directly from the top, so did that mean that she was that bad at managing people?

In three days, Sebastian Taight knew more about her employees and what they needed better than she ever had or ever would have if he hadn't pointed it out to her.

Eilis ripped her piece of paper off the pad and made a notation to look at her tests again with a new eye. Karen beat it. Who knew how many others had? Sebastian had estimated half her workforce could have beaten it, so if it was that flawed, she didn't want it out in the marketplace.

At the thought of Sebastian, of Karen, of Michael and his programmers, an idea occurred to her that she scribbled down before she could forget it. Perhaps the *test* wasn't flawed at all.

No one was at work when she got there, which she had planned. She couldn't face Sebastian's derision or Karen's bitterness, but she couldn't stay away; that just wasn't done. Besides, she had things to do today.

She closeted herself in her windowless inner sanctum and wrote on her single sheet of paper until she'd covered it front and back, and it curled. She had no more lined paper in her office, so she emerged to get another pad or two.

Sebastian stood at the mezzanine window, his hands behind his back. Eilis didn't think he would want to talk to her, so she went downstairs. When she came back with a bundled package of legal pads, he was no longer at the window. Instead, he lay on the sofa in her office, his head on the arm rest, one expensively loafered foot on the floor and the other hanging over the opposite arm rest. One arm was thrown over his forehead and the other dangled uselessly over the floor.

His eyes were open and the only indications he gave that he was even alive was the occasional blink and the steady rise and fall of his chest. She wondered if that was normal for him, because she couldn't imagine this man sleeping, much less resting.

After a minute hesitation, she proceeded past him and sat at her desk. She bent back over her task once she'd opened her package. If he didn't intend to speak, then Eilis would attempt to block his presence from her mind and concentrate on remembering who worked for her. He said nothing for an hour, and Eilis was ashamed to realize she'd marked the time.

"Eilis," he said, "we need to talk."

Uh oh. She carefully put down her pen and folded her hands over her paper. He didn't *sound* angry. "All right."

He didn't move a muscle, except to speak. "Now, you understand that when I go into a business, I don't mess around with the product, right?"

"Yes, I know that." The product usually made the company money in spite of itself.

"I find myself in a unique position with HRP because I deal with people and numbers, but in your case, your *people* are your product. Quite frankly, Eilis, you don't know shit about people."

She swallowed. He still didn't sound angry, but there was a note of—something—in his voice she didn't understand.

"I looked at your list while you were gone and congratulations, by the way, for graduating to paper and pen." She thought she saw a trace of a smile. "It's a nice start. Question: When you came in and saw me lying here quiet and still, what did you think?"

There was no right answer to that. "I don't know what to think about you, Sebastian," she said quietly. "I've never met anyone like you."

He grunted. "Sure you have. You just didn't recognize them. I'll tell you what I was doing. I was working."

Eilis's brow wrinkled. "You were lying there doing nothing."

"Wrong. I was working. Some things require minimal brain power. Some a lot. Most of the time, if I'm sitting doing nothing, I'm working something through, letting my mind wander where it wants, laying the groundwork for the solutions to my next sixty problems. What you need to understand is that lots of people do that. Your product is people, but you've completely disenfranchised that portion of the population that represents the best this country has to offer."

That made no sense.

"Sure it does," he replied when she said that. "This country was built on the back of ADD and its comorbid personality disorders. It's heavy in the general American gene pool because it self-selected. You know, Darwin? Immigrants came here, pioneers. They were of one type, though on a broad spectrum of that type: They were risk takers. They built things. They succeeded. They defied a king and waged war on the most powerful country on earth at that time, and they won. The United States of America is what they built, and my ancestors not only helped win a war and build a country, they made a fortune doing it.

"So back to my unique position. I'm going to mess with your product, contrary to my usual M.O., and I would like to request that you just ditch the screening test altogether."

"It brings in a lot of revenue," she said quietly.

"I know, but it's flawed."

She hesitated for only a microsecond. "I've been thinking about that. I don't think the test itself is flawed. I think the scoring criteria are."

He said nothing and then, "Eilis, I can think of only two people in my very, very large tribe who would pass your test without cheating and that's Knox and Fen, and if he weren't dead, Oliver, either. That's not coincidental."

Eilis struggled to keep her cool.

I'm always willing to look at options if they're presented to me logically.

She took a deep breath and said, "Let me explain my reasoning, please."

He continued to lie still and quiet, so she went on. "I think that the test itself did what it was supposed to do, which was to pinpoint your personality type and learning style. The only thing that was off was the label the program assigned to your score. You only failed because the grading scale said you did. My idea is that if the scoring criteria were based on categorizations, no one would fail; it would only suggest in what capacities those people would do well and where they shouldn't be put at all."

He said nothing for a long while, still staring at the ceiling. Eilis waited and waited. "I'll agree to that," he finally said, surprising her. "But I want you to get it restructured by a psychologist who specializes in personality disorders—and, by the way, I hate that term. It's just convenient to use—as if we need to apologize for or medicate a big segment of the population just because the looters and moochers don't like it."

Looters and moochers? "All right."

He sat up, then stood, shaking out his pant legs. "I'm going to spend the rest of the day and tomorrow talking to people. It's about time someone did," he growled, glaring at her. She truly did flinch that time, but he'd turned by then and started his long stride out of her office, so he didn't see it. "Monday, I'll clean your house."

Eilis breathed a sigh of relief. That wasn't the worst dressing down he could've given her and he hadn't seemed to hate her and he didn't seem that angry, either. She figured she got off light and thanked her lucky stars. She set about researching the type of psychologist Sebastian had specified and started making phone calls.

Sebastian came back to her office at the end of the day with yet another of those pads filled with notes. "When I get finished Tuesday, I want you to administer that test again to those who remain. You'll do that Wednesday before the lunch. You will make it very clear that it won't be scored in the normal way, that it is imperative that they do it honestly and that their jobs depend upon their doing it honestly."

"How will you know if they don't?"

He dropped the pad on her desk. "I'll know. Believe me, I'll know."

She looked into his cold blue eyes and felt herself beginning to think of entirely different things altogether. His scent was odd, one she'd never encountered. One part man, one part expensive cologne, and one part chemical compound of some sort, a solvent maybe. Even with that mixed in, it wasn't offensive in the least bit. In fact, it was so *not* offensive that she was getting aroused. Fortunately, the makeup and contacts would hide that from him.

Sebastian picked up his pad and turned. "I'll see you tomorrow, Eilis. Have a good evening."

35: Knockin' on Heaven's Door

I T HAD BEEN THREE DAYS SINCE GISELLE LEFT BRYCE IN THE PARK, AND SHE hadn't seen him or talked to him. Two unbelievable days, two incredible nights—a completely unexpected turn of events—and then nothing. He would not pursue her any longer. He would wait for her to make a decision and inform him of it, which she couldn't do until she actually made one.

Giselle missed him desperately. They'd been together for less than forty-eight hours and she felt the loss of his presence beside her as keenly as if she'd spent years picking his brain and wandering through his soul; she felt the loss of his body in bed with her as sharply as if she'd slept with him for years. She needed to see him, to touch him, to hear his voice, to smell him, to taste his skin.

Thursday morning she went back to the gallery, to her bodhisattva, and sat in front of him cross-legged most of the day, meditating, turning over and over every second of the time she'd spent with Bryce, every word of every conversation, every touch, every kiss, every orgasm, from that first glance in Hale's office to the moment she'd walked away from him.

Turning over and over what Knox had said. Knox had always had wisdom beyond his years and he gave good advice. He chose to ride the ride each and every time he came across the opportunity to love a woman regardless of the inevitable outcome—but he paid a very high price for it.

Turning over and over what Sebastian had said, his insight, his ability to cut through the bullshit to the core principle. Sebastian, who had begun to inject courage into her soul before she'd graduated from diapers, was angry that she would let her fear hold her back from what she really wanted and hurt someone else in the process.

Turning over and over exactly what Bryce had given her that was as precious as what she had given him. *I don't know when I fell in love with you, Giselle, but I don't remember a time when I wasn't.*

Turning over and over the dreams she'd had before she met Bryce, that he'd fulfilled the most important one, the odds of ever finding that again with someone who wanted children—and how long that would take.

The thought of having to wait another sixteen years made her chest collapse.

Andrew knelt before Giselle in the living room of the house he shared with Knox, his wrist bent back to its limit, keeping him there while she lectured him on how to correctly execute the technique.

Her untied canvas gi jacket floated over her tee shirt and around her hips. Her sleeves snapped the air properly when she moved quickly enough. Knox sat at the kitchen table staring through them as he waited for his study group to arrive. She took Andrew's other hand to emphasize the importance of the ability to do a technique left- or right-handed.

Giselle had put Andrew on his knees again before he knew what hit him and he grimaced in pain.

"See, Andrew, that's why she has the brown belt and you have the blue one."

"Oh, ha ha ha. Screw you, Hilliard."

The front door opened to admit the first of the law students Knox expected. Giselle's attention was distracted for a second—and her breath caught in her throat.

Six-four. Two hundred-plus pounds of solid muscle poured into tight worn jeans, a black tee shirt, brown leather bomber jacket and black cowboy boots. Black hair cut excruciatingly short. Angular face, olive-tinged skin almost as fair as Sebastian's. Small black-rimmed eyeglasses.

Remington Steele.

She continued to talk to Andrew, to explain the finer points, had him recreate the technique on her so she could demonstrate where he needed to change his execution. He did well enough to put her on her knees, but, afraid of hurting her, not well enough to keep her there. Still talking, still teaching . . .

The man had stopped short in the doorway and stared at her with an expression she recognized immediately, for all she'd never seen a man look at her that way before: Lust.

Blatant, unadulterated, hot.

She determined to cut Andrew's lesson short to make certain she had an opportunity to let that man know she reciprocated that lust fully, but out of habit, she checked his left hand.

Sixty seconds. It'd taken her sixty seconds, a glance, to fall head over for a married man.

Turning her attention back to Andrew fully then, she tried to breathe normally, to put aside that stabbing pain behind her sternum, to ignore the sick feeling in her belly. She smoothly maneuvered Andrew so that her back was to the door and she could no longer see him.

How could it be—and at BYU yet? Married men didn't look at women other than their wives that way, or at least, if they did, they successfully kept it to themselves.

More to the point, men didn't look at Giselle *that way at all. Not even Knox did that.*

She left as soon as the time came for Andrew to join the study group. Refusing Knox's offer of a ride home with a wave, she ran the mile from his house on Tenth East to her apartment on First East, hoping to kill some of the pain.

She curled up on her bed, still in her gi, still sweaty. She shoved her fingers through her coarse, frizzy curls with a vicious yank as if the pain would distract her, and let the tears drip silently into her pillow as she confronted the truth of the matter.

Her hand drifted to her pudgy belly, then over her wide hips to explore—not for the first time—the broad expanse of butt that her gi couldn't hide. Strong, athletic, graceful. And fat. She couldn't diet it away; she was already starving. She'd even tried making herself throw up, but that was nasty and worked even less effectively than starving. Sebastian would have a fit if he knew and it didn't matter he lived half a world away. She didn't dare let Knox find out because he'd feed her himself. She couldn't exercise it away; she got stronger, but no leaner.

It didn't matter with Knox; Knox needed her constant presence to mitigate his growing frustration and insecurity because no LDS girl would go out with him once she found out he hadn't gone on a mission—and he didn't want to taint any possible relationships with the details of his inheritance. Giselle needed his constant presence to make her feel as if she weren't, as Aunt Trudy had told her more than once, "the most hideous girl I've ever seen."

Without Knox, she would have no boyfriends at all; with Knox, she had an excuse. It had been enough until that man looked at her like that.

It was more than she could bear, that wedding band on his finger. The only man, a gorgeous one to boot, to look at her as if she had some sexual worth—and he was married.

"How could you?" she whispered, her faith shaken. "I've done everything you asked me to do. How could you do that to me?"

Heartbroken, she touched herself . . . there . . . and, for the first time, did what she knew she should never do.

Nobody else would.

Once three o'clock came, Giselle's head had cleared enough that by the time she got to work, she could do her job accurately and well. Mercifully, after about an hour, she lost herself in it.

But then it was 12:15. She had finished and stopped thinking about her relationship with Bryce. She let her instincts take over and, her heart in her throat, she drove directly to his house.

He lived in Brookside, just off Loose Park, in a three-story pale yellow Italian renaissance revival all renovated and dressed up as a showcase home. The stoop light was on, as well as a small lamp in a great paned window to the right of the front door. She hesitated; after all, most people didn't go visiting unexpectedly after midnight.

Gathering her courage, she walked up to the door and rang the bell. It took a while and another ring of the bell before she heard, "Hold on!" shouted from the depths of the house. Suddenly, the door was yanked open and he barked, "It's twelve-thirty in the morning. What the hell—" And he stopped cold as soon as he realized who she was. "Giselle," he breathed, and opened the door to let her in.

She stepped in gingerly and looked everywhere but at him, hoping once again she hadn't ruined her chance by not keeping hold of him when she had him in her hand. "I— I've thought about it, and— I'm sorry. I—"

"Don't talk," he muttered and kissed her again like he had that first night when he set about teaching her how to fuck, and she lost herself in him for good. She knew she couldn't live without this—this heat, this deep, dark level of carnal experience.

This man.

He gathered her up in his arms as if she weighed next to nothing rather than forty pounds more than what the charts said she should weigh, and carried her up the stairs, to his bedroom, and laid her gently in the massive mahogany bed, into sheets that smelled just like him. He covered her with his body and rolled her over until she lay on top of him. He only kissed her, drinking her in in silence.

How could she have ever doubted that she could live without him, no matter what the future brought? She would ride the ride and see where it went.

She was fully clothed. He wore nothing, having answered the door with a short towel hastily slung around his hips. They lay there together in the dark, not even the nearby streetlight able to pierce the heavy drapes, silent, kissing until they drifted off to sleep.

36: Arbitrage

H I."

"Hi."

Giselle studied Bryce's face in the morning sunlight that streamed through the bedroom window. He studied her in return. She shifted away from him a bit so she could look at his beautifully scarred body, touch it, caress it.

Kiss it.

"I missed you," he whispered and gently furrowed his fingers through her tangled curls as she pressed her lips against the skin overlying his collarbone. Tasted him.

"I missed you, too," she breathed, her hand splayed out over his heart, her thumb stroking his nipple. "I'm sorry I left you in the park Sunday. I—"

He pressed his finger to her lips, silencing her. "No. I'm sorry. I knew what you'd want and I didn't want to think about it. I deserved to be left." He lifted the locks of her hair only to let them slither away through his fingers, then again. And again. "So, kids? Church?"

She shrugged. "I'm here. On your terms."

"Is that going to be difficult for you?"

"Um, *yeah*. It is."

He sucked in a breath, held it, then released it in a whoosh. He looked up at the ceiling and ran his hand down his face. "We need to talk."

"Mmmm, true. But first—"

"Pee and brush teeth."

"Precisely." She rolled out of bed to accomplish those tasks, then stripped. Bryce joined her in the shower as she'd hoped he would. "Don't you have to go to work today?"

"The nice thing about owning your own practice," he murmured in her ear, "is that you can pretty much do what you want."

"What about meetings? Clients?"

"Nothing's ever scheduled before eleven. My assistant rearranges my appointments if I don't show up by nine and my attorneys can step in at a second's notice."

She closed her eyes and sighed, then leaned back into him. His arms around her, they stood quiet in the spray to commune silent, still, through the warmth of their bodies until the water ran tepid.

They bathed, dried, and tumbled back into bed, again skin-to-skin, and cocooned themselves in the fine linens.

"Are you hungry?"

Giselle's ear to his chest, she could feel the vibrations of his hoarse baritone and at that moment, she found that the sexiest thing imaginable.

"No," she murmured. "I don't usually eat this early in the morning. Are you?"

"No." Another moment of silence, though still not awkward. "Giselle," he murmured, "I know we got off to a rough start and we haven't spent any real time together doing things, talking, laying down expectations. You know, doing things by the church's playbook. I told you not to expect a temple marriage, but no matter what, I'm never going to be comfortable having a girlfriend, lover, mistress, significant other, whatever you want to call it."

Giselle's gut began to clench at the possibility he'd had second thoughts after all, that he'd tell her they'd made a mistake and she should go home. "Oh," she breathed. "Okay."

"I *do* want to marry you, just not . . . by the playbook."

Her breath caught.

"Yeah, I know it's weird," he said in a rush when he misunderstood her silence. "Love at first sight and all that—I never believed in that and I still don't. I can't say I love you because I don't know you well enough. I know I'm *in* love with you and in *lust* with you and I'm pretty sure I don't want to live without you. But for right now, that's all I have to offer you. If we don't make it, okay, but I *need* that sense of permanence for as long as we're together."

The pleading in his voice had returned. Still shocked, it dawned on her that he must fear she would say no, that he thought she wouldn't want to commit to him.

"I— Um—"

"I mean, if you want to hold off for a while until we see how this relationship shakes out, I'll respect that."

"No, I—" She cupped her hand over his mouth when he would've continued to defend his position. "Stop. Let me talk." She took a deep breath. "I'm not interested in being a perpetual fiancée, no. But I'm also not interested in going into marriage thinking things like 'if we don't make it.' If I say yes, which I want to, I don't want to always have it in the back of my mind that you've left yourself an out. I'm willing to work at a relationship, at a marriage, with you. I need to know you'll work at it with me."

He caressed the skin of her back with his calloused hands and she waited for him to process what she'd said. His body relaxed, the tension draining from his muscles. "I understand. I can promise that."

"The other thing," she continued, clearing her throat, "is I'm afraid you might one day come to resent me for breaking your covenants with me."

"I didn't get caught up in the heat of the moment, Giselle."

Her eyes widened. Her body tingled. "Oh," she breathed. "So dinner . . ."

"Wasn't part of the seduction. I told you I'd have taken you home that night at the Nelson and I would have. But after Knox summoned me, I took some time to think about it. I decided to talk to you first, to confirm that I wanted to try, to see if we were compatible enough to build something on. If that hadn't gone well, then nothing else would've happened. The reason I wanted to have *lunch* with you was so neither of us could ditch our afternoon commitments in case I hadn't made up my mind, but still wanted to take you to bed. I needed to know where you were coming from, to let you know where I was coming from without the pressure of impending sex."

"I was coming from Rearden. You were coming from Galt."

He laughed and she smiled. "You're not going to let me forget that, are you?"

"Nope."

She took a deep breath and his body tensed again. "Next topic," she said finally, sober again because no matter how ugly, it had to be discussed. "Money."

He started. "What about it?"

"I don't have any. I'm still in debt from my fire, my bankruptcy hasn't been discharged, and I have a ton of student loans. Sebastian says you're as rich as he is and I'm *very* uncomfortable with that. I would feel better if we had a prenuptial agreement."

"I won't agree to that," he said, relaxing again. "You said you weren't interested in going into marriage thinking things like 'if we don't make it.' A prenuptial agreement presupposes that we won't, so no. No prenup. Giselle," he continued when she opened her mouth to protest, "the reality is that even if you tried to take everything away from me, you wouldn't get it. I'd send it offshore and wrap it up so tight it'd take an act of God to break it open. I've already been down that road and I can make it disappear like it never existed. I'm not shy about doing whatever I have to do to keep what's mine. As for how the money would work once we got married, well, everything I have would be yours."

She swallowed in mixed relief, guilt, and dread. "I don't like feeling rescued," she murmured.

"You didn't go under because of anything you did wrong. You went under because Fen's evil and you're lucky that all you lost was your business. That's a completely different proposition from someone bailing you out of your own stupidity. And even if that had been the case— Giselle, you're one of the few women I've ever met who hasn't expected something from me. Before my fire, it was sex and money. After, it was just the money."

"What if I'm putting on an act?"

He laughed then. "You are the *worst* actress in the world. Your face is very expressive and I can read you like a book. I've been chasing you for almost a year because you didn't want to be caught. You could've asked Hale who I was and he would've arranged something; you knew that, but you wouldn't do it. You *knew* Knox would've helped you get to me, but you didn't ask him to. A woman who's after money doesn't do those things."

She sighed. "The money thing is going to take me some time to get used to."

"You live with Sebastian Taight. What's there to get used to?"

"I don't have access to his money. It's his. What I have is what I earn. And you've seen our house—it's a little too middle class for a billionaire, don't you think? He doesn't like living in his money and so it doesn't remind me of what he has that I don't. We're just poor kids from the ghetto and in a lot of ways, we still live like that. Hell, he still drives the old beat-up pickup truck he bought when he was sixteen."

"And a Ferrari," Bryce added dryly.

"So he does, but I don't live with King Midas. I live with my brother."

Bryce grunted. "Well. Okay. Any more issues you'd like to discuss?"

She smiled. "No."

"So *now* will you marry me?"

"Yes," she breathed and pulled herself up his body so that she could kiss him, long and deep. Lazy like a hot summer breeze and sweet like fresh mown grass. She sighed when she felt his palms cup either side of her face.

"I want to give you a nice wedding," he whispered against her mouth as the kiss lightened. She opened her eyes to see him watching her. "But I have no idea how people outside the church plan them."

"Not interested."

He blinked. "That's the last thing I'd've expected Miss Fashionista to say."

"Normally, if we were getting married in the temple and had a huge reception afterward, yes. But we aren't—" He opened his mouth to speak and again she closed it with her fingertips. "—and I've accepted it. This? Between you and me? This is about us becoming lovers before getting married. It's private. I don't want a bishop to marry us, much less any other flavor of clergy. A judge will do. All I want is to be with you. I don't want to spend a year being only your fiancée just to plan a bash nobody's going to care about in six months."

"What about your family?"

"I do what pleases me, not my family. Of course, I want my mom there. Sebastian and Knox. My Aunt Dianne. That's all. The rest of my tribe wouldn't fit in a judge's chambers."

"Is your mother going to resent me?"

Her brow wrinkled. "For what?"

"Because I seduced you."

Her mouth tightened. "Please don't take it all on yourself like I had no choice in the matter. I could've said no and you gave me plenty of opportunity to do so. My decision was as deliberate as yours." He inclined his head in acknowledgment of that. "What makes you think my mother would resent you?"

He stared at her for a long moment, then said, "Because that's how my siblings will feel about you."

She swallowed, hurt to her core. "Oh."

"They would think you must have seduced me and *made* me break my covenants. They wouldn't believe otherwise even if I gave them a play-by-play. But don't take it personally; they aren't too happy with me, either."

"You don't like your family much, do you?"

He shrugged. "It's not that so much as I don't fit in. I was always the black sheep and I don't even look like my siblings."

"Maybe you were adopted."

A chuckle rippled through his chest. "I asked my mother that once and she looked at me funny and said, 'Bryce, I was *there*. For thirty-six hours. Trust me, you aren't adopted.'"

Giselle laughed and thought she might have liked Bryce's mother.

"Do you know how I made my money after the fire?"

She nodded. "You sued everybody who had a hint of a whiff of anything to do with the construction of your house, plus the city for having crooked codes officers."

"Right. Filthy lucre."

"I don't understand."

"Mark and Serena—my siblings—think I'm immoral for having done that."

That blew Giselle's mind. "Why? Your children died."

"Well, you know, the meek inherit the earth. Turn the other cheek. I don't deal with life that way and except for my family and Michelle, the church, I never did. If I showed the proper amount of shame for my work, my money, how I got it, they'd be okay with it, but I refuse to apologize, so . . . " He shrugged.

"Oh, Bryce," she breathed. "I'm so sorry."

"Don't be. It doesn't bother me and they're thousands of miles away. We don't talk. I might as well not have any family for how much we interact."

Giselle had to take him at his word because his voice, which could tell her so much of his feelings, betrayed nothing but statements of fact.

"Well, don't think I won't get my head handed to me on a platter when my mother gets over being thoroughly delighted," she said dryly after a moment.

"Delighted?"

"With you. My mother will *love* you. Once my tribe finds out *the* Bryce Kenard is about to be assimilated, you'll be welcomed like a conquering hero. That filthy lucre thing? We're all about filthy lucre."

He laughed then. "Knox used to say your family was just a hundred-plus people using any excuse to have a party."

"That'll never change."

"He'd talk about it and it was just something I couldn't imagine. Still can't."

"Oh, you'll get plenty of opportunities to see it in action. Every weekend there's something going on, weddings, graduations, funerals, birthdays, baby and bridal showers. Stuff like that. Plus all the major holidays and at least half the minor ones. I don't think we celebrate President's Day. Yet."

Bryce ran a finger across the line of her jaw. Giselle watched. Waited. Finally, he murmured,

"Considering what you said about your jewelry, perfume, and men, I'll assume you want to choose your own wedding ring?"

Giselle blushed and gave him a shy smile then, a warm joy bursting in her soul and filling her. "Yes, please."

"Now," he murmured as he began to nibble at her bottom lip, "we can make love or we can fuck. Pick one."

37: A Little Zen Headed Your Way

THEY LAUGHED AND TEASED EACH OTHER AS BRYCE MADE GISELLE BRUNCH. Kind of. Broiled salmon with parsley and butter, hollandaise sauce, and eggs. The salmon was left over, he apologized, as was the hollandaise sauce, which had broken. She threw it out and made a fresh batch, which amazed him. He did actually cook her eggs to her specifications, which she found incredibly sweet.

"I don't really cook," he admitted finally. "My housekeeper does that for me."

Giselle had begun to set their places at the island when she saw it. Her eyes widened and her jaw dropped at what it must mean. There, at the front of the house stood a glossy black concert grand piano that had yellowing, well-worn music scattered all over it and on the floor surrounding it. *Oh!*

"I want to ask you something," Bryce said, interrupting her wonder. "Why have you stuck with Knox all these years after you broke up?"

"History. Loyalty."

"There's more to it than that, I think."

She thought about it while they gathered their food and sat to eat. After a deep breath, she began, "The proviso is all my fault." At his questioning look, she explained and when she finished, he said,

"So you feel responsible for something you did when you were fourteen and here you are, twenty-something years later, still carrying it."

She shrugged. "You have to take responsibility for what you do."

He snorted. "And you don't think you're honorable. So let's try this again. Define honor. *Your* definition. What are you comparing yourself to?"

She looked at him while she attempted to shake that answer out for herself. "A karate teacher I had at BYU," she finally said. "I know he thought I had a crush on him, but I didn't. I couldn't. He was too out of my league. I was in awe of him. I was so in awe of him, I couldn't *presume* to have a crush on him. He was twenty-two and I was eighteen. I knew the minute I met him I wanted to be just like him. He had *power*. Real power, like the kind where men ten, twenty years older than he paid him deference. He was a true leader. He was a *warrior*. I think of him kind of like Alexander the Great."

Bryce's eyebrow rose. "Twenty-two?"

Giselle nodded, but he released a frustrated whoosh. "What?"

"Aw, Giselle. It took me years to get to that point and then to hear about some punk twenty-two-year-old who had it . . . " He shrugged.

Giselle could empathize with that. "He's the one whose example of honor I've been trying to emulate since. That's why I couldn't define it for you. To me, honor is not a 'what.' It's a 'who.'"

"And I'm looking at her," he returned sharply, and she looked up to see his gaze boring into her. "I don't know where you got this idea that you're not honorable, but get rid of it. Whether you learned it or it was forced upon you or you already had it and just honed it to a science, I don't know. Most people don't earn real respect and admiration when they're children, which, from what little I know, you seem to have earned from Fen. However or whoever you define honor, some nebulous thing you think you can't reach—you did. You're it."

Tears gathered at the corners of her eyes and tickled her cheeks as they tracked their way down to her chin. He smiled at her and reached over to wipe her face with a napkin. "I'm sorry," she murmured, feeling a blush creep up her cheeks. "I cry a lot."

"Takes the edge off the Glocks."

She laughed through her tears. "Yeah, that's not a good thing. Warrior queens aren't supposed to cry."

"They probably don't wear Badgley Mischka and Manolo Blahnik, either."

"How did you know that?"

He laughed then. "Went through your very, ah, *sparse* closet. Reconnaissance."

"Nosy, more like."

"Semantics. So in this whole proviso mess, why didn't you and Knox just get married? It would've been very efficient."

"I was waiting for you. Metaphorically speaking, of course."

A pleased grin grew on his face.

"Something happened my junior year at BYU and it clarified what I wanted, one of those random slice-of-life things that makes you take a good look at what you want."

"Which was?"

"It's stupid. I saw a dude. A glance. That's all. He looked at me like he wanted to shove me up against a wall and fuck me. But then I saw he had a wedding band on, so it didn't go beyond that. I mean, we're at BYU so I'm going to assume he's LDS, which doesn't necessarily follow, but the odds are good, right? He's married and he's looking at me like *that*? That's some powerful mojo right there. It was like Hank Rearden incarnate. And I wanted that."

"So you waited for it."

"Yep."

Bryce's mouth twitched. "Which explains the vibrators and the erotica."

She gasped and her mouth dropped open. "You *know* about that?"

A roar of laughter exploded from him and she huffed. "Knox told me," he finally said once his humor had wound down a bit and he had wiped the tears from his face.

"That *bastard!*"

"You hid it very well. It took me a while to find your toy box."

The heat rose in her face and she ducked her head. She felt his fingers on her chin then found herself nose to nose with him. "And I'm telling you right now. You're gonna read for me, and then you're going to use those toys while I watch."

Giselle bit her lip, aroused and amused despite her chagrin.

Smirking, he released her and went back to his salmon. "So are there any other reasons you and Knox didn't . . . ?"

She looked at him speculatively for a moment. "Are you feeling threatened? Still?"

His smile dimmed and he hesitated. "Yeah, a little bit, I'll admit."

"You don't need to."

"Indulge me."

She supposed she could respect that. After all, she had to deal with Michelle's ghost and she'd welcome any information that would help her do that.

"Well, I don't know how to describe it. Knox *builds* his women and he couldn't do that with me."

"That makes no sense."

Giselle took a deep breath. "He knows precisely what he's looking for in a woman, which is a little teeny spark of fire hidden deep in her soul. Knox only ever falls in love with a woman's soul. Once that happens, he overwhelms her, manipulates her, makes her vulnerable, breaks her down to expose her spark so she can take over when she's ready to progress on her own terms, to fulfill the potential she already had."

"Leah," Bryce breathed as comprehension grew in his expression.

"Leah. She was sad and lonely and had never known passion in her life and she didn't even know it. Knox saw her as a passionate woman, vivacious, and charming. He knew it the first time he saw her and that's what he turned her into."

"And you were already built, so it was a non-starter."

"Between understanding what I really wanted and that, yes."

"So what happens to his women once he's built them? He gets bored and moves on?"

"Oh, no. *They* move on to accomplish great things because he taught them how. His gift is his curse. He loves them, but none of them love him enough to stay with him. Leah never loved him the way she loved her late husband, but she loved how he made her feel. And that was okay with him as long as she stayed with him."

"So all his attorneys—they go to him, they learn from him, take everything they can, then leave him for bigger and better."

"Yes."

"But that, he doesn't resent."

"Actually, I think he does, but he's never said. The only two people who've ever stuck with him are his wards."

"He has wards?"

"Not in the legal sense, no, but he took care of them like they were his own."

"He never told me that."

"No, he wouldn't have."

"What about the prodigy pundit he's in love with?"

"Justice? I don't know and I don't think he does, either. He fell in love with her three weeks before he was supposed to get married. I don't know how he would've dealt with being married to one woman and in love with another, especially if he happened to be teaching any of her classes during her time there."

Bryce's brow wrinkled and he looked off into the distance, tense, troubled.

"Oh, please don't think badly about him. He feels really guilty about that."

"Um, no," Bryce said slowly, looking down at his plate then, picking at his food. "I don't, it's just— I'm having a lot of empathy for him, but I don't know why." It was Giselle's turn to be confused and Bryce waved a hand. "I lost some of my memory because of the fire or the coma; I don't guess it matters which."

"Oh," she breathed. "I'm sorry."

He shrugged. "Eh. If it's that important, I'll either remember it or it'll come back to bite me in the ass when I least expect it to. It's happened before."

She watched him for a moment. "Tell me about your fire."

He barked a humorless laugh. "I'll get you the trial transcripts."

"I read them already. I want to hear it from you."

"No."

Giselle sucked in a long breath and stared down at her now-empty plate. She felt his hand cover hers.

"Giselle," he breathed as his other hand tucked a stray curl behind her ear, "I can't relive it. I had to once when I was arrested and I had to a second and third time for two juries. I can't do it again. You read my testimony. Please let that be enough."

She swallowed, knowing she would respect that even though it hurt. She nodded and looked up at him, only to have her mouth captured by his with a hot kiss that made her breath catch in her throat. She closed her eyes and plowed her fingers through his hair to bring him closer to her.

The kitchen was silent except for the sound of their kissing, Giselle's gasps and Bryce's low, throaty growls. "I will never get enough of you, Giselle," he whispered against her lips. "I can't imagine living my life without you in it."

"Ditto," she whispered back, then drew away slowly. "But I'm scared. I don't have any real experience with relationships."

"You? Afraid of something?" he asked, caressing her cheek with a crooked finger.

"I'm only here because Sebastian kicked my ass."

She could see the surprise that flickered in Bryce's beautiful eyes. "Kicked your ass?"

"He does that a lot," she returned wryly. "He gets into Fix-or-Raid mode with me and I never get fixed. Just raided."

Bryce burst out laughing and sat back in his chair. "Really."

"Yeah, and Knox agreed with him, so I'm sure Armageddon will happen any day now."

"Remind me to thank them."

"You'll have to do it twice," she muttered. "They also kicked my ass to seek you out in the first place." She speared him with a glance. "So knowing that, are you feeling threatened anymore?"

He continued to chuckle and finally said, "No, guess not." He stood and took her hands, pulled her off the bar stool and enfolded her in his arms. "Let's go get rings and get to the courthouse before it closes."

38: Son of a Preacher Man

SEBASTIAN SMIRKED WHEN GISELLE LED BRYCE INTO THE HOUSE AND SWEPT her with a glance. "Oh, so you're wearing Kenard's clothes now. I'm guessing he ripped yours to shreds." Giselle stuck her tongue out at him and he laughed. "Kenard, come with me. You're useful."

Bryce smirked and followed Sebastian into his office. Finally they finished plotting to take over the world— "Pinky and the Brain," Giselle muttered dryly and Sebastian howled. Then Bryce took her to Tivol.

"That's not really a wedding ring," Bryce pointed out once she'd selected a platinum spiral band inset with diamonds. Three square-cut emeralds lay in a diagonal across the three threads of the spiral.

"It is if I say it is," she returned smartly, then smiled up at him. "Matches your eyes."

The crookedness of his grin told her that pleased him. In response, her soul blossomed with that indescribable joy she had when she looked at him, touched him, knowing he was in love with her, knowing she could make his eyes gleam like that.

"The god of the UMKC School of Law," she breathed.

"What?"

She laughed. "You have no idea how this town sees you, do you?"

"What are you talking about?"

"At school. The litigation professors worship the ground you walk on."

"Whatever."

"I'm serious. And my tribe—Morgan's gonna have an orgasm when he finds out I'm marrying you."

"Morgan?"

"Ashworth."

"The economist? On the short list for Fed chairman when Bernanke retires?"

"Yeah, that one."

He stared at her. "Isn't Ashworth related to Étienne LaMontagne?"

"Yes, the inventor. Our pet name for him is Edison."

Bryce wiped a hand down his face, chuckling in bemusement. "Shit, Giselle. You *do* swim in a sparkling gene pool, don't you? This isn't a marriage; it's a financial and political alliance. And you thought I'd be worried about your taking me for a ride. You should be worried about my motives."

"Pffftt. I'm broke."

"You can't tell me your tribe wouldn't bail you out if you asked."

Giselle hemmed and hawed for a moment, then admitted, "Okay, well, that's true."

"And I'll even bet they've offered and you've refused." A blush crept up her cheeks and he chuckled. "That's what I thought."

Kevin Oakley saw her and Bryce at the courthouse getting their marriage license. After he'd congratulated them and gone back to his office, Bryce muttered, "So besides my motives for marrying your *family*, I'm marrying the model of the most infamous Ford painting yet who happens to have a senator in her pocket."

"I'm not the one funding his campaign," Giselle murmured, coy, and he burst out laughing. "Bryce," she said once he'd handed her into his SUV and climbed into the driver's seat, "I forgot to ask you if there's anyone you'd like at our wedding?"

He shrugged and spoke as he maneuvered through the late Friday afternoon downtown traffic. "Geoff Hale. He's my friend as much as he is my lawyer and I think he'd be offended if I didn't."

She caught her breath. "He hates Knox. He'll fire me when he finds out we're so close."

Bryce cast her a strange glance. "No, he won't," he said slowly, "but you *do* realize you don't have to work now, right?"

Oh! "Um, well, I hadn't really thought about it, no."

He shook his head.

"Okay, but what about your siblings? I mean, I know you said they aren't particularly happy with you and won't like me, but don't you want them to come? Or at least tell them?"

He shrugged. "I don't want them there, no. Besides, they have health issues and neither of them would be able to fly." He paused. "We have nothing in common, nothing to say to each other. They were angry that I didn't go to our parents' funerals until I said, 'Oh, hey, by the way, I was in a coma and my children died and I was arrested for murder and why don't you know that?' Even then, they had a hard time letting go of their assumptions. Being disappointed in me is a habit."

Giselle closed her eyes and shook her head, figuring it didn't matter if people like that liked her or not. *"How* did you come out of a family like that?"

"Don't know, but it was a hard row to hoe. I was always trying to be good, to be Peter Priesthood, but I was too intense, too—"

"Passionate?"

"No. Savage. That's the word Knox used. My father was very mild-mannered, very quiet and unassuming. He didn't understand me but I wanted to please him, wanted to be like him, wanted to live up to Mark's example, step into his shoes. When I was young, sports and school took care of that and all anybody saw was a good kid who excelled. But when I went to UCLA, it started slipping out. I tried to keep a lid on it, but it became harder and harder as Knox kept telling me there was nothing wrong with me. I wanted to believe him, but I didn't, not really. Then I got married and got angry, so add that to intense and savage and—" He shrugged.

"After that, the courtroom took the edge off and I started making my reputation right off the bat. I played a lot of racquetball to work through the rest of it, but nothing was going to cut it significantly enough that I could be comfortable. It helped when I started my own practice because there was so much more to do than I had to do as an employee."

Giselle sighed. "And all anybody saw was a hard-working man with a picture-perfect Mormon family. Did you decide to take a job here to get away from your family? So they couldn't see what was happening to you?"

Bryce didn't answer for a while, then, "Maybe. I never thought about it that way. My dad was proud of me, what I'd accomplished, but it was all in the abstract. I had a good education, good job, married in the temple to someone he thought was a good woman, had kids. I was on my way up the church hierarchy and he figured I'd be a bishop by the time I was thirty-five, like my brother. I was on the fast track and he was very happy with me."

"Did you tell him you were getting divorced?"

"No. He would've been disappointed in me for not trying to make it work. I didn't know what I was going to say, how I was going to explain it once it was done and over with. Mark and Serena still don't know I was getting divorced."

Giselle shook her head, unable to comprehend a bit of that. "I think that's really sad," she whispered, looking out the window then, her mouth tight.

"Giselle," he said, "they're a whole *generation* older than I am. They don't really figure into the way I think about my life, my childhood. When I was in Scotland, I did some genealogy and I found out that I come from a long line of highland warriors. I never made the connection as to why I felt so at odds with my family. I think if I'd understood that in college when Knox was yelling in my ear, it would have been a lot easier for me to accept."

"And the Apache?"

He shrugged. "Don't know, can't find out beyond the fact that there is some on my mother's side. I have to assume I get some of it from that bloodline, too."

Giselle said nothing for a moment and then, "The grandmother I was named after, Celia. She was a privateer in the American Revolution. She reported directly to George Washington."

Bryce looked at her sharply. "Your grand*mother?*"

She nodded. "My grandfather was a pirate. Elliott Raxham, Earl Tavendish. He was lucky to get out of England without hanging."

"*Why* doesn't that surprise me?" He was still laughing once they'd pulled into the driveway behind his house and gone into the back door. He threw his keys on the kitchen counter and pulled her into the living room. He dropped onto a leather sofa, one leg outstretched and one foot on the floor. He indicated that she should snuggle up between his legs and she was only too glad to do so.

"So I'm a savage," he whispered in her ear, melting Giselle completely. "Scot, Apache, whatever, and I'm proud of it. I never thought anything in my life could top how I feel when I go to war, how I felt after I'd had my revenge, accepted that this is who I am. But then I fucked you."

Giselle's body tightened with heat and need. She felt like her chest had collapsed and she couldn't take another breath. His hand swept up her body and cupped her breast through the fabric of the large Oxford shirt she'd snatched out of his closet that morning and hadn't bothered to change. He worked at the shirttails that she'd tied in a knot just under her breasts, all the while kissing, nipping, licking her neck, her collarbone, her shoulder.

"I've fantasized about a woman like you for years—" he rasped as he pulled the knot open and began to work the buttons loose, "—one I could talk to, who could function on my level, autonomous. A woman who didn't manipulate, who was educated and interesting. I wanted a woman who wasn't afraid of me, of what I wanted to take from her—a woman I could fuck, a woman who was nasty. A woman who'd understand my dark side that I fought most of my life until I couldn't anymore."

He had finished opening the shirt and dragged his hand lightly up from the waistband of the jeans shorts she wore—also his—across her belly, to her bra clasp and undid it.

Giselle caught her breath as he cupped her breasts in his hands and flicked her nipples with his thumbs. She dropped her head back on his shoulder and closed her eyes, listening to—*feeling*—his words, his hands on her breasts and his arms wrapped around her and his chest at her back. She sucked in a breath—of desire? of fear that she could fail this man? She didn't know, but he continued,

"One in each hand. Gunshot wounds. Threatening Fen at gunpoint. You have no idea how hard that makes me. I wanted that warrior. I wanted her on her knees in front of me. Sucking. My. Cock."

Bryce continued to lick and suck at her ear, her throat, her chin, her shoulder, her collarbone. Giselle panted and she felt suddenly empty. She gasped over and over again with the adrenaline that coursed through her, hot, loose, and clean.

His breath came short and fast, too. His mouth trailed up her neck and again nestled in her ear.

She couldn't stand the emptiness anymore. She had to feel him inside her, moving, filling her, emptying her, emptying himself inside her. She turned then, rising above him to her knees. She stared down at him, he whose green eyes gleamed as he stared right back at her.

She leaned down and in to kiss him, which he took away from her again to direct and command her. She sucked in a long, sharp breath and broke the kiss, standing to take off the shorts she wore. His large shirt still hung from her shoulders, over the bra that also hung.

"Take off your clothes," she murmured, hard, her own voice commanding. "I want to fuck you, Kenard."

"No," he returned as he swung around until both feet were on the floor. He lifted his hips and ripped open the button fly of his jeans, letting his cock free. She stared at it, at him, wondering what he meant, what he wanted from her.

"You. Get naked," he demanded, fast and harsh. "Me? Not so much."

"No," she snapped. "You get me like this or you don't get me at all."

His eyebrow rose and his mouth twitched, then began to stretch in a smile. Suddenly, he reached out and grabbed her shirttails, jerking her so she fell on top of him, between his legs. He wrapped his hand around the back of her neck, his fingers cradling her head and forcing her to kiss him.

"Climb up here and spread your legs," he muttered against her mouth. "Sit. Down."

She could feel his cock against her belly. She didn't know how much longer she could play this game before she gave in. In this game, winning was losing; losing was winning. She could play it for the rest of her life and not get tired of the uncertainty of winning or losing. This erotic tug-o-war was something she'd never really thought she'd get and she would enjoy every second of it.

"I'll do it when I'm damn good and ready to," she whispered against his mouth and he broke the kiss to laugh.

"You're baiting me."

She raised her eyebrow. "And you like that."

"I'm stronger than you."

"Prove it."

He did. He ran his hands over her shoulders, down her back, until he cradled her buttocks in his big hands. His shoulders bunched under his shirt as he jerked her up and spread her legs. She gasped and bit her lip, closing her eyes when he positioned her, then dropped her on his cock, filling her. Hard. Giselle's head back, she cupped her breasts and panted.

"*Now*," he said, lazing back into the couch and lacing his hands behind his head, his face smug. "You may fuck me."

The feel of his jeans on the tender skin of the inside of her thighs, the visual of his body fully clothed and hers nearly naked—it was almost enough to make her come, but she wasn't interested in moving. She just wanted to feel him filling her, stretching her. She rocked a little bit, ground a little bit, but apparently it wasn't enough to satisfy him.

"Giselle," he said warningly, "move."

"I decided," she said between breaths, between her rocking and grinding, "to fuck myself *on* you."

That was when he grasped her hips, sat up and stood all in a flash, forcing her to wrap her legs around his hips and her arms around his neck, or fall. In three strides he had her against a smooth wall, her head thumping back against the plaster, one hand cupping her buttocks, the other wrapped around her wrists, pinning them to the wall far above her head.

She came with his first thrust and matched him in every one thereafter until he came, hard, inside her and filled her the way she wanted to be filled.

"I guess," he said as he kissed her jaw and neck between breaths, letting go of her wrists, "that'll teach you to sass back at me."

Giselle chuckled. "Yes, I intend to do more of that."

He laughed then, a great, rolling laugh that made him move inside her. She came again unexpectedly and she clung to him, crying out, as he laughed and laughed.

"Keep fighting me, Giselle. Keep fighting me."

39: The Strength in Your Hands

RYCE HAD ARISEN BEFORE SHE AWOKE. SHE SMILED AS SHE GRABBED HIS pillow and sniffed deeply. Once she had showered and dressed, she went downstairs to find him.

She couldn't and the house was quiet. Then she heard water running, possibly from a garden hose, and the sounds of squishing and metal on metal. She followed it out the back door to the long veranda and saw Bryce, clad in short denim shorts and steel-toed boots, most of his body exposed. His back to her, he mixed mortar in a wheelbarrow with a hoe. Nearby were two pallets of flat stones.

The muscles of his back and arms bunched and unbunched under all those beautiful battle wounds. So. He was a stonemason in his free time. She leaned against the column of the porch, her arms crossed, and just watched him work.

He never turned around, never saw her watching him while he worked the cement and sand and water, and she wondered if he used this to exorcise some demons or frustrations. Troubled then, as if she had peeped at something private, she went back into the house to see what she could see and make herself useful.

She knew he had lemons because she'd made the hollandaise sauce with juice she'd squeezed. She found some strawberries to puree and use as sweetener. They'd sweeten it enough for her, but probably not enough for Bryce, so she poured a quart of the lemonade for herself, then dumped a cupful of sugar into his jar and hoped she'd estimated well enough.

When she finally went outside with the glasses, she saw him scoop mortar with a trowel, having begun his project while she'd made the lemonade. He barely glanced up at her before finishing his first course. She sat down on the top step of the porch and sipped her lemonade, watching him heft stone with one hand, slap mortar on it with the other, set precisely, and then tap gently, patiently, until satisfied it lay perfectly.

No wonder his hands were so rough, so calloused. No wonder he could lift her so easily and put her wherever he wanted her.

Her arousal crept up on her as she watched him twist and lift, set and level stone. She studied his hips and his ass and the outline of his cock where it nestled in his groin, all covered by a mere scrap of very tight, very revealing denim. She took a long look at his musclebound legs that disappeared into white socks, then the brown high-top boots. She sighed when she thought of what that body could do to her and had done to her and what more she'd like for it to do to her. What she wanted to do to it. She couldn't stop staring.

He was beautiful. And he was hers.

Now, for the first time, she actually studied how much of his body was burnt, scarred, and grafted over. She couldn't imagine what kind of physical pain he'd suffered, much less heartache over the loss of his family and the legal battles that had loomed in front of him at the time.

She remembered the transcripts she'd read, the criminal trial of the electrical contractor whose work could most generously be described as shoddy and the city codes officer who'd passed the wiring—for a price. He had recounted every excruciating, horrifying detail for two juries.

How he had pulled three of his four children out of his burning house, one dying in his arms from smoke inhalation and the other two just days from death. How his oldest child, Emme, had preceded him out and had fallen through the floor just in front of him. How it had taken him every ounce of strength to keep himself and his beloved cargo from falling into the same hole and to find another way out. How his wife had died somewhere else in the house. How he had been discharged from the hospital a year later, about as perfect as they could make him, then arrested and charged with arson and five counts of first-degree murder.

"What are you thinking about?" he asked quietly, shaking her out of her reverie. He stood at the foot of the stairs, one hand holding a trowel and the other wiping the sweat off his mouth.

"You. Your body. Your fire."

He grimaced as he climbed up the stairs and swung himself around and down to sit beside her. He picked up the glass meant for him and chugged most of it. "Thank you."

"Too sweet?"

"Mmmm, coulda used a little more sugar."

"I have a hard time gauging that. I haven't consciously had refined sugar in five years."

"What about all that chocolate you licked off my cock?"

"Food consumed during sex doesn't count. Everybody knows this."

"Oh *really?*"

"Yes, besides, all that protein I swallowed canceled it out, like pizza and diet Coke." He burst out laughing then and she smirked, happy that he was happy. "You didn't tell me you worked stone," she said once he'd calmed a bit.

He shrugged. "Physical therapy. Plus, it's the only thing my dad and I did together that we both enjoyed. It's something of him I can hold onto."

"You really loved him."

"Yes. He was kind and gentle with everyone. He was very proper. I don't think I ever heard him raise his voice or curse. My dad was the perfect example of what a Mormon man is supposed to strive to be. Everyone loved him. Somewhere in my gut, I always knew I was never going to be anything like him, but I tried."

"Knox said you were a very good father."

"It's different with your kids. They're small, helpless. The only thing I knew I'd do different from my dad was not to expect them to be someone they weren't."

Giselle said nothing for a long while and neither did he. "You know, good LDS men come in a lot of different personalities. Take my bishop, for instance. He owns a construction company and he's kind of rough and gruff. He and I have very, ah, *interesting* conversations at times."

Bryce slid her a look. "About what?"

"Um, well, I have a tendency to say what I think, which occasionally doesn't go over well with a few people in the ward and they complain. He tells me I need to stop ruffling people's feathers, but then he asks me what I actually said to ruffle those feathers and that's when the theological games begin."

"Uh oh."

"Exactly. He can be a real hard ass. At least, he is with me sometimes. Now, maybe it's just because it's me that he doesn't see a need to go the kind'n'gentle route. But he doesn't do kid gloves very well even when he should. He hurts a few feelings himself occasionally."

Bryce pursed his lips and then said, slowly, "I've never met a bishop who could be classified as a hard ass."

"Takes all kinds. That's my point."

"I just can't visualize that. My dad, he— He wouldn't have approved of a bishop like that."

"Bryce," she said hesitantly, "are you really okay with this? With us not being married first?"

"I *wanted* it this way, Giselle. Are you having regrets?"

"No, but you seemed so wistful about your dad that I wanted to check and make sure."

"What would your bishop say about us?"

She sat for a moment, quiet, her mouth pursed. "Well, he knows me and he knows how much I've struggled being single and attempting to be chaste—and for how long. He knows how many other women in the church have the same problem. And before you and I had sex, I never thought about how much *worse* it must be for the divorced women and the widows." She paused. "So, yeah. For all he jumps down my throat for spewing unpopular opinions, he'd understand. He wouldn't like it, naturally, and the hard ass in him would feel obliged to mete out some punishment, but he'd understand."

Bryce glanced at her then. "He would? Really?"

She nodded. "Yes."

"But would he understand your porn collection?"

Giselle gasped and shoved at him when he laughed at her. "Cut that out. It's not porn. It's *literature* that happens to be a little erotic."

"Uh huh. He doesn't know, does he?"

She flushed and buried her face in her drawn knees when he laughed so hard he started to cough. Once he'd calmed a bit, he tugged at her until she looked at him. He smirked at the smile she worked to contain, but couldn't. "I love teasing you. Would you and your *literature* move in with me some time today or tomorrow?" His amusement seeped away until only intensity remained. "I need you here with me, not just in my bed, but here, all around. Your clothes, your jewelry, your perfume, your stuff. Your presence. I need to know you want to be with me, that you want this to be your home. I feel like if you go home, you won't come back, that this was all a dream. Please," he added, as if it pained him to say it, as if he hated begging but would do so if only she would stay. The pleading and pain and need had grown evident in his face.

Giselle saw the man inside the warrior, who needed her, who still ached and bled, no matter his protestations to the contrary. She laid her palm atop the scars of his face and caressed him. "You hurt."

He hesitated. "Sometimes."

She needed to know. "Were you hoping I could heal you?"

"I don't know. Maybe."

"I can't heal your pain, Bryce," she whispered. "I can only promise that I'll do my best to make you happy in the here and now, in the future. I can't take away what's done, but I will listen when you need to talk and I'll snuggle with you when you hurt. That's all I can promise you."

"That's enough." He paused. "Giselle? What can I give you?"

"Talk to me," she murmured. "Tell me what happened to you. Trust me. Please."

He took a deep breath, held it, then nodded as he released it in a long whoosh. "Give me a few days, okay?"

She nodded and they met in the middle, but it wasn't a kiss of desire or arousal. It was a kiss of understanding, of shared burdens and ended as quietly as it had begun. Bryce wrapped his arm around her shoulders to pull her close in. They stayed that way for what seemed hours, but the sun only marked about an hour, if that.

"Your mortar's drying," she murmured.

"I can mix more."

"Tell me about the piano."

"Physical therapy, like the stone work. If I miss even a day, my left hand gets stiff and numb."

"You missed a couple of days when you were with me."

He laughed. "I was doing other things with my hands, in case you weren't paying attention. That was just as effective."

Giselle blushed—*again*—which made him laugh even harder, and he kissed the tip of her nose. "I love that you blush so easily."

"Shut up," she muttered and he chuckled. "When did you start playing?"

He hesitated a moment, thinking. "Maybe, I don't know, five or six? It was my mother's dream that she'd have one child who played. That was the only area where I outshone my siblings. I played a lot of jazz improv in high school, got away from it in college. When my therapist found out I could play, she thought it would be the best thing for me, so I bought a piano. She was right."

"What's your favorite?"

"Anything that requires a very long hand span."

"Will you play for me?"

"Tonight, when I usually do. Question," Bryce said slowly. "You said you didn't have enough money to reopen your bookstore. Is that something you still might want?"

She hesitated a moment because not a day had gone by that she didn't want it, but . . .

"I don't think so," she replied slowly. "That's done and past. I wouldn't do it without Maisy and Coco anyway—and I don't think they'd be up to starting over. It'd be like trying to get back together with an ex-boyfriend, where it never quite works right. And I didn't spend the last five years and oodles of money just to go down the first rabbit trail that looks interesting simply because I can now."

They were silent for a while, then, "When do you graduate?"

"May."

"I want to take you on a honeymoon. Do you have anyplace special you'd like to go?"

"Paris," she said without hesitation or thought. "I'd like to see it with my lover, not my brother."

"Mmmm, that can be arranged. I talked to Hale this morning while you were asleep. He wants to move you into practicing when you're done with law school."

She started. "He does?"

Bryce nodded.

"Oh, I'd *love* that. He's been really good to me. I didn't want to know what he'd say or do if he found out about Knox."

Bryce shrugged. "He likes you and he thinks you have a lot of potential as a trial lawyer. He's not the type to cut off his nose to spite his face and he's been planning to offer you a position for the last three years."

More warmth. More fuzzies. Giselle hadn't ever been this happy, this contented.

He said nothing for a long while and Giselle could tell he chewed on something big. "I've been kicking around an idea for a while that I hope you— Well, that you might be interested in," he said slowly. When she said nothing, he went on after drawing a deep breath.

"I'd like to build a foundation for burn victims, to give them the resources they need from, oh, a place to stay for however long they need it, medical care, therapy, further convalescence, money, legal help, plastic surgery. Pretty much a one-stop-shopping experience for burn victims once they're discharged from the hospital— all the things I needed to rebuild my body and my life that I didn't have and had to spend time coordinating once I found them. Say you get discharged from the hospital with nowhere to go and the hospital sends you straight to me. I give you a place to stay and put you back on your feet. Or, say, you're in the hospital and your family needs a place to stay, legal, financial help, whatever. You come to me. And when you run into trouble down the road, you can come back for whatever help you need."

Giselle pulled away from him and looked at him in awe, again feeling that joy that had nothing to do with desire. "I think that's wonderful," she said.

He started. "Really?"

"Absolutely."

His brow wrinkled. "I hadn't articulated it yet. You're the first person I've told."

She sucked in a sharp little breath and felt a smile split her face.

Bryce looked at her then and said, "What?"

"You gave me your idea before you gave it to anyone else. That— It's a gift."

"Not as precious a gift as your virginity."

"Yes, it is."

He didn't smile. "I didn't choose you for my mate, Giselle," he murmured, tracing her jaw with a finger. " You chose me, and I'm honored and grateful for that."

40: Three Kings

I TAKE IT YOU'RE GONNA WANT YOUR SECURITY DEPOSIT BACK?"
Bryce heard Sebastian Taight's bellow when he followed Giselle into her house
the next evening. "If you're giving money out, I'll take it," Giselle hollered back.
"You know how poor I am."

She led him down the corridor by the hand, then up the stairs to the conference
room platform. Beyond that lay an expanse of living room he hadn't seen before.

"There was a wall here Friday, wasn't there?"

"It's retractable," Giselle said. "We usually keep it closed."

Sebastian and Knox sat watching a Chiefs exhibition game, Knox on the sofa and
Sebastian in a club chair, both with their feet up on the coffee table. Knox ate cheese
popcorn from a large tin and had a gallon jug of orange juice on the table between his
feet.

Sebastian, a bottle of wine in one hand, attempted to read but kept getting
distracted by the plays. Neither looked up or around.

"Here," she said, letting go of Bryce. "You're my mate, so you're officially part of
the pack now."

"Aren't you supposed to be at work?" Sebastian called after her as she disappeared into her bedroom.

"No, Mom. I got the day off."

Bryce sat in the club chair opposite Sebastian.

Knox passed him the popcorn, looked straight at him, and said, "You *are* going to
marry her, right?"

"Friday. Two o'clock. Jackson County Courthouse."

They both stared at him. Simultaneously they said,

"No bishop?"

"No big wedding?"

Bryce shook his head. "Nope. She didn't want anybody but you guys, her mother and aunt, and a judge. Oh, and Geoff Hale."

"Great," Sebastian and Knox muttered at the same time.

"Uh, problem with Hale?"

"Hale hates me," Knox said, "which you know and I don't know what he's going to do to Giselle when he finds out she's my cousin—"

"Eh, I gave him the rundown and smoothed it all out."

Knox started.

"Chill. It wasn't anything he hadn't already suspected."

"My problem," Sebastian volunteered, "is my mother. I'm going to get my ass kicked for being the major contributor to Giselle's delinquency because nothing is ever *her* fault."

Bryce looked at him speculatively, his eyebrow raised. "You're what, forty? And your mother still kicks your ass?"

"She taught me everything I know about money, so I figure it's only right to let her amuse herself at my expense."

"Really?"

"Yup. She's one sharp cookie. Actually, that whole batch of Dunham girls—all nine of them—brilliant. Grew up poor as church mice, but Grandpa Dunham made damned sure they were educated."

Knox demurred. "My mom . . . not so smart."

"Yes, she is," Sebastian returned. "*Your* mother is an amoral bitch."

"True."

Bryce ditched any vestige of etiquette to indulge his curiosity. "'Taight. What makes you decide to fix or raid?"

Knox barked a laugh. "You would ask that right off the bat."

Sebastian grinned. "Trade secret."

"Knox, do you know?"

"Whether I do or not, you can file that under attorney-client privilege."

"Of course," Bryce said sarcastically.

"I do a few things that could be construed as, ah, slightly shady," Sebastian said, "and I need Knox to tell me if I'm venturing into felony territory. As for the Fix-or-Raid policy, I have very stringent criteria, but if everybody knew what it was, the whole exercise would be pointless."

"Go on."

"Basically, I won't let a badly run business stay in business even if that means I take a loss—that's what's got everybody up in arms and might still get me into some serious trouble if Kevin doesn't beat Fen. Congress is pissed because they can't figure out how I decide. I'm not sure how they intend to use that information, but I know it'll be bad for me and my cronies, and I'll go to jail before I give it up to that pack of looters."

"Businesses fail all the time and if they were already on the rocks . . ."

"It starts getting iffy when you get things like pensions involved," Knox offered. "There's always the people who end up getting laid off. They might have kept their jobs another year if he hadn't been called in, but by that time, the leadership's digging into the pensions anyway."

Bryce nodded. "So it just looks bad."

"Yeah," Knox said. "It doesn't matter that Sebastian's innocent of anything they can charge him with, he's still going to end up on the hot seat if there are enough congress-critters who have a vested interested in seeing him there."

"Even if I told them, they wouldn't get it and they sure as shit wouldn't be able to duplicate it," Sebastian added. "It all depends on a company's leadership. They have to be teachable. They have to be able to figure out what it is they've done wrong on their own, though I'm massaging things in the background."

"Then they think you just stood around and watched."

"Hell, I don't care. They have to learn and be willing to do things differently. If I can see that they're not going to come to this epiphany on their own, I give them a detailed list of what's wrong and how to fix it. If they don't get it after that or they refuse to do what I tell them to do, I take it. I give them about a year, maybe two at the outside. Hold off their creditors, give them room. I want a solution that lasts and that's how I get it."

"So what about Jep Industries? That went down in a month."

"Oh, I'm not going to fuck around with bullshit like that. I knew the pensions were in deep trouble and I wasn't going to wait for Oth's light bulb to come on before I shut it all down to get the employees out with their funds. So I threatened to get the feds on Oth's books if he didn't hand it over to me for the price of its debt. He would've been indicted because everything was set up to point to him, but I knew he wasn't smart enough to pull off something that complex. He knew it, too, so he took the deal."

"What about the dependent businesses?"

"Mitch Hollander— You know who he is?"

"CEO of Hollander Steelworks?"

"Same. My best friend. He would have gone belly up without Jep's products, so he bought it from me after I'd dismantled it to the ground. He assimilated it into his operation piece by piece, including employees. So now he supplies Jep's products to the other businesses that need them."

Knox snorted. "*Except* for OKH. Turns out Fen decided to run for Senate after Mitch refused to do business with him. Another stake in OKH's heart, because Fen needs Jep's products, too, just not as badly as everyone else. Fen can work around it, but not easily."

"Fen would've taken Jep over if I'd given him half a chance; he was in a helluva lot better position to do it than Mitch was."

"I never heard about any of that."

"Yeah, that's because we kept it quiet. Mitch is squeaky clean and I didn't want Oth to start taking jabs at him like he takes at me."

Knox waved a hand. "It won't stay quiet for much longer now that Oth's having to account for himself. The press will follow that."

"Oth's only real crime is that he's a self-entitled old-money idiot and it serves him right to have to start answering questions about why he'd called me in the first place. I'm not going to let arrogant fucks like him make me their whipping boy."

Bryce looked at Knox then. "Speaking of whipping boys . . ."

"Don't," Knox snapped.

But he did. He always had. "*Why* would you open your mouth about Tom Parley to your bishop?"

Knox sucked in a sharp breath, his jaw grinding. "I notice you didn't ask me why I did it," he finally muttered.

Bryce raised an eyebrow.

Knox shrugged and looked away. "I was stupid. Idealistic. Believed in the system."

"Do you regret it?"

"No," Knox returned, swift and sure. "Too many lives at stake. I wouldn't have been able to live with myself if he'd killed one more person. Justice at all costs."

Bryce remained silent for a moment, then murmured, "You should never have been let near that case. You were too green."

"Arrogance of youth. Thought, 'No problem.'"

"He didn't go to the bishop voluntarily, you know," Sebastian offered. "He was called in during the investigation and asked point blank. He went in thinking the bishop would find it justified, but . . ."

"Shit, it was a done deal before I got there, so I kept my mouth shut."

"They should've gone along with the government's party line and called it good," Sebastian said and Bryce couldn't disagree.

He'd sat in the gallery watching as, each day, the fun-loving surfer he'd always known got chipped away and the ruthless and corrupt Chouteau County prosecutor had emerged—trying a serial killer who'd won acquittal on a technicality.

Sebastian pointed at Knox and said, "But since that made him untouchable *and* he was no longer accountable to his bishop, he decided to go off the rails. Exhibit A: Claude Nocek ousted at gunpoint."

Knox shrugged.

"Exhibit B: Leah Wincott blackmailed into bed."

Knox curled his lip, but didn't dispute it, his face betraying guilt. "Yeah, okay, I went off the rails. I'd been hung for the sheep, so I figured the Lord wasn't going to begrudge me a few lambs. At least I haven't sunk to Sebastian's level of promiscuity."

"Let's see," Sebastian drawled. "Fucking a lot of women. Killing and blackmailing people. Somehow not getting the sex-is-worse-than-violence concept."

Knox harrumphed.

"I have no guilt," Sebastian muttered as he took a sip of his wine. "I like being a manwhore."

Bryce pointed to the wine, a definite sign a church member had gone astray. "What's your story?"

"Don't have one," Sebastian said. "I just got tired of the mission field bullshit. The pecking order, the poor kids being treated like crap. Kids being sent on missions to straighten them out. Half my companions went out carousing, leaving me to work and calling it teamwork. I figured I didn't need that kind of teamwork." He pointed at Bryce. "You know exactly what I'm talking about."

Bryce nodded. "Yup."

"Didn't like having to rely on members for meals. For some reason I don't know, everybody in the mission assumed I was poor and being supported by the church, so I was at the bottom of the totem pole. Nobody thought to ask why I—and any companion I was with at the time—ate better than everyone else and always had money for the subway. I didn't bother telling anyone that I was paying for my mission out of the interest I earned on my margin account in Paris and that I had immediate access to unlimited funds and it wasn't daddy's money, for sure.

"My breaking point came when I had this one companion—super good kid, hard worker, true believer. He really was poor and being supported by the church. By the time he got put with me, he was a basket case. Being with me was a respite for him, but it only postponed the inevitable and his next companion sent him over the edge."

"Went home early?"

Sebastian nodded. "Medical. His stomach ate itself. Nine months in, I decided I'd had enough. Called my mom, told her I was done and to wire the rest of my assets into my European accounts because I was staying for the foreseeable future.

She was pissed. Packed up, left the apartment without a word, went straight to St.-Germain and found a bedsit, dumped what I wanted to keep, mailed the rest home. Went to Spain and fell in with a bunch of degenerate bullfighters."

"In fact," Knox said, "that guy who went home? Mitch Hollander."

Sebastian nodded. "He's still active in the church; in fact, he's a bishop. And his wife's dying. No matter what happens to him, he *still* believes." He looked at Bryce then. "What about your mission?"

"I was somewhere in the middle most of it," Bryce said after he thought a while. "I wasn't the low man on the totem pole, but I was never going to be a favorite."

Knox started. "Your dad was a stake president. You should've been ruling the roost."

Bryce grimaced. "We had our share of slackers and partiers who were all too willing to fall in with the village girls. I ended up kicking a lot of ass, which pretty much shit-canned whatever advantage I'd get because of how far up my dad was in the church hierarchy." He looked at Knox. "Did you ever find out why Fen wouldn't let you go on a mission?"

"He didn't want me to spend too much time sucking up doctrine like philosophical manna."

"Which you do anyway."

Knox threw up a hand.

"So, Kenard," Sebastian said warily, "now, uh— Giselle— That was a complete one-eighty for you. You're just out of the church altogether?"

Bryce pursed his lips. "Yeah. I'm done."

Knox studied him for a moment. "What, you just woke up one day and decided you didn't believe in it anymore?"

Bryce said nothing, unable to answer that because he didn't know exactly when he'd noticed that his faith left.

"*The Miracle of Forgiveness* isn't doctrine. I thought you'd have gotten over that by now."

Bryce swallowed at Knox's statement, one he'd made countless times in the four years they'd lived together—the one that had earned Knox the hatred of Bryce's father. *The Miracle of Forgiveness*: Almost three hundred pages of every 'thou shalt not' ever imagined, written by a church leader William Kenard had idolized. Bryce could recite the list of sins major and minor in his sleep, and had felt the fires of hell reaching up out of the floor to punish him for committing them, even if only in thought.

"But apparently you didn't get over it. So instead of rethinking one man's puritanical rant, you decided to dump the church altogether? You know," he went on, "I'm not going to argue the fact that the church has a lot to apologize for. It does, and that book's one of them because it's done a lot of damage over the years. It just has no bearing on what the Lord's really about."

Bryce wished he could believe that, now more than ever, but he didn't. He had the scars to prove what the Lord was really about.

"So I guess that means you don't care that you broke your temple covenants," Sebastian said finally.

"The Lord broke that agreement first, so, no, I didn't feel obliged to keep up my end of it. And look, I got what I wanted, so what am I supposed to conclude?"

"Oh, shit," Knox murmured with not a little shock. "That's— Whoa. The *Lord* didn't do anything of the sort. *You* wouldn't follow your instincts and *you* fucked up and *you* compounded that by not kicking that bitch's ass to the curb as soon as possible. How long did it take you to figure out I was right? A month, maybe?"

Bryce reacted like he always had when Knox challenged him and he didn't like it, but Knox saw it and pointed at him when Bryce opened his mouth. "Shut the fuck up," he barked. "Answer this: Do you like who you are *now*? Who you've become since the fire?"

He glared at Knox, who glared right back at him until his anger dissipated when he began to understand. "Yeah," he finally murmured. "Yeah, I do."

"You've *always* liked women like Giselle. Fact of life: You'd be lucky to get her to flip you off if you weren't who you are right now. So think about that when you're getting all bitter about what the Lord did or didn't do."

"My kids—"

"You know where they are," he snapped, "and you know they're happy and well cared for. They don't have to stumble through life getting battered and bruised and roughed up and *their* salvation is assured."

Bryce's jaw ground, because Knox was right—as usual—and he hated that.

"Yeah, that's what I thought," Knox said. "You didn't stop believing. You just got tired of that list of bullshit rules your dad pounded into you."

"I want to know something," said Sebastian after a tense moment of silence. "Have you two always communicated like you're about to blow each others' heads off?"

"Yes," Bryce and Knox said at the same time.

"And you managed to live together for four years without killing each other."

"Yes," they again said in unison.

Bryce said nothing for a moment, then said, low, "Knox was the only person who'd tell me the truth whether I wanted to hear it or not."

Sebastian looked at Knox expectantly, who dropped his head back on the sofa.

"And Bryce was the only one who thought I surfed well enough to get endorsements and then kicked my ass until I got a few."

Bryce grunted. "You never gave yourself enough credit for being able to succeed at anything doing it the easy way."

"And *you* never gave yourself enough credit for being a good guy without feeling compelled to attain perfection by the end of the week."

Sebastian looked between them, then said, "Huh. Well. Kenard, I want to give you *Rape of a Virgin* for a wedding present."

Bryce, shocked, took a deep breath and swallowed. Hard.

Kindnesses from Giselle's ruthless family. Knox he'd known for almost twenty years, but never really understood how he ticked until now.

Now, almost twenty years of hardship behind him, he wasn't intimidated by Knox's strength; he wasn't jealous of Knox's conviction of who he really was; he wasn't stymied by Knox's ability to go to church and study doctrine, ignoring culture and tradition, uncaring what anybody thought of him. Bryce would never pass judgment on the choices Knox had made because Knox had always been courageous in seeking truth and justice, and Bryce had had to be backed into a corner to find his courage.

Now, almost twenty years of hardship behind him, he was comfortable with himself, with how he'd evolved. This group of people—this woman, these men, their tribe—were his people. Now that he knew who he was, he could relate to them and they could relate to him. These people wouldn't leave him to deal with his dark soul alone.

Once my tribe finds out the Bryce Kenard is about to be assimilated, you'll be welcomed like a conquering hero.

"Thank you," Bryce finally said, his chest so tight with gratitude and humility he couldn't express it.

Giselle finally came out of her bedroom and went into the kitchen after putting another box on the pile outside her door. Bryce watched her as she stopped to glance at mail, look in the fridge, get something to drink, and do the regular things a million other people do around their homes. And tonight, she'd be doing those things in his home, their home—sifting through the mail, digging in the fridge, pouring a glass of water or that . . . pink stuff.

He swallowed at her beauty, and for only the second time he realized how small she was. Five feet and five inches of explosive strength and overwhelming spirit and will that he could tuck under his chin. One hundred sixty pounds of solid muscle (and enough padding where it counted) packed into that little body that looked like one-twenty-five dripping wet.

White shorts that didn't hide the gash in her thigh. Sunny yellow bikini top that showed her scars. Gun stuck in the waistband at her back, which she finally remembered was there and put on the kitchen counter. Ponytail with a white ribbon. Plain white canvas tennis shoes. Not a speck of makeup; not a hint of jewelry except the ring she'd chosen.

To match your eyes.

Soft, patrician face. Fair skin. Barely-there freckles. She finished her tasks and skipped down into the living room. Bryce sat up so she could sit on his lap.

"Why are you guys so melancholy?"

Nobody had an answer for that and Sebastian got up to go to his office. Giselle huffed and snuggled into Bryce, wrapped herself around him and pressed her lips to his cheek. He'd never had this; never had a woman simply . . . love on him, snuggle him, touch him just because, without wanting something from him.

He wrapped his arms around her and looked at her, enjoying her spark, her nearness. She smiled at him for absolutely no reason he could fathom, as if he'd brought down the heavens and gift wrapped them for her, which he would if he could.

Sebastian came back soon enough and slid a printout and a brand new checkbook in between Bryce's nose and Giselle's. "That's for you, Giz."

Giselle took it, read it, then what little color she had dropped. "Sebastian, what—?"

Sebastian went to his chair and plopped in it. "You paid rent for five years. I figured it was better served in investments. That's your principal plus interest."

"But—"

"Suck it up, princess. I asked you to pay rent because I wanted you to save. You wouldn't take any help and you would've spent every last dime you earned paying off your bankruptcy. You'd have been out of debt but no better off when you were finished—and you were bankrupted because of the OKH proviso. It's a miracle you didn't die in that fire." Bryce felt his gut tighten and his breath come short. Apparently, no one noticed and for that, he was glad. "Hell, it was a miracle you survived your shooting. I've tried to take care of you since your father got sick and now I won't anymore. So, there's your dowry, so to speak. You've more than earned it."

Once he'd caught his breath again, Bryce got a glimpse of the statement and his eyebrow rose. "Maybe I should let you do my investing," he muttered.

"He takes a hefty fee," Knox said. "Ask me how I know."

Sebastian slid Knox a look. "Your operation's so complex I can barely follow it. I earn every penny of that and more, so shut up before I raise it." He gestured toward Giselle. "I mostly put her into art. She's owned a lot of nice pieces over the years and she still has quite a collection. Let me know if you want to hang any of it."

"Thank you, Sebastian," she whispered.

Sebastian smiled, and Bryce could see the love and pride of an older brother in his face, and it warmed his heart on her behalf. *How* could he ever have mistaken Sebastian for Giselle's lover?

Bryce looked up at her and saw tears running down her cheeks. He brushed them away gently with the pads of his thumbs. She gave him a watery but happy smile and curled up into his body.

He could get used to this. Nothing sexual about it; just warm, loving, good-smelling woman sitting in his lap, lying against his chest. In love. With him.

After a while, Giselle said, "I need to show you the Den of Iniquity."

Knox burst out laughing, but Sebastian lost all softness and growled, "Oh, no you don't."

Bryce stared between them all, intrigued. "Den of Iniquity?" he asked slowly.

"I just want to *show* him," Giselle protested.

"No," Sebastian snapped. "Not happening. He takes one look at that and your DNA will end up all over my bed."

"Oh, please. Six forensics labs couldn't sort out how much DNA is in that bed. They only wouldn't find *yours*."

Knox was laughing so hard he began to cough.

"So help me, Goldilocks, if I find out you've been fucking in my bed—"

"Knox has."

Knox choked. "Giselle!"

Sebastian's jaw ground as he slowly turned his gaze on Knox. "Is that true?"

"I don't remember," Knox said blithely, unsuccessfully trying to keep a straight face, and Bryce laughed.

"Sebastian's going to Italy next week," Giselle whispered in Bryce's ear while Sebastian glared between them. "I'll show you then."

"And if you think I'm not going to change the door codes when I go to Italy next week, you've got another think coming."

"He won't change them," she whispered. "He'll forget."

Sebastian began to rant at Knox, who smirked and let him do so, flinging back barbs that hit their targets a little too often. Under all that, Giselle murmured, "I don't have much and it's in the hallway. Can you help me—?"

He would do anything for her; everything for her. And once he got her boxes and bags loaded in the SUV, he felt suddenly light, as if a great weight had been lifted off his shoulders that he hadn't ever known he carried.

41: First, Dust

SEBASTIAN SAT AT THE MASSIVE TABLE IN EILIS'S HUGE CONFERENCE ROOM directly across from Eilis's private office. The officers and tier two executives, the contract employees, were gathered around the table as Eilis gave a brief summation of Sebastian Taight's presence, though everyone already knew. They were nervous but confident that even if they were on the block, they had their golden parachutes.

He had to admit that after all his silent bitching, her Jackie O. persona was a particularly effective weapon and he wouldn't have believed it if he hadn't seen it.

She spoke at the same volume all the time—loudly enough that people toward the front heard well and softly enough that it forced people in the back to be very quiet and pay attention. She had her inflections down to a science. Not monotone enough to bore; not dramatic enough to be a caricature.

Her costume, as badly fitting and unattractive as it was, and in such a bad color as usual, allowed her to blend in with the background. Only her luscious fuck-me voice (was he the only one who noticed this?) and her very well-prepared presentations carried her business deals. She always anticipated every question so that she didn't have to answer any. She left *nothing* to chance. She made sure no one could think of any questions or raise any objections she hadn't already thought of and prepared for. She had an answer, an option, an alternative, or a workaround solution to every conceivable nasty situation.

She was about six steps ahead of the game, especially if it was her game.

Of *course* she didn't understand ADD. She was an analyst, a preparer. She did *not* improvise. She didn't fly by the seat of her pants and she wouldn't put herself in any situation where it might be required of her. She looked at things from every angle, she planned everything down to the most minute of details of each of those angles, and internalized her plan so deeply that it became part of her soul.

Friday, he'd shared with her Knox's reasoning for her ability to rescue her employees' pensions, and that her marriage to David was necessary: It was fate, inspiration, karma, divine intervention, whatever she wanted to call it. Serendipity had saved her company; what would surely have been an otherwise very foolhardy decision made in the face of a national trauma had turned out to be the deliverance of two hundred and fifty people's savings.

Eilis could never have saved all those 401(k) accounts if she hadn't lived with Webster, found his stray doodlings, watched him, caught his little slips, stayed with him long enough to find and fix what he had done to her employees.

But she didn't buy his explanation; it didn't fit into her paradigm. On the other hand, no one else believed him, either. He could talk until he was blue in the face about the good things, things he could work with, but people only saw the bad. He supposed that was a human condition and Eilis was no more or less human than any other business owner who was in trouble they couldn't climb out of alone.

Sebastian started when his Blackberry began to vibrate: **SEC APPV 6% BUY DONE**

"Thank you, Jack," he muttered under his breath, then almost smiled when the numbers flashed at him. Fen was going to shit a gold-plated brick when he got the SEC's paperwork granting one Bryce D. Kenard approval to purchase six percent of OKH stock.

Sebastian didn't know who had hated whom first, but Sebastian's instincts about Fen had borne fruit over the years. He would've moved in on OKH Enterprises long ago just to crush Fen if he'd known how Knox had dreaded taking it over all these years, and Sebastian had to admire Knox for knowing his limitations. He was no kind of manager, that was for sure. He didn't manage his prosecutors; his executive AP did that. He didn't manage the inn he half owned; his business partner did that.

Given that the SEC had spanked Sebastian and sent him to his room, he'd had to recruit another partner in crime to keep the OKH stock plunging. Fortunately, Kenard had been all too willing to play a little tag-team chess. Sebastian couldn't be happier that the man had fallen in with their war and would be thoroughly assimilated into the tribe by the time he became a Dunham on Friday.

"Sebastian will now present the first step in our reorganization."

Eilis thought he wasn't paying attention, which was true, but he'd sat in too many of these types of meetings not to know his own drill. He stood and looked over the table filled with people who looked arrogant and smug in their own indispensability. They thought they knew his reputation, but they also believed that whether they stayed or went, they'd be just fine.

Heh.

He stood silent, looking at each individual, examining them, assessing them one by one until they'd lost that smug edge and began to squirm. He did this every single time, with every single company he salvaged. It shifted the power a little more his way at a time he needed every ounce of his reputation for ruthlessness. He cocked his eyebrow, which he knew made him look positively satanic.

It was time to clean house and Eilis was present and accounted for. He had to give her a lot of credit for that, especially since she did care about her people.

Sebastian looked at one man in particular. "Jason Hearst." That man shifted in his seat nervously, suspecting what was about to hit him yet confident in his severance package.

"You're vice president in charge of product development, right?"

"Yes."

"Tell me something. When you're in charge of developing products, how do you go about actually developing those products?"

Sebastian waited patiently until Jason's miserable speech filled with corporate doublespeak bullshit jargon was over, then he said, "Okay. What products have you developed in the last five years?"

"The screening tests."

"Wrong. That pre-dates you. Try again."

He flushed a bit, his confidence taken down a notch. "The check printing module of the HRP Full Management System software."

"And how much direction did that, ah, project require from you?"

His face flooded completely then. Sebastian could feel Eilis getting squeamish and he didn't care. She'd always needed someone who could clean her house for her because, for whatever reason, she hadn't been able to.

I like to do things in their proper order.

Yes, that explained everything. Nothing else could get done in this company unless and until this happened, and was exactly the reason she hadn't done anything else. Well. She'd chosen the route guaranteed to cause the least amount of damage, given her inability to fire anyone—which was exactly what he would have expected her to do.

"Under the terms of your contract, you were to produce five new products per year for three years to qualify for your golden parachute clause. You didn't do that; hence, you've broken this contract." For effect, Sebastian held up the contract and tore it in half slowly, deliberately. "No golden parachute for you. As we speak, Security has packed your belongings and is waiting at the front door to escort you out. Don't bother trying to get unemployment. I'll fight you for it and win. Hand over your security badge and get out."

Truth be told, Sebastian loved this part. Not that he liked firing people, per se. What he liked was streamlining operations, throwing out the clutter, getting rid of the moochers. He did not like clutter, but he despised moochers.

Jason Hearst exited without a speck of dignity to his name. Heaven forbid someone should expect that they do what they said they could.

"Who wants to be next?" he asked blithely, looking around at the collection of now terrified upper management. Of course, today he was enjoying himself all that much more because these people had mooched off *Eilis* for years. That was as much her fault as theirs, but he couldn't very well fire *her* for not firing people.

"In the interest of saving my time because I have a lot to do today, I'm just going to tell you who gets to stay."

Michael Pritchard, the CIO, that funny MIT kid who tripped over his shoelaces and refused to use screening tests and knew exactly what he was looking for in programmers. He knew computers and software and somehow managed to herd the cats that programmers were.

Karen Cheng. Naturally.

Sheila Navarre, the accounts manager, who was responsible for getting money in the door and did it very well. She had a deft hand with clients. She knew how to massage pissed-off people and coax money out of lagging payers.

Conrad Fessy, the head of the accounting department, who also had an eye for good staff and desperately wanted some input on the accounting portion of HRP's proprietary software package. He had ideas coming out his ears and he used the screening test religiously—it was perfect for him.

"Okay, you four—" He pointed to them and they started. "You move on back to the back of the table there. Eilis, next group, please." He looked at her then and the only emotion he could determine was a slight hesitance to bring the next flock of lambs to the slaughter.

The bloodbath continued all day. He was going to dress her down but good when he was done. This was all part of being a CEO and she needed to man up. Not only did she not know people, she had a weak heart for firing and it was part and parcel of human resources.

Contract after contract had been torn up and he was down to the next level of management. Manager after manager was escorted to the door. No severance. No unemployment. He'd made sure his lawyer was downstairs checking people off as they left and was ready to fight any and all claims. Some he'd lose, but that was okay.

He'd saved millions of dollars today.

It was 6:30 P.M. before Sebastian had finished cleaning out the top-heavy corporation. He still had more to go, but those were legally sensitive. They were people who got things done and were not in any way candidates for firing. However, they were unpleasant people to work for and/or with. Sebastian didn't like morale killers any better than he liked superfluous people.

By this time, the last few dozen who were questionable or definitely on the block had been sent home to await tomorrow. The remaining employees had been asked to go to the small theater on the second floor that was used for big presentations. He escorted Eilis down there to address them all. He'd just fired two thirds of her employees today and by tomorrow night, he'd have fired three quarters. He didn't give a fat rat's ass what Eilis thought about it, either.

"Tomorrow," Sebastian boomed to Eilis's now skeleton crew because he hated microphones; way too officious, "we're going to further winnow this operation until it's as clean as can be. However, I need your honest opinions. You're still here because you've proven your worth and I trust what you have to say. As of tonight, none of you have job titles or descriptions, except for Sheila, Michael, Karen, and Conrad—for now. Sheila, you'll need to continue to serve the customers and keep the hubbub outside these walls to a minimum. Go put your phones on voice mail because you've got meetings all this week. Have a good evening."

It was 7:30 P.M. before the building was empty except for security.

"So," Sebastian said once he and Eilis were back in her office suite and he was putting his things in his backpack, "are you going to yell at me now or wait until you get home and change, then call me to kick my ass?"

She was quiet, so he looked up to see her at the window staring down at the maze of empty cubicles.

"Eilis?"

"Thank you," she said, so softly he almost thought he'd imagined it.

He approached her hesitantly. "What'd you say?"

She cleared her throat and looked over her shoulder, but down at the floor. "I said thank you. It was long overdue three years ago."

Color Sebastian shocked. "Well," he said gruffly, "I would've fired you, too, if you weren't the CEO."

"And I'd deserve it."

Sebastian wondered how hard to come down on her, since he'd already been down this road and he didn't like repeating himself. But.

"You specialize in HR services, Eilis. What kind of image do you present when you can't manage your own human resources issues? This is your product. It needs to be a model operation. I would suggest you hire someone who can fire people if it makes you that squeamish."

She said nothing for a moment. "I didn't know who to fire, where to start. It got so complex, so out of control. I was going through the trial and trying to keep HRP together at the same time. I couldn't pay attention to it and I had to trust that they'd at least keep it steady. I didn't have time to figure it out before Knox put me in receivership and he didn't ask me if I had a plan before he did it."

Oh. Hmm. That explained a lot.

"I'm curious," he said softly. "What happened to the ruthless bitch who built this place?"

Her body didn't move; she didn't betray anything. He waited for her to calmly query him as to why he'd been so vulgar. Again.

"I had to change," she finally said, still no passion in her voice. "I couldn't make the deals I really needed to because my reputation preceded me, but I didn't have enough leverage or power yet to get anything that way."

She stopped speaking and Sebastian continued to watch her carefully. "So now you're a lady of excruciating propriety—very effective weapon, by the way—and somewhere along the line you bought your own act and stopped being a hard ass when you needed to be."

"Yes."

"Which do you like more?"

She didn't reply for a while, then she said, softly, "Some happy medium I can't figure out how to get to."

Sebastian's fertile mind filled with images of how that would manifest and he couldn't help his arousal: a blonde bombshell in a little black dress being a completely brilliant businessbitch at the front of a conference room. *Yummy.*

"The people you fired today are going to talk."

Oh, he supposed he'd let her change the subject. "I know and it'll hurt HRP's reputation here in town for a little while, but Wall Street will love it. This ship has to be tight and working like a well-oiled machine with good products before we can take it public."

"Please don't do that to me," she murmured.

There went his arousal. "Eilis," he said harshly, wrapping his hands around her arms and turning her to face him, "do you know *why* Knox asked me to take this receivership?"

"I think so."

"Uh huh. Well, I'll save you the embarrassment of being wrong and just tell you. He picked me because he likes you, which, by the way, is very rare so treasure it. I am the only man from Denver to Chicago who can do what he wanted done with this company and *not* take a piece of it or all of it. He knew this was a salvageable company. He thinks that you're teachable and cooperative, and he knows how my Fix-or-Raid policy works. So now I want to ask you something: How would you have felt if Fen Hilliard had been appointed your trustee?"

She stiffened slightly.

"That's what I thought. Lucky for you that *Knox* and *I* are at war with Fen, but don't think Fen didn't try to make an end run around Knox to get this receivership for himself. Knox asked me to do this because Fen won't dare cross me."

Well, that and to give him first pick of the art.

He had her complete attention and a very queer expression streaked across her face. Considering she never showed emotion when she was in costume and her face makeup hid most of whatever she did show, Sebastian's gut started to churn, which only meant one thing: The CEO—any CEO—was hiding something from him.

"Fen tried to get this receivership?" she asked slowly.

"Yes, he did. He went to a lot of trouble to get it."

"And you and Fen aren't secretly working together?" she asked even more carefully, pulling herself back into character.

"No." He released her, though he didn't really want to. "To answer your question. The alliance that apparently nobody's figured out is me and Knox."

"He really is your attorney?"

"Yes."

"Nobody I know believes that."

He grunted. "I don't know why. The press has made that very clear."

"Sebastian, the news changes hour to hour concerning you, Knox, Fen, and OKH. The fact that you don't talk makes it all very confusing and it makes you look very bad."

"So I've been told," he muttered wryly. "Why do you think Senator Oth got off my back?"

"I assumed you got a publicist."

"Mmmm, sort of. That's Knox's good ol' boy off-the-record schtick in action. OKH will be mine whether he fulfills the proviso or not because he's not interested in it. He—we—just don't want Fen to have it beyond the date it was promised to Knox. I despise Fen Hilliard."

"You do?"

"Yes. I always have and I would have taken him down long ago if I'd known Knox didn't want it."

Her reply was immediate. "All right," she said in a rush. "I'll agree to the IPO."

Sebastian was stunned and very suspicious. As soon as he got to his car, he pulled out his Blackberry and texted Knox: **FIND LINK-HRP&OKH**

42: Then Vacuum

THE NEXT DAY WAS MORE OF THE SAME. HE HAD HIS EMPLOYMENT ATTORNEY on hand to tend to the firings of the morale killers, which was billed officially as layoffs for financial reasons; for these, Sebastian wouldn't fight unemployment. They got severance and their unused vacation and sick pay. No muss, no fuss.

All in all, he'd done a good job. Out of two hundred fifty employees, seventy-five were left to carry the weight that ninety people could carry around comfortably. The folks who thought fast on their feet and enjoyed doing it would take up the slack.

Eilis stood at the front of the auditorium to outline Sebastian's four-point plan, the first point of which Sebastian had done himself, so he sat in the audience with everyone else. The mood was lively and the beach ball someone had brought bounced gaily around the room. Sebastian almost smiled.

"We have two products," Eilis began and the shushing commenced, to be followed by the silence of scratching pens and paper. There were no handouts or fancy presentations today, no podiums, no microphones. Just the down and dirty work.

"We have two products," she began again, "that are ones we offer as add-ons to the customers who use our services either at their locations or ours: software and psychological screening tests. Both of these are far superior to what is out on the market right now, so we're going to mass market them."

Sebastian was gratified when Karen jumped up, her fists in the air and shouted, "YES!" Everyone laughed and Eilis even smiled. It had been Karen's idea to present these to the general business marketplace and Eilis had stonewalled her on that.

"Next, I'm going to sell the art collection, so when you come to work next week and see the bare walls, don't panic; we haven't been robbed."

And Conrad Fessy, following Karen's lead, did the same. The mood lightened even more. Sebastian had never seen such a happy bunch of people in his life.

"Third, we're taking the company public."

The room roared as people jumped up, and the beach ball went flying overhead. Eilis looked at Sebastian, because nobody was paying attention to either of them, and she smiled. Sebastian smiled back.

"Okay!" Sebastian stood and boomed again after he thought a sufficient time for hilarity had gone by. "Party time later. Work time now." He flipped the sheaf of papers in his hand and began passing them out, with pencils. It took a while for everyone to settle back down, but the settling went quick once the screening tests began to go down the rows.

Eilis began again. "Today we're going to do something we've never done before. We're going to re-administer the screening test. I know that at least one of you has beaten this test—"

Sebastian and Karen exchanged a glance and he winked at her because her paranoia was showing again.

"—so that leads me to believe that a good percentage of you might have also. What I want you to do is answer honestly. You are here because you're the cream of the crop, but if you don't answer honestly, it will mean your job. I won't be able to tell, but Sebastian assures me he will know who is faking and who is not—and at this point, I believe it.

"I'll tell you up front that what we're looking for are the personality traits to best match your interests with the work that needs to be done, how much work it will take to keep you interested and engaged, and what your weaknesses might be. It's in your best interest to answer as honestly as possible. We—Sebastian and I—want to make HRP a fun place to work.

"We'll score these this afternoon and assign job duties tomorrow. Right now, our most pressing need is to staff and service the clients we have. Sheila, you'll be on point for that. Business as usual outside this building. And Sheila—" She looked straight at Sheila.

Good for you, Eilis.

"—you have a free hand and an open checkbook. You also have first pick of staff."

Sheila's eyes grew big as saucers and Sebastian smirked.

The IT department required no changes. The CIO ran it the way he saw fit because his way worked. Even Eilis could see that. She only had to tell him what she wanted when she wanted it and somehow it always happened. So she did.

"Michael, the HRP Full Management System needs a small business version with a thirty-day free trial lockout. I want a beta in six months."

"Okay." That was all he said. It was all he had to say.

"With regard to the mass marketing of the screening tests outside our client base: I will be contracting with a psychologist to restructure the scoring, which I hope will happen some time in the next month. After that, we'll begin the process of reprogramming our scoring software and then we'll begin distributing it. Karen—"

Sebastian could see that Karen, still paranoid, held her breath. Too bad Sebastian hadn't been able shake that out of her.

"Karen, I would like you to work on the marketing campaign or campaigns for both the test and the software while they are in development so that by the time they're launched, we will have saturated the market. You may put any other marketing schemes into place as you see fit. And, like Sheila, you have a free hand, an open checkbook, and second pick of staff or, in the alternative, you may hire at will. You won't need my approval for anything."

Karen gulped and even from across the room, Sebastian could see the tears.

"Sebastian has given us one year to be in the black and pumping money through here like adrenaline before we start the IPO process. The rest of the week will be devoted to rearranging staff, applying new titles that mean something, and giving out raises across the board."

There was a collective gasp and the delighted murmurings began.

"Monday, you'll all start working like fiends to get the money flowing. Today, lunch is on me and you have the afternoon off."

That done, Eilis, feeling very good about life in general, went to Sebastian with a smile. "Thank you," she said and watched as his face softened and he smiled back at her.

"You're welcome, Eilis."

"Now, about that vacation . . ."

His face didn't change at all, but his body tensed and his eyes took on the same definite chill she'd seen Monday when he was slicing and dicing. "After the auction," he said tersely. "It's set for February fifth. I'm sorry, Eilis, but you're needed here and after Friday, I won't be. I'll come in every Friday at three to see how things are going, but I need to get back to my own projects."

Eilis felt like she'd just been sent to the principal's office, though she wasn't really sure why, and she swallowed. "Okay."

"I'll go collect the tests and then put them through the scoring machine myself," he said as he turned and strode up the aisle to pick up the papers. He was waylaid more than a few times by handshakes, thanks, and hugs. Eilis almost teared up when Karen gave him the biggest hug of all and he returned it, genuinely, honestly, and for a long time.

Then he strode out of the theater without a backward glance at her, leaving her a lot unhappier than she had been just minutes before.

Vacation. So she could find Ford. So Ford could paint her. So Ford could fuck her—oh, 'scuse him—*make love* to her.

Sebastian was getting very, very tired of Ford. He was getting the definite impression that there would be no competing with Ford at all.

As usual.

She had her little fantasy, fed by her ownership of *Morning in Bed*. She probably gazed at that damned painting as she went to sleep and then saw it first thing when she woke up, and nothing was going to get in the way of the Ford she'd created in her mind.

He wanted to tell her she couldn't keep it. Letting her keep it had been the worst miscalculation of his career, he was quite sure, but he didn't want her to know that he was jealous of a man who didn't exist.

He locked the door of the scoring room because he didn't want to talk to her, see her, touch her and know that he had no chance with her.

For the rest of the afternoon he fed the tests into the machine one by one and collated the results sheets. It was something mindless he could do that was productive and would still allow him to brood.

43: The Shit Hits the Fan

WELL, YOUR MOTHER WAS RATHER ACCEPTING OF IT, ALL IN ALL," BRYCE murmured.

"I told you she'd love you. I noticed Hale was civil to Knox and thanks for inviting Kevin."

"Did you invite Ashworth and LaMontagne?"

"Yes. Do you mind?"

"Not at all."

"They couldn't believe how sensible I was as to my choice of mate, so they wanted to come see for themselves and make sure I said 'I do.' I think Morgan would've had a gun in my back if I'd hesitated in the least."

Bryce chuckled and looked at the sheer numbers of people in his—and now Giselle's—house. The "Dunham Tribe" had invited itself over for an impromptu party once it made it through the grapevine that Giselle would be getting married on Friday. Bryce didn't know which fact had shocked them more: That she was getting married at all, that it *wasn't* to Knox, or that she had "managed to find the sweetest-smelling rose in the flower shop." Bryce still found Ashworth's congratulatory spiel before the wedding hilarious.

Even though he'd spent years hearing about Knox's enormous yet close-knit family and Giselle had predicted that her family would know Bryce by name and reputation, that they would welcome him with open arms, he hadn't believed it. He couldn't imagine a family like the one they'd described, but then her prediction had come true. This sense of belonging, of family, of across-the-board approval—it had never occurred to him to fantasize about having that for himself, to wish for it. He had never had any hope of belonging to a family like this in his entire life. Lilly, Giselle's mother, who seemed to understand Giselle a whole lot better than Giselle thought she did, had the potential to be every man's dream mother-in-law.

Though a full third of Giselle's tribe had left the church or otherwise flouted church teachings, they were every bit as welcome and loved as those who had remained faithful. Of course, his father wouldn't have approved of this family any more than he had approved of Knox or would have approved of Giselle. Certainly, his siblings had taken his news badly, but Bryce had found that unexpectedly amusing.

"Are we going to have to get a bigger house for your family?"

"No!" Giselle said, horrified. "If we had a bigger house, more of them would come."

True to form for a family of Mormons, along with the people came the food, most of which Giselle didn't touch. He had met more people today than he could count, and, to Bryce's consternation, even Fen and Trudy had shown up.

"Giselle. They're *in our house.*"

"They always come to everything, although I'm not any happier about it than you are," Giselle said. "I guess I should've warned you. I wish Knox had come, just this once, but Trudy, you know. And, hate to say it, but some of the tribe make him very aware of the fact that they would rather not have to claim him."

Bryce sighed. "Just like the rest of the city."

"Yeah. Sad, huh?"

"He doesn't think he deserves any better."

"Oh, you noticed that."

"I lived with him for four years. Kinda hard not to."

"Trudy did that. She broke him over her knee like a dry twig when he was still in single digits."

Bryce shook his head.

"But," she added, "I do think he would've come if he weren't in the middle of a trial. I'm just happy he could make it to the wedding."

Fen's nose had a pronounced bend in it now and Bryce grinned to himself. When he approached Giselle and Bryce in his usual jovial manner, he took them aside to speak a bit more privately.

"Well, Giselle," Fen said with great affection. "Congratulations. I must admit that I'm very, very pleased with you."

"I'm sure you are," she murmured wryly.

"You didn't invite me to the wedding, though. I'm hurt."

"What, did you want to walk me down the aisle and give me away?"

He rocked back on his heels with a chuckle, then pulled a tiny velvet jewelry box from his pocket and gave it to her. "Since you have taken the trouble to send me a statement every month demanding three times reparation for Decadence—ballsy vig, by the way—"

Bryce blinked, then began to chuckle.

"That," he pronounced, "is the key to a safe deposit box where you'll find the cash—couldn't give you a check for obvious reasons. So, I'm sorry and paid in full."

He has an unfortunate tendency toward half-assed contrition.

"Did you also pay the statements detailing Maisy and Coco's losses? With vig?"

"Yes, I did—though of course not personally."

"Natch," Giselle returned as she took the box, seeming not in the least bit surprised. "Thank you, but this doesn't really pay for trying to kill me twice."

"Oh, so you *are* still sulking."

"Fen, it was a wee bit traumatic. You were there both times; you saw what happened. Surely you can appreciate it from my point of view."

He grunted. "Well, now that you put it that way, I suppose I can."

"All right, Unk. I guess between this, your broken nose—you're welcome—and our deal, we're square."

"Maybe you two lovebirds are," came Sebastian's voice as he joined their conversation, "but I can still demand my pound of flesh."

Fen remained surprisingly calm and cheerful, yet Sebastian smirked. "I see you're appreciating the unintended consequences of my last move, but I heard you got your funding from someone else anyway. Congratulations."

"Ah, Sebastian," Fen purred. "So glad to have a chance to chat. I hear the drums starting back up in Washington."

"I don't, but of course we don't run in the same circles," Sebastian said blithely. "Not to worry, though. I have an attorney who understands paper trails very, very well."

Fen snorted. "Of course you do. At my expense, might I add."

"Yes, thank you for that. Say, have you heard Senator Oth lately? I swear the man went from wishing me dead to having a spot open at his dinner table for me."

Fen speared Giselle with a disgruntled glance. "I don't have to guess who cooked that up."

She smiled sweetly and Bryce chuckled, squeezing her shoulder. Now he *did* have the right to be proud of her.

"Indeed, you do not," Sebastian said. "But remember, I do own twenty-one percent of your stock, which means I can still muster up enough votes to be a pain in your ass. Now, about your deal with Giz," he continued. "You do realize you would've been better off if she'd married Knox, right? There was always a better-than-fifty-percent chance she wouldn't have gotten pregnant in time, given how ancient she is and no time to get through the adoption process. But now . . . "

When Fen looked at Sebastian like he'd lost his mind, Bryce laughed outright. "Well, now that I'm not a *squatter* anymore, I've thrown my hat in the ring," he said. "You'll be getting my paperwork soon. Six percent for me and actively buying. With Taight's twenty-one, together, we're the majority shareholders of OKH Enterprises. Right. After. You."

Fen's color dropped.

"Fen," Sebastian drawled, "you're getting squirrelly in your old age. You should've seen that coming a mile away. I can only think you were under the impression that Kenard wouldn't involve himself in our little war. Given the fact he enjoys a good *jihad* and you've tried to kill his wife twice now, you probably should've thought a little bit ahead."

Fen's expression betrayed nothing more and Bryce felt an overwhelming sense of satisfaction, though he did manage to keep a straight face when Sebastian turned to him and said, "Kenard, when's Oakley's press conference?"

"Uh, Tuesday. I asked him about that before the wedding."

"Fen," Giselle said conversationally, "did you know Kevin Oakley's going to announce his run for Senate?" Fen stared at Giselle then. "I like him. I'm sure you understand why."

"Ah, yes," Sebastian murmured, "between me and Kenard—and oh, Holland-er—" Fen's lip curled. "—he'll have a hefty war chest. Justice McKinley's already given him the third degree and she's on board. It's a lock."

"Boss Tom Pendergast, Part II," he snarled.

"Libertarian version," Sebastian added smugly. "But also not my idea. You can blame your little catnip Giselle over there for that, too."

Bryce slid a look at Fen, who didn't bother to hide his anger as he glared between Bryce and Sebastian. "Your move, Fen," Bryce murmured, staring at him with a cocked eyebrow. "Make it my wife, I'll make you wish she'd killed you when she had the chance. I'm not that merciful."

Fen looked at Giselle then and nodded, brusque. "Godspeed, Giselle."

She nodded in return with a wicked smile. "Uncle Fen."

Once he had stalked off to find Trudy and drag her out the front door, Bryce looked down at Giselle to see her chuckle. "I find your relationship with him very disturbing."

"So do we," Sebastian muttered, "but I must admit he *is* entertaining. Giz, what happened to his nose?"

"It ran into my fist."

"See, now that's funny. Has your mother read you your pedigree yet?"

"No. She'll save it for the next time I piss her off."

"Well, my mother got an earful, which, of course, she felt compelled to share with me in a very, ah, aggravated tone of voice. Yet *again*, you bear absolutely no responsibility for your own behavior. Your lack of purity and inability to get married in the temple is all my doing, what with my profligacy. They seem to think I drugged and stripped you, strapped you to the bed, and offered you up as a blood sacrifice to whichever demon I worship."

"Do you mean to say they *don't* think I was sleeping with Knox?"

"No, they do think that, but he is, apparently, as much a hapless victim of my Svengali-like control as you are."

Giselle laughed. "Okay, but did you get blamed for my strapped-to-the-bed nudity on display?"

"Uh, no, come to think of it, I didn't."

"Ah, sweet irony."

Bryce burst out laughing and Sebastian smirked. "I heard you got a drubbing, though."

"It was worth it."

Sebastian snorted his amusement and wandered off.

The party wound down and Giselle excused herself. "I'm really tired, Bryce," she murmured. "I'm going to go to bed. Can you make my apologies?"

He nodded, then leaned down for a gentle kiss. She'd disappeared very early that morning and she hadn't allowed him to get any more intimate than a kiss or two. He'd fantasized about a night like this for years: A wedding night with a gorgeous woman who was intelligent, well educated, and wild in the sack.

And she was tired.

Bryce walked heavily up the stairs after everyone had gone, wondering if, now that they'd tied the knot and ceased to sin, the magic would dissipate. He hadn't thought it possible until she had left the party early.

He realized that he had feared that about their relationship more than just about anything else—his first wedding night had begun the same way and he'd failed to see it as a warning sign.

When he walked into the bedroom, it was mostly dark, the drapes drawn, a small night light on in the bathroom. He could see the silhouette of her body in the bed, absolutely silent, absolutely still.

Bryce sighed and turned to head to the bathroom.

"Take your clothes off, Kenard," she demanded with the same fire in her voice she had had the night they'd met and kissed.

His head dropped back. Relieved and aroused at the same time, he nearly laughed as the tension left him.

"Turn around."

He did and she snapped on a small lamp on her side of the bed. He sucked in a quick breath when he saw her. The skin of her breasts and belly, her thighs and her hips, were adorned with an elaborate copper-colored henna tattoo—which explained her mysterious disappearing act.

Bryce rocked back on one heel just to look at her and take in the woman who lay in his bed.

The tattoo, oh that tattoo! He found it surprisingly, *achingly* erotic, paisleys wrapping around her nipples and belly button and down her thighs, over her thighs, around her hips, and back up her ribs and belly. The gunshot wounds in her shoulder and her hip had been specially decorated.

Her eyebrow rose and she smirked. "I said, take off your clothes. And don't talk," she added when he opened his mouth.

He figured he'd go along with her for a while to see what she had in mind. He started with his shoes and socks, throwing them in a corner somewhere.

"Did you know," she murmured, drawing a finger across the icons around one nipple, "that paisley is the female counterpart to the phallic symbol? Don't talk."

He grinned as his hands went to his shirt. He watched her watch him as he obeyed her as slowly as possible. She didn't object. Once his feet and torso were bare, his hands went to his trousers; he unbuckled, unbuttoned, and unzipped, slowly and deliberately freeing his hard, very erect cock before letting his clothes drop to the floor.

When he took his arousal in his hand and slowly, deliberately stroked up its length, then back down again, she drew in a harsh, shaky breath and shifted in bed, the leg on top drawing up and pressing into her other leg. She slid her hand between her legs.

"Usually," she whispered shakily as she manipulated her clitoris, "I don't do this by hand. But you make me want to."

He quirked an eyebrow and smirked at that, but she only acknowledged it with a slow blink and that not-smile-not-smirk she had. Then she withdrew her hand and rose out of bed slowly. She strutted toward him, then stopped and put her hands flat on his chest, softly kissing his sternum. Butterfly kisses, tiny touches of the tongue, sharp nibbles. He felt his cock rub against her belly and he nudged his hips forward a bit to make his point.

"You are a god," she whispered, awe tingeing her voice. "Ares, the god of war." He stopped smiling, his heart pounding from the impact of her words, her regard. This was so much more than he had ever hoped for and he gulped. Then she slid down his body.

"And I'm on my knees. In front of you. Sucking your cock. Isn't that where you wanted me?"

He gasped when her tongue first twirled around the head of his cock. He palmed the back of her head to pull her closer to him, his head falling back once again. He couldn't think, couldn't move. He had to trust her to know how to use those lips, teeth, and tongue, bold and clever.

Bryce fisted his hand in her hair and swayed from the feel of her mouth around him. She licked and sucked and twirled, her hands clutching the back of his thighs to keep him close to her. His hips began to move and he pressed her into him. His head dropped back, his eyes closed in ecstasy, his back arched. She opened her throat when he thrust harder, faster. He couldn't think. He pumped himself into her mouth and groaned when he came.

When she'd sucked him dry and licked him clean, she pulled away from him and looked up.

"Thank you," he whispered, grateful and very, very touched.

"It was the only wedding gift I could afford on short notice," she whispered back. "I have—well, I had—nothing before it started raining money on me."

"It was more than enough," he said, pulling her up off the floor and kissing her. "That first weekend, the blow job you gave me then—that was the first time for me."

She sucked in a breath. "You never—"

He shook his head slowly. "No. Never."

"I— That's— Oh, my."

"I never dared ask and she wasn't volunteering. You, I didn't even have to ask. I can't tell you how much that meant to me."

He pulled her close and lifted her, wrapping her legs around his waist then taking her to the bed. He lowered her gently and pulled her knees apart, sliding backward down the bed until his face was between her legs. He looked up at her. "Also something I'd never done before you."

She sucked in a quick breath and dug her fingers in his hair to pull him into her. "Drink me, Bryce."

And he did until she came, arching her back and clutching his face into her. He rose then, slowly, and buried himself inside her, having gotten hard again as his tongue played with her clitoris.

Giselle sighed, and sighed again. She came again, softly, and then he did, once more.

He stayed inside her as long as he could, her legs wrapped around him, bearing his full weight. He didn't know how she could do that, but it filled him with joy.

"I lo—"

He clapped a hand to her mouth. "Don't say it," he said softly. "Not in bed. It means nothing to me in bed, when we're coming down off that adrenaline rush. It needs to mean something when things aren't so rosy downstairs or outside or during any number of things that need attention that don't have anything to do with sex. Giselle, I have never had an experience like this in my entire life and I just want to enjoy it, to enjoy you.

"Please quit your job," he continued, a pleading note in his voice as he pulled his hand away her mouth. "I need you here in the evenings with me. I can't stand a quiet house and I can't stand being alone, especially after dark."

She smiled. "I didn't have to. This morning, Hale told me not to come back until after I'd passed the bar. He put me on leave of absence."

Bryce rolled them over until she lay atop him. They kissed for a long time, slowly, enjoying the moment, enjoying each other, until they fell asleep.

44: The House at Pooh Corner

ILIS DIDN'T KNOW WHAT SHE'D DONE THAT HAD MADE SEBASTIAN SO ANGRY with her that he was barely civil, but every Friday at three, he came by, looked at her reports and spoke as little as possible. Only on Fridays did she stand at the window and look down upon Cubicleville, which thrummed with the excitement of Sebastian's three o'clock visit. Because he stopped to talk to everyone who wanted to chat, it took him about thirty minutes to walk the hundred feet from the door to the mezzanine steps.

How did no one in the cadre of CEOs she knew and associated with see what he did? Why was he considered Satan himself? No, he didn't smile or laugh. Yes, he looked like the most beautiful demon she could imagine. No, he didn't take any bullshit. Yes, he was ruthless.

But he understood people. He brought hope to them, faith, optimism, and validation. He made impossible situations look possible. He made work fun. He made the pain and the paranoia go away. He taught and in the teaching, he left better people behind.

Still he delayed the trip up the stairs to her office. She wasn't sure if he did this because he didn't want to speak to her or if this was just his way, but she felt bereft, as if her lifeline, her support, her savior, had disowned her for an offense she hadn't known she'd committed.

The reports he wanted to see every week were on the table between her office and the conference room, waiting for him. She turned away from the window once he'd disappeared to climb the stairs and then he was there.

"Good afternoon, Eilis," he said, remotely cordial as always. He immediately sat down and began inspecting the reports she'd laid out for him. He'd come in looking as preoccupied as he always did on these visits, but was now completely focused and writing with his right hand. She thought both the preoccupation and focus might be a dodge, but she couldn't tell.

She'd learned a lot about people like Sebastian since he'd come into her life and what she'd always seen as deficiencies were not deficiencies at all. The employees who had scored close to what Sebastian had done had been slotted according to their interests and given more work than any human could possibly handle. They had done exactly what Sebastian said they would do. They chugged through their projects at a frightening pace yet managed to spend a lot of time staring at nothing, playing with executive toys, surfing the web, and shooting the breeze over their cubicle walls.

It had taken her a great deal of control not to crack down on that, but Sebastian had noticed and said, "Are they getting the work done?"

"Yes."

"Are they doing it well?"

"Yes."

"Then leave them alone. All you should care about as CEO is the result. The only thing about the process you need to worry about is if they meet their deadlines with quality work. Don't micromanage."

She didn't understand it, but she couldn't argue with it because it worked. If Sebastian Taight couldn't pass her test, if he spent time gazing at nothing and working on his own timetable, then she'd been doing something wrong all along, because he was one of the most successful people she knew personally.

The one time she'd worked up the courage to try to break through Sebastian's shell, she'd asked, "You said most of your family wouldn't pass my test. Do they work like you do?"

Sebastian had stopped reading the reports, stopped writing. He stared off into the distance a little while, then said, "Everybody has their tricks, their coping mechanisms; just because they wouldn't pass the test doesn't mean you would be able to tell they're like me."

"And Knox and Fen?"

"They're both schemers. They plot every scenario and plan every detail out to the nth degree the same way you do and they don't leave anything to chance. The more elaborate the scheme, the better; for them, it's like working puzzles. Knox only understands how I work because he's watched me do it for years. Fen's never been able to figure out what I do, not that he hasn't tried, but he doesn't have the temperament for it. Knox's father was a planner too, so I'm thinking it's a Hilliard trait."

Eilis's stomach turned over.

"Problem was, Oliver didn't have a managerial bone in his body and OKH almost went under before Fen got complete control of it. Fen's a born manager."

"So they don't need the little tricks and toys."

"Sure they do. Fen plays a lot of golf. Alone. I'm sure he's done deals that way, but he doesn't like to. He uses golfing to think. In fact, OKH has a nine-hole course on the property. I don't know what Oliver did."

"And Knox?"

"Knox has a photographic memory. He remembers every word he reads. If he's paying attention—which he doesn't do very much because he'd go nuts—he'll remember everything he sees and every sound he hears. When he's stuck or needs to work something out, he starts reading. Anything. Everything. He doesn't care. It just has to be something he hasn't read before because he needs a bigger fund of knowledge to draw from than what he already has, and he needs to lay new paths to make different associations."

"What's your trick?"

"If it's business, I stare at walls. If it's personal, I paint."

He would say no more after that, and Eilis felt both enriched and bereft, especially when he went back to being barely civil.

From the day Sebastian had left after making all the changes he'd made in two weeks flat, her company's growth had boomed. She wasn't out of the red yet, but they were making steady progress on getting all the bills paid and paid on time.

Karen was a marketing genius.

Sheila was a rainmaker.

Conrad knew where to spend money and where not to.

Michael delivered product.

Sebastian had known this about them, had exploited them for it, and, also as he'd predicted, they thanked him for exploiting their talents and rewarding them well for it.

She had exactly four executives, which was twenty-one fewer than she'd had before Sebastian came. The salary savings alone had allowed them to get out of the most pressing of her debt.

Eilis cleared her throat, uneasy in the silence. "I found a psychologist who's developed a categorization method for the tests. Michael's coding the scoring software himself."

"Good," he said without looking up.

The speed at which Sebastian processed information was astounding to her.

She'd had to fight for every grade, every inch of square feet in this building, every calculation, every data analysis. Math, analyzation, data, statistics: Not her strong suit. She'd chosen the hardest path possible in order to make something of herself in spite of her past, to escape from the reality that was her life.

"Are— Are you a genius? A real one?" she asked, hesitant, and hating that she betrayed any emotion at all.

"Yes," he said shortly.

Oh, she was tired of this. The silent treatment was not fair. "Sebastian."

He stopped what he was doing and was still. Then he raised his head and his cold blue gaze bored into hers. "Yes, Eilis?"

"Why are you angry with me?"

"I'm not."

"I see."

He sighed and put his elbow on the table, then put his forehead in his hand. "It's my problem, Eilis. I'm sorry."

"What did I do?"

"Nothing. I'm sorry if I've been a little cool toward you."

"And I apologize for whatever I did."

Sebastian didn't know how he had let this get so completely out of hand. He remembered the Eilis he'd met at the Ford exhibit, and not only was she still wearing that hideous costume, but she was determined to find Ford. There was only so much a man could take. So he decided to go for broke and looked up at her. "Would you have lunch with me tomorrow?"

As usual, Eilis betrayed no emotion, but he could feel the sudden tension in her body. He felt just as tense; asking her out on a date had been the furthest thing from his mind when he'd walked into this building. "Lunch? Why?"

Sebastian's mouth thinned. Why. "People have to eat, Eilis," he returned gruffly. "Maybe some people would like to not do that alone."

He watched her inscrutable face in case he could tell anything of her thoughts, but she never once dropped her façade.

"All right," she finally agreed, "but I choose the restaurant. You may pick me up at twelve-thirty."

Sebastian felt both elated and dismayed. He wasn't sure why either, all things considered. "Uh—dress?"

"Very casual," she murmured and turned away.

He had all the access in the world to her files, so he didn't bother asking her where she lived. It didn't surprise him that she lived in nearby Chouteau Woods, just ten minutes south of the airport, only two miles away from Knox as the crow flies (and of course Knox would have neglected to mention this to him). HR Prerogatives stood in an office park halfway between her home and the airport.

When he drove through the massive wooden gates of her driveway the next day, flanked by two equally massive four-foot square stone pillars and up the drive to her door, he wasn't sure what he'd expected, but he had to admit the place suited her.

A big brown-charcoal-tan brick boxy Tudor revival with a multicolored blue-green slate roof and two chimneys, it couldn't be seen from the secluded and relatively dark side street that itself didn't invite traffic. An eight-foot-high iron fence hidden by an immaculately trimmed hedgerow surrounded the entire property, which was almost twice as big as Knox's acre plot, the difference being that this was rolling terrain. The lawn was a few shades of the richest greens and nearly perfect. He wouldn't have been surprised to see a few head of sheep trimming it.

There were old, old oaks, maples, and white birch trees dotting the property, which would give the whole expanse shade in the summer, and had not yet started to turn. It had been a long, hot summer and October thus far had been unseasonably warm. This should be a lovely flaming display in two weeks and in four, a nasty mess to clean up when they all dropped and the November rains began.

There was a roundabout in front of her door with a shoulder-high black granite obelisk fountain in the middle of it embedded in chunks of tumbled black glass. Between the roundabout and the front door was a small brick courtyard bordered by a low brick wall and fronted by layers and layers of flowers, which, suiting the house, was a perfect reproduction of an English country garden that was starting to wind down for the late autumn. The chrysanthemums were on full display and brilliantly arranged by color. There were a couple of ornamental apple trees, pear trees, and dogwoods around the perimeter closer to the house that were still green, though they should have been turning and dropping.

"Wow," he whispered to himself as he got out of his truck to walk around and inspect them more closely. Her garden had surprised all the irritation out of him. He wondered if she had done this herself or if she paid someone.

If *she* had done this, he was in awe of her talent as a master gardener. He couldn't help the smile that grew when he imagined her digging in the dirt, planting, weeding, and fertilizing. He touched the last-gasp cosmos of magenta and tangerine. He noted a stubbled bed of what he thought would be irises and wondered if he would find a Georgia O'Keeffe on one of her walls.

Unfortunately, he didn't have a chance. She opened the heavy, rich mahogany plank door with a curved top and three long black strap hinges across its face. Once outside and locking it behind her, she said lightly, "I figured that if I didn't come out, you'd stand me up for these ladies," and swept her hand over her garden.

Sebastian started. "Was I that long?"

She laughed, and he loved that. "Yes. I was starting to get jealous of my own flowers." Then she came across the courtyard and he caught his breath again at her beauty. The first time she had ever looked completely comfortable to him, she had on jeans and a navy rugby shirt, most likely because she thought she should have to hide that magnificent bosom. And her hips! Sebastian groaned when she turned away to smell a tea rose topiary in a large urn. Her waistband didn't touch her waist. She bought her jeans for her hips and he appreciated every millimeter of difference between them. Her ass was the most incredible thing he'd ever seen.

Then she turned back to him, smiling, and she took his breath away. A simple dime store headband held her hair back from her face, which didn't have a lick of makeup. She had no jewelry on. She wore old beat-up penny loafers.

She pointed to his truck. "Are you a millionaire or a billionaire?"

He looked over his shoulder at the old beat-up Ford pickup truck he loved. "I've had that since I turned sixteen. I find myself having to haul stuff around often enough that I keep it. Otherwise, you said casual, so I took you at your word. Warning, though: Air conditioner doesn't work."

That made her laugh and he did so love it when she laughed.

"Did you do this, Eilis?" Sebastian asked. "This garden?"

"Yes."

"I'm— This is— Breathtaking," he whispered and while he wasn't looking for a reaction, he happened to catch the look of amazement that glanced across her face.

"Would you like a tour?" she asked, hesitant, as if she didn't trust his sincerity.

"Do we have reservations somewhere?"

"No."

"Then yes, I would love one."

She didn't seem inclined to talk and neither did he. He took in every bit of color and he knew she watched him for a reaction. At this point, he didn't know if he wanted more to stare at Eilis or Eilis's garden.

In the back of the house was a swimming pool, rare enough here where one could only be used half the year and brought property values down, not up. Cobbled paths wound around the property and served as a simple framework for various beds of autumn flowers that ringed the trees. Stacked stone formed the walls of some of the beds and, on the hills and in the dales, some flower beds had no boundaries whatsoever.

One path diverged and meandered through the lawn, then turned and disappeared into a small glade. Sebastian wanted to take the road less traveled by.

The trees cast an incredible shade, even now at midday. Mourning doves and other birds called. Frogs croaked from somewhere, so there must be a body of water nearby. He drew in a long breath and confirmed that by scent.

Around the bend of the path, a very wide stone bridge spanned a creek. In the creek, she'd planted rushes and lemon grass to keep mosquitoes away, and had strategically placed rocks so as to get a gurgling sound that she could probably hear on a still night and to clean the water as it went through. Minnows and tadpoles could thrive in the small standing pools.

"We don't have to go across the bridge if you don't want to," she said softly. "My greenhouse is back there as well as my compost pile."

He didn't answer, but crossed the footbridge eagerly, absently noting that her stride matched his. The back of the property wasn't quite as tidy as the front. In fact, it was a downright mess. Here, a four-runner with a garden trailer behind it. There, a lawn tractor with an enormous bag and vacuum hose behind it. The greenhouse looked more like a storage shed, and the biggest compost pile he'd ever seen covered a lot of ground. She had a small Bobcat backhoe with its bucket buried in the pile.

"I have to turn the compost quite a bit. I make a lot of compost tea and my worms have to come up for air occasionally."

"Vermiculture? Really?"

"Yes. It's difficult for me to find a convenient time to get horse manure. Worm castings are almost as good. You know about gardening?"

"Not really. What I do know came from spending a week at the Royal Botanical Gardens in Edinburgh trying my hand at it."

Eilis gasped and he looked over at her, not down, which very much pleased him. Her hand was over her mouth. "You've been there?"

"Yes, Eilis," he said softly. "I've been around the world several times. I could go around it another hundred thousand times and not see everything I want to. I always find the gardens."

She blushed a little and turned away from him. "My little garden here must not compare."

"Eilis," he said earnestly, his attraction to her only increasing exponentially at this display of artistry and skill, "you're a master gardener. I might not know much, but I do know that. You've done this magnificent work yourself and I—" He stopped and looked around. "I'm awed. I could spend days lost in here."

She sniffled and he went around her to find her with her hand to her nose.

"What? What did I say?" he asked, almost panicking because he thought he'd said the exact wrong thing.

"My—" She gulped. "David— My ex-husband. He thought it was a waste of time, but it was one of the only things that pulled me through my marriage. Allowed me to stay with him long enough to do what I needed to do."

Sebastian decided to talk to Knox about this David Webster person pronto, then gripped her arms in his hands. "Eilis, look at me." He knew she didn't want to, but she did anyway.

"The man embezzled almost a hundred million dollars from you, half of which Knox wasn't able to recover. Why would you care about his opinion?"

"I don't *care*, exactly," she said, "but I had to redo my entire garden because it reminded me of what he did to me."

"Eilis, this is a work of art," he murmured. "I've been to the best gardens in the world and this—this work you have created with your own two hands—rivals them all." He could see that she *wanted* to believe what he said, but didn't really. "Eilis," he continued, saying her name every chance he got. "I speculate in art. I know greatness when I see it. *This* is a great work of art, whether you want to believe it or not."

This time he didn't ask permission first. He enfolded her in his arms, the back of her head in his palm, and kissed her. Lightly at first, he felt her acquiesce; deepening the kiss, his tongue teasing hers, pleading with her to come play with him, he felt her melt into him. If he thought Knox wouldn't crack his head open for it, he'd lay her down in a bed of dying wildflowers and make love to her right then and there, amongst the wonder she'd built and nurtured.

Sebastian drew away slowly and searched her face for some sign of healing. He ran a finger down her scar and murmured, "I'll do that however many times it takes for you to remember *my* opinion of your garden and forget his."

That made her smile, but the moment was interrupted by the loud rumble in her belly. Embarrassed, she pulled away and tried to laugh, but . . .

"Time to eat," Sebastian pronounced, deliberately killing the mood so he could feed her. He hadn't forgotten how she had reacted to his offer of food at the Ford exhibit, nor had he missed the way she'd eyeballed the remains of the pizza he had shared with Karen. He couldn't count how many times he'd heard her stomach rumble, but he did know how many times he'd seen her eat: zero. "Where are we going?"

"On a picnic, apparently, since you're so hellbent on being a lawn jockey."

Sebastian laughed out loud then and caught her staring at him. "What?"

"You look—you look so different when you smile and laugh. The difference is amazing."

He continued to chuckle as they walked up the path to the driveway and led her to the pickup truck that seemed to amuse her. Sebastian helped her in and closed the door behind her. "Now, I wasn't kidding about air conditioning. I didn't think I'd have to worry about it until spring. I hope you don't mind."

"I grew up without air conditioning."

"So did I. Here's to growing up piss poor. Now, you know," he said after he started the truck and before he let off the clutch, "we can't go anywhere unless you tell me where that is."

"Seventeenth and Brooklyn."

Sebastian thought his heart had stopped. "You're kidding."

"Nope. I feel like getting some nasty, dirty barbecue."

And again he laughed at the surprises she held. When she began to laugh because she apparently liked what happened to his face when *he* laughed, he didn't even try to hold back. He leaned over and kissed her again, softly as before, touching her lip with his tongue to make sure she remembered the one in the garden. While he kissed her, he looked straight at her and she him. He could tell the minute she decided to go with it, but she never closed her eyes—and he liked that. He liked her two different eyes, liked watching the play of emotion across her face.

"I decided not to ask today," he said as he drew away, "in case you said no again."

She flushed a little. "I still think it's not a good idea. I'm not very good at judging men."

His eyebrows rose as he started to follow the roundabout, then up the driveway. "Does that mean you think I'd be a bad choice or that you don't trust yourself to make good decisions?"

"I don't even know why we're having this conversation. Stop a minute."

They had passed the gate and Sebastian stopped the truck, this part of the driveway barely sunlit. She had pulled out her Blackberry and thumbed in a command that made the gates close behind them.

"You're my court-appointed babysitter," she continued dryly once she indicated the property was secure, "and I'm the teenager who can't be trusted with the house to herself."

He laughed again. "Okay, okay. I get your point."

45: Supercalifragilisticexpialidocious

SEBASTIAN DROVE UNERRINGLY TO BRYANT'S. ONCE HE TURNED ONTO Brooklyn, however, she said slyly, "So. I'm not the only fan in this wreck."

"Oh no," he murmured as he looked for a parking spot and found one—a block away. He helped her out and they began to walk. He was careful to walk on the outside of the sidewalk, his fingers lightly touching her back. "Bryant's is a rite of passage. I end up getting Bryant's almost every Saturday while I'm out and about. Some time I'll take you to get the best homemade kielbasa ever."

"Are you talking about that broken-down little grocery just south of the Truman Road viaduct? Peter May's?"

He groaned. "Oh, no—you're a native."

"Oh yes. I know all the good little spots. Although I will say that the Strawberry Hill povitica isn't as good as mine."

He slid her a look. "Not possible."

"Is too. I roll the dough thinner, more like baklava than cinnamon rolls. I also use more filling."

"Now I just can't surprise you."

"Maybe not with food, no."

Sebastian's eyebrows rose. That was packed with innuendo and he'd like to think she'd said that on purpose, but he couldn't tell.

From the outside, Bryant's looked like a typical mid-century diner with red awning-covered glass facing west. On Saturday afternoon, at least half a dozen of the city's movers and shakers stood in the line that went back half a block. Eilis tapped him to point them out, and they traded amused glances.

Sebastian knew why she'd brought him here; she wanted to test his barbecue tolerance as a measuring stick of his worthiness. He knew this because he'd done the same thing with the few women who'd ever consented to a date. Sharp and vinegary, grainy with spices, Bryant's sauce was not for the faint of heart and those who preferred ketchup-with-molasses were suspect in Sebastian's milieu.

"You know all about my company," Eilis said suddenly. "Tell me about yours. What's it called?"

"Taight, Inc."

She chuckled. "That's simple to remember. What kinds of things do you do?"

"Oh." He waved a hand, unsure how to describe it. "It's a hodgepodge of things that interest me. I have an office, but I work at home a lot. I'm a serial starter."

"Let me guess—it's that ADD thing."

He flashed her a grin. "Never underestimate the commercial value of mental illness."

That comment drew laughs from several people around them, as well as Eilis, who was the only person he cared about entertaining. "How did you get started?" she asked.

"If I tell you, do you promise not to think badly of me?"

She nudged him with her body. "Too late for that, Sebastian."

He grinned. He'd never thought he could be this relaxed with a woman he desired so badly, talking business, being personal, not picking her up to take her directly to the Den of Iniquity. He'd never thought he'd meet a woman who wanted to know about him, who he was, how he ticked—and he wanted to enjoy it for its own sake.

Maybe he'd been wrong about her fixation with Ford. She was here, with him. She was smiling and laughing, going along with the flow of the afternoon. She was asking questions, and he hadn't made any gaffes. Yet.

"My family was very poor, but my mother understood how money worked. She just didn't have much to work with because my father had a tendency to give away what little we had to people who had even less than we did."

"Oh, how sweet."

"No, it's not sweet," he returned sharply, surprised at her comment and surprising her with his sudden sharpness. He backed off the sharp and held up a hand to apologize and soften it. "It's stupid. You can't help anyone if you have nothing and there is no value in teaching your children that being—staying—poor is a virtue."

She remained silent, so he went on.

"I made my first loan—a whole quarter—when I was ten. My father chastised me for demanding repayment. He said, 'If he was destitute enough to ask, he needs it more than you do.' My mother waited until my dad went to work the next day and set me straight about that. She said, 'Not only do you demand repayment, you *never* loan money without getting paid for it.' She explained to me how interest worked. She taught me how to barter: what was valuable and not, what might be valuable and why. She taught me to read the stock tables. She taught me what good debt and bad debt were, when, and how to tell the difference."

"Well, if your mother knew all this—" Eilis began.

"I'm getting there."

Eilis laughed then. "She had a shoebox."

"She did. She made *me* my first loan out of it when I really began what she called 'enlightened usury.'"

"What's that?"

"In principle, it's just supply and demand. You charge exactly what people are willing to pay. If Johnny Rich Daddy needed a loan—which is what my mother loaned me money for—I'd ask for some outrageous vig and nine times out of ten, he'd agree to it.

"So she made me this loan and charged me twenty percent." Eilis gasped. He noticed he was drawing some attention, but that didn't faze him. He wished the whole world could understand how he made money and occasionally, he didn't mind sharing his methods and reasoning.

"She said, 'I don't want to know how much you plan to charge that boy, but I'll be very disappointed in you if you charge less than double.' So I charged him fifty percent. When it was all done and I got my money back with interest, I paid her back. Then she sat me down with a pencil and paper and showed me how it worked and how much money I'd really made."

"Margin."

"Right. She didn't know any of those labels, though, so it was rough on me for a while when I actually went to business school. I had to completely reorder my language so I could understand the labels the people in my classes already understood. On the other hand, they didn't have a dime to their names and by that time, I'd made my first million, so definitions didn't bother me too much."

"You made that kind of money loan sharking?"

"Oh, no. I made odds."

"You were a bookie?" Eilis demanded in a whisper because she'd finally noticed that people were listening very intently, and she began to fidget. So he winked at her and she began to relax with a slow smile.

"My mother would have killed me. People who gamble are stupid. I never gamble; I play to win. I don't play games where the odds are against me and I just happened to have a talent for being able to figure rough odds on the fly. So that was a lot more lucrative than loan sharking."

"If you lived in a poor area, how did you get so many customers?"

"Oh, Knox. I wouldn't have made near as much money in my neck of the woods alone, so I ended up loaning money to all Knox's private school schlubs. They're also the ones who'd gamble away their trusts given half a chance."

"How did you make sure you got paid back?"

He slid her a look but ignored the question, continuing with his story. "So, I had, oh, twenty-five thousand dollars by the time I was sixteen. Then." He shuddered. "My mother made me get a job."

The line burst out laughing and Sebastian shook his head. Feeling very . . . odd . . . in a good way . . . about people listening to him and laughing at what he said, he continued to act as if Eilis were the only one listening. "That was the most miserable period of my life—strike that, the second most miserable period of my life. I was a busboy at Shoney's. It was hard work, paid next to nothing and I was completely stymied by why what I'd earned didn't match what the check was for."

"Ah, taxes."

"Bastards."

By this time, Sebastian had the line rolling and no longer trying to hide the shameless eavesdropping. The movers and shakers in the line had recognized him, but simply smiled and nodded. They wanted to be normal people on Saturday as much as Sebastian did. They should've recognized Eilis because they would know her, but they didn't have a clue who this gorgeous blonde was, and suddenly he wondered how so many smart people could be so collectively stupid.

"I was livid," he went on, still talking only to Eilis. "She just laughed at me and said, 'Welcome to normal people world, son,' and I decided that just wasn't for me. She made me stick with it because she said I needed to know what it was like for ninety-nine percent of the population."

At that, the crowd applauded and Sebastian couldn't stand it anymore. He doffed a nonexistent hat and made an elaborate bow to the crowd.

Eilis gasped in delight. "You're a ham! I never would've guessed."

"Me neither," muttered Sebastian, who, for the first time in his life, understood what it was like to not have people back away from him, to have people value what he actually said instead of assuming just enough to be mad at him for what he hadn't said.

"Excuse me, sir?" came a small voice from below him and he saw a black boy no older than ten or so. "Can you teach me that? What you were talking about?"

Suddenly, his mother appeared and snapped, "Christopher! You get over here this instant and don't bother that man. You can see he's talking to his wife."

Sebastian's eyes widened. *Eilis. Wife.* That felt kind of sort of . . . good . . . but he'd think about that later. "Ma'am," he said, his hand on her arm, "please don't rush off."

Sebastian squatted in front of the boy so he was at eye level. He pulled his wallet out of his back pocket and pulled two business cards out and gave them to him.

"My name is Sebastian Taight—" and he heard a couple of gasps in the somewhat trendy crowd, which still eavesdropped. "You give one of these cards to your principal at school and tell him to call me. You keep this one for yourself. If your mother says it's okay, you call me and I'll take you around and teach you everything you ever wanted to know about money. The more people who have money, the better for everybody because money really *does* grow on trees."

He knew that was too metaphorical for the boy to understand, but he wasn't eager to stifle children who understood what they wanted but didn't have the means to get it.

Sebastian rose and smiled at the boy's mother. "Nice to meet you, Mom of Christopher."

"Thank you for being kind to my son," she said.

"Mom?" Christopher said, looking up at her pleadingly. "Please, can I call him?"

"May I," she corrected.

"Tell you what," Sebastian said. "I have to go to the Board of Trade Monday. Would you and Christopher care to accompany me?"

She swallowed, her eyes wide. "I don't even know what that is."

"They buy and sell wheat there, Mom." Sebastian looked down at him, as shocked as his mother. "Please, Mom? Please may we go?"

She looked down at him and caressed his face. "All right." Sebastian's smile deepened when she looked back at him. "My name's Christina Van Horn."

"Nice to meet you, Mrs. Van Horn. If you'll call and leave a message with your address and phone number, I'll pick you up Monday morning at seven. That all right?"

"Yes, thank you," she whispered and hesitantly offered her hand to Sebastian, which he shook firmly. She and Christopher turned then and walked up the street, across the street toward the gated and fenced rattletrap neighborhood of pale blue townhouses.

"That was nice," Eilis murmured.

"Naw," he murmured in return. "It helps my bottom line to teach people how to make money."

"How?"

"Money isn't a zero-sum game. The pie gets bigger as more people have money and therefore the pie has the opportunity to gather more people. It's a cycle. People making money, not being in debt, letting their money do all their work for them, putting it back into the economy by investing? Good for me. Companies working at their best, hiring, putting out good products? Good for me." He stopped then. Generalities, principles, beliefs, he'd share. Specifics, no, and especially not with a crowd packed with people who could and would take detailed notes in their heads.

So he wrapped his hand around her neck to bring her close to him—oh, she smelled divine, like almond and cherry blossoms—and whisper in her ear, "I don't think I'm going to be able to have a decent conversation with you now with all these people listening. Do you want to go somewhere else?"

"Oh, no," she said in a normal conversational tone, grinning, eyes sparkling, arms crossed over her chest. "I'm enjoying myself immensely. Where did you go to business school?"

Sebastian squirmed because at this point he was more on display than he wanted to be—especially now that everyone knew who he was—and he had just passed uncomfortable. On the other hand, he wanted so very badly to amuse Eilis and he was doing a *very* good job. "Harvard."

"What did you do between your horrible job and Harvard?"

"I lived in Paris for six years and studied art at the École des Beaux-Arts."

Eilis's mouth dropped and several people turned around to stare at him. It didn't help matters that now that he and Eilis were in the threshold of the doorway, the whole of the restaurant was listening—and it was a tiny place.

"Really."

"Yes, really," he repeated dryly.

"I— I'm—" Eilis laughed then, her fist over her mouth to try to control it, but couldn't.

"It's part of the ADD thing."

She laughed until she cried and he wanted to see her that way forever. Other than his only actual lover, Vanessa, he had never spent more than a few days at most fucking any one woman and this one—ah, this one he wanted to take to his bed and keep her there for as long as she wanted to be there.

He decided not to speak again until the restaurant patrons had begun to mind their own business, and, fortunately, Eilis understood without having to be told. However, the little nudges in his ribs from her elbow didn't make him stop wanting to amuse her.

"What did you do in Paris besides study art?" she asked later, low, once they'd gotten their butcher-paper-wrapped soggy white bread and brisket-piled-to-the-ceiling sandwiches complete with equally soggy fries and a mess of pickles.

"I discovered wine and absinthe—"

She gasped. "You drank absinthe?"

He grinned. "I *love* absinthe. Anyway, I listened to a lot of good music, saw a lot of nice gardens—" He smiled when she flushed and picked at her sauce-drenched beef. "Fu—er, met a lot of nice women, ate a lot of good food, wore a lot of nice clothes, and basically partied my way through school, Louis XIV style."

"Not like frat boys here, huh?"

"Oh, no. Paris is where I got culture. Knox introduced me to a lot of things, but it was nothing compared to what I could get in Europe. I loved it. Here," he said when it seemed she meant to stop eating after just a couple of strips of brisket. He loaded up his fork, slathered the load with sauce, and said, "Open your mouth."

Confused, she did as he said. Her eyes widened when he popped that bite in her mouth. "Eilis, if you don't eat, I'll feed you myself."

He suddenly wasn't joking and it only took a nanosecond for her to get it.

"I'm not as hungry as I thought I was," she whispered around the food, a sudden desperation in her eyes.

"Yes, you are. You've been hungry for the last ten years."

If it was possible, her eyes got even bigger. "How— That's not true."

"Oh, sure it is. And I'm not going to argue about it. You show me you can eat like you haven't eaten in two weeks and then maybe I'll think about not holding you down and feeding you myself."

"No, you don't underst—"

"What I understand," he murmured, narrowing his eyes, "is that you have a body Rubens would have sold his soul to paint and you don't need to fix it."

She swallowed the mouthful of food. "Rubens painted fat women," she whispered, obviously horrified.

"Bullshit. He painted goddesses. Now eat like one and quit trying to be something you're not."

Eyeing him warily, she took one bite, then another. With a little further urging on his part, she finally allowed herself to eat her fill. She couldn't eat the whole thing, but he didn't expect that. As far as Sebastian knew, only he and the other men in his tribe could put away a whole sandwich *and* the fries. Morgan and Kenard could eat two. Certainly his female cousins couldn't do it and even the Protein Princess could only eat a whole sandwich because she abstained from the bread and fries.

As they cleaned up their mess and left the restaurant into the relative heat of an early October day in Missouri, Sebastian thought he'd push his luck, so he found Eilis's hand and laced his fingers through hers. He smiled and watched her out of the corner of his eye as she started, looking at him in shock. He didn't say anything and she didn't pull away.

"Mr. Taight! Mr. Taight!"

Sebastian and Eilis stopped then and turned to see a woman and two men jogging toward him and he sighed. There went his day, right down the tubes.

"Mr. Taight, I have some questions for you if you wouldn't mind."

"Yes, I do mind." He turned his back on her and continued to walk, Eilis in hand.

"Mr. Taight, wait!" The woman ran around him and spoke into a recorder. "Is it true that Kevin Oakley's bid for the Senate seat was initiated and is being funded by you and Bryce Kenard?" She stuck the recorder in his face.

"No comment."

"Mr. Taight, how do you feel about your growing reputation as the second incarnation of Boss Tom Pendergast?"

The questions all began to run together and Sebastian only wanted to get away from this pack of rabid hyenas.

"Mr. Taight, do you know why Senator Oth is backing off his anti-Taight rhetoric?"

"Mr. Taight, is your defense counsel your cousin, Chouteau County prosecutor Knox Hilliard?"

"I know who all my cousins are, thanks," he snarled and refused to say anything else. They'd spoiled the mood and now Eilis wasn't amused anymore. The reporter kept after him even as he handed Eilis into his wreck of a pickup and then went around to his side to climb in and start it. It was at that point that cameras began to flash. Sebastian let out the clutch and nearly hit some of the reporters in front of him—and he would've been okay with that had it happened.

He was furious and he wasn't even fit company for himself.

"I'm sorry, Eilis," he said before they got back on the highway and wouldn't be able to hear each other at all given the open windows and the loud engine.

"Is it like that all the time for you?"

"If any reporters are around, yes. I should've known better than to say my name out loud where someone could call one to the spot."

"Boss Tom?" She snickered, but tried to hide it when he slid her a look.

While he was happy she was still amused . . . "Yeah, I'm not thrilled about the comparison. It was funny the first sixty-two times. Now, not so much."

Then they were on the highway, and Sebastian only knew one way to salvage everything. He passed Eilis's exit, the engine's roar making it possible for him to ignore her yell that he'd gone too far. He took the next exit and pulled into the drive-through of a frozen custard stand behind three cars.

"Okay, Eilis, what's it gonna be? Chocolate, cherry, strawberry, banana, or what? 'Cause I'm going to hold you hostage until you eat whatever I choose for you if you don't make a decision."

She stared at him like he was nuts. "Okay, look. You made me eat half a brisket sandwich, but I am not eating any ice cream."

"You are too."

"No, I am not!" she repeated heatedly.

At that point, he leaned toward her until his nose touched hers, looked in her eyes and said, very quietly, very deliberately, "If you don't eat at least half a small concrete, I'll take you home and strip you naked. I'll smear ice cream into every nook and cranny in your body and lick it all up. Then I'll put you in a shower and soap you down myself—and possibly lick that off, too, if it smells as good as you do."

Her eyes widened and she pulled away from him.

"Was that a 'Yes, Sebastian, I'll have some ice cream' or a 'No, Sebastian, please lick ice cream out of my nooks and crannies'?"

"I'll have some ice cream," she whispered.

He smiled and sat up. "Very good. Pick a flavor."

"You're a bully, you know that?" Eilis said finally once they'd settled at a wrought iron table on her back patio, eating ice cream and enjoying the garden she'd built that Sebastian loved.

"That's what the Journal tells me," he replied smoothly, very, very pleased with himself for having a nice date and not making a fool of himself, for amusing his date instead of pissing her off or scaring her half to death.

Except for that ice-cream-licking thing.

"Did you have any big rebellion like most kids do?"

He smiled. "Oh, sure. A couple of them, actually, but they weren't like normal rebellions so I wouldn't actually classify them as that."

She waited a beat or two. "Well?"

"Oh, you wanted me to tell you what they were."

She rolled her eyes and he laughed.

"The first one was the oddsmaking, but my mom never found out about that. The second was art. I wanted to study art and she thought that was an extremely unproductive thing to do. She doesn't like that I speculate in art, either, even though I make money at it. She doesn't understand that I need the art as much as I need the game of money."

"How did you get to Paris in the first place? Did you run away?"

He drew in a deep breath and wondered how much he wanted to tell her. "I was a missionary for my church and that's where they sent me."

Eilis looked up at him sharply. "You're Mormon?"

"No," he said, hoping she'd take the hint and not push, but she didn't.

"Okay. Were you Mormon *then*?"

He grunted. "Yes."

"And? What happened?"

"Not quite sure," he finally said. "Several things went wrong and then I just got tired of the politics of the mission. So I left after almost a year."

"Left? Like left, how?"

"I mean, like I left the apartment I shared with my companion one day without a word. That was my third rebellion. I called my mom, told her I was done with it and why, that I was going to roam Europe and to wire the rest of my money into my European accounts."

"And she actually sent you the money?"

"Of course she did. It was my money and my mother is nothing if not scrupulously honest. She was seriously pissed that I'd left, but she wasn't going to withhold my own money from me. Well, I went and saw Europe and learned enough to know that not only did I find the whole process hypocritical, I wasn't even sure what I really believed."

"Then what?"

"I got done with the rest of Europe, though I spent a lot of time in Seville because I finally got seduced." He laughed again. "Twenty years old. I guess better late than never. So anyway, I went back to Paris and pretty much ate, slept, and lived in the Louvre and at school."

"Didn't you stand out there, an American in Paris?" she asked, a quirk to her mouth.

He laughed. "You'd think so. The black Irish look doesn't do well in Paris unless you can speak French like a Parisian, but I passed for a native because of my accent."

"Did you do those little sidewalk chalk drawings?"

"Oh, yes. I wanted to see if I could actually earn money as an artist. Only I didn't do the normal reproductions like they did. I picked odd things to rip off and did a little of my own work."

"Did you make money?"

"Not enough to support myself in the style to which I wanted to become accustomed—" Eilis rolled her eyes and he chuckled. "—but enough to buy basic necessities. Didn't need it because I had a bank account and money sitting in it collecting interest, but it was validating and I made an attempt to live on it. That wasn't hard because I spent so much time out of my apartment I didn't need anything to put in it except art supplies, good bread, good cheese, good wine, and absinthe. I made more money than the students who did the reproductions. I'd be damned if I was going to spend my entire time there drawing the *Mona Lisa* three times a day for ignorant tourists."

"What did you draw then?"

"Well," Sebastian said, looking out at the garden Eilis had built, beginning to remember all he had done twenty years before. It'd been a long time since he'd talked about Paris and now, in talking about it, he missed it. "Have you ever seen *Mary Poppins?*"

"Of course."

"I did the same chalk drawings that Bert did when they went riding the carousel horses through the animation—only much, much bigger and much, much better."

He was gratified when she let out a little squeal of laughter and put her feet up on the edge of the wrought iron table, completely forgetting that she hadn't wanted to eat the concrete and slurping happily along.

"Why didn't you stay in Paris?"

"I was homesick."

She looked at him and tilted her head as if she found that fascinating. "Really?"

"Really. I didn't pay much attention to European politics, so it didn't bother me until they began to mess with my investments. I took my ball and went home."

She looked at him, an amused question all over her face, so he answered it. "My basic philosophy is Objectivist and maybe, if I'm having a particularly practical day, Libertarian."

Sebastian could tell she still didn't really understand because those labels weren't common conversation fodder. "I know Libertarian," she said. "I didn't know there was anything beyond that."

"Ayn Rand?"

"Oh, *The Fountainhead*. Yes, I understand now. Excellence, reason, enlightened self-interest, egoism."

"Right. The concept is best explained in *Anthem* and the nitty gritty of it's more understandable in *Atlas Shrugged*, but yes. It's one of the reasons I'm starting to get pissed off about the Pendergast references."

"The comparison's unavoidable, Sebastian. No, you're not a politician and no, you don't have the entire police force as your thug patrol. But setting up a senatorial candidate . . . ?"

Sebastian snorted. "If Kevin hadn't wanted to run, he'd have said no. He was recommended to me as someone who wanted to get on with the next phase of his career. He just happens to have politics that I can live with, if not thoroughly embrace. He's not a puppet and he figured out the entire game plan the minute he was approached about running. My goal and his goal just happened to be mutually beneficial."

"And your goal is to make Congress think twice about demanding your presence unless Fen is actually sitting in Congress."

"Ooh, you're kinda savvy that way, Eilis."

She laughed delightedly and Sebastian thought he could watch her laugh forever. Her eyes sparkled like sapphires and emeralds, and her tear-track scar glimmered spectacularly in the sunlight. "When Knox assigned you to me as my trustee, I spent all night on the computer, googling and sifting for information; I had to build a flow chart to figure out what was fact and what was fiction. There were a lot of holes in the story I pieced together from that, but now you've filled them all in."

Sebastian shook his head, then took another bite of his concrete—mint chocolate chip. "Not all of them, no."

"I'm guessing murder's a part of it." He started and looked at her. She grimaced. "Do you know if Fen— I mean, Knox's bride? Did Fen really—?"

"Yes," he sighed, and explained. Then, "Fen really kicked my ass with his Senate bid. I didn't know what to do."

"I find that hard to believe."

"In case you haven't noticed, Eilis," he drawled, "I live in my own little world." She snickered. "Practical politics don't register. Ideals? Yes. Principles and concepts? Yes. The everyday nitty gritty bullshit? No. Which is why I came home from Europe."

"Okay. I can see that. So you came home from Europe and went to Harvard. How'd you get into the MBA program with an art degree?"

"They thought it was very, ah, chic to admit a twenty-six-year-old self-made millionaire with an art degree from a European school." He took another bite. "So, all right, Eilis. I've talked more about myself today than I have in, well, *ever.* Your turn."

Her smile faltered infinitesimally, and her laugh was a bit stilted. "Not a lot of highlights. You know, your ordinary poor kid from the ghetto stuff."

Secrets. Interesting. He wondered how far in he could get until she shut him out.

"What about your folks? I told you about mine."

She hesitated. "You didn't say much about your father. I'm guessing he wasn't in the picture much?"

Very good, Eilis. Distract and redirect. I'll go with it. For now. "My father died about ten years ago, but he was always around. Just very distracted." Eilis chuckled. "ADD. He had the potential to be a great artist, but he couldn't afford more than number two pencils and typing paper. And even if he had, he would've had no idea how to capitalize on his talent and further, I'm not sure he would've if he could've. It would've taken away the magic of the creative process."

"Ah, so that's where you got it and why your mother thinks art's a waste of time."

"Yep. He wasn't any happier that I left the mission than my mother was, but he was happy I'd shown the good sense—in his opinion—to go to art school instead. It was one thing he and I could relate to because he certainly didn't appreciate my bank account and how I grew it—*especially* after I offered him enough to retire early and comfortably, and to send him to the KC Art Institute with paint and canvas."

Eilis's brow wrinkled. "I don't understand that. Money's useful. More money is more useful."

"Yes, my mother knew that. All he saw was the need around him. He didn't know that I was making money hand over fist and, by extension, how much of that my mother got. She socked it away, played the market very well once she had enough to work with, hid it from him. But . . . the food got better and the cars got more reliable and the house had a few repairs it couldn't have had before. He never noticed.

"I loved my dad, Eilis, don't mistake me," he said. "He was a hard worker, very wise in other ways, and generous, which I greatly admire. He loved and guided Giselle and Knox as much as he loved and guided me. He taught us all a lot about generosity of both money and time, but I wasn't willing to work as hard as he did for as little money as he made. None of us were."

"What did he do?"

"He worked for the KC parks department doing the crap jobs nobody else would do because they were disgusting or physically difficult, which was very typical for him. His philosophies weren't well thought out nor were they in the least bit practical. If someone had asked my mother for water from a well, she would've let them have the water if they drew it themselves, but made them leave a deposit for twice the value of the bucket and kept back a little of that for a rental fee. My father would've drawn the water himself, given it to them, and told them not to worry about bringing the bucket back, leaving no way for us to draw our own water."

"Did you resent that?"

"No. I didn't understand it until I was older and had money. By then, it was irrelevant because I didn't have to live that way. I talked to him about it a few times and he just couldn't give up the idea that having a lot of money when other people had none was evil. Worse, he didn't understand the concept of teaching a man to fish. I like to think I got a good mix of my mother's basic business sense and my father's philanthropic bent and artistic sensibilities."

"That sounds like a great source of contention between your mother and father."

"It was, but if nothing else, my dad had a strict moral code and a firm hand on the household, so my mother had to sneak. They each had the best interests of the family at heart, but they approached it from opposite points of view and they weren't reconcilable."

"And you don't have any siblings?"

"I had two stillborn brothers." He speared her with a glance. "Do you?"

She ran her tongue over her teeth, again hesitating. "I have a half brother."

"Do you get along?"

"Well, yes, I suppose you could say that."

"What's that mean?"

"It means," she said slowly, "that when he and I have reason to interact, we get along very well. He's always been very kind to me."

"And you have little reason to interact."

"Yes."

"It sounds to me like you'd like to interact more."

"Very much so, yes."

"He's not interested?"

She took a deep breath. "He, ah, doesn't know he has a sister, much less that I'm it."

Sebastian said nothing for a moment, thoroughly shocked, letting his mind run through all the implications of that. "So . . . your parents?"

"My biological parents don't acknowledge me unless it's expedient for them to do so."

Holy shit. Sebastian could feel Eilis's retreat from him the deeper he drew her down into her past, and that was the last thing he wanted. Plenty of time to delve into her history when she felt more comfortable with him. Changing directions, he said,

"How did you come up with the concept of an outsourcing human resources company? You were way ahead of the curve."

She smiled a genuine smile and he could feel her coming back to him, even if only a little. "I was an administrative assistant in an HR department and everyone there was overworked, between managing the health insurance issues and the 401(k)s, plus hiring and such. I did a lot of work I wasn't supposed to be doing and never got paid for. Nobody would let me implement my ideas because I was *just* an administrative assistant, so I decided—" She stopped, chuckled, and said, "I took my ball and went home."

Sebastian laughed.

"I knew I could do a better job than they did and that I could become independently wealthy doing it."

"And you did."

"Yes." She licked a stray drop of ice cream off her lips and at that moment, Sebastian though he'd never been so hard for a woman in his life—and talking business! "I didn't sleep much those first two or three years. I was either working or worrying."

Sebastian had almost scraped the bottom of his cup when he decided that since she wasn't going to welcome his questions as to what made her tick, he'd talked about himself all he could stand, and she probably wouldn't respond well if he simply picked her up and took her to bed, it was time to quit while he was ahead.

He wanted to *amuse* this woman, *seduce* this Rubens goddess, *lure* her into his bed to stay awhile, maybe a very long, long while—a lifetime or so would be a good start.

You don't seduce. You overwhelm.

Giselle's words came back to him in a flash; he realized that in this area of his life, he had never followed his own axiom: *If what you're doing isn't working, think of something else.*

Slow. Easy. No freight trains allowed. As long as he could keep the door open, he could draw her out little by little.

Once he had set his course of action, he stood and stretched. "Well, Eilis, I'm going to head home."

"Where's home?"

"Plaza."

Her mouth dropped open. "You drove all the way up here to take me to lunch, which was way back down there again?"

Sebastian came down from his stretch and saw his opening. He dropped, bracing himself on the arms of her chair, and he kissed her, deeply and long, tasting maraschino cherry flavoring on her tongue, until she sighed and kissed him back, then continued kissing her a while longer for good measure. Finally, he drew away from her slowly, watching her as he straightened to his full height.

"Sure did." He turned toward his truck. "And I'd do it again, too," he called over his shoulder before he climbed in and drove home.

Once there, he pulled up the website of his favorite vendor, ordered the supplies he needed for a new project for delivery to the old falling-down barn at the back of Knox's property. He would inform Knox later that he had appropriated his barn for an unspecified period of time and his services as an artist's assistant.

Maybe he had a chance of squeezing Ford out of her mind after all.

Eilis went to bed that night and looked long and hard at *Morning in Bed*.

Usually she fantasized about what it would be like to be painted by him, that dark and dangerous, beautiful nude man, made love to by him.

She remembered when she'd bought the painting: In Spain, years before, at a gallery that had only had it for three days. She'd already begun collecting Fords by then and she knew with the certainty of a connoisseur that though the subject was male, Ford *had* painted it. The strokes were off, though, different somehow, slapdash, as if the artist had some measure of contempt for the subject.

Her *obsession* with the painting hadn't begun until she'd married David, lived through the hell he'd visited upon her, felt her self-esteem shred with each cruel word David spoke—knowing she had to stay with him until she figured out how he was stealing from her and where he hid it. She might never have survived that time, much less emerged quasi-victorious, but for her garden and *Morning in Bed*.

Somewhere in the back of her mind during that time, she'd known Ford would find her beautiful, would make love to her to give her that precious flush of orgasm, then paint her and present her to the world as beautiful.

Rubens . . . painted goddesses.

So did Ford. While she didn't like the Fords that displayed rubenesque women, she did take comfort in the fact that he loved them well, painted them, made them beautiful.

Valued them.

She still wanted that, but she was no closer to finding Ford than she ever was; she had private investigators in Chicago and Atlanta and New York, LA and Taos and Seattle searching—and had for three years—to no avail.

It occurred to her to expand her reach to Europe, but tonight it didn't seem quite as important while snatches of her date with Sebastian—had she agreed to a real date?—kept interrupting. She smiled when she remembered the kiss in the garden, when he had told her she was a master gardener and that what she had created was a work of art.

The old beat-up pickup truck he drove surprised her, but more than that, the sight of Sebastian in old faded jeans over battered black cowboy boots, with a plain white tee shirt tucked in his waistband, had made her catch her breath. She'd stood at her window watching him flirt with her flowers, muscles rippling under his shirt. His jeans rode low on his hips and caressed his tight butt with a lover's touch. His tousled hair shifted colors from black to iridescent navy in the sunlight as the breeze played with it.

He was forty, her age, and looked thirty, yet she'd seen the white scattered amongst the black. He would never go completely white, but ease into a salt-and-pepper perfectly suited to that sculpted face and those ice blue eyes that randomly darkened to lavender, then violet and back to ice.

She'd seen a weapon, a matte black gun, in his waistband at the small of his back. She hadn't asked about it and he hadn't volunteered any information, but after their incredibly enlightening conversation concerning the fate of Knox's bride, it made complete sense. She wondered if he had worn it while in her office building and decided it didn't make any difference; he was who he was and for some reason, she found herself feeling . . . Safe. Warm. Protected.

She knew Knox carried a weapon. During the course of David's trial, she'd noticed that all the attorneys in his office did and she wondered if that happened in the other counties in the metro or just Chouteau County.

She gave Fen a cease and desist order at the point of a gun.

Then there was this mysterious cousin Giselle who carried, to whom Sebastian had briefly referred as "Boudicca with a Glock" with more than a little affection of the brotherly sort in his voice. Eilis felt bereft at that. She craved that sort of affection from her brother, a man who didn't know he had a sister—and would hate her if he did know.

Eilis had never met anyone who could stand Fen Hilliard down on any level. She knew CEOs who cowered at the thought of incurring his wrath—certainly Eilis was one of them—and yet this family, Sebastian and Knox and Giselle, had declared war on him with no trace of intimidation. She wondered what it would be like to not fear Fen Hilliard.

She knew Sebastian had never married and it didn't take a high IQ to figure out why: looks and money. She wondered if he had ever been pursued by a woman for his brain, but somehow she doubted it. All that genius and sensibility wrapped up in pretty paper and a handsome bow, going to waste.

Today, she'd had a nice date with a nice man. Not King Midas, not Sebastian Taight, not anything but an interesting and attractive man who made her laugh, made her think, and made her tingle . . . there. She hadn't met a man who'd made her do that in . . .

Her brow wrinkled and her lips pursed.

Well, not in a long time, she supposed. David had done her no favors and she barely remembered any one of the long string of lovers before him. She swallowed. No, not *lovers*.

Fucks.

Meaningless, worthless, some of them nameless, and, worse—not fun or pleasurable enough to make up for the transience. Eilis couldn't remember when or even if she'd ever truly enjoyed sex with anyone other than herself.

Not worth remembering, particularly as compared to Sebastian.

Who had only kissed her.

Three times.

Slow and easy, in a way she had never been kissed, and her breath caught again at the memory of how he made her feel.

But now she also feared that about him, how he made her feel. He was dangerous to her in ways she had not expected, in ways Fen Hilliard wasn't.

Yes, Sebastian would sell her paintings, but she would have done that anyway had she had time to clean out her staff herself. Their salaries would have decimated the proceeds from the sale of those paintings and the good cash would've been thrown after bad. Pointless. He comprehended that decision based on her inability to get rid of her dead weight and respected her for it.

But no, he didn't want to take her company or hand her over to Fen, as she'd originally assumed. He wanted her company to recover from what David had done to it, wanted to put her back on her feet. He *understood* her.

Sebastian threatened her with his warmth, his magic.

As far as her nonexistent experience with actual relationships went, she suspected he wanted one with her. She dared not fall in love with him, though she feared it would be only too easy to do so—if she'd even recognize it for love, since she didn't know what that felt like.

From everything she could gather, when a woman was in love with a man and began a relationship with him, she shared herself, her life, her past. The one thing Eilis dreaded most in the world was Sebastian's rejection if she opened her soul to him. Sebastian would despise her for what had happened, what she'd done. Any normal man would.

As a matter of fact, Eilis had no wish to share her past with *anyone* and she'd buried it as deeply as possible. She simply lived as if those years had never existed.

She had never cried over her childhood, her adolescence. She had cried once in her biological mother's presence, begging for some acknowledgment, and had been sneered at, slapped, for her weakness.

I'll not acknowledge a girl who snivels and grovels for what she doesn't deserve. If you'd come here proud, demanding, I might have considered talking to you for a moment. I could have respected that. But you're weak and I despise weakness.

She had cried once in Knox Hilliard's office when she related every second of her marriage and, again demonstrating that he was not the man the city vilified, he had taken her in his arms and hugged her for a long time. She had felt no threat from him, no interest in her as anything other than someone who needed some protection and a measure of vengeance. He was the only one who could give her both and he'd done as well as he could.

She'd never shared a moment of anything before she'd testified to David's evil at his trial, and had refused to talk about anything before David.

Yet she almost couldn't regret telling Sebastian what little she had.

She glanced up at *Morning in Bed*, seeing it shadowed on the wall in the dim moonlight.

Ford.

Ford was the key, because he wouldn't care. If she found him, if he deigned to see her, he would make love to her, he would paint her, he would make her look and feel as beautiful as she wanted to feel, and then he would send her on her way, prepared to meet any man romantically on her terms.

He would throw the final shovel full of dirt on the grave of her past.

46: Morning in Bed

December 2006

I T WAS FRIDAY, SEBASTIAN'S DAY TO VISIT, AND GOING ON THREE O'CLOCK. Eilis was very nervous today. She intended to do something she'd never done before. Ever.

He walked in the building a little after three and stopped at nearly every cubicle if its occupant caught his eye or ear. It was the same way every week and his journey from the front door to her office was going on an hour. Nobody wanted to ask advice; they just wanted to thank him for what he'd done, chat a little, joke around, share food. And he accommodated everyone with ease and grace. She couldn't help feeling some jealousy. They didn't treat her like that—and it was her own fault.

Her persona had been easy when she'd had to make deals she couldn't get as anyone other than the excruciatingly proper Miss Logan. Now with enough credibility to drop the charade, powerful allies, a decluttered staff, and a happy workplace, she missed what she'd never had: a camaraderie with her employees.

Sebastian still never smiled or laughed when he was in a suit, but it didn't seem to matter. He radiated warmth and humor like a cat's purr. How did the financial world not see this? Why had she never heard this from a CEO he'd rescued? All she'd ever heard was how dangerous he was.

Of course, he'd been very dangerous the day he'd threatened to smear her with a cold concrete then lick it off. She closed her eyes and breathed deeply. She almost wished she'd been courageous enough to call his bluff, but that was too risky.

Fridays now were a treat because alwaysalwaysalways, Sebastian took her into her wood-paneled private office to greet her with a kiss, then left her with a kiss. Sometimes it was short and sweet, a drop on the forehead, on the back of her hand, in the palm of her hand, butterfly kisses. Sometimes it was playful and sweet, not too deep, not too flippant. Once, and only once, he had wrapped his arms around her and kissed her long and deep, searching, sucking her soul, devouring her senses. Every week was an opportunity to hope for another one of those.

Little by little, he was seducing her, pulling her into a relationship she didn't want, but Eilis wasn't quite sure he wouldn't do it anyway no matter how hard she resisted. He *was* ruthless after all and he tended to turn into a bulldozer when he was opposed.

"Good afternoon, Eilis," Sebastian said cordially as he dropped his backpack on the table, then entered her office and closed the doors. "I hope you've had a good week."

Eilis smiled, wondering what would be in store for her today. Alas, today was a kiss on the cheek. She hid her disappointment as he returned to the table outside her office doors.

"I think so," she said evenly, drawing up every ounce of her persona to help her through the next couple of hours. As usual, the reports were prepared and he sat to look them over. All was quiet as he read, flipped through papers, scratched out comments in red.

"Well, Eilis, you've done well." Same as usual. He pulled a piece of green paper, folded in thirds, out of his suit coat's inner pocket. It was the checklist he'd written and worked from so long ago—had it really been only four months?—and opened it. He looked it over, red pen in hand.

"Your client sales are picking up a little here, a little there. I suspect you may have tapped out that market, but who knows? It seems the management of the 401(k) plans is exceptional."

"Yes, thank you for getting us in with Blackwood Securities. Quite a few of my colleagues are amazed and jealous."

Sebastian looked up at her, a twinkle in his eye. "Jack Blackwood's a miracle worker, isn't he? When we go to New York, I'll introduce you, but I warn you, he's different."

"I've spoken with him on the phone several times. I can only imagine."

"His wife kicks his ass and his CFO keeps him from floating off into the stratosphere."

"Melinda Newman?"

"Yes. Brilliant woman. She saved my bacon a few years ago when Jack was, ah, unexpectedly incommunicado for a week. Now *that's* a story. I expect that once word gets out about how well managed those accounts are, that's where you'll get most of your business. That and managing the health insurance issues." He looked back down. "The screening tests are out on the market and selling," he said absently, then crossed it off the list. "Your revenue from that is picking up and I'm impressed with the success you've had with it. I've been hearing rumors of its effectiveness, so very good."

Eilis preened under his warmth and regard, even though he couldn't tell because she was "on."

"The beta for the small business software is due in three months. How's that coming along?"

"Actually, Michael has an alpha version right now. I expect it'll be in beta testing next month."

"Oh, very good. The auction is on February fifth and I think, from looking at these numbers today that after the auction, with or without the beta software, you'll be in the black and we won't need to wait until August to start the IPO process. In fact, if the auction goes well, we can start it while we're there. Jack's ready for it whenever we are."

That surprised her. "Really?"

"Yes, really. All you needed was a little time and a little help."

She turned back to the window and watched the hive below her, afraid to ask. Afraid he'd say no. Afraid she may have alienated him somehow that she didn't know, kisses notwithstanding. He joined her at the window then, just as he had the first day.

"I have a present for you, Eilis," he said, low.

She started. "You do?"

"Yes, but I'll have to deliver it to you. When would you be free and have a couple of hours?"

Eilis paused. "Tomorrow, but— I had something to ask you. A favor," she said in a rush. "I was wondering if you'd help me decorate my house for Christmas? You know, climbing ladders, heavy lifting, that sort of thing. I haven't dressed it since September eleventh."

"Of course I'll help you, Eilis. I love Yule, but I don't decorate because I have the Plaza lights out my front windows. When would you like me to come over?"

"Well, since you're coming over tomorrow, maybe you could make a day of it? I'll make a povitica. Blueberry cream cheese is my favorite."

She knew he was looking at her, but she couldn't look at him because she was so embarrassed about having had to ask for help in this particular matter, from a man, and from a man who'd rescued her once already.

"Povitica sounds good. Do you have any mulling spices?"

"No."

"Okay. I'll bring the wassail."

She did glance at him then. "Yule? Wassail? You sound like you're from merry olde England."

She felt, rather than heard, his laugh and he still hadn't smiled, but his mouth did quirk a little. "I'm pagan, Eilis."

"But I thought you said—"

"I didn't say I hadn't found another way, did I?"

"No."

"What time would you like me to show up with my present? Remember, a couple of hours."

"Nine-ish, I guess," she said, feeling as if she'd just missed something important about him.

"Okay. Dress in your warmest worst clothes."

And he was gone.

Without kissing her.

She was waiting in the courtyard once she had opened the gate for Sebastian's old pickup, then closed it after he was through. As he drove closer, she gasped and clapped her hands over her mouth, then began to laugh.

"You brought me horse manure!" she squealed and knew she should be embarrassed about being delighted about feces, but she wasn't. The entire bed was full and piled high with horse manure, a blue tarp over the whole thing.

"I did," he said as he leaned over the seat to open the passenger door for her. "Let's go get it unloaded."

There was a box of wines, juices, and spices on the floor of the passenger side and she said, "Hold on. I'll take this in."

Quickly enough, she was back and had hopped in. He drove down the path to the compost, then over the stone bridge. She told him where to park so they could unload it where she needed it to go.

"Shovels?"

"Oh, no. Bobcat."

Sebastian grinned as she went to the backhoe, climbed in, started it up, and drove it the very short distance to the bed of the pickup. He leaned against the truck to watch her and she felt rather nervous all of a sudden. He had never seen this side of her and she was a little embarrassed. She set the levelers, then lowered the bucket carefully so that she didn't damage the truck—not that anybody'd notice—and scooped up a good portion of the pile. The cab swung around and she dumped it.

It took ten scoops to get all she could, then she lifted the levelers and drove it around to a different spot and parked.

"Eilis," he said, a corner of his mouth turned up, "I never would've thought I'd get turned on by the sight of a beautiful woman shoveling shit with a backhoe."

She blushed and ducked her head, then he laughed. "Shovels and brooms now." When she came back from gathering those, he was thumbing through a CD sleeve. "I don't work without music," he muttered, "but I can't decide what's good for such an auspicious occasion. Here." He gave her the sleeve and took a shovel.

"This is all classical," she said.

"I very rarely listen to anything not classified that way, except for zydeco. *Carmina Burana*'s my favorite."

"Well—"

"Not that," he said shortly. "That's for another time. When you hear it, you'll understand."

"Okay, then. Old Christmas chestnuts. *Messiah* or *Nutcracker?*"

Sebastian pursed his lips. "*Messiah.*"

She blinked. "For a pagan?"

"Good music's good music and spirituality is spirituality. I have no problem with Jesus of Nazareth. It's religion I don't like. It's said that *Messiah* is the most perfect score ever composed. Not sure I agree because there's just way too much perfect music out there, but it *is* divine." He paused. "No pun intended."

Eilis laughed and she marveled at how easy it was to laugh with Sebastian, a man reputed never to laugh at all. It was her own delicious little secret, to know Sebastian Taight laughed and that he laughed with her.

The music began to pour out of the truck's speakers and they began to finish unloading the manure. There was much left that the backhoe couldn't get, but that was better than having to do it all by hand.

"So you won't get your air conditioner fixed, but you have a state-of-the-art sound system."

"Of course," he grunted and heaved. "I have my priorities straight."

"And the zydeco?"

He slid her a glance and his gaze flickered over her hair. "*Jole blon,*" he said, then began to speak in what seemed to her *very* lazy French.

"What *is* that?" she asked, interrupting him.

"Cajun French. Fascinating patois and culture. I *love* it."

"What did you say?"

He smirked. "It doesn't translate, but trust me, it was vulgar."

She blushed and turned away from him when he laughed.

It didn't take nearly as long as Sebastian had predicted and it would've taken even less time had they not gotten into a manure flinging contest. Sebastian actually played to win, but Eilis bided her time and finally smacked him square in the face with an entire shovel full. "Okay, okay, uncle," Sebastian groaned, trying to pick pieces of hay from his tongue. "You don't play fair."

"Of course it was fair. You should've known better than to take me on on my own turf."

The last of it was swept out of the bed and they climbed back into the cab to go up to the house.

"Come in this way," Eilis said, leading him across the back patio and around the house where there was a large atrium with an outside door. It was a bathroom.

He cocked an eyebrow at her. "Floor to ceiling, wall to wall glass in a bathroom?"

"Who's going to see? Besides, the hot water makes it steam up fast. Go ahead. I'll wait since," she smirked, "I didn't get a face full."

Sebastian curled his lip at her and she laughed as she went back to the truck to get the change of clothes he'd brought and had asked her to retrieve.

While she was in his truck, she snooped. Shamelessly. On his key chain was a Ferrari key, which wouldn't have surprised her before she saw him driving his ancient pickup. Nothing in the ashtray. Nothing under the seats. It was probably the cleanest rattletrap truck she'd ever seen, in fact. It was in the glove compartment she hit pay dirt. There was a hardback sketchbook and a case with pencils in it. It seemed there were very few blank pages left. She opened it and her soul filled with wonder.

Page after page of his visual impressions of people, places, and things. There were many pages dedicated to Paris: women in various stages of undress, the Moulin Rouge, the Seine, Notre Dame, a small café with a very old man and a concerned child.

A bedsit with a full-size bed, a small table with a paper-wrapped loaf of bread, a bottle of wine, a small wheel of cheese on a board with a small knife. Apples, lemons, pears, grapes. A stack of clothes folded neatly on a chair pushed up against a wall. Canvases scattered around, an easel.

It was a travelogue of Europe and she knew these drawings were twenty years old, done through the eyes of a twenty-year-old boy with an extraordinary talent. If he had been that good then, she wondered what he'd have turned into if he'd pursued it professionally.

She flipped through the book and saw sketches of Kansas City: Bryant's, May's Grocery, a ghetto neighborhood honestly but lovingly drawn. There was a portrait of an older woman she assumed to be his mother, and a portrait of a devilishly handsome man with a peaceful aura and a blinding smile, yet he was haggard and worn, old before his time. His father.

There was a candid drawing of a young Knox Hilliard passionately kissing an even younger girl. Eilis's breath caught in her throat and she thought she'd cry, so she turned the page quickly.

There was another picture of a twenty-ish Knox Hilliard in a courtroom giving a speech to the jury. This, too, was a study of a face: young, confident, and beguiling. Directly across from that page was the same picture, only the face was different: hard, cynical, and cold. Eilis felt tears well in her eyes again at the difference in the two men.

Still only halfway through the thick book, she kept going, seeing the world through Sebastian Taight's eyes. More random people in random circumstances, some funny, some touching, some heartbreaking. She skipped over the pages of that terrifying September day in 2001.

There was another drawing of the girl Knox Hilliard had been kissing, only now, an adult and much more serious. Her hair was in a ponytail tied with a ribbon in a bow. She stood holding a gun in each hand on two faceless men. That drawing was a study of her face—ferocious, lethal, the face of a warrior. Giselle, the cousin who had threatened Fen with his life. Eilis shuddered and turned another page.

There were only a few pages left and she turned one only to gasp. It was her, Eilis, the way Sebastian saw her. And the way Sebastian saw her was . . . beautiful. It was her as she had been the day they'd gone to Bryant's and he'd stood in line entertaining not only her but the entire line of people. He'd caught her in a laugh, the early afternoon sun bright, white, her hair swirling around her face on a breeze.

Somehow, he'd captured a sparkle in her eyes and he'd managed to make her scar and her nose look attractive. He'd made her eyes actually look two different colors— in pencil.

The next page was her again, as she looked in costume at work, which was definitely not lovingly drawn. He must despise the way she dressed for work. She almost let a tear loose then, but she turned the page quickly—but then she couldn't breathe, couldn't move. She felt desire well up within her.

This was what he imagined Eilis must look like naked, which, she had to admit, was dead on. He'd drawn her nude, lying on her side in one of her flower beds, asleep. If she hadn't known it was her, she'd have thought he'd drawn a fertility goddess. But she knew that though the proportions were right, right down to the pooch in her belly, that wasn't her.

That woman had—something—that Eilis didn't see in her reflection. She didn't know what bothered her more, that he'd never seen her nude but had been able to draw her accurately or that he'd bestowed upon her a mysterious something that made this woman beautiful, but that she didn't have.

"Eilis! Where the hell did you go?" The bellow startled her and she put the book back in the glove compartment. She picked up his backpack full of clothes, then scurried toward the house.

Sebastian smiled to himself when she came around the house in a huff. He figured he'd given her enough time to thumb through his sketchbook pretty thoroughly. He wanted her to know how he saw her. Not that she'd believe him, he thought wryly.

"Geez, Eilis," he groused as he took the backpack and she led the way into the breezeway where it was warm, "took you long enough. Standing there freezing my ass off, yelling at you." She wouldn't look at him. He didn't know if that was because he only had a towel on or because now she knew how he saw her.

"My turn," she murmured and brushed by him through the inside doorway to the bathroom, slamming and locking it behind her.

He dressed as quickly as he could. The last thing in the world he needed right now was for her to see his nude backside.

47: Gris Gris

ELIS KNEADED SWEET BREAD DOUGH WHILE DIRECTING SEBASTIAN AS TO which paintings he should take downstairs to her vault to make room for decorations. As he'd suspected, she had not one, but two Georgia O'Keeffes and he didn't care what Georgia said, those weren't just irises.

Once down in her basement, he saw that she had a pretty thorough understanding of how much money hung on her walls. The vault was an actual bank vault that held millions of dollars in art. He wasn't sure why she just hadn't sold a few of these to get her company out of hot water, but then he was startled to see what it was she had. He understood.

Valuable, yes, but probably not what she'd paid for them and certainly not enough to make much difference in HRP's situation. She was waiting for a market upturn on specific artists before she sold them so she would at least not lose money. Some of these would never regain value.

"Eilis!" he called and it was a minute before she came to the top of the stairs. "Can you stop and come down here a minute?"

"Hold on. I have to set the bread to rise." It wasn't too long before she entered the vault. "What?"

"I know you didn't ask for my advice," he began, "and I'm probably going to offend you, so fair warning, but—" He flipped through the canvases, culling as he went. "These are worth as much as they're ever going to be worth. I suggest you sell them as soon as possible. We could slide these in the lot going to Christie's in February."

He glanced up at her and her mouth was tight, her eyes hard.

"Uh oh. I'm in trouble."

"No," she murmured. "Those were David's picks. I don't like them and I didn't think they'd appreciate at all, but he was insistent."

"All right," Sebastian said, releasing his breath in a whoosh. It helped to know she hadn't been the one who'd selected those. He continued to pull out canvases and put them in a separate stack. "These are questionable. I wouldn't buy them, but you could get your money back if you wanted to. I doubt they'll go up in value."

"I agree."

He looked at her again. "Why haven't you done this yourself?"

She swallowed and looked away. "I haven't been down here since David lived here."

"Why?"

A slight hesitation, then, softly, "He raped me here."

Sebastian's breath caught. "Oh. I— I'm sorry. I won't keep you."

"No, it's okay if you're here. That's why I asked you to help me. I couldn't come down here myself. I suspected you might start sorting through things, but I didn't expect it of you. I only needed you to bring the Christmas decorations up the stairs."

"Do you want to stay?" he asked gently, not daring to touch her.

Eilis looked around then and didn't answer. She stepped outside the vault and looked at the rest of this part of the basement that was used for storage of things that weren't valuable. She motioned him to join her outside the vault and took his hand to lead him across the room to an outside corner. She put her finger on a dark spot that was about six inches in diameter and wrapped around the bead of concrete that was the corner, covering both walls. Sebastian knew that was blood before she spoke.

"That's where he broke my nose and gave me this scar," she said tonelessly. Sebastian could feel horror rise up in him at what she'd suffered personally.

No wonder she'd not been able to salvage her company or take the time to get to know her employees. She'd been too busy trying to survive, trying to save their pensions, trying Webster. Trying to salvage her own soul.

Suddenly, he realized that he hadn't taken the time to get to know her the way he'd gotten to know her employees. If he'd known any of this, he'd not have reprimanded her so sharply and he felt sick to his stomach about that fact.

"Eilis, you don't have to tell me this," Sebastian murmured.

"No, it's okay," she insisted. "You know every detail of my company, what he did to it. And you fixed it."

Maybe you can fix me, too. The unspoken wish hung heavy in the air, and he was only too glad to see what he could do about that.

He laid his hand on her cheek and drew her face around so she was looking at him. Then he laid his other hand along her other cheek.

"Eilis," he whispered, intent on her scar and her nose, both of which he thought were lovely and made her even more beautiful than she would have been without them. "David. Is. Dead."

Her eyes popped open. "What? When? How do you know? I wasn't notified."

"Monday. Knox must not have gotten around to telling you yet. Did you know David had a heart condition?"

"Yes. He took a lot of medication for it."

"Apparently, he just keeled over at mess. Heart attack. Knox thinks it's very . . . *possible* . . . that the infirmary screwed up his meds, but they won't admit it."

She looked at him for a long time, and he waited for whatever she was going to say. She took a long breath. "Thank you," she whispered, "for . . . *telling* . . . me."

"You're welcome," he said with a warm smile and gathered her into his body when she began to cry. He let her continue until she hiccuped, then finally, he pulled her down to the floor and leaned back against the wall. He sat her in his lap and let her cry some more until nothing was left and she simply sat between his legs and pressed her cheek to his chest.

It was a while. Sebastian ran his fingers through her pretty pale butter-blonde hair and caressed the nape of her neck. He rubbed her back and arm.

"Oh, shit!" she said and popped out of his lap to sprint upstairs.

Sebastian sat confused until he heard the slap of bread dough on the counter, and then he chuckled. He spent the next hour sorting her vaulted art and assumed that he'd be the one to broker these for her if she wanted. He found paper and pen, then began to catalog them according to his breakdowns and what he thought they might fetch at auction.

"Eilis, are you done up there?"

"Just a minute."

When she came back downstairs, she had two more canvases. She showed them to him and without a word, he pointed to which piles they should go and marked them on his scratch paper.

"Any more?"

"No. That's it."

"Okay." He went back into the cleaned-out vault and said, "Come look."

The minute she entered the vault, he again framed her face with his hands, but this time, he kissed her. He would kiss her until she forgot what had happened here, what David had done to her.

"Mmmm," she hummed into his mouth, her eyes closed. He watched her face as he kissed her, unable to not watch her flush with desire.

Then the kiss slowly ended and her eyes fluttered open.

"Look around you, Eilis," he murmured and let go her face. She looked. "Remember this. It's clean. Your good art is coming back in. Your bad art is out there and going to auction with your Fords. And remember, your Fords are only going because the corporation owns them. When Christmas is over, I'll help you undecorate and you'll have all your good art to put back. Bonus! You have been well kissed."

Her gaze went everywhere, touched every crevice. Then she looked at him and kissed him on the cheek. "Thank you," she whispered. "You fix everything for me."

"It's all part of the Fix-or-Raid plan," he said dryly and she laughed. Together they put the good art back, then stacked the bad art toward the front of the vault for safekeeping until auction. He'd see about getting them crated up as soon as possible and stored with the Fords so as to get them out of her house.

"Okay," Sebastian said. "Point me to the Christmas decorations and a ladder, and go finish that povitica you promised me." She bounded up the stairs with a laugh and he watched that beautiful ass all the way. "I'd rather have raided," he muttered to himself with a sigh. He picked up the first two of a dozen or more tubs and headed up the stairs after her.

Sebastian requested a stockpot and once that was produced, he poured the wines and the cranberry and apple juices in it. After that he threw in the mulling spices, which were wrapped in cheesecloth, cut up some oranges and threw them in the pot with cinnamon sticks. "Bring it to a boil, then turn to low and then put a lid on it. I'll start putting up the high stuff."

They worked another couple of hours putting up Christmas decorations. When Sebastian would have turned on the radio for Christmas music, she said,

"Do you know who Alison Krauss is?"

"No."

"Okay. I want you to listen to what I listen to."

Sebastian listened to the first strains of this music and recognized the genre—bluegrass, zydeco's English older sister—and though it carried a recording studio polish, it retained its Appalachian authenticity. It was complex yet earthy, the voice divine, the lyrics engaging.

"It's really melancholy."

"Yes."

He speared her with a glance. "Eilis, music can lift the soul or it can destroy it. Melancholy music doesn't do anything good for a soul that's hurting."

She turned away and said nothing, so Sebastian didn't push it except to say, "Next Friday, bring your Alison Krauss to work and I'll trade you for The Wild Tchoupitoulas and Professor Longhair."

They stopped halfway through the decorating to fix a late lunch and dress the povitica, then they sat down with the wine and sandwiches.

Sebastian had never had a worse sandwich in his life.

"What the hell is on this thing?!"

He picked up the bread and looked at the thin coat of mayo or—whatever it was—the fake cheese, the fake bread, the fake one slice of ham. The only real thing on it was the lettuce.

Eilis looked stricken when he finally looked up at her, but he wouldn't let up. He'd had enough of her food and body issues. He got up and went to the fridge, stood there with it open for quite a while, looking at the kind of food Giselle would call "frankenfood."

"Do you have anything that's *not* fat free?"

And, as he'd done to her company and her art, he began to declutter. He dragged the trash can over to the fridge and began throwing everything that said "fat free" out. "Get a pen and paper," he instructed. "We're going shopping."

He knew she wouldn't dare protest. After all, he'd made her eat half a Bryant's sandwich and a whole concrete on threat of licking. Just *today*, he'd seen her eat one bagel for breakfast with—he dug back in the trash—yep, fat-free cream cheese.

She would never believe he wanted her as she was and she wouldn't stop this idiotic diet of hers unless she was forced.

She did what he said. As he dictated, she wrote. "Steak. Eggs. If there's one thing I've learned from my cousin— Lettuce. Peppers. Mushrooms. —it's that protein is king, lots of green vegetables the queen, and fat their prince. Butter. Mayo. Cauliflower. Broccoli. Bread and sugar are the devil. Chicken. Salmon. Fresh tuna. This fat-free shit? Look how much sugar's in that." Eilis looked at the label and gasped. "It's the second ingredient right behind water. No wonder you're so hungry all the time."

"But—"

"No buts. The point is to not be hungry. Giselle fat-free'd and starved her way to two-hundred-something. Then she started to eat like that—" He pulled his head out of the fridge to point at the list he was making, then stuck his head back in, "and she dropped fifty, sixty pounds like a hot potato. Oh, and spuds are verboten, too. Strawberries. Blueberries. Raspberries. The thing was, she wasn't hungry anymore. I don't know who you're trying to impress, but if you were *my* woman, this bullshit would not happen." And no matter how hard she fought him, she *would* be his woman.

He closed the refrigerator door and started in on the freezer, still ranting. "I don't think Giselle's way works for everyone and she still craves things, but I'd rather see a woman put on a few pounds than go hungry reaching for some unrealistic, unattainable view of perfection that's skewed to begin with."

Eilis's voice was hesitant when she spoke. "How tall is your cousin?"

Sebastian snorted. "Short. Maybe five-four, five-five."

"That still makes her overweight."

"You haven't met her. The girl's rock solid muscle, which is heavier, denser. Lots of muscle can go in a really small space," he muttered, throwing out peas and frozen boxed meals. "Crap," he said as he tossed a fat-free TV dinner over his shoulder and it sailed right into the trash can. "All crap. She lifts weights. Looks about thirty pounds lighter than she really is." He shoved the freezer drawer shut, then poured the skim milk down the drain. Then he raided her cupboards and pantry. He needed two more trash bags. When he was done, he said, "Get your coat and let's go. You drive."

Sebastian was startled out of his pique when he saw her car: a vintage British Jaguar.

"Eilis," he purred, "you and your rides. Bobcat. Jag with right steering. You got a Harley in there somewhere?"

That made her laugh. "No. Not that brave."

Then he saw the very respectable luxury car that looked like everything else on the road. "Uh, the Jag?" he said when it became clear she didn't intend for them to take it.

"Groceries, Sebastian."

Of course.

"Let me guess," he said dryly once they were on the way. "You don't drive your Jag to work because it doesn't fit the Miss Logan persona."

"Exactly."

Once at the store, he directed her to the magazine section first and tossed a paperback in the cart. "Read that."

She sucked in a breath, her eyes wide. "Dr. Atkins? I can't—"

"You will," he said, his tone hard, and she gulped.

He saw her wince at everything he threw in her cart except for the berries and vegetables and he didn't care. That hungry thing of hers had to stop. He didn't know how she could stand upright.

She finally protested, but it took longer than he thought it would. "You're awfully bossy today."

"I make my living being bossy," he muttered, looking at the marbling on the steaks and trying to figure out what Giselle would buy. So he called her, explained the situation, and followed her instructions to the letter.

"Sebastian," Eilis said, a desperate edge to her voice once he'd closed his phone and put it back in his pocket. "I'm going to gain a lot of weight if I eat all this."

He stopped and stared at her, making his face hard and cold so she would know he meant what he said. She looked away. "Read that book," he growled as he approached her. "I don't know what it says because I don't eat that way. Nobody cares about the weight, Eilis. It's about you starving yourself while also kicking yourself in the ass over an arbitrary number on a scale.

"I watched you at the Ford exhibit," he continued, softly now, getting closer to her so that her shoulder was in his sternum and her hip was in his groin. He wanted her to know he had a hard-on for her, even standing in the middle of a grocery store talking about food. Her eyes widened and her face displayed innumerable emotions in rapid sequence, none of which he could pick out. She swallowed.

"You were repulsed by the women who look like you and attracted to the women who looked like the Virgin. I can only think that you're repulsed by your own body, which, by the way, there's nothing wrong with."

He pressed his mouth against her ear, wrapped a hand around her other hip, pulled her closer to him so she wouldn't mistake him. She closed her eyes, breathed deep.

"You want to lose weight," he continued on a whisper, his other hand now wrapped around the back of her neck so she couldn't pull away from either his words or his cock. "What you're doing is not only *not* working, you're always hungry and miserable. The definition of insanity is doing the same thing over and over again and expecting a different result. Do something different. Do you trust me?"

Her eyes closed, a tear ran down her cheek, tracking her scar. "Yes," she finally whispered.

"Then trust me on this. Read that book. Do whatever it says, which I don't really know. I only know how Giselle eats and which book she consults. Now, let's check out and go to Subway."

Eilis couldn't believe this was happening to her, what he was making her do—yet she always had a choice.

What you're doing is not working.

That was true enough. The less she ate, the more she gained. Slowly. Insidiously. An ounce or two per month.

Do you trust me?

Implicitly. He could fix anything.

You were repulsed by the women who look like you.

Yes, she was. She was repulsed by what she saw in her mirror, but the pictures in his sketchbook told her everything she needed to know about how he saw her. And he'd made sure she knew he wanted her by pressing her into his body, hard, ruthless, the way he did everything when he wasn't getting his way.

It was evening by the time they got to her home and she felt . . . good . . . with a full stomach. Sebastian gave her permission to eat—no, he *demanded* that she eat. So she got the sub she'd always wanted but never dared get. She ate half, savoring every bite.

"Well, don't have an orgasm in the middle of Subway, Eilis," he'd said dryly after she'd taken her first bite, and she could only laugh.

"You're a chubby chaser, Sebastian."

"Mmmm, yeah, sometimes. Except you're not chubby." She blanched in fear he would feed her until she gained another thirty pounds. "And I like you the way you are, in case you didn't get that in the store."

She could feel the heat flood her face and she ducked her head.

"Yeah, that's right. I've got a hard-on for you, Eilis, but what I'm trying to do today is to get *you* to like you the way you are and also not be hungry."

Once they emptied the car and put away groceries— "I'll have Giselle write you up a list of herbs and spices she uses—the spice cabinet in my house is huge and smells incredible. Then we'll go to Planter's in River Market."

We'll go?

"Sebastian, I don't have time to cook."

"Then hire someone."

That had never occurred to her, not once. It was the perfect solution.

"What about the povitica I just made?"

"We eat it for breakfast tomorrow. And then you won't have to worry about it when you change up your eating plan."

For breakfast tomorrow?

Sebastian built a fire in the massive fireplace and turned down the lights. Christmas music began when she turned on the radio and he brought the mulled wine that had been simmering all afternoon. Outside, it began to snow. He sat on the floor, his back to the couch in front of the fire and gestured that she should sit between his legs. Eilis hesitated. It was too intimate, too cozy and comfortable. She knew how he saw her, what he wanted from her. He was her trustee! And he expected to spend the night?

"You're not sleeping with me tonight," she blurted.

"No, I'm not," he agreed with alacrity, an inscrutable expression on his face. "I figured you must have an extra bedroom or five."

"I didn't invite you to stay."

He looked at her. "Do you want me to go?" he asked softly. "I will if that's what you want."

"No," she whispered without thinking, unable to bear the thought of his leaving now. Then she cleared her throat and attempted to cover with, "We didn't finish the decorating because you got distracted rearranging my life."

He patted the floor in front of him again and this time she sat. "Chalk it up to the ADD."

"You use that as an excuse for everything, don't you?"

"Why change what works? Now hush and drink your wine."

Eilis didn't know how long they sat like that: Christmas music, firelight, snow outside, and a Christmas tree only half decorated. She felt warm and safe in a way she had never felt before.

David Webster had stolen everything from her: Her company, her body, her self-esteem, her soul—things she'd worked so hard to regain when they'd been stolen from her before, time and again. He'd stolen her nose and her face.

Sebastian was hauling her out of bankruptcy. He'd cleared out her art and with it, her bad memories, so she could go into her vault again. He'd cleaned out her refrigerator and had possibly set her on a path that could alleviate the constant hunger that made her so nauseous and dizzy. He'd drawn her as he saw her, which was beautiful, and he'd made it more than clear that he found her desirable.

He was a very, very beautiful and brilliant man who wanted her.

May I kiss you?

Furthermore, he wanted a relationship with her; that could be the only explanation for his behavior: No man who just wanted sex would treat her the way Sebastian treated her and no man had ever treated her that way before.

Do you trust me?

He'd made her think of her garden as a work of art, rendering it a haven again and, in essence, giving her that back, as well. And he'd brought her the one thing she wanted for her garden that she had such a hard time getting.

Her biological parents had taken her life from her. Life had taken from her. David had taken from her.

Sebastian gave. Then gave more. He filled her soul with humor and hope.

The wine was long drunk by the time her grandfather clock chimed one, and she felt a light touch on her neck, then another. Sebastian was kissing her, butterfly kisses on her skin, and she closed her eyes, tilting her head, letting him taste her skin with his tongue. At that moment, she'd let him do anything he wanted to do to her, in front of the fire, cliché and all.

He ran his hands over her hips and up her ribs, gathering her sweater over his wrists. She gasped at the touch of his hands on her bare skin. She raised her arms when prompted and he took her sweater off, slowly, gently. He caressed her belly and ribs, then his fingers went to the clasp between her breasts. She let him take her bra off. He continued to barely touch her neck and shoulders with his lips and tongue, even as he hefted her breasts in his big palms and they didn't overflow his hands.

Sebastian pushed her away gently then and took off his tee shirt. Pulling her back against him, she sighed to feel his bare chest on her bare back. They sat like that, Sebastian caressing every inch of her bare skin either with his lips or his fingers, her juices flowing, her heart pounding, her mouth dry, until the clock chimed 1:45.

"If you can tell me which bedroom I can sleep in, I'll let you go to bed. Alone," he whispered in her ear.

What if I don't want to go to bed alone?

"All right," she whispered. "Up the stairs. First door on the right."

Again he pushed her forward gently and then rose, holding out his hand to help her stand, then turned her around. She was mortified that he would see her naked torso, even though she knew that he'd already drawn her nude and had imagined her correctly. She attempted to cover herself anyway.

He pulled her hands away from her body and looked at her fleshy hips, her squishy belly, her big breasts. He reached out and took one in his hand; she gasped, but she didn't move away. His touch was too exquisite, too . . . right.

"Perfect," he whispered and her heart stopped when he caressed her tightened nipple with his thumb. She looked away, down, uncertain what to make of his approval of all her faults.

"Look at me, Eilis," he murmured, and she did, reluctantly. "No, look at my chest. Look at my body." So she did and she gasped. He was cut, as she'd imagined, complete with six-pack, but he had scars criss-crossing it. Lots of them, some more obvious than others, some fairly thick and at least one that seemed to have developed a small keloid.

"What happened?" she breathed.

He grinned proudly, wickedly. "Angry husband. And assorted other back alley battles."

She didn't know why that was funny, but a lot of things were only funny after midnight. She laughed and put her hand to her mouth because she knew she shouldn't laugh.

"The husband. Were you . . . ?"

"Oh, yes," he murmured. "Caught us dead to rights. It's all part of the Parisian artist thing."

"How old were you?" she asked, tracing a scar with her finger, unable to say why that scenario was arousing to her.

"Oh, twenty-three or thereabouts. I actually didn't know she was married. Not that it would've made any difference." He looked back at her torso, her breasts, and she caught her breath again. He'd made her forget she was half naked. "Eilis," he murmured. "Don't ever let anyone—especially you—tell you you're less than perfect." He leaned in to drop a kiss on her forehead. "And I know from perfect."

They ate the povitica for breakfast and drank the rest of the wine. Eilis let Sebastian feed her, not because he was forcing her to eat, but because she was beginning to like it when he fed her from his own hand.

"Okay, you're right," he said. "You've spoiled me for anyone else's povitica."

She felt warmth suffuse her at his praise. "Thanks."

They spent the rest of the day finishing the decorating, but it was slow going on purpose, because soon Sebastian would leave to go home, she'd have an empty house, and she wouldn't see him again for a week.

After the sky had dropped six inches of snow, Eilis took Sebastian out to her greenhouse and showed him how to put the plow blade on her lawn tractor. She let him plow the path from the greenhouse to the driveway, then the whole of the driveway. She laughed and laughed at how much fun he was having. Once that was done, she went in to flip a switch and said,

"Sebastian, watch the driveway."

In about fifteen minutes, he started to laugh again. "You've thought of everything, haven't you?" he asked as what remained of the snow melted away and the driveway dried as if no snow had fallen at all.

She smiled. "I tried to. Usually when it starts to snow, I go ahead and flip it on low. It's very expensive, but worth every penny."

Sebastian left late that night after a kiss that scorched her everywhere. "Thank you, Eilis," he whispered against her lips. "Thank you for the nicest weekend I can remember."

And then he was gone in his old truck, which backfired once, the gates slowly closing behind him. She didn't know whether to laugh over the wonderful weekend or cry because he was gone.

48: Not Happy Enough Medium

IT WAS FRIDAY. SEBASTIAN WOULD BE IN HER OFFICE TODAY AND SHE BIT HER lip when she stared at herself in her bathroom mirror. Every time he looked at her in disguise, his lip curled a little bit and she was beginning to hate that look. She knew he hated it and he had since he'd picked her out so easily at the Ford exhibit.

Since then, they'd been on that wonderful date to Bryant's, and then that weekend in December when he'd caressed her bare torso in firelight, snow outside, mulled wine in their bellies, Christmas carols playing at just above a whisper in the background.

He'd pressed her against him to make sure she knew he wanted her, yet he hadn't taken advantage of her weakness in the firelight. She didn't believe that he didn't know she would've gone to bed with him that night if he'd pushed just a bit.

He knew what she looked like and he thought she was *perfect*. Why couldn't she just take that and run with it?

She knew what her biological parents looked like. Her mother was one of the most beautiful women she'd ever seen. Her father was handsome, distinguished. Her half brother was what she would regard as extremely handsome. Whatever bad genes they had floating around in there, Eilis had gotten.

A tear tracked down her cheek when she thought of that look Sebastian gave her every time he saw her in Chanel. She remembered his sketch of her dressed that way, and though he'd never said anything to her about it, she knew he despised it. His face was very expressive once one knew his moods. If one didn't, it was his body that radiated humor and warmth. It was that cat's comforting purr of his.

He did not purr with her when she was in Chanel.

She sighed and went to re-do her makeup because the tear had riven a track through it. Then she goofed and had to wipe off more.

The image in the mirror was pathetic, half made up, half not. She gulped.

Without thinking about it, she took out her brown contacts and wiped off the rest of her makeup, then reapplied just as much as she knew would flatter her.

Without thinking about it, she unpinned her hair and brushed it until it gleamed the palest of blondes, like freshly churned butter with only a splash of color.

Without thinking about it, she undressed and threw the Chanel in the corner of her bedroom, then chose a dress she had never worn once she'd left the tailor's shop.

Black linen sheath. Low, wide, square neckline. Hem three inches above her knees. Sleeveless. Eilis's tailor had begged her to let her create this for her; even as she fit it, Eilis stood wondering how she'd allowed herself to be bullied into having something so outrageous made. It clung to every curve, emphasized everything about her body she hated.

Only . . . Something was very, very wrong with it because it certainly didn't fit the way the tailor had intended it to. Eilis ran to the scale and she gaped in astonishment.

She didn't know whether to squeal for joy or dread telling Sebastian, "Hey, you were right." Again.

And she wasn't hungry.

Eilis decided to go with it. She shrugged on the plain black velvet bolero jacket—also loose—that went with it. Though possibly a little too cocktail for work, she didn't care. It had just become her new favorite dress. As soon as she had a chance, she'd go back to her tailor and have it taken in.

Stepping into a pair of very expensive, very high heels, she looked into her full-length mirror and caught her breath. She had never looked at herself and thought she was even plain. Today, she was . . . pretty.

Her mouth tightened. Coco Chanel was dead to her now—

—and she slid into the right-hand driver's seat of her Jaguar.

Between the weight she'd lost, her favorite dress, her Jaguar, and the . . . new lightness of heart that Sebastian had bestowed upon her, she walked into work with her normal long stride that wasn't evident in the Chanel skirt. She ignored the looks, the gaping jaws, the one programmer who dared whistle at her only because he was so caught up in his own world he didn't know who she was.

She went directly to Karen's office and whatever she interrupted, oh well. Karen's mouth dropped open.

"I'm sorry," she said quietly.

Karen gulped. "For what?"

"For not trusting you. For not knowing you. For not letting you do what I hired you to do. I've owed you this apology for a long time and I was too ashamed to approach you."

Karen smiled then, a gleam in her eye that made Eilis *feel* forgiven. "Thank you."

"How's your daughter?"

Then Karen told her. Eilis sat down in a chair across from her and just listened. The girl's doctors didn't expect her to live much longer, and Karen didn't expect her marriage to survive the child's death. Eilis quietly told her that when the time came, she would pay for the arrangements.

They parted ways with a hug and then Eilis took a deep breath and started meeting her employees. It was a long time coming.

Eilis spent the entire day on her feet. After the first hour, she'd taken her shoes off and carried them around looped in her fingers. She went from cubicle to cubicle, talking to her employees as herself, not that Chanel woman.

She asked them specific questions about their lives now that she knew who they were by name and by sight, her knowledge augmented with overheard conversations and sly queries of Louise who, it seemed, knew everything about everyone.

Plenty of people were suspicious of her, but she left them alone with a smile and a gentle hand on the shoulder.

At three, she was so deep in the labyrinth of Cubicleville that she didn't notice Sebastian's arrival. At quarter of four, she had gotten drawn into an extended discussion with a charming programmer who had no particular bias for or against her. She started when she heard Sebastian's voice behind her.

"Excuse me, miss?"

She looked over her shoulder to see him as achingly beautiful as always. It seemed the entire staff had followed him to watch his reaction to this very strange Eilis Logan.

His gaze swept her head to toe and back again, and though he didn't smile, she felt his humor and approval. He stuck his hand out for her to shake and when she took it, he said, grave as usual, "Hi. I'm Sebastian Taight. Who are you and what do you do?"

"I'm Eilis Logan and I'm the CEO."

The whole place roared. He did then smile, that heartbreaking smile she'd seen so often that weekend he'd reorganized her life. He turned and offered her his right arm, which she took. The whispers behind them were just loud enough for her to hear,

Damn, they look fine together.

"What happened?" he asked once they reached her office.

She drew in a deep breath. "I don't know. Maybe I got tired of the way you look at me when I'm wearing Chanel."

His eyebrow cocked. "Oh? How do I look at you then?"

"Like you despise it, like you might despise me for wearing it."

"You're right. I do despise it. I get very angry and short with you whenever I see you in it because I know what you look like."

Nude.

The word hung in the air and Eilis stared at Sebastian. His eyes darkened to purple, but he only said, "Well, I must say it's a very pleasant surprise. Come into the conference room, please. I need to talk to you about something."

Her smile dimmed and her gut clenched at how dire he sounded, but once the doors were closed and—locked?—he wrapped his palms around her face and kissed her hard, hot, urgent, his tongue begging hers to play. She sighed and entwined her fingers with his where they clutched her face. She matched his tongue stroke for stroke.

Sebastian slid one hand down her shoulder, then her ribs, then over her buttock, hers still entwined with it. He pressed her against him so she could feel his arousal. She moaned softly as his hand kneaded her, pressing her tighter and tighter against him.

Then, in one swift movement, he picked her up and plopped her on the massive table, then climbed up after her.

She slid backward until he was over her. She lay down flat and he dove for her mouth again, still on his hands and knees above her.

"I could fuck you right now," he growled, hot, intense, as his lips skittered across the skin of her chest.

"Oh, please *do*," she whispered, and he stopped cold. He stared at her and said, "What about Ford?"

Eilis had no idea where that came from, but she didn't appreciate the interruption. "What about him?"

"You've been pining after Ford as long as you've had that painting. You asked me for vacation time to have him paint you. Is that something you still want?"

"Yes, of course, but—"

"You know what? Forget it," he said as he lifted himself away from her and hopped down from the table.

"What?!"

"I said forget it," he said roughly as he straightened himself out. Eilis shrank from his glare. "I want you, Eilis, but I'm not going to compete with a man you don't know and can't find and who might not do what you think you want him to do for you." He strode to the conference room door, but turned before opening it. "I'll forego looking at your books today. I'm sure they're excellent, as usual."

Then he left, slamming the door behind him.

49: Jole Blon

THE WALDORF ASTORIA'S RESTAURANT WASN'T THE BEST PLACE IN THE world to have an argument, especially one over inappropriate attire, so Sebastian controlled his anger as he watched Eilis navigate the tables. Once she reached him, he murmured, very calmly,

"Eilis, if you think I'm going to be seen at Christie's with you in that getup, you've got another think coming. I can't stand that rag, which you know very good and well, so either go back upstairs and change or go back upstairs and stay. I don't care which."

She drew herself up and Sebastian knew that if she weren't in costume, she'd have taken him on at that moment. A month. He hadn't seen her in a month since he'd had her underneath him and willing. He still remembered how stunning she'd been that day, in cocktail black, all that gorgeous blonde hair down and around her shoulders, one green eye and one blue eye, an expressive face flawless with that scar and nose he loved. Blonde bombshell businessbitch. *Yummy.*

And the first time he'd seen her in a month, she showed up in Chanel.

When she opened her mouth, Sebastian snarled. "Don't. Whatever you have to say, save it until you look presentable. I won't be manipulated, Eilis. I don't play those games, especially not with women, and *most* especially not with a woman I want to fuck in the worst way. Your little stunt of not uploading reports to me on time as I requested? Manipulative. Knox has less patience with it than I do and he wasn't a happy camper."

So saying, Sebastian went back to his breakfast, dismissing her. She stood for another couple of seconds before she decided not to test him. Sebastian's anger was so thick within him, he could chew on it. He'd never taken this much guff from a woman. Ever. He didn't know why he let Eilis get away with it.

He didn't know why he acted so differently with her than with any other woman and/or client. From the very beginning, he'd treated her differently. He'd let her keep that damned painting—bad idea. He'd pulled her pigtails to make her façade crack, then harder and harder when she didn't respond. He'd spent time with her, getting to know her on a level he'd never gotten to know any of his other female clients, *especially* the beautiful ones.

With Eilis, he thought about sex and money at the same time, and she had tripped both sides of his brain *and* his cock immediately, *with* the getup on.

Unlike his other clients, he didn't coddle Eilis. He met her head-on because that was what she understood and he wanted Eilis Logan to understand him *very* clearly.

Apparently, she wanted him to understand her, too, because when she finally came back, she took his breath away. Again.

She wore an ankle-length maroon skirt that flared out wide when she walked and turned. Its waistband overlapped half again around her waist, covering only the most important parts if the skirt lay just right. A prim white Victorian shirtwaist was tucked neatly into the waistband, its collar high under a short maroon silk jacket with Dolman sleeves. Not a bit of skin showed except when her skirt felt inclined to fall open, which it did at that moment.

Sebastian hardened at the sight of a long length of leg, set off nicely by her sky-high heels and the lace top of her white thigh-high stocking—but it disappeared again with the next step.

He gulped. Maybe he should've let her wear the Chanel.

"Do I meet your approval *now*, O Omnipotent One?"

Sebastian bit back a smile at her attitude, happy now that the Eilis he wanted— the one of fire and passion, the ruthless bitch with the wounded soul she wanted to hide from him, the one who'd apologized to her employees when she'd understood what Sebastian was trying to tell her—was now present and accounted for.

And boy, was she pissed.

"Not quite," he said shortly, unable to give quarter until he'd had his way. "Siddown. Eat."

She sat without a word. Sebastian took choice bites from his plate and put them on hers. She looked at it, then pushed it away from her. She put her elbow on the table and propped her chin in her hand. She looked away from him and around at the other restaurant patrons.

"Eilis," he said. She didn't move a muscle, but then he saw a tear streak down her face. At that moment, he'd have given anything to take her upstairs and make love to her until she didn't feel like crying anymore. "You don't have to do this. I can go take care of it myself."

"No," she said tightly, still not looking at him. "I deserve this."

Sebastian sighed and finished his meal. He didn't agree with that, but this wasn't the time to discuss it. He arose and took a step, holding his hand out to her when she didn't move. "Eilis, if you're going to do this, we have to go. The auction starts at nine."

She looked up at him, heartbreak and despair in her eyes, and he didn't know how he would pull her through this. He was responsible for bringing her here, forcing her to do one of the things she should have done to begin with when she could have saved her company without receivership.

And he didn't feel a bit of guilt for that, either.

"Eilis, cowboy up," he snapped.

She gulped and put her hand in his, stood, then took his left arm when he offered it. Once out of the hotel, he hailed a cab that took them to Christie's, not a word between them.

This was a high-profile auction and every überwealthy person in the country, possibly the world, had agents getting numbers, prepared to buy at least one Ford. Sebastian had come to watch, not bid personally, as he usually did. He saw his own agent, nodded slightly, let the man go about his business.

People treated Sebastian deferentially wherever he went. In the worlds of business and art, he rarely ran into someone who didn't know who he was; thus, the surprised glances he and Eilis garnered on their way to the saleroom were not for him.

They were for Eilis, who turned every head she passed and left varying expressions of lust in her wake—not that she would believe him if he pointed it out.

He wrapped his arm around her waist on the pretense of guiding her through the press of people to get to the VIP entrance; he could touch her the way he wanted to without damaging his pride any further. He refused to take second place behind Ford and he had no intention of pursuing this relationship as long as Ford stood between them—even if he was in love with her.

Apparently, she didn't notice that he had his arm around her, so he took the opportunity to caress her hip while her mind wandered.

"Eilis, do you want to sit or stand?" he asked quietly once they were in the mostly filled saleroom.

"Stand," she said. "I'll feel like a coward if I sit."

Interesting. She chucked up her chin and stared straight ahead once he'd chosen a fairly inconspicuous spot on the back wall. Between them, they didn't have a chance in hell of being inconspicuous, so he didn't know why he bothered.

He took his arm from around her waist and she said, her voice breaking, "Please don't."

Against his better judgment, Sebastian nevertheless wrapped his arm farther around her, then pulled her back into his body as he leaned back on the wall. He sighed and wrapped his other arm around her, too.

While he wasn't sure if she noticed, his cock sure as hell did. This would be pure hell until the money started flowing.

Finally, it did. All the bad art he'd sorted from her vault and had had crated here with the Fords went up first. He was pleasantly surprised to know that most of them had gained in value, if only a buck or two. That was a good chunk of change, right there.

Then the Fords came up and the crowd stirred in anticipation. The first one went to an unassuming man halfway back and toward the center of the room.

So did the second.

And the third.

Eilis shuddered with each clap of the gavel. Then the calls began in earnest as phone bids rolled in, and agents were ordered to pay whatever they had to pay to get one.

The unassuming man halfway back and toward the center continued to bid quietly, driving up the prices but dropping out early, usually about three-quarters to its end price.

It was the sixth painting at which Sebastian felt moisture on his hands and he realized Eilis was crying, her head bowed, her tears dripping onto his skin. He'd been so caught up in seeing how much the lot of them would fetch, he'd nearly forgotten that he had his arms around one very heartbroken woman.

"Hey," he said softly, shaking out a handkerchief. He caught her chin and pulled her face around until she looked at him. He gently wiped her tears, then turned her in his arms so she couldn't see—and she took him up on that immediately. She clung to him, her hand wrapped around his neck, her fingers in his hair, and sobbed quietly in his neck.

Eilis's pain was so great that Sebastian felt no satisfaction that the eight pieces had fetched fifty-five percent of her debt. Now, if she'd only put *Morning in Bed* up, too . . .

At least Sebastian had managed to buy her three favorites.

The room emptied and still she leaned on him. Her face was a mess, but she wasn't crying anymore.

"I'm sorry to have made you do this, Eilis," he murmured. "It was for the good of your company and your employees and I'm proud of you for putting them first."

"Sebastian," she whispered, "make love to me, please."

Sebastian's breath caught in his throat and his eyes widened. "Eilis, do you *remember* how you ended up in the saleroom at Christie's?"

She hiccuped. "Yes, but I trust you."

He grasped her upper arms and set her just far away from him enough so she could look in his face and see just how angry he was.

"Do you take me for a fool?" he hissed and her tear-streaked face betrayed her complete and utter shock. "Dammit, Eilis, what do I have to do to knock some sense into your head? You don't want *me*. You want comfort sex and any cock will do." She flinched and he didn't care. "I'm tired of being your fan club, Eilis. I won't be the stopgap between nobody and this asshole you have in your head who *does not exist* who you want to give you something you can't define. Whatever it is you're looking for? Not here. Not in my pants. Not in my bed.

"Vacation? Done. One month. I'll take over your job so you can find your precious Ford," he snarled as he released her. "Maybe *he* can fix whatever it is I can't reach and you're apparently not willing to." He walked away from her without a backward glance. She could find her own way back to the hotel.

That night he paced his hotel room, his headset practically melting from the heat of his rage, barking orders at Giselle and getting angrier every time she tried to talk him down, to plead with him not to do what he planned, to tell him it'd backfire and he'd be sorry.

"I'm going to *kill* that bastard!" he roared at her before hanging up on her. "And you're going to help me. You *owe* me, Giselle."

"I love you," she sighed into his mouth, his cock sliding easily, oh! so easily in and out of her, the weight of his body comforting and not at all heavy.

He chuckled. "I love you, too, Eilis."

The snow under her naked body was not cold and the December air didn't sting her skin. Snowflakes melted on his body as they landed. She opened her eyes, but his face lay in shadow and shade. Beside her, crocuses and hyacinths, tulips and daffodils sprang up in her line of sight and she thought she had never seen such a beautiful thing in her entire life: tulips and daffodils in the snow.

She ran her hands up his body, from those buttocks she knew so well, up his rib cage, to his shoulders. She was about to come and the shadow passed from his face. For the first time, she would see him, who he was—

Eilis awoke abruptly, her hand between her legs, and she came. When her breathing had calmed, she buried her face in a pillow and sobbed. It was the same every time she had this dream, only the locales changed. She would awaken on an orgasm she'd given herself and never remembered initiating.

Only tonight, she'd seen his face and she was horrified. It was everything she had never expected. Terrible. Frightening.

Sebastian's face. Ford's body. *How* had that happened?

First her company, then her garden, then her vault, then her fridge, then her diet, then her body, and now her dreams. Would that man leave *nothing* of hers untouched?

Eilis clicked on her bedside light so she could look at her painting, her *Morning in Bed*. She wished she could bleach her brain so she could get rid of that visual.

She didn't want them mixed. It was . . . *wrong.*

Ford she had wanted to do a specific thing, once.

Sebastian she needed. For a long time, maybe forever, if she thought he wouldn't turn away from her on learning of her past.

But she had burned that bridge because she never suspected he resented Ford until he left her on her conference room table. She certainly wouldn't have known *how* deep his resentment of Ford went until he'd lashed out at her at Christie's.

In retrospect, she saw it clearly: Chanel and Ford—the two things guaranteed to make Sebastian's expression freeze, his body tense, his temper flare.

Her breath came short in panic when she thought of the look on his face, the anger of a man utterly betrayed, and in that moment, she understood how foolish she'd been not to take what Sebastian had offered her to begin with.

But had he offered her anything, really?

Shouldn't she expect that a man who wanted to offer a woman something would *talk* to her, let her know his thoughts? That he hated how she looked in Chanel? That he hated her obsession with Ford? That he wanted to be with her and he found these things hurtful?

Shouldn't she expect him to open his mouth and speak? In *words?*

She didn't know because she had never had a relationship like that, nor, apparently, had Sebastian.

Hurt to her soul, she sighed. It didn't matter. He'd turned his back and wouldn't listen to a thing she had to say at this point.

She knew because she'd tried. Every phone call she made, she got voice mail. When she'd shown up at HRP to talk to him, he disappeared. Every email and text message she sent, she got the same auto-reply: **YOU'RE ON VACATION**

Now she had nothing to hold onto but Ford.

50: Time to Say Goodbye

ILIS SAT ON THE FLOOR WITH A MAGNIFYING GLASS GOING OVER EVERY inch of the painting leaned against the wall. She sighed. If this portrait contained any clues as to Ford's identity, they were too cryptic. After years of studying it, she suspected the rumored "clues" simply didn't exist. The only option she had left was to hire an art historian, but the thought made her uneasy.

After several long teleconferences with the private investigators she had spread out over the country, the truth had started to gel: Ford didn't exist. His ephemeral trail stopped in Chicago.

Eilis dropped her forehead in her palm, at her breaking point. She *must* find Ford.

Soon.

After that dream, she'd barely slept again and spent every waking moment playing Sherlock Holmes. In the last three days, she had managed to doze off only far enough for the dream to start again. She couldn't remember the last time she ate; it wasn't important.

Frustrated, she gave up for the time being and dressed to go turn her compost, something she could do in the dark by the light of the floodlights. She headed out the back door only to stop when the phone rang. At first, her heart thudded, but then she remembered: She'd dismissed her private investigators at their last conference call when each agreed Ford could not be found and they all had better things to do. She nearly ignored it, but she'd never ignored a ringing phone in her life.

"Hello?"

"Um, hi. Is this Eilis Logan?" said a woman whose voice Eilis didn't recognize.

"Yes. Who's this?"

"I'm an agent for the artist Ford. You can stop looking for him."

Her heart thundered and her breath caught. Her mouth was so dry she could barely speak.

"What does that mean, precisely?" Eilis asked carefully.

"It means you got his attention. He'll paint you."

They'd done it. Whichever PI had done this would get a nice fat bonus.

Eilis paused. "Is this a joke?"

"Unfortunately, no." The woman's voice was hard, flat. "If you really do want him to paint you, you'll be picked up from your house and taken to his studio blindfolded."

"He's here?" Eilis whispered. "In Kansas City? I thought—"

"No. You've been looking in all the wrong places. And F-Y-I—there aren't any clues in the painting, either. If you want Ford to paint you, these are the terms. You won't be able to find him on your own."

"Does he even know what I look like?"

The woman gave an unamused bark of laughter. "You have your people. He has his. So. Can you be ready in an hour? Eleven o'clock? I'll pick you up. I'm driving a silver-blue BMW."

An hour! "What— I can't— Not that fast."

"You have an hour," she repeated. "And pack a bag. You never know with him."

Eilis dropped the phone and looked around her kitchen like she'd never seen it before. She couldn't breathe, couldn't think, couldn't move until she walked like a zombie up to her room to shower and pack.

Then she closed up her house and sat down in her courtyard to wait, her bag by her side, unable to do anything but stare at the cleverly lit obelisk in her roundabout, wondering what she had set in motion and why she felt so . . . not thrilled.

Sebastian's words came back to her: *Do you remember* how you ended up in the sale-room at Christie's?

And so now, instead of having sex with and then marrying David in the aftermath of a front-row seat to September 11, or begging Sebastian to make love to her after watching the sacrifice of her precious art, she intended to go to an unknown place blindfolded with an unknown woman presumably to be painted by an unknown man who painted pictures of nude women. After he'd had sex with them.

She knew her judgment was severely stunted and she figured she'd deserved to lose those paintings. Still here she sat, willing to play this through to the last hand to see if she could win anything back.

You're not a good gambler.

Not when she gambled on emotion, she wasn't.

Like tonight.

Soon she heard an engine outside her gate and opened it. As promised, a silver-blue BMW drove up to the courtyard and obscured her view of the obelisk. A woman emerged, and Eilis stood to walk toward the car, bag in hand.

She stood much shorter than Eilis and had a very compact body, muscular yet slightly curvy. Wisps of her shoulder-length curls flickered different shades of a rich blonde in the light from the obelisk, but then she turned—"You— You're the Virgin," she whispered.

"Yup, that's me. Only not a virgin anymore. Got your stuff?"

Eilis breathed a sigh of some relief, her unarticulated fear of a hoax laid to rest.

The Virgin, who didn't seem particularly happy to be there nor inclined to tell her her name, picked up her bag and put it in the trunk. She gestured to Eilis to get in the car and then she did. Once they reached the end of the driveway, she stopped for Eilis to close the gate. That done, the Virgin tied a wide black scarf around Eilis's face, making sure she could see nothing.

Eilis tried to track their course from the map in her head, but after the first turn north and the first turn east, a curve threw her. She'd lost her bearings.

The ride was a long one.

Eilis didn't speak because the Virgin didn't until— "Eilis, do you *really* want to do this?"

What an odd question from the model of the most infamous Ford painting since *Morning in Bed.*

Eilis swallowed. "Yes. Why?"

"Mmmm, seems to me you could go about gathering enlightenment in a less dangerous way."

"And . . . you're different from me how?"

Jealous I'm taking your place?

"Ha! That's funny. He badgered me into it."

Eilis blinked, not having expected such an answer. "Did you— Him—" Eilis stopped. It was rude and no, Eilis didn't really want to know.

"Not on your life," she replied anyway. "Dude doesn't do anything for me. Eww."

Eilis bit her lip. "*Morning in Bed.* Is that really him?"

"Yes."

A thrill ran through her, curiosity hard on its heels. "And he doesn't attract you?"

"Absolutely not," she said flatly. "Does it look like he fucked me?"

No. Which was why it was notorious.

Eilis started when she felt the Virgin's hand lightly cover her clenched fist. "Eilis," she said, her voice softening. Eilis was only too eager to listen to any conversation because she couldn't see. One more second of silence would crush her. "That painting happened because I had met a man I thought I couldn't have, so it made me ache for the rest of what would come with a man, a lover, a husband. So I was in pain. And he wanted to capture that."

Eilis let that settle. "It is devastating," she murmured. "I almost cried when I saw it."

"I guess that's a common reaction. Neither of us thought it would be that powerful."

"What—what's the significance of the books on the bed? It was a Bible and— I don't remember the other one."

"*Intercourse*, by Andrea Dworkin." The Virgin took a deep breath, then expelled it with a whoosh. "Religion and radical feminism have one thing in common: They seek to denigrate women for wanting sex with men. In religion's case, woman is the enemy, the sinful Eve figure if not the Lilith one, the succubus, the seducer of right-eous men into evil deeds. It presupposes that men are without evil inclinations in the first place. It's the thinking that positions a rape victim as asking for it because obvi-ously, the rapist was just an innocent bystander. A woman should have only one interest in sex, and that's to procreate.

"In the case of radical feminism, man is the enemy because, of course, all men seek to dominate and entrap women into indentured servitude or worse. While this is true for *some* men, it isn't true of all men and not all women want the same things from a sexual relationship with a man. A woman who wants sex with a man is seen as unenlightened at best and weak at worst. It gives no quarter for women who, you know, maybe want sex with a man because they like it and maybe want to have a baby. And that's not even getting into any kink. I knew what I wanted and that painting was a statement on the fact that I couldn't get it."

"Was all that symbolism your idea?"

"Between us, we narrowed it down to those two factions and those two books, but he already had a solid idea of what he wanted to do. Ford can cut through bullshit faster than anybody I know and distill everything down to its essence. He looked at me and that painting is what he saw."

"What's he like?" Eilis whispered, eager to know more about him, more about the way he thought, more details that would give her two-dimensional painting its third dimension.

"Not sure how to answer that. He just is. He's different things to different peo-ple. I mean, he's pretty much always the same; it's just that people see him differently according to context and their own issues."

"Everybody sees everybody else like that."

"Mmmm, yeah, but with him? You know how people say, 'Actions speak louder than words'? Not true with him. His reputation—undeserved—speaks way louder than his actions. So loud that nobody sees what he actually *does*."

Eilis suddenly felt like they were talking about someone else; Ford didn't *have* a reputation. She opened her mouth to ask more, but the car stopped and died. "We're here. Don't take off your blindfold or I'll take you back home right now."

She sat in the car until the Virgin came around to help her out onto a steeply sloped sidewalk. The Virgin walked on the downside of her and guided her to a door that opened to cool air reeking of turpentine and oil paint.

The Virgin came back with her bag and closed the door behind her. "Okay. You can take off the blindfold now."

She didn't know what she'd expected Ford's studio to look like, but this wasn't it.

It was an enormous concrete rectangle with harsh fluorescent lights overhead. A heavy canvas tarp haphazardly covered most of the concrete floor. Boxes of art supplies were piled high along an entire stretch of wall beside which stood a large cabinet with an enormous sink. Five-by-five-foot canvases lined another wall. One very large tarp-covered canvas, perhaps ten feet wide and eight feet high, leaned against a different wall.

A magenta Victorian velveteen chaise, the only furniture in the room, stood in the center of the room. Just ahead of her, a switchback staircase rose into darkness. To the right of that, eight wide, richly carved cherry panels with elaborate filigree iron wheels at the top and bottom floated between tracks in the ceiling and floor.

"Come with me," said the Virgin and led her to the cherry panels. She pulled back two panels and turned up the lights. Eilis stopped and gasped. The Virgin stepped aside to allow Eilis to take in details.

A massive dark cherry four-poster bed, hung with velvets and chiffons of green, gold, and purple, sat on a broad two-step dais at a diagonal. A footstool sat on the floor to its left. The linens, the pillows, neck rolls, shams of all sizes and textures, and decorated with beads, fringe, and tassels, perfectly matched the fall of drapery from the bedposts. In the corner above the deliciously carved headboard of the bed hung a matching shelf, both color and carvings. Candles of all different shapes and sizes, in all the colors of the room, jockeyed for position.

The walls were painted a rich purple and dotted with gold-leaf fleur-de-lis. The crown and base moulding were also gold leaf. The carpet, a dark, rich green also dotted with gold fleur-de-lis, oddly, didn't clash with the purple walls.

Feathered masks of all descriptions decorated the walls and ropes of green, purple, and gold beads draped and looped haphazardly. No other art. A bookcase on one wall was bursting with books whose titles she couldn't read. A sleek machine she assumed to be a sound system hid in the shadows, hung at eye level.

"You'll be spending the night here with Ford," the Virgin murmured and Eilis swallowed. "Possibly more. Are you ready to see the salon?"

"Yes, please," Eilis whispered.

A set of dark cherry French doors, whose sandblasted glass panes allowed some light, separated the bedroom from the salon. When the Virgin opened the doors toward them, Eilis gasped anew.

The opulence of 1920s art deco came to life in deep reds and golds. Deco sconces glowed warm, yet only bright enough to read by. The carpet was a plush, deep, rich gold with acanthus leaves sculpted into its surface. A large round table of burled wood punctuated by ebony inlays sat in the center with four parsons chairs upholstered in the same rich red as the walls.

A very large mirror hung over a dark, carved cherry sideboard, which boasted a silver tray with a silver-labeled dark blue bottle flanked by two oddly shaped glasses, two wide slotted spoons, an empty water carafe, and a bowl of sugar cubes.

A fully-stocked liquor cabinet of the same cherry dominated an anteroom that could be seen through a narrow arched doorway. Following that, she found a gorgeous kitchenette with refrigerated drawers, wine cooler, ice maker. Beautiful glasses hung over one counter.

The Virgin led Eilis out of the kitchenette to the far side of the salon and opened another set of French doors.

Yet more surprises.

It was a bathroom, stark white and brushed nickel, the floor tiled in 1920s hexagons. Subway tiles rose from the floor halfway up the walls. In one corner sat a luxurious claw-foot tub and an enormous shower at the opposite corner almost disappeared because it was glass. There were two sinks, over which were two mirrors. Fresh towels and a plush bathrobe, all in white, hung next to the sinks.

All the expensive scents, body powders, lotions, soaps, shampoos, conditioners that a woman could want nestled in white baskets placed randomly about the room. The pretty bottles and labels gave the room its only splash of color, but delighted the senses because of its scarcity otherwise.

The only other color in the room was cradled in a wall vase of brushed nickel between the mirrors, which held a peculiar plant of dull purple bells, black berries, and golden stamens. It took Eilis a minute to place it and then she bit her lip.

Atropa belladonna. Deadly nightshade: Poison. Deception. Danger.

She swallowed and felt the Virgin's gaze on her.

"I'm going to leave now. I'll be back when Ford calls me to come get you and take you home. Eilis," she said, grasping Eilis's hands and looking up at her, her peculiar blue eyes piercing, "do you understand what's going to happen here tonight?"

"I—I think so," she whispered, not at all sure now.

You'll be spending the night here with Ford.

Belladonna.

Besides her uneasiness, she had a vague sense of guilt she didn't understand.

"Is he— Is he dangerous?" Eilis whispered.

The Virgin looked suddenly horrified. "Oh, *no*," she breathed. "Never think that. It's just— I don't— I don't think this is a good idea. For either of you. I don't know you, but . . . " She raised a hand then dropped it, as if helpless and without words.

"Okay," she said with a deep sigh after another few seconds. "Get undressed and go out to the chaise out there. Here's a sheet." She went to the door, and turned, looking at her with that oddly concerned look. "Eilis," she said slowly, "don't assume *anything*. Ford is not what you think. Good luck."

Eilis drew in a deep breath as the Virgin closed the door behind her quietly. She heard footsteps on a staircase above her, leaving her alone somewhere—she didn't know where—with instructions to strip down and lie on a couch in a harsh studio.

Eilis, do you really want to do this?

No. She was frightened, she felt guilty and she didn't know why, and she wanted to go home.

But she lifted her chin. She'd wanted this, searched for it, spent time and money and energy seeking it. If she asked to leave now, she'd always regret it, always wonder what if— She took off her jeans and tee shirt, elegant lingerie, and went into the restroom to freshen up because yes, she would be making love with Ford tonight.

A man she hadn't met and knew nothing about.

In a place she didn't know.

Without allies, without help, without transportation.

Where am I? How far from home am I?

She screwed up her courage and left the salon, the sheet wrapped around her body and trailing behind her.

The studio was dim and cold. She sat on the edge of the chaise and suddenly, bright, bright lights above her blinded her. They heated up nearly immediately, so she knew the air wouldn't stay cold.

She looked out into the darkness and saw the vague outline of an easel, then a shadow moving beyond it. She gasped and a low chuckle came from that direction.

"Good morning, Eilis." It was a hoarse, grainy whisper, as if he'd smoked too many cigarettes in his lifetime.

"Good morning," she whispered.

"Well," he said at that volume in that rough voice, "I'm glad to finally meet you."

He spoke slowly, but clearly and precisely, as if it hurt to speak, but he would say what he needed to regardless of the pain. He snapped on a small light that lit only his canvas "Let's get started. See that round pillow? I want you to lie back on the couch and tuck it under the middle of your back."

She did as instructed. "No, the other way. Your head needs to be at the foot of the chaise." She clutched the sheet to herself and laid down, her heart thundering and her stomach roiling. The bright lights blinded her, and she put her arm over her eyes.

"Very good. Now lift your left leg and drape it over the back of the couch."

That was no stretch for Eilis's long legs, but the couch's finely carved back dug into her calf.

"Right foot on the floor."

She caught her breath. He was spreading her out, arching her back, the way she would look while making love.

"Drop your right arm off the edge."

She did that.

"Take off the sheet."

She began to, but she must have taken too long because:

"Do you want to be painted or not, Eilis?" he demanded gruffly, impatience heavily lacing his voice.

"I think so," she murmured into the half darkness, uneasy with not being able to see him. She wanted to see his face, the person on the other end of the conversation.

"Part of being painted nude is being uninhibited. You wanted this. What did you think was going to happen? I paint nudes. You have to be nude."

"Yes, but I thought—"

"What did you think? That I was going to stroke you and woo you and make sweet, sweet love to you to get you to look like a Ford painting?"

She blushed, embarrassed. She snatched up the sheet and covered herself, then swung her leg off the back of the couch to leave.

"If you leave now, I won't give you another chance. I have very little patience for women who act like little girls."

Stung, she gaped in his direction.

"You've been watching too many tortured-artist arthouse films. I don't work that way. I expect my models to be able to call up their own sexuality."

Eilis didn't believe that for a second. She'd seen those paintings—she'd owned eight of them once upon a time. Every single one of those women had been well fucked.

Confused and feeling betrayed, not understanding why, she simply stood there. She didn't have enough confidence in her own body to call up her own sexuality in front of anyone, much less a man she didn't know; she had come here depending on him to make her feel beautiful enough so that she could.

Although she hadn't intended to tell him that.

His bark of laughter shattered her in a way she had never known. "Is that right?" he purred. "Do you think I'm the great Maker of Fertility Goddesses or something?"

Well, yes, she had thought that, but she kept her mouth shut.

"I see," he murmured when she remained silent and still. "Well," he said, louder this time as he got up and completely disappeared into the darkness.

The overhead lights blinked out and the only remaining light came from a candle in a sconce on a far wall. She waited for what seemed a long time, then started when she heard his raspy whisper in her ear and felt his hand drawing her sheet away.

"Since you seem to have such a high opinion of my skills as a lover—an opinion that you whipped up out of nothing, might I add—maybe I should take the opportunity to test your opinion."

In the darkness, she could only smell him, a mixture of Ivory soap and turpentine, and *feel* what he did to her. She shivered at his touch. Gentle, so gentle. He paced around her slowly, his fingertips brushing across her shoulders, running through her hair, caressing her neck. He laid his palm flat between her breasts, his broad hand splayed out over her skin, his thumb flicking her nipple before he bent and caught it between his teeth.

She closed her eyes with a soft moan, dropped her head back. The brush of her own hair on her back and the brush of his hair on her breasts. His lips pulling at her nipples and sucking, licking. She sighed and wrapped her fingers in his satin hair, *Ford's* hair.

Light as a feather, his fingers caressed her skin, his mouth following his fingers everywhere. Eilis felt her arousal as it began to flow and she felt him take in a deep breath against her skin. She gasped when his hand trailed down between her breasts, down her belly, through her pubic hair until he slipped his fingers up inside her, then pulled them away.

"Eilis," he whispered in her ear as he brought his fingers to her lips, "taste yourself." She did, shocked at *Ford's* fingers on her tongue, wet from her— "That," he continued, so softly she could barely hear him, wrapping his hand around the side of her neck, his mouth in her other ear, "is the nectar of the gods."

"I want to see you," she whispered. "Let me look at you. Tell me who you are."

"No."

He drew his fingers along the line of her jaw so that she smelled herself on him——and choked.

Pulled away.

"I don't want this," she whispered.

Silence. Still, deadly. "What. Did. You. Say."

"I don't want this," she repeated, her voice stronger now.

She'd never said no to sex before—even when she didn't want it.

And she regretted that.

She'd never trusted that part of herself enough to say no. She'd thought that she would want sex with Ford, that he would be different from all the other men. Yet she didn't want sex with Ford and her instincts now told her the same thing they always told her when she put herself in these situations.

The definition of insanity is doing the same thing over and over again and expecting a different result.

"I can't do this. This was a mistake. I'm sorry."

"You've had investigators looking for me for years. I brought you to me to give you what you want. What's the problem?"

"I— Things have changed in my life," she said in a rush, not knowing where the words came from, but knowing that they were true. "I don't need you to make me feel beautiful anymore."

Another long silence. "What changed?" Funny. He didn't sound angry, just curious.

"I think— I think I'm in love with someone, but I don't know because I don't know what love feels like. But if this is what love feels like, then I can't betray that. He already doesn't trust me and he's very angry with me. I don't have a chance with him now."

"How can you be in love with someone who doesn't trust you and who is angry with you? What are you betraying if there's nothing to betray?"

"Myself," she whispered.

"What's this man's name?"

"Sebastian," she whispered, trembling, ashamed to her core that she spoke Sebastian's name to a man with whom she betrayed him. "I didn't know until you touched me. Please forgive me."

"Don't you want to be painted?"

"Sebastian's an artist. I know how he sees me, and *he* thinks I'm beautiful."

"And you just now figured this out."

"Yes. I'm . . . ashamed," she said, her voice breaking as tears gathered in her eyelashes. "Please let me go. Please."

A long intake of breath. "All right, Eilis." And then he was gone.

The harsh fluorescents came up and the air grew colder. She looked around her, seeing for the first time how dreadfully *wrong* she'd been to pursue this when she had had a real man in front of her, who was beautiful and magical, who fixed her soul because that was what he went through life doing: fixing things.

How had she missed it?

Shame of a different type of betrayal overtook her, the kind of betrayal she had never experienced before—not the shame of having trusted, then being betrayed, oh no. It was the shame of having betrayed.

Eilis wouldn't have to worry about telling Sebastian her past, because she had no future with him. With that thought, she sat on the chaise, the sheet covering her, her knees tight together, and curled in on herself and began to cry:

For all the things in her childhood that she'd lost.

For all the things she'd been made to do.

For all the betrayal and pain and anguish that had only stopped when she walked out of a courtroom at fifteen, a jaded emancipated minor, having more than proven that she was better off on her own than with any available adult at her disposal.

She sat on the chaise and curled into herself and cried:

For all the bad choices in men she'd made.

For continuing to search for something that didn't exist.

For always using sex to assuage her pain, which only made it worse—and she'd never known that until this moment.

The definition of insanity is doing the same thing over and over again and expecting a different result.

Yet again, Sebastian's voice, Sebastian's guiding hand, Sebastian's ruthless will had saved her—from another bad decision in men.

That man, who wanted her so much, yet would rather let her go than compete with someone who didn't exist. Who cared for her feelings so much he had let her keep a painting she loved, a painting he should never have let her keep. He had every right to his mistrust and anger with her. He had reason.

Never before had she had anyone who might feel betrayed by her.

She had decided to do something different tonight. If she couldn't have Sebastian, she would have no one.

You want comfort sex and any cock will do.

Not anymore. Sebastian or No One. And tonight she had chosen No One because Sebastian was no longer an option.

"Eilis," said a soft voice above her. The Virgin.

I don't think this is a good idea. For either of you.

Eilis couldn't fathom why Ford would suffer.

She picked up Eilis's hands and pulled her gently off the sofa, then wrapped her in a soft robe. "Come with me. I started the shower for you."

Eilis went willingly, her eyes burning so badly from her tears that she could barely process anything. The Virgin sat her down in the bathroom on a soft bench she had not seen before. She began to gently brush Eilis's hair as if Eilis were five years old and this woman were her mother. She took her hair and slowly, carefully, braided it. Eilis began to sob again at the kindness and the Virgin patted her shoulder. She didn't deserve such kindness for what she had done here tonight.

She urged Eilis to rise, pulled the robe back off Eilis, and led her to the shower. She murmured, "I'll be back in a bit and take you home when you're ready. I've put your bag in the car."

Eilis nodded and closed her eyes against the hot comfort of the stinging water.

Sebastian flinched when he heard the basement door slam closed and the angry footsteps coming toward his bedroom, where he sat on the edge of his bed, naked, his face in his hands, both elated and deeply ashamed.

"What in the hell did you do to her?"

"Almost nothing, Giz," he croaked, his throat sore from trying to maintain that low rasp. He cleared it. "I swear. She wanted to stop before I was ready to stop for her."

"You weren't going to fuck her?"

"No. It would have been rape."

"Then why is she crying?"

"She thinks she's betrayed me. She's ashamed."

When he looked up after too much silence, Giselle was staring off, out the window, chewing on the inside of her mouth, thinking.

"There's a lot of pain there, Sebastian. I don't know what, don't know how deep. There's something going on inside her that she doesn't understand."

"She's been waiting for Ford to fix her."

"And as usual, Sebastian gets the short end of the stick for patching people up and setting them on their feet." Giselle turned and sat on the bed beside him. "You have to start doing something different, Sebastian. You're about to get called to *Congress* because of how you do what you do."

"I don't know how to do it any other way."

"Does Eilis know what you've done for her company and that *you* did it and that she *didn't* do it?"

"Yes."

"You *must* have treated her differently."

"I thought it was because of the court order. She didn't call me and she already knew what had to be done, what I was going to do. Between the trial and keeping her company together, she didn't have time to untangle that knot of executives and cut through the bullshit before I got there. That had to be done first and she knew that, but she never got the chance to do it herself."

"Sebastian, you obviously haven't pissed her off if she's in love with you. *What did you do differently?*"

He sighed. "I did what I do with you. I wasn't her invisible hand. I let her see my anger and I was very blunt."

"Why?"

"I wanted to get her through her receivership as fast as possible so I could seduce her. I couldn't do that while I was her trustee and fixing things invisibly, waiting for the epiphany, is a very long process. She didn't *need* an epiphany. She just needed a third party to help her get the looters off her back."

"And now?"

"I can't even bear to look at her because I want her so badly and I know I can't touch her. The Ford thing's always been holding me back and now she's ashamed she betrayed what to her was already a dead relationship."

"Did you ever ask her what *she* wanted or did you just *assume* she'd prefer Ford over Sebastian because Sebastian can barely get a date, much less a lover? Did you *talk* to her? Tell her what *you* wanted? That you wanted a relationship with her and would she please be so kind as to forget Ford and concentrate on Sebastian?"

He groaned and dropped his face back in his hands.

"Oh, I see. And you got in *my* face for being a coward for running away from Bryce. Congratulations. You're as fucked up as the rest of us."

He could say nothing for a long while as he thought back, all the times he'd gotten angry with Eilis because he couldn't see past *his* fixation with Ford, a man he hadn't set out to become and couldn't seem to get rid of.

"Tell me what to do, Giz," he whispered.

"Act like nothing happened. Act like Sebastian Taight, HRP's trustee, who doesn't know that she loves him, who doesn't know this happened tonight, who's still trying to get her through her receivership for the same reason. Act the way you have always acted with her before you left her at Christie's. You have to tell her who you are, but wait until you're on equal footing again."

"How can I face her with the truth? I've betrayed her more than she thinks she's betrayed me. She's never made a secret of the fact she wanted Ford, but she has no clue I *am* Ford. I've left her hints, I've dropped her clues. She doesn't even know there's a crumb trail, much less that it leads straight to me. At the very least, I expected her to recognize you from my sketchbook and put it together on the way here. I wanted her to figure it out and she never did. She never will. He was too much of a fantasy for her to connect to a real man."

"*Talk to her, Sebastian!*" she shrieked. "You should have told her. You have to— Quit hiding behind Ford." She stopped, took a breath. "You have to cut open your soul. Take it from a woman whose man hides his soul from her."

He choked.

"Do you remember what you told me when I was ashamed for deceiving Bryce?"

"No."

"You said, 'So? It's not like you pulled off some elaborate scam and made a fool of him.' On a scale of one to ten, this is about a five. It's recoverable. Just be patient and let her work through it at her own pace—and help her do that. As you. She loves *you*, Sebastian. She chose *you* over Ford. Don't throw that back in her face."

51: Mother's Day

THE VIRGIN WAS SO KIND, EILIS THOUGHT AS SHE WRAPPED THE BLINDFOLD around her head. Too choked up to speak, Eilis couldn't protest and she didn't want to see. She didn't want to know where she had sunk so low, to know the shame of a betrayer. If she knew where she was, every time she drove past or heard the name of the suburb or neighborhood, it would remind her of this night.

The Virgin helped Eilis down into the same soft, cradling bucket seat she'd sat in so expectantly on the journey here. Once the car was started and they were moving, the rich voices of Sarah Brightman and Andrea Bocelli floated to her ears, but it only made her cry more.

"I'm sorry," the Virgin whispered and turned the music off. She stopped at a drive-through and got her a drink. She didn't bother asking if Eilis wanted food, which meant Eilis didn't have to speak or explain that food was the last thing she wanted. She sipped her diet cherry limeade in the silent darkness.

A numb peace settled over Eilis during the long drive, then:

"Okay, we're here. You can take your blindfold off."

She did. Once the gate opened, the Virgin drove in, parked, then turned off the motor while the gate slid closed behind them. But she just sat there, unwilling to move, staring ahead, tears rolling down her face.

The Virgin opened her door, and tugged on her arm until she could maneuver her out of the car. Eilis went with her, all too willing to be cared for by this small woman with the strength of a man.

She took Eilis in, up the stairs to her room, undressed her, and tucked her in bed. She even brought her a drink of water.

"Eilis," she said softly, "I'm going to take down your painting. Where would you like me to put it?"

Eilis couldn't speak, couldn't fathom a moment when that painting wouldn't hang on her wall where she could see it the minute she opened her eyes in the morning.

"Well," said the Virgin after a while. "I'll just put it on the floor then."

Eilis heard her take it down, turn it around, and lean it against the wall. Then she felt the Virgin over her, felt the soft kiss on her temple, the hand smoothing her hair.

"I'm sorry, Eilis. I'm so sorry," she whispered, and Eilis felt her tears drop on her face, the shift of the bed where she sat, and fell asleep with her mother's soft hand stroking her hair.

Eilis awoke, unable to tell the time of day because her heavy drapes—the ones she never used—were drawn. Her clock had disappeared. *Morning in Bed* stood on the floor, face to the wall, and for that, she was glad. She arose, wrapped a thin robe around her so she couldn't see her body in the mirror, and went downstairs to do . . . something.

She wasn't quite sure what.

Startled when she heard sounds coming from her kitchen, her heart began to race. There were people in her house!

"Thank you, Ares," she heard from where she stood on the landing, out of sight but not out of earshot, a woman's voice. The Virgin. Why was she still here? "Will you come back tonight?"

"If you're here, I will," said a male voice, hoarse, raspy, much deeper, more damaged, than Ford's. "I won't sleep alone again."

"It was rough on me, too."

Long silence, and Eilis peeked around the corner to see the Virgin's legs and arms wrapped around a very tall, very broad and well-dressed man with black hair and fair yet olive-tinted skin, who kissed her hungrily.

She was married, Eilis realized in wonder. Yes, she wore a wedding ring, Eilis remembered now.

Their kiss softened and deepened, and the Virgin whispered, "I don't want you to go."

"I don't want to go." Not long after that, he let her slide slowly down his body and set her on her feet. "See you tonight. Have a good rest of the day."

"I'll call you."

He left. Eilis watched as the Virgin watched her husband until his SUV was out the gate then activate the switch to close the gate behind him. She turned, her fingers to her mouth and a soft, dreamy smile on her face, then went back into the kitchen, out of sight.

Eilis walked down the rest of the stairs, suddenly feeling bereft. Again. Ashamed. Guilty. For what she had done to Sebastian, what she had done to herself, what she'd not be able to have with Sebastian now. She reached the kitchen and saw that it was one o'clock in the afternoon. The Virgin stood over a double boiler, whisking the contents half to death. Curious, Eilis approached slowly to look over her shoulder.

"Good morning, Eilis," said the Virgin softly as she whisked.

Eilis sniffled. "What's that?"

"Hollandaise sauce. For the steak and eggs. How are you feeling?"

"Not well," she whispered, a catch in her voice and her heart because of the gentleness and kindness of this woman whom she did not know. "My soul hurts."

Eilis didn't know where that came from but the Virgin stopped whisking and looked at her, solemn, her eyes glittering with moisture. She swallowed. "What's your name?" Eilis whispered.

The Virgin hesitated for a moment, went back to whisking, and then said, "You don't need to know that."

"Why are you still here?"

"I thought you could use someone to take care of you for a while. I— I, um— I can go if you don't want me here . . ."

At the thought of that, someone to take care of her, Eilis shook her head and began to cry. Lunch was forgotten.

The Virgin took her to the living room sofa and sat with her. She rocked Eilis and sang lullabies to her, stroked the hair that had stayed in its braid all night. This woman, the Virgin who wasn't, was her mother yet again.

And Eilis needed a mother so very badly. She began to pour out her soul to her mother. Her life, her history, the things she'd never told anyone, the things she could never tell Sebastian—would never have the chance to tell Sebastian. She didn't refer to her biological parents by name because she hated them too much to validate their existence by speaking their names aloud.

She kept talking, telling her everything that she had experienced and done, what had been forced upon her, even the most shameful of things that no one should ever know about her, the things no one did know. She told everything to her mother who had no name, who was here to take care of her and for no other reason, who would stay with her until she was stronger.

Her mother cried with her and for her and over her, all through Eilis's tale and when she was through, she said,

"Sebastian fixed me."

The Virgin hiccuped. Sighed. Hiccuped again. Finally her mother said, "Do you love this man, Sebastian?"

"Yes, I do."

"Because he fixed you?"

"No. Because he brings me hope and joy. He brings me peace and quiet. He makes me believe that pain and failure don't exist, that anything's possible. He makes my past irrelevant to me."

"What do you do for him?"

"I don't know. Nothing, I guess," Eilis said and began to cry again. "I'm too needy, too— I betrayed him. I can never look at him again. I'm so ashamed. I bring him nothing but anger and distrust, and he's right to be angry and distrustful. I should have abandoned my fantasy when I had the chance and now it's too late."

"I think you should not underestimate this man's feelings for you, Eilis."

"I could never tell him what I've told you today. He would hate me."

The Virgin took a long, shuddering breath. "You *don't* know that," she said with a surety that struck Eilis as odd. "He fixed you; why would you think any of this would change his feelings for you?"

"Because it's horrible."

"And mostly none of your doing."

"I'm—" Eilis choked, "damaged."

"*Everyone* is damaged. He may have secrets he's keeping from you. You don't know."

Eilis had nothing to say to that.

The Virgin sat quiet for a long time, except for the sniffles and an occasional hiccup. Then she said, "Eilis, I want to tell you a story. About when I deceived a man. When I hid from him for eight months because of my shame. And I ached over him, the way you ache now. I thought he would never, ever forgive me for the wrong that I had done him. And I waited eight months because of my shame. I went to him because my brothers said I should, and I confessed to him. I thought he would yell at me and tell me what a horrible person I was and look at me with contempt and walk away from me, but he didn't."

"What did he do?" whispered Eilis, entranced.

"He married me."

Eilis and the Virgin sat at the table doing a jigsaw puzzle together, not a word between them, when that man, her husband she'd called Ares, called at the gate and Eilis let him in. She had never seen an uglier man in her life, the left side of his face and his left hand all scarred and twisted; the Man Without a Face. Pain radiated from those scars and Eilis felt it in her own skin. She wondered if his entire left side had been burnt. What an extraordinarily handsome man he must have been before . . .

But there was kindness in that face, a peace that put her immediately at ease in spite of the name the Virgin had called him. She could see no war in him. She saw nothing but empathy and generosity of spirit.

Eilis left the room because he lifted the Virgin up into his arms; she wrapped herself around him in greeting and they kissed. Long. Passionately. But she watched around the corner of the staircase landing with the kind of envy that is wistful and bittersweet.

"I missed you," the Virgin whispered to Ares, and Eilis eavesdropped shamelessly because she had never known married people who loved each other and were in love with each other. She didn't know what it looked like.

Until now.

"I missed you back," he said, his voice raspier and more hoarse than it had been earlier, though so full of fire and desire she could hear it across the distance. Love, lust, a whole host of things said in four little words: *I missed you back.*

"How is she?" he asked quietly, still holding her wrapped around him.

"A wreck. And now I am, too. I love her and I don't even know her."

"That's the way it is with you. You love everyone you protect."

I love her.

You love everyone you protect.

Eilis went to her room and lay down to cry. After a while, the Virgin came bringing her food and drink on a tray.

"Eilis? Do you want me to sit with you?"

"No," she replied, sniffling. "I need to think."

"All right."

The Virgin stayed for a week, Ares coming every night to sleep with her, though not speaking much to Eilis. It was as if he thought if he spoke to her, she would break. Once, she tiptoed out of her room to listen to them make love because she needed to know that married people did that and it didn't hurt and it wasn't a chore and it could be pleasurable.

But when she heard Ares's harsh, cruel voice, it startled her and distressed her, frightened her, even; it triggered horrible feelings in her she never wanted to feel again.

Go get my tie.

Turn around and put your hands behind your back.

Get on your knees.

Suck my cock. Harder.

Stand up. Bend over the bed. Open your legs so I can see your pussy. Wider. Wider.

I'm fucking you so you'll stay fucked.

The Virgin burst out laughing. "You had to break out the Henry Miller, didn't you?"

Ares chuckled warmly. "Yeah. Haven't finished the *Story of O* yet."

"I've corrupted you."

"Not completely. Come to bed, Wife."

And though Eilis could clearly hear that the man was smitten with his wife, and she with her husband, she *hated* their way and it gave her no peace.

She tiptoed back to her room.

I went to him because my brothers said I should, and I confessed to him.

What did he do?

He married me.

52: *Full Disclosure*

G ISELLE FINALLY GRADUATED FROM LAW SCHOOL—NOT WITH HONORS, but she didn't care about such things. It was more important that, except for her last two semesters, she'd worked her way through without using student loan money to live on. Now, today, it was enough that she had become an attorney and could practice once she passed the bar. Though she still occasionally mourned her bookstore, she had a job waiting for her in two months and a long-term goal.

Justice McKinley graduated *summa cum laude* with the name she'd made for herself in political circles. She'd probably head out to Washington to play pundit on TV or conservative talk radio. Giselle smiled to herself, knowing that once Knox's birthday passed in a year and a half, that girl would open her door the next day and find him on her stoop. Then all would be right in her world.

And his.

When Giselle pointed her out to Bryce, he thought Knox had lost his mind. "Not that I have room to talk, mind."

"Remember," she said, "I told you Knox falls in love with souls. He probably hasn't noticed what she looks like at all other than the red hair. Trust me, there's a faery princess underneath all that frizz and bad fashion."

Giselle's entire family, save Fen and Trudy, appropriated a large section of the bleachers to see her graduate. "Trudy won't show up on Knox's turf," Giselle told Bryce. "UMKC is the only place in town he can come and socialize and be treated well."

Knox stood on the stage with the other professors, resplendent in full academic regalia. When Giselle crossed the stage to get her diploma, he grabbed her to give her a bear hug and a loud smack on the cheek. He laughed at her shock, and the rest of the graduates hooted and whistled, the strange hostilities between Professor Hilliard and Giselle Cox apparently over.

Bryce's presence in the audience, along with Sebastian's, Morgan's, and Étienne's, was duly noted. Sebastian kept people away from him with his trademark scowl, substantially more threatening than usual. Morgan glad-handed anybody who walked by and chatted *at* people with great enthusiasm. Étienne argued vehemently with a professor who dabbled in "making stuff," and Giselle shook her head at the man's foolishness. Bryce cast baleful glances at her across the auditorium when he found himself surrounded by professors and graduates clamoring for his attention. She smiled at him and blew him a kiss.

"He had no idea he was so popular around here, did he?" Knox said, appearing beside her to watch.

"I told him. He didn't believe me."

"Good job, Giselle. I'm proud of you."

"No thanks to you," she groused.

He let loose a wicked laugh. "I love poking at you, especially in public. *Priceless!*"

She huffed, but when he abruptly stopped laughing, she looked up at him. His mouth tight, he stared into the crowd and she followed his line of sight. There, *summa cum laude* Justice, alone and unnoticed, walked out of the auditorium, her head bowed. She felt Knox's fist clench and unclench against her and tension radiated from his body. She stopped him with a hand on his forearm when he took a step to follow her out.

"Don't," she murmured. "Just eighteen more months. You can do this."

He took a deep breath and muttered, "I'm outta here," before stalking off in the other direction, ripping his cap and hood off as he went, his gown billowing out behind him.

Giselle had to fight her way through the crowd around Bryce, collecting angry stares along the way, but once she reached him and he wrapped his arm around her to kiss her, deep and hot, the anger turned to astonishment.

"Pass her over this way, Kenard."

Sebastian picked her up and hugged her, handed her off to her mother and Aunt Dianne, Morgan, then the rest of the tribe.

It took awhile for her family to disperse and work its way toward the exits, but once it had, Giselle found herself semi-alone with Bryce save the last of the litigation groupies. He took her hand and brought it to his lips for a kiss.

She blushed.

He laughed, but glanced up over her shoulder. His smile faded.

Once again Giselle found herself following someone else's sight line until she saw Fen at the entrance of the auditorium. He simply smiled at her and nodded his approval before turning and walking right back out again. She sighed.

"What was that for?"

"Last year, when I went to his office, he told me he always wanted to be my father. He's proud of me."

Bryce said nothing to that for a moment. Then, "Is *that* what your relationship with him is all about?"

"A good portion of it. Plus, you know how easily entertained I am."

That made Bryce laugh.

"I think Fen felt Sebastian was a rival for my training and wanted to see if he could superimpose his will over Sebastian's."

"Sebastian was a child; Fen wasn't. It's an easy leap to make."

"I s'pose."

"You love him, don't you?"

Her brow wrinkled. "Love? No. I don't know what it is, but I'll miss him when he dies."

"You mean when Knox ends up killing him."

She hesitated, then sighed. "Yeah, I guess that is what I meant."

Sebastian had offered to host Giselle's graduation party and it was in full swing when they arrived, several of her cousins having availed themselves of Sebastian's liquor cabinet and someone else had brought coffee. "And that's why," Giselle explained wryly, "we almost *never* have any parties at Sebastian's house. It's one thing for my aunts to know people go astray; it's another for them to see it happening in front of their faces."

"Where's Knox?"

"Probably on his way to the Ozarks to spend the weekend working out his Justice McKinley issues."

"Ozarks? Oh, the inn he owns in Mansfield."

"Half." She nudged him with an elbow then. "Now say, 'You were right, Giselle.'"

He glanced at her sharply. "About what?"

"O god of the UMKC School of Law with groupies galore."

He burst out laughing then. "That embarrassed the hell out of me."

"How many professorships were you offered?"

"Uh, three, I think."

"And?"

"Oh, hell no."

"How many resumes got slipped to you?"

"Seven or eight."

"And?"

He snorted. "I only hire from Knox's office or if he sends someone directly to me."

"Did you two dance that dance even when you weren't speaking to each other all those years?"

He hesitated a moment, then grinned sheepishly. "Yeah, we did."

The party ran late into the night and finally Giselle couldn't take it anymore. She found Bryce up on the rooftop deck lazing back in an Adirondack chair, looking out over the Plaza, shooting the breeze with half a dozen cousins. She dropped in his lap. "Bryce, I want to go home. I'm exhausted."

Once in the car, Giselle leaned her head back against the seat and watched the scenery go by. Neither of them spoke for most of the quick ride home. "Wife?"

"Mmmm?" She was nearly asleep, her eyes beginning to close, basking in the warmth and love that surrounded her, not only with Bryce, in that car, but in Sebastian and Knox, her mother and her Aunt Dianne, the rest of her tribe who had shown up the day of her wedding to congratulate her, who'd shown up to see her graduate from law school, supportive as they ever were. Even Fen. A hundred-plus people using any excuse to have a party because they *enjoyed* each other.

She figured she probably ought not take that for granted, especially because Bryce so loved and needed her family. The pack, the tribe—they accepted him, loved him, validated him and fed his soul.

"Tell me about that night."

Her eyes opened slowly and she saw that they were pulling into their driveway. Her mouth twitched in thought and she released a great puff of air. She didn't have to be told *which* night he wanted to know about; in fact, it surprised her that he hadn't asked earlier. She'd never told anyone about it because she hadn't had to.

"All right," she murmured as he turned off the car, "but I'm going to take a shower first. I need to relax. It's late and this isn't going to be easy for me."

He nodded and they went into the house. She spent her time in the shower ordering her thoughts, trying to wash away the damage, the blood, before she spilled it again in the telling. She slowly dressed in a set of white cotton men's style pajamas and wrapped her wet hair up in a towel. Bryce waited for her when she emerged from the bathroom, lounging in a club chair in the sitting area of their bedroom and reading a book. He'd changed into his preferred at-home attire: denim shorts.

Sitting across from him, she looked left out the window without seeing anything, wondering what he'd think of her once she'd told him the nitty gritty. She drew a deep breath and began. "Four years ago, I was working at a bookstore on the Plaza. Two guys came after me with guns and I . . . " She shrugged. "Killed them."

53: 47th & Broadway

GISELLE STOOD IN THE BREEZEWAY OF THE BOOKSTORE HOLDING THE door open, *waiting for her boss, a late-middle-aged woman with a completely reasonable fear of walking to her car late at night. Once they had sandwiched themselves between the inner and outer sets of locked doors, Giselle bent to dig in her backpack.*

"That's just unreal," Judy muttered as she watched Giselle perform the same ritual she performed every night they closed together: Ripping the Velcro. Wrapping the wide elastic bands tight around each thigh. Checking to make sure rounds were chambered.

Giselle chuckled as she stuck one Glock in each holster. "You know what they say. Better to have and not need than to need and not have."

Judy snorted. "I s'pose you're right. I needed those last summer and didn't have."

"I'm sorry, Judy," Giselle murmured. Finished with her task, she straightened and shrugged into her backpack and Judy unlocked the outer doors. Giselle preceded her out into the oppressive heat and humidity of a July night in Kansas City. "I do appreciate your understanding about this."

"Opinions change once you've been assaulted. I just don't want to get dragged into—" She waved a hand toward Giselle's legs and shuddered. "Whatever it is you're involved in."

Giselle chuckled. "I'd tell you the story, but you wouldn't believe a word of it."

Judy laughed, and with the snick of the lock and the arming of the security system, they set out toward Judy's car. Giselle walked on the outside of the sidewalk and at Judy's pace. By the end of a twelve-hour shift, Judy could barely make the two blocks to her parking spot.

"Judy," Giselle said gently, "maybe it's time for you to find something different to do."

"Ah, I can't, Giselle. I'm trapped by my salary and benefits. I couldn't make this kind of money anywhere else and I have to have health insurance."

Giselle said nothing; she certainly knew what it meant to be overeducated, overqualified, underemployed, and with few immediate options. She laughed wryly. "I'm a Post-hole Digger, working second shift as a clerk at a bookstore."

"Mmmm, I know what you mean. PhDs in literature don't leave you a lot of choices if you won't head straight back into academia."

"I would, but the publishing part gives me hives."

"Same here."

Giselle's humor faded and the familiar melancholy of all she had lost overcame her, interrupted when Judy gasped. Giselle glanced at her. "What's wrong?"

Judy gestured weakly ahead, her body stiff with fright. Two men sprinted toward them and Giselle said, "Judy, you've met them. They're my cous—"

Tingle.

Giselle whirled, whipping her Glocks up out of their holsters and into her grip.

There, a man crossing the street and striding purposefully toward her, his hand behind his back to pull out a weapon.

"Don't even think about it," Giselle snarled, both guns pointed at his chest; he stopped short in surprise. A dark figure to her right caught her attention. She snapped that gun in his direction. One gun in each hand, she stood for a microsecond, her arms outstretched, her feet spread wide, instantly calculating distance and height. She saw a flash out of the corner of her eye and pulled both triggers.

She hit the ground conscious, but twisting and in agony. She took in the whole scene, dissociated and watching the aftermath of what she had done as if in a dream. Two men, dead. By her hand. It had taken only a second, possibly three, from the time she'd turned to the time she'd pulled the triggers to the time she'd gotten blown off her feet.

Somewhere behind her, her terrified boss cowered and sobbed at the base of a wall.

Somewhere above her, a bullet had embedded itself in the tree trunk behind Giselle, probably the same one that had bored through her shoulder.

Somewhere beside her, Knox flipped open his cell phone and called 911.

In front of her, Sebastian ripped off his tee shirt, dropped to his knees, and frantically wrapped the fabric around her shoulder, held it tight, made her hurt worse. She groaned.

"C'mon, Giz," he murmured when she couldn't hold her eyelids open anymore. "Stay with me, baby. C'mon. Hey, do you remember that kid who bet long odds on the wildcard spot for the '83 NFL playoffs and couldn't pay up?"

Yeah, that wasn't something she was going to forget. Ever.

Knox now squatted behind her, working to get another wad of cloth between her right hip and the sidewalk. She grimaced when he lifted her and whimpered when he gently settled her weight back onto that hip.

"What happened to him, Giselle?" Knox asked, stroking her hair.

Sebastian took a baseball bat to his knees.

"What? I didn't hear you. Talk, Giselle. Stay with us."

"S'b's'n broke legs," she whispered, her teeth beginning to chatter. "Cold."

"Shit, she's going into shock," Sebastian muttered, "and so's her boss. Knox, go see if she's hurt." Giselle missed the warmth of Knox's body behind her, his hand in her hair. "How much did he owe me on that bet, Giz?"

'Ten thousand dollars.

"What?"

She swallowed. She could barely move her mouth. "Ten K."

Sirens wailed through the night, coming closer and closer. She still couldn't open her eyes, though tears began to leak out.

"Hurts."

"I know, princess. Stay with me now. We'll get you to the hospital, get you warm. What was my most outrageous vig ever?"

A hundred and seventy-five percent on three days.

"C'mon, Giz, talk to me. What's the answer?"

"Uhnse'nfye, free."

"Right. Good."

She had a vague awareness of the sound of an ambulance parking and people rushing, but underneath, she heard Knox hiss,

"Shit. Fen was watching."

She felt Sebastian start. "What?"

"Look. That's his Alfa. He was up on the garage roof. He must have seen the whole thing."

I'm gonna kill him.

"Don't say that again, Giz," Sebastian whispered in her ear just as the paramedics shooed him away from her. "At least not where some random cop can hear you."

She was covered with a blanket, lifted onto a gurney, raised into the air, wheeled to the ambulance, slid inside with a thump or two.

"Do you guys want to go with her?"

"Yes," they answered simultaneously.

"Oh, no, you don't, Hilliard," barked an unfamiliar voice from far away. "You're staying right here and help me sort this shit out."

"Yeah, and you— Get rid of the piece. No firearms in the bus."

She opened her eyes enough to see Sebastian sitting near and he picked up her hand again. She had never seen his handsome face so . . . not handsome. Old. Haggard. Like Uncle Charlie.

"Jooey?" she whispered.

"She's fine," Sebastian murmured, his voice tight. "Scared. In shock, like you."

He's taken everything I have away from me, Sebastian.

"Not important right now, Giz. Concentrate on getting through this. Just think, you'll have some nifty new scars to brag about later on."

Oh, that's true.

"She's still got a slug in her hip," said another voice. "She's going to have to have surgery to get it out."

Sebastian said nothing else, but squeezed her hand. It was a fast trip to Truman Medical Center's emergency room—

—and an equally fast trip to the Jackson County prosecutor's office once she was discharged three days later. Executive AP Wells had denied Knox's request to take her there himself, so she was cuffed and stuffed in the back of a squad car, her hands in front of her only because her arm was in a sling.

The prosecutor was in court, so Wells took it upon himself to put them in a conference room and annoy the hell out of Knox. In the presence of two other APs, he began to run down what Giselle would be charged with. She only watched and listened with detachment, half asleep, too drugged with pain medication to speak and too tired to care. She'd take a jail cell cot at this point if it meant a few hours of sleep.

Finally, Knox said, his voice as hard as she'd ever heard it, "If you charge her, I'll defend her and I'm quite sure that's the last thing you want."

Two of the APs in the room reared back, away from Knox, but the executive's face lit up with the scent of challenge.

Even in her dazed state, she understood what a political nightmare that could turn into: the elected prosecutor of one county representing a criminal defendant in a neighboring county.

Knox leaned back in his chair. "Oh, I get it now. You want to make your name on me. Okay. I'll play that game with you and I'll even play it on your terms. But. Think of it," he said. "Beatrix Fucking Kiddo. Bet you got a hard-on looking at the pictures and thinking about what she must've looked like that night. Lemme tell ya, she was hot. I got a hard-on watching her whip out those big guns and pull the triggers. And now that she's survived two gunshot wounds, think what a jury will do when I get finished drawing the whole picture for them in Technicolor—the men'll come in their jeans and the women'll all start carrying Glocks on their thighs."

The EAP reddened and gulped. Knox laughed wickedly.

"Wells!" barked a man from the doorway. "What the hell is wrong with you? I specifically told you I'd handle this personally. Get out."

So. This was the prosecutor. He came in and shook Knox's hand like the old buddy he apparently was and sat, flipping the file open on the table to read it. His remaining two APs watched their boss warily for a long few minutes.

"Okay. She can go."

"Owe you, Kevin."

"Save it." He slid a look at the two APs and they left at a jerk of his head. Once the door had closed, the prosecutor looked at Giselle and said, "You managed to get a couple of thugs I've been trying to put away for three years now."

Knox fell back in his chair laughing. Giselle felt about as much satisfaction as she could muster, given her condition.

"Miss Cox, you'll need to stick around town until the investigation's wrapped up—" He speared Knox with a glance and Knox nodded his acceptance of the responsibility. "—but otherwise, you're free to go. I don't expect we'll find anything different from what your boss told us."

"Giz," Sebastian said the minute Knox brought her home, "don't do anything. Let me take care of him my way."

She said nothing for a moment, then whispered, "I'm tired and I hurt."

Knox herded her into her bedroom and carefully undressed her, then turned her bed down and helped her maneuver into a comfortable position. Sebastian raided the Den of Iniquity for extra pillows. Knox brought her a glass of water. "More," *she said once she'd finished that. He looked at her for a moment before coming back with two fresh liter bottles. She finished off one completely.*

"I want my mom," *she finally whispered, tears welling in her eyes and running down her cheeks. He finished tucking her in then and she closed her eyes.*

"She'll be home from Alaska tomorrow. We're going to tell her you got caught in a drive-by."

"Judy?"

"I got her a job up in the county clerk's office. Pay's not quite as good but the hours and benefits are better and it's a desk job."

"My guns?"

"Still in the property room at KCPD. I'll go pick them up this afternoon."

"My job? Hospital bills?"

"I have a line on a couple of jobs for you. Fen'll take care of your medical bills and he put you on OKH's health insurance."

"That's so fucked up," *she sighed and fell asleep.*

Silence.

Giselle stared at her bare feet, which she'd propped up on the broad ottoman between her chair and Bryce's, wondering what he must be thinking, not daring to look at him, afraid of what she would read in his face. It was one thing for him to know "one gun in each hand," to see and love her scars, but quite another for him to hear details.

Finally, "Giselle."

She couldn't decipher his mood with two syllables, and she slowly lifted her gaze to see him lounging back in his chair, his elbows on the arms and his fingers steepled under his chin. The cocked eyebrow, the tightness of his mouth . . . Her eyes widened a bit.

"Strip."

Giselle swallowed at his unexpected reaction, then felt her juices start to flow. "Make me," she whispered, aghast and aroused and relieved all at the same time.

His eyebrow arched and she felt the fire in the pit of her belly begin to kindle and flare. "You know, I don't think you want to challenge me on this, Wife."

That only meant she'd have to fight harder and she was more than prepared after the draining day she'd had. She needed that hit of adrenaline and testosterone.

"Really, why?"

"You're not stripping," he said, his voice hard. He slouched in his chair, unmoving, watching her. "Why?"

She rose then and, as she passed him, she said, "Maybe I'm tired."

"Oh, really?" He arose and stepped behind her to wrap his hands around her arms, and she smiled. He turned her around and she crossed her arms over her chest, watching him look at her.

His hand went to the towel on her head and he ripped it off, letting her damp hair fall free. His hand went to her pajama bottoms and ripped the drawstring and waistband with one swift yank. His eyebrow rose. "Take 'em off."

"Make me."

Like lightning, Bryce swept her off her feet and threw her at the bed. She bounced. Her legs far apart, she propped herself up on her elbows and laughed.

His face darkened and he approached her, stealthy, ever the predator. He grasped her ankles and straightened out her legs with a jerk. Then he ripped her pajama bottoms right off of her with one pull. He knelt on the bed slowly and crept over her until he had her trapped under him, his thighs straddling her and one hand on either side of her face, the way he'd had her in front of the bodhisattva. She stared up at him, then grasped his face to pull him down for a long, slow kiss.

"When I tell you to get undressed, you get undressed," he growled into her mouth.

"No."

His eyes widened and his nostrils flared. His kiss plowed her down into the mattress and she returned it with the same ferocity, then she put her hands flat against his chest and pushed as hard as she could.

Surprised, he rose enough for her to roll out from under him and off the bed. Her chest heaving, she watched him warily as he slowly unfolded his big, lithe body to step onto the floor.

He stripped off his shorts in one smooth movement, so he stood naked before her, his cock hard, erect, proud. Long, thick. She sucked in a breath at how beautiful he was, but then turned away with a flounce to drop into the club chair.

Giselle relaxed back into the cushion, then hooked her knees over each arm of the chair, opening herself for him. She gestured to the floor. "You know what to do."

He shifted his weight to one foot and crossed his arms over his chest. "No, I don't. Tell me what you want."

"You. On your knees. In front of me." His eyebrow rose. "Eat. Me."

He waved a hand. "And . . . you think that's all it takes."

Staring at him, she ran her hand down the inside of her thigh and spread the folds of her bare vulva wider, then dipped two fingers up inside herself. He sucked in a sharp breath, but he didn't budge.

"You know," she said matter-of-factly as she brought her hand to her mouth and licked her fingers, "I taste pretty good. If you don't want to service me, I can always go find one of my toys—"

Giselle jumped when he dropped to his knees in front of her, wrapping his big hands around her thighs. Her head fell back when she felt his tongue on her clit, then up inside her. She sighed and threaded her fingers through his silky hair, feeling every stroke of his tongue, his lips, his hands wherever he touched.

With every lick and caress, her orgasm built until her body tightened, her chest heaved, and she shrieked his name because she felt it there, right there, but not . . .

"My queen," Bryce murmured reverently against the inside of her thigh just before he jerked her out of the chair and lay back onto the floor so that she straddled his hips. She took his cock in her hand and guided him into her all the way, slow and easy.

She closed her eyes. Sighed. Stayed that way to feel him inside her, filling her to overflowing. He gently wrapped his big hands around her hips to keep her still. After a long moment of savoring the stillness of their connection, she opened her eyes to see him watching her, a seriousness on his face she had never seen before.

"What?" she whispered.

He swallowed. Opened his mouth.

"I love you, Giselle."

Her heart thudded in shock that not only had he said it, but under circumstances he'd forbidden.

The tears came. She bit her lip. She shifted to lie full upon him, wrap her fingers in his hair, bury her face in his neck. To cry. She felt his arms cradle her.

"What—?"

"Thank you," she hiccuped, only vaguely aware their bodies weren't connected anymore, his erection gone, but it didn't matter. She kissed his scarred face, his ear, his jaw over and over again. "Thank you, Bryce, thank you so much."

"Giselle—"

"My whole life," she murmured, still kissing him, her tears smearing over his skin, making the crevices of his scars glisten in the dim light. "My whole life, waiting for a man I love so much to say he loves me too."

She could feel him relax, his hold tighten around her. He brushed her ear with his mouth and whispered, "My queen."

54: New World Man

THERE HE WAS, ALL SIX FEET AND ONE INCH OF BIG-BONED MUSCLE, JUST the way she remembered him. Maybe a couple of new crow's feet here and there. Raw masculinity encased in a gray suit, the jacket open to reveal a crisp white shirt and contrasting tie, with fine Italian tasseled loafers on his feet. Mere approximation of civility for a man who looked as if he'd be more at home in a Chiefs uniform.

He had a quarterback's body: long face, square jaw covered by a five o'clock shadow even though it was only three, and a neck that fell straight from his ears to his shoulders without curving in. His nose was long and straight, his mouth hard. His ice blue eyes did nothing to diminish his aura of imminent danger. His short golden hair contrasted sharply with his tanned skin and made his pale eyes seem sharper, more omniscient.

He walked with an easy grace, a relaxed purpose to his long-legged gait that would allow him to stop on a dime or slow to accommodate the shorter stride of a person—a woman?—he respected. Or loved.

Justice sat on a bench in the hall just outside the Chouteau County prosecutor's office and watched him stride toward her, each step screaming leashed power. Her throat clogged as he got closer, and her heart pounded in her ears. She prepared what she thought must be her most captivating expression and witty conversation, so that when he stopped to ask her to dinner using that devastating grin he possessed, she would not seem at all as immature and gauche as she had three years before.

Each self-assured step brought him closer to Justice and her smile grew with each one. Any moment now, he would see her and be taken aback in sheer delight that she was here. He would tell her that he had not forgotten about her, that he had waited until she graduated from law school before attempting to find her, that he'd read every word she'd published, that he followed her blogging—and wasn't it lucky that she had found him instead?

However, as he drew closer, Justice's smile dimmed, for he glanced at her, or more precisely, *through* her, then proceeded past her without a glimmer of recognition. Her mouth turned down in a full-fledged frown as the faint scent of the cologne she'd never forget wafted to her nostrils in his wake. Her bottom lip trembled as she watched him round a corner, out of sight.

Well, heavens to mergatroid! *What* had she expected? Justice scolded herself with a sternness she reserved only when she caught herself squeeing like a prepubescent girl over a boy band. He was a busy man, with lots of things on his mind. Justice would wait until the time was right and speak to him, give him the opportunity to take the first step toward a relationship.

"Miss McKinley?"

Justice's gaze snapped up to her left to see a not-so-expensively dressed but very tall and handsome black man lean out of the threshold of the prosecutor's office to call her name. She gulped, a pre-interview attack of the jitters assailing her. Standing, she smoothed her best business dress, a printed cotton chintz of cream and blue and green, and hoped that her tight French braid held her unruly hair in check.

Once she had her messenger bag over her shoulder, she took a deep breath and chucked her chin up a notch for the appearance of courage. The man's smile of approval dazzled her and she took heart. "Okay," she murmured.

"Come with me. Eric Cipriani is the one who'll be talking to you today. By the way, my name's Richard. Richard Connelly."

"Nice to meet you."

"Same here. And don't worry. You'll do fine."

"Thanks," she said, the word released on a tremulous sigh.

Justice followed Mr. Connelly through a maze of desks in the open-area office, garnering barely a notice as men of every age and race imaginable, some dressed expensively and some not, buzzed this way and that, talking, shouting, cussing and discussing. Deputies, troopers, and KC cops roamed freely in and out.

Not a woman in sight. Not even an administrative assistant.

She lowered her eyes as she followed the man to a desk separated from the others by a rickety thigh-high railing that wouldn't hold up under the weight of a small cat.

Richard Connelly pulled a chair out from under a man who was about to sit in it. He left the poor man cursing on the floor to seat Justice with a gallant flourish and told her he'd be right back with her interviewer.

"So," said the man who had had the misfortune to try to sit in the wrong chair. He propped one hip on the absentee Mr. Cipriani's desk. He was clad in a designer suit comparable to the one Mr. Hilliard wore, but he was not nearly so handsome, with his bald pate and mushy belly. He took her in from head to toe and back again. "*You* want to work in the Chouteau County prosecutor's office?"

"Yes," she said slowly, beginning to get the feeling that, her plan to give Knox Hilliard access and time to fall in love with her aside, this might not be the best idea she'd ever had.

"Okay," he breathed and whirled away; Justice could *hear* the man's eyeballs rolling in his head.

Justice stood as Mr. Connelly came back with yet another expensively-dressed man, as handsome as Mr. Hilliard, but much younger, taller, and darker. Carved, angular, and olive-toned features; black eyes, close-cropped black hair. He rolled the sleeves of his fine white shirt up to his elbows and his tie was a little too loose. He flapped the latter to straighten it as he sat without having either looked at Justice or acknowledged her outstretched hand.

She swallowed. Adjusted her bag awkwardly. Smoothed her dress under her as she re-seated herself.

"So. You're Justice McKinley. Quite the rising star," he said conversationally, a slight smile at the corner of his mouth, though he never looked up from her CV.

"Well, I don—"

He looked up at her then, and she abruptly quit speaking at his searing glance. "I do the talking, Miss McKinley. When I ask you a question, then you may speak."

Justice gulped. Should she say *yes, sir* or not?

He went back to perusing her credentials. "*Summa cum laude*, very good. Two articles in the UMKC *Law Review*. Published many times over in the *National Review* and other conservative journals. You're a regular contributor to several prestigious conservative blogs and you're quoted all across talk radio. Your endorsement of Kevin Oakley was influential enough to put him ahead in the polls—and you only graduated from law school last week. I'm confused. Your emphasis is in litigation, but your field of interest is constitutional law and commentary. Why both?"

She cleared her throat. She had expected this question, practiced it in front of a mirror, but she couldn't seem to quell her unease and hoped it wouldn't come out in her voice.

"I would like to try cases, but I also enjoy studying and publishing on the Constitution; I guess you could say it's a sideline."

Mr. Cipriani pursed his lips and said, "Well, that seems reasonable."

He sat back in his seat and clasped his hands behind his head. Stared at her.

"Miss McKinley, I understand that you are eager to work here."

She nodded.

"Why? I can't imagine you haven't had offers from every conservative think tank from here to DC. I'd be surprised if you haven't been approached about your own talk show. You have a certain, ah, cachet in conservative circles."

At the moment, Justice wished she'd given all those offers more than a cursory glance because she had no backup plan—and now she might need one.

"What I do is theoretical, academic," she said without hesitation. She knew she'd be asked this question, but she couldn't very well state the real reason. "I want to learn the practical side of things and I want to train with Knox Hilliard."

"Do you know how many several dozens of other baby lawyers want to be trained by Knox Hilliard? What makes you any better than they are?"

"My CV makes me better than they are."

Mr. Cipriani's eyebrow rose. "That's an arrogant thing to say."

That confused her. "It's not arrogant; it's a fact."

Clearly he wasn't going to belabor the point. "Well, now that I know you want the same thing everybody else wants from this office, what can *you* do for *us*?"

"I can help you help people find justice."

Mr. Cipriani gave a bark of amused, cynical laughter. "Your idealism is showing, Miss McKinley. We don't help people here. We put them in jail. See that sign on the door?" He pointed to the glass door and Justice turned to look behind her.

PROSECUTOR'S OFFICE

"That," he said, and Justice turned back to see him in the same relaxed pose, "means that we're the bad guys. We make sure that people who need to be put in jail are. You understand that?"

"Yes," she said in a small voice.

"Okay," he continued as he sat up and rifled through the papers on his desk. "I only have a few other questions for you, since your reputation precedes you and your background check came up—ah—*excruciatingly* clean." He nearly sneered at her, and Justice decided she didn't like him very much. He rested his elbows on his desk and leaned forward, his voice and expression hard. "Do you know how we work here in Chouteau County, Miss McKinley?"

Mr. Cipriani's tone let her know that if she didn't, she was the biggest idiot in the world—

There're plenty of lawyers coming out of that office talking about the mysterious cash that gets passed around.

"Yes," she murmured, her nerve endings tingling.

No women.

The tone surrounding her presence here.

It's a racket. He's a racket.

Lots of expensive suits.

Subtext galore.

"Would you be willing to work with us to ensure that the integrity of this particular office is upheld?"

"Um— Yes?"

"Up to and including the necessity for keeping complete and total confidentiality as to what goes on here?"

One big fucking conspiracy and all the rednecks up there love him for it.

"Ah—"

"Okay, Miss McKinley, let me be honest," he began, and Justice breathed a sigh of relief. He glanced past Justice, then back at her. "I'm not going to offer you a posi—"

He broke off suddenly, his attention snapped back to that same point beyond Justice. He bounded out of his chair, his hand behind his back as he bellowed, "KNOX!"

Justice, confused, swiveled in her chair to see what had happened, why utter silence suddenly cloaked the room—except for the ominous clacks of rounds being chambered in semi-automatic handguns. Her eyes widened at the scene unfolding before her. Through the circle of men all aiming guns at the same spot, she saw a man with his arm wrapped around the throat of the man who had rolled his eyes at her, a gun pressed against his temple.

"Put. It. Down."

The dark voice of Knox Hilliard echoed off the walls. Justice looked over her shoulder to see him in the threshold of his private office, a gun in his outstretched left hand. He advanced on the thug and hostage like a lion stalking prey. "Put it down and let him go before I blow your head off."

The only reason he keeps getting elected is because he killed that guy.

Justice couldn't breathe and her heart raced in fear. She knew she should've left after she'd put together the expensive suits and no women, gone home to construct plan B.

"I'll kill him, Hilliard, if you come any closer."

"What do you want, Jones?"

"I've paid my payments to this office for years to keep a good track record and I haven't won anything important since you forced Nocek out. What are you doing with my money and why aren't you holding up the deal?"

"I never made that deal with you, Jones. Claude did. Take it up with him."

"He's *dead!*"

"And the world's a better place. I don't fix cases. Everybody else got the memo. How come you didn't?"

"Then give me back my money."

"Fuck no. If you were fucking stupid enough to hand it over, you're too fucking stupid to know how to spend it if you get it back."

Justice gasped as the man turned his gun on Knox Hilliard, but everything happened too fast. She jumped at the deafening boom. She wanted to close her eyes, but couldn't. The man lay on the floor halfway out the threshold, his eyes open, the back half of his head missing where it had splattered on the wall.

Nobody spoke. Nobody moved.

Except Knox Hilliard.

"Get CSU up here to clean this up," he muttered as he stuffed the gun in his waistband at his back, then stepped nonchalantly over the thug's corpse. "Just what I need—more feds and more paperwork. You all right, Hicks?"

Hicks was not all right; he trembled and he could barely stand. "Oh, yeah," he said on a forced chuckle, toughing it out. "I'm fine."

Knox Hilliard nodded once, curtly, then turned on his heel before stopping abruptly when his gaze met Justice's. She knew terror shone from her eyes and she knew she should suppress it, because fear could be smelled. She couldn't look away from him, even though she wanted to. She wanted to run away from the horrifying reality of what she had just witnessed.

I should've googled.

"Who the hell are you?" he barked, making Justice jump out of her skin yet again. She blinked and began to shake as she clutched her messenger bag to her chest, glad now that he didn't remember her.

Justice struggled not to look past him at all the blood and shredded flesh. Her tongue and throat were frozen and all she could manage was an "Um—"

"Justice McKinley," Mr. Cipriani answered calmly, as if that should say everything—because it should have.

"So? Who is she? Why is she here?"

"She's the girl you told me to interview, remember?"

He cocked one hip and planted his hand on it. He swiped the other hand down his face. "Shit," he muttered as if he were merely disgruntled. "Now I have to hire her."

That moved Justice's vocal cords immediately. "No! No, that's all right. I'll go." She fairly leaped out of her chair, her briefcase still plastered to her chest and turned, but froze when he spoke.

"Sit. Down."

She did, but she couldn't look at him.

"Well, Miss McKinley, welcome to the Chouteau County prosecutor's office. I'm Knox Hilliard, your new boss. May I assume you know how to keep your mouth shut?"

Justice closed her eyes and a tear escaped.

"I asked you a question."

You have to walk barefoot through fire on broken glass.

"Yes," she choked.

"Good. I expect to see your ass planted in that chair over there at eight o'clock tomorrow morning. If I have to come looking for you—and I will—I will be *very* pissed off. Got that?"

She gulped. "Yes."

"And heaven help you if you aren't a decent lawyer."

Justice wanted to cry when she looked at her watch: 8:30 and she couldn't budge the last lug nut on her flat tire. An enormous dark green SUV pulled up behind her on the shoulder on I-29 and *he* got out. She flinched when she heard the door slam.

"Miss McKinley."

Her eyes closed and she choked back a terrified sob when she heard Knox Hilliard's voice behind her. Would he remain angry once he saw predicament? She said nothing as she went on trying to loosen the stubborn thing. She felt him sit on his haunches beside her and stiffened at the current of electricity that shot through her when his knee made brief contact with her hip. Cars whizzed past them at eighty miles an hour and at the moment, Justice imagined that death wasn't the worst thing in the world.

"Need some help?"

Justice didn't respond to his facetious question. What could she say to a man she'd seen kill another man? "Go away" was *not* a conversational option.

She gave the tire iron another good yank and heard the rusty parts scrape together as the nut loosened. Expertly, she held the iron in one hand and spun it so fast it blurred. Almost immediately the lug dropped onto the ground, and she put it with the others.

"I'm impressed," he said after a second, while Justice arose. He rose, too, and she dusted off her dress.

"I don't care," Justice muttered, almost to herself. She hated his superciliousness after what had happened the day before, but she didn't figure it mattered much if the man took a notion to kill her. Surely, this wasn't the man who had championed her all those years ago, caressed her face with his fingers, connected with her?

She pulled her tire off the car and turned to *him*. "Excuse me," she murmured. "I need to put this in the trunk."

He didn't move, regarded her with speculation. That worried her.

"Do you mind?" she snapped, feeling reckless all of a sudden. "It's very heavy."

"Give it to me."

She stared at him a moment and, driven by that same recklessness, she tossed it at him. He caught the tire easily but scowled at her, and she swallowed as he put it away and dusted himself off.

Justice turned and picked up her full-size spare, put it on, quickly and efficiently put the nuts back on, tightened them, and tapped her hubcap back in place.

"Where'd you learn how to do that so fast?" he asked as she let the car down and put her jack and tire iron neatly in the trunk.

"I live on a farm," she muttered as she wiped her hands on a rag. She looked down at her dress. What she wouldn't give to be able to go home, shower, and change clothes. Fortunately, her chintz dress was busy enough to hide any smudges of dirt. Her white collar and hose were not so lucky.

"So . . . are you saying that people who live on farms know how to change tires better than people who don't?"

Justice stared at him. "No, that's not what I meant at all," she replied in confusion.

"Then your leap in logic doesn't bode well for your courtroom skills."

She gulped at the rebuke and felt, curiously, worse than if he'd just told her step out in front of speeding traffic. "I didn't know junior attorneys went into the courtroom at all for a while."

"That's not the way I train my people, Miss McKinley. I have a staff of trial lawyers. That's what we do—try cases. I throw my attorneys into the deep end as soon as possible and as of seven o'clock this morning, you have a stack of files on your desk that would scare most juniors and you're due to arraign your first defendant in—" He looked at his watch. "—five minutes."

Justice's eyes widened. He went on. "I wasn't planning to hire you, but I do have a backlog of work I need to get off my other attorneys' backs. It's scut work— jaywalking, speeding, shoplifting, bad checks—but that's your job now and I expect you to do it and do it well. Got that?"

"Yes," she whispered.

"Good. And one more thing." He leaned closer to her and she retreated only to be brought up short by her car door in her back. She gulped when his nose came within millimeters of hers and he braced himself against her car, one big hand on either side of her. "I hate tardiness," he whispered. "It's on my top ten list, right *before* people who turn a gun on me and expect to live."

Justice held her breath as he pushed himself slowly away from her. His gaze caught on her shoulder and he scowled. She didn't—wouldn't—flinch when he reached out a hand and attempted to scrape a speck of grease off her white collar.

She couldn't help her shiver.

"Watch out, Justice," he murmured. "Animals sense fear. Be very, *very* careful how you react to me because I could attack at any moment." He looked at her head to toe, taking his time. "But then, you might like the things I'd do to you."

Justice gulped, fully expecting him to do something horrible to her, but he only turned and walked to back to his truck. He climbed in without another word and sped off down the highway.

55: Midwest Farmers' Daughters

"JUSTICE? JUSTICE, WHERE ARE YOU?"

"In here."

Justice continued to muck out the stall even as her father invaded the gloom of the barn, but Justice didn't stop or slow her rhythm as set by the pounding drums of Rush.

"How was your first day at work?" he asked in a tone Justice recognized.

"Okay, I guess," she muttered, intent on forgetting about it. Forget about the cleaning crew still scrubbing the floors and walls clean of the blood. Forget about the crush of people in and out of the office before Knox had barked at her to get her ass downstairs to court and do her job. Forget about the fact that the rest of the prosecutors and county employees had simply shrugged the shooting off as if it were one of Knox Hilliard's more minor idiosyncrasies.

"Turn that music down. You know I can't stand that shit."

Without a word, she dropped her pitchfork and stomped over to the stereo—a foot from him—to turn it off.

"You don't sound very happy." He did.

"I'm just tired, is all."

"Why don't you go to bed, then?"

That was a stupid question and she very nearly said so. "Too much to do."

"Suit yourself, then. I don't care. What's the problem?"

"I don't want to talk about it."

He cackled suddenly. "That asshole prosecutor not what you expected, huh?"

Justice's pitchfork halted in midair. How did he know that? It wasn't like he paid much attention to anything about her life, other than what chores she needed to do.

"No, he's not," she finally murmured before continuing with her work.

"Look for another job."

"I can't."

The next logical question, of course, was *Well, why not?*, but he wouldn't ask it. He wanted her to fail. She could see his point of view, looking at all this work and not enough money coming in and needing her.

He'd flip his lid if he knew about her life that was secret to him only because he didn't pay attention.

He didn't know she had any "cachet" at all anywhere. He wouldn't understand her political world or her place in it. He wouldn't understand why the prosecutor of the second largest county in the state of Missouri had requested her endorsement of him as a senatorial candidate. He wouldn't know why anybody would pay her money to express her opinion. He didn't know she *had* an opinion about anything.

"So what did you do today?"

He didn't care; he wanted to gauge how long it might be before she stopped all this lawyer foolishness and came home to stay and work. "Well," she grunted as she tossed a pitchfork full of hay and manure onto the flatbed trailer in the middle of the barn, "I arraigned and plea bargained and reduced charges."

There was a long pause. "What's all that?"

"It's stuff I shouldn't be doing for another six months or so." Not only that, but her boss hadn't seen fit to let anyone guide her through the county's protocols and culture, so she'd had to wing it. Some great trainer.

"Like?"

She stopped and sighed. He hadn't a clue and she didn't know how to explain it. "I just . . . I did what lawyers do, Dad."

"Well . . . how did you do?"

Justice stood and thought, surprised by the question. She'd been so busy feeling sorry for herself that she hadn't evaluated her own performance. Neither had her new boss, except to drop another stack of files on her desk and walk away without a word.

"Okay, I guess," she finally replied, her work pace picking back up again. "I didn't embarrass myself in front of the judge or anything."

In fact, Judge Wilson, a kindly old man with half glasses perched on his nose, had only had to nudge her through a couple of rough spots and later had complimented her on her first day's efforts.

And only a week out of law school, yet. You listen to Knox, little lady. He'll turn you into a fine prosecutor, just a fine litigator. He's the best trainer in two hundred miles. Of course, he's careful to hire bright people—that's a lot of it. He may not say much to you at first, but don't worry about that.

Justice snorted. She'd *pay* for her boss to ignore her. There was only one reason she was in that office and that was to keep her from talking about what she'd seen him do the day before.

If she were honest with herself—and Giselle Cox had told her explicitly that she *must* be honest with herself—she had to concede that what her boss had done was in no way murder, illegal, unethical, or anything else wrong.

But he'd been so blasé about it, with no remorse, stepping over the body like nothing had happened—that rattled her badly. Yet there was no crime in that, either.

"Well," he finally said when Justice didn't reply, "if you're that unhappy, maybe you should just hang it up and come back to the farm."

That was his answer to everything.

He ambled off when she didn't bother replying. She worked in the stalls long into the night, turning up the Rush and, when she got tired of that, Nugent, Pink Floyd—things nobody her age listened to or even knew existed.

It was almost midnight when she put her pitchfork away and got ready for bed. She opened her laptop and, for the first time that day, smiled when she read the comments made in response to one of her random glimpse-of-life blog posts:

hamlet writes:
name that quote j- Any property that's open to common use gets destroyed. Because everyone has incentive to use it to the max, but no one has incentive to maintain it.

JMcKinley writes:
Neal Stephenson. That was way too easy, hamlet. I'm disappointed in you.

hamlet writes:
doing things the easy way doesn't give you a sense of accomplishment - adversity is what makes life worth living - try this one: is not this the true romantic feeling—not to desire to escape life, but to prevent life from escaping you?

JMcKinley writes:
Okay, that took me a while. Tom Wolfe.

hamlet writes:
admit it, you googled

JMcKinley writes:
Busted.

Going on two years now, that particular fan arguing with her, challenging her assumptions, encouraging her and making her laugh so much she felt she knew him. And suddenly, she wished she had the courage to email him, to lay out her situation for him, see what he would advise her to do because he'd always displayed a curious wisdom.

But no. She'd emailed him once and he hadn't replied. No matter how much that disappointed her, she had other things to do, a gazillion other things to think about, and didn't have time to indulge in an online . . . well, *anything* with individuals. As long as she could hold on to hamlet and his little game of quotes to illustrate his philosophies, she thought she'd be okay.

She didn't dare go through the rest of her nightly routine because then she'd feel the lack of her daydreams all that much more acutely. She knew that her days of staring mindlessly at her wall and sending herself off to slumberland by spinning images of Professor Hilliard gently, sweetly slipping into bed with her in the dead of night were over.

The Chouteau County prosecutor had killed a man yesterday.

And he didn't care.

56: Walk Don't Run

THE FOLLOWING FEW DAYS DIDN'T DIFFER MUCH FROM THE FIRST. SHE doggedly worked her way through the files Eric gave her, because as executive assistant prosecutor, he controlled assignments and workload. Nobody paid her much attention or even seemed to know who she was, especially Knox. He came and went, spending his days in court, as did half the staff—and that was okay with her.

Richard Connelly, the man who didn't wear expensive suits and who had been kind to her, was the only person who talked to her more than he absolutely had to. After he had watched her eat alone her entire first week, he had invited himself over to her desk to eat with her and tell her how the office worked.

The staff consisted of no more than eight assistant prosecutors. Four were core staff: Thomas Hicks, the man taken hostage, was close to retirement. At thirty, Eric Cipriani, the executive assistant prosecutor and staff manager, was the youngest member of the core staff by far. Patrick Davidson, affable enough with everyone else, had not yet seen fit to speak to Justice. And Richard had become her lifeline.

New law school graduates filled the other four staff slots, the current attorneys in various stages of their course in the Chouteau County prosecutor's office. It ran a bit like a medical school residency; in fact, those attorneys were actually called "residents." They usually left around their second or third year and went on to do other things. If they wanted to stay they could, but nobody ever did.

Three residents would leave soon; one had three years, another two, and the third a little over a year, but he was a quick study. Justice had replaced the fourth, who'd left to work for Bryce Kenard, a name she'd heard over and over again since her first week of law school. If she hadn't wanted to work for Knox so badly and had not been tempted by the various other plum offers extended to her, she might have considered commuting to Kenard, PC after all the great things she'd heard.

Amongst all these people, nobody said anything about her work, good or bad, so she had to assume that if she'd screwed up, somebody would've yelled at her by now.

People came and went constantly: victims, witnesses, defendants; county deputies, state troopers, Kansas City police officers and detectives; defense counsel. Justice drew a lot of surprised looks, especially from the female officers and attorneys, as if she were a mirage; she supposed she could understand that, since she was the first and only female assistant prosecutor Chouteau County had ever had.

"Why aren't there any women here?" Justice asked Richard, low.

"Because the sheriff is a pig. Raines," Richard explained after he caught her puzzled look, "likes to harass anything with two X chromosomes to call her own and he's not shy about it. He got elected during Nocek's time, did Nocek's dirty work, and still gets elected every cycle. Either Knox hasn't figured out a way to get him out or doing it will just bring more heat down on his head. So . . . he doesn't allow women in the office. He can't control the hiring anywhere else in county government, but he can here."

Dirk Jelarde, Chouteau County's most sought-after defense attorney, popped in and out of the prosecutor's office several times a day on various cases, but occasionally to talk to Eric about a karate studio they co-owned. Justice found it very odd that two men would own a business together then meet each other as adversaries in the courtroom.

"They went to college together," Richard said when she'd questioned him about it. "They're sparring partners and they balance each other out."

"I understand sparring partners; they do that in court. It's the *business* partners I think is weird."

"This is Chouteau County, Alice," Mr. Davidson said as he passed by, the first thing he'd ever said to her. "Welcome to Wonderland."

Richard laughed, and Justice did have to smile.

"JELARDE!" Knox bellowed from his office, then appeared in his threshold, glaring at Dirk, his hands on his hips and his suit coat gathered back and over his wrists. "You're representing Rachel Wincott now?"

"Yeah. Too bad Nocek kicked the bucket. Now she has a lawyer who isn't terrified of the Badass." Knox's expression darkened and Dirk's pretty white smile flashed in his pretty black face. Dirk was just . . . pretty . . . and Justice realized she had never seen a *pretty* man before. "Sucks to be you."

"Get your punk ass out of my office, Jelarde. You want to talk about the dojo, do it on dojo time."

Dirk did leave, but not without a healthy laugh floating after him.

"That wasn't about the dojo, Boss," Eric intoned, but Knox snarled at him before slamming the door behind him.

Everyone found that hilarious, but Justice only thought the whole exchange very strange. "Dirk," Richard told her between chuckles, "likes to poke at lions. Rachel Wincott is the thorn in Knox's paw and Dirk took her as a client just to push it in a little deeper."

"Why?"

"Probably because he was bored. He does a lot of crazy things when he's bored."

"No, I mean, who's Rachel Wincott and why is she a thorn?"

"She is a woman Knox put in prison for armed robbery. She also almost became Knox's stepdaughter."

Justice blinked.

"Oh, he wasn't happy about it, but he loved her mother, so . . . " Justice's gut tightened. "And if it hadn't been for Rachel, he'd have never met Leah in the first place."

"Why almost?"

Richard suddenly speared her with an odd look. After a moment's hesitation, he finally said, "Leah . . . died."

"Oh," she breathed.

"On their wedding day," he added carefully.

Justice's eyes widened. "Oh, how *sad*."

Richard continued to stare at her with that strange expression for a moment longer, then released his breath in a whoosh while shaking his head. He said nothing more and Justice figured that topic was closed.

Justice wondered what it would mean to be loved by Knox Hilliard. She couldn't imagine it would be easy to be with him; in fact, now that she'd worked in the same office with him a week or so, she couldn't imagine him with anyone at all, particularly anyone who might need a little tenderness once in a while.

Actually, no, she couldn't imagine that Knox Hilliard could love *anyone*.

Knox was . . . cold, cruel. She should've understood that her third day in law school, when he'd defended her, touched her, but she had assumed it to be righteous anger, noble in its purpose. Never had it occurred to her that his kindness might be the true anomaly. Betrayed by her naïveté, she felt vulnerable because now she couldn't trust anything she saw, felt, or deduced.

The only thing she knew she could trust her eyesight for: the money.

Endless streams of crisp banded bills, all thrown around like candy. On Wednesday of her second week in the prosecutor's office, Mr. Hicks tossed Justice a banded pack of fifty one-hundred-dollar bills. She caught it reflexively, but dropped it like a hot potato and stared at it as it lay on her desk. The office grew as quiet as it ever did and she looked up to see him, Eric, Richard, Mr. Davidson, and the residents all watching her expectantly.

"Um . . ." She gulped and her chest felt like it had collapsed as her gaze returned to all that money. She thought about the things it could buy: Better feed for the cattle, repairs for the tractor, seed to sow. She thought of all the things it could go toward: shoring up the foundation of the house and a new roof, a new car . . .

"Take it or don't," Knox barked at her from his office threshold after what Justice realized must have been a long time. She looked up at him, feeling bereft and betrayed once again. "Whether you like it or not, this is who we are, so you can either benefit from it or you can cut off your nose to spite your face. I don't give a shit one way or another."

"What's it for?" she whispered.

"It's your free hit."

She gulped and picked it up, then handed it to Richard with a flush, refusing to look at anyone else. The office went back to its usual activity, apparently having satisfied its curiosity as to which side of the divide she'd chosen. Out of the corner of her eye, she saw Richard toss it back to Mr. Hicks, whose indecipherable smirk unnerved her.

"Yo, Tommy," Eric called. "Lemme have it if you're giving it out."

Justice gulped when he laughed and chucked it at Eric's head, the rest of her illusions shattered and gone by her eighth day of working in a prosecutor's office.

"Where does all this money come from?" Justice whispered to Richard one day almost three weeks after she had turned down the money, her curiosity hanging over her like a dirty cloud.

"Don't know. As far as I know, nobody else does, either, including the feds."

"How do the other new hires deal with it?"

"Different ways, but most pretend to not see it. Usually after a while, they get used to it and then do as the Romans do. Whatever he's doing, he's hiding it very well because his books and our files have been gone through meticulously several times over. He's as untouchable as Nocek, but Nocek had to work a lot harder at hiding it." The note of reluctant pride in his voice unnerved her, but at this point, she couldn't pass judgment; she wanted some of that money every time she drove onto her property and saw her house.

"When Eric interviewed me, he asked me if I knew how *this particular* office worked. I always thought it was just a rumor."

Richard shook his head. "I can see why you might, but no. Nobody in ten counties wants to take Knox on and the governor has better things to do than reinvent the FBI's wheel. The feds even tried to get him on Leah's death, but that didn't stick, either."

Her mouth dropped open. "But— *Jones.*"

"Justice," he said sternly, "you saw what happened that day and he did the right thing, whether your sensibilities were offended or not. And," he went on, gathering steam for his chastisement, "*you* of all people should know better."

She gave him a surprised look.

"We know who you are. We just don't care. You're popular because you're a novelty, not because you're saying anything original. Not that you won't mature, but you need time and experience to sift your idealism from reality."

That accusation had hit her in print more than a few times, but it shocked her how bald it sounded face to face.

"And," he continued, "most of us don't agree with the rest of your politics, either."

She shrugged and took a bite of her sandwich. "I don't care if anybody agrees with me," she said. "I have as many friends in the liberal blogging communities as I do the conservative ones, possibly more."

"And you wonder how Eric and Dirk can be business partners and adversaries at the same time."

Her gaze flickered to his. "I never thought of it that way."

"They're your colleagues, no? You talk? Email privately?"

She nodded. "Yes, we do. I guess that's exactly what they are."

"Look, Justice, I know you're having a hard time and you'd rather be anywhere else, but you haven't been treated any differently than any other new resident we've ever had."

"Yes, I have!" she protested on a hot whisper. "He came looking for me that first day when I was late."

"You aren't the first; doubt you'll be the last. He *really* doesn't like tardiness and he does that to make a point."

. . . you might like some of the things I'd do to you.

Justice decided to keep that part to herself.

"You have a lot of potential and it would be foolish to waste your time here. Do your job. Do it well. Be on time. Do what we tell you to do and how to do it because in this office, you have no name. You're just the latest junior AP fresh out of law school."

She sighed, but saw the truth of what he said. Too much attention to her political status—which meant nothing here anyway—could only hinder her training as a litigator and, much as she hated to admit it, every lawyer in the office was superb at his job. Any of them could turn her into a stellar prosecutor.

"Eric will tell Knox when you're ready for more. If you can immerse yourself, get better, learn from Knox, you'll settle in here just fine." He gathered his things and stood. "Thank you for buying my lunch, Justice."

"You're welcome."

"One more thing," he murmured, leaning down to whisper in her ear. "Quit thinking about Knox *that way.*"

Her eyes widened and she pulled away from him.

"It's written all over your face every time you look at him. You're too young, too naïve, too—" He waved a hand, looking for the right word. "—conceptual. He likes women who are much older than he is—"

Older!

So. She'd never had any chance at all and the irony of that stabbed her somewhere deep in her chest. Now she was stuck with no reason to be in the Chouteau County prosecutor's office at all, nowhere else to go, and no way to get there even if she knew where *there* was.

Richard was still speaking. "—street smart and experienced, and you need to put—whatever it is—away."

She gulped and her stomach churned with a mixture of embarrassment and hopelessness. "I thought I had," she whispered.

"Nope. Get rid of it. He's getting irritated and I don't think he'll tolerate it much longer."

"Richard, I have to get out of here. I can't *stand* it."

"That's not going to happen, either. Part of the deal with Knox is that if you're hired, you stay until you're well trained and ready to have his name on your CV. Period. Nobody's ever tried to leave earlier than he allows. Believe it or not, we *want* you to succeed here. We're interested in watching how this experiment's going to turn out."

He straightened then and patted her back before he left. "Remember what I said."

57: Will the Circle be Unbroken

FOR THE FIRST TIME IN HER WORKING LIFE, GISELLE DIDN'T HAVE A JOB. SHE didn't have to be anywhere. She didn't have to do housework or cook. She and Bryce had spent three weeks in Europe just after she graduated and would have liked to have stayed all summer, but Bryce had too much work to do to stay away from his practice that long.

Thanks to Sebastian's investment of the rent she'd paid him and Fen's reparations for her bookstore, she had her own money, no debt, and a new car. She didn't feel too much the moocher since she could live off the interest her money earned.

Bryce grew very impatient with her money issues, but something just didn't sit right with her about a poor, debt-ridden woman marrying a very rich man— especially without a prenuptial agreement—and he wouldn't understand that. She suspected Bryce had instructed Sebastian to move money from his account to hers, as her interest had begun to outpace normal earnings, even under Sebastian's stewardship. While that annoyed her, she decided not to call him on it.

They had enough adjustments to make, even now after having lived together for nine months. They were both moody and short-tempered, and he had yet to fulfill his promise to tell her about his fire, his family.

Some days Giselle thought their long conversations and the incredible sex were the only two things holding them together.

Until Bryce would hoarsely call his children's names in his sleep, mostly Emme's, plead desperately with the Lord to help him get them out of the house alive, to not let them die, then jerk awake in a cold sweat, chest heaving, bury his face in her hair while he caught his breath. Wrap his arms around her and pull her close to him. Whisper, "Help me, Giselle. Please help me," over and over until he went back to sleep. He didn't seem to remember what happened in the wee hours of the darkness or realize why some mornings he woke up exhausted and grouchy.

Until she suddenly began to think about the prospect of actually *being* a lawyer, standing up in court in front of people, her growing fears that she wouldn't be able to do the job, that she wasn't cut out for it. Her family scoffed at her insecurities and told her to suck it up, princess, but Bryce listened to her. "Giselle," he'd say gently, "if it turns out you don't like it or you get bored with it, I'll support you in whatever you want to do. But if you quit lawyering, it won't be because you're not good at it." He never failed to tell her how beautiful she was, how simply looking at her turned him on; he *understood* why she'd posed nude, why she needed to hear him say it. No *suck it up, princess* from Bryce.

So they had their problems, but for the moment, she decided to enjoy the time off. She spent her days lying in the shade in Loose Park with her mp3 player, lost in the worlds her favorite authors built for her. That got old in about two weeks, but she had more than a month to go before she was due to show up at Hale and Ravenwood, no longer a transcriptionist, no longer in that stupid cubicle, no longer with those infernal buds in her ears. She spent her evenings with Bryce going places and seeing things, the symphony, the zoo, the movies, outdoor concerts, Shakespeare in the Park.

"Say, Wife," he purred one evening as he approached her from behind, wrapped his arms around her, and slid two tickets down her neckline into her bra. "Think we're too old for a Mötley Crüe and Aerosmith double-header in October?" Giselle had squealed in delight.

Every night she lay on the couch in the candlelight, drinking in her lover's music with her whole body as he poured his passion, his strength, his anger, and his skill into the keys of their concert grand piano. He saw what he did to her with his music, stroking her, seducing her with it as effectively as hours of foreplay.

Once he had heard *Carmina Burana* in its entirety, he had fallen in love with it so that he'd bought the chamber score to learn it.

"This is like nothing I've ever heard or played before," he muttered one night as he struggled over what he said was a deceptively difficult passage. "I don't know whether I like it on its own merits or because it was what was playing our first night together."

"Sebastian only plays it when he's lonely or he's got a woman on his mind. He says it fucks your ears."

He smirked and abandoned the piano to slowly lower himself over her on the couch, on all fours, the way he did every time he wanted to conquer her, when he wanted her to give him a fight. "I'm not interested in fucking your ears right now, Wife," he murmured and kissed her harshly.

The next day, Bryce came home from work in a more foul mood than usual. "Giselle," he barked, "when you look at me, what do you see?"

She looked up from the club chair where she slouched reading *Fanny Hill*. Her brow wrinkled. She could've answered that six different ways, but she didn't quite know which one he wanted, and she told him so.

Bryce was insistent. "I want whatever you have to say."

She gulped, searching her memory for her impressions, not wanting to get this wrong because it was the first sign she'd seen of any willingness to talk about it. "I see an extraordinarily strong body that got that way with physical labor, not weights. I see graft scars, most of them healed now, but I don't want to see your scars." He flinched and paled. "No!" she said, impatient with herself and searching for words. "When I see your scars—you know, *see* them—I see pain and suffering. I see children who died and a little bit of my heart dies."

She arose and went to him, pulled his shirt out of his trousers, unbuttoned it, took it and his undershirt off his body. "Like, here," she said, caressing a particularly vicious wound just under the lowest rib on his left side. "That looks like something sharp went in there."

"A broken floorboard."

"Well, and then here—" She unbuckled his pants, let them fall, then knelt to take them off of him. Shoes, socks went, too, so that he stood completely naked before her. She touched his ankle where began a wicked scar she knew very well. It streaked up his calf and thigh until it stopped at his hip. She lightly drew her fingertips up the length of the scar as she arose. "It looks like fire burst all the way up your leg from the floor."

"It did," he whispered.

"Your arm," she said and, with a fingernail scraped the mat of scars on his left arm where he had no hair. "When I see this, I think about the child you carried there, that your arm was on fire, and that the child was on fire."

"Andrea," he croaked.

She knew that from his transcripts, but she didn't tell him she heard his anguished rants during the nightmares that plagued him.

"Your face— Your shoulder— Here," she said as she touched a spot on his neck that was still intact and stood out more for it. "This is where another child hung onto you—Luke? Because he was strong enough to hang on? His arm protected you there because he was on fire, too."

His voice broke. "He was."

And Randy, the three-year-old he'd carried in his other arm, had died of smoke inhalation. Giselle tried not to choke up herself.

"I don't want to see that. Every time I do, I feel pain, but that sounds stupid when I say it out loud because I didn't go through it. You did."

She said nothing for a while as she looked, inspected, touched. He tensed everywhere she put her hands, and she knew he held himself together only by the barest of threads. She wasn't doing much better.

"When I look at your body," she whispered, "I see strength, protection, safety. I see a man who nearly died to save his family, who not only survived that but took on and conquered everyone who was responsible for it. This," she said as she wrapped both hands around his upper arm where muscles lay underneath the scars and her fingers didn't wrap but halfway around. "I see the beautiful stonework outside, the flower beds you've built for me, the fountain you put in one of those beds just because I fell in love with it—the one that took *two* men to put in the truck when you bought it for me."

She walked around his body and ran a finger down his spine, then splayed her hands out along his lower back, and he dropped his head back as he released a pent-up breath.

"So what else, what else." She slid her hands around his body until she felt his cock and cradled it. "There's this," she whispered, massaging him, but he stepped out of her arms and turned.

"Okay, no. Keep talking."

"Why?" she asked, bemused. "What happened?"

He took a deep breath. "A man came to see me today. He'd been burned in a flash fire. He came to me *because* of my fire, not in spite of it or coincidentally. He had the same medical team I'd had and they insisted he contact me. I looked at him and I— I didn't *want* to look at him," he said low. "And I'm ashamed of my reaction to him; how could I, of all people, want to look away?"

Giselle thought about that while she studied him and felt his urgent distress. "Okay. You know when I said that I don't want to see your scars because I feel pain?"

"Yes."

"I really do. That's why I want to not see. It hurts to see someone else in pain, especially someone you love. But for you, it's worse. You already know what that's like and you reacted to him more strongly than you would have if you had not gone through that yourself. I'll bet what you actually felt was physical pain and you wanted to look away so your body would stop hurting. It's not revulsion; it's *empathy*. What do I see when I look at you? I see a warrior god."

He grasped her upper arms and looked at her for a long time, searching her face for—what? She didn't know. Then he gathered her to him, wrapped his arms around her as if he would never let go, and rasped, "Thank you, Wife."

She snuggled into his embrace, so glad he had trusted her with that, and said, "You talk about your dad, about how his kindness and gentleness was the first thing people felt, how you think you don't do that. You don't. You make people feel safe. Cared for. Protected.

"The day I sought you out at the courthouse, I heard the pain in your voice when you gave your closing; it was your client's pain. It was genuine. I remember how you held her while she cried into your chest. You weren't her lawyer; you were her rock, her strength. She felt safe and comfortable. Protected. Was she ever afraid of you?"

He swallowed. "No," he admitted after a moment. "She looked straight at me when I first met with her and she never flinched."

"Don't think that just because your kindness doesn't manifest the way your dad's did that you aren't just as kind. Bryce," she murmured, "could your father have pulled three children out of a burning house while being on fire?"

His eyes widened and he stared at her. "No," he whispered. "He would have figured the odds and accepted it as the Lord's will and died, let them die."

"And you chose to fight the odds because of who *you* are. I wish you could see how people react to you. Nobody else sees or feels your anger; they only feel peace and warmth. Either you hide your anger for others' benefit or you aren't angry at all when you're with other people."

"What does that say about how I am with you and the pack, the tribe?"

"We're your kindred spirits, Bryce. *We* are savages. We know you for who you are and we love you *for* it, not in spite of it and you embrace us and our savagery." She paused, then said slowly, "You came home to us."

He swallowed and his face tightened with emotion, tears he didn't want to shed, wouldn't shed.

"I think it's time to start drawing up plans for that foundation of yours."

"Ours," he rumbled. Giselle smiled at the immediacy of his response, for it must have weighed heavy on his mind for some time.

"Ours."

58: Ride of the Valkyries

KNOX DROPPED A THICK FILE ON THE DOCUMENTS THAT LITTERED THE conference room table, right in front of Sebastian's face. Then he dropped a banker's box full of more files a little farther down the table.

"I don't know what kind of a link between OKH and HRP you're looking for, but in all of this, there is no link that can be found. It's, ah, *interesting*, but nothing to do with OKH."

Vaguely disappointed, Sebastian drew a deep breath and opened the file. "I know there's something going on there," he muttered. "I can feel it in my gut." Then he looked up at Knox. "Do you know that CEOland thinks you and I are at war over OKH?"

"Well. We are. Kinda."

"Yeah, pushing it off on the other doesn't count. Eilis told me that's the impression everyone's got. She was surprised when I told her it was us versus Fen."

Knox pulled out a chair and sat. "I find that odd. Why would she think that when I gave her to you?"

"She had to rearrange her assumptions PDQ, but then she didn't know where to put them. The minute I told her that you and I are allied against Fen, it was like the sun came up. She couldn't wait to agree to the IPO."

Knox didn't respond and Sebastian began to read the information in front of him. Pages and pages of social services reports documenting a life of foster care. "Interesting indeed," Sebastian murmured before he got into the meat of it.

```
The child continues to display an unwillingness to
cooperate with current family; suspect abuse. Spot
check 4/13.

Child taken to ER for spiral fracture of ulna. Placed
with different family.
```

Sebastian sat, his mind numbed with the very first two paragraphs he'd read. He wiped his mouth, wondering if he wanted to continue reading.

```
Child bonding with foster mother and father but
application for adoption denied at child's request.

Application for emancipation of a minor approved.
```

"She was an emancipated minor at fifteen," Sebastian murmured.

"Yes. Did you notice what's redacted?"

No, he hadn't noticed and he flipped through the pages. "She had her last name changed when she was emancipated."

"Yes, and I can't find out what it was."

Sebastian pursed his lips and went back to reading.

```
Child placed with Klewezewski family 6/30. Child
requests transfer to Reyes family. Transfer 7/4.

Child taken to ER, spontaneous abortion.
```

Sebastian checked the date, her recorded birth date, and sucked in a breath. He felt a pain behind his sternum that he didn't recognize. "Eleven years old," he whispered. "Fuck."

"Yeah."

"I can't do this," Sebastian said and began to close the file, but Knox's fist slammed down onto the pile of paper and he rose up over the table.

"You will," he snarled, and Sebastian pulled away from him. "Don't make her tell you this. You *will* read it and I'll stay here until you do. Reading it can in no way compare to the fact that Eilis Whoever-Logan has suffered through it. Read it, feel whatever pain you're capable of feeling, then maybe you can begin to understand what the rest of the population feels."

"What the *fuck* does that mean?!"

"You avoid pain like the plague, that's what the *fuck* that means. You take shots at me for going off the rails, always doing things the hard way. You take shots at

Giselle for shit-canning a temple marriage after waiting so long. You take shots at Bryce for shit-canning his entire life to fuck a woman he knew less than a day, poking at us because we're hypocrites and you're not. Shit, no, you're not a hypocrite. You decided you didn't believe anything so you could go do whatever the fuck you wanted to do without being accountable to anybody."

Sebastian just stared at Knox, wondering where the Chouteau County prosecutor had suddenly come from. "Where is this coming from?" Sebastian asked. "What have I done?"

"How long has it been since you talked to Eilis?"

"March, but I've emailed—"

"No. The beginning of February, when you got pissed at her and ditched her in New York in an auction house where you'd just made her sell off all her most prized possessions."

Sebastian swallowed.

"And then you cooked up that bullshit Ford stunt and *humiliated* her. *Ford* saw her in March. Giselle told you what to do, told you to go back to being who you were before you took *your* issues with Ford out on Eilis. And did you do what she told you to do? No. Eilis hasn't seen you *once* in five months and she's sitting up there at HRP soldiering on alone with a weekly email that's copied to me. What she really needs is the same coddling you give everybody you fix. But no. You *must* love her, because you're treating her like shit."

Sebastian stared at him in pained wonder. "You think I'm a complete bastard."

"Yes, I do." He waved a hand toward the documents he'd brought. "I did what you asked, got these records. So I finish reading all this bullshit this morning and go see her, take her to lunch, maybe talk to her about it if she wants, ask her her birth name, see how she's doing, if there's anything I can do for her, and I find what? The trustee I assigned has all but abandoned her and mind you, *she* didn't tell me this. Her new CFO—"

"Conrad Fessy," Sebastian whispered.

"Yeah, him. He asks me when you're coming back because you haven't been there since Eilis got back from her vacation. And she was as calm, cool, and collected as she always is. Shit, she could give *Epictetus* lessons."

Sebastian blanched.

"And you know what? Before today, I never really noticed that you haven't had a whole lot of pain or failure in your life."

He opened his mouth.

"If you say your mission, I'll put your head through the fucking table."

He snapped it shut again and watched Knox, his cousin, his brother, in a rage

Sebastian had never seen directed toward family.

"Giselle's already gone through this with you, but apparently you didn't get it, so here I am after I had to threaten her with a subpoena to get a full accounting of what went down with *Ford*. You're a fucking *coward*, Sebastian. You've always been a coward, starting when you bailed on your mission because it was *hard* and you had *no* control and you had to follow someone else's rules and you were *afraid* of failure."

"But Mitch—"

"Yeah. Mitch Hollander. Couldn't hack the mission because it was full of stupid pricks who shouldn't have been there. Not his fault. Came home early. Got mocked, laughed at, called weak. Accused of fucking around. Couldn't get a date for shit because he wasn't a 'returned missionary.' Lucky to find a girl to marry him at all. I went to BYU so I could find a wife. Ask me how many nice LDS girls ever went out with me—a guy who didn't go on a mission at all. That would be a big fat *zero* and I came home single when I thought I'd be coming home married with kid.

"So Mitch did what? Went back to Pennsylvania and built the country's biggest fucking steel mill and put the *entire fucking industry* back on its feet *single-handedly. Then* he absorbed Jep Industries to save the industry all over again. *While* his wife was dying, *while* his kids were little, *while* he's a bishop. Pain, Sebastian. Pain and adversity and failure build people. You have *never* known that and you have no patience with or empathy for people who have—*especially* the people you love."

Sebastian didn't know if he would be able to catch his next breath. Knox stared at him with a mixture of rage, deep hurt, and contempt.

"You didn't paint Giselle to help her when she thought she had no hope with Bryce. You painted her to make your name rise another notch—'going into his symbolic period,' my ass—and she doesn't know that. She thinks you were being sensitive and altruistic to *her* pain. Not only that, but you don't even know *why* she consented to be painted nude in the first place.

"There is no honor in remaining detached from life, from its hardships and its pain. The only reason you've been able to do it is because you've always had money, always had power, always had leverage. I want you to understand pain and failure— even if it's vicarious. Eilis has spilled her soul to Giselle and don't you dare make her do it again. If you love this woman, and you might, insofar as you are capable of feeling that kind of love, read it. If you don't love her, then okay, just say so and I'll release you from her receivership and appoint Blackwood because she trusts him."

Sebastian's eyes widened and his gut tightened. "You've already talked to him."

"I have and he's willing to do that for her. I've been thinking about this for a while now, thought if Jack was her trustee, that would free you up to pursue a relationship with her. If all you wanted was to fuck her, I probably could've lived with that if you'd waited until you were finished, but you *humiliated* her and now I just want to protect her from *you*."

There was that stabbing in Sebastian's chest again. He didn't know what it was or which direction it was coming from. Eilis—what he'd done to Eilis—Mitch, Knox, Giselle, Kenard. He watched the Chouteau County prosecutor sit back down calmly and fold his arms across his chest and prop his feet up on the chair next to him, as if he hadn't just ripped him to shreds.

When Knox saw he still stared, he curled his lip and slammed his fist on the table again and bellowed, "READ!" with an expression Sebastian had only seen once. In a courtroom. Questioning a serial killer.

So Sebastian read. And he sank into darkness, a darkness he had never known.

```
Child (age 5) taken to ER. Broken collarbone

Child (age 13) taken to ER. Spontaneous abortion

Child (age 14) taken to ER. Spontaneous abortion

Child (age 9) taken to ER. Cigarette burns

Child (age 12) taken to ER. Prescription drug overdose.
Suspect suicide attempt. Admission to psychiatric unit.
Update: Suicide attempt ruled out; suspect poisoning

Child (age 7) reported doing well in school, but
withdrawn

Spot check on Reyes family. Child (age 15) laughing
and eating with family
```

Sebastian couldn't breathe. He couldn't contain whatever it was that was happening to him and finally, he shoved his hands through his hair and stood, bellowing something he didn't understand. He picked up a chair and swung it through one of the frosted glass walls, shattering it.

"That's right," Knox sneered. "You go ahead and throw your little tantrum. You have the luxury of being able to replace whatever you destroy. Sit the fuck down and shut the fuck up. Keep reading."

Sebastian's chest heaved with anger and something else that hurt. Really, really hurt. Eilis's past, her suffering. His family's contempt. The fact that everything Knox said was true.

He sat and continued to read. High school transcripts. Straight As. College transcripts. Penn Valley Community College, a business vo-tech school, three different small and very un-prestigious urban liberal arts colleges. Straight As. Bloch School of Business. Straight As. MBA.

Married and divorced once. No mention of any more pregnancies or children. Court transcripts from Knox's prosecution of David Webster.

KH: Mrs. Webster, did you know what your husband was doing to your company?

EW: Yes.

KH: When did you find out?

EW: Two weeks after he moved in with me.

KH: How did you find out?

EW: I found a tiny scrap of paper on the floor by the dresser and I picked it up.

KH: What was on the paper?

EW: The combination to my office safe.

KH: Had you ever given him that combination?

EW: No. I'd never given it to anyone.

KH: How did he get it?

EW: I don't know.

KH: What was in your office safe?

EW: The key to the safe deposit box where I kept the access to the cash reserves.

KH: Didn't you ever check the statements?

EW: No. I thought they were untouchable so I let David reconcile those statements and I didn't ask to see them.

KH: What was your first thought when you saw that small scrap of paper?

EW: That he'd been in my safe. That he had access to everything. That there was only one reason he'd want to be in my safe.

KH: What did you do when you realized this?

EW: I started watching him, hacking into his computer files, trying to figure out how he was doing it, where it was going.

KH: How long did it take you to figure it out?

EW: About five months.

KH: Why didn't you call the police when you found out he was stealing?

EW: He'd set it up so all the clues pointed to me. I needed to dig deep enough to find out where the trail began.

KH: Okay and then why didn't you call the police?

EW: I only found the proof I needed when he began the transfer of the employees' 401(k) plans to a plan that was a front for his own account. The transactions were going to go through faster than the police could have gotten to my office, so I waited until I could block the transaction.

KH: Where were you when you did this?

EW: I was on my computer at home. He couldn't get to me.

KH: When did he find out that you'd done this?

EW: When the police showed up to arrest him.

KH: So in effect, you saved the pensions of two hundred and fifty employees on a moment's notice?

EW: Yes.

KH: Thank you, Mrs. Webster. Your witness.

RS: Good afternoon, Mrs. Webster.

EW: Good afternoon.

RS: I only have a few questions for you. What had you done the evening prior to the day you say you locked yourself in your house to stop these alleged transactions from processing?

EW: I'm sorry? I don't understand.

RS: Oh, okay. Let me ask more directly and please forgive me for being insensitive. Did you not make love with your husband just the night before?

EW: No.

RS: Oh? Are you saying the deposition Mr. Webster gave is false? That he was lying?

EW: I'm saying it wasn't making love. It was rape.

RS: I see. I suppose you'd consider it that, with what you suspected.

KH: Objection.

BW: Sustained.

RS: Thank you, Mrs. Webster.

KH: Redirect. Mrs. Webster, do you know what these are?

BW: Let the record show that people's exhibit 19a is entered into evidence. Witness may answer.

EW: Those are medical records.

KH: From what?

EW: From the night he broke my nose and gave me this scar.

KH: What else do these records say?

EW: That I was raped.

KH: Thank you, Mrs. Webster. And I'm sorry for your pain.

Sebastian read long into the night, Knox sitting guard, never letting up. Never letting him escape this hell that, he suspected, he would not have felt if Eilis were any other woman. Not the woman he loved and was in love with.

"Now," Knox said, calm, as the sun rose and shone bright in the kitchen and cast its rays onto the tabletop, "however deep you feel that is however deep you're going to feel it. But if you have any inclination to come down on her for her choices—" Knox held up a hand when Sebastian opened his mouth in outrage at the thought. "Sebastian, you give no quarter to the people you love. You expect us to function on some level of perfection that only you know and then you turn into a hard-ass motherfucker when we don't perform to your standard. I don't know why; maybe it's just your way. If you love her, if you want to stay with her, do not treat her that way. You treat your clients with kid gloves and they invariably end up despising you for it."

Sebastian wanted to curl up in a ball and stare out the window.

"I'll take all this with me because you'll burn it just to get it out of your sight. If you test me on this—if you do anything else to hurt her—I'll give her receivership to Jack and I'll hand every bit of it over to Bryce and let him deal with you, and he's already not happy with you about this. I think he's the last person you want in your face, eh? Of all the people in the world Giselle chose to bring into this family, it would have to be one of the only men *in the country* who could actually destroy you."

Sebastian dropped his head in his hands. "Just shoot me," he whispered and meant it. It wasn't as if Knox couldn't or wouldn't if he felt like it.

"No. You don't deserve that much mercy."

As soon as Knox left with that mess of paper, Sebastian curled up in a ball on his bed and looked out the window at the street, trying to block the visuals his fertile mind tortured him with. A movie, a horror movie. His mind filled in details.

A child, a girl. He remembered Giselle at ten, busy swinging in trees and balancing and twirling on high ledges. She'd wrestled Knox, getting stronger and wilier every day until she could pin him right before he hit his growth spurt. She'd flipped through fashion magazines and sighed over all the pretty clothes she dreamed about fitting into, read *Tiger Beat*, trying to decide if she wanted to marry Knox, or Bo or Luke Duke. Sebastian had put a gun in her hand the year before, taught her to use it, when, where, and why.

Eilis had been raped and impregnated when she was ten. He let himself feel the pain a small girl must have felt being abandoned to a foster care system that was criminal at worst and negligent at best.

Giselle at thirteen had accompanied Sebastian on his nightly jaunts to collect on his loans and bets, always armed, always confident, guarding his back—then he would watch her at church where she drowned in a gaggle of mean rich girls, thoroughly bewildered and intimidated by the cruel manifestations of jealousy she didn't believe, understand, or know how to combat, convinced that being able to fit into a pair of Jordache jeans would solve all of her problems.

Shit, Giselle, suck it up.

Giselle at fourteen, and Knox at fifteen, slept in the same house, down the hall from each other, had discovered how to kiss with tongue, and that was about all they'd discovered by that time.

Eilis had been raped at least twice more, had had two more miscarriages by the time she was fourteen years old.

Broken bones. Cigarette burns. Poisoning made to look like a suicide attempt. He only had facts, but Sebastian thought in images.

This was the antithesis of everything he believed now or had ever believed before he'd turned his back on the church. No god or goddess Sebastian had ever read of or believed in had taken care of Eilis Logan and Sebastian loved Eilis Logan.

. . . insofar as you are capable of feeling that kind of love . . .

How did she live with this?

For that fact, how did Kenard—a man Sebastian most definitely did not want to piss off—live with his pain? A fire that killed his four children, a year of agonizing pain in a burn unit, charges of arson and five counts of homicide, the erased memories, the scars that ensured that Giselle would be the only woman on earth who'd find them attractive. Everyone, most *especially* Kenard, knew why he'd been unattached when he'd met Giselle—except Giselle. All she saw was the god of war, which greatly eased Kenard's pain but it didn't make his ugliness any less obvious to the rest of the world.

How did Knox live with his pain—and for Knox, which pain was worse: The horrors he'd had to study to try that case? The fact that he'd lost that trial and had to see a serial killer go free? Or the fact that he'd gone out that very night with the fury of gross injustice and executed a man? He'd only been twenty-five years old when he'd lost his soul and died, only to be resurrected as the hated and feared Chouteau County prosecutor.

Sebastian had never known why Knox had defied Fen to go to BYU, leaving with a law degree but not what he really wanted. How many other slings and arrows had Knox taken that Sebastian didn't know about? And why *did* he always do things the hard way?

And Giselle? He had *no* idea what pain she lived with now. No, wait—

Take it from a woman whose man hides his soul from her.

Sebastian groaned. Knox had been right about why he'd painted her hurt so graphically, and Giselle *didn't* know that. Why *had* she consented to become a Ford, knowing her nude body would be displayed all over the world in perpetuity?

Mitch Hollander, his best friend, a companion from his mission when Sebastian still believed but had become disheartened, disillusioned, and sickened by what ostensibly honorable Mormon boys did. Mitch, whose naïveté had broken with those same deeds, who had gone home early and suffered the stares and derision of not having made it all the way through. Yet now he was one of the wealthiest men in America, powerful, feared—and had kept his faith so much that he was a bishop of a ward and on the short list for stake president.

Sebastian dropped his head in his hands.

But Eilis! What Sebastian had done to her . . . Oh, *Eilis!*

You treat your clients with kid gloves and they invariably end up despising you for it.

He wanted to weep, but he couldn't. He didn't know how.

59: Freewill

G ISELLE, I DON'T WANT TO DO THIS."

Giselle watched Bryce as he paced the kitchen floor.

"It's done. I already told him we'd do it and we will."

Bryce had come inside from his current stone project for a drink of water and overheard her on the phone making plans with Knox. Since this required Bryce's cooperation, too, she'd informed him of it the minute she hung up.

He was furious.

"*We* don't have to do anything. It's not *our* problem; it's his. That's my point. Knox is a grown man. He can figure out how to—" Bryce waved his hand in the air, searching for the word.

"Make over."

"Yes, make over a girl who shouldn't be in his office in the first place. Just because you want to get this mess over with and getting him married off is the last thing on the to-do list doesn't mean you personally have to cross it off. This isn't your project anymore."

"You think Knox is a *project* for me?"

Bryce laughed, totally without humor. "No. The *proviso* is your project because you feel responsible for it, you feel guilty for Leah's death, and your whole life would still be about managing that project if I hadn't damn near fucked you on that bench a year and a half ago. Am I arrogant to demand you let it go? No. That's my right because you married me." He held up his hand, then pointed at her when she opened her mouth again. "No, Giselle! Let Knox clean up his own messes."

"So we take the girl in for a week, cut her hair and buy her some nice clothes—on his tab, I might add. What's wrong with that?"

He began to pace again, his hands on his nearly bare hips. "This is all his fault and he needs to take care of it. She shouldn't have been in his office for any reason whatsoever."

"Oh, yes, she should've!" Giselle shot back. "She needs a spine and he can give it to her—in weeks, not years. Umpteen years from now, she's not going to be sitting in a junior attorney chair wondering where her life went and how she became irrelevant because she didn't have the balls to stand up for herself in real life."

Bryce's teeth ground. "You know what? That's not Knox's job. He does *not* have carte blanche to just force anybody he wants into his personal blast furnace just because he thinks they need hardening. Now *that's* ego."

"This was *my* idea, Bryce. I would've waved a magic wand over that frizzy braid years ago if I thought it wouldn't drive Knox out of his mind to see her on campus all drop-dead gorgeous or make him compete for a woman he couldn't have for another four years."

"Then let *him* make her look like what he wants her to look like. Wasn't he the one who taught *you* how to walk and talk and dress like a debutante?"

"This is not for *him*. He couldn't give a shit what she looks like as long as her hair's red and her IQ is higher than his. It's for *her*. She looks like she's still in high school and nobody's going to take her seriously as an attorney of any type. Whether she stays in his office or not, she needs to look professional and she doesn't."

"That doesn't wash, Giselle. The girl could go to the Cato Institute and they'd let her show up in a bikini as long as she drew an audience and cash. No!" he roared when she opened her mouth to protest that. "I don't buy that. All you're doing now is cleaning up the mess he made with her. And by the way, why are you always cleaning up after those two? If it's not this crisis, it's that crisis. You—we—cleaned up after Sebastian and the mess he made with Eilis and we're *still* dealing with the fallout from that.

"And Knox tore Sebastian a new one over that, but he can't talk because he trumped Sebastian's bullshit a hundred times over. So we get to put *Knox's* woman—strike that, *girl*—back together again. Both of them fucked up royally and there you were, at the crook of a finger, to pick up Sebastian's pieces and here you are now, at the crook of a finger, getting ready to pick up Knox's pieces. I don't want *my* wife spending her life cleaning up after another man's—*two* men's—messes!

"I've thrown in with the rest of you against Fen. I'm an adult. I have means. I'm invested. I chose for myself *and* I can choose to bail at any time. That girl is young, has no means, and isn't being given any choices whatsoever, which is bad enough, but she's got the most to lose all the way around—*including* her life. That's just fucked up."

He stopped his angry pacing and glared at her, pointing at her again. "No. It's not fucked up, it's *immoral*, Giselle. Do you get me? Immoral. *Evil.* He took her *freedom* and her *choices* away from her. He's pulled some pretty shitty stunts in his time but I *never* thought I'd see the day he'd go this far.

"*Justice* is a *girl.* She has a *crush* on him. She's not even experienced enough to get past a crush to an adult emotion, and I don't care what the hell she writes or how influential she is or what a genius she is—when it comes right down to it, she's just a *girl* with a *crush* on a man who's almost old enough to be her *father,* and who is exactly what she *didn't* fantasize about."

"But he—"

"I don't care 'but he.' But he's a selfish bastard, is what 'but he.' If he *really* loved her, he wouldn't do this to her. Do you not remember what Fen's done already? Oliver and Leah are *dead,* Giselle! He burned your bookstore to the ground and you were supposed to go with it. He sent *two* men to kill you—and you have the bullet holes and blood on your hands to prove it. Do you want to have that girl's blood on your hands, too? If *anything* happens to her, it'll be on all three of you and it'll be innocent blood."

"Fen knows what'll happen to him if he bothers a potential bride."

"But then the deed's done, isn't it? You know, I get a hard-on that you threatened him at gunpoint. Love the scars, love the Glocks. Girls with guns. Totally fuckable. Not so crazy about the actual murder part. So she's dead, Fen's dead, you're in prison. That makes it all better how?"

Giselle drew in a deep breath, angrier than she could remember being in a long time. *Why* wasn't he willing to understand this?

"He wasn't going to hire her, much less force her to stay. He just wanted to see her before he sent her on her way. That's all."

"Yeah, and what happened to the grand plan to wait until after his birthday and go get her?"

"Someone turned a gun on him is what happened!" she yelled. "It just—happened!"

"That's *bullshit.* He should have let the investigators interview her and sent her on her way. He's just using it as an excuse to keep her there and accessible so he can seduce her because he couldn't *bear* to wait another year and a half. You can't look me in the eye and tell me that wasn't the first thing you thought when he told you."

She had thought that, in fact. She didn't like it any more than Bryce did, but she'd seen Knox's agony, watched and felt his torment over the last three years, understood his motives.

"To wit," he snarled when she remained silent.

Then, so angry and hurt, confused and torn, she couldn't do anything but clench her fists and let out a howl. She only wanted a release valve for all that raw jumble of emotion, but suddenly, she found herself crushed to Bryce's chest and her mouth filled with his tongue. He kissed her hard and held her tight to him, one arm wrapped around her body and his hand clutching, caressing her buttocks. The other hand gripped the back of her head and held her still.

Giselle squirmed, but into her mouth, he growled, "Don't move. Just feel." Once he'd said that, of course, she did feel. She felt his bare chest crushing her breasts, his jersey shorts no better than a fig leaf for the cock that pressed hard against her belly. She felt the urgency of his mouth as he kissed her. She felt the hand that kneaded her as it slid down between her legs to knead there, too. She could barely breathe for the lust that coursed through her, competing with the anger and confusion, each feeding off the other, getting hotter and more intense.

He pulled away from her, tore her shorts off of her with a rip that resounded through the kitchen, then picked her up and plopped her on the counter, her knees spread wide. He had shoved his shorts down and had driven his cock inside her before she could say a word.

She was wet and she didn't know when or why that had happened. He filled her, stretched her. She planted her hands on the smooth granite, spread her knees wider, hooked her heels on the edge of the counter. Her eyes closed. Her head dropped back against the cabinet.

"*Look at me!*"

She obeyed slowly, snarling at him and he her. He was so close they could kiss, leaning against her, his hands braced on the counter on either side of her hips. His whisper was harsh, hoarse.

"I'm that man you were looking for way back when to fuck you like you want and need to be fucked, to love you like you want and need to be loved. But you aren't always in this with me one hundred and ten percent and I resent that. I will *not* compete with your pack and you are *not* the alpha. Just like I didn't get a pass on fucking you and leaving you in the morning, you don't get a pass on keeping little bits of yourself from me and giving it to them."

Then he drew away from her and she gasped at the force of his first thrust. His second.

"I. Am. Your. Lover."

His third.

"I have always been your lover."

Fourth.

"And I will always be your lover."

His voice was so raw he dropped words, matching his thrusts to his cadence.

"You married *me*.

"Your loyalty should be to *me*.

"You are *mine*.

"*All* of you."

She gritted her teeth. Used the counter for leverage. Matched him thrust for thrust.

Rode their angry fucking to its end.

Came screaming his name.

His back arched and he roared as he drove into her one last time.

She collapsed on him, her chest heaving.

He wrapped his arms around her, buried his face in her shoulder, tried to catch his breath—

—and sank his teeth into the crook of her neck, making her shudder with the intensity of her response to that.

Silence while their breathing returned to normal.

Savages.

Giselle sighed.

"I'll let you do this," Bryce whispered in her ear finally. He held her close, his fingers curled in her hair. He licked her skin where he'd bitten her. Kissed. Nipped. "But not because of Knox. This is for her. She's going to need every bit of strength and courage you can pump into her in a week. But once she goes back to that office, I'll give him a week to do the right thing by her and then I'll go in there and pull her out myself—and don't you *dare* say a word to him about that before I do.

"After this, no more. I'm tired of sharing you with two other men, family or not, loyalties or not, Fen or not. *Proviso* or not. You changed loyalties when you married me, and I'm going to hold you to that."

He pulled away from her then and held her face gently between his hands. She could see that his anger was gone, but his face betrayed deep hurt and weary resignation. "They will *never* love you like I love you, Giselle."

She swallowed, ashamed that she had hurt him so badly, that she had caused that pain in his face, and whispered, "Okay. I'm sorry."

60: To Sip from a Devil's Cup

JUSTICE WAS LATE. AGAIN. THIS HAD NEVER HAPPENED TO HER BEFORE. ALWAYS prompt, always prepared, she hated the fact that now, five weeks in, she had acquired a reputation for tardiness. She could only chalk it up to her dread of facing another day in the prosecutor's office, dragging her feet out the door every morning.

She'd arrived late twice after her first day. Knox hadn't known about it either time and Eric had only given her a scowl.

Today, her luck only extended to the fact that she'd straggled in *so* late, everyone else was in court.

Except Knox.

"MCKINLEY!" he roared at her when she came in at exactly 9:13, harried, overwhelmed, and terrified. "In my office. NOW!"

Justice stepped into Knox's office, her heart thundering. She knew she'd get reprimanded for her extreme tardiness, but she could bet he'd also make good on Richard's prediction that he'd call her on her mooning.

Her spine tingled in horrified anticipation and she swallowed. Hard.

He walked in behind her, slammed the door, and brushed by her on the way to his desk. She stiffened at the slight touch of his body against hers, but she couldn't squelch her strange reaction to a man she feared.

She took a deep breath.

Knox dropped himself in his chair and relaxed, his loafered foot on the edge of the desk, his chair tilted back, his elbows on the arms of his chair, his fingers steepled under his chin, his face carefully blank as he studied her. She started when he spoke.

"That's the fourth time you've been late in five weeks. Care to explain yourself?"

There was no excuse.

She knew it. He knew it.

"I can't," she finally said.

"If you're late again, I don't know what I'm going to do, but I guarantee you won't like it."

"Yes, sir."

"Now, one other thing."

Justice knew what was coming and she swallowed, already mortified.

"I know you've been hankering after a piece of my ass since you got here so all I want to know is where you'd like to have it. Here, now, or later when I can take you home and do you up proper?"

Her mouth dropped open.

"Ex—excuse me?" she stammered. She felt herself flush and her blood thump madly in her ears as she stared at him in morbid fascination.

"I asked you where you wanted me to fuck you. Here or at my house?"

She squeaked.

"Yes, Miss McKinley, you heard me right. Pick a place, any place. I'm yours."

"No!" Justice cried and closed her eyes against her rising horror. Her fists clenched at her sides until she felt calm enough to look at him, she opened her eyes slowly to find his face carved in mocking amusement.

"Miss McKinley—hello. I'm still waiting for an answer."

"No," Justice said again, as forcefully as she could manage.

Knox pursed his lips and looked at her in speculation. It was a lion's look, right before he tore into his prey's throat. Justice felt a trickle of anger of a type she didn't recognize. "That's sexual harassment."

She jumped at his bark of laughter, then scowled as it turned into a rolling guffaw. It took him a while for his amusement to subside, and he wiped his eyes and chuckled every once in a while. "Sexual harassment," he crowed. "That's hilarious. Sweetheart—" he said, then paused to chuckle. "I've been investigated for every felony in the book—*six times*. Do you think anybody's going to pay attention to a little sexual harassment? Sexual harassment doesn't exist here. I give the orders. You take 'em. That's it. End of story. *Fini*. If that means I point at that couch and tell you to lay down, that's what's gonna happen. If I tell you to go make coffee, you do that, too. If I tell you to make coffee *bare-ass naked*, that's what I expect to see. You understand that?"

He'd offended her deepest philosophies, and for that, she'd face any fire. She drew herself up with a dignity and courage she didn't know she possessed. "I quit."

His amusement fled. "No one quits this office before they're trained, Miss

McKinley," he said low. "I will not have my name on someone's CV who hasn't earned that right. If you have to stay here ten years before I think you deserve my name, then that's what's going to happen. And I *will* come looking for you just like I did that first day you were late—and I *will* find you."

She didn't doubt it.

"Now, you have two choices: You can be a good little attorney and do your work the best you know how, or you can be a bad little attorney and take all the harassment you can handle—sexual or otherwise. You're here to stay and to do what I say. Get used to it."

Justice's mind raced. There had to be a way out of this. There had to be. Who could she contact? What agencies would care enough to bust a small-time prosecutor in a small-time county?

"And oh, if you're thinking about trying to set the feds on me yet *again*, good luck with that. They keep looking and they keep not finding."

"You're just a two-bit bully," Justice whispered, afraid of Knox Hilliard as she'd never been afraid of anything in her life, yet thoroughly angry with him.

His face stretched into a calculating smile that chilled Justice to the core. "No, Justice," he murmured, "I'm worth much more than that. Perhaps, six bits. Shall we discuss where and when again?"

"No," Justice said, her nostrils flaring. "I can't imagine any woman going to you willing, without being *paid*."

He catapulted out of his chair and around his desk, and Justice, feeling very stalked, whirled to open the door, to get away from him. With a powerful hand, he shoved it closed so hard she thought the wood would crack. And she was trapped—trapped between the solid door and the large, hard body of the Chouteau County prosecutor, whom she'd just called a thug.

She pressed closer to the door in an effort to get away from him, but he pressed closer still. The warmth of his flesh seeped into her, made her super aware of him, and her breath came harder and faster.

"What do you think now, Justice?" he whispered warm in her ear, his sweet, rich butterscotch breath tickling her cheek. Her body, palms, and other cheek pressed flat against the door, and she could feel his arousal against her backside.

She swallowed when she allowed herself to acknowledge its presence against her and what it meant. What it meant to *her*.

His large hands caressed the curve of her hips as his lips caught at her earlobe. Justice gasped at the contact, not because she didn't expect it, but because she didn't expect it to be so . . . *gentle*.

And she certainly didn't expect the sharp pang that shot through her body and settled between her legs, in a place that suddenly seemed empty and wanting for— She closed her eyes, horrified that she wanted what Knox had and that Knox was perfectly willing to give it to her.

"What was that you said about having to pay for it?"

His voice was liquid warmth, hot spiced cider, melted chocolate. His mouth closed softly over the skin of her cheek here and there, butterfly kisses. Justice's eyelids drooped and she felt a soft sigh pass over her own lips. She was vaguely appalled at her own reaction, but could no more stop it than she could make Knox leave her alone.

Even if she wanted to.

Her buttocks tensed when Knox's fingers spread out over her hips and his thumbs caressed her chintz-covered skin even as his mouth moved to her neck and throat. Her hands, flat against the wood, curled inward as Knox's masculine scent wrapped itself around her, beguiling her senses, making her want more.

How could a man so utterly despicable make her body feel so many wonderful things?

Things she'd really never believed happened to a woman with this intensity.

Things she'd wanted from him for three years.

It wasn't until Knox's fingers began to gather up the front panels of her skirt, and his palm touched the inside of her nylon-covered thigh that Justice was shocked enough to realize how . . .

Lush

Verdant

Exquisite

. . . he made her feel.

"Leave me alone."

"Not an option," Knox murmured into her ear as he continued to nuzzle her there. "You've made it very clear that this is what you want and I *will* give it to you. Don't doubt that for one minute."

It was when he kissed and sucked the underside of her jaw that Justice realized he was absolutely right, and that yes, she would go willingly.

"No, please, don't," she finally whispered. "Let me go. Please. I don't want this."

He stopped, pulled away from her slowly. She glanced at him over her shoulder. He didn't smile. His sapphire eyes gleamed. He breathed heavily. She flinched when he reached a hand out to caress her cheek, a feather-light touch. "You're a hot mess," he murmured. "Go sit on the couch a minute."

He wheeled away from her then and went to a small fridge she hadn't seen. He took out a small bottle of water and tossed it to her. "Your face is red."

Of course it was red. She was embarrassed and aroused. Embarrassed about being aroused. She looked down and away from him, then stepped toward the couch, where she sat on the edge of it, primly and properly smoothing her dress under her, keeping her knees perfectly together and aligned, the hem dropping a respectable two inches below them.

She looked down at her hands. Opened the bottle. Took a couple of small sips. Pressed the bottle against her face.

Knox leaned back against his desk, his ankles crossed, his arms over his chest. He just watched her.

"You can't keep me here."

He reached behind his body under his suit coat, then withdrew his hand and placed his shiny silver semi-automatic pistol on top of his desk very deliberately, never taking his eyes off of her.

"Can't I."

Justice felt like her chest had collapsed, completely unable to comprehend the enormity of what he'd said with that one simple gesture.

"But I'm not going to have to work very hard to give you what *you* want, am I?"

She closed her eyes in deep, deep shame.

"Stand up and straighten out your clothes, then get back to work."

61: Elton Live

THE FUTURES TRADING FOR THE INITIAL PUBLIC OFFERING OF HR
Prerogatives was out of control. Eilis stood at the podium with Sebastian at
the New York Stock Exchange, feeling him watching her. Eilis was nervous
as she readied herself to strike the opening bell.

Jack Blackwood, CEO of one of the most powerful investment banks on Wall
Street, and Melinda Newman, the CFO of Blackwood Securities, stood with her.
Blackwood Securities had underwritten HRP's IPO on the strength of Sebastian's
work and word. Once Eilis rang that bell, Sebastian would no longer be her trustee
because Knox would consider that the end of the receivership. All it would need
then would be for him and the judge to sign it off.

It would be done. She would be free of what David had done to her, free of a
court order, free of her babysitter. Not free of her shame, and she could barely stand
to look at Sebastian because of it.

The sweet ring of the bell that morning signaled the end of her road with David.
And Sebastian. Confetti flew, the roaring began, the boards went crazy, and her
symbol, HRPS, was the first across. She looked down at the trading floor and back
up to the ticker, joy and delight swelling her soul to bursting, but tempered with
melancholy.

Sebastian had given her this.

And then he would leave for good, not even a weekly impersonal email copied to
Knox.

She looked up at him to see him still watching her, the corner of his mouth
quirked.

"Congratulations, Eilis," Sebastian said and held his hand out for her to shake. She did, hesitantly. It was the first time he'd touched her since February, when he'd held her in the saleroom at Christie's. "Your bills are paid. With the sale of *Morning in Bed*—very wise decision—you have significant cash reserves. You have a good staff. Your receivership is over, and it took just under a year."

Then it was Jack's turn, who hugged her. Melinda she hugged too, but tight, like a sister, and she sniffled back bittersweet tears. It was Melinda who'd shepherded the process, thus had been with Eilis every step of the way. The chairman of the NYSE and all the rest of whoever she'd been introduced to but didn't remember all gathered for handshakes.

Eventually they wound their way outside to Wall Street on their way to Jack's office, chatting a bit before Eilis and Sebastian went to their hotel and Jack and Melinda went back to work. After that, the rest of the day could only be anticlimactic.

Once they reached the marbled lobby of Blackwood Securities, one of Jack's assistants accosted him and drew him aside to speak frantically. "Sebastian," Jack said low once he returned to them, "not to horn in on Eilis's day or anything, but Fen's in town."

Eilis looked at her watch. "And running late," she muttered, then realized she'd spoken too loudly when both Sebastian and Jack turned to look at her. Melinda stared at her with one eyebrow raised.

Finally, Sebastian said, "Out with it, Eilis. You've been hiding something from me about OKH and Fen from the minute I proposed this IPO."

She took a deep breath, then reluctantly opened her mouth to explain—

A deep male voice boomed, "Sebastian!" The sound echoed off the marbled walls of the cavernous space.

Eilis knew that voice, had anticipated it because he would want to take this golden opportunity to do what he'd spent years trying to do—and failing at every turn.

She watched Fen Hilliard stride toward them, elegant and grand as always. Eilis stared at him and he stared at her. "Sebastian," Fen said again without looking at him, cordial, always cordial, yet his voice contained an underlying note of hatred with which he had *never* spoken to Eilis. "Jack. Ms. Newman."

Neither Jack nor Melinda said a word.

"Fenimore," said Sebastian, who had not missed that he wasn't today's target.

"Eilis, congratulations on your IPO," Fen said expansively, offering his hand to her, which she refused.

"Fen," she murmured, feeling her Inner Bitch begin to creep over her, to cover her, to protect her, "you're late. I expected you five minutes ago."

Sebastian started, but Fen laughed. "Of *course* you did, my girl, of course you did."

"So how much did you buy?"

"Nine percent."

"And you flew all the way to New York to do it personally," she said, calm now that her beloved Bitch had returned. "I'm flattered."

"I had to thank you for so graciously handing yourself over."

"Fen," Sebastian said, "shouldn't you worry about your own stock instead of hers? It's a little late to be playing raider—and on a company as small as hers? That makes no sense."

He turned to Sebastian then. "Why, Sebastian, my dear nephew, of course it makes sense. It isn't my problem you obviously don't know *why* it makes sense. Right? Eilis?"

Rage.

Rage she had known long ago and thought she'd put away. Rage that strengthened her, empowered her. It burst through Eilis's soul and she allowed herself to ride the wave.

"I'm glad you're here, Fen. It gives me the satisfaction of knowing you couldn't get to me unless I gave you a way to do it. God knows, you've been spinning your wheels for the last twenty years. But you knew I'd be here with Sebastian, so all things considered, I'd think you'd want to keep this private."

"It's as private as it needs to be, Miss *Logan*," he said, smug. "Your house of cards is safe with me."

"You built that house, Fen. You and that evil cunt you sleep with."

Before she could move or say anything more, Sebastian had Fen's wrist clasped in his big hand, caught as he'd been about to slap Eilis. Jack and Melinda stepped back, horrified.

"Fen," Sebastian said with careful civility, "I would've thought you'd learned your lesson about slapping women when Giselle broke your nose. Please try to remember that you're only alive because Knox has politely requested she not kill you—and for no other reason. He does have a breaking point and then you'll find out exactly how merciless she can be."

Fen swallowed.

No matter that she had killed any hope of a future relationship with Sebastian, she knew she wouldn't have to fight alone anymore. She had powerful allies now and because of that, she had nothing to lose.

She could go home clean, start fresh. Done with David. Done with Sebastian. Done with Ford.

Done with Fen.

Her Bitch roared within her.

"Fen," Eilis said, hard, her life rolling up into a ball inside her and exploding in that rage that kept coming and coming and coming—a barrel of gasoline thrown into a bonfire, "since you're so dead set to still not do what you should've done forty years ago, why don't I go ahead and tell Sebastian what your interest in me is?"

Fen gulped.

No, he wouldn't have anticipated this, wouldn't have planned for it.

She turned to face Sebastian, looked him straight in the eye. No more shame. No more deceit. Just rage.

"Fen and Trudy Hilliard are my biological parents."

Eilis had no words to describe the look of shock that went across Sebastian's face. She could only presume Jack and Melinda were equally shocked.

She looked at Fen then, whose arm was still in Sebastian's strong grip and he looked . . . frightened.

"I'm sure," she went on, "that you think you're very clever, buying up a controlling interest of my company at its IPO. I expected that, but remember this: The enemy of my enemy is my friend."

His Adam's apple bobbed.

"You go ahead and consider me part of whatever war Knox—my *brother*—and Sebastian have waged upon you. Jack," she said, turning to her underwriter, "when the SEC refuses to allow Mr. Kenard to purchase any more OKH stock, which I expect will be any day now, please put it in my account. I'll take over from there."

Then she turned back to Fen and slapped him across the face so hard it snapped his head a full quarter of a turn.

With that, she turned on a heel and walked out of Blackwood Securities, down Wall Street, and hailed a cab to take her back to her hotel.

"Jack," Sebastian said calmly, still holding Fen's wrist in a grip that he tightened steadily until Fen winced, "call Kenard. Let him know what's happened and see what he wants to do. And keep your fat mouth shut about this. I don't want it all over Wall Street." Jack and Melinda broke into a run toward the elevator banks.

Fen couldn't get any paler than he was. Sebastian dropped Fen's wrist and his lip curled. "You're pathetic."

Sebastian decided to walk back to TriBeCa. He needed the air. And time to talk. He flipped his phone open and punched two buttons.

"You got a minute? You're not going to believe this."

He went straight to his room once he got to the hotel and changed into his most comfortable clothes before knocking on Eilis's door.

She was in there, he knew, because he could hear her moving around, and then the sounds came closer. She didn't ask who it was before opening the door wide and then turning to walk back into the depths of the suite. He didn't feel like yelling at her for that and he came in and closed the door quietly behind him.

Dressed in a fuzzy robe with a towel all wrapped up around her head, she sat at her table and calmly read the paper. Eggs Benedict, no bread, sat uneaten on the room service cart. Sebastian dropped into the opposite chair without a word and just looked at her. This was the woman he had shamed in order to destroy a man who didn't exist. This was the woman about whose horrible life he'd read—a direct result of Fen and Trudy's selfishness that they gave her up for adoption instead of at least asking one of Trudy's sisters to take her in and keep their secret. Sebastian's mother—any one of his other aunts—would have welcomed her with open arms and passed her off as her own, without ever telling a soul. This was the woman he'd brought here, to this day, to this hour to put a capstone on his work of fixing her company.

This was the woman who'd taken his heart and his soul.

He didn't speak for a long time and just played with the utensils while she calmly read and ate, drank water and generally acted like the goddess that she was, not deigning to speak to the mortal who'd come to beg an audience.

"Knox is thrilled," he finally said. "Shocked as hell, but thrilled."

She said nothing, gave no sign that she'd even heard him. But then he saw a tear track down her scar, and he almost smiled.

"I knew his reputation. I thought that if I told him, he would hate me, throw me to the wolves for being Fen's daughter," she said matter-of-factly. "I would like to think I know him well enough now to know he wouldn't have done that. But," she continued, "in spite of his reputation, in spite of what he could have done to me— what any other prosecutor in Kansas City would have done to me—he didn't charge me and he gave me to you to fix me. Because he knew you could and he liked me enough to want to see me fixed."

"I guess kin knows its own."

"Are you going to yell at me now?"

"No," he said, knowing he couldn't very well throw stones when he had his own deceptions that, in his mind, were much, much worse. "It might have been nice to know this, yes, but it wasn't crucial to anything. I thought you handled him very well."

"The Bitch is back," she said low in her throat.

"And I *like* her."

She was silent for a long time and then put down her paper. She wouldn't look at him. Almost three months after that night and she still couldn't look at him.

Ah, well, it was mutual. He could barely look at her.

Today, on the podium at the New York Stock Exchange, was the first time Sebastian had seen Eilis since the night she'd come to Ford's studio.

Eilis swallowed. "I need to tell you something."

Sebastian remained silent.

"I went to Ford. I—I wanted him to paint me and to make love to me and make me feel beautiful." She turned her head, away from him. "I was naked and I let him touch me, and he was very gentle, but—I couldn't do it. I didn't— I left. I just couldn't do it."

"Why?" Sebastian whispered, every word that fell from her tongue stinging his soul for making her do this because he was a coward.

You've always been a coward, starting when you bailed on your mission because it was hard.

She opened her mouth to say whatever it was she was going to say, but then Sebastian raised a hand and said, "You know what? Never mind. Don't. Don't say anything. It doesn't matter why. Eilis, I have my own secret and I need to have you come back to Kansas City before I can tell you, show you. Whatever it is you think you've done doesn't begin to compare with what I've done. Put it away for now, Eilis. I want to enjoy my time here in New York with you."

"But— How can you even stand to be near me?" she asked. "I've betrayed your trust."

"No. You didn't. You couldn't have because I never gave you enough of myself to betray. Please, Eilis. Let me show you New York. Get rid of the guilt and let me give you some memories before you get rid of me."

She looked at him then, fully, her expression hopeful, a spark of life, of her passion, coming back into her one green eye and one blue eye—but tinged with confused sadness. "Why do you think I would do that?" she whispered.

"I won't tell you now, but trust me when I tell you that you have good reason to."

62: The Look of Love

THEY STROLLED THROUGH THE HOTEL LOBBY TOGETHER HOLDING HANDS, their fingers interlaced, both clad in denim shorts, tee shirts, and hiking boots because they would walk wherever they went. It was June, sticky, and hot and Eilis had decided to wear her hair up in a ponytail. Though Eilis wasn't sure where Sebastian intended to take her, he apparently had an itinerary in his head.

She noticed stares of both genders aimed at them and grew uncomfortable. One man grew quite bold in his perusal of Sebastian, and Sebastian chuckled, vastly amused, and shook his head. "I never get used to that."

Eilis was acutely aware of the female stares of blatant lust Sebastian garnered and that those stares turned to surprise and disdain when they looked at her. They were beautiful women, to the last one, women Eilis wouldn't be able to compete with—and she knew it.

"They're jealous," he said in her ear. "Men who appreciate truly beautiful women wouldn't give them the right time of day and they know that. Don't pay any attention."

She automatically protested. "They think I'm too ugly to be with you—"

"No, that's not what they think, Eilis," he said low. "They're insecure because they can't touch you for beauty. Be who you are; accept that you're a *bomb*shell, and revel in it." They walked out into the bright June afternoon sunlight and Eilis felt a warmth suffuse the pit of her belly.

"Sebastian," she said on a whim as they turned right and walked—to where, she didn't know, "don't you think those women are beautiful? They're thin, they're elegant."

"I thought we addressed that thin thing at the grocery store," he muttered.

"Yes, but—"

"No 'yes buts.' For one thing, I don't like fake body parts. For another, they're clothes hangers. Yeah, they can carry the fashions well, but you get 'em naked and you risk being impaled on one of their bones."

She laughed with Sebastian for the first time since that magical December weekend, oh so long ago, ever so aware that he hadn't let go of her hand. He looked at her and smiled; she caught her breath. This was Sebastian Taight, the most feared and respected financier in the Midwest? He was coldly handsome when he didn't smile, but when he did, he was warm and magical.

"You?" He stopped and spread her hands wide as he looked her up and down. "You were made for love."

She blushed and looked away, and he laughed as he pulled her forward again.

"Have you ever thought about modeling?" she asked.

"It's been suggested to me now and again," he admitted.

"And?"

He shrugged. "I'd just as soon be behind the camera if I absolutely had to be in that industry. I'm not that vain. It takes a lot of time and effort to maintain that kind of vanity and—as you know, I live in my head." Then he slid a look at her. "Have you ever thought about it?"

"I'm not the type Madison Avenue wants to see."

"That's probably true," he mused, and her gut clenched in pain. "More's the pity." Then the pain went away and her gut unclenched as he continued to talk.

"Men instinctively go for women like you. It's an evolutionary response. That they don't allow themselves to acknowledge or follow through with their desires is more a result of brainwashing by popular culture and porn than a true desire for the Barbie dolls. I'd be willing to bet that most younger men don't know what they want because they've been fed a steady diet of video vixens who have identical faces and look like boys with fake tits. They're all interchangeable. MTV didn't even exist until I was seventeen and even then I was too busy making money to watch it. I got time and experience to figure out what I liked without being fed pablum from the time I was four."

"You don't— Porn—?"

He sneered. "I despise pornography. I like beautiful women. I like looking at beautiful women naked. I like making love to and having sex with and fucking beautiful women. Pornography is a perversion of both art and sex."

"I don't— I've never met a man who didn't . . . uh . . . "

Sebastian shook his head. "I'm related to a host of men who don't. Knox. Bryce,

Giselle's husband. My uncles. My dad would've beat my ass with a belt if I'd brought anything like that into the house. The other fifteen of my male cousins. Can't even imagine Fen wasting his time on it."

Eilis's brow wrinkled in confusion; this completely upset her worldview of men and their appetites. "Why not?"

Sebastian laughed. "Well, in Bryce's and Fen's case, too busy fucking the real women they've got and—" he continued huskily, "in Knox's and my case, too busy thinking about the real women we'd like to be fucking."

Eilis blushed and looked away and he said, "Not to touch a sensitive topic for both of us—but do you think Ford objectifies women?"

"No," she said immediately. "He worships women."

"That's right, and it's very clear that he does. Pornography does the opposite and women buy into this artificial construct. Women have all the power. If they valued themselves the way they should, as who they are, then there would be much less porn and men wouldn't stand for the crap they're getting. They'd start to demand a better class of woman."

He stopped and turned to her. She watched him as his hand reached out to draw a line down her face from forehead to chin. "I like your nose, Eilis. I like the way it gives your face character and definition. I like your scar for the same reason. I'm sorry you came about them the way you did, but to me, they're . . . part of the work of art that is your face. I love your eyes, one green, one blue. I've never seen anybody with two different colored eyes before. No, you don't look like the women in that lobby; you stand head and shoulders above them. You should be proud of it and carry it like a badge of honor."

Eilis said nothing to that because it was so profound, so—validating. But then, that was what Sebastian did. That was his purpose in life, not just for her, but for Karen and everyone else he came in contact with.

She realized that they had gone quite a way when she asked, "Where are we going?"

"Mmmm, I don't know. Where do you want to go?"

Just then her stomach gurgled and she laughed. "I want to go get something to eat; I didn't eat my lunch."

"Okay, and I know just the place to take you."

Sebastian and Eilis still ambled along, their fingers entwined, and he said, "Have you ever been to Central Park?"

"No. I've never been here to *see* anything. It never occurred to me to look at things while I was here doing business."

"Every time I travel for business, I book at least a week on the back end for sightseeing. It's kind of a drag by yourself, but I want to see and experience the world.

And obviously," he muttered wryly, "since I can't show you anything new about Kansas City, I had to bring you to New York."

He stepped over and bumped into her so she stumbled, and then she laughed when she saw his wicked smile. She bumped him back and he grabbed her around the waist, picked her up, and spun her around until she was squealing with laughter. He stopped abruptly and her head spun, which made her laugh more.

Eilis found herself sliding down Sebastian's body slowly and she stared at him when they were eye level again. She thought he was going to kiss her and she bit her lip, but then he tickled her and she broke away from him, laughing. She ached from laughing.

And desire.

Sebastian took her hand and began walking again, a crooked smile on his face. They didn't speak again until Sebastian stopped at a hot dog stand and got several. "Eilis, you're gonna have to help me here."

So they ended up juggling hot dogs, topping them off with condiments, then they picked out pop and water, sticking the bottles into pockets and waistbands. And they picnicked in Central Park as the sun got lower in the sky.

"Why did you come back to Kansas City?" she asked. "You could live anywhere in the world and do what you do."

He didn't answer her for a long time, eating while he thought. "Kansas City's in my heart. I grew up there. I explored every single alley with my cousins. My comfort food is there. I learned about money and art there. My family is there. Nowhere in the world is going to have *that* place in my heart. So I stay to soak up the comforts of home and family. When I get tired of that, I leave for a while."

Eilis could understand that. "What neighborhood did you grow up in?"

"I went to East High School. You?"

She laughed. "Northeast."

"Ghetto kids. Why don't you leave?"

"I'm afraid," she admitted with alacrity, somehow knowing that he wouldn't make fun of her. "I feel safe and secure. I don't want to go somewhere else to live by myself, no friends, not knowing the local spots, not knowing how to find the local spots, not knowing how business is done there, who to talk to, how to get things done."

"That's why you hire an agent."

She shrugged.

They ate for a while, not speaking, then Sebastian asked quietly, "Do you want to go to Ground Zero tomorrow?"

"No," Eilis whispered. "That was the beginning of the end for me. I— I was here that day. I saw the planes crash into the towers. I— Um, David and I— We— That's why—"

"Don't," he said sharply. "It's gone, past. You're done with what he did to you and he's *dead*. Let that be enough."

She looked up at him and watched him look at her with an intensity that wasn't passion, but something warm she didn't understand. She nodded. "You're right."

"Good. Do you have clothes for the opera and Broadway?"

"Yes," she said, delighted, her soul coming alive at the thought of seeing such things with a man, a man who did care for her.

Sebastian laughed at her. "There's a little girl inside there somewhere just dying to come out and play, isn't there?"

Eilis threw back her head and laughed a great rolling laugh that had been building inside of her all day long. It washed away the stain of Fen's intrusion. It washed away her shame and guilt. It washed away all the bad things in her life because she was laughing with Sebastian, and to laugh with Sebastian was to experience life to its fullest, to have no pain, no failure.

And then she was in his arms and he was kissing her, his lips and tongue thoroughly engaging hers and she watched him kiss her, watched him watch her as they kissed. He deepened the kiss, pulled her down to the soft grass of Central Park so she lay half atop him, kissing. His hand cupped her buttock and caressed her, there where her buttock met her thigh, and she sighed.

"Eilis," he whispered, "I want to make love to you so badly I can't stand it, but I won't until we get home and I show you my secrets. Then you can make the choice. Will you trust me?"

"Yes. I trust you, Sebastian," she sighed.

63: Morning & Evening

HE NEXT DAY THEY WENT TO THE METROPOLITAN MUSEUM OF ART AND
held hands again, which she still found oddly and deliciously endearing and
oh! so twelve years old. That night, Sebastian took her to the Metropolitan
Opera to see *La Bohème*, which, he said, was his favorite.

The day after that was the American Museum of Natural History, which amazed
Eilis and without doubt, she could feel Sebastian watching her wander around in
delight, unable to hide it. "Someday I want to take you to the Smithsonian," he
murmured in her ear.

Someday.

That night, Broadway, and he asked her to choose. *Phantom of the Opera.* They
walked back to the hotel, Sebastian's arms around her and holding her tight, then
stopping to kiss her every so often. It was difficult parting company at their respective
hotel room doors, but Sebastian was insistent.

Every evening, Sebastian took her to a different hole-in-the-wall ethnic restaurant.
The night they went to the opera, they had Thai. The night they went to the theater,
they had Greek.

The day after the theater, they went to the Central Park Zoo and their only
evening plans consisted of meeting Jack Blackwood and his wife Lydia for dinner at a
cozy place in Little Italy.

Jack wrapped his arms around his wife, took every excuse to touch her, looked at
her as if she were the embodiment of everything wonderful in the world. She
returned his affection shyly, as if they'd just met. Every once in a while, though, she
glanced at him as if she resented every minute she couldn't spend in bed with him.

The contrast between Jack and Lydia, whom he called Daisy for no reason either of them would explain, was stark: He, five-ten, dark, half east Indian and half English; she, shorter than he, fair, with a mop of old gold curls and blue-gray-purple eyes that seemed mystical. With a breath, she could transform herself from a cute-cum-pretty woman to a great beauty and get any male within speaking distance to do her bidding. "I call it her magic trick," Jack murmured wryly. "It doesn't work on me."

"Which was why I married him," Lydia returned smartly.

Jack and Lydia Blackwood were gorgeous together and suddenly, Eilis wondered if this was how people saw Eilis and Sebastian, that dark male and sunny female. She ached to know if that was true.

She got her chance to find out the next night, their last together in New York, when Sebastian took her to the ballet. Eilis didn't bother to lie to herself that she wasn't dressing for Sebastian. He loved her body, loved her face, and he made sure to let her know as often as possible.

. . .*accept that you're a* bomb*shell, and revel in it.*

Even if she didn't really believe that, she determined to fake like she did. She went to the hotel's salon and got her hair curled and pinned up. The cosmetician could not stop exclaiming over her unique features.

Then she returned to her room and put on the dress.

Kelly silk charmeuse and chiffon. A very low-cut pleated silk charmeuse bodice that emphasized the size and curve of her breasts, with halter straps that tied at the nape of her neck. Empire waist, from which flowed a generous cut of chiffon-overlaid silk to the knee. Very high heels with straps that crossed over the top of her feet. Pearl studs.

Eilis couldn't remember ever having shown this much skin or even wanting to. She certainly had never dared to wear a color so striking and vivid that it would attract attention all by itself. She looked at herself in the mirror and didn't really believe that the woman looking back at her was . . . her. All she wanted was for Sebastian to look at her the way he'd looked at her the day he'd had her on the conference table.

She dug out the sterling silver repousse purse that she had fallen in love with oh so long ago, but had never used. She didn't know why she'd brought it with her, but tonight was worth it.

One final check in the mirror and she was ready to meet Sebastian in the lobby, where a pianist played the Rach Three.

The look on Sebastian's face when he saw her was beyond anything she had ever dreamed, ever hoped for, ever wanted from him. She wished she could paint, so she could remember that moment forever.

In his trademark crisp black, he strode toward her and met her more than halfway. Uncaring that they were in public, in a five-star hotel in TriBeCa, he wrapped his big hands around her face, his fingers in her hair, and kissed her. Deeply, passionately. The way people in love kiss.

And she kissed him back with everything she had, so pleased she'd made this beautiful, notorious man, whom every woman and some men in this place lusted after, desire her. Publicly.

"*La fée verte,*" he whispered into her mouth before he continued to kiss her. "*Ma chère, si c'était pas pour peur de la loi,*" he murmured heatedly as his lips skittered across her cheek to her ear, "*je me dresserais un chevalet . . . te déshabillerais . . . peindrais ton image . . .*"

She gasped at his mouth, trailing kisses down her neck and across her shoulder, whispering to her, hot, rapid. She didn't understand a word he said and she wasn't even sure he realized he was doing it.

"*Et puis,*" he whispered as his teeth nipped her earlobe, "*je te brouterais le cresson devant toutes ces personnes . . .*"

Her head was back and her eyes closed, Sebastian licking, nipping, and kissing in a line from her collarbone up her throat and chin, back to her mouth, speaking to her in the language of love. She didn't need to know the language; she knew what he meant.

The complete lack of human voices in the lobby, which underscored the pianist's exquisite playing of the urgently romantic piece, finally soaked into both their brains around the same time. Sebastian stopped speaking, stopped making love to her neck. They opened their eyes together and turned their heads slowly, to see the entire population of the lobby staring at them agape.

"I'm so embarrassed," Eilis said, feeling her face flushing and turning her face away from the largest cluster of people.

"Why?" Sebastian asked, looking back at her and tilting her face up to look at him with two gentle fingers on her chin. "Eilis, you're beautiful. Of course, they're going to look."

"You're far more beautiful than I," she whispered, staring into his purple eyes, "and everyone here knows who you are anyway. It's not me they're looking at and I only dressed for you," she admitted.

He grinned then, lopsided, and studied every feature of her face. "You are so wrong, but that's okay. Come with me."

Sebastian turned then and offered her his right arm, and she took it, though glancing at him questioningly. He looked only at her, his eyes sparkling and that same lopsided grin never dimming. "I use my right hand when I think in numbers and money, my left for images, language, and sex. That's why I offered you my right arm."

Eilis couldn't look away from him, either, but she was acutely aware of the stares they still garnered, although most everyone had gone back to their conversations.

"And the French?"

"What do you mean?"

"You were speaking in French." She couldn't help the delighted smile that spread across her face. "I didn't understand a word you said."

He looked genuinely intrigued by that. "I did? Really?"

"Yes. You threw in an English word here and there."

Sebastian chuckled. "Stands to reason, I guess. I learned how to make love in French."

He stopped then, drawing her around until she saw that they faced a mirror. There was a gorgeous couple there. Tall. Well built. The man was behind the woman, his arms wrapped around her waist, his chin on her shoulder.

The man had a heart-*stoppingly* handsome face, his eyes purple, alive, sparkling. Fair skin, blue-black hair sprinkled with white, broad shoulders, long legs, strong body. Crisp black suit and crisp white shirt.

The woman had a face with character and interest, one green eye and one blue eye, both dancing. Lightly tanned skin, sunny blonde curls piled on top of her head, pretty shoulders and arms, beautiful breasts, long and well-shaped legs whose musculature was defined sharply by the height of her heels.

The contrast between them was striking and she sighed. *What a beautiful woman.*

Sebastian chuckled. "Yes, she is," he whispered in her ear. "Eilis, that's you. Do you not know that?"

There were people milling all about, but suddenly, they faded. Eilis sucked in a breath when she realized that, yes, she was looking at herself and Sebastian. And they looked divine together. As divine as Jack and Lydia Blackwood.

"No, Sebastian," she whispered. "That can't be me."

He bent his head and, as she watched him in the mirror, he kissed her shoulder, then worked his way up her neck to her ear, his eyes closed. His big hands stroked down her hips and she shuddered with the exquisite sensations that pulsed through her. He partook of the corner of her jaw with lips and tongue, making love to her there, in front of this mirror where she could watch.

"She is you, Eilis," he whispered when his mouth returned to her ear and he opened his eyes to look in the mirror. "Remember this always, Eilis, because no matter what happens between us, this is how I see you. This is how I've always seen you, will always see you. You are a goddess, Eilis, a goddess. Never, *ever* forget that."

64: Blood & Water

THEY GOT INTO KCI AND DROVE SOUTH STRAIGHT TO KNOX'S HOUSE, AS he'd requested. She was surprised to know that he lived so close to her and not in Chouteau City, which was a twenty-minute drive.

"He hates Chouteau City," Sebastian told her. "Plus, he needed a place to hide and he can do that where he lives. You won't find it on Mapquest and the satellite images won't help."

"Hiding from Fen?"

"Yes."

"Fen killed his father. Why doesn't he just . . . ?" Eilis couldn't bring herself to say it.

"Kill him? Knox would rather Fen go to jail, preferably on death row, and the whole world know what he's done. If Fen forces his hand, then . . . Yeah."

Knox had secured his home almost as well as Eilis had hers, though one could see his entire property through the plain iron fence. An iron gate stood open, awaiting them.

Eilis was nervous. She hadn't seen Knox since he'd unexpectedly dropped by her office last month to say hello and check on her progress—a kindness that had made her cry after he'd left. Now, for the first time, she would be meeting him as family, as a brother who hadn't known she was his sister, but liked her and cared about her anyway.

Who didn't hate her for being Fen's daughter.

Eilis stepped out of the black Ferrari when Sebastian opened her door and offered his hand. She turned to find Knox striding toward her determinedly, in jeans and tee shirt, looking a lot less intimidating than he did in a designer suit. She walked around the front of the car hesitantly, but before she knew it, she was engulfed in Knox Hilliard's arms.

She began to cry, then sob. Finally. Family who wanted her and claimed her.

"I knew I liked you," he murmured, holding on to her as if he would never let go. She wanted to hold onto him forever, to make sure that he never went away, that he would never leave her alone and without family.

But finally he released her and said, "Come in and we'll eat and talk."

Eilis looked around at Sebastian, who leaned back against his car, his ankles crossed and his arms folded over his chest. He looked very . . . pleased.

Knox had ordered pizza and Eilis laughed when Sebastian groused at him for not having any alcohol in the house. "You should know better than that," Knox retorted. "If you want booze here, pack it in and pack it right back out again."

"I tried to keep some here and the next time I got here, he'd poured it all down the drain," Sebastian told Eilis wryly. "It was expensive, too."

They all sat around the table and eased into the conversation with small talk.

"So," Knox said once they'd begun to decimate two large pizzas amongst them, Eilis letting Sebastian goad her into eating her fill, "how is it that you're Fen and Trudy's daughter?"

"I honestly don't know," she said. "All I know is my birth date and their names. And that I'm almost three years older than you are."

"That was during Vietnam," Sebastian observed, around a mouthful. "Knox, didn't your dad go? Fen did."

"Yeah, he did."

"You'd have to work out dates, but I can see how that could've happened."

"If that was the case," Eilis agreed. "I have my original birth certificate. I was supposed to have been adopted—several times, actually—but they all fell through and then I was past the age when people wanted to adopt children. I was luckier than most of the kids in foster care. I had a fairly decent caseworker who'd consider my requests and honor them more times than not."

She didn't miss the look that passed between Knox and Sebastian, but decided to keep her curiosity to herself.

"I found refuge in school. Math wasn't my strong point, so I set out to conquer it."

"And succeeded very well," Sebastian said, and she smiled, warmth spreading through her. "What was your strong point?"

"History. English. I love Shakespeare."

Both Knox and Sebastian broke out into great bursts of laughter at that, and though she knew they weren't laughing at her, she was still uncomfortable.

"Shakespeare," Sebastian chortled. "Giselle has a PhD in English lit. I'm passably versed. Knox knows and adores every word the man ever wrote—but don't get him started. He'll start reciting his favorite soliloquies and expect everyone to stay awake."

"Really?"

"Guess that runs in the blood, too."

"So Fen— I don't understand," Knox said. "He deliberately didn't claim you?"

"Yes. I made the mistake of going to OKH for a job when I was in vo-tech learning how to be a secretary. I was nineteen. I put my real name on my application to see if that would help me get the job. Not only did it not get me a job, Fen showed up on my doorstep to tell me flat out that he wouldn't claim me and not to try to pull that stunt again. I was the right age. He took one look at me and knew I was his daughter."

Sebastian nodded. "I can see why. Knox'll look exactly like Fen in twenty years and sitting together there, you can tell. Apart, though, no one would put you together."

"He told me that since I'd gone to all the trouble to change my last name to use it. He was very upset I hadn't changed my first name, too, because it's so distinctive. I never told anyone and requested my records sealed after I'd gotten copies of everything I needed."

Knox and Sebastian speculated for quite a while on why Fen had chosen to show his hand when Eilis went into receivership. Eilis ate, listening to their theories, waiting—

"Eilis, do you know?"

"Yes." They looked at her expectantly. "He watched me build HRP. He sabotaged every business deal he could, told people what a ballbuster I was. So I started trying to think like Miss Manners, you know: What would Miss Manners do? It threw people off just enough that I got an edge and it discredited his opinion of me."

Sebastian chuckled. "So nobody realized you were still busting their balls?"

"Or they enjoyed it," Knox muttered wryly.

Eilis smiled, thrilled to finally be able to talk about it with people who cared about her, who would understand and approve.

"Things started going my way, which took a lot longer than it should have because he had his fingers in every pie I needed. But I was getting around him, so then he started buying up as much of my debt as he could, and he'd call the loans immediately. He nearly bankrupted me a couple of times."

"And he couldn't do anything with HRP as long as it was in the middle of a criminal trial," Sebastian murmured.

She nodded. "All these years, he's been working behind the scenes, but he came to my office after court the day after Knox assigned Sebastian to me— I panicked. I didn't know who was allied with whom."

Knox sighed. "You thought Sebastian would give you to Fen."

"I didn't know what to think. He said if I told either one of you who I was, he'd find a way to finish the job David started."

They were silent for a while, both Knox and Sebastian lost in their own thoughts, then Knox asked softly, "Eilis, why didn't you just tell me you were my sister some time during the trial? You and I spent hundreds of hours together going over your testimony and the paper trails."

"I thought you would hate me for being Fen's daughter and charge me in retaliation. You don't have the best reputation in the world. I never understood why you have that reputation, but I wasn't going to take any chances. Then after you put me in receivership— Well, I didn't know who to trust. I only knew I couldn't let Fen get his hands on HRP."

Sebastian ran a hand down his face. "Which was why you never went public."

"I've wanted to go public forever, but I didn't dare. He'd do to me what you've done to OKH. After I found out you hated Fen, it didn't matter because I could count on you as an ally who was stronger than Fen. He came to New York to declare war on me and didn't think I'd call his bluff."

"Eilis," Knox asked slowly, "why does Fen hate you so much?"

Eilis pursed her lips, the familiar hurt deep in her soul not as sharp as usual, more of throbbing ache than a stab. "He . . . doesn't." Both Knox and Sebastian started. "I don't think. Trudy does. Well, she hates that I exist. I think he's just desperate to keep her secret from coming to light."

Eilis stopped, felt her eyes well with tears, bowed her head. Sebastian drew her to him and into his lap.

Knox looked away, Eilis noted, pale beneath his tan, and she saw a tear track down his cheek and his jaw tense up. "I hate that bitch," he murmured. "I've always hated her. Even when I still lived at home, I used Giselle's mother as my emergency contact."

Sebastian grunted. "Pardon my saying so, but that little ménage à trois that is your parents is seriously fucked up. At least Oliver wasn't as whipped as Fen."

Both Eilis and Knox laughed through their sadness, yet Eilis felt so much better for knowing that her hatred of her mother was shared by her brother, that she wasn't in this alone anymore.

"Knox," Eilis began softly, not wanting to know but needing to ask, "will you take me to meet our sister?"

Sebastian's hand abruptly stopped caressing her arm. Knox stared at her, puzzled.

"What sister? You mean there's another one?"

"Uh— I don't— All I know is, when he came to see me last year, he said, 'I have another daughter. You will *never* measure up to her.'"

Knox and Sebastian both sucked up long, shocked breaths and they stared at each other, wide-eyed, mouths open. Knox swallowed. Sebastian's body shuddered.

"Oh, shit," Sebastian breathed. "*That's* what that's about."

Eilis watched them both work through something that was apparently tremendously significant.

"Gi— Fen's, uh, *daughter* didn't take the news well," Knox muttered at Sebastian as his jaw clenched. "I called Aunt Lilly right after I hung up with you. She was *pissed*. She told me not to tell anyone because she wanted to wait until Étienne's fortieth birthday bash to announce it to the tribe at large."

Sebastian froze. "She knew very good and well what would happen."

"Aunt Lilly said Gi— That she slugged Fen a couple of times, but then went after Trudy. Backhanded her so hard it put her on the ground a foot away. It took Bryce *and* Morgan to pull her off Trudy."

"Shit. Morgan's as big as Kenard."

"Broke a couple of bones in Trudy's face. Broke her arm and at least one rib. Left bruises around her neck. So the ER called the cops and the cops called me. By then, Morgan had already given me the visual, so . . . "

Eilis sat and listened to this tale in silence, completely confused. This daughter, Eilis's sister, the favorite— Punched Fen? Beat Trudy nearly to death? On Eilis's behalf?

"Got no phone call from Trudy wanting to press charges, so I figure she knew what I'd do—or wouldn't."

"And Fen?"

"Oh, he got off light. Nose broken the other way and a few bruises. She was gunning for Trudy."

Sebastian sighed and shook his head. "What a mess."

"Who," Eilis asked slowly, "is this other daughter? And why would she do this? She doesn't know me and Fen made it very clear she was his chosen one."

"Fen doesn't have another daughter," Knox snapped, his cold eyes glittering at Eilis. "He never did. It was a fantasy he built around a girl he couldn't control and he loved her for it. She doesn't respect him, but she does think he's funny and so she's indulged him for years. When Aunt Lilly told the tribe about you, she just— She lost it."

"Man, I wish I'd been there to see that," Sebastian muttered.

"Me too. Right now I'm fishing around, see if Fen's looking to retaliate. Again."

Sebastian sucked in a breath and released it on a long whoosh. "He'd be a fool to try that now."

Eilis still didn't really understand. "So who is this woman?"

Neither of them said anything for a moment. "I think," Sebastian finally murmured, "that's best left for another time."

Knox sighed and searched for words. "Fen lied to you, so for a year, you've been thinking you had a sister he loved, but threw you to the wolves. You need time to get used to the idea that it was a lie. When you meet her— You need the chance to get to know her and love her. *She* deserves that chance. It would hurt both of you if you met her knowing this and possibly resenting her for it. We don't want this to color your opinion of her. Please, Eilis. Trust us. "

"Please, Eilis," Sebastian repeated. "Please trust us on this."

She looked between them. The pain and sorrow, the pleading, on their faces was too real, too deep. Whoever this "daughter" was, these two men loved her and didn't want her *or* Eilis to suffer. And right now, Eilis could afford to be generous with the woman: She wasn't Eilis's sister, favored or otherwise, and she had taken unexpected and violent vengeance on the two people Eilis hated most in the world.

"Okay," she finally said. "I'll wait." She paused for a moment, looked down at the table because she didn't have anywhere else to look while she said what she needed to say. Sebastian's arms surrounding her helped, but not much. "Knox, I'm sorry my father killed yours."

She felt fingers on her chin and realized that Knox was lifting her face so that she would look at him. "Eilis," he murmured, "it's not your responsibility. You had nothing to do with it and I don't want you to take that on yourself."

"Eilis, I want you to know something else," Sebastian said. "If anyone in our tribe had known about you, I can guarantee you, there would've been eight families clamoring to take you in and give you everything you ever dreamed of as a child. I promise you that."

Knox reluctantly chuckled. "Well. They're clamoring right now. They may not be able to wait until the Fourth of July picnic. Aunt Dianne's threatening a welcome-home party."

"Dammit," Sebastian muttered. "A hundred-plus people using any excuse to have a party."

"Your tribe— Are they all Mormon?"

Knox and Sebastian looked at each other as if calculating that out. "Maybe two-thirds?" Sebastian finally said. "We all grew up in the church, so you won't be able to tell who is and who isn't by the way we talk, although by and large, the ones who aren't drink alcohol."

That confused Eilis to no end. She had had very little exposure to religion in her life and none of what she knew about any particular religion impressed her enough to find one for herself.

"I have employees who're Latter-day Saints," she said, vaguely proud that she could say that, that she could remember such details about them. "They don't like the word 'Mormon' and they don't act like you all do."

Knox looked away and Sebastian sighed. "I don't believe what the church teaches, but it *is* possible to have a faith and not live it. Knox and Giselle, Kenard— They're the minority of about five or six people in the tribe. They believe, they have faith, but they don't live the way they believe. Then there's the majority, the believers, and they're just like the Mormons who work for you."

"We're, uh—" Knox cleared his throat. "We're not normal."

Sebastian handed Eilis into his car long after midnight once she had drunk in every drop of information she could get about Knox, her family, their family, aunts, uncles, cousins. Her head spun with too much information, too much that was significant. They were almost to the highway when Sebastian spoke. "Eilis," he began hesitantly, "I told you I had something to show you and I do. What I'd like to know is, do you want to see it now or would you like to wait until tomorrow?"

She was tired, but curious as to what could be so bad that he'd made her wait until he'd shown her, especially after the night she'd worn that kelly dress. "Tonight, I guess."

He sighed. "Okay. I do have a guest room or five."

Her mind stopped on that and she said nothing for a moment. "Um, guest room?" she asked slowly.

Sebastian didn't look at her. "I'm not holding out any hope that you'll forgive me, Eilis," he murmured after a moment. "It'll be up to you."

Everyone is damaged. He may have secrets he's keeping from you. You don't know.

Eilis sighed as the Virgin's words came back to her and began to tremble at what he could tell her that would be so bad.

Silence cocooned them on the thirty-minute drive to the Plaza, though it didn't feel uncomfortable. Sebastian had retreated into his head and Eilis had too much to process not to do the same. Finally Sebastian pulled into an alley behind what looked like a big black concrete box perched high on a steep incline on the west side of the Country Club Plaza. From what she could tell, the house followed the contours of the ground and had three levels. The top level held the garage and it was mostly underground once one drove up the alley on the west side of the house. They parked right next to Sebastian's old Ford pickup.

The garage door closed behind them and he helped her out of the car, then opened a door and led her down a flight of stairs to another door that led into the house. "Eilis," he said as he stopped in a corridor with a stark white wall on her left and an open maple platform that was mid-thigh height on her left, "you've had a lot of shocks today, a lot of stress. This is going to be another one."

"Sebastian, you're scaring me," she whispered.

"I'm sorry."

He led her down the corridor where it turned right at a ninety-degree angle, past two doors on the left to a third. He opened the door and it swung inward. The smell of turpentine wafted up the stairs.

"Oh, this is your studio."

"Yes." He went down the switchback staircase first, and she could see almost nothing because it was so dark. He drew her into the room and then turned on the light. She flinched at the suddenness of it, but as her eyes adjusted and she looked around, her breath caught in her throat.

Her mouth went dry. She swallowed. Hard. She had no words for the mixture of emotion that swirled within her in a tornado.

Anger

Joy

Fear

Desire

Betrayal

Love

Shame

Happiness

There, in the middle of the room sat the magenta chaise she had lain upon. Before she'd changed her mind. The whole room looked just it did that night, with the exception of a few new paintings covered in tarps.

"You—" she whispered. "You're Ford."

"Yes," he murmured, "I'm Ford."

"You— You were going to— On purpose."

"No, I wasn't going to. I was going to send you home because I couldn't do it. It would have been tantamount to rape if I had made love to you as a man you didn't know, but was me, deceiving you." He stopped, then began again. "I had planned to tell you at Christmas, but . . . I didn't know if you would ever look at me as me, Sebastian, or as Ford, that guy you dreamed up in your head, which guy is not me and which expectations I could never fulfill, even if I knew what they were."

She walked around touching things, and he said no more. She didn't know what to say, what to think, what to do. Sebastian Taight *was* Ford and she had been too stubborn to let herself see that because she'd been too invested in the Ford she'd fantasized about all those years. The clues he'd dropped:

His training in art.

His anger at the mere mention of Ford and her desire to be painted by him.

His sketchbook, which he most assuredly meant her to find.

His Ford pickup truck that he'd bought when he was sixteen.

He'd *wanted* her to figure it out on her own and she hadn't. Now Eilis didn't know if she was more angry with him or with herself. He'd fooled her with the same transparency that got all the CEOs he'd ever rescued, only for her, it was in his artist's life. It was so obvious.

She walked to the deep, dark alcove, its heavy cherry panels drawn back, where that magnificent bed stood on its dais in the darkest corner and almost could not be seen at all. He turned up some of the lights in that room and she saw it again in a new light. This was Sebastian's bed.

There was no Ford.

"I like Mardi Gras," he whispered in her ear and she shivered with a mixture of desire and anger. "I try to go every year. N'awlins is the most decadent city in the world."

To her left was the set of oversized French doors that led into that red and gold salon and to the hedonistic bathroom in stark white.

"Eilis, please go around the room and take the tarps off the canvases."

She looked up at him, unable to say anything. In his face she saw worry, pleading, and uncertainty—three things she never thought she'd see in Sebastian Taight's face. In his voice, the same things. So she did as he asked and left the bedroom to go around the studio.

A tarp-covered canvas, eight feet long by five feet high, leaned against a stack of blank five-by-five canvases. She uncovered it carefully.

Her jaw dropped. It was *her*. And she was beautiful. It was his nude sketch of her come to life in vibrant colors and textured oils.

Eilis looked around at the other tarp-covered canvases and she went to each one only to find herself, some nude, some not, all beautiful, the way he saw her. At work, in her home, in her garden.

And then there was that big canvas, a radical departure from his public five-by-five hallmark. She uncovered it to find her garden, every detail down to the last flower. And there was no nude to be found.

"You've never painted anything without a nude in it," she whispered.

"Not true," he said from directly behind her, and she felt his arms wrap around her. "I just made my name in nudes. What I have never done is paint a woman nude more than once and now I can only paint that one." He pointed to one of the canvases of her, none of which were on five-by-five canvases; some were smaller, some were bigger, but none five feet square.

Eilis knew what that meant: She was special, unlike the rest.

"I don't know what to say. I'm really angry. I'm so happy I could burst. I'm shocked. I'm feeling betrayed and shamed all over again. I'm—confused. It was so out of context that I couldn't—well, wouldn't—pick up on it. I thought you hated Ford."

"I do. I hate the one that lived in your head. I couldn't compete. Wouldn't compete."

"You exaggerated his importance to me."

"I'm sorry. It never occurred to me to ask you point blank. All I heard was that you wanted a vacation so you could find Ford, have him paint you, make love to you."

"So you destroyed him."

"That was the intent, yes."

"These," she said, indicating the canvases of her. "Are you going to hang these?"

"Only with your permission. I want the world to know what a perfect woman looks like. Eilis," he murmured reverently in her ear, "I have never, in my entire life, seen or painted a woman so perfect as you. You are my finest work."

Once again her breath caught in her throat, and she was simultaneously aroused and so very deeply touched.

"In one day," she whispered. "In one day I met family who likes me and claims me, and I saw how Ford, how you, see me as I've never seen myself. In one day—the most incredible day of my life."

"Better than opening bell at the stock exchange?"

"I think— Much better."

"Come lie with me, Eilis," he whispered in her ear. "Come and be worshipped by me, Sebastian, the man who's been in love with you since the first time he saw you."

65: Nessun Dorma

WHATEVER SHE THOUGHT FORD COULD'VE GIVEN HER, SEBASTIAN DID. He was luxuriant, sensual, giving. He took her to his bedroom upstairs, into a hot shower naked, tall and cut—a man who could bear her weight with ease.

He took her hand and turned her around so that they were touching from knee to collarbone. Their hands locked with fingers entwined, he devoured her skin. Her neck, her throat, her collarbone, her shoulders, her breasts. He got on his knees and devoured her belly, then lower and lower. He turned her around again and devoured the skin of her back, the skin of both her buttocks, the crease where her thighs met her torso.

He bent lower, licked and sucked and nibbled on the backs of her thighs, then the backs of her knees. Again he turned her back to face him and he worked his way up her legs until his hands gently parted her legs and he kissed her most private of places. His tongue licked and his fingers slid through the folds of her and she thought she'd die.

Eilis wrapped her hands in his hair as his tongue did so many marvelous things to her that she had never expected a man would ever do to her. Her head fell back and she panted for air, and she knew she was going to fall over the edge—but he drew away just as she got to the top of the mountain, and she felt cold, bereft.

She opened her eyes and looked down at him. He stood, sliding up her body, his hands trailing, touching wherever they moved. He smiled at her, a crooked smile that, under other circumstances, would have melted her heart a little. Under these circumstances, it made her ache inside and feel her emptiness just a bit more acutely.

Sebastian picked her up slowly, raising her far above him so he could look up at her for a moment. She looked back at him and what she saw astounded her: A man in love. With her.

Then he lowered her slowly and took a step forward so that the shower wall was at her back, supporting her.

He wrapped her legs around him and slid his hard length up into her. Immediately she gasped and clenched him. Her mind froze as her body took over, quaking, the sensations like nothing she had ever experienced. Exquisite pleasure, so fine and ephemeral, like the delicate undulating lace of sunlight through leaves. Her eyes closed and her head dropped back against the wall. She could only feel his skin against hers, his big hands wrapped around her hips, his body inside hers stroking in and out.

Building, building. Just as she began to slip into orgasm, he held back, making her nearly cry with frustrated joy. "Sebastian," she whispered, agonized. "Please."

"Please what?" he whispered back.

Eilis arched her back in an attempt to draw him closer, to persuade him to release her tension for her, but he held back. A low moan escaped her when he began to move again, grateful for anything he would give her until she sucked in a sharp, surprised gasp: Sebastian had sneaked up on her and she began to come when she least expected it and oh, it was divine—

—Sebastian grasped her buttocks and pushed her back against the wall, his hand up high on the wall, supporting himself. He crushed her mouth with his while he thrust into her, coming with a tortured groan that Eilis heard as harmony to the melody of her own moan of utter bliss as she came with him.

Finally, Eilis opened her eyes and stared at him as water sluiced over his head, down his face, making his skin glisten. His ice blue eyes had darkened to violet and he watched her intently, a small smile on his face that made him look like an ordinary man. She smiled at him, then, delighted that he *was* just an ordinary man, not King Midas and not Ford.

Neither said anything for a while, listening to the sound of running water and feeling it drench them, looking into each others' eyes and feeling each others' bodies. Finally, the water that ran down Eilis's face had nothing to at all to do with what was coming out of the showerhead.

Then he murmured, "Was that Sebastian or Ford?"

"There is no Ford," she whispered in return, choking. "Only you." She held his face between her hands just to look at him, to study him.

He stared at her. "Are you crying?" he asked, wondrous.

"Yes," she replied, then laughed through it. "That was the first time I have ever made love, Sebastian. It was the most joyous experience I have ever had. *What* blessed magic have you worked on me?"

"What magic have you worked on *me*, Eilis Hilliard?"

She swallowed, another first bursting in her soul: The first time she liked hearing her birth name, because it had been said by Sebastian and Sebastian took pain away.

He pulled her away from the wall. Still inside her, her legs wrapped around him, he turned off the shower and carried her to his bed. He turned and sat, then lay back so that she was on top of him, straddling him. She felt him harden again inside her again.

"I want to paint you like this," he whispered. "On top of me, with me inside you. I want to see you pregnant with a child I put there, my child, and paint you like that."

Her eyes widened and she sucked in a breath. "You didn't use a condom."

"No, I didn't, and I have never *not* used a condom in my entire life."

"Why?" she whispered.

"Didn't want to litter the world with a bunch of little me's that I'd never know about. I never intended to use a condom with you."

"You want to get me pregnant," she murmured, slow.

"Yes."

"Pregnancy results in things that are a tad more long-lasting than an architecturally interesting belly. What would you do with them?"

"Love them," he said simply. "I left my childhood religion behind long ago, but one thing I do know is that the Man who created this—"

He gestured to her body, running his hands down her ribs, inspecting her with both a lover's and an artist's eye, with awe and reverence. He hefted her generous breasts and laid his palm flat on her flatter-than-before belly and swept down, caressing the hair of her pubis. His hands gripped her generous hips and still he studied her, his gaze caressing every part he touched as he touched it.

"The Man who created this is a master artist and craftsman and he loves and is in love with a Woman, a fertility goddess. He loves her so much that he wanted to immortalize her. So he made you, a replica of her, his woman, in all the variations he could think of. And because you are his tribute to his Goddess, he loved you and he loved you so much that he made you his assistant. And as his assistant, he trusted you with his best work, which is *Homo sapiens*.

"There is a Woman, the Fertility Goddess. The Master Artist, her lover, worships at her feet, and whatever he gives her, she gives to us, her children. The only thing I can do as a man and as an artist is attempt to outline a child's character—to pencil sketch what I see and set the child loose to finish the painting himself. The sketch will tell me when my part is finished and to let the child have the brushes, even when my mind, my heart, tell me I'm not ready to let him make free with the paint.

"I want to make and raise children with you, Eilis. I want to bind you to me forever."

Tears ran down her face at his reverent soliloquy. She throbbed with the passion he infused through her, the spirituality that ran so deep it couldn't be seen unless he chose to show it.

She swallowed. "Sebastian, I'm forty-one and I— I don't even know if I want children. I don't— Not because I don't like children, but I don't know what kind of mother I'd be. Maybe not a very good one, I think."

He looked at her for a long time and she was afraid to look away in case she would blink and he would be gone. "Eilis," he said, "I don't agree you wouldn't be a good mother, but I love you. I'll take you any way I can get you and if that means no children, that's what that means." He lay his hand flat over the tiny pooch of her belly again and caressed it. "You are *my* fertility goddess and if the only way I can immortalize you as the Master immortalized his Goddess is to paint you, then I'll take it and be grateful for it."

66: Le Cygne

WHY DIDN'T WE SLEEP IN THE BED DOWNSTAIRS?" EILIS ASKED LATE THE next day as they ate together in what Sebastian called the conference room. She wore one of Sebastian's Oxford shirts and nothing else.

Sebastian wore only a pair of very short cutoff jeans shorts that rode low on his hips and showed off his body in a way Eilis had never seen it. He hadn't bothered to button the fly and she couldn't keep her eyes off the trail of black hair that disappeared into the V of the plackets. He took her breath away.

He caught her staring and cast her a wickedly lusty grin. "Giselle calls this my Parisian peacock look."

Eilis laughed, delighted, because it was true. "I could look at that for a while."

Chuckling, he said, "The bed up here, where we slept last night, is where I sleep alone, where I dress, where I get ready for the day's business. I have never had a woman in that bed before you and I wanted our first time together to be in that room, Sebastian's room."

Eilis blushed and felt warmth suffuse her.

"The one downstairs is for love and sex and fucking. I've never slept in that bed alone." Eilis's smile dimmed a bit, but he went on in a wry tone, "It seems my family makes frequent use of it. Apparently, my cousins who know I'm Ford bring their spouses on a rotating schedule timed for my out-of-town trips. I came home early from Italy and caught Giselle and Kenard *in flagrante delicto*."

"They slept in your bed?" she asked, aghast.

"No, they didn't *sleep* in it," he grumbled. "That's my point. Mind you," he added, "that's going to stop because I don't intend to sleep upstairs again anytime soon. I haven't slept in that bed for five years and I'll be damned if I just turn it over to my family."

Eilis's eyes widened. "Five years?"

He nodded. "Yep. Giselle is the only woman I've painted nude in all that time and there was nothing arousing about it. It was a statement on her conflicted sexuality, so it doesn't count."

"Why haven't I met her yet?"

"You have. She's the Virgin."

"That's Giselle? The one Fen's terrified of?"

"Yes."

"Oh," she breathed, re-experiencing the warmth and love the Virgin had surrounded her with. "She's *wonderful*."

There was a pause and Eilis looked up to see him studying her with an inscrutable expression. "How do you mean?"

"She took care of me that night," she said, clearing her throat, remembering. "She put a robe on me and helped me to the shower. She brushed and braided my hair. She took me home and undressed me and tucked me in bed. She took my painting down off the wall and put it on the floor, face to the wall, so I wouldn't have to see it when I went to sleep and woke up."

Sebastian was dumbstruck. "*Giselle* did that?"

"Yes. She stayed the night in another room. She took care of me the next day, too. She cooked for me. She rocked me and sang me lullabies, and I poured out my soul to her and she held me while I cried on her shoulder, and she cried with me. She brought me dinner in bed. For a week, she was the mother I never had.

"She wouldn't tell me her name. I never called her anything. We didn't talk a lot. We did a jigsaw puzzle together that first day. Her husband came every night to sleep with her because he couldn't stand to sleep alone. He brought more puzzles. And it didn't matter that I didn't know who they were. All I knew was that she took care of me until I could do it myself. I never met the Giselle you talk about and even her husband called her 'warrior queen.' I don't understand that."

"Sometimes," he said slowly, "I think Giselle has no place in this world. She takes the church seriously, but she's steeped in the eastern ideas of war and honor and justice, and she's sensual to her core. She doesn't even try to reconcile them all and she won't choose one over the other, so they've torn her apart most of her life."

"I never saw the warrior."

Sebastian took a deep breath and stared at her for a long time as if trying to decide what to say. "Giselle is the one Fen referred to as his daughter."

Eilis felt the bottom drop out of her world and her breath catch in her chest. She wondered if she would ever be able to breathe again. "I— I told her everything, all about my life," she whispered, swallowing, panicking. "Things I've never told anybody, things I don't ever want to talk about again. What must she think?"

"She apparently thought enough of you to knock Fen senseless and break Trudy's face," he muttered. "She didn't want me to bring you to me that night. She really tried to talk me out of it, but I didn't listen to her and I played on her sense of obligation to me and guilt to make her do it. I wasn't at all honorable about it. Before she took you home, she came up here and chewed my ass but good. She told me what to do to salvage that mess I made, but I didn't listen to her. She hasn't spoken a civil word to me since."

Eilis blinked. "She— I don't understand why she'd care for me, defend me. She doesn't know me."

He shrugged. "That Giselle you described to me, who cared for you and cried with you? *I* don't know *her*. I can't tell you why she did what she did. Knox would know." His voice had a strange hollowness she didn't understand and she looked up at him, but he looked away from her. She didn't press the point.

"Her and Fen—"

He cleared his throat. "We never understood her relationship with him until you said he had another daughter. Fen respects her, loves her in his sick and twisted way, but he's always resented that he couldn't control her the way he controlled Knox. They always got along well as long as Fen amused her and hadn't pissed her off, which he did a lot. I'm positive that Fen doesn't care that she beat the hell out of him. His punishment is that he can't redeem himself in her eyes now."

"She would forgive him trying to kill her but not for having abandoned me?"

"She can take care of herself and she has all the power in their relationship. An abandoned child can't take care of itself; it has no power."

Eilis's head swum and she laid her forehead in her palm.

"I'm so confused. She was so gentle."

"You'll have to introduce me to that woman some time. I'd like to meet her."

"But her husband knows this."

"He would have to, I guess."

"She calls him Ares."

Sebastian gave a short laugh. "The god of war. He caught her where she lives and breathes, which is on the battlefield and as far as I can tell, their bed is their battlefield."

Eilis could feel the heat rising up in her face. "When they were at my house, I heard them. He's— When they— Um . . . "

"Vicious?"

"Yes. It bothered me. Well, bothers me. I— No, I *hate* it," she burst out. "He's twice her size. I thought he would— I almost called the police."

"Given what David did to you, I can understand why that shook you up." He paused. "That's who they are, Eilis. It was what Giselle was looking for and it works for them. They don't act that way outside the bedroom and you caught them in a private moment, so . . . "

Eilis digested this for a moment, recalling how Ares—Bryce—had tiptoed around her that week as if afraid he might say or do the wrong thing, but always helpful, always thoughtful.

She sighed and admitted, "He was very kind to me. I shouldn't have let that color my view of him— Of them."

"He makes Giselle happy. He's Knox's best friend. He fits in with the tribe and he's become a good friend to me, so that's really all I care about."

She took a deep breath. "What did Trudy do to Knox?"

"Kicked him out of the house with nothing but the clothes on his back. He was fifteen."

Eilis sighed. Her mother hadn't wanted either of the children she bore; she just couldn't dispose of the second as easily as she had the first.

"It wasn't as bad as it sounds," he added, as if reading her mind. "He went to live with Aunt Lilly and Giselle. I mean, it wasn't like he didn't have anywhere to go. He was the golden boy of the tribe. Good kid, did what he was told, didn't drink or smoke or do drugs—basically your regulation Mormon kid in spite of Trudy. Cheerful, optimistic no matter what. He liked going to church and someone in the tribe made sure he got there every week, without fail. Sometimes Oliver would take him if he wasn't busy. Wanted to go on a mission. Trudy made sure he was educated and cultured. And he had an adventurous streak I'd compare to Tom Sawyer, Huck Finn."

A faint sadness underpinned Sebastian's matter-of-factness.

"What happened to him?" she asked softly, although she had a pretty good idea and Sebastian's next words confirmed it.

"Losing that trial. He was fresh out of law school, naïve and he had to study things—photos, autopsy reports, you know—that no human should ever have to know exist. It did something to him— I don't know how to put it. It raped his personality. His *joie de vivre* was gone. He was never the same after that and he . . . lost it. Totally spiraled out of control. He's a completely different person now."

"I remember the news then," Eilis said softly. She would never forget the publicity that surrounded him at the time. "That's when I found out I had a brother. After that, I always paid attention if I heard his name." She had never wanted to believe— Yet she was glad that— "Knox didn't really . . . ?"

Sebastian raised his eyebrow at her. "Sometimes what's moral and just is very, very ugly."

"Did your church teach you that?"

"Shit, no. It's one big reason why I left."

She hesitated. "So . . . David—?"

"Eilis, we do what we think is right. No, I haven't done a lot of the things Knox and Giselle have done, but don't doubt for a minute I wouldn't. I carry on the off chance Fen comes after me, but I haven't had to use a gun since I was a teenager and I certainly haven't been presented with the situations Knox and Giselle have. We— the three of us—are a pack of fighters and we believe in justice at all costs. Then we got Kenard, who's just as ruthless, with his own brand of justice."

Sebastian studied her for a long moment until she squirmed. Then he opened his mouth and said, very deliberately,

"And now we have you."

Her eyes widened.

"I've never met anyone with an iron will like yours, Eilis," he said with reverence. "Very few people in the world could build something like HRP, beating Fen back at every turn. You stayed with a man who'd raped you so you could save your company and the livelihoods and life savings of two hundred and fifty people. You sold your paintings to keep those people employed. How you handled Fen in New York was *magnificent*. If that's a glimpse of the ruthless bitch I'd heard about, then I'd sure like to see more of her come out to play."

Then she realized: Sebastian Taight—King Midas—didn't simply love her, desire her, want children with her; he *respected* her as a businesswoman, a *fighter*. Eilis thought she'd never catch a breath.

He stood then and held his large hand out. She put hers in it and felt his fingers close around hers gently to pull her up and out of the chair, then to the basement door. He led her down to the studio where she'd found shame in her fantasy and for betraying the real man. He flipped some switches so that they had enough light to see their way to that decadent bedroom.

"Do you remember," he murmured as he led her into his other bedroom, and she began to feel desire course through her when she understood that he was bringing her into Ford's bed now that she'd been in Sebastian's, "at Christmas when I told you you'd understand why I didn't want to play my favorite music for you when you heard it?"

"I remember."

"Have you ever listened to it?"

"I didn't remember the title."

Sebastian held her hand as she climbed up the step stool into the bed, then he closed the velvet and chiffon drapes surrounding it before getting in the other side. She gasped as the first chord rang out. Sebastian sat cross-legged on the bed, then reached out for her.

Sebastian ran his hands through her long blonde hair and he pulled her close so that she was lying on her belly, looking up at him; she had never had to look up to look him in the eye.

He lowered his head, almost kissing her, but not quite. He studied her and she studied him.

"Welcome to my other world, Eilis Logan," he whispered, his words arousing her to such a degree as she had never imagined words—and so few!—could do, "my world of decadence and hedonism and Bacchanalian pleasures. I'll give you the best the world has to offer in music, wine, food, literature, and the arts; the finest silks, the deepest velvets, the smoothest cottons, the roughest linens, the loveliest furs; the most splendid gardens, the sweetest of flowers, the most fragrant of oils.

"Today, tonight, for the next few lifetimes, you're here in my studio, my bed, my world, a world where only fine things live. I'll teach you every wonderful thing about sex and love and fucking that you never knew existed." His whisper became a breath. "But the finest, most decadent, most perfect thing in my world is you."

"Sebastian," she whispered when finally he kissed her.

67: Dulcissime

EILIS HAD BEEN DRUGGED AND THAT DRUG WAS SEBASTIAN TAIGHT. He brought her chocolate and strawberries, exquisite cheeses and breads and wines, grapes and oranges and tropical fruits of every type—and fed them to her, caressed her body with them, squeezed the juices into the most sensitive areas on her body and licked it all up. Lazy. Slow. Hot.

He brought her champagne that she drank straight from the bottle, then shared with him in a kiss. He poured it over her belly and sipped from her navel.

He brought her absinthe and they shared it in glasses that were a hundred years old. He taught her how to pour ice water over the sugar cube cradled in absinthe spoons that were at least as old as the glasses.

He brought her mint chocolate chip ice cream and he drizzled it at the apex of her thighs, in her "nooks and crannies," then leisurely licked it off, all the while whispering to her that mint chocolate chip ice cream *was* her name, and he said her name over and over again, reverently, like a whisper on a breeze.

He read to her from the Song of Solomon, the *Rubaiyat of Omar Khayyam*, Ovid, *The Canterbury Tales*, The Decameron, *Fanny Hill*, *Lady Chatterly's Lover*, *Delta of Venus*, Sextus Propertius.

He whispered to her in French when he made love to her.

He played for her all the operas of Puccini and Rossini, and *Don Giovanni* and *Faust* and *Carmen*; he played for her Rachmaninoff, deBussy, Smetana, and Orff. He played for her Gershwin and murmured in her ear of the things he had done and seen as an American in Paris. He made love to her to Delibes, "The Flower Duet" and again to Albinoni, "Adagio in G minor" and again to Liszt, "Sospiro."

He brought her exquisite, delicate oils of jasmine and orange blossom that he rubbed into her skin, every square millimeter, every pore, and where he oiled, he kissed.

He brought her a blindfold and, while she was blinded, he drank from her the nectar of the gods.

He slid strawberries up inside her, then ate them before sliding in himself and loving her.

There was only one thing Eilis could do for him that he had never had a good experience with, and she was shocked when he told her.

"I spent my life learning how to give," he murmured to her once she'd swallowed everything he gave her and rose above him to then settle beside him, lying half atop him, her legs entwining with his. "I was under the impression that wasn't something women wanted to do, so I didn't ask and the only volunteers didn't make it worth my while. I didn't figure I was missing anything. Silly me."

She didn't know how long she'd been with him in that dimly lit bed of velvet and silk, cotton and chiffon, in the corner of an equally dim alcove. There were no windows, no sense of day or night, no clocks, no sound except the music and the ventilation system, and absent that, the gasps and cries of their own passion.

They made love and slept in the bed whenever they felt like it; they took meals and drank the absinthe in that hedonistic red and gold salon she now realized was rife with sexual imagery; they showered in that sparkling white bathroom that had its own stark sensuality. It seemed Sebastian had an endless supply of clean sheets.

The fourth time they'd changed the linens, he said, "I like to eat in bed, in case you hadn't noticed."

She'd laughed in sheer delight.

Time had stopped.

Sebastian slept very little, she noticed, and certainly not on any pattern she could discern.

"What are you thinking about?" she asked when she awoke slowly to find that he was, again, awake.

"I'm thinking about the present I got you at Christmas."

Her brow wrinkled. "Why didn't you give it to me at Christmas, then?"

"Look," he whispered as he pulled a pair of black French silk stockings out of a small box she hadn't seen. Her eyes grew wide and her juices began to flow, hot and thick, like lava. "And this," he said as he let a black silk garter belt dangle from his fingers. "And these." The highest pair of fine silk sling-back heels she had ever seen. "Go sit in that chair. I want to watch you put them on."

She put the garter belt on as she sashayed across the room to the deep chair, looking over her shoulder at Sebastian, who had the look and tension of a hungry wolf about him.

She sat facing him and rolled the stocking over her thumbs, then raised her leg. She slid the first one over her skin slow, languid, because she had nothing to be shy about now. She carefully rolled the next stocking up her leg, fastening it slowly, carefully to the garter belt. Once she'd finished rolling both stockings over her legs, she leaned back and spread her knees so that he could see everything between her thighs.

He sucked in a long, shuddering breath.

Lifting her leg high again, she put one shoe on, then repeated the process for the other foot. Then, standing, she modeled her new clothes, coming close enough for him to barely touch, then prancing out of reach once again. Sebastian sighed. He sat on the edge of the bed, then, his legs splayed out. He lay back until his torso was supported by one elbow. He grasped his hard cock in his hand and he slowly stroked himself while he watched her strut around in front of him with an intensity that made her even wetter.

So she sat and threw one knee over the arm of the chair, then the other knee over the other arm. She put a hand between her legs. Sebastian sucked in a deep breath, his eyes wide.

Eilis felt her own hand do to herself what she had done a thousand times before, what Sebastian had done to her almost that many times. She watched as his hand moved faster and faster, but Eilis decided she needed to be filled. She abruptly got up from the chair, pushed Sebastian roughly onto his back, straddled him, and slid down his cock, making them both groan in ecstasy.

And she fucked him, her legs strengthened by years of gardening and who-knew-how-many days of unrelenting sex. She felt every rub of every fine rib of her silk stockings between her skin and his. She didn't go to bed without them on again.

Sebastian painted her as he would have painted her to begin with. Languid and dissolute from his lavish debauchery, she called up her own sexuality over and over again while he painted her.

"That," he murmured to her when he'd finished, "is not getting hung anywhere but our bedroom."

Our bedroom?

"Is that our bedroom?" she asked, pointing to the Den of Iniquity as he drew her up, twirled her around, and walked her backward.

"Do you want it to be?"

"We're both rich," she murmured as he slammed her up against the studio wall. "We'd never have to work again."

"Ah," he said as he stroked slowly in and out, her legs wrapped around his hips, "but I need the numbers and the game as much as I need the art; I won't stay sane without both. And you, who've had to work and scrabble for everything you've built, would become very, very unhappy with this life soon enough and gardening alone wouldn't fulfill you. Work without pleasure means nothing. Life without work means even less."

"I'm bored with HRP," she told him breathlessly, tightening her legs to encourage a faster pace. "I want to do something different now."

He obliged her, pounding into her until she came almost violently. "I've never been able to fuck a woman while talking business. I'll never look at money the same way again."

Some time after they had changed the sheets (again), showered, and slept, Sebastian took her to the magenta chaise and, his chest to her back, pressed her body forward until her hands found the carved wood on the back of the couch.

Eilis felt him slide slow, easy, inside her and she dropped her head down panting, bracing her body, preparing for the hard thrusts that she wanted but that didn't come. His big hands wrapped around her, but his hips barely moved as he stroked her, long, slow strokes she could feel against her pubic bone.

She had no idea what he was doing to her; this wasn't like anything she'd experienced before. She loved this, she couldn't deny it, but it was foreign—the sensations were different. It felt richer, deeper in its subtle and never-ending buildup. He slid one hand down and around to her clitoris, but instead of manipulating it, his hand cupped the whole of her mons and pressed her firmly back toward him and then she understood.

Eilis came as slow and easy as he was stroking her, filling her, sandwiching her pubic bone between his cock and his hand. She raised her head and breathed deeply, pulling all the air into her lungs that she could, which only deepened this burgeoning . . . thing . . . that she never knew existed.

She sighed as it went on and on, never quite satisfying her but not wanting to let go, until at once her legs trembled. It didn't burst so much as bloom and make her feel like she had had an epiphany. She clenched around him and pressed back against him for more, more.

Sebastian pushed back hard enough to make her cry out as her body gave her what he had promised. He began to move then, both hands back on her hips, pulling her to him, thrusting into her the way she'd expected to begin with.

And as his strokes got shorter and harder, faster and more urgent, she came again, the way she'd expected the first time, with flash and energy and the lovely, familiar sensations in all the familiar places.

He buried himself in her and shuddered as he came, his fingers digging into the flesh of her hips and pulling her back to him as he emptied himself inside her.

"What *was* that?" she breathed.

"That," he replied, hushed, "is the elusive and infamous G-spot. It's what I want-ed to do to you the night you came here to Ford. I wanted to make love to you so badly that night, Eilis, to tell you it was just me, tell you I loved you. I was afraid you'd be disappointed that it was *just* me, that I wasn't the man in your head."

"I'm so sorry, Sebastian," she breathed. "I—"

He put his fingers over her mouth. "Don't. We both made mistakes, but we're here now, so it's all good."

They awakened when footsteps sounded overhead and came down the stairs to the studio. Sebastian's mouth curled in a wicked smile, his eyes still closed.

"How long have we been here, Sebastian?" Eilis asked, curled up against him, his arm around her.

"I have no idea."

"How did they get in the house?"

"Knox and Giselle, a few more of my cousins, are free to come and go as they please. They have codes for the keypad at the front door."

"Is this a sign that we've been missed and need to get back to our lives?"

"I'm guessing yes. Or else they want to use the bed."

Eilis laughed. "Perhaps you should padlock the studio door."

It was only a minute or two before a woman's voice rang out. "I found them." Then, "It's been a week and a half, you two. Wall Street burned you both in effigy three days ago. And Sebastian? Air this place out. Even the turpentine can't cover the smell."

Sebastian only chuckled and raised his voice above a murmur for the first time in days. "All right," he croaked. "Get us some clothes."

Not long after that Eilis heard the thwack of clothes on the floor at the foot of the staircase.

A long, slow shower and an even longer exchange of oil massages, all the while snickering and laughing at the thumps and squeals, giggles and groans directly overhead.

"Freaks," Sebastian muttered with a wry chuckle.

Eilis's jeans were loose, surprising her; she'd not really noticed how her body had changed since Sebastian had cleaned out her refrigerator.

He noticed, however, and quirked an eyebrow at her, unhappy about that state of affairs. "I'm going to have to take you to Subway twice a week for the next few weeks," he groused as he followed her up the stairs. "How much have you lost?"

"I don't know."

"Too much is how much. I wanted you to stop going hungry, not lose weight."

"So you made very clear," she said with a chuckle, unexpectedly pleased with both her weight loss and the fact that he'd rather she have more padding.

It was nine o'clock in the evening. Which evening, Eilis didn't know; Giselle and Bryce still hadn't emerged from wherever they had gone.

Eilis heard a loud gasp, then a moan from behind the other door in the corridor.

"Deviants!" Sebastian yelled as he pounded on the door, then led the way up to the kitchen.

Eilis helped Sebastian scrounge leftovers from their retreat from society. Strawberries. Flat champagne, which he made her drink and she did, straight from the bottle. Exquisite chocolate that he fed her, then followed with deep kisses so that they could share it.

The Virgin and her husband emerged from the bedroom while she and Sebastian kissed. They were rumpled and breathless, but jovial. "You guys inspired us," she said as she bumped Sebastian out of the way of the refrigerator with her hip, uncaring that Sebastian had his tongue in Eilis's mouth. Her husband came up behind her, reached between her legs, and squeezed. She screeched and hit her head on the freezer door.

Everybody laughed except Giselle, who rubbed her head and pouted.

"Well, Sebastian," she finally said as she snatched berries from Eilis and leaned back against Bryce, who wrapped his arms around her and kissed her on the top of her head. "I guess you managed to spring the news on her without her keeling over." He rolled his eyes.

Eilis had something to say. "I want to thank you so much for your kindness that week."

"You needed it," Giselle murmured with a warm smile. "I get the feeling you haven't had a lot of TLC in your life."

Somewhere down deep inside, Eilis's soul hurt, because she didn't know she'd missed it until it was pointed out to her. Sebastian pulled her into his arms. She dug her nose into his shoulder and smelled him: one part soap, one part him, one part turpentine. After she'd collected herself, she turned to look at Giselle again and whispered, "No. Not like that, no. Never. You were my mother."

There were tears in Giselle's eyes and her mouth trembled. Eilis didn't think she could have spoken without letting it all out.

"What day is it, anyway?" Sebastian asked.

"Sunday," Bryce said. "We wouldn't have bothered you at all, but late Friday, the SEC approved a buy order Fen had made for HRP." Eilis's gut clenched and her eyes widened. She felt Sebastian's huff of impatience. How soon their time together had come to an end. "On the other hand," he added, "I took it upon myself to match him share for share. The SEC just cut me off at the knees with OKH, so Jack's been putting whatever he can find into Eilis's account. Kevin's campaign is getting national coverage now and Oth's former anti-Taight buddies are refusing to talk about you at all. What with OKH and now HRP wrapped up in it, people are making connec-tions left and right. At this moment, the whole country's just sitting back, eating popcorn, and enjoying the fireworks. The Journal actually called us Pendergast Friday, so you owe me ten bucks."

Sebastian grinned. "Well, that only means I'm not the only thug in this room now."

Bryce barked a laugh, and Eilis looked at him, sorry that she had eavesdropped on them, sorry that she had thought so badly of the way he and Giselle expressed their love for each other. "Thank you," she whispered.

Bryce shrugged. "No skin off my nose. I don't like bullies."

"He didn't count on you joining up," Sebastian said. "Some days I wonder where that man's long-term planning went. How much OKH has Jack gotten for Eilis?"

"Two percent. I got another four before I got shut down."

Sebastian's eyes widened. "Holy shit. That much! OKH stock's getting a little sparse around the trading floor now."

"Jack can wring blood out of a turnip. Fen's got thirteen percent of HRP and I'm there with him at thirteen." He laughed again, and Eilis watched him carefully, beginning to understand what Giselle saw in his face; the beauty of a warrior's battle scars, the mark of not only survival, but utter dominance.

Where Bryce was Ares, though, Sebastian was Dionysus, the god of wine, bringing an end to care and worry. "I've been enjoying myself and entertaining my interns and juniors with this all week long. They're getting quite an education. I bought you as much time as I could before I figured you should be rousted out of your honeymoon for business tomorrow."

"Let me get this straight. You have ten percent of OKH and Eilis has two percent."

Bryce nodded.

"I have twenty-three," Sebastian said, "so thirty-five percent amongst us. Fen controls fifty-one percent himself, which means his board and employees probably own the other fourteen percent."

"They're bailing."

"It's about damned time. Well, I think we can sit on that and wait him out another year and a half. Are you up for going to shareholder meetings now?"

Bryce chuckled wickedly. "I'm all for the games. I vote Eilis comes too."

"Yes! Oh, yes! I would love to!"

"It's the HRP we've got to concentrate on now," Sebastian said to Bryce. "How much more can you get?"

"Probably as much as I want."

"The SEC's keeping me on a leash and if it weren't for Kevin beating Fen's ass in the polls and Oth and company backing off, I'd've been called to Washington by now. I'm not going to try to get away with buying any of her stock. You wouldn't happen to know if Knox and the judge signed off on the receivership yet, would you?"

Bryce started. "Oh, right. Yes." He reached into his back pocket and handed Sebastian an envelope. "Knox drew it up and had it signed after Fen started buying shares at the IPO."

Sebastian opened it and read it, then nodded and handed it to Eilis.

"But," Bryce added, "don't worry about HRP. I'll take care of it."

"I'd appreciate that," Sebastian muttered absently, his gaze on the ceiling. "I need to think a while. He's not going to let this go no matter how many ways we put him in check."

"Other than Bryce buying up HRP shares," Eilis said, "I can't see why anybody needs to do anything now but wait. Business as usual."

Sebastian looked at her speculatively, then said, "Except for making ourselves a general pain in his ass, that's true. Next OKH board meeting is a week from Wednesday, nine o'clock."

"Got it."

"I can't wait to see his face when all three of us walk in," Eilis growled, feeling her Inner Bitch come back, and now, perhaps, she would stay.

"Okay, then. Time for us to get going," Giselle said and pulled away from her husband's grasp, wiping her strawberry-sticky fingers on her jeans as she turned. Eilis's eyes widened when, for the first time, she noticed a gun sticking out of her waistband.

"She never leaves home without it," Bryce told her when he noticed the look on her face. "Especially now that she's laid a hand on Trudy."

"Fen'll forgive anything but besmirching Trudy in any way," Sebastian observed.

Giselle looked down and away, her arms crossed over her chest, and Eilis could see the muscle working in her jaw. Eilis studied Giselle, beginning to understand what Sebastian had told her. Ares and the Warrior Queen.

Their power overwhelmed her.

"What happened?" Sebastian asked Bryce quietly.

Bryce shrugged. "Lilly made the announcement and all hell broke loose."

"She had to know that would send Giselle up the tree."

"Well, there's a reason for that," Bryce murmured. "Lilly needed to set something right with Giselle, too."

Eilis looked at Sebastian, who seemed as confused as she.

Giselle sniffled and, at a loving nudge from Bryce, reluctantly began to explain her relationship with Trudy, her cheeks flaming.

Three children. Eilis thought she could never hate one woman so much, nor be so ashamed that that woman had given her birth. Her time in foster care suddenly didn't seem so bad by comparison.

When she finished, Sebastian whispered, "You never told me that."

"I thought you'd tell me to suck it up," she muttered, and Eilis felt Sebastian flinch.

"What did your mother have to do with that?" Eilis asked.

"After Étienne's party, my mom told me— I didn't know—" Giselle gulped and dashed tears away with her fingertips. "When Knox brought me home that day, my mom didn't know what to do. Fen helped her for years after my father died. Trudy didn't know that he helped us at all, much less how much, and Mom knew she couldn't support us on what she made. So she never confronted Trudy. Fen didn't know how cruel Trudy was to me and Mom didn't want to tell him. Mom springing that on me—the tribe—the way she did, knowing what I'd do, was as much her apology to me as it was to punish them for Eilis."

Silence.

The tension, the sadness.

"What was everybody else doing?" Sebastian finally asked.

"Watching," Bryce said, clipped, hard. "Listening. They needed a little dose of reality, in my estimation."

There was a long silence and Eilis snuggled into Sebastian's arms.

"I'm sorry, Eilis," Giselle whispered suddenly without looking at her, her gaze still away and down. Eilis felt her throat clog with sorrow. Bryce wrapped his arms around Giselle and laid his cheek on her head, rocking her gently. "I didn't know how Fen felt about me until about a year ago."

"Giselle," Eilis whispered, "please don't. It's weird for me, too. You can't help how he sees you any more than I can help how he sees me."

She took a deep breath and she looked over at Eilis, and Eilis didn't know how she could have resented this woman for even one second. The pleading and hope in her face was plain, and it *wasn't* her fault. No, Giselle wasn't her sister.

She was the Virgin, Eilis's mother.

68: Un Bel Di

ILIS WENT BACK TO WORK THE NEXT MORNING, TWO WEEKS LATER THAN intended, dreading what she'd find. It had occurred to her in the depths of that dark velvet bed, when Sebastian had one of his rare naps, that she'd just gone through receivership and an IPO successfully, only to let her company go to pot the minute it was done.

On the other hand, she thought with a dreamy smile, it would have been worth every single second spent with Sebastian, being coddled and pampered, laved and loved, seduced over and over again. She had never known that that existed, that people really did that, that sex wasn't a series of nameless, meaningless fucks.

That there were men who gave instead of took.

Eilis . . . I love you. I'll take you any way I can get you.

Oh, yes. *That* was making love.

In reality, though, she could never expect that he wouldn't have other women. She didn't trust that what he said in the heat of the moment would be how he'd feel in a day, a week, a year from now. No man as sensual as that, who loved women that much—Ford—could really believe in or live things like fidelity, monogamy. She wasn't going to presume that he'd even entertain the idea of marriage.

On the other hand . . . *I want to make and raise children with you, Eilis. I want to bind you to me forever.*

She really couldn't think of anything that said "commitment" more than that.

Her heels clacking on the sidewalk, she walked into the building to find the usual hive of activity. She couldn't tell any difference between the collective activity of the one hundred employees she had now versus the two hundred fifty she'd had before

Sebastian had taken a chainsaw to it.

The floor was humming along so nicely, in fact, that she wasn't noticed and that was a first. She looked up when something caught her eye. There were blinds covering the mezzanine's glass walls—and they were drawn!

She climbed the stairs to her office and nodded to her assistant, who was on the phone. Louise gave her a thumbs-up, which surprised her. What really surprised her was the roundtable of six executives gathered in the middle of her office. Karen was giving an informal presentation and Eilis decided to take a seat and watch.

Why had she never noticed Karen's genius, her leadership ability? Well, she amended, why had she not noticed the extent of it? *Because I'd squelched her, that's why.*

Once given the authority to act on her responsibility, she'd blossomed like a hothouse orchid. Sebastian had known this about her. How? *Because he talked to them. He got to know people. He gave them what they needed to succeed.*

She knew where the blinds had come from now, and why. Karen had put them in place, to keep this roundtable together, short, on time. No distractions. It wasn't for the benefit of the employees in Cubicleville. It was for the benefit of the executives.

Finally, Karen's portion of the meeting was over and Sheila stepped up to the plate. Ditto Conrad Fessy. Then Michael! *How* had they gotten him to speak more than two words strung together and in front of people, yet? Eilis looked around her and realized that there was one superfluous person left in her company and it was her.

Somebody passed her the financial report going around the table. She'd caught the tail end of a comment about not making a bunch of copies for people when all they did was throw them away. Things got printed once, passed around the morning roundtable, initialed, then filed for future reference. The digital copies were always available on the server.

Conrad's idea, she was quite sure. He hated waste.

Eilis glanced through it and gulped at the amount of money flowing like whitewater through this company. All of the ad campaigns Karen had launched were working like a dream.

The money coming in from the IPO shares was incredible.

She started when the chair beside her was pulled out and she looked up to see Sebastian there, sitting and leaning back to listen, just as she had. She initialed the report and passed it to him. He looked as somber as usual and a bit of her cheer dimmed when he looked straight at her without a change in expression.

Until he winked at her.

She couldn't help the wave of desire that went through her. The chocolate and the absinthe. The oils and the music. The poetry and the blindfold. The silk stockings and stiletto heels. It had begun all over again after Giselle and Bryce had left last night.

He flipped through the pages, nodding approvingly, then initialed it—right-handed—and passed it on. Her staff never missed a beat. They didn't acknowledge either of them in any way, though everyone was aware of their presence. They had too much work to do to interrupt the flow. Eilis realized that this was a daily routine that must have begun when she went to New York with Sebastian for the IPO.

Her employees were invested now and they acted like it.

The meeting broke up at nine on the dot and everyone scurried to their offices with rushed greetings to her and Sebastian as they scattered. In two minutes flat, the office where she'd spent the last twelve years basically alone was again empty, save her and Sebastian.

Neither spoke until she said, "I think I need to be laid off."

"Eilis, you're in a position most CEOs can only dream about. Enjoy it. Now. I need to talk to you in the conference room, please."

Her heart stopped and her breath caught because she didn't know if she was in trouble. She preceded him in and he locked the door behind him. His face took on a predatory look and she backed up against the table. When he got close enough to touch, she hoisted herself up onto the table. He grabbed the back of her head and brought them together for a hot, hard kiss.

Oh, yes, she was in trouble all right.

"I could fuck you right now," he growled as he climbed up on the table.

"Please do," she whispered, sliding herself back and lying down.

"What about Ford?" he asked once he was on his hands and knees over her.

"Who?"

That made him laugh and they spent an hour in the conference room. Nobody interrupted and Eilis wasn't sure that their presence was even a tickle in anyone's thought process.

"My house or yours?" he whispered to her much, much later after he'd shown Eilis how good hard and fast could actually be. Twice. "I need a bed; my back and my knees are killing me. I'm not getting any younger, you know."

She laughed. "Yours. I love your dungeon."

"My dungeon? You make me sound like I'm the Marquis de Sade."

Eilis made a face. "Eww."

"Yeah, my point exactly. Okay, then. Meet me there; here's a code to the front door."

"What are you going to do?"

He gave her a slow grin. "I have to pick up a few things."

"A few things" meant more fruit. More exotic wines and champagnes. More ice cream. Different oils. Toys.

And a very wide emerald and sapphire choker set into platinum filigree.

She gasped when she opened the black velvet box he gave her once they'd made love hidden away in that incredible bed yet again. Her hand was on her mouth and tears began to well in her eyes as she picked up the exquisite piece with reverence.

Sebastian's gaze was upon her as she studied it, and she turned it over and over, taking in every detail. It called to her; it was familiar. She got out of bed and walked around the room with it, looking at all the canvases that were wet, half finished, fully finished, and then she came to the enormous canvas of her garden and she realized what it was.

The platinum filigree that held the gems was the layout of her garden and the sapphires and emeralds were her flower beds. The clasps were her stone bridge.

She heard him chuckle and say, "I knew you'd figure that out pretty fast."

"You're a genius, Sebastian," she murmured.

"I know. Come back to bed so I can lick you."

They'd finally decided to eat a real meal at a table in an actual dining room and were across from each other at the conference table. Eilis, now an expert in the preparation of the perfect rare steak, exquisitely spiced, cooked while Sebastian went to his office for some documents, which he piled on the table beside his plate.

Once they'd settled in to eat, Eilis took a deep breath and blurted, "I'm not going to tell you about my past, so don't ask."

Then she saw the flinch, the slight twitch of his muscles, the slight glance to the side before he closed his eyes for a microsecond. She sucked in a breath and could say nothing.

He knew. Somehow— No, she knew how he knew and she began to feel a little sick.

"I— Um—" He swallowed. "I wanted you to tell me, but . . . " He trailed off. "I had hoped you would trust me with it."

"It wasn't that I didn't want you to know," she said with a shrug. "Exactly. It was that I didn't want to tell you myself. How much do you know?"

He sighed heavily. "Your foster situations. Your pregnancies. Your poisoning. The abuse. I mean, I have no way to know what I don't know. Eilis, I grew up in the ghetto, same as you, and I never saw anything like that. And that Fen and Trudy—

Why they just didn't hand you over to one of my aunts . . . I don't understand. Do either of them know any of this?"

"No. I've never told anyone until I told Giselle. Everything. Every detail."

Apparently he heard the slight bitterness she couldn't keep out of her voice, because he said, "Now wait a minute. Giselle hasn't said a word of it to me. She *never* betrays confidences."

Eilis blinked and her nausea began to seep away. "Then . . . how—?"

"When you were so quick to jump on the IPO idea after I told you that Knox and I were at war with Fen, I knew you were hiding something from me. I asked Knox to see if he could find a link between OKH and HRP."

"You didn't find it."

"No. But Knox brought over a carton of documents and made me read every last one of them. That's the first time I've ever actually been afraid of him, the way most people who don't know him are afraid of him."

"Why did he do that?"

"He said I needed to know real pain, your pain, the way everybody else experiences it. He says I've never known pain or failure, and I have no mercy, no empathy."

"Oh, Sebastian," she breathed. "I would hope that you *never* feel pain the way other people feel it."

His eyes widened a bit and his fair skin paled. "What do you mean by that?"

Eilis had no idea what was going on but there was a roiling whirlpool inside that big chest of his. She didn't know if there was anything she could say that would fix it, but the only thing she could say was what she thought.

"You make people believe that pain and failure don't exist because for you, it *doesn't*. Because you haven't known pain, it must not exist and so then the people you're with believe that pain—their pain—doesn't exist, either. You infuse people with your passion, your fire, your joy. You give people hope that no cause is ever lost if they look at it the right way. You make people believe in themselves and give people exactly what they need to succeed, without a sense of failure, without a sense of pain."

He stared at her for a long time, then said, low, hoarse, "Knox and Giselle think I need to know pain. They think I did you a great wrong by bringing you here to Ford."

Eilis pursed her lips. "I wouldn't have known that I had fallen in love with you if that hadn't happened," she said quietly, watching him, wanting him to know it was important for both of them that she experience Ford the way Sebastian had made her experience him. "I wanted something that didn't exist and that's what little girls do."

She reached across the table and laid her hand over his, white-knuckled around his fork. "When I'm with you, it doesn't exist. None of it does."

He swallowed. "Knox is mad at me. Giselle hadn't spoken a nice word to me since the night you came to Ford."

"Funny. Didn't seem too mad to me."

He said nothing for a long time, studying her, watching her face. She stared back at him, hoping he would understand that she felt free. "I guess they didn't, did they?"

Eilis smiled at him. "Eat," she murmured. "I have plans for you later."

He burst out laughing then, and did as he was told.

"What's that stack of papers there?"

"Oh!" Sebastian muttered around his bite. He swallowed and leaned across the table toward her. "Were you serious when you said you were bored with your company and wanted something different?"

"Yes. I told you this morning I thought I should be laid off."

"I want you to leave HRP and take over OKH as CEO on Knox's fortieth birthday."

Eilis's mouth opened and her eyes widened. There was a jumbled mess of emotion behind her sternum and she couldn't think.

Joy

Apprehension

Elation

Fear

Sebastian apparently leaped to some conclusion about her feelings, and said quickly, "You don't have to. I think it's a win-win for everybody. You get to take what Fen has. Knox doesn't have to take what he doesn't want. Kenard and I don't have to run what we're not interested in. Knox turns his shares over to us because we've purchased so much of it and goes off and does his thing. You get out of HRP and into something more challenging.

"I'd buy HRP from you or something, I don't know—haven't thought that far ahead. The only thing is that you'll have to rebuild OKH from the ground up."

"Why?"

"For one thing, Kenard and I have managed to sabotage quite a bit of its growth, which we needed to do to drive the stock price down."

"And for a second thing?"

"Because I'm going to finish the job we've started and destroy it."

Her brow wrinkled. This wasn't like him. "Why?" she asked slowly.

"Because Fen has destroyed us. The sacrifices we've made can never be paid back and he needs to know I'm not kidding. He *killed* people. If that means I have to tell him I'm going to raze what he built to get some justice, I will."

Eilis sat back in her chair and looked at him. "OKH is a very successful and well-run company, Fen or not. *Why* would you destroy something like that?"

"I told you. Justice."

"What about all those employees who aren't fluff? Fen doesn't have an ounce of fat in his organization."

Sebastian waved his fork. "Collateral damage."

Something inside Eilis's soul died just then. "Well," she said on a breath. "I just don't know what to say to that."

"What do you think?"

She looked at the table, at the grain of the wood, at the gloss of the finish while she tried to sort out the nastiness inside her. What could she think? She couldn't think at all.

"I—" She gestured with her hands because she had no words.

"Sorry about your having to reinvent the wheel and all."

She put down her fork. "Maybe you do need to learn some empathy after all," she said quietly. His head snapped up just then as she raised her hands to take off the necklace he'd given her and lay it quietly next to her plate.

"Eilis?"

She arose from the table and gathered her things. Somewhere downstairs more of her things littered their—his—Den of Iniquity. Too bad; she'd buy more.

"Eilis, wait. What'd I say?"

"You said 'collateral damage' about thousands of people you'd put out of work to spite one man. Cleaning my house was one thing. Laying off Jep Industries employees to save their pensions—understandable. And creating a way for them to get their jobs back was genius. Razing an entire working organization with thousands of employees for vengeance on one person is—" She searched for the word. "Vile. Immoral. Evil. I don't know. Pick one."

"Eilis, no, wait. I didn't really mean it like that. It's just, that's the only way I've ever thought about it. Maybe I just didn't think far enough ahead, maybe I just stuck my foot in my mouth; I don't know. I've never put people out of work for nothing."

"OKH is a whole different animal to you, Sebastian," she said, on the verge of tears and unable to look at him. "It's a thing; property. It's not a living entity like every other company you've ever salvaged. You're a doctor; doctors don't kill patients they don't like. I hate Fen more than you ever will and I wouldn't do that just to spite Fen."

"No, Eilis, please. I wouldn't really!"

"No, Sebastian. It's too late. That you even thought about putting all those people out of jobs just— I'm— I'm appalled."

She opened the front door.

"Eilis, please! I didn't think about it. I just wanted to destroy Fen. It's the only thing I've thought about for the last seven years whenever I've thought about OKH."

"That's little better," she said softly, having stopped to stand in the threshold.

"Eilis!"

She could hear the desperation in his voice but she didn't know which he was lying about: putting all those people out of work or not, just to get on her good side again.

"I'm not talking about this any more, Sebastian," she said. "I never would have guessed that the Sebastian Taight I've come to know and love, the one who cleaned out my life, would be so heartless as to devastate the lives of so many people."

"*Eilis!* It's not really like that!"

He hopped off the platform to catch her arm, but she pulled away from him and still she couldn't look at him. Her eyes filled with tears and they dropped on the floor as she thought of what she had endured to save her employees' jobs and savings. And to think Sebastian would— On a whim—

"You're lying to me about one or the other. I don't know which," she whispered. "You can 'not really mean' what you very clearly said or you can really mean it. You can't do both and I'm not going to stick around to find out whether you're a liar or a bastard."

She closed the door behind her and ran down the stairs to her car, her tears nearly blinding her. Before she could get in, she heard the most soul-destroying thing she'd ever heard in her life.

Sebastian roared her name and she could hear it outside the concrete walls of his home. The front door opened and she dropped in her car.

She watched him in the rearview mirror as she pulled away from the curb and he ran after her. She sped up, and he pounded the trunk of her car, but he wasn't fast enough.

He dropped to his knees in the middle of the street, holding his head as if it were going to explode and howled to the sky.

"EILIS!"

69: But I Did Not Shoot the Deputy

July 2007

JUSTICE QUIETLY WENT ABOUT HER BUSINESS AS SHE HAD THE TWO WEEKS SINCE her boss had propositioned her, taking calls, making deals. She said nothing about it to anyone, including Richard, but took his advice, setting herself to the task of learning how to be as fine a prosecutor as her colleagues. As each day passed with a string of successfully negotiated deals behind her, she gained confidence and comfort with her job duties and her environment, if not her boss.

As ever, money flowed like water through the office, always fresh, always banded, always in twenties and hundreds. Mr. Hicks must have read the want and need in her face, because he taunted her with a bundle every day until Eric snapped at him to stop.

"She's made her choice. Respect it. If she changes her mind, I'm sure you'll be the first to know."

Richard puzzled her. He had three teenagers, and a sick wife who required chronic and very expensive medication. He needed the money more than anyone else, but he wouldn't take any. Most days he didn't seem to notice it, but occasionally she saw his longing. No one teased him with it, though, so for that, Justice was glad.

But he was proud to be in the Chouteau County prosecutor's office, to work with Knox, to say he had had a hand in Knox's training. He didn't seem to hold Knox's corruption against him, nor did he seem inclined to blow the whistle on him.

Not like it would do any good. As Knox had so succinctly informed her, nothing had ever come of any investigation of the office. He dropped a brown paper bag on Eric's desk at least once a week no matter who was in the office—deputies, troopers, or attorneys not of the prosecutor's office.

Knox's arrogance was mind-boggling.

He hadn't spoken to her or given her one glance askance since that day in his office, except to request the status of whichever case she had that interested him. It was as if nothing ever happened—

—and she resented the *hell* out of that.

Her eyes widened and then closed.

Her deepest feelings, her gut instinct, her body's reaction—couldn't care less who and what Knox Hilliard was. They wanted him anyway, and at home, in bed, in the small hours of the darkness, she indulged her body and refused to acknowledge it in the morning.

She crossed her arms on her desk and dropped her head on them, near tears. No matter what he said or didn't say, what he did or didn't do, he still caught her breath and stopped her heart, made her lower abdomen tingle and caused that wetness between her legs that only happened when—

Stop it. It's wrong. He's a bad man.

She ached in her soul whenever she remembered what she'd thought before she'd walked into that office for an interview. For three years, she'd held an image close to her heart: That magical moment when Professor Hilliard had touched her face and connected with her. She'd built a whole white-picket-fence fantasy around him and now she had to face the reality she had avoided for three years.

Justice laid her hand over her heart to hear the comforting crackle of a ragged, faded, soft, and worn piece of paper she had carried close to her heart for months. The gift Giselle Cox had given her. She didn't have to read it to know what it said.

> *. . . come to it on your own, through hardship and fear*
> *. . . know who you are and what you believe . . . take stock of that every day*
> *. . . walk barefoot through fire on broken glass*
> *. . . stand up to people who frighten you under conditions that terrify you*
> *. . . be honest with yourself about what you really want*
> *. . . be willing to fail*

That day almost a year ago, the day she'd caught Giselle Cox in the restroom of the Jackson County courthouse. She'd known Giselle was in an awful hurry, but Justice couldn't wait another second once she'd finally screwed up enough courage to talk to her and ask her for what she wanted.

And Giselle had given it to her, with kindness and grace. The minute she'd left the room, Justice had written it all down, as fast as she could. She knew she hadn't gotten every word, but she'd done her best.

For the last eight weeks, it had been the only thing she had to hold onto. "I need that," Justice would whisper to herself like an affirmation. "Whatever she's got, I need it." Justice had to take her example of strength and run with it, develop it *somehow*.

But Justice didn't have that kind of strength or courage, and not for the first time, felt envy curl through her at what *she* had that Justice didn't and *still* didn't know how to get. She could gain comfort from Giselle's soliloquy, but she couldn't put it into action.

Nor could she put down her memory of what Knox had done to her that day in his office, how breathless, how hot he'd made her, how hot she grew every time she thought about it. She could only hope that either she didn't telegraph that to the entire Chouteau County jurisprudence system anymore, that everyone was too kind to remark upon it, or that no one noticed or cared. Surely Richard would let her know if she were still doing it . . .

Every day she left the office having lawyered well, she went home and did the manual labor that she'd neglected while going to school and studying. It needed doing and she needed the energy-sapping exertion. Once she'd had all of that she could take, she stayed up late into the night writing articles, answering emails, blogging.

> **darrylm writes:**
> j whatcha up to these days

> **JMcKinley writes:**
> Plugging along at my new job.

> **tropsicle writes:**
> share

> **JMcKinley writes:**
> You know better than that, trops. I never write about my personal life.

> **thefaithful writes:**
> you wrote about law school

So she had and now that she didn't write about her new job, her regulars had gotten suspicious about her well being. She was actually tempted to blog about the Chouteau County prosecutor's office and Knox—without naming names—but Eric did read her and he'd take it straight to Knox and then . . .

Justice shuddered as a chill overtook her.

That had made her laugh for the first time in days.

She sought her solace in sleep now. She *must* be able to fall asleep the minute her head hit the pillow, so she worked harder than she ever had trying to wear herself out.

If she didn't, she'd lie in bed and relive that day in his office over and over again, ashamed that she had felt *such* pleasure. She'd curl up into a little ball to try to crush the feelings that bloomed in her lower belly, to still her hands—unsuccessfully. *What had Knox done to her?*

And in those few moments nearly every night when she tossed and turned, resisting temptation, she heard a little voice in her head: *He wants you. Take him up on it.*

Some nights, the sun couldn't rise fast enough.

Fingers snapped above her head. "McKinley. Earth to McKinley." She looked up to see Eric glaring at her. "Get to work and quit gathering wool."

Justice sighed and made another phone call. She had just hung up when a woman angrily strode into the office like she owned the place, her hair flying out behind her like a flag. She looked neither left nor right and proceeded directly to Knox's office, shoving the door open so hard it banged back against the wall.

"Knox Hilliard, you'd better make it worth my while, dragging my ass up here to this pigsty of a county *today*," she barked. "Do you think I exist to cater to *your* timetable? And by the way, Bryce is pissed as hell at you about this."

It was *her*. Wha—?

Justice, confused, looked around to gauge her coworkers' reaction. A couple of the residents looked as aghast as she felt, but Eric, Mr. Hicks, and Mr. Davidson sat back in their chairs to watch, amused. They tossed wry comments back and forth, making it clear to Justice that this didn't happen very often, but when it did, it was a treat indeed.

That it happened at all blew Justice's mind.

"Good morning to you, too, Giselle," came Knox's voice, heavy with sarcasm and what Justice had come to recognize as extreme irritation. "I see Kenard hasn't managed to put a collar on you yet."

"As if."

"Oh, so you're fair game. Then how about a piece of that fabulous ass up against the wall over there?"

"Pffftt."

"No? Damn."

Eric choked on a laugh. Mr. Davidson and Mr. Hicks cackled. Justice's eyes widened and she thought she'd die.

Older.

"C'mere."

Knox's chair scraped rough on the wood floors and footsteps sounded loud as they came toward the door. Like everyone else, Justice watched his door as if it were an especially riveting movie, so she was surprised when *she* emerged from the office first, followed by Knox, who looked straight at Justice. Then Giselle looked at her, their ice blue eyes eerily similar. Knox waved a hand toward Justice. "There she is. Take her, do whatever."

Justice's eyes got wide and she felt her color drain. Mr. Hicks, Mr. Davidson, the residents all stared at her, amusement gone, as shocked as she. What, exactly, was Giselle Cox supposed to *do* with her?

She watched as the irritation on Giselle's face melted away and she gave Knox a delighted smile. "How long can I keep her?"

Knox grunted and flipped her two fresh bundles of cash. "One week tops." He looked down at Giselle's booted feet, her leathers, then raked his gaze all the way up to her gold hoop earrings. His lip curled and his jaw clenched. "Don't—" He gestured to her clothing. "Just—don't. *He* might like your fetishwear, but— No. Just— No."

Giselle laughed then and he scowled at her before he whirled back into his office, slamming the door behind him.

"AND NO TATTOOS!" His bellow could have been heard through that thick wood door all the way downstairs.

She looked back at Justice, still laughing and wiping tears from her eyes. "C'mon, Justice. Get your stuff and let's go."

She was unable to do anything but what this woman said whether she wanted to or not, whether she now felt deceived or not. She grabbed her purse and briefcase and followed her out of the office, down the hall, and down the stairs. She had trouble keeping up with Giselle, she was so discombobulated and so . . . disillusioned. She didn't think it possible to be more disillusioned than she already was.

Giselle had been her constant or, rather, what she imagined Giselle to be had been her constant and that, too, had been taken away from her with one glimpse at Giselle's obviously intimate relationship with Knox.

Justice stopped suddenly on the stairs when she was confronted by Sheriff Raines, the "pig." Giselle was so much farther down the stairs than Justice that it must have appeared to him that they weren't together.

"Well, well, well," he said, rubbing up against Justice, his—thing—hard and touching her thigh between their clothes. Her heart in her throat, nauseated, she backed up against the wall and she thought she might puke. That wasn't the way it felt when Knox had done that to her. "Where you goin' all in a hurry?"

"I—"

"Knox ain't gonna be happy about you leavin'."

There was a clack in Justice's ear, from below her and the sheriff. "I suggest," said that woman in a terrifying voice Justice had never heard out of her before, "that you get your pathetic excuse of a penis out of her skirt before I blow a hole in your chest."

Sheriff Raines turned and saw her then, on the stair below him. She was leaning against the wall and pointing that gun at his chest.

"Do you know who I am?" he grated.

"Actually, yes. I know exactly who you are. Do you know who I am?"

"I know you're begging to get arrested and nothin' tellin' what could happen to you in *my* jail, pretty girl like you."

Giselle flipped open her cell with one hand while keeping an eye on Raines, punching in two numbers with her thumb. "Yeah. Would you charge me if I shot your sheriff?"

"WHAT?!" The roar, broad, deep, and impatient, louder than his previous bellow, resonated through the halls and, simultaneously, from Giselle's phone. She flipped it closed and smiled sweetly.

Sheriff Raines had gone ashen; whether it was from Giselle's threat to shoot him or Knox's roar, Justice couldn't tell. Footsteps sounded and came closer and closer until Knox was at the top of the staircase, looking down. Justice could see that he deduced pretty much what had happened instantly. He crossed his arms and looked at the sheriff.

"*She*," he said, nodding toward Giselle, "is my right hand. If she shoots you, just consider that I shot you. I don't know exactly what you did, Raines, but you offended *her*, so you offended me. And *she*," he continued, nodding toward Justice, "is my AP. I catch you fucking around with her again, I'll kill you myself." Raines's eyes widened and he gulped. "Get lost."

He did, scrambling down the steps as fast as he could as the three of them watched until he disappeared from sight. Knox turned and strode away from them. "Arm her, too," he threw over his shoulder as he disappeared back into his office.

Giselle stuck her gun in the back of her waistband and looked up at Justice, her face softening into a smile. "I don't think you'll have to worry about him anymore."

70: Some Other Woman's Shoes

JUSTICE'S NERVES, ALREADY STRUNG TAUT, WERE NOT SOOTHED IN GISELLE'S presence. She didn't make small talk and she seemed a thousand miles away, but once they were in her low-slung BMW and on the way, Justice couldn't contain her curiosity. "You— Knox— I thought— You *know* him?"

Are you his lover?

Giselle smiled. "He's my cousin. We grew up together."

Justice blinked, unable to process that completely. She couldn't imagine Knox as a baby, a boy, a young man, or anything other than what he was now. She couldn't imagine that the woman she knew as his bitter enemy was his friend, his family.

Justice felt utterly helpless, her image of Giselle Cox having been betrayed by the fact of her association with Knox, her willingness to do what Knox said. If nothing else, she had needed Giselle's example to get through each day, and now . . .

She is my right hand.

"What are you going to do with me?" Justice whispered.

Giselle shifted gears, looked over her shoulder to change lanes, and proceeded to zip around the southbound traffic. She drove like a demon just released from hell, though she sat relaxed in the seat, with one hand on the gear shift and the fingers of her other hand lightly draping the steering wheel.

"I," she said, "am going to pull a Pygmalion on you. You're a beautiful girl, make no mistake. However, if this dress is anything to go by, your wardrobe came straight out of Sunday school, circa 1983. There's nothing wrong with it, really, but it's not appropriate for court. You look sixteen."

Justice gaped at her. A *makeover?* Perhaps she'd rather be shot dead. That wouldn't have hurt as badly as knowing Knox thought she needed a *makeover*. She thought she might cry, but Giselle reached her hand out and touched the clenched fist Justice held stiffly on her knee.

"Enjoy yourself, Justice."

"I'm not interested in a makeover. I just want him to let me go. I want to get away from him. *Please* help me."

"Oh, Justice," she murmured, and withdrew her hand to shift again. Her humor had vanished and she seemed . . . sad. A bit. But Justice didn't know why that would be. "You don't get away from Knox. Nobody does. He's a tornado and everybody who comes in contact with him gets sucked in. Don't get discouraged and don't show your fear. Trust me. I promise you, there will come a day when all this will have been worth it and you'll be glad you persevered."

Justice swallowed at the odd answer. There was so much more going on under the surface and she didn't trust this woman anymore.

"I don't—" Justice hesitated because she figured her pleading would be in vain, would more than likely get her in trouble with Knox, but she couldn't not ask. "I don't want to be there."

Giselle looked over at her, her sorrow seeming to deepen. Justice had never met anyone she could read so well, but then, it might all be an act. She took a deep breath and said, "Give it one more week, Justice. Just one week from the time I take you back home. Can you do that?"

Was this a promise of rescue? Could Giselle possibly be powerful enough to forestall—

"He threatened to kill me if I left. I'm really scared."

Giselle sucked in a sharp, deep breath and looked out the window. "I'm sorry."

"Would he really do that?" she whispered.

"Well," she said finally, "he's not going to kill you to*day*. Or any time this week. He just sent you on a week-long all-expenses-paid vacation, my dear, and our first stop is the spa."

Justice's head spun. Knox—the *same* Knox—had sent her with this woman so she could go to a spa? "I— I don't understand," she whispered.

Giselle chuckled. "Yeah, that's a common reaction when it involves Knox. He plays his cards close to the vest and makes no sense most of the time."

"That's why you took that money? To buy me clothes?"

"Yes."

Appalled and outraged that she would be wearing the dirty money it took her so much to resist, Justice said, "Do you *know* where that money comes from?"

"Yes," she replied immediately, this time with a bit of a steel edge. "I know *exactly* where that money comes from."

That was not the answer Justice expected and she blinked, but she dare not ask the next logical question. Yes, Giselle *was* easy to read, but that served the same function as the rattle at the end of a snake's tail.

"Justice," Giselle said with purpose, "my goal is to help you be as comfortable in real life as you are online."

Justice started. Swallowed.

"Being comfortable with who you are when you're behind a computer and being lauded and paid for your opinions, and courted by prestigious institutions where you could hide away and write? Not the same as being comfortable in your own skin. Being comfortable in your own skin *no matter where you are or what you're doing* and knowing what you want are the first and most crucial steps to power.

"You have opportunities that most women your age would kill for and yet— You're an AP in a backwater county on the outskirts of Cowtown. Why? Is what you wanted in any way similar to the reality?"

"No," Justice murmured, ashamed that Giselle Cox thought she was hiding away from the world.

"Do you really know what you want?"

"I did, once."

"I'm guessing that didn't work out for you."

"No."

"Perhaps you should think about what you want now. Take some time to think about what you've learned in that office." She paused. "You asked me to teach you to be powerful and I told you I couldn't do that."

Justice nodded.

"Knox can and he will if you let him. If you choose to stay with him, he'll teach you everything you ever wanted to know about power."

"I didn't choose to stay," she snapped. "I can't choose to leave."

Giselle made no reply and the silence went on, as she had apparently said all she wanted to say. As usual, Justice felt the silence uneasily.

Though the minute she began to get comfortable with it, Giselle spoke again suddenly, and Justice jumped. "Do you know anything about guns?"

"Rifles and shotguns, not handguns."

"Knox wants you to start carrying a weapon. Of course, if you turn it on him," she said, her voice suddenly hard and cold like iced marble, "I'll make sure that's the *last* thing you ever do. However," she went on, back to her usual humor, "you need to carry a weapon like everyone else in that office. Knox can't protect you from Raines every minute of every day. You're in the roughest part of Chouteau County now and he wants to keep you safe."

Justice's head spun. "Safe?" she squeaked. "Who's going to keep me safe from *him?*"

Giselle slid her a glance and said softly, "You may enjoy not being safe from him, Justice."

. . . *how about a piece of that fabulous ass up against the wall over there?*

Justice thought her chest had been kicked in. "You and, and—"

"Oh, heavens no," she said. "We weren't meant for each other."

Which simply confused Justice even more.

"You'll be our house guest for the next week, my husband and me, I mean. I'm going to teach you how to dress and how to walk and how to present yourself to a jury. Henry Higgins had six months to turn a Cockney flower girl into Hungarian royalty, but I don't have to teach you diction or proper manners. Well, I don't know about the manners. We'll go somewhere and try you out. This is the part of power I *can* teach you, Justice. Women don't just get power from character. We get it from beauty and presentation."

"That's manipulative," Justice sniffed, looking out the window.

Giselle chuckled. "You could look at it that way, yes, but consider this: When you *know* you look fabulous, you'll feel powerful and then people will assume that you are. They will give you respect and then that will in turn feed your power. It's a cycle. And besides," she added, "why would you want to look a week-long shopping spree in the mouth?"

Well, truly, Justice did want to relax and enjoy herself, but couldn't bring herself to that. Knox would be livid if he knew she was having fun. Giselle promptly disabused her of the notion.

"Believe me, he doesn't care how it happens. All he cares about are results. Your having fun or not having fun doesn't even register with him."

Finally they reached a high-end spa on the Plaza. For the rest of the morning, Justice was massaged, mudded, oiled, lotioned, exfoliated, manicured, pedicured, and generally pampered. Once the strangeness of being nude in public—or pretty close to it—and being cared for as if she were a baby wore off, she relaxed and enjoyed it.

"Hair is next."

"But—I like my hair."

"Needs a more flattering cut."

Justice was silent because Giselle's statement was final and if Giselle was offended, Knox was offended. The last thing Justice wanted was to offend Knox.

It took a while to cut Justice's hair once her waist-length braid had been unceremoniously cut at the midpoint of her shoulder blades, then packaged up to be sent to Locks of Love at Giselle's behest. That done, she instructed the hairdresser in a tone that brooked no argument,

"You will not color, straighten, curl, or otherwise chemically alter her hair. Take out all that bulk, cut it so it flatters her face, and for crying out loud, give her a hot oil treatment or three and a good shampoo."

When he turned Justice around an hour later to look at herself, she gaped.

Her hair was short but very full, very shaped, and didn't look as short as it felt. Where before was frizz, frizz, and more frizz, there were fairly large, smooth, sleek curls all over her head that bounced. It was long enough in the back to barely brush her collar, then it curved softly up around her face. Where before was a dark red mahogany was a burnished red-copper that gleamed. She would have never suspected that her hair could look like that, that *she* could look like that.

Justice wondered how she could have gone her whole life without thinking to do this herself, never mind that she'd never had the money to do it or maintain it.

"Makeup."

The cosmetologist and Giselle were giddy with the abundance and rich copper color of the freckles on her cheeks and over her nose, but Justice was mortified.

"You can't be serious," she said when they both agreed that she should never, ever cover those up ever again. But Giselle would have her way and Justice knew it would be pointless to argue—

—but when she saw the finished product, she couldn't stop staring at herself. "That's me?" she whispered.

Giselle swung down and got in her face, a wide grin on her face. "Yes! Aren't you gorgeous?"

Yes, that girl in the mirror was gorgeous. Justice didn't know that girl.

"Lingerie."

Justice thought she would die of embarrassment at the things she picked out.

"Justice," Giselle finally said, frustrated, "you cannot wear cotton granny panties for the rest of your life. No matter how good you look on the outside, cotton granny panties will kill your confidence every time. It's just not—" She looked for the right word. "It's just not *done*." She shuddered.

"Tomorrow, clothes," Giselle said as they dropped into her car, bags of shampoos and conditioners and oils and lotions and lingerie having been dumped in the trunk. "I'll loan you something to wear tomorrow. Tonight, you get to sleep without dreading working for Knox in the morning."

Justice shifted uncomfortably, because she still wasn't sure that everything she said wouldn't get back to Knox. Giselle laughed. "Knox is a bastard. I sure wouldn't work for him."

Giselle lived in a beautiful house, pale yellow, white trim, with an iridescent green barrel-tile roof and three gables. She parked in the back and they walked up flagstone stairs onto a deep covered veranda that spanned the width of the house.

"This is beautiful," Justice whispered, looking at the stonework that defined flower beds in front of the porch. She could only dream about living in a house like this.

"My husband built the flower beds. He likes to play in the mud on the weekends."

Once inside, the entire expanse on Justice's left was open, front to back. Three different areas were delineated by rugs and furniture placement. Closest to the back was a desk. In the middle was a grouping of leather sofas, club chairs, and a coffee table in front of a fireplace over which was a TV no thicker than a painting. At the front of the house was a black grand piano.

But the most wonderful thing about that room was the fact that the entire wall, save the fireplace and the TV, was covered in floor-to-ceiling bookcases filled with books of all types. The ceiling was twelve feet high and so there was a ladder and track to reach the higher books. There wasn't one spot of blank wall or shelf that could be seen, and Justice stood and stared in awe.

"Pick anything you want," Giselle said as she bustled by to dump some of Justice's bags on the stairwell landing. "Bryce will be home in a bit and I asked him to pick up dinner. I guarantee it'll be Greek."

I see Kenard hasn't managed to put a collar on you yet.

Justice shot a look at Giselle, unable to believe what she thought she just heard.

"Bryce? As in, Bryce Kenard?"

Giselle released a resigned chuckle. "Oh, please don't tell me you're a groupie too."

"Yes! How—? He's all anybody talks about at school."

"Tell me about it."

"You can't have told anybody. You didn't have people hanging off of you all the time."

Giselle burst out laughing then. "Nobody knew I'm related to Knox, either, did they?"

Justice released a breath, unable to hide the stars in her eyes now. Bryce Kenard. Never in a million years had she thought she'd ever encounter him.

"Well, don't have an orgasm, Justice," Giselle said wryly. "He'll be home in a bit and you can fawn all over him in person. But come upstairs for a minute. I'll loan you some clothes and a robe. I want you to take that dress off right now because it needs burned."

Justice's mouth dropped open, stunned out of her delight. "Burned?" she squeaked. "This is my favorite dress!"

"You'll get a new favorite tomorrow."

"No! I worked hard to buy this dress!"

"Fine. I'll get it framed. Hand it over."

"I will NOT!"

"Oh, leave her alone, Giselle," came a deep hoarse voice from the archway to the kitchen. "How would you like it if someone took your favorite dress away from you and burned it just because they didn't like it?"

Justice gasped and her hand went to her mouth at the sight of the man in the doorway, his head down as he sifted through mail. He was badly disfigured, the entire left side of his face matted with scars, as was his left hand. And he was huge, bigger than Knox. She took a step back from him, but he'd turned and set the mail on the kitchen island, walking out of sight while taking off his coat and tie.

This was Bryce Kenard?

She'd never had to do a class assignment on him, but she'd heard enough lectures, enough stories, to know his name and respect his genius. No one had *ever* mentioned this.

Justice knew Giselle hadn't missed her reaction to her husband and also knew she had every right to be offended at her. She sighed and turned to Giselle. "I'm so sorry," she murmured. "That wasn't kind of me."

"You're right," Giselle agreed readily, but without anger. "Lesson number one: Don't let appearances deceive you—good or bad. You miss getting to know a lot of good people that way."

"Lesson number two," called that gravelly voice from the kitchen, though she couldn't see him. "Never, ever let people know your first impression, good or bad."

"Especially since he just saved your dress for you," Giselle muttered, that undertone of humor back in her voice. "Come on. Let's go eat."

And as Justice turned, she caught a glimpse of a very large painting over the staircase and she sucked up a breath, her mouth opening slowly as she looked up, up, up.

Her eyes wide, she studied it. She knew Giselle was watching her, but she didn't care. Her hostess was laid out nude on a bed, strapped to it, but that wasn't what got her. What got her was the symbolism of the locks and the keys and the books.

She put her hand to her mouth and she could feel tears begin to roll down her face. "Oh," she whispered. "Oh." Justice swallowed. "Oh my. You— It *didn't* come easy to you."

Giselle went to her and hugged her. "No, it didn't," she murmured and led her to the table where dinner awaited. "It still doesn't."

71: What a Girl Wants

JUSTICE SAT UP IN THE MOST LUXURIOUS BED SHE HAD EVER SEEN, MUCH LESS slept in, reading a Georgette Heyer novel Giselle had given her.

"Why don't you give her *Sleeping Beauty*, Giselle?" Mr. Kenard had drawled slyly, which, to Justice's astonishment and delight, made Giselle choke on her food and blush furiously.

"The fairy tale?" Justice had asked doubtfully.

"Anne Rice's interpretation," Mr. Kenard offered helpfully, almost eagerly. "Google it."

"No, don't," Giselle muttered.

Justice watched her in astonishment, never having seen her flustered before this evening, which Mr. Kenard seemed to do with ease and great regularity. As soon as she got to her room that night, she pulled out a piece of paper and wrote, "*Sleeping Beauty*, Anne Rice."

Justice didn't feel like cracking her laptop open; she simply wanted to enjoy this sudden and welcome break from the blogs, the writing, the constant analytical thinking. She was a warmly welcomed guest in a beautiful home that she imagined could only be superior to the best hotel in the world, a large library at her disposal, no work, no school, no farm chores.

When she'd called her father to tell him she was staying with a friend for a week, she'd expected to be given the silent treatment at best and a good drubbing at worst. Instead, he'd said simply, "Okay."

That was suspicious.

But she'd forgotten it as they ate and then the evening deepened. The three of them sat around the table for hours talking about politics and constitutional theory, both as interested in her opinion as she was in theirs. The subject of Kevin Oakley appeared to be off limits, though, which disconcerted Justice to no small degree.

She didn't dare ask how Mr. Kenard had gotten his scars, though she could see now that they were burns. She felt so very sad and regretful that she had had a bad initial reaction to him, that she had been so rude. It made her feel small and undignified.

"In the interest of full disclosure," he'd told her wryly, his voice rough, "Giselle breaks a lot of her own rules. I knew exactly what she thought the first time she looked at me because she *wanted* me to know what that was."

Giselle laughed. "It's a little different when you take one look at a man and all you can think about is what it'd be like to be on top of him."

Justice could feel the red creeping up her cheeks. Mr. Kenard chuckled and patted her on the back.

She took the liberty of staying up late just to read for pleasure, because that itself was such a luxury. She was in heaven and—

Knox had done this for her.

The thought sobered her.

Why? Giselle was his cousin; didn't he know what would happen? Had he meant for her to be here having fun, being pampered and cosseted by two of the nicest people she had ever met?

Troubled, she had a hard time getting back into her book. At midnight, she went downstairs to raid the fridge of some blueberries she'd seen there—Giselle had told her she was welcome to anything—poured some cream and sugar over them, and took them back to her room.

As she passed the master bedroom door, she heard a series of long, low moans that startled her and she stopped, unable to not listen. She heard a sharp gasp, a giggle, and then a low, grainy chuckle.

Low voices talking. More laughter, more gasps and moans.

"Ares." It was only a whisper, heavy and dripping with desire. "Do that again."

"Say, 'Please do that again, Ares.'"

"Oh, *please* do that again, Ares."

Justice closed her eyes and swallowed. She swayed, thinking of that day in Knox's office. She knew. For the first time in her life, she had felt real passion, real desire. It was nothing like she had read or imagined. She wanted what the Kenards had, but she didn't know how that would happen or even if it would.

Then Justice's eyes popped open and she blushed, deeply embarrassed for having eavesdropped on something so intimate. She scurried back to her room and sat down on the bed, confused, and feeling very, very young.

When had she turned into such a stupid, *stupid* girl? She lay down and curled up, closing her eyes to relive that day in Knox's office when he'd seduced her.

She wasn't ashamed for wanting what the Kenards had, but only a fool would still want it from *Knox Hilliard* after everything he had done to her.

"Today, guns," Giselle pronounced three days later, once Justice had arisen and gotten ready for the day in a pair of Giselle's jeans that fit more like capris, and a tee shirt that stretched a little too tight across the chest and revealed more of her midriff than she liked. "You can just wear my regular clothes until you get home."

Giselle hadn't bothered with such things because every girl had sixteen dozen pairs of jeans and a billion tee shirts, she said.

"The reason Knox wants *me* to do this," she pronounced on the way to the shooting range, "is because he doesn't trust your sheriff up there not to give you defective equipment, which would likely get you killed. Either it won't fire when you need it to or it'll misfire and kill you. And he probably doesn't want you anywhere near that shooting range. He'll take you shooting somewhere else later."

He would? Justice gulped with both dread and tingling anticipation.

Justice proved to be a better marksman than Giselle had hoped and Justice allowed herself to be proud.

"Unfortunately," Giselle said, "I can't teach you anything about hand-to-hand in four days. I don't buy into those short-course women's defense seminars because they just give women a false sense of security. In my opinion, they do more harm than good. It took me four years of martial arts for me to get half as good as I felt I should be. So that's why I carry a gun. No fuss, no muss, and people get the point."

"Why do you carry a gun at all?" Justice asked.

"Oh, it's just one of those things," Giselle said airily, meaning she wasn't going to tell her. Just like Kevin Oakley. "A thigh holster isn't going to help you if you're wearing a dress, so we'll get you the standard shoulder holster the men wear. You need to wear one or the other at all times along with your badge, except when you're in court, just like the men do."

Justice had three days at the range, which was equal to the time it took to get a new wardrobe. In that time, she got really good at drawing from both holsters, shooting with two standard grips, shooting with one hand, and with her hand turned over in what Giselle called "gangsta grip."

"Don't use that if you can help it. It's unstable and inaccurate as hell, but it's very intimidating because of its gang association. Now, let's do it all over again, only with your left hand this time."

"But—"

"You have no idea how important it is to be able to be as good with your non-dominant hand as your dominant one—and both at the same time. Trust me."

It was in the car on the way back to Giselle's home that Justice put her foot in her mouth.

"Have you ever used a gun?"

Giselle pursed her lips. "Be more specific."

"Have you ever used one on someone?"

There was a long silence. Then Giselle drew in a deep breath and looked away from her, out the window. Suddenly, Justice understood. "Oh, I'm sorry. Never mind."

But by the time they parked in the driveway late that evening, Giselle had begun lecturing again as they walked into the house, like nothing had happened.

"You never draw a gun on someone unless you're prepared to shoot them, but—as Bryce so kindly pointed out—I break a lot of my own rules. I do attempt to aim for something nonessential to life."

"If you consider the head nonessential," Mr. Kenard called from somewhere in the house and Giselle laughed delightedly.

Justice spent the rest of her time there feeling as if she were being prepared for something. There was something going on that ran much, much deeper than her having shown up at the courthouse for an interview one day and witnessing a shooting. Justice knew she was in over her head and had no idea how she'd gotten there.

The deafeningly silent answer Giselle had given her probably shouldn't have shocked her so much. Giselle was Knox's "right hand."

Justice had already seen what Knox's left hand could do.

72: Living in a Fisheye Lens

S HE CLEANS UP NICE," MR. KENARD COMMENTED, POPPING A HANDFUL OF nuts into his mouth as Giselle put the finishing touches on Justice to go to the symphony the last night she would be with the Kenards.

"Yeah, she does," Giselle commented absently, fiddling with Justice's hair and some very nice costume earrings. "Pretty sure Knox doesn't want me buying you pearls and emeralds straight out of the gate," she'd said earlier that day when they'd passed by Tivol.

Justice didn't say anything. After almost a week of trying on and buying tons of clothes and shoes, learning how to wear them and walk in them, how to hold her head and sit and cross her legs, how to apply makeup and fix her hair, Giselle had declared her a quick learner and said they'd go out.

"You don't really have a need for a formal evening gown," Giselle had told her, "but every woman needs at least one—if only to make herself feel better. That, a semiformal dress, and a couple of cocktail dresses ought to be sufficient.

"I'm not sure Knox would consider pants appropriate for the courtroom, so we're only going to get a couple pairs. I think that pants in the courtroom diminish a woman's power but then, Knox doesn't like my leathers, so what do I know? If I had legs like yours, I wouldn't hide them in pants. Okay, let's go."

At the Lyric Theater, there was a good mix of people milling about in the lobby and gathering at their seats in various dress, from jeans and tee shirts to formal. She noted that the people in jeans sat way up in the back and the people in formal wear sat down in the front, center.

Mr. Kenard had offered Justice his left arm and held hands with Giselle on his right. Justice garnered many looks that night, which made her anxious not because she was getting them, but because they were entirely different from the looks she'd always garnered. Men looked at her appreciatively and women looked at her resentfully. Giselle got the same attention, but seemed oblivious to it—as always.

Then Mr. Kenard spoke to her, low. "Don't let on that you see people looking at us. I'm a very ugly man with two very beautiful women, so people are going to stare. If you were here alone, they'd stare anyway. It's just part of being a beautiful woman. You need to understand that you are one and get used to the attention. Stand up straight and walk like you own the world—because at this moment, you do."

"Does Giselle—?"

"Oh, believe me, she knows *exactly* what's going on. And she doesn't care."

Justice wore a short-sleeved cheongsam made from an iridescent green silk that looked black when it lay a certain way. "It's woven with two colors," Giselle told her. "The warp is green; the weft is black. The silk itself has a sheen, so when it's all put together, it shimmers."

It had black piping and frogs and stopped just below her knees and looked like it was a lot tighter than it really was. It fit well, emphasizing her long legs and what Giselle called her "hourglass figure." Her copper hair emphasized the green sheen of her dress while the green sheen of her dress exaggerated her hair color and her freckles to outlandish proportions. Her hair was not specially dressed.

"Your freckles dance and your curls bounce when you walk. It's *very* dramatic." Justice wasn't a dramatic person, so she was uncomfortable with this and she *still* wasn't happy about the freckles. Her legs were wrapped in almost-nude nylons and her feet were shod in black heels.

"... in until lights down."

"... be so stupid. You see fin anywhere?"

"No."

"Are we done cleaning up his messes?"

"Do we have to talk about this right now?"

Justice only caught bits and pieces of Mr. and Mrs. Kenard's low conversation, but it meant nothing to her.

Mr. Kenard and Giselle took their seats, leaving Justice on the end, with one empty seat between her and the aisle. Once the lights dimmed and the emcee had begun to speak, she felt the seat next to her shift and depress. She looked up and gasped.

"Justice," Knox murmured as he inspected her from head to toe, but it was dark so she wasn't sure how he could tell anything about anything. "I guess you'll do."

Anger exploded in her chest and she sucked in an angry breath. She'd *do*?

He smirked at her, then settled back in his seat to listen to the orchestra while she fumed. She couldn't even enjoy it because of him—and she'd only had time during law school to go to one symphony concert.

Gradually, though, she relaxed when Knox did nothing. He shifted every so often, but other than that, he didn't talk to her, didn't touch her except when they brushed at the arms a few times. Yet at the moment she'd decided to let her guard down and enjoy the rest of the program, his arm stretched across her shoulders and he began to play with her curls.

She gasped and shot him a look, and he looked straight back with a calculating but endearing smile, daring her to say anything.

Justice gulped and decided there were worse things than having one's hair played with by a devastatingly handsome blond man in a black suit—and he never wore dark suits at work—at the symphony.

Though she refused to look at him if she could help it, she did feel every twist of his fingers, every touch of his thumb brushing her ear.

Gradually, she got used to the feeling of the warmth of his body next to hers, his hand in her hair, the occasional touch of his shoulder to hers, the feel of his thigh next to hers when he moved his long legs to a more comfortable position. She didn't even get angry with herself for resting her elbow on the arm they shared and leaning (just a little) toward him. This—this was what she had fantasized about oh, so way back, when she was still a law student.

Suddenly she felt fingers on her chin. Surprised, she looked at him and found herself caught in a kiss that took her breath away.

Knox's tongue swept into her mouth and she thought she was falling off a cliff. Her belly turned and churned. That empty spot between her legs was suddenly wet and she tingled all over.

Who was this man beside her tonight? Was he the same man who'd calmly put the gun on the desk to let her know she wasn't leaving? Was this the same man who'd not-so-forcibly nuzzled her in his office that day? Was this the same man who, except from that moment in time to now, had ignored her completely?

The kiss went on and on, and Justice thought she might cry with the sheer beauty of it.

Then he wasn't there anymore.

The lights came up to reveal an empty seat. She was left flushed, her mouth wet, her heart thundering in her chest, and bereft.

Lost.

Alone.

She missed him. Inexplicably. She touched the cushion that was still warm and felt a tear slide down her cheek.

73: Not Your Daddy's Shotgun

JUSTICE WALKED INTO THE COURTHOUSE MONDAY IN ONE OF HER NEW OUTFITS, turning every head as she went. She wondered if it was because she was pretty now, because they didn't recognize her, or because she looked *so* different. She did *not* like all this attention, and she didn't care what Mr. Kenard said.

She tried to walk the way Giselle had taught her, with a slight swivel to her hips—not too much as it would be trashy and not too little because it wouldn't be noticed. The high heels helped with that because she had to walk that way just to balance on the darned things.

On the other hand, the leather shoulder holster complete with Glock under her left elbow, and the badge attached to her holster did take quite a bit of "gorgeous" edge off the outfit, for which she was grateful.

Looking in the mirror that morning, with no Giselle there to fuss and pick over details, she had been struck nearly dumb with this new person who looked back at her from the glass. That girl—woman—*was* beautiful and that was one thing Justice had *never* been. Her father had looked at her in a way she didn't understand, but left her vaguely uncomfortable.

"I don't know where you got the money for those clothes, Justice," he said gruffly, "but you better not have gotten it from the farm account."

He didn't really seem interested in the money, though, and she'd left as quickly as she could.

The dress was almost straight, plain, lightly tailored; it had short sleeves and a square neckline that dipped a little too low for her comfort. The hem was too short in her estimation, but Giselle had assured her that, as it stopped only an inch or two above her knees, it was a proper length for court and, if pressed, could do double duty for a cocktail party if she didn't have time to change.

A harvest gold color, it nearly disappeared, giving her the illusion of nothing between her face and her feet. Her red-copper hair overwhelmed the color, but in turn, it made her freckles pop and her hazel eyes glimmer amber the way Giselle wanted them to. She still didn't like deliberately emphasizing her freckles when she'd spent her entire life trying to fade them and hide them, but Giselle said it made her unique and memorable. It would make people focus above her neck, she said, which was a good thing to dress her body down and her face up.

Her sandals matched her hair. It was just enough color to contrast, Giselle told her, but not too much.

"The essence of pulling all this off," Giselle said, "is knowing what's just right. It's subtle and very tricky. You'll get better with practice."

So here Justice had arrived at the courthouse, hoping she wasn't too much and wasn't too little, trying to remember how to walk in high heels, thinking everyone would laugh at her, and desperately trying not to think about the scandalous (albeit lovely and sensuous) lingerie she wore underneath it all. Giselle had threatened to tell Knox to check her for cotton granny panties if she didn't promise to wear her new things and Justice had no doubt she would follow through with that.

She dreaded Knox's reaction. Not that he would hate it—oh, no, but his "you'll do" at the symphony was a slap in the face. On the other hand, she trembled every time she thought about his hand in her hair and his smile at her.

And his kiss.

She just didn't know how she was going to deal with this, looking at him, knowing he wanted her, that her three-year fantasy didn't have to remain one.

As she climbed the steps with no incident, she gathered her courage in a steam and walked into the office, hoping to approximate a slow version of how Giselle had stormed into it.

Everything came to a halt before she'd taken three steps in and because it did, so did she. Uncertain and very nervous, she looked around at her coworkers, who looked at her in shock.

"Davidson!" came a shout through the door of Knox's office and he jerked the door open, looking down at a file, and stepping through. He glanced up to look for Davidson and he stopped dead in his tracks when he saw her there, standing right in front of him in the middle of the room.

His jaw dropped. His eyes widened. His nostrils flared. Justice felt sick. "What the hell did she do to you?" he barked after he'd collected himself. "I have a good mind to send you home to get something decent on. Get in my office. NOW!"

Trembling, unable to squelch her fear and forgetting everything Giselle had ever said to her, she did as she was told without a word and he stepped aside to let her.

She had to wait a few minutes for him to finish his business with Davidson and when he had, he returned, that angry scowl still on his face. She closed her eyes and gulped. What *had* Giselle done to her?

The door slammed and she flinched, but she didn't open her eyes until she felt Knox's hand on her chin, forcing her head up—and he kissed her.

It wasn't a nice, sweet kiss like the one at the symphony, oh no. It was firm, demanding, and way too much for her limited experience with men—well, limited solely to Knox, that was. He didn't touch her other than for his hand on her chin and the kiss that she was falling into, her libido picking up where it had left off the night before last.

She sucked in a breath, her body strung as tight as a violin string.

He drew away from her and she opened her eyes, but didn't look at him because he had been so angry earlier. She didn't understand what any of this meant. Her head was a jumbled mess.

"Congratulations." She gasped at his cruel tone. She looked up at him and his face was hard, cold. "You're getting married today."

"What?" she whispered, confused.

"You and I are getting married today. Judge Wilson's on his way up the back." He slapped the files he had in his hand on the desk, one single paper on top wafting in its own breeze. He pointed to it. "Sign it. That's the license."

"What— I don't understand. Are you serious?"

"I'm dead serious," he snarled.

She had indeed slipped down the rabbit hole and Knox was the Mad Hatter.

"I don't have to marry you. You can't make me."

He cocked an eyebrow. "No?"

"No."

He turned and sifted through the same files, then pulled out a professionally taken zoom shot of her father going about on the farm. "Look at that, Justice. Imagine it with cross hairs."

She sucked in a breath. "You wouldn't," she whispered, dread clutching at her throat.

He leaned toward her, his face hard. "Do you want to try me?"

"Why?" she whispered, choking on a sob. "Why me?"

"What's it gonna be, Justice? Marriage or a dead dad?"

She swallowed and said nothing.

"Marriage it is, then," he said, and stood over her while she signed the license. He picked it up, stared at it, then looked at her. "What is that?" he barked, pointing to her signature.

"My name," she whispered. "My name is Iustitia."

"Is it on your paperwork like that?"

"Yes."

After staring at her for one more moment, he went to the door and threw it open. "Cipriani. Connelly. Davidson. I need you."

The three of them came into Knox's office and closed the door. She looked around her. They actually seemed to know what was going on and their attendance had been anticipated.

"Justice," Knox said, low, "you are to speak of this to no one. Do you understand me?"

She gulped. "Yes," she whispered.

Judge Wilson came in quietly through another door in the back of Knox's office. He said the minimum he felt he needed to. Eric and Richard signed the certificate with alacrity and seemed to know, but not care, that she was doing this under duress. Judge Wilson took the file with him. He nodded grimly at Knox and left the way he came.

"Everybody back to work," Knox barked when the evidence was gone, and he turned his back on her. "You too, Iustitia," he said, sarcasm dripping from his tongue after Richard, Patrick, and Eric had closed the door behind them.

She felt like she'd been run over a truck, but she determined that she would not cry. What would Giselle do? she asked herself, and she stood up tall, all five-feet-ten-in-heels of her and she stared at him until he looked up at her to see why she hadn't gone yet. They stared at each other for a long moment, then Justice gathered herself and spat in his face.

His eyes glittered as he stared at her, wiping her spittle from his face without saying a word. That was much more frightening than anything he could've said and she gulped.

Finally he bent down to write something on the back of his business card. He stood then and walked toward her. She trembled in fear, but refused to back up when he got within a centimeter of her, their noses nearly touching.

He pulled at the neckline of her dress and slid the business card unerringly into her lacy, almost nonexistent, bra, staring into her eyes the entire time. "That's your new address," he said, his voice filled with things she didn't understand. "I'm going to send you back to your farm and you're going to change into something a little less— Blatant. Once you've done that, pack your things and take them to that address and make yourself at home. Be back by one o'clock, because I want you in the courtroom."

"I hate you," she murmured, her voice steady in spite of her fear, which gave her some more badly needed confidence.

"Uh huh. I can tell by the way you kiss."

Her nostrils flared and her eyes narrowed.

"You slap me, Iustitia—" *Why* was he calling her that? "—and you'll regret it, I guarantee it. I need a child from you and I need it by Christmas of next year. You do that and on New Year's Day, we'll call it square. You only have to put up with me for a year and a half."

Could it get any worse? She couldn't decide if she wanted to be angry or confused. "A child? What will you do with it after you get it?"

"Keep it, naturally."

"I would not abandon my child to you."

"Then you're welcome to stay with me, too."

"How are you going to get this child if I don't let you—"

He stepped as close to her as he could, his body touching hers, because she wouldn't back down.

What would Giselle do what.would.Giselle.do.*whatwouldgiselledo?!*

"Not only will you let me," he whispered, barely touching his mouth to hers, his eyes open, "you'll be begging me. I know how you respond to me and I'm going to take every advantage of it." His lips on hers were light, butterfly kisses, gentle. He caught her bottom lip and touched his tongue to it and she gasped because she was letting him do this to her and she did like it and she hated him *and* herself for that.

Then he let her go and she darted back to her desk as fast as she could.

74: Weak Enough Not to Choose It

SOMEHOW, BETWEEN THE MOMENT KNOX HAD TOLD HER TO GO HOME, change, and pack, and the moment she actually got ready to do so, he must have changed his mind, because he emerged from his office and grumbled at her, "Put your stuff down and get to work." He dropped another stack of files on her desk, as Eric was in court. "Your files backed up while you were out stripping Halls and Armani bare." Justice's eyes widened and she wondered if this was when he would start holding her "vacation" against her. It seemed so far away ago now, even though it had ended only yesterday.

His mouth quirked as he looked at her. "She has champagne taste and a husband who lives to drench her in it. I know where she shops."

Justice nearly wilted in relief and she did get to work. She noticed throughout the day that the men looked at her and treated her differently—not in a sexual way, but like an adult, a professional, as opposed to a teenaged girl playing prosecutor. She regretted that Giselle had been right about that.

The defense attorneys who covered the speeding tickets, DUIs, and other such revenue-enhancing offenses of the county, who had gotten to know her when she was still in her sixteen-year-old-girl Sunday school wardrobe, did a double take and didn't treat her quite so cavalierly. In fact, they acted like she'd actually graduated from law school. On Giselle's advice, she watched what the female defense attorneys wore and while Justice was pretty sure her neckline was a tad too low and her hem a little too high, it wasn't in any way inappropriate.

The women also looked twice and their attitudes changed. Before, they'd been kindly amused with her, even compassionate that she was stuck with Knox for a boss.

Now they were out for her blood. Perversely, this heightened Justice's confidence in a way that the men's treatment of her didn't. It meant they saw her as a threat—not as a girl who needed gentle handling.

. . . comfortable with who you are when you're behind a computer . . .

She'd never been comfortable anywhere else and she suddenly realized that all these years, people had patronized and condescended to her.

Except Knox.

That realization wasn't immediate. It took half a day to remember that from the first moment he'd touched her and talked to her all those years ago, to when he'd hired her, to when he'd found her on the roadside, to when he'd pressed her up against the door, to when he'd threatened her father—never had he patronized her.

She knew how to spot online condescension and deal with it effectively, but in real life . . . Knox's blatant cruelty had heft and definition. She could catch most of it and throw it back at him even though he frightened her. Condescension and patronization were nebulous weapons she had never seen, but now that she had, they only became more effective because she didn't know how to deflect them.

You— You're powerful and— And I want to learn that.

With each defense attorney she met, each file she dispatched in her favor, she grew more confident in herself and her work. It snowballed and she cleared her inbox faster and more efficiently than she thought possible. She was so pleased with herself, with the changes within her that she almost forgot she'd gotten married that morning at gunpoint—

—then remembered the minute Knox appeared at her desk with a speculative look on his face. He said nothing. She looked at the clock and saw it had passed seven; everyone was long gone—and she hadn't noticed.

"You did well today, Iustitia," he said, his voice strained from being in court all afternoon. Suddenly, she realized that he was very tired.

"Thank you," she said warily—because what else *could* she say? And why was he *still* calling her that? Her mother was the only one who'd ever called her that and at that moment, she missed her mother very, very badly.

"Pack up your stuff. I want to go home and go to bed."

Her gut clenched and she swallowed. It wasn't as if she had forgotten this, precisely. It was more that she had just refused to think about it. She had lost herself in this newfound confidence and respect from her coworkers and opposing counsel, had enjoyed herself and her work—and because of that, she hadn't had room in her brain to be afraid of Knox, of what would happen if she defied him.

And what would happen if she *didn't* defy him.

Right now, though, she did as she was told because she didn't figure she had a choice. However, she lectured herself very sternly, if he wanted anything from her, he'd have to rape her to get it; that way, she could lay all the blame on him.

But in her soul, she knew that wouldn't be necessary and that was what she feared most. The memory of that night when she had passed by the Kenards' bedroom door and heard them making love flashed across her memory and she blushed. Fortunately, she was turned away from Knox, so he didn't see her face.

He said nothing as he followed her out the door and down the stairs. Sheriff Raines glared at her, but she ignored both him and the frisson of fear that ran through her. She walked toward the AP's parking spot she'd appropriated—and stopped.

Where was her car?

She turned, panicked, and nearly ran into Knox's chest.

"You're coming home with me," he rumbled, steadying her so she didn't fall backward, "and your car's gone for good. It was a piece of shit."

But it was *her* piece of—crap. She'd paid for it with money she had worked very hard for and suddenly, she was very angry. She hadn't even had a chance to fight him for her car the way she'd fought for her dress. Even then, Giselle would have had her way if Mr. Kenard hadn't interceded on her behalf.

Her nostrils flared as she looked into his eyes. With three-inch heels, she could look Knox in the eye and she liked the equalization. He stared right back at her, daring her to say a word.

So she did. "You have taken everything I have away from me," she said low, enunciating every word with haughty precision.

"Not everything," he murmured lazily, his eyes hooded as his gaze raked her from head to toe. "Not yet."

Justice sucked in a breath, her eyes wide, her mind in turmoil.

The breeze lifted her curls and released one from a loose pin. It flipped across her face and he lifted his hand to smooth the wayward curl from her face and tuck it behind her ear. Then he turned and walked farther down the sidewalk, expecting her to follow. On the one hand, if she did, she'd be capitulating. On the other hand, if she refused, he'd force her. Either way, it would be humiliating.

He'd reached his SUV and had opened the passenger door. He turned to look at her, waiting for her to make up her mind whether to go with or without force.

Finally, resigned, she walked toward him slowly. She might have even dragged her feet if it wouldn't have ruined her shoes. Surprisingly, he did help her up and in, took her briefcase and closed her door. He opened the back door and put both his and her briefcases there, then proceeded around to the driver's door. He got in and started the car, then looked at her sideways. "Seatbelt?"

That made her mad all over again. If he'd read anything she'd written, he'd know how she felt about that.

"No," she said shortly. "I resent that law; I resent most laws that regulate what someone can do with his own property, and by that I mean his body, too."

Knox sat back and looked at her for a long time, but she refused to look at him.

"Abortion?" he asked quietly and she wasn't surprised. It was the next logical question, though considering that what he wanted from her was a child, it had much more impact. She was tempted to lie, but couldn't bring herself to voice an opinion opposite what she truly believed—and if he'd read her, he'd know this too.

"The child's rights are protected by the Constitution," she muttered, and she hated that she sounded so sullen.

Knox said nothing for another long while and she finally looked at him. He was leaning back against his door, his face propped on his fingertips, his elbow on the door ledge. He watched her carefully, not a hint of mockery on his face. Other than that, she couldn't tell what he thought.

"The argument is that it's not a human being," he finally said. "That it's just a part of a woman's body and her body, being her property, is free to do with as she wishes."

She snorted. "I don't think anybody actually believes that."

"Yes, some people actually do believe that."

She looked at him sharply. "Do you?"

"We aren't talking about my opinion. We're talking about yours."

"Okay," she said, engaged now, and she turned toward him, her knee crooked in the seat. She leaned toward him, suddenly completely dismissing who he was and why she was in his car. "Why is it that in an abortion clinic, a fetus is being terminated and in the NICU down the street, a baby of the same gestational age is given all sorts of heroic treatment to save its life? Where's the logic in that? Who decides that one is a person worth saving and the other's just a part of the woman's body and how do they decide that? The mother decides: A human being or a mass of tissue, depending on her circumstance. If puppies were terminated that way, PETA would be all over it. And why is it that in some jurisdictions, killing a pregnant woman is charged as two murders, but abortion isn't a crime? If choice is such an issue, why couldn't a woman choose to use birth control?"

"Rape? Incest? That's not a woman's choice."

She drew in a breath and it was a long time before she admitted, "I don't know. I haven't been able to sort that out in my head yet. I try to think what I'd do and I just— I don't know."

Knox stared at her and she returned it until she remembered who she was talking to, where, and why. And when she did, she opened her mouth and snapped, "But it looks like I might have to start thinking about it, huh? I might have to rethink my whole position."

His jaw tightened, but he didn't respond; he simply turned to back out of the parking space. She noticed he hadn't put on his seatbelt, either.

The ride to his home was absolutely silent, which reminded her of Giselle's penchant for silence. She had so many questions for him, left over from when she'd still held him in such high regard, but wasn't really interested now. What could he say that would bring back her opinion of that man who'd touched her in class and defended her and set her firmly on the path to political punditry?

Justice began to pay attention to where they were going once Knox had turned off the highway. The streets that wound deeper and deeper into his neighborhood were tree-lined and secluded. He had about an acre of ground at the back corner of a very old subdivision built when acre plots were the norm, the only plot on a small street that probably wasn't even on a map; in fact, it didn't even have a street sign. The whole property was bordered by a high wrought iron fence with the gate across the driveway, which was closed.

The house was a 1960s-era low brick ranch with a steeply pitched roof, what she thought was classified as French provincial. The brick was painted cream, and black shutters flanked the windows. The big mullioned windows in the front sparkled, their small beveled diamond panes catching the last rays of the setting sun through the thicket of trees that bordered the west side of the property. The foundation of the house was camouflaged by low yews.

This was not what she would have thought Knox would choose to live in. She had him figured for a federalist or Georgian style, but understood that the seemingly nonexistent address would appeal to someone like Knox.

To the right of the driveway were two well-worn ruts, which circled around the house and disappeared. It was the only thing that marred the otherwise flawless turf and she thought it . . . odd. Just beyond that to the west was a windbreak of trees that ran from the front to the back of the property. The east boundary of the property was bordered by old scrub pines.

A gate across the driveway slid open and he drove into the garage. Once the door began to close behind them, Justice closed her eyes and sighed in resignation, fear and—something else. She dropped her head back on the head rest.

Justice felt him touch her neck. She opened her eyes and turned to him before she realized that he had closed the distance between them. He kissed her, gently, quietly, before deepening it. Without thinking about it, she closed her eyes and laid her hand along the side of his face.

It went on for many moments as he taught her how to kiss, how to be kissed, how to tease and nip and lick.

Knox drew away from her slowly and she opened her eyes. Suddenly she flushed hot, ashamed that it had taken nothing at all for him to make her forget— everything.

"This'd be a whole lot easier on both of us if you didn't fight me," he murmured, his voice husky.

"What else am I supposed to do?" she muttered, looking at the floor, more angry with herself and her own weakness than with him. "Why should I make this easy for you?"

"Well," he said, pulling away from her and opening his door, "when you put it that way, I see your point."

He opened her door for her and bustled her into the house. When he spoke again, that hard edge in his voice was back. "Here's the deal, Iustitia. We can eat first or have sex first. Your choice."

Justice looked at him for a long time because what he said and how he'd said it was so jarring. She didn't know what to say to that, but she must have waited too long. He stepped toward her and she backed up a step. He took another step, and another until he had backed her up against a wall. His body touched hers as he braced his forearm against the wall and caught her earlobe with his teeth.

"Or," he whispered menacingly into her ear, his finger tracing her collarbone, "you can just forfeit your choice right here and right now."

She said nothing. There was no choice. She would take whatever Knox had to give her and bear the consequences of her shame later. Her eyes closed when his hand traced lightly down over her breast and stopped, stayed, his thumb finding her nipple through her clothes. She sucked in a breath and gulped.

He still nibbled on her ear and he pressed closer to her, letting her know that whatever her wishes, he would get what he wanted tonight—and he wouldn't have to take it by force.

It occurred to her that she was married to him now and that she had every right to him. While that was a heady thought, he wasn't an honorable man and he'd forced her into this.

You assume too much.

Giselle's sharp reprimand came back to her; she hadn't known what it meant then and she didn't know now. What she did know was that taking her freedom, making her a prisoner, was *not*, by any definition, honorable.

"Stop thinking," he growled in her ear. "I want you to feel it, feel *me*, feel what I'm doing to you."

He was right; she had stopped feeling and started thinking and maybe if she thought of the Supreme Court—

"I'll talk to you," he whispered. "I'll tell you what I'm doing and how and why, just to keep your brain occupied, if that's the only way I can keep you with me—because your IQ *is* going to come with me, even if I have to drag it kicking and screaming. I'll fill your mind with *me* until it stops fighting your body."

Justice swallowed again. Her palms lay flat on the wall behind her. Her eyes were closed. She stiffened because he had read her so easily and that he had such a simple way of counteracting it.

"You're mine now. I *own* you."

Her eyes popped open as she sucked in a deep breath. She looked at him and snarled, "What did you say?"

"I. Own. You."

She slapped him across the face, hard, furious that he would again take her deeply held philosophy and turn it against her. Her eyes narrowed and she saw his face darken. "Don't you *ever* mock me like that again," she hissed, her teeth grinding together.

Knox's eyebrow rose and he touched his face where she'd slapped him. His voice was rough when he finally spoke. "I told you never to hit me."

"Hit me back and see how long you live."

His nostrils flared and his stare matched hers second for second. She wouldn't back down and she didn't feel fear. He'd imprisoned her and for him to throw that back at her was vile.

Justice could see that they'd reached a stalemate. Knox slowly pushed himself away from the wall and turned, taking a few steps away from her. She had taken two steps away from the wall when he pounced.

He grabbed her around the waist and pulled her to him, crushing her, crushing her breasts, crushing her mouth against his. Knox's tongue crushed hers, one hand crushed her buttocks, the other hand crushed her hair.

Enraged, Justice fought, but she was no match for his strength. He picked her up, kicking and hissing, and strode down a hallway into a bedroom, where he threw her on the bed. She bounced and immediately rolled off to stand on the other side of the bed, taking deep gulps of air while surreptitiously slipping her heels off.

"If you want anything from me, you're going to have to take it by force."

"Don't think I won't," he gritted as he ripped off his tie, then unbuttoned his shirt with lightning speed and took it off.

"I'll fight you."

"At this point, I'm counting on it."

She really had no way out; she knew it would happen in the end, but she wasn't frightened or intimidated. She was livid and unwilling to give him the satisfaction of winning too easily. She couldn't remember ever being this angry in her entire life.

Justice didn't care that he was Knox Hilliard, ruthless, untouchable. She didn't care that he'd trapped her here by his threats and his far stronger body. She didn't care that she would end up underneath him somehow. She just had to make her point.

You have to walk barefoot through fire on broken glass.

Justice didn't remember it so much as feel it well up inside of her, come alive, give her energy and strength. And she ran.

She bolted around the end of the bed and made it past him through the door.

"Ow! *Shit!*"

Whatever he'd done to himself, it gave her enough of a head start to get out the back door. And she flew.

Justice could run like the wind; she knew this, she took pride in it. She also knew that there were very few people who could run as fast as she could, especially if they were built like quarterbacks and not running backs. She was gambling that Knox wasn't one of those few people.

She lost.

He tackled her, wrapped his arms around her waist and took her down into the soft grass. He twisted to land first, and she fell on top of him, both of them rolling and rolling. Then, rolling her over before she could do anything else, he was braced over her, most of his weight pinning her to the ground. His chest heaved.

She said nothing, because she, too, was winded and she gasped for breath; it was made more difficult by his weight on top of her.

Neither of them spoke as they caught their breath, but Justice wouldn't look away from him first. It was too important. Her jaw gritted and her eyes narrowed. Her adrenaline was pumping hot and swift through her body, and she was not going to back down.

"You're an evil son of a *bitch.*"

"And you want me anyway."

Knox kissed her then, hard. She was caught between wanting to fight him and wanting to get sucked into his tornado. If he spoke to her—

"I can kiss you till you come," he panted when he broke off the kiss and let his head drop so that his mouth was again at her ear. "I can stroke you till you scream. I can suck your nipples until you beg me for more. I can talk to you until all you can think about is when I'm going to slide inside you. You can run from me, Iustitia, but if it means the difference between making love to you and not, I'll catch you every time."

Her brain was engaged and she nearly sobbed with—relief? Anger? What was that feeling? He *had* caught her, and he'd used her only weapons, philosophy and intellect, against her. Her name had even betrayed her. Her body she could command, if not control, but once she was fully engaged—

And he wanted her. As much as she'd wanted him for the last three years.

Knox rose to his feet then and pulled her up to him harshly, again holding her tight and kissing her with force. She returned his kiss with equal force, but every time she thought she'd had enough of this, he talked to her, told her what he'd do to her, kept her from thinking about anything but him. He had her dress off of her before she'd realized he had begun.

"I'm going to take your bra off," he whispered, hot, when she was beginning to get some control, "and I'm going to take your panties off, and I'm going to lay you back down in the grass and you're going to wrap your legs around me. You're going to feel every inch of me, skin-to-skin."

She snarled at him but didn't resist, still panting, though from her run or from what her body was doing to her, she didn't know. The corner of his mouth curled in victory as he let her go just long enough to finish undressing.

Justice's hands wrapped as far around his arms as she could and dug her fingernails into his muscles to have something—anything at all—to hold onto so she wouldn't collapse. He held her and nuzzled her throat until she couldn't breathe at all. Overloaded with adrenaline and overwhelmed with what he was doing to her, she could do nothing but stand and let him strip off her barely-there pantyhose and scandalous underwear, his large, warm hands stroking, caressing every inch of her buttocks and thighs, calves, and feet on the way down.

He rose and her bra came off as if by magic, his mouth again raided hers, and she gasped at how wonderful it felt to be skin-to-skin with a man; she had never imagined anything like this.

She started. No, not just with any man!

She was skin-to-skin, knee-to-shoulder, with *Knox Hilliard*, kissing, having sex, his naked arousal pressed into her bare belly. When, in the last three years, *hadn't* she dreamt of this moment?

From the first day she laid eyes on him—

I bet she wants to fuck Knox Hilliard as much as I do . . . She wouldn't know what to do with him if she had him . . .

Justice gasped, her eyes popping open. Surprised, he stopped and drew back, looking at her questioningly. She studied his dark blue eyes and that gorgeous face for a long moment, remembering that day in class when he'd touched her, defended her. The day she'd fallen in love with him to begin with.

Then she threw her head back and laughed. When she looked back at him, his face betrayed his shock and, still smiling at the irony, she took his face between her hands and kissed him the way he'd taught her.

She felt him smile against her lips, then she gasped when he rolled her back onto the ground, taking the hit on his shoulder.

"Iustitia," he murmured, hoarse, still out of breath. She felt his hand between her legs, drawing gently up the inside of her thigh and she trembled. "Never let it be said that I can't or won't give you what you want."

She drew in a deep breath, her eyes wide, and arched her back when his fingers slid inside her and his thumb flicked her clitoris. He lowered his mouth and caught one of her nipples in his teeth and she moaned aloud, then again and again.

Justice was beyond thinking. This is what she'd wanted for three years, what she'd been taunted for wanting. His hand, where hers went when she thought about him, and his fingers, doing what hers did.

She felt her muscles contract around his fingers and she spread her legs wider. In the middle of it all, her back arched again and her body exploded. She sighed with the rhythm of his hand. Her muscles moved around his fingers and clenched rhythmically against them as she panted. He slid them in and out while he nipped and sucked at her nipples and never once did she forget who this man was.

Knox's mouth found hers then and she pulled everything she could out of him, again her hands on either side of his face, holding him to her. Her knees fell wider apart as if of their own volition, as if they hadn't already gone as wide as they could already, and his fingers withdrew from inside her.

Then he moved away from her, shifted—

Then *yes!* He was between her legs, the insides of her thighs hypersensitive to the feel of his naked hips, and he was balanced over her. She looked up into his eyes, which were that same dark, dark blue even as she wrapped her legs around his thighs.

"Kiss me, Knox," she whispered, her fingers in his coarse blond hair so that she could bring his face down to hers if he was not inclined to do so.

But he was and he kissed her with a tenderness she didn't expect.

"Make love to me, Knox," she whispered into his mouth, then felt his soft answering sigh,

"I will, Iustitia, I will."

She felt him, much bigger, much heavier, and much longer than his fingers, ready to fill her body and she desperately wanted him to. His mouth left hers so he could nuzzle at her throat as he made his first impression in her virgin body.

And she screamed.

Her eyes popped open and she fought against him, surprising him.

"Iustitia?"

"Get off! Get off! You're killing me!" she cried. "Please, please don't. It hurts. Oh, it hurts so bad."

Her sudden sobs shocked even herself because she wanted this, but his body in hers was so foreign and painful, she couldn't stand it. *Never* had she expected—

She choked as she tried to stem the flow of tears through her tightly clenched eyelids, but once begun, she couldn't stop the river of tears that poured down her cheeks.

"It goes away, Iustitia," Knox whispered even as he withdrew from her. "I promise it goes away."

It barely registered in her traumatized mind that his voice was heavy with a pleading that was just as foreign as his body inside her. She didn't care. She hurt too badly.

"Go away," she sobbed. "Please don't make me do this. Please," she begged.

She cried harder when she felt Knox's head fall to her chest and his sigh caress her flesh. She felt moisture between her legs and she wanted to put her knees together, but couldn't. He was still on top of her, between her legs.

Knox shifted so that he lay half on and half off of her, one leg still between hers. He caressed her face and ran his fingers through her curls while she cried, in pain and humiliated beyond belief. "I'm sorry, Iustitia," he whispered into her ear a thousand times if he whispered it once. "I'm so sorry. Please forgive me."

She closed her legs as far as she could. She turned into him, curled up, holding onto him even though he was the one who had caused her pain, and sobbed into his throat until she hiccuped, then hiccuped until she fell asleep in his arms, naked in the grass under the stars.

75: Snake Eyes

SEBASTIAN ACHED IN WAYS HE DIDN'T REMEMBER EVER HAVING ACHED. HE knew he had no hope with Eilis now. It had been an unrecoverable gaffe that had hit her in her heart, which lay with her employees.

Yet every night he drove to Knox's to continue with the project he'd begun after his first date with Eilis, when he'd stood in awe of her garden and seen her beautiful face in the noonday sun on Brooklyn. The materials had arrived in November, after which he and Knox had spent the winter out in the barn hammering, stapling, painting.

Knox shared an exit with Eilis, but they lived on opposite sides of the highway. Every night, he looked longingly to the left to see if he could see one speck of her property, house, anything. But she was too well secured to let that happen. She had millions of dollars of art in that house, though many millions less than before *Morning in Bed* had gone through the private sale Sebastian had brokered to fund her cash reserves. He had not bought it. He couldn't stand the damn thing, but couldn't bring himself to destroy it. He'd even sold the three he'd bought back for Eilis—at a hefty profit—figuring she'd not appreciate looking at nude women who weren't her, who didn't have her body type, whom *he* had painted, all the while knowing precisely how they'd acquired that freshly-fucked look.

He drove into Knox's driveway and he continued on around the house, through the lawn where he'd cut a path with his rickety old truck down to the barn.

Knox had grumbled about Sebastian appropriating his barn and having his lawn wrecked by the workers who came to reinforce the building enough so that it wouldn't fall down on Sebastian's head. Once the structural work was done, the makeshift electricity and plumbing done, lights and space heaters installed for the coming winter, and an elaborate pulley system rigged to Sebastian's specifications, the rest had to be done by Ford and his assistant—

—who had bitched and moaned the entire time he'd helped prep the space and the canvases: twelve feet high and twenty-four feet across total, in three sections clamped together. Sebastian and Knox had used gallons of gesso and painted it with rollers. They'd strung the cables through the pulley system to haul it off the floor and lean it back against the hayloft, then they'd assembled the scaffolding. After that, Knox had declared himself officially done as an artist's assistant and told Sebastian if he wanted anything else, he'd have to recruit a different cousin, do it himself, or hire it done.

That night, after he'd parked, Sebastian plucked a very heavy five-gallon pail out of the pickup bed and took it into the barn. He flipped on the switch and half blinded himself, then turned on the music and looked up the canvas. Most of the top quarter was finished and he had to admit he hadn't done badly. He had a hard time painting himself for several reasons, mostly because he didn't like to. It necessitated professional photography and then painting from the photo, which he didn't do so well.

He pulled out the paint he needed, a tray intended to hold drywall mud, and a putty knife, then opened his pail.

Clear diamond chips. He'd already gotten the little bit of ruby, emerald, and sapphire chips, not to mention the yellow diamond chips and gold filings that he needed for different parts of the painting. It was time to work on her body.

An entire tray full of titanium white, teensy bit of chrome yellow, teensy bit of cadmium yellow. Then a fairly generous scoop of diamond chips. He had no idea if this would work on a painting this large. It had sort of worked on a five-by-five, but he'd experimented until he had the paint so thick with diamonds, the paint barely held it all together.

That night as he worked, he grew more and more despondent as he remembered the sight of Eilis pulling away from him, leaving him, and began to understand a little bit of the pain Knox and Giselle wanted him to feel—what Eilis didn't think he should have to feel.

A goddess. She was his Goddess and he was the artist who loved her and he was going to paint her in diamonds.

. . . don't bother that man. You can see he's talking to his wife.

Almost a year ago at Bryant's, Eilis and "wife" in the same sentence had felt good. Right. Mrs. Van Horn occasionally asked about the pretty blonde he'd been with the day he'd met his little protégé Christopher. Just this past Sunday after dinner, after all the Van Horn children had been sent out to play, he'd sat at their table across from Christina and told her what he'd done to kill the fantasy Ford. He'd flinched at the disappointment in her chocolate eyes when he'd admitted that he hadn't taken responsibility for it, that he hadn't done what Giselle told him to. Christina's husband had looked him in the eye and said, "You're a durned fool."

Tonight, the idea of Eilis being his wife didn't seem just good and right. It seemed like an opportunity to bind her to him with paper and ring, which he had fucked up. He wanted to marry her, to be faithful to her, to give children to and take children from her if she was inclined toward that.

And now he wouldn't have the chance.

He hadn't told Knox about their argument, nor Giselle. He wanted to stay in their good graces as long as possible. Since Eilis was so enamored of the fact she had a brother who liked her and claimed her, and a cousin-plus-husband whom she thought of as her spiritual and financial bodyguards respectively, she'd probably end up telling them all herself.

Picking up his paint and four different sizes of drywall knives, he climbed up the scaffolding and began. An experienced muralist, he knew exactly what he wanted to do. He thwacked on the first plop of paint and realized that if he weren't careful, the diamonds would slice the canvas.

More paint, just to soften the edges of the diamonds.

He painted for a long time. Tired. Sebastian couldn't remember ever being this tired. He hadn't slept since she left him; he'd sat in his living room drinking, which had given him a hangover, but hadn't put him to sleep. He didn't know it was actually possible to get a hangover without sleeping because he'd never, ever gotten drunk before. Getting drunk was so . . . gauche.

Maybe Knox would let him crash on his couch tonight, because he sure didn't think he'd be able to make the thirty-minute drive home.

The tray was heavy. The spackling knife was heavy and he didn't dare try to paint with his right hand to even out the load. No matter. This was a labor of love; the labor of an artist who loved his goddess—

—who could not have her.

76: One Soul Shall Not Be Lost

JUSTICE AWOKE NOT KNOWING WHERE SHE WAS FOR A MOMENT. HER EYES blinked in the all-encompassing blackness until she could make out silhouettes of furniture—not hers.

Not a dream.

She stiffened a bit, unwilling to turn over and see Knox in bed with her, but after a moment of utter silence and stillness, she realized she was alone. A thimbleful of disappointment suffused her; after all that and he hadn't slept with her? Curious.

On sitting up, she winced at the soreness in her hips and legs, triggering the memory of the details of what had happened only hours ago. She gulped, unable to think about it right then.

She looked down to see that she wore an enormous pale blue Oxford shirt that smelled like Knox and a pair of soft gray boxers. Once she stood up, she realized that the boxers would have fallen off but for her hips. She took a step and winced.

A wide yellow rubber band of the type used in offices and around newspapers held her hair back. She reached down between her legs to rub her sore muscles and the scent of soap drifted up to her nostrils. Her brow wrinkled. He'd *bathed* her? Well, sponged her off, anyway. She was pretty sure she'd remember if she were given an actual bath. Curiouser.

She sat back down on the edge of the bed and closed her eyes, her body tense, her fingers curled into the edge of the mattress. She relived every second of what had happened out there in the yard, confused and . . . *angry* . . . for the wrong reason. *Why* had it hurt? For all her lack of opportunity to practice with another human being, she knew what sex was about, what she should expect and not. A woman wet, ready, wanting a man should *not* have pain. She didn't expect to have had pleasure her first time, but never had she imagined having such pain.

And she *had* been wet, ready, wanting. She'd *begged* him, just as he'd told her she would.

Heat suffused her face at that, her embarrassment mitigated only by the fact that he hadn't gloated, that he had been equally stunned. His voice hoarse with a touch of desperation, he'd apologized. Over and over again while he stroked her hair and held her close and kissed her ear and cheek and temple while she cried. *Why* had he done that? That wasn't the ruthless and cruel and untouchable Knox Hilliard she'd come to know.

He'd given her a glimpse of the power he had over her when he'd slipped his fingers inside her and his thumb had manipulated her clitoris just *so,* and she'd come with a fire she'd never known by her own hand. He had great skill to make her want things from him that she should *never* want from a man who'd taken away her freedom, her choices.

She felt shame for that, for giving in to him up until the point he hurt her, to the point where even now, though her body felt empty and sore and ragged, she wanted to try again, to know what it was like to have him fully inside her, making her pain go away. If he hadn't hurt her, she'd still be with him, in this bed, still feeling— acting—as if she were there of her own free will.

Justice stopped thinking and rose to waddle to the bathroom, hoping to walk it off.

Once there, she saw a dim glow coming from the backyard where they had— what? What *had* they done? He'd given her an orgasm, an entirely inadequate word for *that,* but it wasn't sex. Wasn't making love. Wasn't rape. Wasn't the F-word. She didn't know how to label it and Justice was all about labels.

Something had happened, for sure, but—what?

Out the bathroom window, she could see an old barn back there lit up like a Christmas tree. It was some distance away, maybe half a football field; she vaguely remembered seeing it on her mad dash out the patio door. Her brow wrinkled. What was he doing out there?

She had to talk to him, to beg him to let her go—from this marriage, from this house, from that office, and she would go to Washington, which wasn't far enough away from Knox Hilliard to suit her. She couldn't live or work this way: Without her freedom, yet wanting to be with him.

What would she do if he wouldn't let her go? Was she willing to take the chance he'd really kill her father if she left him anyway?

Once she'd made up her mind about seeking him out, Justice didn't hesitate to walk outside in the nighttime barefoot, the grass wet and spongy under her feet.

Strange music—classical? opera?—with a thumping beat floated over the distance to her ears. There was something familiar about one phrase of it, but she was pretty sure she hadn't heard any of the rest of it. She wasn't even sure she liked it, and she liked pretty much everything, especially if it had a driving bass rhythm.

The barn itself looked like it was about to fall down. Light sprayed out from in between every vertical clapboard and every piece of wood on that barn was the odd gray-gold-green-silver color of disintegration. The roof wasn't much better, and she could see that a blue tarp or six had been strapped down over it.

It took her a minute to find the barn door, thrown open wide to let the summer night breezes cross through to the other end, those doors also open. She flinched. The music nearly deafened her and the light nearly blinded her. She put one arm over her eyes and the other hand over one ear so they could adjust.

There, in the middle of the barn stood a canvas twelve feet high and at least twenty feet wide, leaning back on the edge of the hayloft. A man—not Knox—was on a high scaffold in front of it, painting. Odd. In his left hand was a large drywall knife, and in his right, a spackling tray full of paint.

Through the scaffold, she could see that not much of the painting was done, only the dullish gray torso of a man visible and complete. She got caught up in watching the artist work and in this music she didn't know if she liked but attracted her anyway. The paint shimmered in the light and cast sparkles over the opposite wall. After a while, she decided to step into the barn and sit, with some pain, her knees drawn up to her chest and her ankles crossed, enthralled with this process.

Justice had no artistic talent; she wished she did. Her talents only lay toward scholarship and lately, she didn't seem to do that very well, either. She'd never had the opportunity to observe someone creating something so lovely instead of always seeing or hearing or reading the end result.

After a while, the man—a huge man with black hair and pale skin who wore only an old pair of cutoff denim shorts—began to slow, then sag. He gripped his left shoulder with his right hand and rotated it, then rolled his head around on his neck. He stretched, yawned, then turned—and jumped back when he saw her.

He grabbed a remote and turned the music off. The sudden silence almost nauseated her and her ears rang most annoyingly.

"Who the hell are you?" he barked, nearly identically to Knox, but he didn't scare her. How could he? Knox had scared every bit of fright out of her already.

She looked into his ice blue eyes and knew that he too was related to Knox, thus to Giselle. Probably not a brother; they were all too disparate, so she would assume he was another cousin.

"Justice," she said. "Who are you?"

Staring at her for a long while, he finally said, "Ford. Or Sebastian, take your pick."

Huh. She didn't understand the Ford reference, but *that* was not what she'd expected Sebastian Taight to look like.

"What are you painting?"

He looked at her strangely before turning and wiping his face on a discarded tee shirt, then drew it over his head. "What time is it?"

"I don't know. I woke up and saw the light, then came out to see."

"How long have you been here?"

"Half an hour, maybe."

"No, I mean, how long have you lived with Knox?"

"Oh. Just today." Not even that, really.

He climbed down the scaffold and began to clean his knives and brushes in a makeshift sink connected to a garden hose. His back to her, he threw a question over his shoulder.

"When'd he marry you?"

She blinked. How did he know that? "Today," she murmured. "Er, well, yesterday. I guess."

"Not too happy about it, huh?"

"No," she said flatly.

"I'm guessing that means the wedding night wasn't terribly successful."

Justice blushed and looked away.

"I see. Well, I'm sorry."

She was silent for a moment and then said, "I didn't know you could paint."

He looked over his shoulder, his brow wrinkled. "What's that supposed to mean?"

"It means that I've never read anywhere that Sebastian Taight painted anything ever."

He dropped his knives in the sink and turned, his arms crossed over his chest. He looked at her for a long while, then, "That's because Sebastian Taight *doesn't* paint. Ford does. How much do you know about me?"

"I started hearing about your 'Fix-or-Raid' policy when Senator Oth got upset with you. I like it, even if it is rather . . . Randian."

"You read Rand?"

"Everybody reads Rand at some point. It's kind of a political rite of passage, like Marx, but most people grow out of it."

"I take it you're not a fan."

"No, but it doesn't take much to see you're a devoted disciple." Sebastian laughed.

"I'm curious: What made you interested in raising up Kevin Oakley for Senate?"

"You *are* full of surprises, aren't you?"

"I guess that depends on what you assume I know."

"Oh, you've got a smart mouth. You'll fit in with us just fine." She smiled, comfort and warmth spreading through her inexplicably. "I'm going to go ahead and *assume* you know the answer to that question and you're just fishing."

She pursed her lips and realized she liked this man. He was warm and funny; she needed that right now—but more importantly, she had a lot to say to him. She picked up a random twig and played with it, studied it, while she spoke. "In *Atlas Shrugged*, when Hank Rearden was put on trial for being a 'greedy enemy of the state,'" she began and, out of the corner of his eye, saw his body stiffen in shock, "he had already decided to destroy his company and his metal for the sake of Galt's revolution. I didn't like that. I think it was childish for all the producers to destroy their own work to prove a point, then ride off into the sunset.

"I know what Congress wants from you and why. They want to know why you make some companies better and why you take some companies completely out of the picture. They want to turn that on you and use it against you and people like you. Don't give it to them. If they haven't figured it out by now, they don't deserve to know.

"On the other hand, don't just take your ball and go home to Bora Bora, either, because people need to know people like you exist and they need your strength and example to become you. You need to teach those people for your own benefit, to better *your* bottom line and *your* strength as an entrepreneur—not theirs. Stay in the game. Keep doing what you do and thumb your nose at the looters. The moochers are unavoidable."

Justice had the satisfaction of watching his incredulity grow as she spoke, though he did recover himself enough to say, "Well? How do I decide?"

She laughed. "Three of the five senators who were calling for your head are ones whose companies you took and destroyed or handed over to someone else to run after you took them and fixed them. They're bad leaders. They're stupid. They're arrogant in their place in life and feel entitled to it."

"Of course they do. They're old-money back-room Republicans."

She inclined her head. "Yes. So I'm going to assume that they were the same way as businessmen. Put that together with your very obvious worship at the altar of laissez-faire capitalism and any fool can see exactly what you do and why you do it."

Sebastian threw back his head and laughed. After a moment of utter hilarity, he calmed and said, "Well, Justice, I have to tell you—you're the first outsider who's figured it out from scratch."

"Kevin's not going to be able to protect you from congressional hearings, you know. He'll have no position of power when he gets there and it'll take him years to build that kind of clout. So that's what I'm asking. What do you think he can do for you the minute he gets into office?"

"It's not what he can do for me once he gets there. It's about what he can do for me just by running. I'm stalling for time."

Justice pursed her lips and thought about this for a moment, looking at it from every angle she could think of, then laughed and gave him a small salute. "Very clever."

He looked at the floor and fidgeted, then looked back up at her. "So since I'm not assuming what you know, what do you actually know about Fen Hilliard?"

"I know he's Knox's uncle and that you definitely don't want him to win that Senate seat."

Sebastian nodded absently, then said, "What do you think of OKH Enterprises?"

Justice's brow wrinkled at the odd question. "Hilliard's the CEO and I'm not impressed with his politics. Why?"

He glanced at her, then at the floor. "No reason, I guess."

He turned back to his cleaning, and at that moment, Justice felt more normal than she had since she'd come to the Chouteau County prosecutor's office.

She jumped when she first felt, rather than saw, Knox sit on the floor beside her, so close up against her that her shoulder overlapped his, and she looked at him. He wore only a pair of gray jersey biking shorts. He didn't look at her, but stared at the enormous canvas mostly hidden behind scaffolding.

"Did you tell her who you are?" Knox asked hoarsely, and Sebastian threw another quick look over his shoulder before continuing to clean his tools.

"So nice of you to join us. Yes, I did. She doesn't know Ford. Or the proviso."

Knox sucked up a quick breath, held it, then released it with a soft, "Oh, *shit*."

"Yeah."

Justice didn't bother questioning him about this turn of the conversation, as she knew she'd get no answers. She simply tucked the information away in the file drawer of her mind; it could wait until she'd sorted out the most pressing points of her situation first.

"Iustitia," Knox murmured and she blinked. He reached a hand up to smooth some of the hair out of her face, and his mouth thinned when a stray tear tracked down her cheek. "I'm sorry."

She flushed a little. This was the Knox who'd defended her, given her her name and her first kiss, sent her to Giselle's for pampering and coddling, done those . . . indescribably magical things to her out in the grass.

He was also the one who'd forced her to stay in the prosecutor's office and marry him at gunpoint. Force. It was a word she used often in reference to Knox.

"You knew I was a virgin," she said low, pretty sure Sebastian couldn't hear over the distance and the running water. "The whole *world* takes one look at me and knows I'm—was—a virgin, but I certainly never expected it to hurt. My mother— She didn't want me to get mixed up with boys until after I'd done something grand. So I didn't. It didn't matter anyway. I never had any time to learn anything about it first hand, never had anybody to talk to or ask. I never had a boyfriend, I never went to a prom. I never participated in any of the university activities and never dated.

"I had work to do and books to study and articles to write and blogs to keep up with." Justice didn't attempt to hide the bitterness in her voice because she *deeply* resented that he didn't know who she was. "I didn't have time to read for pleasure and certainly never had time to think about what other girls think about. Last week, at Giselle's—thank you, by the way—was the first vacation I've ever had and I got to read what I wanted to read and that was the nicest thing about the whole week."

She drew a deep breath and decided to lay it all out for him. It wouldn't make any difference anyway; she couldn't be more humiliated.

"You come at me and do things to me I don't have any experience with. Yes, I'm almost twenty-five and yes, it's pathetic that I'm like this, but I can't help it. You're so much older than I am and I'm scared. I'm scared of you, scared of what you make me feel, scared of what you've made me do, scared to know why you've made me do it, scared of what you'll do to me or my dad if I don't do it. That night at the symphony? That was my first kiss. Ever."

His eyes widened a bit and she could see his Adam's apple bob when he swallowed. Then he reached across her and touched her chin, the same way he had done three years ago, and gently guided her face around to his. He leaned over to her, his wrist brushing her hip as he put his hand on the floor to brace himself, and kissed her. Softly. Slowly.

She closed her eyes and sighed, kissed him back the way he had taught her, because— What else could she do? She hadn't forgotten that she had come out here to beg him to let her go, but she didn't seem to want to do it right now.

All she wanted right now was this man to keep kissing her.

"Hello! Does anybody remember I'm still in the room? Dammit, Knox, you couldn't have taken your time and slowly seduced the girl, could you? Oh, but wait. I forgot. That's not your style. It just wouldn't be the same if you didn't terrify her *first* and then seduce her. You're a bull in a fucking china shop, as per usual."

"Shut up, Sebastian, and mind your own business."

"She *is* my business."

She blinked. And how was she this man's business?

"Isn't it past your bedtime?"

Sebastian ignored that. "Any blind man can see the girl's naked as the day she was born. Why couldn't you have just done it *her* way instead of dragging her along doing it *your* way? And why couldn't you have just *told* her up front and let her decide? That would've been the honorable thing to do."

"Sebastian," Knox said slowly. Justice realized his temper had blown and fortunately this time, not at her. "Shut. Up. And. Go. Home."

"Fine," Sebastian snarled, and stalked around looking for something until he found his car keys. He walked to the other door, then turned for a parting shot.

"You're a piece of work, you know that? You were *so* disgusted at Giselle's cowardice that she kept Kenard on ice for almost a year, and it wasn't a month ago you pounded my head into the table for being a coward, but now you have way less room to talk than either of us. You're so much of a coward you'd rather sink to the lowest evil than risk being turned down if you asked for what you wanted with a modicum of decency and sincerity. Shit, and here I thought what you did to Leah was fucked up, but she *did* have a choice. So the next time you feel like getting all self-righteous and indignant, you remember this. This—" He pointed at Justice. "Makes you no better than Lucifer himself."

"You don't believe in Lucifer," Knox snarled in return.

He stared at Knox, his eyebrow cocked. "I do now. The Lord might forgive you Parley, but this— No."

With a click, the lights died and Justice couldn't see at all. Then headlights pierced the blackness but were gone when the car—an old battered pickup—drove away.

Justice and Knox sat there on the barn floor in the dark and the silence. For the first time since she could remember, she did not mind the silence; in fact, it seemed rather comforting, like a soft blanket fresh from the dryer on a cold day.

She turned the situation over in her head, looked at it, took it apart and put it back together again seventeen different ways. A few incomplete hypotheses later, she realized that she couldn't deduce the bigger picture because she didn't have enough information or experience or both.

The only thing she could deduce for a certainty was that she had been handpicked to be Knox's wife and the mother of the child he needed, and that *she*—no one else—was crucial to their situation. She could also conclude that no matter who had chosen her, she would've ended up here one way or another. She'd just saved everyone the trouble by showing up on Knox's doorstep.

"You're thinking again," Knox said quietly, interrupting her thinking, which annoyed her.

"Why did you choose me for this—this *Handmaid's Tale?* Why this elaborate farce?"

"There's a method to my madness, Iustitia."

"You should've just asked me. I would have given you anything after that day in class when you touched me and defended me—if you had just asked."

Knox arose. "No, you wouldn't have," he said, his voice suddenly hard.

Justice gulped. The Knox of the soft kisses and the Knox who had held her and apologized over and over as she sobbed her pain into his chest was not the only Knox inside that beautiful body of his. She must do better to remember that.

But that didn't stop her from taking Lucifer's hand and allowing him to gently help her to her feet. She also didn't protest when, as they walked across the lawn back to the house, that his hand splayed lightly across her back.

At least she could now conclude that he did, in fact, remember her and that day in class.

All the way home from Knox's house, Sebastian thought about his visit with Little Miss Kingmaker, his unwitting partner in crime.

She'd shocked him, that girl, the most magnificent redhead he'd ever seen in his life sitting quietly on the barn floor watching him paint. With her arms wrapped around her knees, she'd been lost in the hugeness of Knox's clothes and she looked so very sad, so very alone and bewildered. And *very* young. She reminded him of someone, though he couldn't figure out who.

Obviously the poor girl had been threatened, probably at gunpoint. She had looked a tad on the roughed-up side, so he guessed there'd been no wedding night ecstasy.

Sebastian sighed.

He vaguely regretted he hadn't met that girl before he'd met Eilis because wouldn't it be a kick to have a matched set of the three women in his life? But no, Knox would shoot him if he even suggested painting her.

Sebastian knew Knox's taste in women and Miss McKinley clearly rose head and shoulders above any woman Knox had ever had in his bed. In fact, he thought absently, if Eilis weren't in his heart and soul, filling every corner of his mind, he'd have taken that girl home, stripped her down, painted her, and then fucked her himself, mind and body, Knox be damned. She was that beautiful, that brilliant.

She had large tousled mahogany copper curls that framed and accentuated her face, then fell to her shoulders. Her face was pure pixie, the freckles, amazingly, screaming "fuck me!" and freckles *never* said that. Her skin was as pale and almost as iridescent as the paint he'd tried to mix with diamonds. She had amber eyes that she probably classified as hazel, but would glow gold when she laughed.

Copper and gold. Copper and gold.

That girl was a simmering teapot about to blow. With rage or passion, he couldn't tell, but he'd sure like to be witness to it. She looked like she was about to morph from a timid wee folk into a sword-wielding virago if Knox pushed her hard enough—and Knox would definitely do that. He could clearly see this girl had spirit and was ripe for the training she'd need to take on Fen if she had to.

On the other hand, Knox had given her no choice, and what had seemed rather innocuous in theory was, in reality, truly evil. It went against everything the Dunhams believed and practiced, and Grandpa Dunham would have kicked all three of their asses for it. He felt shame rise in him again as he thought about all the bitching he'd done about his involvement in OKH, constantly riding Knox to get married.

He was enjoying the hell out of every minute of this takeover, especially once Giselle had drawn the blueprint and Kenard had thrown his checkbook and influence in the ring. Likewise, Oakley had figured out the entire plot the minute Knox had told him, "We want you to run for Senate" and agreed with a hearty laugh; then the rising star conservative pundit had been persuaded (albeit covertly) to give her endorsement to Kevin, however reluctantly.

When Little Miss Kingmaker had set about lecturing Sebastian, he'd seen her true colors in a blinding red, white, and blue fireball. He might have had a good friend and ally in her if they hadn't been willing to take her freedom, make her a prisoner, manipulate her and use her youth and naïveté against her.

Yeah, it'd been easy in the abstract.

He'd pressed Knox to this. All Knox had wanted to do was wait until after his birthday, go find that beautiful girl—with too much knowledge and wisdom for all that selfsame youth and naïveté—hat in hand, and ask her out, woo her, court her, charm her so that she never, ever had to see who and what the corrupt and murderous Chouteau County prosecutor was all about.

In a flash of insight, Sebastian understood what Knox had really wanted with Justice: To feel like the good Mormon kid he'd been before he'd traded his personality and his salvation—his *soul*—for the lives of people he didn't know, when he'd been looking for a nice LDS girl he could take to the temple. He could have approximated that feeling with Justice if he hadn't been able to use Sebastian's constant bitching as an excuse to justify his impatience to have her, to have that with her.

He had borne Sebastian's mockery for years for being faithful, for believing what Sebastian considered a senseless doctrine. He would have thrown Knox a party after his excommunication if Giselle hadn't pitched one of her better fits.

First Fen wouldn't let him go on a mission like he wanted, which made him completely untouchable to the single female population of the church. And now he's just lost his priesthood, his membership, and most of his family—the most important facets of his life—in one fell swoop. You're damn near an apostate and everybody in the family still loves you; he's a true believer and he's been disowned. I swear, you can be such a fucking asshole sometimes.

Sebastian never thought he could feel *more* miserable than he already did.

When Sebastian had stood at the sink cleaning his knives and Knox's voice had come out of nowhere, he had looked over his shoulder to see Knox seated on the floor beside the girl, snuggled up against her as if to beg forgiveness for whatever he'd done or hadn't done. Sebastian had gone back to cleaning but strained to hear their quiet conversation, then turned again when they'd stopped speaking to see them making out like teenagers. He watched them together and sure enough, Knox had lost ten years off his face, that cruel edge it had acquired during Parley's trial.

And her! She was a woman in love, lost in a daze of sensuality and seduction, taking anything and everything Knox had to give her, wanting more.

Sebastian was pulling into his garage when it crossed his mind that though Justice would have gone to Knox willingly if he'd told her the truth and asked her, Knox would never have believed it even if he'd been told straight up, thus, he hadn't bothered to try. Then Sebastian's eyes widened with devastating epiphany.

So *that* was why Knox did everything the hard way. *Oh.* Sebastian swallowed. Hard.

Mab.

That was who Justice McKinley reminded him of.

Faery Queen Mab, bringer of dreams.

77: A Problem With His Power

LAST NIGHT *HAD* BEEN A DREAM. IT HAD TO HAVE BEEN BECAUSE KNOX WAS no different today than he was yesterday. Or the day before that. Or any day since she'd walked into the courthouse. The only reason she knew it wasn't a dream was because she was very sore and very stiff and she was in his car, going to work with him.

He hadn't slept with her. Once in the house, he'd clipped down the stairs to the basement without a word, leaving her to journey on to the bedroom alone.

He still hadn't answered her questions nor, given the way the day started out, would he anytime soon. Didn't matter. Justice could barely look at him.

He was irritated that he had no extra toothbrushes and so had lent her his after nuking it for thirty seconds or so.

He was irritated that she had nothing new to wear but what she'd worn the day before, which necessitated a trip to Wal-Mart for a change of clothes: a simple black skirt, crisp button-down shirt, and a pair of basic black pumps, her beautiful gold dress and pretty shoes stuffed in a crappy plastic grocery bag.

He was irritated by the fact that when they rolled up into the parking lot— late—there were the usual swarms of people about and quite a few who took note of the fact that she had come to work with him. He commenced to railing at her about the dependability of her piece-of-shit car and her perpetual tardiness, which put everyone back in the right mindset about why she had arrived with him. Once he finished thoroughly humiliating her over a nonexistent situation, he stalked off ahead of her and left her alone to walk the gauntlet of people who smirked at her for being the prosecutor's most long-lasting target to date.

He was irritated all morning and took it out on not only her, but everybody in the office, too. He snapped at her to put her shoulder holster on and snarled at her for leaving it at the courthouse instead of taking it with her when she left—but there were no semi-amused glances askance at her today because Knox spread the love equally and generously.

Justice decided to conduct business in an empty jury room downstairs. Everyone else who didn't have court scattered as well. Two residents ended up in the same room with Justice and the rest found other empty rooms in which to work.

Predictably, Dirk and the rest of the defense attorneys found this hilarious.

At lunch, she told Richard she had to take care of some things. She grabbed her laptop, went to hide in a dusty, nearly forgotten storage office, and began googling.

Ford: A recluse artist whose true identity no one knew, whose paintings were world famous and worth millions.

Sebastian Taight: Nothing she didn't already know, except that he speculated heavily in art. No surprise to her now.

Fen Hilliard: Nothing she didn't already know.

Knox Hilliard: She'd googled him a gazillion times since she'd started working for him, so she didn't know why she bothered. She saw nothing new, but she kept going back pages and pages and pages. There must be something to find since Sebastian had all but given her a roadmap.

What do you think of OKH Enterprises?

She doesn't know Ford. Or the proviso.

"Knox Hilliard," she whispered as she typed into Google. "OKH Enterprises. Proviso." Bingo, the first hit on the first page, a three-year-old article in the *Wall Street Journal* entitled, "OKHE bride murdered, groom suspected."

She read. And as she read, her stomach began to roil as she got deeper and deeper into the long story.

> To date, Knox Hilliard's wedding and announcement of a birth are the most anticipated social events on Wall Street and financial quarters across the country, especially as the deadline, Knox Hilliard's 40th birthday, looms. If he fulfills the terms of the proviso, his net worth could increase by as much as a half billion dollars.

Justice barely made it to the restroom before she threw up.

He was still irritated at the end of the day when he had to go looking for her because she wasn't at her desk. She looked up from her stack of files when he appeared in the door and leaned against the jamb, his arms folded across his chest. He stared—well, glared—at her and she shrunk into herself.

"Here," he growled and tossed something at her. Reflexively, she caught what he'd thrown and was confused to find a set of car keys, brand new, with all the bells and whistles on the ring. "It's in your usual parking spot. Go back to River Glen and pack for the week. You can take the truck Saturday and finish up then."

So many questions, but he was turning away. "What am I going to say to my dad?"

He stopped, but didn't look at her. "I took care of him."

Her eyes widened and her breath caught in her throat, wondering how bad it was and what she'd find when she got to the farm. Dreading the next few hours, she went upstairs to put away her work. She dragged her feet on the way to the parking lot, not understanding anything, being thoroughly confused. There, in her spot, was a dark silver Toyota Corolla, brand new. Not flashy, it was a nice starter car that a young prosecutor could afford. It would attract no attention at all.

There was a pain behind her sternum so deep, so sharp, that she wanted to clutch at it and fold into a little ball, cry, and then die because this was a nightmare. *Trust me*, Giselle had told her.

She did *not* trust Giselle and at this point, she didn't like her, either. There was just something very nauseating about knowing one had been watched and speculated upon for years before being forced to play a game one had not asked for nor understood when dragged into it.

And all it had taken was one semi-coherent speech one day in one class three years ago to attract their attention.

"Hey, Justice, I see you got a new car."

She turned to see Richard approach her. She looked for Knox's SUV, but it was gone. "Knox gave it to me," she said low, once he had caught up to her. His mouth tightened. Then she did something she'd never done before because she'd never had the opportunity: She confided in someone. She hadn't even said too terribly much to Giselle because she wasn't sure what would get back to Knox and what wouldn't.

"I found out about the proviso."

Richard's mouth pursed and he looked at her suspiciously. "How did you not know about that before you came here?"

"I— Um, I heard things. At school. I didn't want to believe— If I had just—" She wanted to cry because of it, but she swallowed and sucked up a breath. "I'm so stupid."

Richard's face softened then. He wrapped his arm around her shoulder, and hugged her close to his side. "No. You're just young and naïve. It's kind of charming, really, and it's one of the reasons people read you."

"Richard, if I could leave, I would."

"How did he get you to marry him?"

"He said he'd kill my dad."

He raised an eyebrow. "And you *believed* him?"

She stared at him.

He threw up a hand in disgust. "Of course you did."

"Why *me?*" she whispered.

He studied her for a moment, as if deciding how much to say. "He's attracted to you," he said flatly.

Justice's breath caught and she tingled. She knew he wanted to have sex with her, but to hear it stated another way . . . *attracted.* And by a third party who'd noticed . . .

"None of us realized that until yesterday, but he couldn't hide it. Considering you wear your heart on your sleeve, I don't know why he didn't do it the easy way." She sighed and he gave her one more squeeze before releasing her. "I wish I knew how to help you, but I don't. He can be a crazy sumbitch and I don't understand why he does half the things he does. The best I can do is lend an ear when you need it."

She sighed. "I'd better get on with things."

They parted ways and Justice unlocked her new car. She took the time to inspect it. It had a few features she didn't think came standard, like a manual transmission (how did he know she'd want that?), moonroof (wow), remote keyless entry (admittedly nifty), and satellite radio (all Rush and Nugent and Steely Dan all the time), and a GPS system (no more paper maps to re-fold).

She put her forehead down on the steering wheel and choked. Why had he done this? How and when had he done this? She couldn't fathom his motives and she knew he wouldn't explain himself anytime soon.

She finally, resignedly, sat up and started the car. A strange song boomed out from the obviously state-of-the-art sound system (how did he know she liked good sound?), one she'd never heard before. She nearly turned it off, but began to listen to the lyrics.

. . . I'm gonna hunt the hunter . . .

. . . Cook my dinner while I shine my gun . . .

Her eyes closed as she began to go with the rhythm, the beat, the empowering lyrics, then it was over and she punched the CD player. Imani Coppola. *Chupacabra.*

"Legend of a Cowgirl."

Taking a long breath, not daring to think about how that got in the CD player and, better yet, how the stereo got programmed to repeat it, she headed north to River Glen and wondered how Knox "took care of" her father. She needn't have worried. Once she'd parked and gone in the house, her father confronted her directly.

"You need to move out," he stated baldly.

Justice backed up and blinked. "What?"

"You need to move out," he said again.

"How are you going to work the farm by yourself?"

"Hired some help."

"Hired? We don't have money for that."

He smirked, then Justice understood. Knox had *bought* her from her father.

I. Own. You.

She sucked in a sharp breath, then noticed that he still looked at her the way he had the morning before. Her eyes widened when she realized what it was and why he looked at her that way.

Knox had looked at her like that last night.

"Justice," he said in a tone she'd never heard before. She swallowed and backed up a bit more when he took a step toward her, his hand outstretched. "You look just like your mother when she was your age."

Whatever had happened, she had to get out of here. The shoulder holster that she wore, the gun firmly under her left elbow . . . Suddenly she was very glad she had it.

And that sickened her.

"I'm going to pack a bag. If I can't get what I want tonight, I'll be back Saturday with Knox for the rest of my things."

She didn't dare come back here without him, and she turned to dash up the stairs.

She closed and locked her door when she heard him start up the stairs after her, though he simply went into the bathroom. It occurred to her that she was more afraid of her father now than she was of Knox. Knox had threatened her, had taken everything she had away from her, had forced a life upon her she didn't want—but she liked what Knox did to her, that he wanted her, that he had begged forgiveness for hurting her. And now she knew his threats to be sheer bluff.

No man would pay money to get what he wanted if he could follow through on the kinds of threats Knox had made.

She happened to glance out her window at the car Knox had given her, then she did a double take. A brand new car. Money in the bank and credit cards. Her laptop and purse. Gun and badge. The enormous new wardrobe.

She could leave. She could leave Knox, her father, this farm, the Chouteau

County prosecutor's office.

Her heart soared as she thought about it and she changed clothes as quickly as she could. Jeans, tee shirt, boots. Badge, thigh holster, and gun (she wasn't going anywhere without that for a while). When she finally dragged her suitcases stuffed with nearly every piece of clothing she had, a few cherished mementos of her mother, birth certificate and other documents she'd need to start a new life, she opened the trunk.

In it she found a small fireproof safe. She looked on her key ring and picked out a small key that unlocked it. It was loaded with documents. Confused, she picked it up and went to sit in the back seat of her car to sort through it, and her breath caught in her throat.

- title to the car: Iustitia Jane McKinley
- insurance and registration for the car in her name
- notarized copy of her marriage certificate
- letter of reference signed by Knox Hilliard
- ten thousand dollars in worn hundred-dollar bills
- annulment documents drawn up by Eric Cipriani and signed by Knox Hilliard

She put a hand to her mouth and laughed in disbelief.

Knox was letting her go and he'd given her everything she needed to leave him and go to DC like she should've done in the first place. Only now, if she went, she looked right and walked right. She'd spent eight weeks in the Chouteau County prosecutor's office learning how to talk to people, make deals, negotiate plea agreements. She had a coveted letter of reference from Knox Hilliard.

And an annulment. All she had to do was sign it and drop it in the mail when she got to wherever she was going.

She looked for a note to her, then realized that the CD was it.

After all that and he was letting her go. Maybe he did have a shred of honor in his soul after all. Well! She wasn't going to look a gift horse in the mouth. She threw her stuff in the trunk, went back for the rest of her clothes, and tucked a couple hundred dollars in her pocket, then locked everything down tight.

She did a little jig and let out a giggle before she got in the car, and she knew that her father watched her from the window. That didn't faze her now and she didn't bother to say goodbye. She turned south when she got to the interstate and passed the exit that would take her to Knox's house with utter glee. In Blue Springs, she stopped and got something to eat and to top off her tank.

Annulment!

After eight weeks of captivity, she was free.

78: Thy Will Be Done

S HE WASN'T SURE WHEN THE GLEE SLOWLY FADED AND SHE REALLY STARTED
to analyze the situation, but it wasn't long after Blue Springs. Knox Hilliard
had let her go after a wedding at gunpoint, less than two days of marriage,
money having changed hands between him and her father, a week with Giselle being
made over, armed, and prepared for—

Fen Hilliard.

Fen Hilliard had killed Leah Wincott. Justice knew that as certainly as she knew
her own name. It only spoke to his cunning that the only man in the world who had
any reason at all to see her dead could cover that up so well.

She rested her elbow on the window ledge and rolled up her fist against her
mouth, her mind churning and burning as she drove.

The question wasn't why Knox had let her go. That was obvious. The question
was why he'd made her a target in the first place—and why he'd employed such an
elaborate scheme to do so.

Occam's Razor: The simplest explanation tends to be the correct one. That was
her starting point for everything she had to spend time to puzzle out and now was
no different.

The simplest explanation was that Knox had wanted to marry her.

He's attracted to you . . . he couldn't hide it.

Indeed, that was a simple enough explanation, but it could not be the correct one.
All he'd had to do was ask her.

I know you've been hankering after a piece of my ass since you got here . . .

I would have given you anything after that day in class when you touched me and defended me—if you had just asked.

No, you wouldn't have.

What twisted logic led him to think she would've turned him down?

. . . why couldn't you have just told her up front and let her decide? That would've been the honorable thing to do.

Yeah, Knox, why couldn't you have?

Have you ever used one on someone?

Silence.

How many people knew? How many people were in on this?

Giselle.

Mr. Kenard.

Sebastian.

Kevin Oakley? Somehow, she doubted that.

Fen Hilliard, out next year on December 27 whether Knox fulfilled the proviso or not.

OKH, a lock for Sebastian.

Fen, losing his campaign.

Congress, backing off Sebastian.

Justice groaned as the entire situation exploded in her head. "I should've googled."

She reached Columbia after eleven and stopped to get gas. While it pumped, she opened her trunk and her safe again. Retrieved the annulment documents. Eric had written it so she was the petitioner and Knox the respondent. Basis: fraud.

She sighed as she put it all away again, locked it up, and went to pay for her gas. By the time she'd gone to the restroom, picked up a pop and a bag of chips, slow tears had begun. The clerk, who was about her age, did a double take when he looked at her and attempted to flirt with her. He was deliberately slow so as to lengthen the one-sided conversation.

"It can't be that bad," he said, indicating her face, which was probably blotchy.

It was horrible. It was wonderful. Choices. She had choices now. Knox had taken away half her choices when he'd forced her to stay in the office, then the rest when he'd forced her to marry him.

She shuddered, then sniffled. "Everything's fine."

"Are you from town or are you a Mizzou student?"

She tightened her lips and said, "I had the gas on pump six."

"What's your name?"

"I'm married." It just slipped out. She hadn't meant to say that, but she caught her breath, horrified when she realized how much she'd enjoyed saying that because of who her husband was. She suddenly felt she'd lost something she'd never really had.

The clerk looked at her bare left ring finger and his mouth tightened.

By this time, she'd gathered a lot of attention because he was holding up the line for flirting at her. Then she noticed that people were staring at her thigh holster. A pair of state troopers on break and foraging for dinner was there. They approached her when she had finally paid for her gas and got a receipt and change.

"Miss?"

She stepped out of the way of the other customers and took the officers aside.

"I'm an assistant prosecutor in Chouteau County," she said quietly to them before they could go any further, showing her badge as a courtesy to them.

Both sets of eyes widened a bit. "Isn't that Knox Hilliard's county?"

"Yes. He's my boss." *My . . . husband.*

"Can we give you an escort to wherever you're going? East or west? We'd be glad to, you know, speed things along for you."

"No, thanks," she murmured. "I'll be okay."

They tipped their hats and went about their foraging. One hundred fifty miles east of Chouteau County on her way to Washington, DC, Knox Hilliard's name preceded her, protected her, garnered deference and respect as one of his attorneys. How much more would it have garnered if they knew she was his wife?

She was married to a notorious man and his name would protect her all the way to DC should she care to invoke it.

It took another two hours to get to St. Louis and find a cheap motel room. She had a lot of driving ahead of her but all the time in the world to do it, as long as she husbanded her money carefully.

East or west?

The question had plagued her since Columbia and she could only come to one conclusion:

Both choices were wrong. Or right. But she didn't know which or why.

I will choose a path that's clear: I will choose free will.

Free will? She'd had none of that the minute she'd seen Knox shoot Jones in the head and he'd used it as an excuse to keep her there. Yet after having had eight weeks of dealing with criminals and getting to know Hicks as a rather lovable curmudgeon, Justice figured Jones deserved what he got. Maybe more.

She managed to get twelve hours of mostly troubled sleep and awoke after noon.

I wonder what Knox is doing right now.

Without her. Eric would know why she hadn't shown up for work; she wasn't sure about Richard or Patrick. Hicks had court today and wouldn't notice.

Why was she thinking about that office? As of six o'clock last night, she didn't work there anymore.

She got out of bed and cracked open her laptop to check her email and her blogs. No hamlet. She sighed, more depressed than the situation warranted.

Justice went out for food and found a hole-in-the-wall diner. As she ate, she caught herself looking at her cell phone, expecting it to ring. Why? She checked it for messages: None.

Vague disappointment. Why?

Justice finished her meal and went back to her room, then spun the Rush from her laptop and sat on the bed in the dark, the blinds drawn.

Only twice in her life had she done this: Once to give her strength to stand up to her father and go to college, the other to give her strength to stand up to her father and go to law school.

Now she needed guidance because she didn't know what to do to quell her uneasiness with going east *or* west.

"Speak to me, Geddy," she whispered as she lost herself in meditation; three songs passed with nothing catching her ear or her mind.

Being comfortable with who you are when you're behind a computer and being lauded and paid for your opinions, and courted by prestigious institutions where you could hide away and write? Not the same as being comfortable in your own skin.

Okay, then. Who was she?

Justice McKinley, granddaughter of Juell Pope, widely respected legal philosopher.

Justice McKinley, wife of the OKH heir and Chouteau County prosecutor Knox Hilliard.

Justice McKinley, writer of political and legal philosophy and theory—

—and that was all it was: theory. Based on nothing because her life experience consisted of working on a farm until she'd gone to work for Knox and Richard's words ran through her mind: *You're popular because you're a novelty, not because you're saying anything original.*

She'd learned more about herself in the last eight weeks than she had her whole life.

Who was she *really?*

Just a lonely, confused, nobody baby lawyer sitting on a bed in a motel in St. Louis, Missouri, armed, ready and able to take on the world, but with no path, no direction, no plan.

Who was she? Wait, no. That was the wrong question. Who she was would always be in flux as long as she didn't know what she wanted to be—

Her eyes popped open.

—and had never known until she'd met Giselle Cox.

Powerful.

I can't teach you how to be that . . . You have to come to it on your own, through hardship and fear . . . Power is acquired, earned.

Justice had had a very short and sweet taste of power standing in the middle of Missouri in a QuikTrip, armed, paid deference by two state troopers because of whom she represented.

She liked it, but she'd like it a lot more if she could command that kind of respect on her own. It would take her years to acquire that kind of power without guidance, a shoulder to lean on occasionally, some validation.

What you wanted from me was to teach you to be powerful and I told you I couldn't do that . . . Knox can and he will if you let him.

The enlightenment she sought began to bloom in her mind like a lotus. It unfolded and spread until it supported the whole of her soul. She began to shake it out, distill it.

Knox was her guidance.

. . . you haven't been treated any differently than any other new resident we've ever had.

With regard to her training as a lawyer, no, she hadn't. She saw that clearly now. He wielded his scalpel with exquisite precision in a relatively safe environment where he could catch his baby lawyers if they fell under his sharp edge.

Everything he had done and said to her from the moment he hired her had been designed to break her down, force her to work against him to make her stronger, like a muscle. He'd goaded her, baited her with increasing intensity to make her focus on him, to keep her from disengaging or cowering in fear, to keep her in the fight, to make her comfortable with confrontation and, in her case, sexual confrontation.

She'd thrown a tire at him.

She'd threatened him with a sexual harassment suit.

She'd spit in his face.

She'd never backed down when he'd gotten in *her* face.

She'd thrown his tyranny back at him.

She'd slapped him for making her a slave and dared him to hit her back by threatening his life.

She'd made him work for her acquiescence out in the grass, but her breaking point had come as a shock to both of them. He'd backed off immediately, cocooned her in his warmth, apologized, kissed away her pain; bathed her, dressed her, put her to bed.

Knox had taken away everything she had, given her everything she needed to be the woman she wanted to be, then set her free with years of training he'd packed into eight weeks.

You have to be honest with yourself about what you really want.

To work in the Chouteau County prosecutor's office. Check.

To be powerful. Check—or at least getting there with a good push in the right direction and all the tools and trappings she needed.

To have some sort of personal relationship with Knox Hilliard. Check.

East or west? She still didn't know, but she couldn't stay in a cheap motel in St. Louis indefinitely. She had to make decisions because she had no backup plan. Now she had too much disparate information, her options too numerous and foreign to sort through efficiently.

West:

To fight a good fight with people like Sebastian Taight and Giselle Cox and Bryce Kenard against a man who had murdered an innocent woman to keep what rightfully belonged to Knox. They thought her their equal, worthy of their regard, capable of joining the fight and taking on Fen Hilliard if she had to.

East:

To flee from a man who would kill her if he knew Knox had used her to fulfill half of the condition of his inheritance. For whatever reason, Knox had changed his mind and sent her away, given her back the freedom he'd taken from her. She could take back her life and everything he'd given her to continue east to do wonderful things, perhaps change the world.

You have to be honest with yourself about what you really want.

Justice sucked in a deep breath at that and closed her eyes again when she finally stumbled into the heart of it. Yes. The truth will out.

She still wanted Knox as her lover, in spite of everything.

She gulped.

. . . if it means the difference between making love to you and not, I'll catch you every time.

And Knox wanted Justice to be his lover.

His kisses. His hands in her hair. His mouth on her breasts. His naked body against hers. His fingers inside her, making her arch her back and feel that glorious blossom and pop. His husky baritone rolling over and over in her mind, telling her what he wanted to do to her, what he wanted her to do to him, fanning the flames, making her want him in spite of everything else he had done to her.

She sighed and shrugged, opened her eyes, turned off the music. Trapped between Fen and Knox Hilliard, between what she wanted and who she wanted to be, she again found herself with no choice whatsoever.

Her mind and her soul at ease, she slept like the dead.

79: I Already Bought the Dream

J USTICE WALKED INTO THE CHOUTEAU COUNTY PROSECUTOR'S OFFICE AFTER
lunch. All conversation stopped and Eric's jaw dropped. Ignoring everything, she
went to her desk and dumped her stuff on it as if nothing were different about
today than any other day she arrived late to work.

Knox strode angrily into the office and she got a chance to study him for a
moment: his haggard face, his strained voice, the exhaustion that underlay it all. He
went straight to Eric's desk to begin a rant, and Eric ignored him, still staring at Justice.

He slammed his palms down on Eric's desk and barked, "Cipriani! Pay attention!
What the *fuck* is your problem?"

Eric's gaze went to Knox's then and with a small jerk of his chin, he said, "Look."

Knox's head whipped around and his eyes widened when he saw her. Nobody
spoke, nobody moved.

"I'm sorry I'm late," Justice murmured as she sat and began to sort through the
files she'd left behind two days before, not daring to look up at him. "It won't happen
again."

Knox unfolded to his full height slowly and turned to face her. He sat back on
Eric's desk and crossed his arms over his chest, and one ankle over another.

"That's what you say every time you're late, McKinley," he growled. "I oughtta
fire your ass."

She glanced up then and raised an eyebrow. "You can't. You haven't laid any
paper on me and I'll sue you for wrongful termination."

He pursed his lips as he stared at her, then he barked, "Thanks for the tip. I'll
remember that," before he stalked back into his office and slammed the door.

Justice went about her business as usual, expecting that at some point, Eric would—

"Why are you here?" he demanded, leaning over her desk at 4:30 after everyone except Knox had gone home. Knox was downstairs in the sheriff's department yelling at Raines for causing him to lose a case. That happened a lot with Raines, she'd learned; he'd burned every attorney in that office several times with sloppiness bordering on outright sabotage and Knox more than most—which was why Knox unofficially relied more heavily on the Kansas City Police Department and state troopers than he was supposed to.

"He sent you away for a reason, Justice," he snapped when she refused to answer the question. "You weren't supposed to come back and you were supposed to sign your annulment."

"Fen Hilliard's got bigger problems than whether Knox fulfills the terms of the proviso or not."

He backed off and stood to his full height, his black eyes wide. "You know?"

"Yes, Eric," she muttered dryly. "I'm fairly decent at researching, and getting married at gunpoint certainly warranted a little bit of it."

"Fen will have you murdered if he finds out."

Justice chewed on the inside of her cheek and nodded slowly. "I figure so. But. There are worse things than dying over a matter of honor."

He stared at her speculatively and for quite a long while; she returned his gaze, daring him to say it. Finally, he did. "Honor has nothing to do with it."

"Now that you mention it," she snapped, "you're absolutely right about that and you probably knew that from day one."

"I did," he returned sharply. "I don't know exactly why he wanted me to interview you, Justice, but I had no intention of hiring you."

"Got that part, thanks. The right questions are: Why did he marry me? And then turn around and let me go after all that hoopla?"

Eric said nothing for a moment, then sighed. "I don't know. Knox does a lot of things that don't make sense to me."

"Apparently, you're not the only one."

He took a deep breath and stared at her desk, using a fingernail to absently pick at nothing. "Well, for what it's worth," he said, releasing his breath in a long whoosh, relief now evident in every syllable, "you have no idea how happy we are that you came back."

80: Don't Wrap It Up

KNOX'S SUV WAS GONE BY THE TIME SHE WRAPPED UP HER DAY AND DROVE home.

Home. Hers. Hers and Knox's. Together.

She found her way through the labyrinthine suburban streets to the back corner of the subdivision where she lived now. The gate was open and she parked in the driveway.

I bet she wants to fuck Knox Hilliard as much as I do . . . She wouldn't know what to do with him if she had him.

She sighed and dropped her head on the steering wheel, tears dripping down her nose because now she was here by her own choice and she didn't know how this would turn out. She felt sad and amused and melancholy and frightened and hopeful all at the same time. She scrounged around on her key ring for what might be the front door key, but she couldn't find one.

He had never expected she'd come back. To him. To fight his fight with him. To see what could be if she were here freely, to be his wife and his lover and the mother of his children, like she'd dreamed of. She'd been handed her fantasies on a silver platter and she wanted to live in them for however long that lasted.

She popped her trunk and got out, slammed the driver's door, and started unpacking her car.

Her eyes were dry and scratchy. Her brain was tired from working through the tangle of emotions, which she couldn't do until she knew a few more things.

Like why Knox did everything so bassackwards.

She slammed the trunk lid closed and at that moment, she heard the front door open. Well, now she wouldn't have to ring the doorbell of her own house.

Knox strode across the lawn toward her, an expression on his face she couldn't decipher. The setting sun in the west splashed across his hair and his face. When the small beveled diamond panes in the windows caught the sun, they shot gold prisms onto him like raindrops. He *was* the sun.

His well-worn jeans rode low on his hips and did nothing to hide the strength in his legs—the ones that had outrun her their first night together. Likewise, his plain white tee shirt did nothing to hide the vivid musculature of his chest and arms. She remembered what his bare chest looked like, remembered how it had felt against her bare breasts, and she couldn't help those sensations in the pit of her belly.

Knox Hilliard, her boss. Her husband.

Her lover.

He stopped right in front of her and just looked at her. She did nothing but stare back at him. She watched him as his eyes warmed and darkened, then her eyes closed.

It wasn't long in coming. He furrowed the fingers of his right hand through her hair and pulled her to him gently. His kiss was half gentle, half demanding and she vaguely wondered if—hoped that—he would take her to bed right now. Pulling her body to his, he wrapped his other arm around her hips and held her close.

Oh, yes, *this* was why she'd come back, Fen Hilliard be damned.

Knox's arousal pressed against her belly, their clothes doing little to soften it. Justice was drowning in him, falling into whatever magic spell he had cast over her. She ran her hand over his arm, up, up until she had wrapped her arm around his neck and pulled herself as close to him as she could get.

That kiss went on and on and on. Justice loved and gloried in every second of it. He stroked her nowhere else, made no other demands, didn't talk to her. He just kissed her and she kissed him back.

The evening was silent of the man-made sounds of civilization. The birds, the cicadas, the breeze in the leaves were the only sounds, the only music that accompanied their kiss.

"You came back," Knox whispered into her mouth, still kissing her, now butterfly, sweet, light.

"You noticed."

"Why?"

"Because you let me go."

He wrapped his arms around her tighter and buried his face in her neck. She held him close to her, her head on his shoulder and she felt moisture seep through her hair and onto her skin. She found that . . . odd.

After a long while, he said, hoarse, "How far did you get?"

"St. Louis. I stayed there. I had a lot of thinking to do."

She was shaking badly, her thighs trembling as if she had just run the mile in two minutes. Justice wanted Knox to take her to his bed, to keep her there forever.

To love her.

He pulled away from her slightly and sighed heavily. "I have to tell you some things."

Oh. That. "I already know."

He stared at her warily. "Sebastian said you didn't."

"Google is my friend. I found an old *Wall Street Journal* article and drew my own conclusions as to who killed Leah."

Knox's eyes widened then and he pushed her away, though still grasping her upper arms as if he would never let go. "And you came back anyway?" he demanded. "*Why* would you do that?"

She took a deep breath. There were only two reasons, and she wasn't sure she wanted to admit either, but she settled for the less revealing of the two:

"I want to be powerful, like Giselle," she whispered. "You can teach me that."

"So you can go back to Washington the way you were supposed to two days ago," he returned, a note of . . . something . . . in his voice she couldn't figure out.

Justice shook her head slowly, holding his gaze. "I told you I'd have given you anything if you'd asked. Why would you be so *arrogant* as to presume to know what I would or wouldn't do or think?"

"You're a genius, Iustitia. I thought you'd understand this isn't the smart choice." She shrugged. "Taking on King George wasn't the brightest idea anybody ever had, was it?"

Knox's face was so haggard, so worn. He looked every minute of his almost-forty and then some, and to Justice, he was the most beautiful man who ever lived. He stared at her, apparently unable to speak because he kept opening his mouth as if to say something, then closing it again as if it weren't worth saying.

Finally, he lifted a hand to her face and caressed her cheek with his knuckles.

"Do you believe in vigilante justice, Iustitia?" he whispered.

"Yes," she murmured.

His eyes widened. "What about theft versus crimes against the body?"

"Truth is more sacred than life or property," she whispered.

"Revenge?"

"Occasionally serves a purpose."

"Black and white?"

"Truth. Justice."

"At all costs?" he whispered.

"Yes."

He looked at her for a long time, then whispered, "Very good, Iustitia."

They stood looking at each other forever and then, "I need to unpack and iron my clothes. And I'm still very tired. It's been—" She bit her lip and couldn't help that her eyes filled with tears and her mouth trembled. "It's been a very long week. I can't— I can't take much more."

He nodded his assent and he wrapped his arm around her shoulders, holding her close as they went into the house together, his lips pressed against her temple. Justice knew that must mean something, but in her fragile state of mind at the moment, she refused to analyze anything he did.

Knox left her alone to sort through her things as he brought them in from the driveway. She discovered room in the drawers for her clothes. Half the closet was empty, save the ubiquitous tangle of hangers, which meant he had done this before he married her. It made her feel . . . special. No, equal.

He came back just as she finished hanging up the last dress she owned. He leaned against the jamb and crossed his arms over his chest, looking at her clothes in the closet.

Justice had to know. "Why did you send me with Giselle if you weren't going to like how I came back?"

He grunted and looked her up and down. "I love what she did with you," he said gruffly. "I don't like that other men like it. You were pretty before, but I guess it didn't occur to me that you'd come back so—" He stopped, took a deep breath, and released it softly, reverently, his eyes blazing: "Stunning."

Her insides, between her legs, tingled sharply and she didn't know what to say to that. "She said I looked sixteen."

"I know. She made sure to point that out to me very loudly and with much profanity. It was her idea to take you shopping in the first place."

Her eyes widened. "But I thought you—"

He shook his head. "I very rarely pay attention to what women look like, Iustitia. I only care what's in between their ears and in their souls."

So he hadn't thought she needed a makeover. A burden lifted from her heart that she hadn't known she still carried.

"She was right," Justice admitted. "The day I came back, the other attorneys, defense counsel, treated me differently—like I belonged there, like I could do my job. They had been patronizing me all along and then they didn't anymore. I didn't know until I came back different."

He sighed. "I— I never noticed. I'm sorry."

"I have another bone to pick with you."

Knox snorted. "How many more after that?"

Her mouth twitched. "I'll let you know."

"Well?"

"You bought me. You bought me from my father."

He looked away then. "He would have never let you go, Iustitia. You would have been chained there forever by his need for free labor because he's too damned cheap to hire someone, too damned lazy to work himself, always guilting you into staying. I asked his permission, blessing, whatever you want to call it. He wanted money because he thought I had it."

"Why didn't you just threaten him like you did me?"

"He told me point blank he'd call the FBI with some bullshit story and I didn't want to take the chance they could make some oddball charge that would stick, especially since I'd forced you to stay in the office."

"Why *me?*"

He chewed on the inside of his cheek. "I had my reasons," he muttered finally.

Justice huffed, shaking her head as she turned away from him to begin folding and smoothing the clothes that would go in the drawers. "Honestly? I don't know whether to be grateful or to be mad. I—" She stopped, more tears welling. "When I came back from Giselle's, he— He looked at me the way you looked at me out in the grass that night."

Knox sucked in a deep, quick breath. "If I'd known that—"

"I didn't understand it myself at first," she said. "When I went to pack my stuff, I was very happy to have a gun."

"You think he—?"

She hesitated, remembering how she'd felt. "I think it crossed his mind to test the waters. I think if I hadn't had a gun, he might have tried to push it. He said I looked like my mother, so . . . I'm not sure he was seeing *me.*"

"Iustitia," he breathed.

"So," she went on briskly, "I'm upset you bought me, but I'm grateful, too. You pulled me out by a hair." There was a long silence and she looked over her shoulder at him. He was still chewing on the inside of his mouth. "There's, um— There's a petition in the little safe that I don't know what to do with. Could you— Um, could you shred it for me, please?"

He looked at her sharply. "I don't want you here if you're just grateful, Iustitia."

"Give me a little bit more credit than that," she snapped, feeling their balance of power shift and level out for good. She was here of her own will now and he had no more hold on her.

"Okay," he snapped back. "Then why *are* you here? The *real* reason?"

Justice took a deep breath and turned back to her folding. "I— I want to see where this, with you and me, together— Uh, out in the grass, before—" She cleared her throat, embarrassed because of what she was trying to say and stumbling over her words because of it. "I mean, um, I want to know . . . If we— If you and I can—"

She stopped. It wasn't going to get any better.

"I want to try," she whispered.

Deep, ragged breath. More silence. Then, softly, "I'm sorry I hurt you out in the grass, Iustitia."

She reluctantly chuckled. "So you said about a gazillion times."

"I won't pressure you," he muttered. "You come to me when you're ready."

Shocked, she looked up over her shoulder then, and he was gone.

84: The Paragon of Animals

H E'D DISAPPEARED COMPLETELY BY THE TIME SHE'D FINISHED MAKING his bedroom hers, too. There was an intimacy about the task that made her feel like she belonged somewhere, to someone—to Knox. That was just too surreal.

Unpacking and ironing done, she had free run of the house and she was going to take advantage of it. When she opened what turned out to be the garage door, his truck was gone. She sighed.

To say the house had no decorative theme would be generous. What little furniture he owned was a hodgepodge of types, styles, fabrics, woods, and colors, some good quality and some just cheap crap from Wal-Mart, but nothing special and in no particular layout. It looked as if he bought the first thing he saw that fit his immediate need.

Two of the three bedrooms were completely empty except for a closet full of clothes she'd presumed he'd moved to make room for hers.

The kitchen needed remodeling or—something. The cabinetry was almost fifty years out of date. The ovens, original to the house, hadn't been used in years. The electric range top looked like it saw occasional use, but she wouldn't want to cook on it. Her used gas Viking and old Sub-Zero were far better than . . . this. Her lip curled. Clearly, he didn't care. This was a place for him to sleep and get out of the rain.

She opened a door in the hall to find a staircase down to a full finished basement, which was obviously where he spent his time. In one corner sat a large desk littered with papers piled high, falling off the edge and collecting on the floor. One cleared spot in the middle of the desk was big enough for a laptop.

One wall had a huge TV facing a disreputable couch. The blankets and pillow piled on the cushions told her where Knox intended to sleep tonight and she swallowed.

Floor-to-ceiling bookshelves packed with books hither and thither flanked the TV. While he had as many books as the Kenards, his were not perfectly ordered or stacked. These books were haphazard, careless even, two and three layers deep. She looked at some of the titles and her eyes widened. Religious texts of all types, shelves and shelves of them. She lingered until she realized that not only could she not tell from these which faith he favored, she had never heard of half of them.

Knox Hilliard, *religious?*

"That might be a problem," Justice muttered.

He had texts from economics to history to higher math. He owned everything Joseph Campbell and Noam Chomsky had ever written. She found several dog-eared and written-in and highlighted copies each of *The Art of War*, *The Prince*, *Anthem*, and *Lord of the Flies*. Shakespeare alone, various editions of collected works and single plays, took up three shelves. He had dedicated an entire section to texts regarding the founding of the country, the Federalist Papers, and other writings and biographies of the various founding fathers. There were histories and books that deconstructed the battle plans of various wars.

She pulled out a badly abused text on the naval battles of the Revolutionary War; one section, about the privateers who made their fortunes fighting the British, was broken out of the spine, dog-eared, dirty, food-stained, written on, highlighted, and obviously very, very loved. So, he was a kindred spirit in this, and she began to smile as she ran her hand across the spines.

Her watch buzzed nine o'clock. She needed sleep badly, but she was too wired, her mind too chock full and she wanted to take advantage of her solitude. She needed room and time and silence to think.

It was her day to blog, so she took her laptop into the bedroom that had become hers only three days ago. With a deep breath, she sat in the middle of the bed cross-legged, and cracked it open. She had a routine:

Checked her email. She shook her head at the vitriol some *religious* people threw at her for having dared to post *There is no God*. "I'm on your side of the political divide," she muttered, half amused, half annoyed. "Don't know what *your* problem is." Indeed, those nastygrams gave her more ideas than she knew what to do with.

Found the streaming audio archives of the day's talk radio shows and started with Glenn Beck.

Typed, edited, proofed, and posted the article she'd written in her mind. And she had a lot to say about freedom, about bondage and slavery; property rights; living one's convictions; justice, mercy, morality, and revenge. That was about a five-parter, right there.

Surfed the rounds of all the other blogs she followed, read, commented.

Paid bills.

Pulled up the *Wall Street Journal* Online and perused the headlines, reading what interested her, then moved onto the *Washington Post* and *Washington Times*.

JMcKinley writes:
Yo, hamlet, where'd you go?

thefaithful writes:
havent seen him in a while

darrylm writes:
went back & lookd for his last post - a week

JMcKinley writes:
hamlet, name that quote: In the United States there's a Puritan ethic and a mythology of success. He who is successful is good. In Latin countries, in Catholic countries, a successful person is a sinner.

She'd posted that yesterday in St. Louis. It should've drawn him out of the woodwork in a couple of hours at most. Disappointment settled in a knot behind her breastbone.

Lost in her thoughts, she was badly startled when the most humongous cat she had ever seen jumped up on the bed with her and head-butted her elbow.

Knox Hilliard had a *cat*?

"Hey, buddy," she said softly, looking to see if he had a tag and if so, what it said.

DOG HILLIARD

She laughed, a great rolling belly laugh.

Knox hadn't come home by the time she took a shower and went to bed. She looked for his shirt and boxers to sleep in again, but they seemed to have disappeared. She went to his side of the closet and dresser and filched clean duplicates shamelessly. She found a pair of his socks and put those on, too.

She took a whiff of the shirt and sighed, because she couldn't help it.

Justice had her hand on the bedroom light switch when the bed itself caught her eye. She went to it and stroked the elaborately decorated antique wood.

A hand-carved sleigh bed, it was stained a rich dark, almost black, walnut color. Because it was an antique, it was smaller than a queen but bigger than a full. It would require a custom mattress and custom linens; when she turned the bed down, she realized that not only were the linens custom, they were very fine, more so even than the ones on the bed at the Kenards'.

So. In this house, there were only three things Knox Hilliard cared about: his bed, his books, and his cat. As she fell asleep, she vaguely wondered if she would ever be the fourth.

82: Bonfire of the Vanities

K NOX WAS IN COURT ALL THE NEXT DAY, SO SHE DIDN'T SEE HIM, BUT THAT was okay. She did her day's business in the usual manner, although she had a hard time staying awake.

He hadn't slept with her and she'd dozed most of the night, wondering when she'd feel the lifting of the covers and the depression of the mattress. It was nearly time to get up by the time she'd given up and succumbed.

Once home, Knox wasn't there. She was very tired, so she changed into Knox's clothes and decided to take a nap. She awoke with a start only a few minutes later and looked at the clock: two o'clock in the morning and it was dead quiet. No male body next to hers breathing. No rustlings of covers that didn't belong to her.

Justice sighed.

Knox had made himself unavailable for talking—or anything else—so she decided to pad out to the barn.

Sebastian was listening to Rachmaninoff tonight. He cast her a glance when she came in and sat where she sat before. He turned the volume down but kept working high up in the air.

"Where's Knox?" he asked absently, busy scraping and cutting paint, mixing and changing out the sizes of his spackling knives.

"I don't know," she said after a while. "He wasn't in bed when I woke up."

Sebastian cast her a sharp glance. "Really," he drawled, then turned his complete attention back to his canvas. Neither said anything for about an hour, he working, she watching.

"What makes it sparkle like that?" she asked suddenly.

He started and looked down at her. "You can see that?"

"Yes. Look," she said and pointed to the opposite wall of the barn that wasn't lit, where millions of speckles in all colors of the rainbow danced across it.

His mouth dropped and he sucked in a deep, amazed gasp. "Hot damn!" he finally shouted, laughing. "Look at that! Holy shit, I love that! Thank you!" He looked down at her again, still grinning. Then he turned back to her. "Look at the canvas. Tell me what you see."

She tilted her head and pursed her lips, studying it for a long while. "It's skin," she finally said.

"Yes."

"You want it to look like mine, without the freckles."

He started, as if he hadn't expected her to know that. "Yes, kind of, but more ethereal."

"It needs to be thinned out, not so textured. Like a glaze."

Sebastian raised an eyebrow, as if he were quizzing her. "Why do you think that?"

She shrugged, not understanding why he'd ask her such things. She knew nothing about art and cared less. "I don't know. I'm not an artist. You asked me what I thought, so I told you. What's in the paint?"

"Diamond chips."

Diamonds. Her eyes widened as she thought of it, but she remained still.

Another half hour of renewed energy in his painting and she saw what he was trying to do. She watched the wall while he painted, cutting in the jewels with his knife as if he were sketching them there, and the image's main lines replicated themselves in sparkles. He looked back at the wall, a wide grin on his face.

Then it was Justice's turn to gasp. He scraped every bit of white paint off that canvas. Most came off easily; a little he had to chip off.

"*Why* are you doing that?" she demanded.

"I'm going to start over," he said. "I didn't know if this would work and it worked better than I ever hoped."

"That's a lot of wasted effort."

He speared her with a glance. "There is no such thing as wasted effort when you're learning." Then he was done for the night. He climbed down from the scaffold and walked toward her. "You shouldn't come out here too often. Knox is very territorial and would assume the worst."

Her brow wrinkled. "He would just assume that I would— With you—?" She bit it off and blinked back tears.

"Oh, no. He would assume I had taken it upon myself to seduce you, paint you, and hang you in an art gallery for the world to see—and believe me," he laughed wryly, looking her up and down very appreciatively, then again until she blushed, "if I didn't have my mind wrapped around one woman, I'd take great pleasure in seducing you, Knox be damned. And then I'd paint you, but for that, Knox would actually shoot me in the head. And he wouldn't blame *you* for a bit of that."

She flushed again, deeper this time, embarrassed at the thought of being painted nude, but strangely pleased that Sebastian Taight thought her that attractive.

"I googled you. Well, Ford."

He turned and dropped to the floor beside her, stretching his legs out straight in front of him and lying back on his elbows.

"Figured you might. I'd appreciate it if you'd keep the whole Ford thing to yourself, though. It'd really cramp my style if people knew. Did you Google anything else?"

"Oh, yes."

"I see," he said after a moment, when he finally understood she wasn't going to say any more.

"Sebastian?" she murmured, still looking out the barn door. "Why me?"

"I'm not going to answer that," he said immediately, not even pretending to misunderstand. "It's not my place. Knox needs to tell you that himself and he will when he's ready to."

Justice sighed and looked away from Sebastian, toward the back of the barn, her other cheek now resting on her knees.

"He let me go," she said after a while.

"Huh?"

She cleared her throat and turned to look at Sebastian again. "Knox let me go. He gave me a new car, money, clothes, a letter of reference. He let me go. Tuesday after work." Sebastian stared at her, his eyes wide. "And," she added, just for good measure, "he gave me an annulment."

His face drained of what little color it had and he gulped. "Oh, fuck," he whispered and closed his eyes, dropping his head back as if pained.

Well, at least now Knox wouldn't get a drubbing by Sebastian for letting loose his last chance to get out from under OKH. Her mouth tightened now that she had just lost all traces of her enchantment with King Midas.

"Then why are you here?" he asked sharply, suddenly suspicious, his head snapping up and his gaze spearing hers. She knew exactly why.

If he fulfills the terms of the proviso, his net worth could increase by as much as a half billion dollars.

No, she wasn't going to admit why she came back.

"You read my work, right?"

"Yes," Sebastian said.

"Of *course* you do," she said, her newfound venom lacing her tone. "You were counting on me to endorse Kevin. You're welcome." That startled a reluctant, wary laugh out of him. "What I write is rhetoric. Complete theory. I suspect that very rarely in life does one get the opportunity to truly put her money where her mouth is, to choose a fight that's worth fighting even though it has high stakes."

Sebastian said nothing for a long while, then, slowly, "That's the biggest crock of shit I ever heard." Justice started and gaped at him. "You know very good and well Kenard and I have that locked up tighter than a drum. You're in love with Knox and it's written in every freckle on your face. You want to ride this ride with him and see where it goes."

"Well then if you knew that, why'd you ask?" she snapped, disturbed at how easily everybody read her. "It's not like you care why I came back. You're just glad you might not have to plow through that takeover."

He started. "What gave you that idea?"

"Your very obvious disgust at Knox having let me go."

"You assume too much," Sebastian snarled, and Justice stared at him agape. How dare he! How dare all of them!

Her nostrils flared. "Look in the mirror, Mr. Taight," she ground out in return. "In fact, all three of you need to. Talk about making assumptions! If you people would talk to me and tell me what's going on instead of treating me like I'm three years old—and *assuming* you know what I'm going to think or say or do at any given moment—maybe I wouldn't have to assume so much. If you and Giselle are so offended by the assumptions I make about you and your motives, you've no one but yourselves to blame. If Knox hadn't assumed what I'd say if he'd just asked me for whatever he wanted, none of this would've been necessary. And another thing—my assumptions, given how much I don't know, make a whole lot more sense than yours do about me."

Sebastian's face softened then and he looked away. "You're right," he finally said, low. "I'm sorry."

There was a long, though not uncomfortable, silence in the barn that stretched as they each cooled off.

"It's too bizarre," she said finally, softly. "I can't make head or tails of it. I just want to know why me and no one will tell me. All Knox says is he has his reasons. I know it'd all come together if I knew that."

Sebastian sighed deeply. "And that's the one thing I can't tell you. If Knox isn't ready to yet, then you'll just have to trust me that they're good reasons. I'm sorry." He sat up and studied the ground for a moment. "If you stay with Knox and see this to its end with us," he murmured slowly, "do you understand what's at stake for you?"

"Yes. My life is at stake, possibly our child's if we have one. That part I don't like and I don't want to go along with it."

Sebastian grunted. "I can say a lot of bad things about Fen, but he wouldn't kill a baby."

Justice took a deep breath. "Well," she finally said.

"Are you joining us of your own free will?"

"Yes."

"No coercion, blackmail, death threats? Bribery?"

"No." She glanced at him sharply. "You do understand that I could've gone to Washington and immediately made my own fortune on the radio, right? I wouldn't even have had to wait for *eighteen months* and *get pregnant* and *had a baby* to *maybepossiblymight* get it if someone didn't *kill me first*." He blinked and she saw that, no, that hadn't occurred to him. "I turned down three million a year for a two-hour radio show straight out of law school to work for Knox for reasons apparently you and the rest of the world already know. Think about that before you keep thinking somewhere in the back of your mind that I'm a whore."

Sebastian flinched and Justice was inordinately pleased by that. "I'm sorry," he said again after a moment. He rose then and brushed himself off. "But that only means you're not as smart as I thought you were."

That made Justice laugh unexpectedly. "I'm smarter than you are."

He grinned then. "Oh, yeah? What was your major?"

"Economics. I'm betting yours was art."

"Hrmph. Maybe you are smarter than me." He helped her up and looked at her for a long time, his grin fading, then said, "Let Knox work through this in his own way, okay? Be patient with him and don't get discouraged. And now I need to go home and you better go back in the house. Would you like me to walk you there?"

"No," she said. "Not necessary."

"You're welcome to come watch me paint, but I wouldn't if I were you. Your choice."

"Yes, it certainly is. *I* will decide when I want to come watch you paint."

83: Irresistible Object, Immovable Force

JUSTICE WALKED UP THE COURTHOUSE STAIRS MONDAY MORNING, ONE WEEK TO the day of her marriage to Knox, not having seen Knox all weekend. If he had been home since Friday night, she didn't know when. She had spent Saturday rearranging kitchen cabinets, shopping for groceries, and exploring her new home.

Sunday evening she'd decided to scope the desk where Knox paid his bills (with checks and envelopes and stamps, even!). She rifled through his haphazard files shamelessly, assuming that Knox would be thorough enough in his schemes to lock up whatever he didn't want her to see. After a while, the only thing that scandalized her was the amount of useless information he kept and in what disarray. She began to pitch and toss and shred until he wouldn't have a file left to his name when she finished.

"That'll teach you to leave me alone for a weekend," she muttered, then stormed out to the barn.

"What can I do for you, Justice?" Sebastian asked absently as he carved in oils and diamonds.

"Does Knox have a lover?"

Sebastian's head snapped around. "*Shit, no,*" he breathed, horrified. "*Why* would you think that?"

"He left Friday night and he hasn't been back."

His mouth tightened. "He runs to the Ozarks when he's upset."

Her brow wrinkled. "What does he do there?"

"He works. If you want to know more, you'll have to ask him, but don't expect an answer until he's ready to tell you."

"Is he upset with me?"

"Doubt it."

"But—"

"No more, Justice," he said, somewhat harshly. "Whatever's going on between you two, you have to work out. There's a helluva lot more to being with a man than roses and chocolates and candlelight, especially with one who's damn near old enough to be your father. You came back to him in spite of Fen, but you apparently didn't think about the fact that you'd have to work out an actual relationship with him."

She blushed at the reminder of her inexperience and, did he but know it, her fantasies—

He likes women who are older than he is . . .

—and the difference in their ages.

Then his face and tone softened. "Obviously, you can't work at it if he's not here and he's a shithead for leaving you alone. But whatever else you think of Knox, he would never cheat."

Standing in the hallway in front of the prosecutor's office with her hand on the door, she shook her head to clear it of that conversation. She had no wish to go in, wondering if she'd see Knox. She thought it truly pathetic that she, his wife, didn't know what he'd been up to all weekend.

The sound of Knox's bellow through the outer office door let her know he was here, but it made her even less eager to see him. Apparently, he wasn't any happier now than he had been the day she'd come back, when he'd ranted at Eric.

She sighed and opened the door, then stopped short when she heard the answering bellow from behind Knox's office door. *Who* besides Sebastian and Giselle would have the guts to yell at Knox that way?

"You can't just up and decide whose spine you need to replace next!"

Mr. Kenard. Of course.

"Bryce, this is my office. Do you think I'm going to let you come in here and tell me what to do?"

Mr. Kenard yelled over him as if he hadn't said a word. "I've known you to pull some stupid stunts in your time, but this takes the cake. This trumps Leah all to hell and back."

She cast a glance at Eric, who typed away, a smirk on his face. "Why is Mr. Kenard here?"

Eric looked up and pursed his lips at her, trying not to laugh. "I think you're just about to find out."

"MCKINLEY!" Knox roared. "In my office. NOW!"

"Well, hey," Richard said from behind her, "at least now you know he's not going to kill you."

That made Eric and Patrick howl, but Justice only scowled at them and dropped her things by Eric's desk before she opened the door to Knox's private office. Mr. Kenard stood in the middle of the room, his arms crossed over his chest, looking at her with a kind expression that was totally incongruous to his volume just seconds before.

"Justice, Bryce seems to think you'd rather work somewhere else."

Her eyes widened. "I didn't—"

"I know you didn't," Knox said low. "Yes or no. Stay here or go with him."

Her eyebrows rose as if considering the offer because she was angrier than she thought about his having left her to fend for herself for the weekend.

Mr. Kenard spoke before she had decided what to say. "I am giving you a choice, Justice, since *Lucifer* here doesn't seem to get the whole free agency thing."

Knox flinched and she looked between them, feeling undercurrents running wide and deep that she didn't understand. That was the second time in a week someone had called him Lucifer. She knew it wasn't coincidental and she knew it was a religious reference, but she didn't understand the heavy subtext.

"Justice," Knox said then, staring at her with those beautiful blue eyes, "I would like it if you stayed here. You're a good lawyer."

"DAMMIT, KNOX!" Mr. Kenard bellowed and Justice stepped back a bit. At school, she'd heard he could be vicious in a courtroom, but in the week she'd stayed with him and Giselle, she'd seen no evidence of a temper. She might have been frightened but for his unwavering kindness and gentleness toward her. "Make up your fucking mind! Couldn't you have used that approach two months ago? Why do you have to do everything the hard way?"

Knox's jaw clenched, but he said nothing. He continued to stare at Justice and her insides melted. Still . . .

"You're a good lawyer, Justice," Knox repeated. "You'll make an excellent prosecutor. I can teach you how to be one of the best in the country. But you'd make an equally good tort lawyer, and Bryce can teach you how to be one of the best in the country—his name on your CV in civil litigation is just as prestigious as mine is in criminal law. You'll make a lot of money at his firm. You'll never make that kind of money here."

She glared at him, then looked at Mr. Kenard. "I was offered three million dollars if I took my own radio show. Can you beat that?"

He didn't seem surprised, but then she couldn't read his expressions through all those scars. "No. Not until you're bringing in the kind of money that would justify that. Ninety thousand."

There's a helluva lot more to being with a man than roses and chocolates and candlelight.

"Thank you, Mr. Kenard."

Knox started and gaped at her. "Justice!"

"But I think I'll stay here."

Mr. Kenard's eyebrow rose as he studied her. "Sebastian told me Knox let you go."

"Yes, he did."

"And you came back on your own."

"I did." Justice didn't dare look at Knox at that moment for reasons she didn't want to think about.

"And you know about Fen."

"Yes."

"Knox didn't pressure you?"

I won't pressure you. You come to me when you're ready.

"No."

"I gave her an annulment, dammit," Knox grumbled. "What the hell else do you want?"

"Did he?"

"Yes. I shredded it."

Mr. Kenard sucked in a deep breath then and studied her for a moment before saying, "Okay. Just wanted to see for myself."

Give it one more week, Justice. Just one week from the time I take you back home. Can you do that?

He'd had this rescue planned before Giselle had kidnapped her; she had known, had asked Justice to wait a week. She wondered if Knox had known in advance, but she doubted it. She had not thought it possible for Knox to look as if he'd been sucker punched.

And Mr. Kenard, well. Obviously, nobody had banked on Knox just . . . letting her go free, no strings attached, and if they had, no one would have bet on her coming back of her own free will. Suddenly, she felt a bit more forgiving of the Kenards: Willing to ambush Knox, their family, to right his wrong against her, a stranger.

"The offer's always open, so call me when you've had your fill of his bullshit."

"Thank you, Mr. Kenard."

"You're welcome, Justice," he said warmly, his voice hoarse.

She left then, closing the door quietly behind her, but stayed at the door and eavesdropped. It didn't surprise her when she felt Eric behind her, his ear to the door, too.

"You bastard," Knox said, his voice not muted enough to hide the dripping sarcasm.

"You're welcome."

"Lucifer was a bit over the top, don't you think?"

"You know the answer to that, as attached as you are to theology. I figured you'd get the point. Apparently Sebastian thought so, too."

No answer.

"Knox," Mr. Kenard sighed, "not everyone is going to abandon you. You don't have to work three times harder to keep a woman who'd have gone with you willingly than you would to keep a woman who'd have left you anyway." What did *that* mean? "You should've just asked her."

"Get out of my office. And don't pull another stunt like that again."

"You got a lot of nerve, you know that? You're on my case constantly about my dad, but you don't want to hear about how fucked up *you* are. Yet *another* thing that hasn't changed in twenty years."

Twenty years?

"They both need to see a shrink," Eric muttered and grabbed Justice's arm to drag her away from the door—and just in time, too.

Mr. Kenard stalked out through the outer office the way his wife had stalked into it two weeks ago. Knox stood in the doorway of his private office, glaring after him, then glared at Justice where she stood next to her things on the floor by Eric's desk.

"Get to work, McKinley," he snapped. "You too, Cipriani."

Then slammed the door behind him.

84: There's No Place Like Home

AUGUST 2007

"So SEBASTIAN TELLS ME LUCIFER LEFT YOU ALONE FOR THE WEEKEND. Again."

Justice blushed as she held the front door open for Giselle the Saturday morning that would begin her second weekend as Knox's wife, but . . . not. Surprised yet touched that Giselle had come all that way for her, she shrugged, attempting to feign nonchalance. "I guess so," she murmured as she stood uncertainly in the entryway, Giselle watching her carefully. "He didn't come home last night."

Giselle snorted and said, "I could've called and asked if you had plans, but I decided I didn't care. Let's go to the movies." Justice's eyes widened. The movies! Justice couldn't remember the last movie she'd seen and it would never have occurred to her to go by herself. Suddenly she realized that she now had time to do all the fun things she'd missed so much, things other people did and took for granted because they didn't have chores and school and working for actual money all at the same time. "And, oh, hey—pack a bag or something because you're spending the night with us. See? I can be as autocratic as that shit-for-brains husband of yours."

That made Justice laugh, just because someone had said it and made it real. She had a husband and someone other than she knew it, had referred to it as if it were an everyday thing to talk to another woman about her husband. It wasn't mentioned at work; in fact, everyone, including Justice, took great pains to act as if nothing was different about her relationship to Knox than it ever had been.

Giselle drove to the local cineplex, where they went from one movie to the next.

"You have to really juggle those time slots if you want maximum return on your investment of a day," she said as she dragged Justice from one end to the other, only five minutes between the end of one movie and the beginning of the next.

"No more!" Justice finally said after movie number four. "I can't take another one."

Giselle laughed and said, "Couldn't anyway. Gotta get home to the hubster. It'll be dark soon." She glanced to the west. "I think I may have cut that a bit too close."

Justice thought it a very strange thing for someone like Giselle Kenard to allow herself to be accountable to a husband, and her face must have revealed her confusion. "Bryce doesn't like to be home alone after dark," Giselle murmured, almost reluctantly, as she started the car and pulled out into traffic. "After his fire . . . Well, I mean . . . Um, he— He just . . . doesn't like to be alone in the dark."

That powerful man, afraid of the dark?

You were so disgusted at Giselle's cowardice that she kept Kenard on ice for almost a year, and it wasn't a month ago you pounded my head into the table for being a coward.

You don't have to work three times harder to keep a woman who'd have gone with you willingly than you would to keep a woman who'd have left you anyway.

These men, Bryce Kenard and Sebastian Taight and Knox Hilliard—powerful, wealthy men and much older than she—had problems and insecurities like she did? They made mistakes? They had fears? And Giselle Cox, a coward? Justice could barely wrap her head around any of that.

"Penny for your thoughts," Giselle murmured as she drove south on I-29, sliding smoothly across two and three lanes at a time to find any opening she could rocket through. Justice looked at the speedometer edging up toward ninety, then out her window. Yes, they raced the sun, and it was a long way from Chouteau Woods to Brookside.

Justice said nothing for a moment. "I don't know how to put it in words," she finally said. "I guess I thought your husband was invincible. And Sebastian. Knox. You."

Giselle shook her head thoughtfully. "No," she said slowly, "just better at hiding it. You get older, you learn how to protect yourself better. Everybody has their weaknesses, their Achilles heel."

"What's yours?" Justice said before she thought.

Giselle slid her a look. "Before I met Bryce, it was whether I'd ever find anyone who could love me the way I wanted. And then when I did, he wasn't what I'd expected, so it took me a while to come to terms with it."

"And now?"

She paused, as if deciding what and how much to say. Finally, "Well, one thing is that I can't have children."

Justice's eyes widened. "Oh," she breathed. "I'm sorry." And she was because suddenly, she heard a heaviness in Giselle's voice she'd never heard before. Ferocity, yes. Humor, yes. Sadness, easily explained now. Anger, definitely. But this was . . . pain. "That's why that painting means so much to you."

She sighed and looked away from Justice as if hiding something, but she caught the glimmer of something on her cheek and her breath caught.

Giselle Cox cries.

Justice said nothing more as Giselle's foot stroked the accelerator down farther and she glanced between the road and the dusk.

"Hey, kid," called Bryce (he had forbidden her to call him "Mr. Kenard" anymore) Sunday morning when she finally roused herself out of bed and found her hosts in the front yard . . . building a flower bed. He flashed a smile at her that was so warm and welcoming that she felt like she'd acquired an older brother.

"Good morning, Justice," Giselle said as she slapped mortar on a brick with a trowel.

"Not that way, Giselle," Bryce muttered when he saw what she'd done. "Here, like this."

Justice kept her laugh to herself as she sat cross-legged in the grass to watch the two of them together, the way she teased him out of his impatience, the way he teased her into a blush. She sighed then, wondering if she and Knox would ever get to that.

"Not if he keeps leaving me every weekend," she whispered to herself.

"What's that?"

"Nothing," Justice replied, then figured it couldn't hurt to try these people for the answers neither Knox nor Sebastian would give her. She knew better, really, but . . . "Why am I here?" she asked sharply.

Both Giselle and Bryce stopped and looked at her warily, then looked at each other.

"You mean, why are you here on Earth?" Bryce asked slowly and Justice's eyes narrowed at his deliberate misunderstanding.

Giselle laughed and poked him with an elbow. "You're not in Scotland anymore, pal."

He cast her an amused scowl, but looked back at Justice. "Look, Justice, we can try to make things as comfortable as we can for you, but you came back, so you have to ride this ride alone. Either wait until he's ready to come to you and explain, or demand the answers, or leave him for good. I'll be honest and tell you I don't like what he's done to you, any of it, but this . . . Your wedding—" He threw up a hand. "I've known Knox for twenty years, Giselle and Sebastian have known him their whole lives, and none of us can figure out why he did that or what he was thinking when he did it. It wouldn't be fair to you for us to speculate."

"I doubt even he knows why," Giselle added. "He's not always, mmmm . . ."

"Sane."

Giselle nodded when Bryce pulled that word out of the air. "That's it. Sane."

So Fen really wasn't her biggest problem; living with Knox, building a life with him, was, just as Sebastian had already told her. No, that hadn't figured into her imaginings. She didn't quite remember what she'd imagined now, but she was pretty sure it had involved chocolate and roses and candlelight—

—from an experienced man who would lead her through life with him, teach her how to hold up her end of a relationship with him. So much for that.

"I want you to know something," Bryce said then, with that infamous Kenard fierceness, and she understood again that she was not the target of Knox's family's anger. "If we had known Knox was planning to force you at gunpoint, it wouldn't have happened at all."

"I'm sorry I took you back there, Justice," Giselle whispered, biting her lip. "I didn't know how far he'd go. Please forgive me."

Oh. Justice gulped, the remnants of her anger and mistrust slowly seeping away. She looked away, across the street, and waited a few beats just to make the point, then nodded. "Okay."

After a few moments of an uneasy silence, Giselle broke it abruptly. "When's your birthday?"

"August twenty-fifth."

"Three weeks! You'll be what, twenty-five?"

"Yes." Justice didn't want to think about her birthday. Usually, it was just a day that passed by like any other without fanfare or notice. But until Giselle had asked, she hadn't known how much she had wanted and hoped that Knox would know that, would recognize it for her somehow.

"If you could have anything in the world for a present, what would it be?"

For Knox to love me.

She shrugged. "I don't know."

Bryce sighed and turned back to work, but Giselle still stood, her expression one of speculation.

"Don't you have *anybody* in the world?"

Justice hesitated when, for the first time, she realized how alone she was in space and time. "No," she whispered, and looked away. "Just my online friends, my followers. If you can even count that. I try not to, but it's difficult when that's all you've got." She paused. "There's one in particular," she admitted reluctantly. "He— Well, I mean— It's like he always knows what I'm thinking."

"It's easy to get attached to people online, isn't it?"

Justice looked up at Giselle, surprised. "You?"

She shrugged. "Sure. I don't get along with women very well and it's really my own fault. Then I ran across a few female kindred spirits online and when I don't feel like talking or rousing any online rabble, I can just walk away from the computer for a while."

"And they don't get in her personal space," Mr. Kenard muttered absently.

"That's a plus. I read your blogs. Who's your favorite commenter?"

"Hamlet."

Giselle stilled and stared at her. "Really." She exchanged glances with her husband. More subtext. Always subtext with these people.

"I would have liked to have met him in real life. I emailed him once about a year and a half ago, but I don't think he got it because he didn't reply."

"How'd all that happen, Justice? The politics, the blogs?" Bryce asked, looking over his shoulder at her with blatant curiosity as he buttered and set bricks. "You're way too young to have that kind of influence."

"My mother," she began slowly, trying to coalesce her thoughts into some logical pattern. "Her name was Liberty. Well, Libertas. She went by Libby. And my grandfather. He taught me about American history, about the Constitution. He was a constitutional lawyer."

"What was his name?" Bryce asked.

"Juell Pope."

They looked as shocked as she'd expected them to.

"I didn't know until I went to law school. He always joked that he was just an old country lawyer with more time than money." She told them about him, about her mother, how much she missed them both, only vaguely noticing that Bryce and Giselle had stopped working completely to listen to her. She told them about her father, her farm, and how much she *didn't* miss that.

The sound of sniffles broke into her tale and she saw Giselle with her head bowed, looking at the ground. Bryce leaned on a spade, also not looking at Justice.

As the silence lengthened, Bryce murmured, "So you made a name for yourself."

"In print, anyway. The first piece I published in the *UMKC Law Review* I wrote when I was seventeen. My grandfather set me the topic and told me where to look for the information."

"Seventeen," he breathed.

"He— He didn't live to see it published," she whispered. "I hope he was proud of me. I Ie said it was C work."

Giselle lifted her head then and she saw the tears streaking her face. *Giselle Cox cries!* Justice still couldn't credit it. "C work?" she demanded. "That was *not* C work."

"I know that now," Justice said quietly, suddenly proud of what she had accomplished—that she had done it on her own, without ever once invoking her grandfather's name. "He said that because it gave me something to reach for. He was like that. I'd do anything, reach farther than was possible if I thought he might tell me I did B work. What do you have left to do if you do A work all the time?

"He loved the Internet when it came along. He took to it so easily. He loved Usenet and IRC and almost nobody knows how to get there anymore . . . Blogging and IM before their time, I suppose. I was posting before I left high school. I just wasn't doing it under my own name. I was afraid that— And then Knox, he— He defended me. I sent in a piece to the *National Review* that weekend and . . . it was accepted."

A long silence turned longer until Justice squirmed. "You would never have submitted that article if he hadn't said what he did that day," Bryce said, a question more than a statement.

"No."

"And you started blogging and tagging your posts with your name," Giselle said.

"And I linked everything else I'd ever said online. That first article for the law review got me a lot of credible attention through my professors, which is why I just kind of . . . overnight, it seemed. Both academically and online. Knox doesn't know; I'm not even sure he knows what an ISP is, much less wireless broadband, much less follow any blogs. Everything's on my CV. If he read it, it didn't seem to register."

Giselle laughed through her tears, then dashed them away with her fingers. "That's 'cause he's got shit for brains," she groused good-naturedly, her humor seeming to have been restored.

Bryce threw a grin at his wife. "That hasn't changed in twenty years, either."

Then they both laughed. Giselle approached Justice, holding her hands out to pull her up, then drew her into her personal space for a bear hug. "You're not alone in the world anymore, Justice. You have us now. Let's go eat."

85: Personal Space

T HURSDAY AFTERNOON, JUSTICE'S EMAIL CHIMED.

Subject: Come to my house tomorrow night. Pack a bag. nm
Reply-to: cgckenard@haleravenwood.com

Justice snorted. Yes, indeed, she could be as autocratic as Justice's "shit-for-brains husband."

"You must be my new sister-in-law," an unfamiliar female voice called to her Saturday morning from the area of the couch, startling Justice just as she descended the last two steps of the Kenards' staircase. Suddenly, a gorgeous blonde sat up, discarding the book she'd been reading and smiled at her. Justice gasped.

"You look like Knox!"

"That would stand to reason," she said and arose to engulf Justice in her arms. "Considering we share a mother."

Justice hesitantly wrapped her arms around this blonde Amazon who was as soft and lush as Giselle was small and firm. She smelled different from Giselle, too, more flowery and delicate. It suited her, Justice thought, and then wondered what the perfume she had chosen during Makeover Week said about her. Really, she wondered how she fit in with these sophisticated ladies who were so much older than she, who had to know so much more about life, about men and sex.

"I didn't know Knox had a sister," Justice murmured as she pulled away from her, embarrassed about that fact. It only highlighted her sketchy knowledge of her husband versus her vast ignorance.

"Well, don't feel bad about that," she returned. "*Knox* didn't know he had a sister until about a month ago."

Justice's mouth dropped open as she stepped back, noticing only then the scar down her face, her broken nose, and her eyes—her eyes!—two different colors. "How can you not know you have a sister for almost forty years?"

"When your mother's a raging bitch and doesn't tell anyone she had you," she said with genuine amusement. "Giselle and I have been waiting for you to wake up so we can go to the spa."

The spa . . . Justice could certainly get used to this life, Knox or not. Then something else occurred to her. "Does this mean I have the mother-in-law from hell?"

"It most certainly does mean that," came Bryce's deep voice from the back porch as he and Giselle came clattering in the house.

"Trudy Hilliard," said Knox's sister—Justice's *sister-in-law*—said. "Fen's my father."

Justice gasped and stepped back, her hand on her mouth, thoroughly shocked and confused. Had she been delivered here as some sort of sacrificial lamb? All three of them watched her warily as she swiftly discarded all scenarios and all combinations of scenarios that didn't make sense. Then her hand fell and she drew a deep breath as she drew her conclusions and said, "I think I understand. At least in principle."

"Trudy's really the evil one," Giselle offered. "I don't think Fen started out that way."

"Just weak and easily seduced," Bryce said, a wry tone in his voice that made Giselle laugh. "That's how it is with us."

Justice looked at him, confused. "Us?"

"Men. We're all weak and easily seduced." He almost laughed, but Justice didn't find that terribly funny or apropos under the circumstances, considering Knox wasn't around to be seduced even if she were inclined to try. Apparently, her new sister-in-law, whose name she *still* didn't know, found it no funnier than she did.

"Well, shit, I'm sorry," he said with a sigh and turned to go back outside. "I'll just shut up now."

Giselle could barely contain her amusement as she watched him leave, and suddenly the woman beside her laughed. "Justice, my name is Eilis Logan."

"Eilis," Justice repeated slowly, letting that roll out on her tongue. "That's beautiful. How do you spell it?"

She obliged, then said, "I am in dire need of exfoliation. Let's go."

An hour later, Justice found herself soaking up to her neck in a sunken tub filled with orange blossoms while some strange concoction made of cocoa powder did something to her face. Both Eilis and Giselle were arranged thusly, each in her own tub after having chosen different combinations of scents and scrubs. A sense of contentment stole over her as she relaxed and listened to what she supposed constituted girl talk for forty-year-old women: sex—

—about which Justice knew next to nothing firsthand except what she'd always done to herself when fantasizing about Knox, and what Knox had done to her out in the grass.

"Justice," Giselle said, startling her out of her musings. "Did you read that book?"

She didn't have to ask what book. "Yes," she said, a little embarrassed, but amused and trying not to laugh.

"And?"

"And I thought it was the most ridiculous thing I've ever read next to *Atlas Shrugged.*"

Giselle burst out laughing.

"What book?" Eilis mumbled from under her cucumber mask.

"*The Claiming of Sleeping Beauty,*" Justice returned smartly.

It was Eilis's turn to laugh. "Oh, now that didn't turn you on? Not even a little bit?"

"I couldn't suspend my disbelief enough to get turned on," she said airily, though it was the teensiest, eensiest bit of a small fib.

"Suspension of disbelief isn't a requirement for reading erotica, Justice," Giselle said dryly.

"Yes, I know, thanks."

"Well, Giselle," Eilis said, "you're deviant, you have to admit."

Giselle sniffed. "Can't help it." Then her head came up sharply as she gaped at Eilis. "How do you know I'm deviant?"

"You *aren't* quiet about it."

"Boy, ain't *that* the truth," Justice muttered under her breath and she started when both women burst out laughing. She huffed and said the first thing that popped into her head. "And you have a perpetual bite mark on the back of your neck. It's not even a hickey. It's a bite. Do you two turn into cats at sundown?"

Giselle and Eilis screamed with laughter, and for the first time in years, Justice felt like she belonged somewhere, truly belonged. Knox's desertion of her had served a purpose she didn't know needed served and now she didn't resent him for it so much. She wondered if Knox had arranged this, to this end. It wouldn't surprise her if he had.

Justice had family now and they wanted her to be comfortable, to fit in. She was soaking in a tub next to a woman who, six weeks ago, had awed and intimidated her; she hadn't even known whether to trust her or not. Now, today, she had teased

Giselle about her sex life, which made Justice feel terribly liberated all of a sudden. Wanted. Cherished.

"Eilis," Justice said suddenly, "please tell me about your mother."

"Ask Giselle."

"Trudy," Giselle said before Justice could do so, "is beautiful, like supermodel beautiful. None of her sisters are like that, including my mother. She's always used her beauty to get her way and she's never *not* gotten her way, except at home. My mom says she was always rebellious and married Knox's father just to get out from under Grandpa Dunham's thumb. All Trudy cares about is her own comfort and satisfaction. Eilis and Knox inconvenienced her and believe me, all hell breaks loose if Trudy's inconvenienced."

Justice sneaked a peek at Eilis, but could tell nothing of what she was thinking under all that goop. "Eilis?"

"Oh, I have nothing to add," she said with alacrity. "Giselle knows her better than I do."

That stunned Justice so much that the silence lengthened until Eilis began to speak, "just a few tidbits," but that was more than enough. Justice thought she might just die of vicarious pain, but Eilis was curiously matter-of-fact. Justice couldn't help but remark upon that.

"Well, now it's kind of like it happened to someone else. Once I talked about it, shared it with someone who accepted me in spite of it, it became almost irrelevant. My life is in the here and now. What happened then got me here and I like where I am." She paused. "For the most part."

Giselle reached a hand out and patted Eilis on the arm. "Eilis, please," she murmured. "He misspoke. If you'd just let him explain—"

"I don't want to talk about it, Giselle," Eilis snapped, and though Justice wanted to know what all that was about, she kept her mouth shut. Then Eilis took a deep breath and said, "I'm ready for my massage."

The three of them spent the rest of the afternoon in relative silence, each with a masseuse, and Justice had no need to talk during a massage and certainly no need to listen to anybody else talk. She drove home Sunday evening with a promise from Eilis to invite her and Knox over for dinner some time soon. "We're still getting to know each other on a basis other than prosecutor-and-victim."

Sebastian ambushed her as soon as she drove through the gate, yanking her car door open before she got the key out of the ignition.

"Did you see Eilis at all?" he demanded, seeming nearly desperate, but Justice couldn't quite believe that from someone like him.

"Yes," she intoned warily as she stood and led the way to the front door. "Why?"

"Did she say anything about me?"

Justice stared at him for a moment, dumbfounded, her mind clicking through what few faint details she could put together to make some cohesive picture—

"Well?" he snapped. "Did she or not?"

The lightbulb came on.

Justice opened the door and walked through the living room to the kitchen, Sebastian following like a puppy dog. "You know what, Sebastian? I'm not going to tell you. You don't scratch my back, I don't scratch yours."

His mouth tightened.

"There's a lot more to being with a woman than roses and chocolates and candlelight," she said, just to rub it in, at once annoyed with his sudden idiocy and delighted to know that the great Sebastian Taight had the same problem she did. "But I'd have thought a man sixteen years older than I am with, I'm assuming, a little bit of experience with women, would know that better than I would."

"Point taken," he snarled at her before he threw the patio door open, then slid it closed again with an equally vicious slam. After casting her a glare through the glass, he stalked across the lawn, then disappeared around the corner into the barn.

Justice giggled with the glee of a little sister who'd successfully poked at her older brother, then blogged that night on the definition of family. She went to sleep with the same smile, feeling as if she had come home to people who had been waiting for her.

86: Sydney Carton

JUSTICE DRESSED FOR WORK, FOUR WEEKS TO THE DAY OF HER WEDDING TO Knox. Not that anybody'd notice, since she never saw him at home and rarely saw him at work. She didn't know if he'd been home this past weekend and she didn't really care.

Fun. No guilt. No thoughts of what she wasn't getting accomplished back on the farm that she would never have been able to keep up with anyway.

No hurt over being abandoned, or at least, not much since it was possible Knox had engineered that the way he engineered a whole lot of things.

I had my reasons.

She was still lost in "Why me?" though and the richest irony of it all was that of all the women Knox could've chosen, he'd chosen one who had a national audience and political clout—and was ignorant of it. It would take only one well-written letter to the editor at the *Wall Street Journal* to crack the whole situation wide open.

But now it wasn't just Knox at stake if she did that; his family and friends were, too. These people respected her for coming back on her own, staying with Knox, being in love with him, however naïvely, for being willing to fight his fight with him, with them, even though her only real role in it consisted of silently bearing the name of Hilliard. There would be plenty of time for a baby to happen if they decided not to take any precautions against it.

Abstinence works every time it's tried.

Her lip curled and she snarled at nothing.

She arrived home to a silent house yet again. She had grown used to the silence, her only companion a neutered tomcat named Dog. She liked the beauty of silence to think about the day, about how the office worked, about her progression as a lawyer.

She'd settled in to her job and her environs, though now that she had developed a system, the endless stream of traffic tickets and deadbeat dads and bad checks and penny-ante arraignments had begun to bore her silly.

It still unnerved her that large amounts of cash came and went, but now she wasn't so sure that its source was illegal and she definitely wasn't going to believe one way or another until she had proof. But because she couldn't quite work out how it could be legal, she followed Richard's lead and pretended not to see it. Her only personal goal at the moment was to get better at being a prosecutor.

Her coworkers' attitudes had changed for the better when she came back; she had no idea why. It wasn't as if they had a stake in her presence the way Knox's family did. Eric's comment still baffled her and he'd refused to explain it.

Other than that, they didn't care that she was Knox's wife and they certainly didn't care about her writings. They yelled at her like they yelled at each other and the other residents; it was how they communicated all the time, a male bonding ritual that had Justice rolling her eyes and snorting a lot. Yet as she got better, they didn't yell at her so much because they had no reason to. Every once in a while, someone would point out where she needed to fix something—nicely.

Justice hadn't been late once since she'd come back from St. Louis. She wasn't up to her eyeballs in farm chores until one in the morning and it wasn't like Knox was making love to her all night, every night. Oh, no. She had no excuse for not being well rested and able to get to work on time.

I won't pressure you. You come to me when you're ready.

What did that *mean*? Was she just supposed to walk up to him and say, "'Mkay, ready now"? How was she supposed to go about asking him for what she wanted without completely embarrassing herself? She knew he wanted her and would definitely not turn her away or laugh at her, but she was still just too inexperienced and insecure to be able to initiate anything—

Make love to me, Knox.

—and too embarrassed to ask either Giselle or Eilis to give her instructions on the proper seduction of a husband.

For the last three mornings, she had gone to the basement where he slept to see if she could catch him just to talk to him before he turned into At-Work Knox. He was always gone, the couch still warm. She decided that if he wanted to avoid her that badly, maybe she should probably take the hint. After all, if he expected her to come to him, he should stick around so she could do that.

At lunch, Richard pulled up a chair and deposited both his and her lunches on her desk. This had become a ritual with them. She'd pay for his lunch if he went across the street and got hers, too. She'd seen the meager lunch he brought every day while the rest of the men went out. That would be expensive for a married-with-three-teenagers man who didn't dip his hands in the cesspool of possibly dirty money.

Justice had opened her laptop and checked the new comments on the blogs while she waited for Richard to come back. "Darn," she muttered as she scanned them, then sighed.

"What?"

She clucked. "Oh, there used to be a regular poster who followed my articles and he hasn't commented in almost a month."

"So?"

"Well, you know, you get used to people online and then you miss them when they don't show up for a while. This guy, he— He's my buddy. His comments are always interesting and smart, and I like him a lot. He's been following me around the web for two years and then just— Nothing."

Richard didn't get it; he was busy with real life, family he adored. He did things with them and his life was full.

She frowned. "It's like he disappeared off the face of the Internet." She tried to explain it to him again. "Okay. It's like having a pen pal that you get a letter from every other day for two years. Then one day the letters just stop coming. You don't know why; there's no explanation. You only know that your friend disappeared."

She closed her laptop and happened to look up to see Knox watching her, looking at her the way he had that night in the grass, with what she now understood was desire, his eyes dark. He wanted her. His jaw clenched and his nostrils flared. His fingers curled into his palms and tightened.

Her eyes widened. Her heart beat a little faster, her breathing sped up, and she bit her lip.

Take me home, Knox, please.

"You're not sleeping with him, are you?" Richard muttered around his sandwich, having apparently witnessed that exchange, and she reluctantly looked away from Knox to Richard.

She couldn't even be offended; Richard was her . . . girlfriend? She snorted. "That obvious?"

"Quite. He doesn't act like a man who's getting regular sex and you still look at him like a high school freshman with a crush on the captain of the football team."

"Why were you all so happy I came back?"

He looked at her thoughtfully for a moment, and then said, "He was insufferable, the worst I've ever seen him. Then you came back and . . . he wasn't."

That confused her, but it warmed her soul that the office thought her responsible for some improvement in Knox's mood that she could not discern.

Justice sneaked glances at Knox throughout the afternoon when she could; she, like the rest of the staff, was busy in court and meeting with defense counsel making her plea deals—but every time she sneaked a peek, he was looking at her, too.

That evening when she went home, she decided she'd had enough of this. She missed him, the At-Home Knox, the one who'd let her go, the one who had kissed her so well, because kissing seemed to be his favorite thing in the world to do.

Justice awoke to the sound of her alarm. He had to be sleeping at this time of the morning and she was determined to catch him before he went to work.

She opened the basement door and saw a bluish-white glow, the muted sound of the TV, and what sounded like chuckles. It was three o'clock in the morning; didn't he ever sleep?

Sneaking down the stairs, she wasn't sure what she expected to catch him watching—although it had occurred to her that it could be porn—but what she saw wasn't even on her radar.

" . . . pondering what I'm pondering?"

"I think so, Brain, but pantyhose are so uncomfortable in the summertime."

A snicker came from the couch.

Pinky and the Brain?

Justice blinked and shook her head, unable to process that. Knox and cartoons. Another snicker came from the area of the couch at the gag that followed. He hadn't seen her or heard her once she reached the bottom of the stairs and she tiptoed in a wide circle so she could approach him without his seeing her.

Knox lay on his side, clad in very short black cycling shorts and a white tee shirt. A thick tome lay open on the floor in front of him, next to a bucket of cheese popcorn and a gallon jug of orange juice, half drunk. He had his head propped up on one hand and shoved popcorn into his mouth, wiped his hand on his shirt, turned the page of his book, and read a few lines before he chuckled at the TV again.

His golden hair was rumpled and his jaw was frightfully scruffy and Dog sprawled along the length of his waist and ribs, asleep.

At that moment, Justice longed to know more about this man who'd forced her to marry him to get his inheritance, then set her free the very next day.

"Iustitia," he breathed, obviously surprised, and she loved the sound of her real name out of his mouth.

Her gaze ran up the length of his prone body to meet his look.

"What are you reading?" she asked, because she wasn't sure what to say now that she'd gotten his attention.

He shrugged. "Junk."

"And you're eating junk and watching junk."

His face betrayed no emotion. "What'd you expect? The Playboy channel?"

Justice was glad he couldn't see her flush in the dark. She looked away and decided that maybe this wasn't such a good idea after all.

"Iustitia, come here."

She blinked at his gentle tone of voice. She looked back at him with a good measure of suspicion. "Why?"

He burrowed back into the sofa and patted the cushion in front of him. "C'mere."

Justice stared at him, unable to decipher his expression or his mood. She bit her lip and looked toward the stairs. "I really should go back to bed . . . "

"I said, 'Come here.'"

That hard edge was back in his voice. She did think about defying him, but she'd sought him out—and now she couldn't go through with asking him for what she really wanted.

Knox's big hand reached up and gently wrapped around her arm, pulling her around the arm of the sofa, then down. She sat stiffly on the edge of the sofa until he caught the side of her neck. With a force so gentle as to be almost nonexistent, he compelled her to lie in front of him, facing the television so that the heat of his body seeped into her back. He settled his arm heavily in the curve of her waist and his large palm cupped the hip that sank into the cushion. He insinuated his knee between hers and the twining of their legs seemed terribly intimate for so innocuous a position. His chin lay atop her head and his other hand played with a lock of her hair.

He liked her hair. A lot. She sighed and relaxed back into him.

"Hi," he murmured and tiny tendrils of her hair moved on his breath, tickling the skin of her face.

"Hi," she murmured in return, catching a breath when she felt his growing arousal against her lower back. She felt an answering heat between her legs and she closed her eyes helplessly.

"Relax. Watch TV."

"Why are you being nice to me?"

"Because I'm too tired to be an asshole. Enjoy it while it lasts."

Justice smiled a little at the wry tone and shifted a little closer to him.

Knox said nothing else, but continued to play with her hair, watching TV and occasionally chuckling. She liked the way his chest rumbled when he laughed at his cartoons. She felt every breath he took, every absent stroke of his palm as it drifted up and down her skin along the line of her ribs and hip underneath the gray jersey. She hadn't stopped wearing his clothes to bed and had even taken them to the Kenards' to sleep in.

That had not gone unnoticed nor un-smirked upon.

She drew in a breath when his thumb brushed the underside of her breast— every slide of his hairy legs along her smooth ones, every shift of his hips as he tried to adjust his arousal. She vaguely wondered if that caused pain.

She missed him. She missed him the way she'd missed him when he'd left the symphony early, his hand not in her hair, his shoulder not brushing hers, his mouth not on hers. She missed the Knox she thought must be in there but had only had glimpses of.

"You're thinking again," he whispered in her ear.

Justice caught her breath, wondering what he was going to say to her that would make her tingle more than she already did.

"What are you thinking about?"

He didn't need to know that. She leaned over and looked at the book he was reading and flipped it closed yet keeping her thumb at his place.

"Who's Porter Rockwell?" she asked, suddenly intrigued.

"Joseph Smith and Brigham Young's bodyguard."

Justice thought he must be working his way through his religious texts. "As in Brigham Young University?"

"As in. I graduated from law school there."

She gasped and shifted so she could look at him. "You're a Mormon?"

"No." He paused, then said, "Well, not anymore."

"Why not?"

Knox laughed, a mix of bitterness and sadness, but no humor. "You have to ask? Use your head, Iustitia. What religious culture in its right mind would condone what I do? I lie, I cheat, I steal. I blackmail women into my bed. I kill people and I force people to do what I want at gunpoint." She swallowed heavily. "So you tell me why I'd get my ass thrown out."

The depth of bitterness was unexpected from a man like Knox, who thrived on his reputation. "Would you go back if you could?"

"No." The answer was swift, like the sharp blade of a guillotine through a soft neck. "I don't want the responsibility."

Responsibility . . . what an odd choice of words. A choice that implied too much for Justice to sort through all at once.

. . . as attached as you are to theology.

"You still believe in it, though, don't you? I mean, the religion?"

There was a long pause. Justice held her breath in wait for his answer, and waited for a while. "Yes," he finally murmured, then cleared his throat and spoke a little louder. "But not enough to change my life."

"But, Knox—"

"I don't want to talk about this anymore, Iustitia. It's a very demanding religion and an even more demanding culture and I've made my choices. For better or worse. Porter Rockwell," he said, reaching over her to flip the book back to where it was, and that, his body wrapped around hers like that—oh, that!—nearly disengaged her brain. She wanted him to stroke her and caress her the way he had their wedding night; she wanted him to tuck his hand under her shirt and undress her, kiss her . . . "Was a very powerful man. He was called the Destroying Angel of Mormondom. He did things no one else could or would do in order to protect his people and his prophet."

His reverence brought her mind back from her need. "You admire him."

"I do. Very much. I absolutely believe that there's a place in society for men like him, for people like us, me and Sebastian and Giselle. Bryce. Justice at all costs. And since I showed you mine, you show me yours."

Justice thought for a minute, because she'd never been asked this question that she hadn't replied, flippantly or otherwise, "There is no God."

"I believe in the republic and capitalism. The Declaration of Independence, the Constitution, Federalist Papers, Democracy in America—that's my holy writ. Neil Peart writes my hymns and Rush is my choir. Ted Nugent is my Porter Rockwell. You have your prophets and I have mine: James Madison, Alexis de Tocqueville, Walter Williams, Morgan Ashworth. I follow no other faith."

Knox pulled her even closer and ran his fingers through her hair. He didn't seem to be inclined to speak, but—

"Why did Sebastian and Bryce call you Lucifer?"

He tensed and his arm tightened around her, then he sighed. "In Mormon theology, Lucifer thought it would be a good idea if everyone had no choice but to be perfectly obedient, so then everyone's salvation would be assured. Nobody liked that idea, so he got pissed off and left. Or got kicked out. I'm sure it would depend which side you asked. Theoretically, in our hierarchy of sins, taking away someone's ability to choose—anything—is probably the worst."

"Huh. Well, I don't do Judeo-Christian myth. Or any other myth."

He combed his fingers through her hair. "Okay."

"That doesn't bother you?"

"Why would it? I'm a man without a God."

For some reason, Justice found that simple statement, said without a trace of emotion, terribly sad.

"Knox?"

"Mmmm?"

"Did Giselle do something to that girl, Sherry Quails, who made fun of me?"

"Yes. I asked her to."

Justice felt a warmth blossom throughout her body, but after the weekends she'd spent with her new family, she should be used to feeling so cared for.

"I don't know *what* she did to her, though. She never told me and I never asked. You have to understand something about Giselle. She falls in love with the people who need her protection. If she thought you needed her—and you did right then— she would've gone to the ends of the earth to make sure you were protected, that you had a smooth path to walk."

Justice looked at that, took it apart and put it back together again seventeen different ways.

"Bryce— She protects him, too?"

"Oh, no. She wouldn't have married any man she felt she needed to protect, which is one reason she would never have married me even if I'd wanted her to. Bryce Kenard is the last man on earth who needs anyone's protection."

Justice remained silent for a moment. "Do you know he's afraid of the dark?"

She felt Knox start behind her and the hand that stroked her curls stopped abruptly. "Afraid of the dark?"

"Well. Maybe that's not the right word, 'afraid.' She said after his fire that he doesn't like to be alone after dark. So she always makes sure to be home before the sun goes down."

There was a long silence before the tension left Knox's body and his hand began to play in her hair again. "No, I didn't know that," he murmured. "That puts an interesting spin on things."

"Like what?"

Knox drew a deep breath. "Do you know anything about his fire?"

"Not much."

Justice listened as he spoke and her skin began to tingle and warm most unpleasantly. Her body tensed with phantom aches when she visualized Bryce's scars while listening to Knox's words.

"So what do you find interesting about it?" she asked when he had finished.

"His thing about the dark— That could be a symptom of PTSD. I didn't pick up on it, but I should've. We've had enough victims come through the office with it, enough defendants with it. You know what it looks like."

"But he doesn't act like those people do."

"People snap under different stressors. I doubt he's had his trigger tripped, but when he does—" He shuddered.

They lay quietly for a long time, Justice attempting to work up her courage to ask—

"Why haven't you been home for the last three weekends?"

Knox took a deep breath. "I—" He stopped. She felt his shrug against her shoulders. "I had to take care of a few things." She swallowed at that, feeling a bit of grief at what he wasn't telling her, like *I had to get away from you*. What he didn't say, like *I did it so you'd have to go to my family so they could love on you*. He cleared his throat. "I won't leave you alone on the weekend again, Iustitia," he murmured.

"You didn't do it on purpose so Giselle would come get me?"

"No. I didn't think about how that might hurt your feelings or that my family might take it upon themselves to fix it. I'm sorry."

"Did Sebastian or Giselle make you apologize?" she asked, more bitterness in her voice than she meant to show.

"Apologize? No. I thought you would be more comfortable if I left and they did let me know that wasn't the case."

She huffed. "I wish you'd just talk to me. Ask me. Quit assuming things. Sebastian and Bryce both told me I needed to learn how to live with you, to learn how to have a relationship with you. I don't know how to do that, but I can't even try if you're not here, if you don't talk to me."

He said nothing to that, but she felt his acquiescence. Then, "Okay." At that, she began to wonder what tomorrow would bring, or possibly tonight . . .

"Knox?" she finally said, working up her courage to ask what she came to ask. Maybe.

"Mmmm?"

"Why haven't you— Er, um . . ."

He waited, but she couldn't bring herself to finish the sentence, she was so embarrassed.

"Why haven't I made love to you?"

Justice closed her eyes and sighed, her body responding to even that little bit and relieved that he hadn't made her say it. "Yes, that."

He started to speak, then stopped. Finally, "Do you want me to?"

Yes! "I'm not sure what I want."

"Well, Iustitia, I know what I want, so go back to bed before I decide for you."

She did, slowly, but she lay awake the rest of the night, spinning everything he'd told her.

Do you want me to?

Suddenly, she didn't care how she'd gotten into Knox's bed. She just wished she'd had the courage to answer his question differently and that he were in his own cherished bed with her.

87: Battle Fatigue

"M CKINLEY! I WANT YOU IN COURT IN HALF AN HOUR."
Justice looked up at Knox, At-Work Knox, the one who hadn't told her
all those revealing, wonderful things last week when she'd snuggled with
him on the couch, *Pinky and the Brain* on in the background—

—the one who hadn't spent the past weekend on the basement floor in front of the
TV with her cocooned between his legs and snuggled up against his chest, introducing
her to his favorite 1980s movies and sharing a tin of cheese popcorn, with nothing but
a bare ten sentences between them and not so much as a kiss.

We're all weak and easily seduced.

"My butt," Justice muttered.

Knox stared at her, his voice and face hard. "Did you hear me?"

"Yes. I'll be right there."

Nobody blinked an eye when he quit the room in a huff. Knox was always like
this and he was no different with her than he was with anybody else, so she shrugged
it off.

Once seated in the gallery behind the prosecution table, Justice forgot all about
Fen Hilliard, her marriage, OKH. All she could do was watch Knox do what he did
better than everybody in the metro area. She suddenly remembered why she'd had a
crush on him to begin with.

He was a very handsome man with his squared jaw, golden hair, huge body, and
designer suit. He was even more handsome in jeans, bare chested. She would never
forget how she'd felt with his naked body pressed tight against hers. But that wasn't it.

He was a skillful interrogator, drawing facts out of the few witnesses as if he had injected them with sodium pentothal; but then some of the witnesses would lie, and Justice would miss their contradictory statements and nuances, but Knox didn't. He zeroed in on little slips of the tongue easily, remembered verbatim their previous testimony. But that wasn't it either.

He was a charismatic orator, using rural vernacular as eloquently as if he were using the Queen's English in the House of Lords. His normal syntax was precise and clipped but in court here in Chouteau County, it changed. He spoke in lazily finished words with just enough of a country twang. He could flash good ol' boy redneck expressions and mannerisms as if he'd been born and raised in a honky-tonk; he made the jury and spectators laugh on a regular basis. Anyone else would have seemed to be patronizing the jury, but not Knox. Knox had an attractive and approachable personality when he wanted to use it—and he used it liberally in court. Still, that wasn't what reminded Justice of her initial reaction to Knox.

It was his brilliance. Understated legal acumen hidden by a pretty face and easy smile, lazy speech, and a bad reputation. That was why she was there, to watch and learn.

And she found herself crushing on him all over again, as if she were still in law school and he were still her substitute professor, as if she didn't know a thing about him and had no chance with him.

The man on trial had a rap sheet longer than the Missouri River, but not as long as Knox's memory, for Knox recalled every crime he had tried the man for. The thief was a seedy type, a real two-bit thug—as opposed to Knox's high-dollar operation, whatever it was—who liked to steal cars for a chop shop.

Justice looked to her left and saw a woman with four young children. The woman would have stood out anyway because of the children and the way in which she wept helplessly as Knox grilled the man on trial—but the way they were dressed . . .

Worn homespun (Justice didn't even know homespun was still manufactured) and calico, as if she were a prairie woman and her man was about to be hanged for horse theft. Of course, for all the woman knew, that was exactly what Knox planned to do. However, Justice couldn't begin to understand why any woman in her right mind would cry over such a no-good thief.

Knox turned at that moment and deliberately caught her eye; she didn't know what he was thinking about, but his eyes were that warm sky color they turned when he was half aroused. Her eyes widened and she sucked in a deep breath, forgetting all about the woman in the back. Knox went on with his interrogation, then one of the children whispered, "Hun'ry, Mama," and her attention was again diverted.

The children were getting restless, and the poor lady couldn't comfort them because she was so distraught. Justice felt pity for no reason that she could fathom and she decided that maybe her troubles weren't that bad.

Justice cast a glance at Knox and decided that she would risk his wrath and take these people out of the courtroom in order to fill their unnaturally protruding bellies. She rose and went to the woman, touching her on the shoulder to get her attention. Lanky dark hair curtained away from her dirty face, red eyes, and drippy nose when she looked up at Justice.

"Come with me," Justice whispered. "I want to feed you."

She looked back at Justice as if she'd lost her mind or had an ulterior motive or both. Justice wondered how old the woman was. Thirty-five? Forty? Too old to be in this situation.

"Please let me do this."

Justice easily herded the children out with a knack she didn't know she had. The mother, all too willing to let someone else take charge, shuffled along behind Justice and her newly acquired brood. Justice put the five of them in the charge of the metal detector guard and ran up the stairs to the office.

"What are you doing here?" Eric barked.

There wasn't much she could say to that except the truth.

He threw up his hands and said, "Okay, but it's your funeral. And put your holster back on if you're going out."

She shrugged into her holster, stuck her badge on her pocket, grabbed her purse, and accidentally kicked over the wastebasket that was under her desk. She stooped to pick up the trash and her brow wrinkled as her hand encountered what felt like cotton balls. "What in the world . . . ?" she whispered as she picked up a handful of cotton stuffing and brought it up to her face, but she didn't have time to think about it. Those people were hungry.

She met up with the mother and her children a couple of minutes later and smiled at the woman, whose tears had not abated.

"Come with me, Mrs. Barber."

"Oh," she sniffed, "that ain't my name. It's Dawson. I ain't married to Billy, but I been with him nigh onto ten years, since I's fifteen."

Justice was hard pressed to keep her jaw from dropping on the floor. Twenty-five? This woman was Justice's age yet looked like she was about to hit menopause. She blinked. "Well, okay, Miss Dawson—er—"

"Betty."

"Okay. Betty," Justice said as she hefted the youngest child up into her arms. "My name's Justice. Let's eat."

It was fifteen more minutes before the six of them were seated at a table inside the café across from the courthouse.

"Order anything you like, Betty. As much as you want. And for the kids, too."

"You don't mind?" she asked, uncertain but hopeful.

"Not at all. And if I don't think you've ordered enough, I'll order more."

The look on the woman's face was of utmost gratitude and she proceeded to order enough food to feed a starving nation. But of course, these five people were starving. Justice made sure the kids' glasses were kept full of milk and juices and that they ate as much as they could possibly hold. And Justice tried to hold her tongue, though she wanted very badly to pick Betty's brain. Finally, when the devouring of food had calmed somewhat, Justice began.

"Betty, tell me something. Do you love Billy?"

Betty looked up at Justice, her eyes sharp and face hard. "Why?" she asked in a dangerous tone, but Justice went on, undaunted, yet studying her fingernails intently.

"Because I wanted to know why you stay with him and put up with this life when you could do so much better."

The woman swallowed heavily and cast her eyes down at her plate. "That's just it, Miz Justice. I couldn't do no better. Billy, at least he feeds us . . . " But her voice trailed off. "Well, I guess he don't, now do he?" She looked up at Justice, who, though she looked younger, felt older by decades at that moment. "You got a man?"

Justice cast a glance down at the bare ring finger on her hand and—again—felt deeply the loss of something she'd never had to begin with. She nodded. "Yes."

"What's it like to love your man, to know he loves you?"

Justice started, and looked back up at Betty. She stared at the woman for a long while without actually seeing her. "I don't know, Betty," she finally murmured.

"What's that mean?"

"He doesn't love me."

"Do you love him?"

"Maybe. I don't know yet."

"Oh. Well, what's he like? Does he hit you? Or force you ever' night? Does he get drunk and tear into your kids? Does he cheat on you?"

The enormity of Betty's sincere questions and the significance of the answers washed through Justice and she shook her head again. "He, um," Justice cleared her throat. "No, he doesn't do any of that stuff. He takes care of me."

"Then from where I'm sittin', it don't matter whether he loves you or not."

"I can see that."

"Do you like layin' with him?"

Justice swallowed as she remembered the week before, being wrapped in Knox's arms on the couch and feeling so warm and secure, so cared for. That night in the grass. The weekend spent watching movies, sharing popcorn. "Oh, yes," she sighed, then cleared her throat again. "So why were you crying over Billy in the courtroom?"

"Because he's all we got. I don't think I could make it on my own with four kids. We couldn't get up enough money to buy off that bastard prosecutor Hilliard. Shoot, ever'body knows he'd sell his mother down the river for enough cash, but we didn't have it."

Justice's eyebrows rose. "Really. How much did you have?"

"Two hunnerd and seventy-five dollars."

"How much did he say it would take?"

"Three hunnerd. We just couldn't come up with the other twenty-five, and he knew it."

Justice huffed and rolled her eyes. He could be obnoxious, that was for sure, and she wondered if he'd done it out of boredom, frustration, or amusement.

"Betty," she ventured, not sure she wanted to open this can of worms, "he doesn't fix cases. Never has."

"Oh, how would you know anything about Knox Hilliard?" she snapped. "Anybody can tell just by lookin' atcha that you wouldn't know nothin' 'bout him."

Justice just looked at her, confused. "Betty, he's my boss. Why do you think I'm wearing a gun and a badge?"

Betty's jaw dropped as she worked at her vocal cords, but nothing came out besides helpless gurgles. "You—you're— You work— Knox Hilliard?"

Justice nodded.

"You—" she gasped. "You—*bitch!* You—this food an' an' an' bein' nice an' all an'—oh!" She looked around frantically. "C'mon, kids, we—we gotta—" she gulped as she looked at the plate of food she hadn't quite finished. "We gotta go."

"Betty, wait—"

"Don't you touch me!" she screeched. "C'mon, kids!"

"Mama, tell Billy Junior to gimme my teddy bear back," pleaded the littlest one.

"C'mon, Billy Junior! Chad!"

"Mama!" squealed Chad.

Betty continued to bluster disconcertedly as she packed up the children.

"No, please, Betty, stay. Eat some more," Justice pleaded. "I know you're hungry. This doesn't have anything to do with Knox."

"No, I—not with you! I wouldn't take nuthin' from you—workin' for Hilliard! You tricked me!"

"Mama!" the boy screamed.

"Chad, you stop that right now!"

"But Billy took my bear!" he wept, tears coursing down his face and streaking the dirt as he struggled to stand up in the seat.

"What bear?" Betty snapped. "You ain't got no bear."

"I do! I do!" he insisted as he sobbed. "Big gold man gimme bear."

Billy Junior held up the medium-sized brown fur bear by one of the paws. "He ain't no good, though," said the older boy. "He's all crinkly."

Betty snatched the bear, glared at both boys, then tried to scoot out of the booth.

"Wait, Betty—"

"Don't wanna talk to you."

"There's a note on the teddy bear, Ma," Billy Junior intoned. "What's it say?"

Betty looked down at the bear in her hand absently, then her brow wrinkled as she took a closer look. "What'n the hell's this?" she muttered as she plucked at the back of the toy, then gasped as she drew out a piece of green paper. "Oh, my good Lord," she whispered in awe as she held up a soft, worn hundred dollar bill and relaxed back into the booth. She looked back at the animal and poked through it. "It's full o' them puppies. Hunnerd dollar bills." She glared at Chad then. "Where'd you git this, youngun? I won't be havin' you takin' after your pa an' thievin'."

"Big gold man gimme."

There was only one "big gold man" in that courthouse and Justice thought she might cry right there.

"What's the note say, Ma?"

Looking abashed, Betty said, "Well, I forgot my readin' glasses. Don't know what it says."

"I'll read it for you, Betty."

She glared at Justice. "Mind you, I kin read. I just don't got my glasses handy."

"I understand."

Reluctantly Betty handed the note to Justice and Justice gulped at the computer-generated message. "'Dear Miss Dawson,'" Justice read aloud. "'Please take this bear and go away from here, away from Billy. Start a new life. Go to school, get some skills. You don't have to depend on anyone but yourself.'"

Betty sat dumbfounded. "Oh, my," she whispered as tears came to her eyes. "The good Lord's done answered my prayers at last."

Justice didn't even care that she got back to the office at 4:30. Knox didn't give her a chance to explain, so she got chewed up and spit out in front of everybody.

But she held her head high and stared straight back at him while he yelled at her, letting him know she knew what he'd done.

His eyes were a deep blue.

88: Wipeout

FOR THE FIRST TIME SINCE SHE'D MOVED IN, HE WAS ACTUALLY IN THE HOUSE and, better yet, upstairs when she came home. He watched her speculatively, as if he were deciding what to say to her first.

She didn't say a word; she just went about the business of cooking dinner for both of them, since he'd had the presence of mind to show up.

"All right," he snapped. "Let's have it. Where'd you go today and why?"

"We're not at work and you could've asked me that before you started in on me."

"Tell me anyway."

She huffed. "Took the defendant's family across the street and fed them."

He grunted. "Why?"

"Because they were starving and I thought that was more important than watching you do what I've seen you do a gazillion times if I've seen you do it once." He had nothing to say to that, and she looked over her shoulder at him and drawled, "And don't act like you're all mad. You gave them a teddy bear stuffed full of cash."

Knox rolled his eyes. "I have no idea what you're talking about."

"Liar."

He said nothing for a long while and Justice threw the vegetables and meat into a wok. She plugged the steamer in and threw some flour tortillas in it. She heard a low meow and the swish of cat against denim.

"It was a dumb thing to do," he finally admitted.

She tossed the stir fry and glanced at him where he sat at the table, Dog stretched up with his front paws on Knox's thigh to get his face scratched. Knox obliged absently and she bit back a smile. "I don't think so. I thought it was sweet."

"Eh. She'll blow it all and go back to Billy as soon as he's released."

"No, she was pretty graphic about the way he treats her and now she has the means to do something about it. With women like that, it always comes down to means. You pulled me out of a bad situation and then you gave me the means to leave you."

"And you came back. There you go."

She looked at him sharply. "You don't beat me. You don't rape me. You don't get bastard children on me. You don't cheat on me. You take care of me and give me everything I need; in fact, you'd give me anything I wanted if I asked—and don't tell me you wouldn't. Not only don't you make me slave my life away and make me look like I'm forty when I'm actually twenty-five—you pulled me off that farm, where that's exactly what would've happened to me. I can ditch you any time. I'm free to do what I want, when I want, how I want as long as I'm to work on time—and even that's negotiable."

Knox laughed reluctantly, but said nothing else and she finished dinner. She put the tortillas on a plate and divvied up the stir fry, giving herself as much as she knew she could eat and him the rest.

He put his fajita together and took a bite. "This is really good."

"Thanks."

They ate in silence for a moment as he hand-fed Dog bits and pieces of beef and tortilla. Finally, Knox muttered, "I'm sorry I was an ass today."

"Which time? I counted three or four."

He chuckled, again reluctantly.

"I want to know something. Were you born grumpy?"

"No, Iustitia," he said, sarcasm dripping from his tongue. "Believe it or not, I wasn't. I was a semi-professional surfer in college. You can't surf and be grumpy."

Her mouth would have dropped open if she didn't have food in it. She swallowed it so she could speak. "You were?"

"Yes. Surfing is probably the most—" He stopped to think, to look for a word. "—*joyous* experience in the world. Man communing with ocean via fiberglass."

There was so much she didn't know about this man and suddenly, her heart hurt because of that. "So . . . what happened that made you grumpy?"

He paused mid-chew. Then, softly, "I'd rather not talk about that."

"Oh. Okay." They ate in silence that felt tense to Justice because she had so many things she wanted to ask and didn't know where to start. She cleared her throat. "Um, Knox . . . "

Knox suddenly watched her intently, waiting for her to finish.

Justice stared down at her plate as if it would give her courage. "I wanted to know if you would rather not sleep on the couch anymore?"

He said nothing for a long time, but she couldn't bear to look at him. She felt his fingers on her chin, lifting her face so she would meet his gaze. "I don't know if I can just sleep with you, Iustitia. Are you asking me for more than just sleep?"

I want anything you'll give me, but I'm too embarrassed to ask.

"I just feel bad that you love your bed so much but you're sleeping on the couch."

That surprised him, taking him out of the moment. "How do you know I love my bed?"

"It's well taken care of. You have very fine linens on it that are custom made. The rest of your house—" She waved a hand. "It's a wreck. Chipboard furniture from Wal-Mart, even."

He laughed outright then.

"You love your books and your cat."

Love me, Knox, please.

Knox took a deep breath and said, "Probably not, Iustitia. I need to—" He stopped. Cleared his throat. Wouldn't look at her. "Um, probably not."

Justice raised her eyebrow as she watched him, and she pulled in a long, soft breath. Oh! It wasn't about Justice's readiness at all; it was about his, and suddenly, she felt yet another heavy weight lift from her shoulders. The weekends alone—*not about her*. With her curiosity bursting inside her so violently it nearly hurt, she only said, "Okay."

Knox offered to clean up, so she went into her—well, their—bedroom to blog. No hamlet. She swallowed and gritted her teeth, trying to keep the tears at bay. It'd been a month and a half. He wasn't going to come back.

At ten, she heard the driveway gate open and watched out the mullioned window as his SUV backed out and drove away. She didn't have to wonder where he went at night. The evidence was all over the courthouse every morning: the dozen or so discarded orange juice bottles; files that hadn't been signed off on the evening before but were come morning; prosecution tables that had been clean the night before but grew exhibits overnight.

Justice closed her laptop then, not having the stomach for more words. She wandered into the kitchen to get something to drink and saw an old yellowed newspaper on the kitchen table that hadn't been there before.

It was dated August 30, 1994, and in the middle of the page was a picture of a very, very young, though no less hard and cold, Knox Hilliard as he walked into the courthouse. The headline next to the picture read "Prosecutor not charged in slaying."

> Assistant Chouteau County prosecutor Knox Hilliard, 25, was cleared today in the execution-style murder of Tom Parley, 43, after Parley was acquitted of 19 counts of homicide over the course of three years.
>
> Hilliard, who prosecuted Parley for serial murder, was the lead suspect in the FBI's investigation, but federal prosecutor John Riley cited lack of any credible evidence linking Hilliard to the murder. "Our investigation has taken us in another direction," said Riley.
>
> Hilliard, who has been on administrative leave from the prosecutor's office while under investigation, returned to work today. When asked for comments, he said only: "It was a gross miscarriage of justice and my only regret is that I wasn't able to convince a jury of Parley's guilt. I offer my heartfelt apologies to the people of Chouteau County and the state of Missouri for not doing my job well enough."

There was more. Justice didn't bother to read it; she knew what it said. She threw it in the trash and sighed, a tear rolling down her cheek. "Oh, Knox," she whispered. "I'm so sorry."

She went to bed and stared out the mullioned windows at the fractured moonlight. Her age. He'd been her age, just out of law school. So much she hadn't wanted to believe about her husband, so much she didn't know . . . His pain, his joys—if he had any left. A man who loved to surf more than anything in the world living sixteen hundred miles from the Pacific Ocean.

You're an AP in a backwater county on the outskirts of Cowtown. Why? Is what you wanted in any way similar to the reality?

So. Giselle's question to Justice at the beginning of her journey with Knox applied no less to Knox himself.

None of this had figured in her girlish fantasies; she had thought nothing of who he was as a man, a man with almost forty years of life already behind him, a man who apparently didn't have much to laugh about at all, a man with no joy behind that radiant smile he used as a weapon in court, a man who hurt and bled more than most.

Knox Hilliard: Not the most powerful force in the universe. Who knew?

A semi-professional surfer who had come home to spend his best years fighting for an inheritance he didn't want but felt honor-bound to claim because of the lives it had cost.

Dog jumped up on the bed, and she held onto him, unable to sleep. It was 12:30 when she heard Knox come in the house. She listened as he threw his keys on the table, opened the refrigerator door, poured a glass of orange juice (she didn't have to see him to know what he'd chosen to drink), then silence. After a minute she heard the rustling of a trash bag and the crackle of an old newspaper, then the opening of the basement door and footsteps clipping down the stairs. She heard the water run when he turned on the shower in the basement bathroom, then heard it stop a bit later.

At 1:15, she threw the bedcovers back and padded down the hallway, to the basement door and down the stairs. She came to a halt behind the couch where Knox lay, on his side, clad only in his short cycling shorts, asleep in the light from Wakko, Yakko, and Dot's world.

Justice stood and watched him, as she had before. He looked so very young, so innocent as he lay with his head on his outstretched arm, his hand still clutching the newspaper. She took the remote off the arm of the couch and clicked off the television, then touched his muscled shoulder.

"Knox."

His eyes fluttered open and he turned his head to look up at her. "Iustitia?"

"Come to bed."

She sensed his flicker of surprise, but she only turned and walked back upstairs.

The clock had marked thirty minutes before she felt the cool wash of air on her back, and the depression of two hundred pounds of raw male muscle on the bed. She heard the soft thud of four paws on the floor and the baritone voice she loved say, "Go away, Dog."

Justice smiled a little when Knox's arm curled around her waist and pulled her gently into the curve of his body. She felt his face burrow into her curls that lay on her pillow.

"I murdered that man, Iustitia," he murmured, as if she didn't know, hadn't known for three years, hadn't deliberately blocked it out of her mind.

Daring more than she had ever dared before, she reached behind her and spread her hand over Knox's thigh, stroked slowly upward to his jersey-covered hip, and squeezed.

"I know."

They were silent for a long time. Then, "I made him get on his knees and put his hands behind his head," he said, his voice gathering strength and Justice understood that though this was a confession, it was far from an apology. "I put my gun between his eyes and I made him beg for his life. Then I blew his head off."

Justice was very aware of his chest against her back, his ragged breathing, the thundering pace of his heart as he awaited her condemnation—if not for what he'd done, then that he felt no remorse.

"Well," she sighed. "It needed done."

He froze for a second then took a deep breath, released it slowly. His breathing and heart rate eased. His hand drifted across her cheek and into her hair, and Justice felt safe and protected for the first time since her grandfather died.

89: Happy Paper Trails

I DON'T KNOW WHAT TO DO, JUSTICE. I MEAN, I JUST CAN'T SEEM TO MAKE MY paycheck stretch all the way to the next payday. So when I get the next paycheck, half of it's already spent. Alisha's medical bills are paid, but her medicine is sky high. I mean, if I could get a night job or something—just to pay the bills that overlap, get some of them paid off, maybe."

Justice nodded in understanding, her mouth full of a bite of the burger she'd bought. She took a sip of strawberry shake. "I know what you mean about the bills. A farm's always like that. We were always almost barely hanging on." She paused. "Tell me something, Richard. How come you're not interested in the widow'n'orphan fund?"

He snorted and stuffed a French fry in his mouth. "Are you kidding? I see all that money come through here and sometimes morals don't mean a damn thing—especially in the beginning, when Claude was the prosecutor. There've been times when, you know, Davidson will toss me a bundle and I'll look at it and think of all the things five thousand dollars would buy that my kids need. Shoot, even if they didn't need anything, it'd be nice to buy my wife a huge diamond ring just because she deserves it."

"So what keeps you from taking it?"

He shook his head and he stared at his food. He looked up at Justice. "I don't know, Justice. Sometimes I just really don't know." His gaze didn't stray from hers and her eyes flickered in question. "What keeps you from doing it?"

She shrugged. "What's the point in that? I get to keep my whole paycheck and my other earnings. Knox pays for everything, probably with that money. I don't have to clean or do laundry or mow the lawn or fix stuff around the house. He gives me money for the things we need and he'd give me more if I asked. I have all the time in the world to write and for the first time in my life, I'm accountable to no one. If I wanted that kind of money, I'd take a radio show. So . . . I just don't feel a need to. But," she went on, slowly so as to make her point as clearly as possible without saying it outright, "if nobody knows where it comes from, *how do you know it's hot?*"

Richard looked up at her then, and sat back in his chair. "Justice, I never fixed cases when Claude was here, but that wasn't his only racket. There are a dozen illegal things he could be doing. Where else could it come from?"

"Think about it. We presume people to be innocent—well, no, we really don't, but that's the theory. But even if we don't think they are, we still have to prove it beyond a reasonable doubt. So until you can tell me where it comes from, why it's hot, I'm not going to assume anything."

"Justice, I'm telling you. This office has always worked this way."

"Oh, okay. Then what do *you* think he's doing?"

Richard said nothing for a long while, then, slowly, "Knox hated Claude. He didn't bring a dime into this office."

"Did Patrick?"

"No, nor Hicks. I remember when Knox came here. He latched onto Hicks, but all three of us were good at hiding what we were not doing."

"And you're still not. I mean, everyone who puts his hand in the till has to contribute. That's the way a widow'n'orphan fund usually works, right?"

He stared at her. "Are you saying it's all Knox's money and he's just . . . *giving* . . . it away?"

"Follow the money. There's only one reason the FBI wouldn't be able to find a paper trail and that's if there wasn't a paper trail at all. Knox is the best white-collar prosecutor in the state. He would know how to hide money in plain sight."

"He can't possibly make that kind of cash here."

"With Sebastian Taight managing it?"

Richard's eyes widened. "I always forget about that." He looked around the room at the men milling about, yelling as always, turning the air blue. "They've already figured it out," he murmured.

"Right. And they're willing to play whatever game Knox has on the table, especially because it involves free money. The residents? It only matters what they think insofar as they spread the rumors of the nefarious goings-on in the Chouteau County prosecutor's office far and wide, initiated by the thirty-year reign of Claude Nocek."

He sighed. "Now I feel stupid."

"Don't. Occam's Razor."

"The simplest solution tends to be the right one."

"Right. The simplest explanation is that the office is still on the take somehow because it always was and that Knox is just better at hiding it than Nocek was. No one just gives money away, especially with no strings attached and on such a sustained basis. Second, it's just an invisible part of your life, like breathing. You've never contributed and you're so used to it being here, so used to abstaining, you wouldn't notice unless it stopped. Third, you've got so many worries on your mind, I'd have been surprised if you had enough room in your brain to give it more than a passing thought. You have a very sick wife and active teenage kids. You're constantly running. I only figured it out because I live with Knox and I see another side of him that nobody else sees. I have the time and the silence to think about it. If I didn't have that, I'd still think it was hot, too, the way I'm *supposed* to."

"Thanks, Justice," he sighed as he arose to clean up his lunch mess and go to the restroom. She could tell he was distressed by not only the idea that he hadn't picked up on it like the others had, but by the fact that he'd missed out on all that cash trying to be honorable.

Justice sat and contemplated the wall, her chin in her hand, chewing on Richard's situation and how she might help him.

"Why'd you tell him that?"

She started as Knox's low growl sounded behind her. She looked over her shoulder at him and her belly did a little flip when she took in his lithe bigness and golden darkness. She'd ached for him to make love to her every night for the last week as he'd slept curled up around her. But it was her own fault. All she had to do was turn over and kiss him and she just couldn't work up the nerve.

"Why not?" she asked after a minute of staring at him. "He needs the money more than anyone here and you could've just taken him aside and told him, instead of letting him think he was doing the honorable thing at the cost of his family's welfare. Why do you always do things the hard way?"

He paused for a moment and looked at her, an odd expression on his face. "How did you figure it out?" he finally asked.

She swiveled in her chair to face him, relaxed, her elbows on the arms of it and her fingers steepled. "Knox. I realize that your lasting impression of me is that mousy little girl her first week in law school, and that's what you see when you look at me, and that's what you're always going to see. What you don't know is that now, three years later, my name and my opinion have some meaning in the world. If you'd paid attention while I was in law school or read my CV, you'd know that, but apparently you didn't pay attention and you still haven't read my CV. I didn't make *summa cum laude* and a name for myself by being stupid."

"I wouldn't have hired you if I thought you were stupid."

"You hired me because I saw you shoot a man in the head—and that was a bogus reason anyway. My intellect or lack of it had nothing to do with it."

He pursed his lips and nodded. "Well, that's true."

And that hurt. More than anything he'd ever said to her. "Oh, go away," she muttered.

"What did you say to me?"

There was that hardness, that chilling tone in his voice, but because she didn't fall for that anymore, she glared up at him and spoke through her gritted teeth and clenched jaw. "I. Said. Go. Away."

His jaw worked in silence, his eyes a glittering sky blue. Justice simply watched as he braced his hands on the arms of her chair and kissed her. Hard.

Without a thought, Justice returned it, as much to shove his attitude back in his face as to suck every smidgen of pleasure out of his kiss. He hadn't kissed her since she'd come back—and oh, how she missed feeling his lips on hers, his tongue in her mouth.

"You're asking for it," Knox muttered when he jerked away from her suddenly.

"Then why don't you give it to me?" Justice shot back.

"Is that an invitation?" he growled.

"What do you think?" she snapped.

They stared at one another for what seemed like hours, neither breaking eye contact. Justice felt no insecurity, no embarrassment; she just wanted to have an excuse to look at that beautiful face.

Finally, Knox raised a hand to run his fingers through her hair. "You have a lot of guts, Iustitia Hilliard," he murmured. "I like that."

Noises sounded in the hallway and he backed away. Cleared his throat. "Lunch is almost over and you've got work to do." She watched him as he turned and sauntered back to his office. She took a deep breath and began to smile. Well. She supposed she knew what she'd be doing all night tonight, and it thrilled her beyond reason.

Fifteen minutes later she was buried in paperwork. Conversation swirled around her and she easily pulled out comments and questions from the general hubbub that were aimed at her. Justice attempted to keep herself focused on work, which was really a losing battle. Thinking about being naked with Knox in bed, making lo—

"Good God!"

The gasp was somehow able to pierce the thick conversation, and the entire population of the office stared at Richard, whose face had lightened a few shades of brown. He held a manila envelope in his hands and looked down in the gaping space.

"What's wrong, Connelly?" Patrick asked on a forced laugh in order to maintain some sense of joviality in the face of their coworker's astonishment. They all wondered how bad the news was. "You look like that thing's going to take a hunk out of your nose."

He looked up, then. "Okay, who did this?" he asked as he pulled out a thick stack of worn one-hundred-dollar bills and looked around.

One of the residents snorted. "Yeah, like we'd cut you in if we didn't have to." Justice rolled her eyes. Hicks caught her look, then grinned and winked at her. She returned his grin and chuckled to herself.

Richard looked around and realized no one was lying. They all got along well, but their altruism only extended to the sharing of office supplies and trading food. They communicated by yelling and cussing at each other. No one remembered birthdays, no one asked after another's family, and no one bought someone else lunch.

Except Justice, who had done all three for Richard. It was to her he turned.

"Justice?"

And Justice could see the tears of gratitude that shimmered in his eyes and threatened to fall. Now he knew. His initial reaction had been habit and he only needed her validation that taking it was not dishonorable. She shrugged.

He put the money carefully back in the envelope and gulped. "How much?" asked Hicks.

"Twelve thousand dollars," he whispered, because his voice was creaky with tears.

Justice shook her head. She looked up through her eyelashes at Knox, who was engaged in deep conversation with a detective, oblivious to what was going on around him. She smiled to herself and then sucked in a soft breath when he slid her a glance and a sly smile.

90: Occam's Razor

H E WAS NOWHERE TO BE FOUND WHEN SHE GOT HOME AND SHE SCREECHED in utter frustration. She didn't want to crack her laptop open. She didn't want to cook. She didn't even want to go out to the barn to see how much progress Sebastian had made on his painting—he was probably still mad at her anyway, since he hadn't seen fit to speak to her yet.

So she went downstairs and flopped on the couch, flipping through channels. Nothing. Naturally, when she wanted to watch TV, there was nothing on in two hundred and fifty channels.

What she wanted was for Knox to come home and take her to bed. Unless and until that happened, she was going to be restless.

She got up and walked around the library again, looking more closely at the spines. In the section that was dedicated to her favorite subject, the Constitution, there was a box she'd missed before. A battered shoebox was buried in the midst of the mess of books and booklets, pamphlets and stray papers.

Justice pulled it out, opened it, and nearly dropped it in shock. There were copies of the *National Review* that she had written for, copies of the two issues of the *UMKC Law Review* that contained her articles, and printouts from her blog posts. Each magazine was opened back to the articles with her byline. Each law journal article was marked with stickies. They were all dog-eared.

Every word she'd published—print and online—was here, yellow highlighted, written on, circled, redlined, beat to death. The only magazine issues in the box were the ones with her articles; there were no others.

Her hand to her mouth, she half cried-half laughed. She took the box to the couch and sank to the floor, her back to it. She began to sift through them to see what he'd written in his distinctive hand: elegantly stylized block letters, the way an architect would write.

Comments were sparse and seemed to run fifty-fifty on whether he agreed or not, whether he found a logical fallacy or not, whether he thought something was irrelevant or could have been emphasized more.

Then she flipped through the printouts of her blog posts and comments, also marked. What most interested her, however, were the printouts of hamlet's comments. On seeing his moniker, she felt that pain behind her sternum again.

JMcKinley writes:
hamlet, name that quote: In the United States there's a Puritan ethic and a mythology of success. He who is successful is good. In Latin countries, in Catholic countries, a successful person is a sinner.

Underneath that printout he'd written the answer to the question: Umberto Eco.

Justice sucked in a long, shocked breath, held it. Then she giggled and threw her head back to look at the ceiling to squeal, kicking her legs up in the air, feeling her face flush. Grinning, she looked for and found a comment she'd made very early in her official blogging career: *You remind me of a professor I had my first week in law school.*

He'd highlighted that comment in yellow and drawn a smiley face.

Was this why her?

Suddenly the couch behind her shifted and she gasped, looking up to see Knox lifting one leg over her head so that he could sit on the couch with her between his knees.

She didn't know what to say to him, so she didn't say anything. He leaned forward against her, wrapping his arms around her to read over her shoulder. Her insides went all tingly.

"I wondered how long it'd take you to find that," he murmured.

Justice's eyes welled with tears that tracked down her cheeks and splattered on the printouts, smearing the ink.

"Why did you leave me?" she whispered. "I needed you so much."

He said nothing for a minute. "I've watched Sebastian compete with Ford for years—and lose—and the last thing I wanted to do was catch myself in that net, but somehow . . . " He sighed. "It wasn't easy to stay away from you. I knew you felt abandoned and I'm sorry."

"Did you get my email?" she asked, hearing the pathetic plea in her own voice.

"Yes," he breathed. "I still have it. Sometimes I hit reply but I don't know what to say."

"Why me?" she whispered, needing him to spell it out in words because conclusions about such things as these were just too risky.

"Oh, Iustitia. All I wanted was to see you before Eric sent you on your way east, wait until after my birthday and come find you. I never wanted you to see me in my world, who the Chouteau County prosecutor really is. But then I shot Jones and I saw the look on your face, watched your heart break. I couldn't let you go knowing I'd never, *ever* have a chance with you after that. Your being my wife had nothing at all to do with the proviso."

Justice's soul began to fill with light. "Why did you let me go, then?"

"I had become Lucifer."

She thought about that a moment, then nodded in understanding. "And the baby?"

"I *don't want* to fulfill the proviso. Sebastian and Bryce have that under control and it's not dependent on me." He paused for a moment. "Iustitia, I fell in love with you that day in class, the second I touched you. Every day I bantered with you online I fell more in love with you. Every day you were in my office was torture for me. I let you go because I love you and I couldn't stand what I'd done to you. I'd like to have children with you and I'll take any children you want to give me—or not—just so long as I have you."

She could barely breathe. This was everything she'd ever wanted from him. He nibbled on her neck; her eyes closed and she tilted her head so that he had easier access.

"Never," he murmured, "in a million years did I think you'd come back to me. Why? *Why* did you come back to me?"

"I wanted to be your lover. I hoped maybe you might come to love me someday."

"I do. I always have. Come to bed with me," he whispered in her ear, warm butterscotch. "Come make love with me. Please."

91: Hey Nineteen

B Y THE TIME KNOX'S MOUTH MADE ITS SLOW AND AGONIZING JOURNEY
down Justice's belly and between her thighs, she writhed in pleasure. She
gasped when his big hands caressed her hips and grasped them, tilting her up
so he could dip his tongue up inside her, lapping at her most sensitive spots. She
marveled at the scandalous deliciousness of it all, her legs wide, her fingers clutching
his coarse blond hair to bring him into her even closer.

She bloomed and popped with a cry and her back arched. Her hips shot up out
of Knox's hands, then fell back to the bed. She sighed when Knox rose above her,
then sank into her, slowly, carefully. She wrapped her arms around his ribs, then ran
her hands down his back until she clasped his buttocks to pull him deeper inside her.

He shuddered and groaned when she did that, which made her body fall apart,
turn to liquid—and the feel of him sliding inside her so tight, so slick, so . . . perfect . . .

Justice started to wonder why it hadn't been that way before because she'd been
just as wet then as now—

"Stop thinking," he whispered in her ear. "I can tell when you start thinking."

"Mmmm, talk to me," she said, holding his face between her hands and kissing
him, tasting herself on his tongue and his lips and growing even more aroused.

So he talked to her. He spoke in time with every thrust, told her what to do and
how to do it and why. He told her what he wanted her to do to him and when and
why. He said naughty things to her, words she never liked because they weren't
dignified, but in that instant, she fell in love with each and every one of them as he
spoke them, how he used them.

All night, he made her come and come again, turning her over and rolling her on top and doing things she'd never imagined a human could do. She knew what animals did, which she had always assumed people did, more or less, after adjusting for differences in anatomy.

Then her horizons had been widened from the merely mechanical, the ordinary and pedestrian, to the extremes of human sexuality with no stops in between. In one night with Knox, she'd hit her stride and had become rather proficient at a couple of things that, with no more information than she'd had before Anne Rice, she would never have thought to try.

"Professor Hilliard," she murmured as he settled himself beside her, half on top of her, his big hand sweeping her body from breast to thigh and back again.

He raised an eyebrow. "Yes, Miss McKinley?"

"You're a *very* good teacher." She cupped his scrotum in her hand to feel the velvet, the delicate skin there, the stones that lay hidden inside. He closed his eyes and sighed, shifting so she had better access. She stroked his semi-hard length and liked that he was sticky from sex with her, that he wore her scent as she wore his.

"You're a much more willing student than I gave you credit for. My apologies, Miss McKinley."

"I think I could be downright perverted if I had enough practice."

"You *need* more practice, Miss McKinley. You're eager enough, but you're a rank amateur." Justice shoved at him and he laughed. "You give head like a veteran, though. Are you *sure* you've never done that before?"

She harrumphed. "I think I'd have remembered that."

"*Why?*" he whispered as he caressed her cheek, staring at her, making her blush with pleasure. "Why haven't you had a dozen lovers?"

Her brow wrinkled. "Do you want me to have had?"

"I don't care one way or the other. What I don't understand is how you've gone all these years without some man grabbing you and hauling you off to bed. You're extremely sensual, uninhibited. I just— I don't get it."

"I didn't have time," she said simply. "I was too busy trying to survive and get ahead in the world."

He sighed.

"So how many have you had before me?" she asked, trying to remember that she was the one he wanted, so it shouldn't matter.

He tensed just a little, but then relaxed and said, "Five. I was twenty-six the first time I got laid and my relationships were serious and long term."

She struggled to one elbow to stare down at him, incredulous. "You're kidding."

"Before Parley, I was . . . a good Mormon kid. Celibacy until marriage is part of the deal."

She said nothing for a moment and then, "You miss being able to say that about yourself, don't you?"

"Yeah." He paused. "I've left it up to the Lord to decide if I made the right decision and . . . I have faith that he might agree with my choice, even though the church didn't. If he doesn't, I'll take the consequences."

"Oh, Knox," she sighed. "There is no God."

She could feel his chuckle against her body as she cocooned herself in his arms and the warm covers and the wonderfully perfect mattress. Her eyes began to close, too tired to even relive the preceding hours when her beautiful lover had loosed her Inner Pervert.

She started when the alarm buzzed and groaned. "My boss is going to kill me today. You wore me out."

Knox laughed then and caught her mouth in another hot kiss that made her juices begin to flow yet again. "Once you get up and around, that goes away," he whispered.

He was right; once she got to work, she felt more energetic and more able to do her work even though her mind was back home, in bed, with Knox, and she couldn't keep a smile off her face.

Richard pulled up a chair at lunch. "Congratulations," he murmured.

"Congratulations what?" she asked, biting into one of the absolutely divine cheeseburgers from the café across the street.

"Now he's looking at you the same way you look at him."

She choked and then swallowed her food. "So I'm not the high school freshman with a crush on the captain of the football team anymore?"

"I didn't say that. Now the captain of the football team has a crush on the little freshman."

Justice laughed delightedly, warmed to the depths of her soul.

"And—Justice?"

"What?"

"Thank you for the money."

"I didn't give it to you."

"No, but I'm sure you put a bug in Knox's ear."

She smiled and patted his arm.

That night, Knox pounced on her as soon as she walked in the door and she was more than ready to be pounced upon, but she was tired and went to sleep as soon as she'd popped, Knox still buried inside her.

The morning after that, she was late, and Knox yelled at her in front of everybody. She was tempted to yell back that *she* didn't have a terminal case of insomnia and it was *his* fault for keeping her up all night, but she wasn't quite that bold.

"Time to get up, Iustitia," Knox whispered in her ear the third morning as she snuggled herself into the warmth of his naked body.

"Grrr. Can we take a sick day?"

He laughed. "No. Especially not both of us at the same time. But would you come away with me this weekend?"

She opened her eyes to see his face there in the pillow, suddenly with fewer lines, and a serenity she had never seen before. He gave her a crooked grin that made her belly flip over. "Say yes, Iustitia. I haven't asked a girl out on a date in a long time."

"Why do that when you can threaten?" she murmured with a shy smile as she touched her palm lightly to his scruffy face.

"I do everything the hard way, remember?"

"Yes, why *do* you do that?"

"Too early in the morning for psychoanalyzation, love."

Her shy smile widened a bit at the endearment and she felt her face flush, so she buried her nose into the pillow. He laughed as he bounded out of bed and went into the bathroom. "I'd really rather not have to yell at you today. You know I hate late."

"Knox, it's five-thirty in the morning. Couldn't you stand to actually get to work on time instead of an hour early?"

"Old habits die hard," he muttered around his toothbrushing. "Couldn't you stand to actually get to work on time instead of thirty minutes late?"

She dragged herself out of bed, then nearly tripped over the cat, who'd decided that since he'd already been dislodged twice, he wasn't budging again. "Dog," she breathed, exasperated. One loud meow let her know how irritated he was with her, and Knox laughed.

"Guess he told you."

Once in the bathroom, she nudged Knox over with her hip and he protested with a grunt; then she began the task of brushing her teeth. Knox moved around her to turn on the shower and she bent to rinse her mouth.

She gasped when she felt Knox's big hands around her hips. One slid slowly from her hip over and around her thigh until his fingers slid up inside her and his thumb massaged her clitoris. She closed her eyes and sighed as she rose a bit so that her back was against his chest. His other hand caressed her, hip to ribs to breast until it was in his hand, his thumb manipulating her nipple.

"Look in the mirror," he whispered in her ear, deep and gruff. "Watch me make love to you."

Hesitantly, she opened her eyes and saw that girl who surprised her every time, with copper-mahogany curls as messy as they ever were in the morning; with freckles heavily layering her face; with hazel eyes that had never been anything but dull to her until right this moment.

She saw Knox's sunny blond hair, his mouth in the crook of her neck, nibbling, kissing, licking. She simultaneously saw and felt what his hand did to her breast. She watched the muscles in his other arm move in time with what she felt his fingers doing to her.

Her breath came fast and hard even as she watched Knox raise his head and meet her gaze in the mirror, that dark, dark blue they turned when he was aroused, and oh! he *was* aroused.

"Look at your face and your breasts; they're flushing," he murmured, and she looked. Indeed, they were flushing. "Look at your eyes; they're gold." Indeed, they were gold. "Look at your chest, how hard you're breathing." Indeed, she was panting as if she'd run the two-minute mile. "I've waited three years to make love to you, Iustitia, to watch you flush like that and your eyes turn to gold."

"*Why* did you wait?" she breathed, her eyes closing in sheer sensation.

"It would've been longer if you hadn't been in my office when Jones came barging in."

Then Knox slid his hands up and around her ribs, drawing away from her. She opened her eyes again to see that he was inspecting her back and buttocks, caressing her skin slowly all the way down her body until they were again at her hips, then between her legs, parting them gently until at last, his shaft was right *there* and she did so love that.

He pressed her forward a little and then slid up into her, his hands flat on the counter, his big body surrounding her and pressing against her as well as inside her. She released a ragged sigh and closed her eyes.

"Put your hands on mine, love. Wrap your fingers in mine. Brace yourself."

She did, then he began to move and she sighed again, deeper.

"Open your eyes, Iustitia. I want you to see this."

What she was looking at was two people making love, their bodies moving, their breath coming shorterharderfaster, and their skin flushing more.

What she saw was a man who loved her, had loved her from the beginning, and who had finally felt ready to take what she would have given him freely to begin with if he'd just asked.

She couldn't watch herself come; she was too busy feeling, her eyes closing yet again, her head back on Knox's shoulder, until she had come with soft gasps. Then she opened her eyes to watch Knox.

His head back, his shoulders tense, he moved with the grace of a lion and came with the roar of one, too.

He was *magnificent.*

He stilled for a moment, then slowly wrapped himself around her, propping his chin on her shoulder and looking at her, his eyes lightening as she watched.

"So how about it? Romantic weekend?"

"What about being seen together?"

"Not where I want to take you. Whittaker House in Mansfield."

Justice's brow wrinkled. "What's that and where's that?"

"Mansfield's in the Ozarks. Whittaker House is an inn that I half own."

Justice, taken out of the moment, stared at him agape. "You own an inn in the Ozarks?"

He chuckled and moved away from her, then directed her into the shower. "Half."

"That's where you went those weekends?"

"Yes. My ward, Vanessa, is a chef. It's her baby; I just put up the cash. I go down there to unwind and help out. Do the books and whatever legal work needs to be done."

Justice was speechless. "You have a *ward*?"

"Two," he said absently as he bent to lather soap up Justice's legs. "It's a long story. I'll tell you on the way."

She sighed in bemusement at how much she didn't know about Knox and watched him rise to his full height, then duck his head under the spray. His body was strong, his shoulders and arms heavily muscled, his chest covered in a dusting of hair lighter than his skin. Justice didn't know what other forty-year-old men looked like naked, but she supposed she could be happy with what she had.

"What are you smiling about?"

"You're *gorgeous*."

He stilled, stared at her for a moment, and then she gasped, delighted, when he *blushed*. "No one's ever said that to me before," he grumbled when she began to giggle, but he grabbed her and kissed her to shut her up.

"I'm not going to be able to think about anything but this all day today," she whispered against his mouth as the kiss softened.

He gave her a goofy grin she'd only begun seeing after they'd really made love the first time, two nights before. "I've been having a bit of that problem myself, Iustitia."

"Knox? Were you waiting to make love to me until you told me about Parley?"

He stilled "Yes," he finally said. "I needed you to hear it from me, all of it, how I did it—I've never told anyone what I told you. I'm *not* sorry, but I didn't want to feel your disappointment or horror; didn't want to see the same look on your face you had when I shot Jones. And I certainly didn't want you to leave me again. Sleeping on the couch and having you in the house somewhere was better than not having you at all." He paused. "Thank you, Iustitia."

"For what?"

"Believing in me. Coming back to me."

"You made me who I am. You gave me the strength and courage to put my name to my opinions and then defend them. Everything you've done to me, the threats, the intimidation—you wanted, needed, me to stand up to you. Telling me you owned me was the straw that broke the camel's back."

There was that grin again. "Well, I didn't need you to slap me that hard, but yes, I wanted to get you where you live and see what you'd do. Iustitia, you already had it in you; you've always had it in you. I just wanted to bring it to the surface and test its strength."

"Did I pass, Professor Hilliard?"

He laughed then. "Yes and I want to explore that Professor Hilliard thing in more depth with you this weekend."

"Oh?"

"Oh yes," he purred. "That older-professor-nubile-young-student thing is unexpectedly erotic. I don't know how the *hell* I missed that all these years."

92: Little Resort in the Ozarks

JUSTICE FELL IN LOVE WITH MANSFIELD AND WHITTAKER HOUSE THE MINUTE
they drove onto the pastoral property complete with grazing sheep, though it did
unnerve her that Knox's ward, Vanessa Whittaker, was almost exactly Justice's
age and, along with being warm and gracious, she was very, very pretty.

With straight chocolate-colored hair streaked blonde from the sun, vivid turquoise
eyes, and perfect, faintly tanned skin (without even one freckle), Vanessa was drop-
dead gorgeous. Justice had never thought of herself as a particularly jealous person,
but if it had to do with Knox . . .

She looked at Vanessa and those acid-green tendrils curled through her until
Knox wrapped his big hand gently around the back of her neck and pulled her up
against his broad, hard body. He caressed her backside and his mouth brushed her ear.

Justice closed her eyes. Sighed.

"I told you on the way down here, Iustitia. Vanessa's my daughter. She was a
twelve-year-old girl who did a tremendously courageous thing in the name of truth
and justice, then needed someone to protect her from the fallout. I happened to be
the AP who caught that case." He turned her and pointed to a painting of Vanessa
that hung in what was called the grand parlor. "Tell me what you see in that work."

Justice stared at the eight-by-five-foot semi-nude portrait entitled *Wild, Wild West*;
she could feel Knox watching her, waiting . . . Justice gasped, all traces of jealousy
vanishing in a mist.

"Ford," she whispered, recognizing Sebastian's style as well as the flush of
Vanessa's skin as she posed in the classic odalisque style on a magenta chaise, her
hair a chic mess, her mouth curled in a self-satisfied smile and her eyes half closed.

"Vanessa—? Sebastian—?"

"That's right. Neither of them thinks I'm observant or smart enough to figure out how that all went down—no pun intended—so you and I will just keep our correctly drawn conclusions to ourselves, shall we?" Justice opened her mouth to ask more questions, but Knox kissed her, long and deep. "There's a reason I wouldn't have let Sebastian paint you, Iustitia," he murmured against her lips, "and it's not because I don't want the world to know what my stunning wife looks like nude. I could have gotten on board with that as fast as Bryce did with Giselle, but you notice Giselle doesn't look like she's just spent a week in bed having the most incredible sex of her life."

Justice swallowed. "Sebastian told me that if it weren't for Eilis, he'd have—" She paused. "I didn't believe him."

Knox laughed. "Sebastian turns into a completely different man when he sees a woman he wants to paint. He's a freight train and there's just no getting out of that path. Now he's obsessed with Eilis and since Sebastian never lets go of his obsessions, that's not going to change for a couple hundred years or so. He wouldn't paint you now even if asked, in any form, like Giselle's or otherwise, whether Eilis goes back to him or not."

"What was different about Eilis?" Justice asked.

"She went wandering through his mind and his soul. Now, let's go up to our suite so I can wander around in you for a while."

Justice awoke the next morning, alone in a strange sleigh bed in a suite whose opulence she had never seen the likes of. This was definitely *not* her bedroom. It took her a minute to remember where she was, then she relaxed back into the glorious mattress, closed her eyes, and smiled.

She heard an elevator ding and soft footsteps across the carpet toward her. The mattress depressed from underneath her and she caught a whiff of a musky cologne before she felt lips on her earlobe and strong arms wrap around her. She smiled.

"Happy birthday, Iustitia," he breathed in her ear.

Justice's eyes popped open. "You knew! You remembered!"

He smiled at her. "I did."

"Did Giselle tell you?"

"Please give me a little credit for doing something nice without having to have my ass kicked by my family. No, she didn't. Now, I got you something, but you have to get dressed and come downstairs before I'll give it to you."

She pouted. "Bribery is a felony."

"Call the FBI. They might *finally* have something to nail me on." And with a bounce and a laugh, he was gone.

When she stepped off the elevator into Whittaker House's lobby after showering and dressing, she stopped short, her senses assaulted with the sight of hundreds of balloons of every color imaginable clinging to the ceiling and some floating around on strings with weights. Paper ribbons criss-crossed the grand foyer and dining room, and what seemed like hundreds of people stood looking at her expectantly.

She knew it was coming, braced herself for it, but—

"SURPRISE!"

—she still jumped at the roar. Who *were* all these people?

"This," Vanessa murmured as she looped her arm through Justice's to pull her along through the crowd into the dining room, "is about half the population of Mansfield and Ava."

"They don't know me," she whispered.

"No, but they know Knox and they love him; therefore, *you* must be pretty special."

"But what about Fen?"

"Oh. Him. Wright and Davis counties convinced Fen a few years ago that it might be smart for him not to show his face south of Sedalia, and that any random snooping around about Knox would not be appreciated. If he finds out Knox has a wife now, it won't be because of anybody down here. We protect our own."

"Do they know—"

"They don't *know* anything. What they suspect, well . . . That I can't say. But we're pretty sharp and if it looks like it could be trouble, it probably is. If we're wrong, we'll apologize *after* we shoot you."

Justice chuckled, then laughed. Her eyes filled with tears as she looked overhead at the twenty-foot-high embossed copper ceiling covered with balloons and streamers, walking through a throng that thought she was special because they thought Knox was special—special enough to protect him and to welcome an unknown wife with open arms.

Then she saw Knox waiting for her at a table with a cake and a present.

"We didn't know what kind of cake you'd like, so I made chocolate. I hope that's okay."

Justice couldn't respond to Vanessa's whisper before Knox took her hand to pull her down into his lap. She turned into him then, wrapping her arms around him, and began to cry the way she had that night in the grass, but for an entirely different reason.

She didn't know how long she stayed like that, her nose in the crook of his neck, smelling his skin, his cologne, his broad, muscular body against hers, his coarse blond hair in her fingers, his arms wrapped around her.

"Everyone's off eating cake and ice cream now," he whispered after a while. "I wasn't sure how you'd react to the crowd—that, I didn't plan for—but I wasn't going to send them away."

"It's not that," she whispered in return, hoarse. "It's— I— I've never had— Not since my mother died, anyway."

"I wondered," he breathed. "I watched you walk out of the auditorium at graduation alone. You looked so sad and lonely. You don't know how badly I wanted to take you home right then."

And remembering that, Justice began to cry all over again.

"Hey! I didn't mean to upset you. Here," he said and gently pried her away from him. "Open your present."

She half-laughed and half-cried. She tried to wipe her face with her hands, but Knox took a napkin and wiped her face for her. "You're a hot mess," he muttered, and Justice laughed.

"It's a book," she finally said when she picked up the heavy package covered with haphazardly folded and taped paper. "You wrapped this yourself."

"I tried. I don't do that so well. I probably should've had Vanessa do it."

"No! No, you shouldn't have." She carefully unwrapped it, taking her time, knowing she would save the paper because Knox had folded and taped it with his own two hands. Then she saw the name on the dust jacket and her jaw dropped. "Morgan Ashworth!" she breathed and turned the book over and over again. Her brow wrinkled. "I didn't know he wrote novels."

"Nobody else does, either. Yet. Open the cover."

She gasped. On the inside cover, a very upright masculine scrawl said, *To Justice Hilliard, on your 25th birthday. Enjoy it before everyone else does. Morg.*

"How—?"

"No no no. Not nice to ask questions. Let's just say I know people and leave it at that, 'kay?"

"*Knox*," she breathed. "I did my senior thesis on his economic theories. He's a *genius*."

He snorted.

"Do you *know* him? You must because he wrote 'Justice Hilliard.' Can I *meet* him?"

"Not on your life. I'm already jealous."

She was completely, thoroughly delighted with her gift. "Oh, Knox," she said again because she didn't know what else to say. "*Thank* you."

"My pleasure, Iustitia." He paused. "But you know this doesn't mean I'm going to stop yelling at you at work, *especially* if you're late."

She burst out laughing. "I'd have to wonder what was wrong with you if you did."

93: Getting to Know You

JMcKinley writes:
I didn't say I was switching positions on vigilanteism, darrylm. It's just that I'm seeing limitations in the legal system that nobody likes, but can't seem to change.

darrylm writes:
im just relly dsippointed in u, justice

JMcKinley writes:
I'm sorry, darrylm. I'm still thinking about it, still trying to find some moral compromise. There's more of a gap between law and justice than I thought there was and I guess in a fight between them, my first inclination is to see justice come out on top.

hamlet writes:
so justice's position is on top

"What am I supposed to say to that, Knox?" Justice breathed as she raised and lowered herself over Knox's hips, taking her pleasure at her leisure.

"Whatever you want to say, Iustitia," he breathed in return, his big hands around her hips urging her to go faster, but no, she couldn't. Wouldn't. She liked this too much, the languid slide in and out with that depth she got when she was in control.

"I'm guessing you like it on top?"

She snickered and looked down at him, his crooked grin all but making her heart explode. "You better stop flirting with me online—the rest of the crew is going to get suspicious."

"Iustitia, I've been flirting with you for the past two years. You're the only one who didn't notice." Justice's mouth dropped open. "It was cute you never got it."

Justice, jerked out of the beginning of her orgasm, stopped and stared down at him. "*What?*" Knox closed his eyes and lifted her away from him, then pulled her back down on his cock. He arched his back and groaned when he came, and Justice's eyes narrowed. She crossed her arms over her chest and glared at him until he was done. He opened his eyes slowly, took one look at her, and started to chuckle. She truly did see the humor in it, but still . . .

"You just couldn't wait to tell me that until after I came, could you?"

His chuckle turned into a rolling laugh and he slid his hands up her back to pull her to his chest. They lay together in the middle of the bed and she kissed the line of his jaw while he stroked her bare skin. Their laptops had been cast aside once Knox had posted his last comment.

"Well, now I feel a little silly," she murmured. "Didn't notice. Hrmf."

"Iustitia, your innocence is a very large part of your popularity. You see things so simply, it makes others think it doesn't have to be difficult. My flirting with you—and I'm not the only one, by the way—and your not catching it is very . . . " Knox searched for words, which he very rarely had to do, so Justice treasured the moment. "It gives hope that there's still such a thing as innocence in the world, that not everyone is dipped in the acid of cynicism. On the other hand," he said low in his throat as he kissed her; Justice could never get enough of Knox's kisses. "You caught that innuendo fast enough. I might be rubbing off on you."

"You're rubbing up inside me, is where you're rubbing. You owe me an orgasm."

Knox burst out laughing and laughed until he was wiping his eyes. "Damn, Iustitia, you make me laugh. I love you."

"I think I've had enough blogging tonight," she sighed with great smile of contentment.

"You barely got started before you attacked me."

"Oh, don't act like it was a great hardship."

"Don't you still have an article to write?"

"Mmmm, not right now," she muttered. Justice was falling asleep, which she almost always did after making love no matter what time of day it was, orgasm or not. She felt Knox's chuckle as she shifted around to grab the bed linens to cover them.

Neither awoke until morning.

Everything was still normal at work. And except for the occasional snickers or glances askance, like the money, Justice's three co-conspirators pretended not to know that the reason Knox suddenly seemed a lot happier was because of Justice, pretended that she was just a junior AP and Knox was her significantly less disgruntled boss.

Then they got home, in bed. Or in the yard, when she ran like she had the first time and she squealed, giggling, when he tackled her and they rolled over and over and spent hours making love in the grass (with the bug bites to prove it), the heat and humidity of a late summer Missouri night their only blanket—until Sebastian had emerged from the barn one night.

"JUSTICE! Quit howling, dammit! I can't hear myself think. Why can't you two fuck in the house like normal people?"

Justice wrote articles for print, and Knox would mark them up and leave them on her desk at work. He expected her to be better than she was, better than her editors thought she was. He refused to read her work before she turned it in, but once it was in print, he took great liberty in assessing her.

Knox took her to a remote shooting range where they wouldn't be seen together and taught her the finer points that Giselle hadn't had time to.

"I really should have Giselle do this," he said one day. "She's better at it than I am."

"You seemed pretty good the day you shot Jones *right between the eyes.*"

"I had to. Either Hicks or I would've died that day, so I couldn't afford to miss. Giselle *enjoys* it. She's a martial artist so she understands body movement better and she's got a knack for it. I think it's always better for a person to learn something from someone who enjoys it."

"Who taught her?"

"Sebastian. He taught us both."

"I can't imagine Sebastian with a gun in his hand."

"It's not his weapon of choice, no."

"And that is?"

"A baseball bat. And as far as I know, he hasn't used one since he was nineteen."

Justice's eyes widened. "That's . . . that's not normal."

Knox burst out laughing. "*Sebastian* isn't normal."

He made her practice endlessly, left- and right-handed, though he did tell her he thought she was an excellent marksman.

When Knox was in full teaching mode, he was harsh and biting in his criticism, but he was equally effusive with praise. All the residents, including Justice, strove for the moment Knox would grace them with his approbation.

Every other weekend, Knox and Justice left work on Friday and headed south to the Ozarks. Justice was glad to get away, though Vanessa's gourmet kitchen only emphasized how much she hated her own kitchen. She sometimes helped cook Friday and Saturday night dinner, learning various tricks from Vanessa and her sous chef. Justice, however, was much better at pastry than Vanessa, and her cherry pie became a favorite (but surprise) treat of the Friday- and Saturday-night dinner crowd. Knox did whatever bad-guy dirty work Vanessa needed done and tended to guests.

Justice loved watching this side of Knox unfold before her eyes, the wealthy, refined gentleman he was born to be. He was a gracious host to people who thought he hung the moon, his reputation four hours north nothing but a slightly amusing quirk. The towns of Mansfield and Ava adored him, but he didn't seem to notice.

What Justice liked most about going to Whittaker House:

"This is my wife, Justice," he would say to whomever he spoke, a proud note in his voice that thrilled her to the core of her soul.

She loved being with Knox in public, being a regular husband and wife with him without fear of anybody seeing them together, holding hands, whispering, canoodling, kissing—

—slow dancing on Saturday nights to the band that played standards during dinner, its singer's voice a dead ringer for Ella Fitzgerald's. Along with everything else he'd taught her, Knox taught her how to dance, something she had never had the opportunity to do. "You're very good at this, Iustitia," he whispered. It never failed that she and Knox garnered quite a bit of attention as they danced, but Justice wasn't sure why unless . . .

"Knox?"

"Mmmm?" He pressed soft kisses in the curve of her neck.

"Every woman here wants to kill me."

He stilled and looked at her, confused and concerned. "What makes you say that?"

"Because the hottest dude in the state is making love to me on a dance floor." That made him throw back his head and laugh. She huffed. "Well, don't stop just because I pointed it out."

Eric decided it was time for Justice to start being a real prosecutor instead of staying in traffic ticket, deadbeat dad, and arraignment hell. Finally, one day after he'd given her her first fairly big case, she stepped into the courtroom and sat at the table alone. None of her coworkers stayed with her because Knox had forbidden it.

"She goes alone like everybody else does. She wins or loses on her own merits. Nobody in this office is to go into that courtroom while she's trying it. Not to help, not to watch."

She'd prepared to the hilt, memorizing every speck of every detail of the file, and Eric, Richard, and Patrick had drilled her endlessly on the facts. Hicks taught her how to pick a jury and Justice was shocked to learn that he was the one who had taught Knox how to do it long, long ago when he was a junior AP, and Knox still couldn't pick a jury better than Hicks. Patrick and Eric taught her how to prep witnesses.

Knox taught her how to find and draw out nuances on the fly, how to coax and cajole and flatter obscure information out of witnesses. He'd taken her to an empty courtroom three days in a row and made her try the whole thing against him.

He taught her how to walk, when to talk to the jury and not, and went through her side of the closet to pick which outfit she should wear and why. "No pants. A woman has a different power than a man in court and part of that is how she dresses."

"That's what Giselle said."

"Giselle should open a finishing school."

She was amazed at how much she'd picked up just by spending all those hours and hours watching Knox do what he did so well, how well she could imitate him and his inflections. Since he'd never trained a woman before, he had to sit back and watch her to make adjustments. By comparison, he had her watch Eric and the residents try their cases and without exception, they all looked and sounded exactly like Knox.

It took a week of incredibly intensive thinking on her feet to win it. When she came back to the office after the verdict, Knox muttered, disgruntled,

"Shit. Now I have to keep her." The office howled, shook her hand, slapped her on the back, and generally yelled good-natured insults at her across the office until it was time to go home.

"You did very well, Iustitia," Knox whispered in her ear that night. "I'm proud of you."

Things changed for her after she won that case. She was part of the team. They took her writings seriously now and they all argued back and forth across the office about whatever opinion she'd had online or in print. She knew she was persuasive in print and she knew she was persuasive in court, but it never dawned on her that she could be persuasive in her workplace with people who held their own strong opinions, had reasons for them, and had years of lawyering behind them.

She found she had a talent for impeccably timed comedy and very often her wry observations, rapier wit, and cutting asides had the office howling with laughter. Knox had begun to leave his private office door open, she suspected, because he wanted to hear what bomb she was going to drop next.

As she spent more time in Knox's arms and brain, she lost some of her innocence along with her ignorance. She didn't miss either. Occasionally, he'd fling an innuendo at her at work when no one else was around to make her blush, but it made him laugh. Under Knox's tutelage, her language sank into the gutter with the men's and she didn't care; she liked being one of them and she wasn't that girl in the front row her first week in law school anymore.

"I *like* it when you talk dirty, Iustitia."

Justice wrote a blog article about being a prosecutor and the practical versus theoretical. She talked about her colleagues, the different approaches to their cases, her friendship with Richard, Eric's management style, Patrick's willingness to do anything he was asked, and Hicks's sly and irascible humor—although she thought it prudent to change their names and not mention where she worked. Yet.

Knox blew his stack.

"Iustitia, if you mention the Chouteau County prosecutor's office, you're going to get a lot of backlash you don't want, and I'm not even talking about Fen coming after you. You're the golden girl of conservative politics; once you mention me or my office, you'll carry a taint you won't be able to wash off and your career'll be over before it really got rolling. It's also very possible that if Kevin loses this election, you could get dragged into Sebastian's mess. Neither Wall Street nor Washington would take it kindly that *the* Justice McKinley is also *the* OKH Bride and possibly the mother of the OKH Baby."

Well, he did have a point.

"I'm asking you not to write about the office, Iustitia, not just for your career, but for Sebastian's and Kevin's. Your credibility will tank if you're associated with me and if your credibility tanks, so does Kevin's. Sebastian really needs your pull right now. Please, Iustitia?"

Justice was quiet for a moment and bit her lip. "It's really not as simple as I make it sound, is it?"

Knox shook his head slowly. "No. It's not. You may lose your audience as you lose your innocence, I don't know. You may gain audience that thinks you're too naïve now. But you *will* lose your innocence and you chose the quickest route to do it, too."

"Being a prosecutor," she sighed.

Richard coordinated a party when she had somehow managed to come to a newspaper's attention and get her own syndicated column. She'd asked Knox if he had had anything to do with that and he'd been deeply offended.

"Iustitia, if there's one thing you should know about me, it's that I strip people down and throw them in the deep end and let them sink or swim based on their true selves. If they swim, fine, but I don't interfere. I just give them a safe place to hit bottom, then I fish 'em back out again. That's just the way I teach."

Hicks retired and three residents who'd been with the office long enough, respectively, went on to new and better things, as they always did. So now there was the core staff of three, then Justice. Everyone who was left in the office knew she and Knox were married, and Justice figured he'd meant it to be that way.

"Justice," Eric called to her one day across the office when it was just the four of them, "since you're here for as long as Knox is, you're taking Hicks's place. You're going to be part of the core staff now."

"Is this your decision or Knox's?"

"Mine. You know he doesn't manage staff."

"Thank you."

Richard and Patrick nodded and went back to work. She had gone from being a mousy little girl laughingstock to a tolerated coworker to a respected colleague in the toughest county in the ten that made up the Kansas City metro area.

Knox had stripped her down, thrown her in the deep end, and she'd swum.

94: Affirmative Action

J USTICE WAS LATE. AGAIN. AND KNOX WOULD PUBLICLY CRUCIFY HER WHILE THE entire courthouse listened and chuckled. She knew she deserved it, though—and he refused to wake her up in the morning.

"You're an adult and I'm not your mother. *Dammit, Iustitia,* why can't you get to work on time?"

"It's a passive-aggressive response to my asshole boss."

He'd laughed in spite of himself.

Not only had she slept through Knox getting ready for work and her alarm, she couldn't decide what she wanted to wear. She'd grown frighteningly persnickety about her wardrobe since Giselle had taken her shopping and she'd learned how it felt to dress well.

She finally settled on a linen suit: black skirt, discreet black silk and lace chemise, shoulder holster and gun, white blazer, badge, black nylons, black sling-back heels Eilis had given her for her birthday.

Justice decided to test the limits of the incestuous law in Chouteau County and she sped. This was something she had never done before coming to work at the Chouteau County prosecutor's office. Always prompt, never speeding so as to avoid tickets, she'd lost herself in that courthouse. She didn't miss anything Knox had taken away from her because she'd gained so much more, and all of it far superior to what she'd come to him with.

Her reverie was interrupted by the wail of sirens behind her and she nearly swallowed her tongue. Of course, on a day she decided to speed because she was late again, she'd get pulled over.

The state trooper was young and must have been regularly stationed somewhere other than Chouteau County because he didn't believe her when she told him she was an AP.

"Ma'am, I happen to know there is no such thing as a female Chouteau County assistant prosecutor and insisting that you are one is going to make me mad."

She showed him her badge and of course, that made her shoulder holster visible.

He arrested her for carrying a concealed weapon without a permit and impersonating an officer of the court. The only thing she could think of was to say, "Please call Knox Hilliard and ask him."

"Don't need to, ma'am. Everybody in Missouri knows how Mr. Hilliard works. Except you."

Mr. Hilliard would blow his top, that was how Mr. Hilliard worked—and she'd to be on the receiving end of it, very loudly and very publicly. At least it amused her colleagues.

Much commotion surrounded her arrest and Sheriff Raines didn't bother to hide his delight. Defense attorneys looked at her askance, wondering whether to laugh or offer their services. Raines felt perfectly free to book her, process her (in a white blazer!), and detain her regardless.

Knox would probably say it served her right and she wouldn't be surprised if Knox had ordered him to let her cool her heels for being late. So she took off those heels and put them on the bench beside her, slouched against the wall, and folded her arms over her chest.

She was *so* going to blog about this.

An hour passed before the jail cleared and she was the only one left in the holding cell block. Out of the corner of her eye, she saw Raines slip into the deserted area and approach her cell arrogantly, his keys jangling tauntingly in his hand.

"So," he said, looking through the bars and leering. "I see you got yourself all gussied up some time back ago. Trying to catch Hilliard's eye, I bet. I seen how you look at him and mebbe I want you to look at me that way."

Justice gulped. No, Knox would never have kept her here on purpose and at Raines's disposal. When Raines opened the cell door, Justice felt real fear slice through her; Knox didn't know she was here and she had no way to defend herself. Except one.

Surreptitiously, she picked up one of her shoes and stood to meet him. Heart thumping in her chest, throat dry, she felt anger seep through her, replacing the fear.

"If you touch me, I'll kill you," she snarled, surprised that that had come out of her mouth and how viciously.

That did take him aback, this new and different Justice McKinley. He hesitated, then bucked up and chuckled. "Naw, ya won't, girl. You might even like it. Now, you put that shoe down and we can have a little fun before I let you call Hilliard to come bail you out."

She hefted her shoe in her hand, feeling for the right angle, looking at him through narrowed eyes. She couldn't remember ever being so outraged.

You have to walk barefoot through fire on broken glass.

The feeling—it was never a thought—infused her with strength and courage. She fired her shoe at him with such force that the heel drew blood where it hit him in the face, barely missing his eyeball. He howled, clutching at his cheek.

She picked up her other shoe and aimed for his crotch. Once he'd doubled over, she slid across the smooth concrete floor in her stockinged feet and plucked his gun out of his holster. Stepping back, firm on her feet then and pointing it at him two-handed, she said, in a terrifying voice, a voice she didn't know she had:

"You picked the wrong woman, Raines. That girl who walked in here five months ago is long gone. You want me to drag your sorry ass upstairs to Knox and let you tell him what happened or do you want me to blow your face off?"

"No need," came Knox's emotionless baritone from the door to the holding cell block. He stepped aside to allow in a couple of deputies and said, "False imprisonment and attempted rape. I'll figure out what else I want to add to the list and arraign him myself." He looked at Justice, his eyebrow raised. "You're late for work. Again. Get your shit together and get to my office."

He left. Just like that.

She rolled her eyes and collected her shoes, but didn't put them on, preferring instead the stability of flat feet; now that the crisis had passed, her thighs and knees trembled and threatened to buckle. The property clerk handed back her holster, gun, badge, briefcase, and purse. She was still missing one thing.

She looked around the office and saw the trooper who had arrested her. He looked miserable. "You—" she snapped and pointed at him. He barely looked up in time to duck her car keys, thrown at him so hard it put a hole in the plaster behind him, right where his head had been. "Find someone and go get my car."

Every man in that office looked at her with an awe and respect they had never shown her—and she *liked* it.

She shrugged into her shoulder holster and put away her gun. Blazer, badge. She straightened her dress and didn't care who looked at her nearly-uncovered ass when she bent clear over to do it, her hands up her skirt to adjust the lining. She glanced up to see that the state trooper was still there.

"Why are you still here?" she barked, making him scramble.

Justice jogged up the stairs, shoes in hand, purse over shoulder. She strode into the office like she owned the place, her large copper curls bouncing. She looked neither left nor right and proceeded directly to Knox's office, shoving the door open so hard it banged back against the wall. She thunked her shoes on his desk, right on top of the file he was studying.

"The county owes me a new pair of shoes," she demanded, daring him to challenge her.

Knox looked up at her slowly then and she realized why he sat at his desk, not prowling around like a caged lion as usual. His eyes were the darkest blue she'd ever seen them and she sucked in a breath, her own eyes wide, wondering if she could get away with closing the door and staying awhile.

"I'll see what I can do," he muttered tersely, grabbing the shoes, dropping them in a desk drawer.

"Thank you," she said and turned on a heel.

"McKinley."

She stopped, but didn't dare look at him.

"The next time you're late—most likely tomorrow—you better have a better excuse than you had today. And I hope you're not planning to go into a courtroom with bare feet."

"Nope."

And she slammed the door behind her on the way out.

Justice went home that night with a new and profound sense of purpose. Knox had tricked her into marrying him, but she'd chosen to come back—and it had been the right decision.

I promise you, there will come a day when all this will have been worth it and you'll be glad you persevered.

Yes, Giselle had known what would happen to her, how Knox felt about her—had known from the minute he touched Justice in class and sent her out to buck Sherry up against a tree until she nearly passed out.

Now she wanted more. She wouldn't live in that wreck of a house one more second. She really wanted to be his wife publicly, but she knew that wouldn't happen until the handoff of OKH had taken place: Fen would have no reason to hunt her down and Kevin could stay clear of any association with Knox. Justice wanted children with Knox, but not before the deadline. Of course, they hadn't done anything to prevent that.

But for right now, today, she wanted some stability in their marriage and their life together and it had to start in the kitchen.

She walked in the house and yelled. "Knox!"

"What?!" he yelled back from the basement.

"I want to talk to you."

She waitedwaitedwaited and then heard his footsteps on the stairs and waited some more until he was fully present and engaged. "What?"

"I want a new kitchen."

His jaw dropped. "You what?"

"I want a new kitchen. This is a piece of shit and if I had the means to call a tow truck and have it towed, I would. If I'm going to live here the rest of my life, I am NOT—repeat, NOT—going to live in this Brady Bunch monstrosity with chipboard furniture."

He leaned against the door jamb and crossed his arms. "You planning on living here the rest of your life?"

"Yes, I am," she said defiantly.

"What if I want to live somewhere else?"

"Then you'll build me a house to my specifications."

"You're awfully uppity today. Was it the shoes?"

She ignored that. "And also? I want natural gas. Electricity is useless to cook on and I'm just not going to live like this. You might be okay with a bed and a roof, but I want a home. We can keep the bed," she muttered as an afterthought. "I like it."

"Well, you're on a roll; first Raines, then that poor little state trooper you terrified out of his wits, then storming into my office demanding new shoes. And now you want a kitchen."

"And you know what? You'll do it, too, because you love me."

That wonderful sunshine of a grin slowly took over his face. "So what if I do? That doesn't mean I'm going to give you *everything* you want."

"I'll give you a blow job."

That surprised a bark of laughter out of him. "You'd do that anyway. You *like* giving me blow jobs."

"Well, okay, that's true." She turned to go to the bedroom and, over her shoulder, said, "But I still want a new kitchen."

She squealed with laughter when he grabbed her around the waist and spun her around. He put her back down and turned her around to kiss her.

"Knox, did you know I'd been arrested?"

"No. You're never more than a half hour late, so when it was going on an hour, I was starting to get worried. I thought for sure Fen had found out about you and gotten to you. One of the defense attorneys who'd seen you brought in came to me and told me what happened. She was worried what might happen to you in Raines's jail."

"How much did you see?"

"All of it. I would've stepped in if you were in over your head, but I knew you had him dead to rights the minute you picked up your shoe. And you know what?"

"What?"

"You were *hot*. Come to bed."

95: Pixie Dust

JUSTICE AWAKENED AT MIDNIGHT ONLY TO FIND SHE WAS ALONE, AND SHE waited for Knox to come back, but he didn't. Dim light pierced the darkness as usual and she decided to go find him. Not in the basement. Probably out in the barn.

It had grown cold at night now, so she had to put on socks and Crocs and a heavy robe over her nude body before she went trudging outside and across the lawn, the Puccini growing louder with each step. She rounded the corner, not surprised to find him and Sebastian in the middle of a yelling match.

She sighed and marched herself in to break it up, only to stop short when she saw the canvas. She stepped back, looking up and up and up, and gasped, her hand over her mouth and her eyes wide.

The music died abruptly and Sebastian yelled, "Knox, it's none of your business!" and walked across the barn toward Justice. "You like?"

"Oh, Eilis!" Justice whispered, awed and reverent. "She's *beautiful*."

"Yes," Knox sneered as he approached them, "and Sebastian just can't bear to go back to her and beg and grovel for forgiveness."

"Look, I tried to explain. I've emailed her. I've called her but she won't take my calls. She doesn't feel needed at HRP, so she's pretty much stopped going to work except to sign paychecks and nobody misses her. She won't let me in her gate. Giselle won't tell me when she's at their house so I can ambush her. I can't seem to get to a tribe party when she's there because of business and I do *not* want the tribe to know about our relationship since it seems to be dead in the water. I've begged and groveled every which way I know how. What the hell am I missing? Tell me what to do and I'll do it."

Knox wiped his hand down his face and relented with a sigh. "I don't know, Sebastian. She asked me about you."

"Yeah, tell her to talk to me personally instead of mooching information off her brother."

"I did. But. In case you forget, she," Knox went on, pointing up at the goddess, "is as much *my* business as Justice is yours."

"Not true. She," Sebastian said, pointing to the canvas, "can help us. Queen Mab here," he said, throwing his thumb at Justice, "is crucial. She doesn't get pregnant, you're done and then I'm at war. She's the woman you love and gave everything up for and she's the woman who chose to come back, knowing *all* the ramifications.

"I was just fine with doing it your way once Kenard and Oakley threw in with me, but now that you've got a chance at meeting the proviso with her, I'd like you to at least *try* to fight your own fight. There's still the election, although I'm pretty sure Fen's gone through his funds by now and, as Mab continues to remind me, I'm going to end up in the hot seat whether Kevin's elected or not and there's still HRP to deal with."

"A—Bryce is dealing with HRP, so that dog don't hunt. B—You've been enjoying the hell out of this takeover since you acquired cohorts. You're not exactly a martyr. C—It's not like you're going to be in that hot seat all by your lonesome, so go whine at someone else. You get summoned to Capitol Hill, so do I. And Bryce. Hell, let's make it a party and bring the women along for shits and grins because at this point, they're all knee deep in it, too. D—Whatever happens with a baby is up to the Lord and you know how I feel about having one before the deadline anyway."

Sebastian ignored that and speared Justice with a look. "Are you pregnant yet?"

"No."

"Get that way," he snapped and stalked out the opposite barn doors.

Knox looked at her and chuckled, wrapping his arm around her shoulders and walking her to the barn doors where the light switch was. Then he picked her up and took her in the house and laid her down in the bed.

"Why has everyone started to call me Queen Mab?" she asked when Knox kissed her slowly, teasing.

"Queen Mab is a faery queen, the bringer of dreams," he whispered. "Shakespeare refers to her in *Romeo and Juliet*: 'She gallops night by night through lovers' brains, and then they dream of love . . .' I'd quote you the whole thing but you'd fall asleep."

"So?"

"So you look like a faery queen, Iustitia. Queen Mab, bringer of dreams. You brought my dreams to me."

96: Fertile Soil

ILIS GARDENED. SHE DIDN'T HAVE MUCH TO DO AT HRP AND SHE HADN'T yet thought of any other business projects she wanted to pursue, so she went out to her garden and worked from sunup to sundown.

She dug in the hard clay soil by hand, something she hadn't done since she got her backhoe, because she needed that kind of backbreaking labor. On the weekends, Giselle would often come, sometimes with Bryce, to learn about plants. Eilis wasn't sure if she was really interested or if she was faking it for Eilis's sake, though she did seem more interested in cooking herbs than anything else. Either way, Eilis was grateful for the company and support of her family.

Justice and Knox showed up a couple of times a week for dinner; neither she nor Justice could get enough of Knox's tales of the Dunham tribe and the stories of his growing up. Eilis came to know her brother better and like slowly turned to love, the same kind he had for Giselle and Sebastian and Bryce, and filled in the holes in her soul that Trudy and Fen had shot into it. Justice, Giselle, and Eilis spent a lot of time at the spa and it felt good and right to have other women to talk about sex with, who could help her smooth out the few remaining nicks in her psyche.

One Saturday morning, she opened her gate to find a delivery truck idling. As Bryce directed it in, he pointed to a spot where she'd once absently said she wanted something that looked like Hadrian's wall. The truck door slid open and she gasped as five pallets of river stone were unloaded, along with a pallet of cement mix, bagged sand, wood, and other assorted tools that looked brand new.

"Oh," Giselle said brightly as Eilis watched all this in shock, "did I forget to tell you Bryce works stone? Congratulations. You get your wall. Bonus!" Eilis flinched, because that was such a Sebastianism, but Giselle didn't seem to notice. "Bryce has actually studied Hadrian's wall. Personally, I'm glad he has a new project. He's clad everything in our yard and I had to put the brakes on so we'd have a patch of grass."

So Eilis and Bryce spent that day marking out where she wanted it to go, how she wanted it contoured, where she wanted it to curve. On the weekends Giselle and Bryce or Knox and Justice didn't come to see her, there was a tribe party and she had been welcomed with open arms. A hundred-plus people using any excuse to have a party was an understatement. Eilis had suddenly been beset by family she'd never had and she enjoyed every minute of it.

Nobody talked about Sebastian. It was as if he didn't exist and Eilis found herself wishing, wanting, waiting for a word, anything, to know that she hadn't dreamed him up.

When she finally asked Knox about him, he slid her a glance and said, "I don't think you want to know my opinion, Eilis. If you want to know about Sebastian, talk to Sebastian. It's not as if he hasn't been trying to get you to talk to him." She felt like she'd been spanked and put in a corner with her nose to the wall, but Knox didn't seem to hold it against her.

As autumn came on, she slowed down quite a bit but kept her grass immaculate. This wasn't a chore so much as a soothing activity, what with her lawn tractor. Hadrian's wall was coming along nicely, but would have to stand over winter as Bryce wouldn't work stone in the cold.

The last Saturday he worked on the wall before putting it all away for the winter, he came into the living room where she and Giselle lay on the floor poring over fashion magazines as if they were both twelve years old. He dropped into an overstuffed chair and said, "Eilis, what are you doing Wednesday night?"

"Nothing," she said, a little depressed that she didn't have to think about it.

"Good. I'll pick you up at six. Casual."

Eilis looked between a very smug Giselle and a very blank-faced Bryce and opened her mouth, then closed it again, deciding not to waste her breath.

97: Tuatha Dé Danaan

ATRIPTYCH TWELVE FEET HIGH AND TWENTY-SIX FEET ACROSS HUNG BY heavy cables from the high ceiling in Kirkwood Hall at the center of the Nelson-Atkins gallery.

It was titled *The Goddess and Her Lover*, and, by all accounts, it was a magnificent work: explicit in its sexuality, layered with symbolism, bold in its use of color and lines, extraordinarily detailed.

It wasn't for sale.

Buyers offered auction houses tens of millions of dollars for it; Ford, through his agents, had declined to speak of it, much less entertain the offers. He had loaned it to the Nelson-Atkins Gallery for as long as they wanted to display it, with certain conditions for the first few weeks of its debut:

It had to be facing a large blank wall.

It had to be lit to very stringent specifications.

Music had to be playing while the gallery was open, and only select pieces of classical music would be allowed.

The top third of the painting, spanning the width of the panels, was a woman, nude, her skin an iridescent white-gold. When the light wasn't at all right, it was beautiful. When the light was perfect, it sent millions of prisms out onto the wall in front of it and duplicated the contours, shades, and nuances of her body perfectly.

Her eyes were vivid: one green and one blue. Her mouth was full and red, one corner of it tucked in a tender smile. Her hair was gold. Each of those features, too, twinkled in green, blue, red, and yellow on the wall, along with her brilliant body.

Her hair was a rich, vibrant gold, light and airy, floating around her face, shoulders, and arm as if on a breeze. Her pubic hair was only a tad darker. Her face was incredibly detailed and it was wondered at that a woman so perfect had a broken nose and a scar that made her look as if she were crying.

She lay on her side on a bed of clouds. One didn't know where her skin ended and the clouds began; indeed, one breast seemed to be cloud. Her head rested on a lazily outstretched arm that dropped off the left edge of the canvas as she looked down upon the earth, her face etched with great love: the love of a mother to her children. Her other arm dangled over the bed of clouds.

She was very pregnant.

Her bottom knee was bent slightly and her top leg stretched out beyond the right edge of the canvas. Behind her sat a man whose back, it seemed, leaned against the right edge of the canvas, and his shoulders rose above the top edge of the canvas. He was gray and dull, blending into the shadows, his impressive musculature vaguely delineated in slightly darker gray. It seemed his carved chest and ribs, what could be seen of them, were criss-crossed with scars. His arm lay over her broad hip, his huge hand, strong and wide, stretched out across the lower part of her pregnant belly, two of his fingers curling deep into her pubic hair. His knee rose from behind the valley of her waistline and his other arm lay across it, a myriad of paint brushes and knives dripping with vivid colors, laced through his fingers and spearing up out of his fist.

The lower two-thirds of the panels showed the earth in all its seasons. The narrow left panel was winter; fields lay fallow under snow, the watery sun lay low along the horizon. A large stone altar ran bloody with the sacrifice of a boar, a nude priestess raising the animal high above her head. Bonfires blazed behind her and her bloody altar.

The large middle panel was of spring fading into summer over the course of three-quarters of the canvas. Rain poured from beneath the bed of clouds over an immense landscape of spring crops, flowers, blossom-covered cherry trees. A nude woman squatted upon bricks—half of her in the spring rain and half of her in the summer sun, her head back, her face contorted in pain—giving birth, the Goddess's lazily dangling iridescent hand catching the bloody child that fell from the mother's hips in her palm easily, dripping blood through her fingers onto the soil. Under the child's and mother's commingled blood, the grass was thicker, richer, greener.

The summer sun was highest of all and the land was a rich green, simple, restful.

The narrow right-hand panel was of autumn, its fields stripped and barren. A nude huntress drew an arrow back and took aim at something beyond the right edge of the canvas, a slain doe at her feet, bleeding into the ground.

A masterpiece, it was called, a testament of a Man's love for a Goddess and her love for her children.

98: Wanted: One Super-Ego

SEBASTIAN'S HEART WAS BREAKING. EILIS WOULDN'T TAKE HIS CALLS. SHE didn't answer his emails. If she actually happened to be at work, she made herself scarce if he came into the building and her employees were all the warning she needed to know when he came in. She wouldn't let him in her gate. He went to all the tribe parties he could manage, but she was never there.

Now he knew how she'd felt when he'd shut her out after leaving her at Christie's, and he felt sick.

All he wanted to do was explain. If, after that, she still felt the same way, he'd let her go because he hated feeling like a stalker. Sebastian was almost out of options, except for this one.

He needed Giselle in a way that she had never needed him. For the first time in his life, he wasn't in a power position, didn't have any leverage, and wasn't above groveling for her help. He understood why Knox had hung onto her all these years; no matter what, Giselle would never have said "suck it up" to Knox.

And she didn't say it to Sebastian when he hesitantly presented his request. She said, "Ask Bryce." Sebastian raised an eyebrow, but did as she directed. Kenard had shrugged and immediately said, "No problem." Then Giselle had hugged Sebastian and told him things would work out.

That was when he caught a glimpse of the Giselle she kept hidden away from him, that nice, sweet Mormon girl he hadn't seen for years, the soft-hearted girl to whom he'd said "suck it up, princess" to harden her, to keep her from getting hurt so easily, and never respected that part of her that couldn't be hardened.

This was the Giselle who'd taken under her wing a girl who needed her protection and love—without question, without hesitation—and who had protected and loved her from the first day she'd met her.

The Giselle who'd taken care of Eilis with such tenderness and selflessness and love after the shame Sebastian had made her feel, which was the first time Eilis had ever known such kindness from anyone—the Giselle who'd wept over Eilis and with Eilis and was the mother Eilis had never had, who'd braided her hair and rocked her and sung her lullabies. Who'd been the only person Eilis had ever told her history.

"Sebastian," Giselle had finally said, thoroughly exasperated with him for wanting to know what Eilis had told her, "it didn't happen. In her mind, in her *soul*, none of it happened because you decluttered it all and took out the trash, I scrubbed her clean, the tribe validated her, avenged her, and filled her back up with all the love she could take. It's gone. The trash truck has been by and the trash cans are empty. You don't need to carry it any more than she does."

"Well, what about you?"

She shrugged. "I can sympathize. I can remember what she told me. I can cry about it here and there. But it didn't happen to me, so it's like a sad novel I read and put back on my bookshelf with the rest of the books I keep but never read again."

Sebastian supposed he could understand that, when she put it that way.

The Giselle whose warrior soul was fed and driven by her love for her family, for whom she'd sacrificed everything she had—and had nearly sacrificed her life. Twice.

Sebastian's missionary training came back to him in a flash: *Pure religion and undefiled before God and the Father is this, to visit the fatherless and widows in their affliction.*

He felt a deep, deep shame in knowing that Giselle had kept this part of her from him all these years because he would've ridiculed her for it. He remembered the time he'd caught her reading her dog-eared scriptures and praying, alone and quiet in her room, and he'd mocked her for that; he knew she still did it and always had, but she'd made sure he never, ever caught her at it again. She hadn't locked her door the night she'd taken Kenard as her mate, but she'd *always* locked it to study and pray.

That told him more about himself than it did about her. Knox had been right about him. And Knox! Sebastian closed his eyes when he thought of the depth of what Knox had done—for honor and love. He'd sacrificed everything he was, everything he believed in, everything he owned to right the wrong he had done to the Faery Queen he'd married and it stabbed Sebastian in the chest. Whether Knox would yet survive it alone, without help, was anyone's guess, but Sebastian would make sure to be there to pick him up and put him back on his feet if he fell.

Sebastian coddled his clients and was gracious to strangers; he treated them better than he'd treated either Giselle or Knox, who'd both been part of his soul since he was six years old, and they'd loved him unconditionally.

Still deep in his guilt and shame, Sebastian showed up at the appointed time and place, keeping to himself, mostly hidden in the shadows, but people were too engrossed in the art to pay any attention to anything else. Hundreds of people streamed through, gasping, exclaiming and he couldn't enjoy it, even from the shelter of his anonymity.

He couldn't bear to look at that painting, though he knew it was his finest work. Nothing he could ever do now would top that. Of course, he couldn't stop painting, but everything after this would be anticlimactic for everyone. That painting represented his soul, what he believed, who he loved and why.

It was also a catalog of his deficiencies, weaknesses, and character flaws.

One of the music pieces on the short list to be played during exhibition hours was the chamber version of *Carmina Burana*. While the gallery was reluctant, it had complied and the effect had been so powerful that soon after the opening, it had applied to the Kansas City chorale and the percussion section of the Kansas City symphony to perform live on Friday and Saturday nights for a premium price that people were more than willing to pay.

Every once in a while, someone would tap the canvases slightly with a pole to make the prisms dance.

It was displayed as performance art—exactly as he'd intended.

"What are you going to do with it when it's taken down?" Giselle asked him quietly, sneaking up on him—or probably not, since he was lost in thought and the music called to him.

"I don't know," he murmured. "I guess I could store it in Knox's barn, but that's falling down. I have nowhere else to put it and the only places with spaces big enough are in galleries. Maybe I'll leave it here on permanent exhibit. Maybe I'll let it travel. Maybe the Louvre will show it. Who knows?" He looked down at her then. "Giselle," he said softly.

She looked up at him, startled, suspicious, and he hated himself for that. "What."

"I'm sorry."

Softening with confusion, she stared at him. "For what?"

"For mocking you. For being a bastard to you. You're my little sister; I should never have treated you that way."

Her mouth was open and her eyes wide. She blinked. "Oh."

Sebastian took a deep breath, because he didn't want to tell her this, but felt he must. "I didn't paint you to help you with your pain over Kenard. I did it for my career. I was sick of painting random nude women; I wanted to go in a different direction and I used you to do it."

She was silent a moment, then sighed. "You do remember that I'm fairly well educated, right? I can even do double-naught long dye-vision. Did you think I didn't know that?"

He started.

"I *wanted* to be painted nude. I needed that validation, that I—my body—could be the object of desire. But I didn't want to ask you because you'd want to know why and I didn't want to explain because—" She bit her lip.

He sighed. "I would've told you to suck it up."

"Well. Yeah."

"So . . . posing nude was about sticking it to Aunt Trudy?"

She shrugged. "Pretty much. Cheap therapy. Breaking her face didn't cost me anything, either."

Sebastian chuckled.

"*But* I also didn't want to look like just another one of your models you fucked. I did *not* want to be seen that way and I *so* wasn't going to masturbate in front of *you*. Eww." She shuddered, gagged, and made a face that made Sebastian laugh. "So . . . I let you badger me about it for a while, made you sketch it out for me so it wasn't sexual. Win-win."

"Does Knox know this?"

She slid him a glance. "He does now. I didn't know he was going to hit you over the head with it or I would have told him before."

Sebastian chuckled and shook his head. "Tell me something, Giz. What pain do you live with?"

She said nothing for a moment. "I take on other people's pain, Sebastian," she finally said, "and I try to protect them from it. I don't know why I do that. Maybe that's my mission in life, I don't know, but my personal knee scrapes don't measure up to the ones other people go through. Eilis? Knox? Ah, and let's not forget my husband—who won't tell me what his are because he doesn't want to burden me with them. He thinks he's protecting me because he knows what I do. That he withholds that part of him from me is painful. It's not like he unloaded on someone else like Eilis did and then things were better in his world. He hasn't spoken of it to anyone and he carries it like it's a punishment he has to endure. That's painful to watch, knowing I'm not trusted to help him get rid of it or even help him carry the load." She paused, then burst out,

"He says he'll tell me, but every time I've asked, he wants another couple of days to get his thoughts together and that turns into a couple of months. Oh, and then kids? He doesn't want any children with me because of the pain he can't deal with on his own, but won't ask for help. That kills me—the evil *bitch* got his kids, but I don't. That's not even including the whole church thing, which he also won't talk about. Yeah, that hurts."

Huh. She *did* sound rather bitter for all her protestations of having no pain.

They stood there for a while in companionable silence, Sebastian absently looking about for a gold and diamond Viking goddess, turning what Giselle had said over in his head.

"You've always brought stray people home, Giz. I guess I never noticed before."

She chuckled then. "My mom sure did." She paused, then, "Sebastian, you take care of me; you've always taken care of me. You protected me from boys who wanted to hurt me. You took vengeance on boys who did hurt me when I was too small and physically unable to fight for myself, which protected me from anyone else who might have thought I was a good target. You taught me almost everything I know about waging war, being fearless, having courage, meting out justice. You never, ever made fun of me for being fat—and that alone is worth every single 'suck it up, princess.'

"You came to me the night my bookstore burned and you took me home and gave me a place to stay, no questions asked, no deadlines. You invested the rent I paid you and you returned it to me a thousandfold.

"You were with me the night I got shot and killed those men. You went with me to the hospital and you stayed with me the whole time I was there. You started the war with Fen because he'd tried to kill *me*. You've always pulled me out of the rapids when I got in too deep. Yes, you tell me to suck it up, you mock me sometimes, but that's just you; you've always done it; I've always dealt with it. I've always been secure in your love for me. I'll tell you one more thing: Fen greatly admires how you raised me. What you made me is what he loves, why he feels about me the way he does."

That startled him and he looked down at her. She didn't look back and invited no comment or question. So Sebastian waited, because while her words warmed him and lightened his load, there was a "but" in her voice. With Giselle, there was always a "but."

"But. When you have children, don't expect them to suck it up and don't mock them. Listen to their hurts without expecting them to tough it out every time. They won't have the luxury of growing up with you, understanding when you make mistakes, feeling free to mock you back and knowing that in spite of everything, you still love them. They won't understand; they'll think you don't find them worthy to be your children. They won't have the luxury of being able to stand over you all night and force you to face your flaws.

"Your children will be small and helpless. Your job will be to teach them character and honor. Whatever you're apologizing for? Done, forgiven, blah blah blah. But take your epiphany and learn from it and don't do it to the people who will depend upon you most for kindness and understanding. Check your ego at the door of the maternity ward and leave it there."

He was silent for a moment, both more reassured and worried than he was before, but— "I won't be having any children, so I s'pose that's a good thing."

Giselle rocked back on her heels, her hands behind her back. "If you say so." Then, "In case you're wondering, Eilis is with Bryce. He felt it best to let him do the talking. He knows what it's like to be in love with a woman who won't talk to him."

Sebastian nodded heavily. It was a good thought and he appreciated their understanding of what needed to be done.

"I'm not sure you're going to be able to get her over the idea that you would put all those people out of work."

His jaw tightened. "It was a careless remark. I hadn't thought about it because the probability of Knox *not* getting OKH was less than fifty percent. Was I going to destroy the whole company? No, but Fen needs to believe I will and I have to act— *think*—like I will because he knows I bluff. Then I went and shot my mouth off and—I didn't know how it would sound."

Giselle sighed. "Sebastian, why do you think we're helping you do this? *We* know what you meant. And I'll give you credit for having managed to keep your foot out of your mouth long enough to actually have a relationship with a woman. You were bound to piss her off sooner or later."

He looked around again for his blonde goddess and thought he might have seen her, but she wasn't with a dark-haired man.

And then the crowd gasped and stepped back. He heard Kenard roar his name. He and Giselle burst into a run and plowed their way through the crowd, ignoring the calls and yells they left in their wake.

Sebastian's gut clenched when he saw Eilis lying in Kenard's arms—and she was very pregnant. He took her from Kenard, cradling her against his chest, and strode to a private place where he could bow his head over her to weep into her breasts.

He'd learned how.

The first thing Eilis saw when she opened her eyes was marble wall, cold but for the warm glow of hidden incandescent lights. There wasn't a lot of light, but it was enough.

She became aware slowly that she lay cradled in Sebastian's arms; her nose told her that. One part him, one part cologne, and one part turpentine. He caressed her bulging belly.

"Eilis," he whispered, and she looked up at his face, which was streaked with tears. She'd never seen a man really cry before. Of all the men she'd expect to cry, it wouldn't have been Sebastian. "I'm sorry. I didn't mean it like that; I was never going to do it. It was just something I'd said to make sure Fen knew I was serious and that's just how I thought of it. Please, please don't hold a careless remark against me."

She might have, if she hadn't seen that painting—that magnificent creation that had put her on display for the world as a sparkling twenty-six-foot nude-and-pregnant fertility goddess who was loved by a master artist and craftsman.

Eilis sighed and closed her eyes again, letting her mind remember the painting and she began to smile. "I'm pregnant," she whispered.

Sebastian's laugh choked on a sob and he murmured, "Just a little bit."

"Sebastian," she said, opening her eyes and looking straight into his face, "no matter what happens with Knox, promise me you won't put those people out of work."

"I promise."

He was dead serious and she could see that he really never planned to.

"Then I'll take the deal. My company for yours."

He nodded, then said, "I have another proposal for you."

Eilis didn't quite know what he meant, and then her face cleared when he dug a ring out of his pocket, emeralds and bright blue sapphires set in exquisite platinum filigree. He must have had this made when he had the necklace made.

"Will you marry me?"

Eilis's mind blew and her heart stopped. Here was the commitment she'd wanted him to articulate in no uncertain terms, but she said nothing for the longest time, searching her mind, searching her soul. Wondering, doubting. He began to squirm.

"Eilis?" he murmured. "Talk to me. Please."

"Sebastian," she said slowly after another half a minute, "there's one thing I need from you that I don't think I'll ever get. I thought I could deal with it, but now I know I can't."

He swallowed. "What?"

"Fidelity. Monogamy. I can't— No, I *won't* share you with anyone else. I'd rather not have you at all if I would have to watch a parade of women in and out of your studio, in and out of your bed, the one I'd share with you whenever it was my turn. You're *Ford*. You're famous for making women look beautiful because you've loved them so well and I will never believe you made *any* of them call up their own sexuality. No man who loves women as much as you do could stay faithful."

He stared at her, dumbfounded. "Eilis," he whispered, "do you not know you're the only woman I—me, Sebastian—has had an actual relationship with? Ever? I was tired of my life long before I met you, which is why I haven't painted anyone but

Giselle in six years. When I met you—with that hideous rag on, might I add—"

Eilis couldn't help the watery chuckle that escaped her.

"You were the first woman I've wanted in my bed in all that time." He paused. "The only thing Giselle told me about the week she spent with you was that you didn't know what you do for me. That you thought you were too needy for me to truly love you." Eilis's mouth dropped open and felt not a little betrayed by that. He read her expression correctly and shook his head slowly. "No, I needed to know that because *you* need to know what you do for me. So listen very carefully. First off, you weren't afraid of me."

"Yes, I was."

"No, you were afraid of *Fen*, afraid that I'd hand you off to him, which is completely different. You weren't afraid of my size or the fact that I don't smile or laugh when I'm doing business. You stood up to me when I was angry, which only my family has ever done.

"Almost immediately, you started asking me questions about how I work, what I do, and why. You were curious about me and you picked my brain. You listened to what I told you would make you and your company better, and you acted on it. You told me when you thought I was wrong in a rational manner. You noticed that I'm ambidextrous. You went around the Ford exhibit with me and you hugged me with no sexual intent. You're the first woman who's ever done any of those things and I cherish you for that. For the longest time, I couldn't tell if you were attracted to me or not, which has never happened to me before, and I loved that."

"Oh, Sebastian," she whispered, "I almost came the minute you walked in my door."

He grinned then, silly, like a little boy who'd received an unexpected treat. "Really?"

"At the Ford exhibit, I thought about how wonderful it would be to be on top for once because I wouldn't break you." He laughed. "When did you know I was attracted to you?"

"When I kissed you after our date, after I made you eat that concrete, I thought you were attracted enough that I might have a chance at seducing you away from Ford. I went home that day and ordered everything I needed to paint you in diamonds."

Eilis had tears in her eyes. Her heart burst and she hadn't known how much she needed to know this. She wanted to say—

He put his finger over her mouth. "All this time, I've been waiting for a woman who'd talk to me, who'd see me for who I am. And you did."

Eilis pulled away a bit then, saddened. "I didn't see you were Ford."

"Well. That made me mad, I'll admit, but I guess I could've just told you and saved us all a lot of time and misunderstanding."

"I wouldn't have believed you," she admitted. "I've been thinking about that, wondering why you didn't and—" She shrugged. "It was too out of the realm of possibility. I needed to figure it out for myself, the way you make the CEOs you work with figure it out themselves."

His mouth pursed in thought. "That's just the way I do things. It brings a better long-term result." He sucked in a deep breath. "I knew I wanted to have children with you, Eilis, and obviously I got what I wanted. You were the first woman I've never worn a condom with, the first person I've ever wholly explained my faith to, such as it is, the first woman I've ever made love to as Sebastian Taight, who hid behind Ford because I— I never knew how to talk to women and Ford didn't have to talk at all. All the women, every last one—that was *Ford*, who never said the wrong things, who never mumbled and fumbled and tried too hard in an effort to find the one woman who'd talk to me. You loved *me*, Sebastian. You chose *me* over Ford and I have never made love to anyone but you. I promise you everything, Eilis. My love, my fidelity, my children."

Eilis's heart thundered and her breathing came hard. Joy, so vibrant and warm, raced through her until she thought she might not be able to catch her breath at all.

"Hi," he finally whispered. "My name's Sebastian Taight and I fix things for a living. Who are you and what do you do?"

Eilis's chest collapsed with the wonder of this man's love for her, his heartfelt confession.

"I'm Eilis Hilliard Logan," she murmured. "And I'm Sebastian Taight's wife."

99: Priceless!

JUSTICE WAS LATE. AGAIN. KNOX'S YELLING AT HER FOR BEING LATE WAS AN obligatory ritual for everybody. Nobody paid attention, not even Knox, who was apparently resigned to the situation, but couldn't give up his habit.

This day, Eric met her at the courthouse door. "You need to take a long drive. Right now. And don't come back until Knox calls you."

She took a step away from him, alarmed at his tone. "Why?"

"Fen's here."

Her breath stuck in her chest and Eric took her arm to lead her away from the courthouse and they walked in the frigid November morning air.

"What does he want?"

"You."

Justice's mind fuzzed up a bit. "Me? Does that mean he found out I'm married to Knox?"

Eric shook his head. "He thinks if he can get your endorsement, that'll make up for the money he doesn't have and can't get. He figured out where you were, so he's trying to get Knox to turn you over to him for his campaign as his publicist. As far as I can tell, the *only* thing he knows is you've endorsed Kevin and he wants you to change sides and help run his campaign."

"That makes no sense whatsoever on about seventeen different levels."

"I don't understand his rationale, either. Knox is stalling for time so I can send you away, and it's a damn good thing you picked today to be late. Fen must *not* see you and your red hair."

"What's that got to do with anything?"

His gaze bored into hers and he very deliberately said, "Knox likes redheads. A lot. He has never dated anyone *not* a redhead. He's *famous* for his taste in redheads."

She swallowed. "I didn't know that," she whispered.

"On the other hand, Knox also has a reputation for his taste in older women."

Her nostrils flared. "Richard told me that a while back."

"Oh, don't get pissed off. He married you. Be grateful you're atypical for him. It's possible Fen will assume—the way the rest of the county has—Knox hired you because of the political and PR coup of having you in this office. Add to that the fact you're so much younger than he is and no one's blinked an eye. But he still doesn't want to take the chance."

Her mouth tightened then and she wrapped her gloved hands around his arms. Her voice hard, she said, "Eric, I've spent the last six months standing Knox down. I'm not going to wilt now."

Eric's mouth dropped open. "Don't you dare. Knox wasn't ever going to kill you, which you have *always* known. Fen will—and you came back knowing that. He's murdered two people and he's taken out two hits on Mrs. Kenard."

"And yeah, I get it. I'm not her." She glared at him, not bothering to keep the bitterness out of her voice.

Eric paused. "Justice, have you been comparing yourself to her all this time?" She looked away, saying nothing and he sighed. "Don't. If he'd wanted her, he'd have married her years ago."

"That's not why," she grumbled.

"Whatever. Just stop it. *She* doesn't have a national audience who adores her."

"I have a trial," she murmured finally. "I need my things."

"I'll get them for you." He turned to walk back to the courthouse.

"No," she said sharply and he stopped. She marched back toward the courthouse. "I'll do it myself. I have a gun. This is why."

He started. "Uh, no, you will *not*. He'll kick my ass."

"Knox has been kicking your ass since you were seventeen years old and you regularly thumb your nose at him," she said as they jogged up the stairs together.

"Yeah, I've never thumbed my nose at him when it involves his *wife* and her *safety*."

"As long as you keep doing his job so he can stay in the courtroom, nothing's going to happen to you."

Eric chuckled, though reluctantly.

Knox stood in the middle of the open area talking heatedly with the man she knew to be Fen Hilliard. She would have recognized him in any case because Knox looked so much like him; she vaguely wondered if Fen was really his father as well as Eilis's, but her heart thumped so loudly in her ears she couldn't concentrate on that or anything they said.

She calmly strode across the office as if Knox yelling at someone in the middle of it was an everyday thing—which, actually, it was. She went to her desk, dumped her messenger bag and purse, hung up her coat on the coat rack, and sat down at her desk to prepare for that day's testimony.

" . . . tell you what. She's right there—" Knox pointed at her and she looked up; he was furious and he was furious with her for defying him. "Ask her your owndamnself."

"Um, no asking me anything right now," Justice said and buried her nose in paperwork, completely dismissive of Fen Hilliard. "I'm late and I'm due in court."

"Young lady, do you know who I am?" asked Fen in a tone of voice that said if she didn't pay him proper and immediate obeisance, she was going to be sorry.

"Yes, I do, Hilliard," she said without looking up. "You're a dilettante politician."

Justice could hear the jaws dropping on the floor. Knox and Eric barked surprised, disbelieving laughs. Richard and Patrick chuckled and leaned back in their chairs to watch the show, tongues in cheeks. She tried to squelch her answering laugh, because she did so like to make them all laugh, most especially Knox, whose rich guffaws warmed her heart and soul.

She stood then and threw files in a banker's box, then picked it up and headed for the door, brushing past Fen without so much as a blink. At the threshold, she turned and looked him straight in the eye, and eyebrow cocked. "Do you know who I am?"

There was no change in Fen's expression, but she saw the flush that stained his face and felt animosity radiate from him. In response, she felt power emanate from her body, her eyes, her face, and she could tell when he began to feel it, too. He rocked back on his heel just the slightest bit. Oh, oh, *yes*, she could get used to that.

"You're Justice McKinley. I'm here to see you."

She raised one eyebrow. "You *do* understand I'm a conservative, right?"

"Yes."

"And you *do* understand I've already endorsed Kevin Oakley, right?"

"Yes. I was hoping I could change your mind."

Justice shifted her box and rested it on one hip, put her hand on her other hip, and said, "You know, an endorsement's kinda like virginity. It's a one-dude-only deal and I gave mine to Kevin. You're okay taking sloppy seconds off him now?"

Everybody in the office, attorney and random deputy alike, howled with laughter.

Knox laughed so hard, he was wiping tears out of his eyes. Justice somehow managed to keep a straight face, though Fen was clearly livid.

"You're not only wasting your time and mine, but you're stupid. I endorse who I want to and I certainly won't endorse a profligate spender of other people's money. Please bear in mind I have more influence than you do." She paused and pretended to think for a second, just for effect. "Oh, wait. You know that already, which is why you're here to grovel and beg for my endorsement. So since you're going to make me spell it out for you, no. You can't have it. See ya."

Then she walked out the door with her box and clicked down the stairs with the raucous laughter of an office full of men following her all the way down.

She smiled.

The rest of the morning went well. The extra adrenaline boost was quite nice, very brightening to her day. Her power, the power that had come from nowhere, surged through her, recycled, surged again. The case she was trying kept that adrenaline level ramped and she was on her game.

After lunch, Fen came into the courtroom to watch her. Knox came in and leaned back against the back wall, his arms across his chest. There was absolutely nothing out of the ordinary about her boss observing her in the performance of her job, though she didn't kid herself that Fen didn't know exactly what he was doing.

To anyone watching, it was very plain who had trained Justice to try a case; Knox was stamped all over her. While Justice didn't feel the need to dumb down her language or exaggerate the country twang she had, same as everybody else in the county did, she figured that there were worse things than having been trained to look and act just like Knox Hilliard in a courtroom. It gave her as much cachet in the legal world as her own work gave her in conservative politics.

In fact . . .

She started and her eyes widened. She stumbled over a few words and forgot what she was saying for an instant before she smiled to herself and went on.

Fen's presence should've frightened her, but it didn't. She had a cool calm that came through in her voice and her gestures, minor fumble notwithstanding

After the epiphany she'd had that settled so much of what had been troubling her, she actually forgot about Fen and immersed herself in the thrill she always got trying a case.

At 4:15, the judge adjourned for the day and Justice stood to clean up her table. Knox stood in her periphery, talking with Richard and Eric. Patrick was on the other side of the courtroom talking to a deputy. All guns were clearly visible and easily reached.

She nearly choked up. They were *all* here for her, to protect her.

"Miss McKinley," came Fen's voice from behind her, and she tensed. "I'm afraid we got off on the wrong foot."

Taken out of the moment and truly exasperated, she turned around to spear him with a look. "No, we didn't, Fen. I'm right of conservative and you're left of liberal. I've already endorsed who I like. What can you possibly think I'm going to do for you?"

"Most people will do anything for a price."

That pretty much blew Justice's mind and she stared at him as if he'd lost his. "I'm sorry. I must've misunderstood. Did you just attempt to *buy* me?"

"Oh, I wouldn't call it that. People give up good jobs to go to better ones all the time."

"Which part of 'no' don't you understand? I do what I want and I say what I think. I can't be bought."

His eyes narrowed. "I doubt that highly. What if I made it known that you work in the Chouteau County prosecutor's office? That would send your credibility down the tubes—along with Kevin's. And you might find yourself sitting with Sebastian, Knox, and Kenard in front of a Senate panel."

Out of the corner of her eye she could see Knox stiffen, but she didn't hesitate. "Knock yourself out, Fen, but think about it: Every year, hundreds of people compete for a residency with Knox Hilliard and I got a spot. *Why* would so many people risk being investigated by the FBI, risk their careers and possibly their lives, to be trained by Knox Hilliard—that murdering, racketeering, money-laundering bastard? Do you *really* not understand how prestigious his name is? No, my credibility won't go down the tubes. It'll shoot through the roof and so will his, if my name's attached to it. That's how highly *he* is regarded as a teacher and that's how influential I am in conservative politics."

The muscles in his jaw twitched. "Then perhaps you could be persuaded a different way?"

Justice sucked in a long breath, her eyes widening before narrowing to a predatory stare. Never in her wildest imaginings concerning Fen Hilliard did she think he'd threaten her for her *opinion*. He must've gotten a taste for killing when he couldn't get his way. Since he'd gotten away with it twice, and would casually allude to it within the confines of a circle of players who couldn't prove it, he must think he was immune to legal retribution. She leaned forward, her face hard and her voice cold, ringing through the courtroom, echoing, bouncing off the walls.

"I'm going to tell you this once and only once," she declared in a rapid staccato, poking her finger in his sternum. Hard. "You threaten me again and I'll have you arrested so fast it'll make your head spin. And then I'll write about it. If there is one person in this world a senatorial candidate should not want to piss off, it's me."

Fen reared back from her as she spoke. She sat down on the thigh-high wall between them and spun, thunking her feet on the floor on the other side and going toe to toe with him, getting in his face, eye to eye, nose to nose. Her finger still stabbed his chest. He attempted to back off, to bat her finger away from his breastbone, but the bench behind him made that very difficult.

"I have friends. Lots of friends. Lots of *liberal* friends who are credible and influential, whom I respect and who respect me. Don't think I can't take you down from your side of the aisle without ever dirtying my writings with your name, because all I have to do is let them know you threatened me and your campaign's done before you start. Do not test me on this, Hilliard. I can make you radioactive across the Democrat landscape with one click of the SEND button."

He swallowed.

She relaxed and rocked back on her heels, her hands on her hips and an eyebrow cocked. "Now," she said calmly, "you can leave and I'll just forget we had this little tête-à-tête. I suggest you spend your time raising funds so you can get through the last few months of the campaign. Oakley's pounding you into the ground and apparently Boss and Tom and all their rich friends enjoy throwing money at him. I have no idea what you think Congress could or would have me answer for—that pesky first amendment thing, you know—but lemme tell you something: The idea of sitting at the same table with three of the most brilliant men in the country to tell the Senate to shove it up its ass is damn near orgasmic."

Lusty laughter rang through the courtroom from Knox and her coworkers. Justice merely cocked an eyebrow at Fen's barely veiled fury.

"Fen," Knox said, a wide grin on his face and laughter heavily lacing his voice. He stood relaxed, his hands in his pockets. "I'm guessing that means she *really* doesn't want the job."

Fen snarled at her before he left in a storm. Eric and Richard left, chuckling, as did Patrick and the deputy. Knox waited until the courtroom was empty and closed before he spoke to her, his amusement gone in a flash. "Congratulations, Iustitia," he said with heavy sarcasm. "Now he's after you on two fronts. I thought I told you to stay out of his way."

"He doesn't know he's after me on the first front yet and, quite frankly, I'm flattered. He came here looking for Justice McKinley and her political clout, not the OKH bride, and he wasn't going to give up trying to pitch me on the idea just because you sent me out for a brisk walk around the courthouse one morning."

He said nothing for a long moment as he stared at her, chewing on the inside of his cheek, unable to refute that. "Did you mean that about attaching your name to mine?"

"Yes, I did," she murmured as she climbed back over the wall and continued to clean up her things. "I don't think you fully comprehend the strength of your reputation as a trainer, Knox. If you did, you'd understand why people compete over the residencies here in spite of your reputation. Murder and racketeering and all."

That pulled a snort and a roll of the eyes out of him; she chuckled.

"You believe your own bad press," she said quietly as she finished throwing the last file in her box. She stepped toward him, the rail between them. She slipped her hand into his belt buckle to draw him close to her until they were chest to breast, nose to nose. She watched him as his ice blue eyes slowly darkened. Her lips barely brushed his as she continued to speak in the husky whisper she knew drove him crazy. "But you won't believe the good. I don't understand why you can't bring yourself to see you the way I see you, the way the pack sees you, the way Vanessa and Eric and half the Ozarks see you.

"After you told me *why me*, I still couldn't figure out why you'd go to such extravagant lengths to get me to marry you when all you had to do was ask me. But I've been watching you and listening to you. I know why you forced me, why you jumped through all those stupid hoops.

"You didn't think I'd do it any other way. You didn't want to hear me say no because it would've broken your heart." Knox sucked in a sharp breath. "People take everything they can from you and then leave, so you think that must make you . . . what, inferior to any other alternative? You truly believe that the FBI and Wall Street think you killed Leah. Why? Because deep down inside, you think you're bad, therefore, everybody else must think that also and they must be right—and that all the bad things that happen to you, you must somehow deserve. You do things the hard way because you don't trust that you can be successful the easy way, that anyone will *let* you be successful the easy way. On the other hand, get you to Whittaker House and you're all about efficiency. You don't spend so much time in the Ozarks to help Vanessa; you go there to feel loved and valued because you *are*."

"Iustitia," he breathed, raising his hand to tuck a stray curl behind her ear, then absently play with another curl.

"*Everybody* knows you executed Parley. The *feds* know you executed Parley. I don't know how well you covered your tracks or if you bothered to cover your tracks at all, but you notice you're not in prison for it and nobody's crying about it. *Nobody* believes you killed Leah. They just can't prove Fen did."

"They investigated me for fourteen months for that," he whispered.

"No, they waited fourteen months to tell the press that you were in the clear. They probably used that time as a cover to investigate Fen and came up dry. They use you the same way you use them; if they wanted you that badly, they could leverage Parley against you at any time, but they haven't. What does that tell you? Now," she said in a more normal volume since she'd gotten the result she wanted from her micro-seduction. She pulled away from him to fiddle with his tie and brush the palm of her hand down his chest, then back up again, straightening a button here, picking off imaginary lint there, as any wife would do when admiring her husband. "I'm going home. I have a lot of writing to do tonight."

She brushed past him, which wasn't difficult because he was too dumbfounded to stop her, then she turned. "And one more thing. Fen Hilliard is a bad man. He's pure evil. At your core, in your soul, you're a noble prosecutor and law professor who gets justice for people at all costs and defends naïve, idealistic, mousy little girls in the front row. That's who you've always been and that's who you're always going to be. I wouldn't love you if you weren't."

100: Money-Back Guarantee

JUSTICE LAY IN THE DARK, UNABLE TO SLEEP. SHE COULD HEAR AND FEEL KNOX'S slow, deep breathing beside her. Dog's huge body lay under the covers between them, stretched his full length (paw to tail, probably four feet long), his fur warm and silky against her back with a subwoofer purr that vibrated the bed.

Her side of the bed was the one closest to the window, farthest from the door, and she lay looking out the beautiful beveled harlequin mullions at the fractured moonlight and thought about all the storms she was caught up in.

The storm at work never stopped, but it was the same storm all the time, never ending, never changing. She didn't imagine it was any different in any other prosecutor's office anywhere.

Eric spread the big cases out by lottery. She got what she got, like everyone else, even Knox. No trial case was rated by anything other than by case number, so some weeks Justice had a lot of work to do and other weeks, she sailed along. Just like everyone else.

Occasionally Knox would override Eric's system and assign himself or someone else a particularly sensitive case, depending on any one attorney's strengths. Knox took Sheriff Raines's case and dispatched him to prison with great efficiency and much satisfaction.

Eric was actively interviewing and for the first time, she began to see women being interviewed. "Don't get your hopes too high, Justice," Eric told her when she remarked upon it. "I don't plan to hire any women until your name is officially tattooed on his ass. I'm just interviewing to make him happy."

"Why?"

"Because I'm not going to spend my time kicking some chick's ass who decides she needs to be Knox Hilliard's next conquest, that's why, and the last thing I need is for you to be perpetually pissed off. The minute you go by Hilliard, I'll hire a woman, but not until."

She grinned delightedly. "Aw, now I feel all warm and fuzzy inside."

He glared at her for being amused at him. "You're welcome," he snapped and stalked off.

Then there was Fen's threatened publicity about her association with Knox (the one that he knew of, anyway). She had decided to start a back burn.

Where I Work
posted by Justice McKinley, 11/22/07, 9:38 p.m. CST

The Chouteau County, Missouri prosecutor's office. Did you think I'd give up the chance to be trained by *the* Knox Hilliard when the opportunity presented itself? By the way, we have three residencies open. Everyone entering this courthouse must wear Nomex; a fire-breathing dragon lives on the second floor. ecipriani@co.chouteau.mo.us

"Thank you ever so much, Justice," Eric snarled at her when she walked in Monday after she'd posted that.

"What?" she asked, alarmed, glancing at the clock. "What'd I do? I'm on time. Today."

"Look at this," he snapped, slapping his hand on a stack of papers three inches high. "Do you know what these are?"

"No."

"CVs. Hundreds of them. My email box is full of resumes that I have to look through."

Oh, was that all?

"Nomex?" Knox had asked as they sat on the basement floor watching TV, his back against the couch and his body wrapped around hers, both of them snuggled up in a blanket. "Nice touch."

"I thought so." She took a deep breath. "Knox, I want to be your wife."

He started. "Uh, you are."

"Publicly. As in, not just at Whittaker House."

"No. I didn't bust your head open about humiliating Fen—" He started to laugh again. "—twice—*Priceless!*—and I didn't bust your head open for calling Fen's bluff about attaching your name to Chouteau County, but don't push it."

She sighed.

The third storm, the OKH game, was in play. Justice was fully on board with everyone else, although her body hadn't seen fit to cooperate with the baby part of that and she thought that was quite all right.

The pack had begun to meet regularly at Sebastian and Eilis's house on the Plaza for Saturday dinner when the Hilliards were in town. It was the only house with a table big enough for all six of them to spread out and sit comfortably with food, drink, books, laptops, and other references to back up positions they took. ("No, Justice, you can't cite yourself. That's dirty pool.")

They'd talk and debate long into the wee hours of the morning until Giselle and Bryce floated off to Giselle's old bedroom, Sebastian and Eilis went downstairs to that hedonistic delight that had made Justice gape in awe the first time she saw it ("Knox, I want a Den of Iniquity, too."), and she and Knox took the bedroom that used to be Sebastian's until he'd moved downstairs permanently. No one got out of bed until early afternoon and then they ordered in Sunday brunch before going back to their lives Sunday evening.

One Saturday at dinner, during a lull in the conversation, she blithely said, "I got a call yesterday from the dean of the Brigham Young University law school."

Dead silence when five people looked at her, agape.

"So it seems," she went on, taking bites of her dinner, as if she hadn't noticed their reaction, "he reads me. He recognized Knox's name—not like anybody could forget it—and looked him up in their old records. He wanted to know my more in-depth opinion of the way he teaches, so I told him." She took a drink and looked at Knox, whose reaction was complete and utter shock, then smiled sweetly. "He wants you to call him at your earliest convenience."

So now she just had one last loose end to tie up, which had been simmering under the surface for a while. It was this loose end that had her sleepless that night and had for the last few nights and it was time to deal with it.

I. Own. You.

She's the woman you love and gave everything up for.

She'd been bought and she wanted to know what "everything" was.

Justice turned the situation over in her head, looked at it, took it apart and put it back together again seventeen different ways. She came back to the same answer every time: Her father had *never* loved her. She had always been a farm hand to him.

Martin McKinley had used her from the moment her mother died, the mother who'd died of overwork: Backbreaking labor, guilt, recriminations, disrespect. No free time, no books, no study, no education. It had just been his dumb luck that he'd married a closet scholar who'd given birth to a not-so-closet scholar who had a grandfather who wanted to channel and exploit that.

Then she'd come back from Giselle's and he had been intent on changing her purpose in his life. That still made her sick to her stomach.

Knox had paid her father to be able to have her without going to prison. Whether or not her father had sold her as a whore or a brood mare to Knox was irrelevant. Certainly a brood mare was treated better than her father had treated her. A whore, probably not so much. To him, she was a farm implement left out in the rain to rust when not in use, her oil never changed, her tires worn down to the steel belts.

As she lay there in bed feeling the warmth and love of the two most important men in her life (albeit one of them neutered), she hatched her plan. It needed groundwork laid, so she'd begin that tomorrow. She knew that however long it took her to do that, she'd work herself up into a good enough mad for her to be able to carry it out to its end.

Just then, Knox shifted and rolled over, his hand landing in her hair. She didn't think he'd awakened, but he caressed her curls anyway. Didn't matter where he was or even if he was lucid, he found her hair. Always.

She turned over then and saw that he was on his back, still sound asleep, a luxury he could indulge himself in more and more. His face looked so young, so different without that hardness she'd come to appreciate for its own cold beauty. She roused Dog out of his pocket between them and laid herself out along Knox's side, her leg over his, her breast to his chest, her head on his shoulder, her arm across his body. She softly kissed his cheek, his ear, his jaw.

Justice felt his smile and she laid her hand alongside his scruffy face. She coaxed him to turn his head so she could kiss him because she loved kissing Knox.

101: Light of My Life, Fire of My Loins

"HEY, JUSTICE, WANNA GO GET SOME LUNCH?"

"No thanks," Justice returned absently as she wrote, trying to get the exact wording that would make her plan so tight it'd take an appeal to the Supreme Court to break it, and not even then. Maybe she'd ask Patrick for help. He was especially good at this stuff and she'd never cared a whit about contract law.

"Aw, c'mon, Justice. Just across the street."

"Deputy, I'm busy," she said, so absorbed in her task she didn't bother to try to remember the man's name.

"Justice, c'mon. Give me a chance."

"I'm in a relationship. You don't get a chance. Not now, not ever." Okay, which would be the better word choice in that paragraph: *shall* or *must*?

"But—"

Suddenly a big hand dropped flat on her desk and she resisted the urge to chuckle as she continued to struggle over the minutiae of her document.

"Deputy," Knox rumbled, "she said no. How many ways do you need to be told?"

"Well, can you blame a guy for trying?"

"Yes, when the woman says no and you don't take it on its face."

Justice rolled her eyes.

"But—"

"Deputy," Knox said slowly, precisely, and Justice tried not to laugh out loud, "she's married."

Oh, now that was interesting.

"Fine," he muttered and slunk off. Justice still wasn't eager enough to disrupt her concentration to look at Knox.

"This is why I don't like what Giselle did to you," he muttered.

"Curious you staked your claim without actually staking your claim," she said absently.

He grunted. "What are you working on?"

"A personal project. I'm on lunch. I can do that."

"Not on county stationery, you can't."

"Hello? Recycling? I'm using paper from the shred bin for scratch. As usual."

"You've got a smart mouth."

"You liked what my smart mouth did to you last night."

"Mmmm, yes I did. Come to my office and do it again."

Suddenly, she stopped writing and stared at the blank she'd just drawn as a placeholder because she didn't know what to put there. "How much?"

"How much what?"

She looked up at him then, her eyes narrowed because she wasn't so involved in the mechanics of her plan that she couldn't remember and get mad about the reason for it. "How much did you pay for me?"

His expression was somewhere amongst shock, anger, and wariness. "I'm not going to answer that," he said. "That's a sucker's question."

"Of course it is. There's no amount of money that would justify it. An actual brood mare would cost more than I probably did, but a whore wouldn't."

He stiffened and his eyes widened. "A whore? Is that what you think?"

"How much, Knox? Don't act like I don't have a right to draw the worst conclusions or that I don't have a right to know. I have a right to know how much you value me."

His chest began to heave and she knew she was pushing him. She meant to. She wanted to know and goading him for it was the only way she'd get it.

So she poked at him again. "I want to know if I'm a Park Avenue call girl or a 63rd and Prospect streetwalker."

His teeth ground.

"Or, in the alternative, if I'm Secretariat's dam."

His nostrils flared.

"Oh, hey, here's a thought. You know Kelly's in Westport, right?"

Knox's eyes narrowed and he sucked in a breath. Of course he would know about the shackles *still* embedded in the brick walls of a bar that had been used for buying and selling slaves before the Civil War. He knew exactly what she was going to say—

"Two hundred and fifty thousand dollars, Justice," he finally snapped. "Happy now? A quarter of a million dollars and he wanted more. If I could've gotten my hands on any more at that moment, I'd have paid it."

Her eyes wide, Justice gulped as she watched him stalk off, her head spinning. Never in her wildest imaginings would she have thought . . . She couldn't really imagine having that much money, much less that Knox had paid that amount for her and had been willing to pay more if he'd been able to liquidate anything else fast enough.

Maddening, was what it was.

She walked into Knox's office, where she found him pacing, his hands wiping his face and running through his hair. She spoke low, calm.

"I don't know if I'm more pissed at you for not shoving a gun up his nose for daring to blackmail you, or with him for pimping me out. I'm not going to be home until very late tonight and for the next few evenings. I'll also be gone all day Saturday. Just letting you know."

She walked out as calmly as she'd walked in, Knox saying nothing. It was indeed very late when she got home that night. She showered, then climbed into bed beside him. She knew he wouldn't be asleep—he never slept when troubled—so she wrapped herself around him. He pulled her close.

"Do I want to know?" he asked softly.

"No. I suggest you keep your nose out of it until I'm done if you don't want it smashed."

That made him chuckle. "Are you still mad at me?"

"Of course I am. You *so* didn't have to do any of that if you hadn't—"

"I know. I know. Done it the hard way. Sebastian bashed me over the head when I did it."

"Now, about my smart mouth . . ."

Justice drifted off to sleep half on top of him after her smart mouth had licked and sucked everything she could from him, his hands in her hair, keeping her close when he came. She sucked and licked up every last drop, then lay down between his legs, her cheek on his belly. She absently caressed his bare hip and thigh.

I bet she wants to fuck Knox Hilliard as much as I do . . . She wouldn't know what to do with him if she had him.

She snickered. "Heh."

"Thank you," he whispered, stroking her cheek and playing with her curls. "I love it when you do that."

"I love it when I do that, too."

He chuckled, but soon she heard his breathing even out.

Early Saturday morning she threw on jeans and a white sweater and well-worn cowboy boots. She tucked her gun in the back of her waistband and stuck her badge on her jeans pocket. She threw her briefcase in her car, laid her gun on the seat, spun out "Legend of a Cowgirl" (because she needed that little extra kick today), and was on the road before Knox woke up. A bare three blocks from home, her cell rang.

"Not telling you," she said immediately before hanging up and turning the phone off.

Two squad cars pulled her over in Chouteau City, one in front of her and one behind. The trooper in the front car got out, walked back, leaned against the top of the car.

His mouth twitched. His tongue was in his cheek. He was trying very, very hard not to laugh. Justice sighed. "Uh, Justice, Knox has an APB out on you."

"Surprisesurprise."

He snickered. "Where are you going?"

Justice gritted her teeth. "Hadley, you and Knox can kiss my ass."

He chuckled and wiped his hand across his mouth. "You know we're going to follow you. He said you might need backup."

"Bastard," she muttered, and the trooper laughed all the way back to his car.

When she drove up the farm's driveway, she saw a new car. That was the only difference she could fathom. It was December, so the fields were fallow. Between the time she'd left in June and now, nothing had happened here and if it had, she couldn't tell what.

She got out of the car, tucked her gun back in her waistband, grabbed her briefcase, and walked up the porch stairs. With a wave, she signaled the troopers to stay put. Once in the house, she found Martin McKinley sitting in his easy chair, the TV blaring nonsense. He had a can of cheap beer in one hand and the remote control in the other. The place was littered with empty beer cans and fast food trash. It reeked of stale beer and . . . other things she didn't care to try to identify.

She couldn't tell if he'd gone to sleep and awakened that way or if he hadn't been to sleep all night. It was only 7:30 in the morning and she couldn't give him that much credit for getting up that early. He probably hadn't moved a muscle except to get up and go pee. If that.

"You're so pathetic you don't even know what to do with a quarter of a million dollars."

Startled, he struggled his way around in his easy chair to look at her, his face ashen. "Justice. You're not supposed to be here. Go home before— Go home."

"Before Knox gets here to take it all away again?" He didn't answer her, so she continued conversationally. "Knox has no interest in taking anything away from you."

He gave her a wary look. "He doesn't?"

"Naw."

"Are you sure? He's a mean bastard."

"Ah, so you see him differently now that calling the FBI's off the table."

"He *told* you about that?"

"Of course he did. He's my husband."

"So why are you here?"

"I am going to take it all away from you."

He rolled his eyes and released a disdainful puff of air. "Sure." He turned his back on her and relaxed back into his easy chair. He pointed the remote at the old TV he hadn't bothered to replace with something expensive and changed it to a shopping channel. Justice wasn't sure if her level of anger now stacked up to her level of anger at Raines, but it was a close call. How dare he dismiss her!

He'd done that her whole life and she suddenly realized that she'd always thought she deserved it, that she'd always acted like she deserved it so she'd gotten it everywhere she went. She'd accused Knox of thinking he deserved no better than what he got, but who was she to talk?

Knox was the first person ever to not dismiss her out of hand, who'd listened to what she'd had to say. Knox had made her who she was because he'd listened to her and validated her when no one else had.

And she had stayed with Knox. What a pathetic, perfectly matched pair they were.

Justice hefted her briefcase and stood between her father and the TV. He protested with an exasperated whine. With one swift donkey kick, she put the thick heel of her boot through the glass of the TV and knocked it off its rickety stand on-to the floor.

That got his attention.

She pulled a document out of her case. "Sign that," she said flatly and handed him a pen.

"What is it?"

"Power of attorney."

"I don't need that. I'm fine."

"You won't be if you don't sign it."

"Oh, what are you going to do? You're spineless. You've always been spineless."

Justice felt her brain freeze and the warmth in her soul mist away like steam, leaving only darkness and ice behind. Was this how Knox felt when he got that cold cynical look on his face? She calmly reached behind her back, pulled her Glock out of her waistband, and chambered a round. She pointed it at the easy chair, between his legs. "Sign it," she said in her Terrible Voice, the voice that had come out of her at Raines.

He didn't know what to do at first because he obviously didn't know who this

Justice was and she felt the first warmth of satisfaction come back into her body. He began to beg and plead. Cry and moan. Attempt to explain himself.

It took one shot into the easy chair between his legs to convince him she was serious, then she stuffed her gun back in her waistband.

The documents flowed and he signed them all without question, without hesitation. She couldn't tell if he cried and carried on because of her gun or because of what he was signing, but really, he was too busy writing to read. She calmly fed him document after document until her entire folder was done.

After that, she demanded he cough up the title to his new car, which he signed over to her for one dollar. She didn't bother to give him that. She figured his old car would be sufficient to get him to an actual job, provided he got one.

"Your first rent payment, money order, will be due in the Chouteau County prosecutor's office on the first of February, addressed to me," she said as she assembled her things and arranged her briefcase. "If I don't have it, I'll come collecting."

"But Justice, you took everything I have. How am I supposed to come up with rent?"

"I don't know and I don't care, but you have almost two months to do it."

"But *why*? I'm your father!"

"No, you're my pimp."

"But—"

"If you still can't come up with the money when I come collecting, I'll have you evicted. I'll warn you now that every deputy in the county and every trooper on this stretch of highway is either terrified of me or loves me, so I won't even have to file suit before your clothes are out on the roadside. And you should feel lucky I'll let you have that much. Everything on this piece of property is mine now, along with the money Knox gave you."

Justice walked back around his chair, across the living room, and out the front door, her sperm donor dragging behind her like a wet rag. She wasn't surprised to see the troopers gone and Knox casually leaning against the front of the truck waiting for her, wearing jeans, a thick black pullover sweater, and driving moccasins. His badge hung on his jeans pocket and she could see the bulge of his gun stuck in his waistband through his sweater.

His hair gleamed gold in the winter morning sunlight and his thick morning beard made him look delectably wicked and dangerous.

She caught her breath at his beauty, then shook her head to clear it. This was business time. She clipped down the stairs and across the crappy dirt where lawn should've been. She tripped on a clod and sneered at it, comparing it to the smooth, lush (although now brownish) lawn at home. Lazy bastard.

"Howdy, Martin," Knox drawled with a smirk.

"You went back on our deal!"

"Nope, sure didn't. She works her own deals. They teach you how to do that in law school."

"She shot me!"

Justice stopped cold and turned to glare at him. "You're lucky I didn't blast your dick into the floor," she snarled.

"Hilliard! Are you going to let her talk to me that way?"

"She does what she wants and right now, what she wants is to kick your ass, so sorry. Can't help you."

"Oh, I see. Big badass Hilliard's pussy whipped."

"Say. Martin. Should I have my deputies canvassing River Glen for any teenage girls you might've taken a fancy to?"

Justice watched as he paled and gulped. Her mouth dropped open and she drew in a long, slow breath. She felt Knox's gaze on her and she closed her mouth with a snap.

"I don't have time for this," she said to Knox when she'd recovered herself. "Bank closes at noon. Let's go." She climbed into the passenger seat of the SUV.

As Knox got in and started the car, she stared out the window, away from that man on the porch. She thought if she looked at him, she might puke.

Knox escorted her into the bank with a hand on her back. His presence garnered the attention of the branch manager, who helped her himself. She then proceeded to drain every account Martin had and pour it all back into Knox's accounts. Knox made one brief phone call to Sebastian. It wasn't very long before the bank officer, thrilled to have had contact with *the* Sebastian Taight, had an email with an encrypted zip file of all of Knox's account numbers and detailed instructions on how Sebastian wanted the funds parsed up and routed.

Most of the money was still there. Martin hadn't known what to do with it after he'd bought the car. The only thing that money represented to him was a lifetime of easy chair and TV and beer and cigarettes and no work. Perhaps a fifth of Jack Daniel's if he happened to be not lazy enough to get off his ass to go get it.

He'd be able to afford none of that now.

Knox didn't say anything as the documents were notarized. He lazed in the chair beside her, his right ankle propped on his left knee, his elbow on the arm of the chair, his face on his fingertips, watching her, watching the process.

It was after one when she'd finished her business. The bank had been closed for an hour and she didn't care that a few people were inconvenienced.

Once they were back in the car, she said, "Back to the farm that I own now. Gotta pick up my car, plus I want to show you something."

Knox still remained silent for another long while and she finally looked at him. He was leaning back against his door, his elbow on the door ledge. He watched her carefully.

"Did you *mean* to make him a sharecropper?"

"Yes, I did."

"What are you going to do if he doesn't produce anything?"

"Won't matter," she muttered. "He'll be in jail by spring."

Knox stuck his tongue in his cheek. "Gonna follow up on that, then?"

"Yes." Justice swallowed, hard, and wouldn't look at Knox.

She felt his hand on the back of her neck and she turned to melt into his kiss. "I'm sorry," he whispered against her mouth. "I'm sorry I did this, sorry I put you through this."

"I'd rather know the truth, no matter how nasty," she murmured in return, her eyes opening again and watching him kiss her, watching him watch her. "I'll get some deputies on it Monday."

"Yeah. About that."

Justice sighed. "You already did it."

"When you came back and told me how he reacted to you, I started sniffing around."

"I'm guessing you can't make a case?"

"No. I couldn't turn up any underage girls and I couldn't get any of the barely legal ones to talk."

"My mother was underage."

He started. "What?"

"She was fifteen when I was born. My grandfather gave him a choice between marrying her or going to jail."

He stared at her and asked slowly, as if he didn't really want to know, "How old was he when you were born?"

"Thirty-three."

He held his breath and then released it in a long whoosh and wiped his mouth while he stared out the window. "I should've just killed the bastard when I had the chance," he muttered, as if to himself.

"I'm sure my grandfather thought the same many times."

"So you're reliving your mother's history."

"I wasn't underage."

He shuddered. "Close enough," he grumbled, then he chuckled suddenly as he started the car. "Between your father and my mother, we were just fucked from the get-go."

Justice had to laugh at that, considering her earlier realization. "At least I'm not the only one with the in-laws from hell and a reason to avoid them."

"Come to think of it, this is the first time I've ever had to deal with a woman's parents. I always ended up dealing with a woman's teenage, early-twenties children, who weren't exactly thrilled with me."

Justice's lip curled and he snickered at her.

"They didn't like knowing cougar was gettin' her groove back, much less how and with whom."

"Apparently, you got over your vicarious Oedipal complex without counseling."

"Ouch. Did you come up with that yourself?"

"I took psychology like everyone else. Even an econ major like me could figure that out."

"Okay, okay. Got it."

"This has been pointed out to you before, I hope?"

"Giselle says it was a power thing," he replied with alacrity. "So, truce?"

"As long as you remember who's holding whose leash, Humbert."

His warm chuckles filled the car. "Yes, Lolita, my sin, my soul."

They drove back to the farm, Knox's fingers laced through hers, which made her smile. She looked out the window as they sped along, silent, watching the familiar-but-not landscape go by. When they drove back into the bumpy yard, the new car was gone, surprisesurprise, but that was okay. She'd get somebody out here soon enough to repossess it; she may not be able to throw him in jail, but she could make his life miserable.

"He went to the bar in town," she said as they got out and entered the house. "He won't be back for hours."

She tucked her small hand in his big one and led him up the stairs to her old bedroom, which was completely untouched except for a layer of dust. Pink, delicate flowered wallpaper, frilly pink curtains. Child-sized desk and chair. Round table and rickety kitchen chair that were little bigger than the desk. Tiny closet that could barely fit the three 1983 Sunday school dresses she hadn't bothered to take with her. Maybe she'd give them to Giselle for burning. Chipboard dresser propped and repaired various ways so it wouldn't fall down. She and Knox could barely fit into the room together.

An ancient white wrought iron full-size bed that was still neatly made from the day she'd left for work and had unexpectedly had to get married was on the only wall it could be on.

"That," she said, pointing to the table, "is where I found my voice and made my name. It's also where I sat and looked at the wall and fantasized about a law professor I once had."

She felt Knox start, then relax behind her, his hand plowing through her hair. "Oh?"

"Yes," she said briskly as she took her gun out of her waistband and laid it on the desk. Then she grabbed the hem of her sweater and pulled it over her head. She heard his quick intake of breath as she threw it in the corner. She turned and sat on the bed, lifting her feet one at a time for him to pull off her boots. He obliged and tossed them over his shoulder where they landed out in the hallway.

"I fantasized about him coming to my room in the middle of the night. Sometimes he'd sneak in the front door or the back door and magically miss all the stairs that squeaked. Sometimes he'd climb in my window. But he always found me in bed and would slip in with me."

Justice pulled her jeans down and she slid a look between her legs at Knox to see that he'd kicked off his moccasins and taken off his own sweater. Gun on the dresser. He unbuttoned his fly, and she tried not to smile.

"And it was a secret affair, you see, because, while he *had* to have me, he was protecting me and my good name. My father couldn't know because this man had a *baaaad* reputation, but I knew better." Knox chuckled.

Justice shimmied out of the barely-there lingerie Knox *did* appreciate oh, so much, and went to the bed, turning it down. She gasped a teensy gasp when she felt Knox's naked body against her naked back, his arousal hard against her, and his mouth on her neck and shoulders, one big hand splayed out over her belly to hold her to him and one cupping her breast. But she pulled away from him and climbed into the bed, slipped down under the covers, and pretended to be asleep.

"And I would wake up," she whispered, "with him beside me, kissing me awake. He would say, 'I love you, Justice' over and over again while he kissed me."

Justice smiled when the bed depressed and creaked under his weight and the covers floated down over both of them. He wrapped his arms around her and pulled her tight, their naked bodies entwining. "I love you, Iustitia." He kissed her softly, slowly, deeply until her eyes fluttered open. "I love you, Iustitia."

"I love you, Knox."

"Okay, and then what?"

She snickered. "And then what I don't know. He took over from there."

Knox laughed outright, then stilled. She watched him as he studied her reverently. Finally, he murmured, "Miss McKinley, you haven't been a very good student this semester."

"I'm so sorry, Professor Hilliard," Justice breathed. "What can I do to make it up?"

"Come to my office for a conference after class. I may be able to find a way for you to earn some extra credit."

102: Holly Golightly

"Iustitia."

Who was this person attempting to roust her out of the cozy warm depths of sleep?

"Iustitia."

"Goway," she mumbled into her pillow.

"Iustitia."

"What?"

"Santa brought you a present."

"What time is it?"

"Noon."

"Knox," she groaned, turning over, presenting her back to him. "I get to sleep in today without my boss yelling at me. Just because you don't like to sleep doesn't mean I don't like to."

"Iustitia Jane Hilliard, you get out of that bed right now and come see what Santa brought you. How come you're not bounding out of bed and all happy? It's Christmas morning."

She sighed and opened her eyes to look at the wall. "Knox, I told you. Holidays mean nothing to me. I don't care; I never cared after my mother died. And besides which, you know how I feel about that whole Jesus thing."

Knox grunted and the bed shifted, then she screamed when cold air hit her like a blast the instant Knox ripped the covers off of her. He picked her up and grinned smugly when she glared at him. "You need an attitude adjustment."

"Fine!" she snapped and Knox laughed. "Okay, okay. Put me down and I'll throw on some clothes so I don't freeze my ass off."

He did, and trotted off to the basement.

Justice sighed and looked outside. It was dark, for noon. The snow fell thick and fast, which was unusual. It very rarely snowed before January and almost never on Christmas.

Well, whatever fetish Knox had about Christmas, Giselle and Sebastian shared it. Her companions in Christmas Bad Attitude were Bryce and Eilis. That didn't surprise her much.

On Thanksgiving, they'd gathered at the Plaza house to have dinner, along with Knox's aunts Lilly and Dianne, who had started to become regular fixtures at their get-togethers since Knox wasn't welcome with the tribe and Justice had to remain a secret. She wasn't sure how much the aunts knew about Fen, but Knox had assured her that they dutifully swallowed whatever lie the pack told them and kept their own counsel. "The individual families have their own Thanksgiving dinners, then the tribe has a dozen parties all weekend. Giselle and Bryce and Sebastian and Eilis will show up at one or two of those. Christmas is pretty much the same way."

Justice, Eilis, Sebastian, and Lilly cooked; everyone else cleaned up. She felt that was a fair trade. Sebastian made mulled wine for himself, Eilis, and Justice, and mulled cider for everyone else. They all went up to the third floor sitting room he'd created solely to watch the Plaza lighting ceremony on Thanksgiving night.

No one had noticed her lack of delight except Bryce, who sat beside her and seemed very, very far away, then said, "We seem to be the odd ones out." It hadn't been long until Eilis joined them.

"Look at them," Justice said, pointing to Giselle, Sebastian, and Knox, who were practically bouncing off the walls. The aunts weren't much better behaved. "You'd think, in forty years, none of them had ever had a Christmas."

"They," Bryce said softly, "still have their family. I can't get through Christmas without thinking about my kids."

Justice and Eilis nodded. "I like to dress my house," Eilis admitted. "Sebastian made that special for me, but otherwise . . ."

Justice harrumphed.

So Justice pulled on a pair of Knox's gray boxers and buttoned up one of his Oxford shirts, then rolled up the sleeves. She found a pair of his socks and pulled them up to her knees, but they were big and they just slid down and gathered at her ankles.

She sighed, dragged herself into the bathroom, brushed her teeth, dragged herself down the hall and then opened the basement door. Christmas music floated up the stairs, being the golden pipes of Nat King Cole. It was dark down there, with an odd glow that didn't come from the TV. Warily, she walked down the stairs and as the room came into sight, she drew in a breath.

It was a Christmas wonderland and the glow was from the incredible number of Christmas lights on a Christmas tree as tall as the ceiling, as well as from a fire in the fireplace that Knox had never used.

She stopped at the bottom of the stairs and put her hand on her mouth, looking at everything. There was a porcelain Victorian village in fake snow and surrounded by a tiny picket fence. There was a fake-snow bank that had the snowman and the Santa and Rudolph from the only thing she liked about Christmas, which was the Rankin and Bass TV special. There, around the tree, she could now see two tall piles of presents wrapped gaily and waiting for . . . who?

"Knox?" she whispered. "Where are you?"

She squealed when he caught her up in his arms, tackling her from the side and spinning her around while the lights came up a bit, enough to see but not enough to dim the mood.

Her whole family was there, watching her, waiting for her reaction to what they had created for her overnight. *Her* family, the one she'd come back to when she'd come back to Knox. In St. Louis, all the time she had wrestled with what to do next, it had never occurred to her that she might get more than Knox if she returned. All she'd wanted was the man she was in love with and the hope that he might possibly someday come to love her, and the opportunity to become courageous and, also maybe, powerful.

What she got was a group of people to love, who loved her and doted on her. These six other people besides Knox, these people who made up her family were kind and generous, as lavish with their affection as Knox was. "Merry Christmas, Iustitia," Knox whispered and kissed her the way she loved most. Then he planted himself on the couch and plopped her down on the floor between his legs.

And then another surprise. Eilis, who had participated in this scheme and had been up all night decorating with the rest, was pulled down on the floor next to her, Sebastian on the couch next to Knox, surrounding her. Giselle sat on the floor by the bookcases between Lilly and Dianne, all laughing and chatting, while Bryce enjoyed every minute of being the elf.

And the presents flowed. She and Eilis were plied with gifts, mostly duplicates, from the silly (Silly Putty, Slinky, Etch A Sketch, crayons and coloring books) to the fun (handheld video games, jigsaw puzzles, and whole sets of Nancy Drew and Laura Ingalls Wilder) to the sensual (lotions and oils for Eilis that Sebastian had selected, new lingerie for Justice that Knox had picked out: "Yeah, I'm tired of not having any shirts or shorts"), but absolutely nothing cerebral ("Everybody here thinks for a living").

"The point of all this," said Bryce, who still desperately missed shopping for his children, who had had the idea, and who had done most of the shopping, "was to give you the Christmases you should have had as children. You're lucky you didn't get pink Barbie bicycles with training wheels."

Justice and Eilis were both laughing-crying and hugging each other by the time the presents were finished, especially Eilis because she'd known about all this except for the part that she would be getting the same treatment Justice got. Knox had left a few minutes before Justice opened her last present, and then he came back to sit down beside her on the floor.

"Iustitia," he breathed as he snuggled close, "this is from me." He handed her two pale blue boxes, stacked and tied together with a white bow, Tiffany & Co. stamped on the lids.

Justice caught her breath and untied the bow slowly, not believing that a farm girl like her could have ever won the love of a man like Knox or that such a man would ever give her jewelry from Tiffany.

The smaller box held a pair of earrings, diamond and platinum flowers from which pearls dropped, and then her eyes welled with tears and she sniffled. The second box held a matching platinum necklace, studded with diamonds and pearls every quarter inch, all the way around.

She began to sob in earnest and reached for Knox so he could hold her and she cried into his shoulder. He shifted so that she was in his lap, and she cried for what seemed hours until she hiccuped and then stilled. The rest of the family had deserted the basement, but she could hear them upstairs in the kitchen and she could smell the food.

"Thank you, Knox," she whispered.

"I would give you the world if I could, Iustitia," he murmured, his chest vibrating deep with his words.

"I don't have anything for you."

"You came back to me and you stayed with me. You believe in me and you love me. That's all I need."

"But—"

He silenced her with fingertips pressed softly against her lips. "Trust me when I tell you I can never repay you for what you've done for me."

103: Busted

January 2008

JUSTICE DROVE TO WORK IN TEN INCHES OF FRESH SNOW AND WAS GLAD FOR THE combination of front wheel drive and manual transmission. But she had to go back into the house and change into thick socks and hiking boots, then throw her dress shoes in her briefcase.

So she was late. And seriously annoyed. She walked into the courthouse to hear—

"MCKINLEY!"

—bellowed all the way from upstairs. Only new county employees bothered to make note of the time. Everybody else went about their business although occasionally someone thought about it enough to snicker.

He bellowed her name again when she was three-quarters of the way up the stairs, which climb seemed remarkably difficult for some reason, and her mouth tightened because she was married to the man and couldn't say boo about it.

She was irate by the time she walked into the office only to see Knox waiting for her, a hand on his hip, a glare on his face.

"What?!" she demanded.

"You're late."

"I'm *always* late, Hilliard. Fire me." The amused silence amongst her colleagues was palpable.

Knox looked at her strangely. "Get in my office. NOW!"

She went and he followed, slamming the door behind him. "What's up your ass?" he grumbled, brushing behind her toward his desk.

"I could ask the same of you," she shot back. "I'm tired of you hollering my name as soon as I walk in the door—nobody cares and it's a waste of breath—and furthermore, it hasn't been *my* name for the last eight months."

That set him back on his heels.

"That's right," she continued, warming up to the subject. "I'm tired of sneaking around, feeling like I'm just fucking my boss."

"You are fucking your boss."

"Yeah, except there's that little matter of the marriage certificate nobody knows about."

"Nobody knows you're fucking your boss, either. No harm, no foul."

Justice stared at him, her mind completely fuzzed. "Are you blind, deaf, and dumb?" she barked. His mouth dropped open and she went on. "Almost every last person in this courthouse, *including* the sheriff's department, knows we're sleeping together, not to mention every trooper from St. Joe to Grain Valley and the entire KC North Patrol, which means it's probably filtered its way to the Clay and Jackson County patrols. And do you know how they found out? Because the *Chouteau County prosecutor* put an APB out on his *redheaded* assistant prosecutor at *seven o'clock* on a *Saturday* morning starting from a location suspiciously close to *his house.* I knew the minute Hadley opened his mouth you'd blown it wide open."

"*Oh, shit.*" He turned and wiped his hand down his face.

"I will say," she added wryly, "everyone's very grateful to me for keeping you happy, so they're not about to make an issue of it. But who knows what kind of damage it's done to my credibility as a prosecutor? It might make *you* look like the Supreme God of Studliness and Instant Nice Guy, but it just makes *me* look like I'm not competent enough to get or keep this job without fucking you for it."

He gulped. "Iustitia, I'm sorry. I didn't know that."

"Then you need to pay more attention to what's going on around you. Whatever you hoped to gain by keeping our marriage a secret is long gone and now I'm tired of fucking my boss." She could see his distress, but she didn't care. "You make this right by me by the end of today or I'll blog it tonight *and* I'll rip your cover as hamlet to shreds. No, better! I'll call a pack meeting and invite Fen. Maybe both."

His eyes widened and he sucked in a breath.

She went to the door and opened it wide. She said loudly enough so everyone in the courthouse could hear, "And another thing! Until I have a ring on my finger and a nameplate that says Justice Hilliard, you can forget about getting laid!" Then she left, slamming the door behind her. Gales of laughter rang out all over the building.

She stalked to her desk and stewed about that for most of the morning, getting angrier and angrier as she worked. The loud and shameless mirth around the courthouse didn't help, though it did serve her purpose. More deputies, troopers, KC cops, and attorneys than usual strolled in and out all morning, every one of them in an overly jovial mood. Dirk sauntered in to talk to Eric, but cast Justice a smirk that made her want to slap it right off his face.

"Don't get too close," Patrick called to a Kansas City detective who needed to talk to Justice, but could barely contain his amusement. "I hear she bites." The detective burst out laughing and Justice snarled at both of them.

By lunch, though, the office had cleared of all but Dirk and Eric, who had settled in with dojo business, and Patrick and Richard, who brought Justice a peace offering of a chocolate malt to go with her cheeseburger. She glared at them both to let them know it wouldn't work.

Knox had fared no better than Justice had. He strode into the office just after lunch and said, "Hilliard, in my office."

Well, that was new and different. Hilliard. Not McKinley. No storming; no bellowing. She went *hoping* he would fire her. She closed the door behind her to see Knox standing over his desk, digging through a drawer.

"What."

He didn't look up at her. "You want me to proclaim to the world that you're my wife?"

"I thought I made that perfectly clear."

He snorted and Justice gasped when he straightened to his full height, a tiny pale blue box with a white bow in his hand. Her hands on her mouth, she watched as he skirted his desk and approached her with it. "The week you spent with Giselle— I went to New York and got these," he murmured and opened the box for her. In it were two wedding rings of platinum, hers a solitaire princess cut dark yellow diamond flanked by yellow diamond baguettes—"To match your eyes," he whispered. "If you don't like them, we can find something else."—and his a band with eight small matching diamonds embedded in it at equal distances.

She shook her head almost frantically. "No, I *love* them."

Tears ran down her cheeks when he picked up her hand and slid the ring on it, then let her put his ring on.

"I had Judy copy our marriage license and post it on the message board outside her office and file the original where it's supposed to be filed, instead of in Wilson's office. I radioed Hadley to tell him to put the word out to law enforcement and I'll send out a memo later today in case anybody misses it. Are you happy now?"

She looked up at him, wiping away tears, happier than she remembered ever being in her life. "Yes. Thank you."

"I'm sorry, Iustitia. I didn't think how that would look and I would never have done that to you intentionally. Please forgive me."

"Done," she whispered, throwing herself in his arms to hug him tight and bury her nose in his neck so she could smell him. "Thank you, Knox. Oh, thank you."

He set her down and looked in her eyes. "Next year, when this is all over with, I'm going to give you a huge wedding with all the bells and whistles." Then he laughed at her stunned expression and slapped her butt. "Go get back to work."

Justice left Knox's office with a ring on her finger, and the entire metro would soon know she'd never been just fucking her boss. She waved her ring at Eric as she passed his desk. "Okay, you can hire women now. My name is *officially* tattooed on his ass."

They howled, and Justice skipped to her desk, dropped into her chair, and spun, laughing until she was wiping tears away. The jokes began to fly fast and furious at her and each other, which she returned with the best of them—

—until Fen walked in.

The sudden silence was deafening. Justice gasped and felt sick to her stomach. She carefully, quietly put her nameplate face down. Richard looked at her and she gulped as she looked at Fen. Of all the days—

"Well, don't everybody stop having a good time on my account."

Everyone went back to work, sober now, and Justice attempted to make herself very small, though she did take the liberty of doodling Knox's name and putting a heart around it—because she could do that now.

Knox came out of his office, chuckling and shaking his head, a wide grin on his face that died as soon as he saw Fen. His expression flashed from sheer amusement to sheer rage and he stopped, swiveled on his hip and put his right hand on his hip. His voice hard, he said, "I thought I told you not to darken my doorstep again."

"I have a proposition for you that could settle this whole thing."

"There's only one solution I'm interested in, so unless that's it, I suggest you leave before I set your nose for you."

"Don't be so hasty. I'll give you half of my shares of OKH in exchange for *her*," and he pointed straight at Justice, whose eyes widened as she looked up from her doodles.

"I told you to ask her and she declined. What's the problem?"

"Make. Her."

The room was dead silent. Knox looked at Fen as if he'd lost his mind.

"Fen," Knox said slowly, "I don't own her, not to mention the fact that I stopped taking orders from you years ago. Did you not get the memo?"

"I know," Fen replied equally slowly, flat, threatening, "that you run this county with an iron fist and this office no differently. I also know that you aren't quite as willing to make the same, ah, *sacrifices* that I'm willing to make to get what I want. Make. Her."

"Are you out of your fucking mind?" Knox barked. "You threatened Justice in front of my entire office and now you're threatening me?"

Justice's breath caught in a sharp stab behind her sternum at the thought of Knox leaving her, dying over an inheritance he didn't want and the best he could do about it—because he wasn't willing to take the most drastic step—was to weave and bob.

She couldn't imagine her life without Knox in it now—now, when her dreams had come true, that *he* had made her dreams come true. She rose then, tall and proud, her hands on her hips.

"You simian cocksucker," she growled, that Terrible Voice coming from the depths of her soul once again. "What makes you think I'd whore for you?"

Fen's anger was palpable and he took a step toward her. Suddenly, the sound of chairs scraping on the wood floors and four slides chambering their rounds echoed through the office. No one was amused; she'd never seen such expressions of ferocity on the faces of her friends, not even when Hicks had been taken hostage. Eric. Richard. Patrick. Even Dirk, whom she had never known carried a weapon. On their feet with their weapons pointed straight at Fen. Knox's eyebrow rose at Fen's look of shock, his face draining of all color.

"She doesn't want the job, Fen," Knox said mildly. "For the third time now."

Justice watched Fen as he looked around at them all, and then directly at Justice. He stared at her for a long time and she stared right back, refusing to look away first. She'd taken on Knox, Raines, and Martin McKinley and won—Knox's respect, Raines's imprisonment, and property that was hers by right of her labor. She might actually fear Fen's henchmen, but she wasn't afraid of him face to face.

Then his eyes widened and he sucked in a breath. "Red hair," he said slowly. "She has red hair." He looked at her left hand, which she didn't try to hide, then at Knox's. His brow wrinkled. "But she's so young," he whispered in confused awe.

Justice whipped her own Glock out of her holster and pointed it dead at him.

"Here's the deal, Fen," she snarled. "You come after me like you did Leah and Giselle, I'll shoot you where you stand. You go after Knox, I'll sneak up on you in the dead of night and make you beg for your life before I slit your throat. He's my lover and my husband and the father of my children. You will *not* take him away from me without retribution."

Fen sucked in a breath, unable to hide his fear and remnant rage. Knox watched him, his expression inscrutable. "Check and mate, Fen," he said. "You have no way to keep OKH whether Justice and I have a baby or not. I suggest that you clean out your desk on December 26 so Eilis can move in on December 27."

The man's gaze snapped to Knox. "What do you mean, Eilis?"

"She'll be the new CEO of OKH Enterprises." Knox tilted his head and smiled benignly when his face turned red and he snarled. "You can probably also say goodbye to your senatorial hopes, all things considered. And to think: All you had to do to keep OKH was ask me if I wanted it."

Fen stared at Knox warily. "You don't?" he asked slowly.

"No. I never did. I still don't." Fen swallowed and his color dropped. "Furthermore, Sebastian and Bryce don't want it, either." He sucked up a sharp breath and his eyes widened. "We started fighting you when you tried to kill Giselle, although considering how you feel about her, I'm not sure what you hoped to accomplish there except pull her pigtails a bit. She certainly called your bluff, though, didn't she?" Knox tsk'd at him, slapped his back good ol' boy style, and pressed him toward the door, chuckling all the way. "Go home, Fen, and think about that for a while." He shoved Fen out unceremoniously and slammed the door behind him.

Then, leaning on the doorknob, Knox looked directly at Justice, who very calmly holstered her gun and primly straightened her dress. He put his hand on his hip.

"You enjoyed the hell out of that, didn't you?"

"It was orgasmic."

Three weeks passed after Justice had forced Knox to claim her, and each day, Justice's temper grew short, then shorter.

As expected, Justice's sperm donor hadn't made his rent, so she took Hadley and his partner with her to clear out his belongings and padlock the property. Neither trooper dared say a wrong word to her for fear of getting their heads blown off. She glared at Hadley and muttered, "Buncha gossipy little girls, every last one of you."

Everyone, including Knox, began to give her a wide berth, and at home, Justice picked a lot of fights and they had lots of angry sex, which she found Knox liked almost as much as she did.

On the other hand, Knox had grown downright indulgent and cheerful. Two new residents who had gone through law school with tales of Knox's temper whispered in their ears looked thoroughly and completely confused their entire first week.

Everyone pretty much agreed that they *liked* Knox Hilliard now. The older set reminisced about a young AP who'd spent four years in California surfing before going to law school and coming to Chouteau County, who'd said "dude" and "hang loose" a lot, who'd had a breezy, lovable personality.

And wasn't it a shame that that poor young AP had died in the trial of a lifetime when he was too young to understand how to shield his soul from what he'd been witness to? But that young AP had been resurrected by a new, younger AP who'd given him his joy back.

One day, along around lunchtime when Justice had kicked her shoes off and Richard brought her her cheeseburger from across the street, she opened it eagerly to smell its addictive deliciousness—only to be assailed by a wave of nausea so intense she burst out the door, nearly knocking Knox over, and ran down the hall to the restroom, sliding halfway there, her hand clamped over her mouth.

She barely made it before she hung over the porcelain god and sacrificed the meager contents of her stomach. Justice wanted to cry, but couldn't, suddenly simply too tired to do so. She sat on the floor, wiping her mouth and patting her tongue with toilet paper, her back to the wooden stall door (because she hadn't bothered to close it behind her), her knees up to her chest.

Justice felt very, very sorry for herself.

At that moment, she heard Knox's ringing laugh from all the way down the hall and she scowled.

Waitingwaitingwaiting.

Footsteps pounded down the hall, closer, faster. The restroom door burst opened and those footsteps sounded on the tile floor.

"This is the ladies' room," she groused, not looking up at him.

Knox sat on his haunches, his elbows across his knees, that radiant grin wide and his eyes sparkling. "Well, I guess that explains your month-long bitchfest."

"Fuck you," she muttered, and he laughed again.

"I'd kiss you, but you know—"

"Then go get me a toothbrush and some toothpaste," she snapped, and sighed when he arose, taking her hands and pulling her up, enfolding her in his arms.

"Thank you, Iustitia," he said a thousand times if he said it once, raining kisses over her hair and face. "Thank you so much."

"It's too soon," she sniffled. "I'm actually scared now. What if Fen—"

"He won't. Iustitia, I don't think I've ever been this happy. *Thank you.*"

Tears welled in her eyes at the depth of love and gratitude in his voice. "You're welcome," she sniffled. "Are you going to go get me a toothbrush or not?"

104: If You Don't Know Me By Now

GISELLE LOOKED AT THE TWO LITTLE BLUE LINES, HER SOUL BOTH REJOICING and apprehensive. Did she want this? Absolutely. Did she want to tell Bryce and watch him as his swift mind came to the only logical conclusion? And did she want to go through that moment when he'd be forced to confront a development he most definitely did not want? No.

But she remembered how she had avoided him all those months so she wouldn't have to tell him how she had deceived him. It hadn't done her any favors to wait and she'd still been compelled to tell him. If she waited now, it would only make him that much angrier that she hadn't told him up front.

She squared her shoulders and decided to go on the offensive, so she marched herself downstairs to the library where he worked. She slapped the stick down on his desk and said,

"You need to go get your swimmers counted and pronto."

Bryce stared down at the stick for a long while and she could *see* the gears working in his head. She could also see when his teeth ground and his jaw clenched. He looked up at her slowly, his face hard.

Her eyes narrowed. It *was* the only logical conclusion, after all. "Don't you dare," she said, hoping the warning in her voice would give him pause. "So help me, if you accuse me of being with another man, I will walk out that door and you will never see me or the baby again."

Now he couldn't say anything at all unless—

He opened his mouth and she held up a hand.

"Don't try to call my bluff. I *never* threaten what I won't carry out."

His nostrils flared because he would know she meant it.

"I suggest you go get tested as soon as you can and then I will allow you to apologize *on your knees* for thinking what you're thinking and, most likely, will continue to think until a paternity test tells you otherwise. And I *might* think about forgiving you for it.

"I also suggest you get used to the idea, if not totally embrace it. I agreed to your terms, even though I wanted a child and I will not tolerate any thoughts on your part that I somehow trapped or tricked you into getting what I want."

He leaned back in his chair, his hands clasped behind his head as he looked at her speculatively. She waited anxiously for his return salvo, as she had no idea how he could counter that attack.

"You know," he said slowly, "Michelle tried that offense-as-defense tactic on me. Once."

Giselle froze and gaped at him, unable to believe what he'd just said. A part of her soul died and she swallowed, the hurt in her chest so deep she didn't know where it would end, or if it ever would. She blinked to stave off tears, then nodded abruptly. She turned and left him there to go to the bedroom to pack her things. She put them in her car while he watched her out the window.

Looking up toward him, she called, "You just can't let go of the idea that I'm a slut, can you?"

Then she dropped into her car and left.

She didn't cry until she was safe in her own bed in the house that had been her home for five years. Sebastian and Eilis, startled, looked up from their dinner at the conference room table, but said nothing as they watched her bring in a small overnight bag. She slammed her bedroom door shut and commenced to sobbing.

Bryce gulped as he watched her taillights round the corner and disappear, devastated by her indictment of him.

A *slut?!*

No, oh *no*. She couldn't really think—

He dropped his head in his hands. Of course she could; he'd said it once before with the lift of an eyebrow and a smirk. She had suffered in lonely shame for eight months, avoiding him, avoiding his opinion of her. He would never have had the opportunity to redeem himself without Knox's intervention—twice.

Whatever other irritating habits he could lay at Giselle's feet—her mood swings, her still-divided loyalties, her refusal to spend any of his money, her overt yearning to go back to church and to take him with her, her quest to draw him out about his thoughts on matters of theology, his children, his fire, his life before the fire—she would *never* cheat on him.

Because she loved him, only him, and always had. She'd shown it in a hundred different ways, not the least of which in the way she'd thrown herself into the building of their foundation—the way she took care of their burn victims in the same manner she took care of Bryce, never flinching, never looking away, and never, *ever* failing to touch them, love on them, snuggle them if they needed or wanted it.

To draw them into her personal space and invade theirs, to give them human contact, to let them know someone didn't see them as monsters.

As he watched her do this, Bryce had come to understand how significant it was that Giselle had been willing to touch him, to be touched by him, to draw him to her when she didn't know his name. That she had allowed him into her bed, into her *body*, making him her first and only lover, after only a few hours of conversation and without the temple marriage she'd wanted was—

He drew in a ragged breath.

He picked up the all-too-familiar stick and his gut clenched at the thought of another baby—another he would adore with his whole heart and fear losing every second of every day because of who he was, who he wasn't, what he liked, how he liked it. Now, to that list of his sins, he could add the way he had deliberately broken his covenants and disgraced his wife—the one he'd fantasized about his whole life, who gave him everything he wanted and needed and craved and loved.

A baby made in love with a brilliant woman, well educated, related by blood to two equally brilliant men he respected and loved as brothers. Four, really, if he included Morgan Ashworth, one of the country's foremost economists, and Étienne LaMontagne, genius, scientist, inventor. With few exceptions, her entire tribe fell into the pattern of excellence and courage bred by the Dunham sisters and manifested in Knox, Taight, LaMontagne, and Ashworth. She came from good stock.

Though he'd dismissed the possibility of her infidelity nearly immediately and most particularly any infidelity with Knox, he'd been angry that Giselle was pregnant at all. Perhaps it was *her* fault. Perhaps, just by wanting a child so badly, she had magically conjured one up. He knew that couldn't be so and felt humiliation wash over him.

Giselle had every right to accuse him of all those things, but she was smart and had given him an out. Not only had he not taken it, he'd slapped her in the face with both what she'd told him not to say and compared her unfavorably to Michelle in every other way.

He'd called her a slut.

Again.

No excuse. The pain of having been utterly betrayed was clearly written in her expressive face and hit him in his gut. He knew that this might be unrecoverable and he'd lose the wife he adored and his *fifth* child.

With no one to blame but himself this time.

He didn't need his swimmers counted. What he needed was time to figure out how to make her understand that he hadn't meant a word of it, that he had lashed out because of pain he'd thought he'd buried deeply enough and guilt he'd thought he'd left far behind.

The sun was setting and he gulped. He'd be alone in his house when dark fell and he'd go to bed alone. He'd wake up alone tomorrow morning. He'd come home from work tomorrow evening to an empty house. With one intentionally devastating remark, his home had turned back into a house.

Giselle knew. She *always* made sure to get home before he did, even if that meant she had to drag her entire desk home from work, to be there for him because he hated the dark silence so much. In all that time, she'd spent one night away from home, the night she had taken Eilis to Ford then stayed with her, and it had nearly killed him then.

He knew where she'd go, where she always went when she was in trouble. She had a home to go back to—hell, any one of twenty-plus homes, really—and with that one comment that had hurt her so deeply, he'd sent her straight back to the two men who loved her and had always, without fail, picked her up and brushed her off.

He dropped his head in his hands, wracked with guilt, tortured by the irony and the depth of his hypocrisy.

Sebastian Taight and Knox Hilliard would clean up the mess Bryce had made with his woman.

105: What Not to Expect

GISELLE'S ANGER SUSTAINED HER AND SHE SUSTAINED IT SO THAT SHE didn't completely fall off the edge of the cliff. How dare he! He knew very good and well that this child was his; she'd known the second he'd accepted that fact in his heart. Still he'd called her out—and with something worse than she could have ever imagined.

She hadn't had any of what she thought were the usual signs of pregnancy. Because she had believed it to be an impossibility, she had put it away forever.

She'd not suspected that, beyond lack of self-control, there was a *reason* that she couldn't stand the smell of cooking beef and had been irresistibly drawn to chewy pumpernickel bagels with vegetable cream cheese.

She'd thought that her more-easy-than-normal tears were due to some softening of her personality, safe in Bryce's love—emotional growth, perhaps.

She hadn't paid attention to the timing of her periods since she'd begun having the damned things because . . . why? and so she hadn't noticed. Any month without a period was a good month, in her estimation.

She always gagged up her morning vitamins on an empty stomach.

And of *course* she was tired all the time. Throughout the last year, she'd grown to love the courtroom the way she'd loved Decadence. She'd put in long hours preparing and trying cases. She spent equally long hours making love to, having sex with, and fucking Bryce, her appetite for him more insatiable now than ever.

Until Eilis and Justice had handed her a pregnancy test and ordered her to use it, the possibility had never occurred to her. Giselle had rolled her eyes and done it just to prove they didn't have a good grasp of the odds. She didn't relish hearing the smug "We told you so," but once they finished teasing her, she would be able to count on their guidance. What Giselle knew about pregnancy wouldn't fill a thimble.

"Uh, Giz, you've been here three days without saying a word. Wanna share?"

"I'm pregnant," she muttered, and she could see the confusion on Sebastian's face.

"I thought you said he was fixed," he said slowly.

"That's what he thought, too, so you can imagine what conclusion he jumped to when I told him."

Sebastian's eyes widened. "Did he think . . . ?"

"He didn't name names, but in his mind, there would be only one other possibility."

"Oh," he breathed. "Knox will be livid."

"Don't you dare tell him that," Giselle snarled. "I shouldn't even be talking about it to you—" She choked suddenly, then swallowed.

"Giz, I'm sorry. But . . . aren't you happy you get a baby now?"

"He doesn't want any more children at all. How can I be happy about being pregnant with a child he absolutely does not want? A child he doesn't want to believe is his?" She took a deep breath. "You know, I could deal with a broken heart on my own, but with a baby to raise . . . ?"

Sebastian gathered her up in his arms and stroked her hair. She started to cry at his unexpected and uncharacteristic softness. "Give him a chance, Giselle," he murmured. *Giselle.* Not *Giz.* No *suck it up, princess.* She cried harder. "Knox thinks he's got some serious PTSD from his fire and probably from Michelle, too. That's not something you get over just because you wake up one day and decide to leave everything you believe behind."

Giselle said nothing for a moment, then, "He has nightmares about his fire, but he refuses to talk about it."

"Knox says his father beat him over the head with the Rule Book. He thinks that might be at the root of it all."

She blinked and suddenly, it all fell into place. The "Rule Book," their Grandpa Dunham's disparaging moniker for a book he hated. He'd preached against it to the tribe, and had made sure every one of his children and grandchildren knew it wasn't what the Lord nor the church was really about.

"I should've known," Giselle murmured, heartbroken on another level because that had never occurred to her. It wouldn't have; the Rule Book wasn't part of her family's paradigm. "He thinks the fire, his children dying, was the Lord punishing him for not being perfect."

Sebastian wiped his hands down his face with a sigh. "He probably doesn't even know how to begin sorting it all out. I wish my dad were here; he'd know what to do, what to say."

She sniffled.

"I know you're hurt, Giz, but he's going to need you to help him through this."

"But how? What do I do? *He won't let me!*"

"Wait him out. He knows where to find you and he'll show up. The man adores you. Don't throw that away unless or until you determine he's never going to work it out."

So she waited for Bryce to show up at her office or at Sebastian's house and apologize. And she waited. And waited—

—until by the time he *did* show up a week later, she was livid. And in court.

Bryce walked in and sat in the back. She happened to see him out of the corner of her eye when she stood to give her closing argument. Her heart raced when she saw him, her libido went into overdrive, and she bit her lip. She had never given a better closing argument. She could feel her soul fill with passion, infusing her voice with something even *she* had never heard before.

What it was, where it had come from, how to do it again, she didn't have a clue.

Once court had adjourned, she waited until the room cleared, which proved difficult because her boss waylaid Bryce. He finally interrupted Hale's cheerful ramblings. "Geoff, listen, I *really* need to talk to Giselle. Catch you later."

Bryce approached her with some hesitation. "You won your case," he murmured.

"How do you know?" she snapped, feeling the tears already start, too hurt and hormonal at the moment to care about his issues.

"That was probably one of the most brilliant closings I've ever heard. I— I actually didn't know you had such a way with words. It was almost—poetic." She swallowed to try to stem the tide of tears, but they began to overflow anyway.

"I read eighteenth-century literature for fun. I must have absorbed some of it," she muttered. He moved toward her, but she looked away.

"I'm sorry, Giselle."

"I don't want to talk about this here."

He inclined his head, looking at her things spread out all over the table and gestured toward them. "I'll help you clean up," he murmured. "Then would you come with me? Please? I need to show you something."

Neither spoke as they worked to collect her papers and files, then he carried her box to their SUV. They were out of the parking garage and had turned east on Truman Road before he broke the lengthening silence between them.

"When you told me you were pregnant, all my anger with Michelle came back and—" He stopped, wiped his hand down his face.

Her teeth ground. "And you compared me to that *cunt*."

"I'm sorry, Giselle. You're not in any way like her."

"Oh, I see. Michelle was giving other people what you wanted, so that left you high and dry, but oh, so righteous and pure in your indignation. I give you what you want and I *like* it, so that makes me more sinful than you think you are because I don't have any shame for what we did, what we do."

"*No!*" She started at the intensity of his tone. "I do *not* think that. I envy the spiritual freedom you have, that your family has, but that doesn't make you sinful."

Giselle threw up a hand. "Dammit, Bryce, make up your mind. Either it is or it isn't. What we do together can't be sinful for you and not sinful for me at the same time. I swear, I don't know how you can be so *fucking* brilliant in a courtroom but so *fucking* dense when it comes to your idea of morality or lack thereof. You're a forty-two-year-old trial attorney. Did it not, at some point, occur to you that *The Miracle of Forgiveness* was Victorian bullshit?"

He flinched.

"That's not what the church is about, Bryce. It's not what the Lord's about. There are two rules," she snapped, reaching across the car to put two fingers in front of his face. "Love the Lord. Love your neighbor. That's it."

He pushed her hand away. "It's not that simple."

"It *is* that simple and I guarantee you that if you went to our bishop and asked him that, he'd tell you the same thing. That's one of the very few things he and I agree on." Her mouth tightened, her tears having dried with her anger. "My grandfather would have knocked your father's head off for teaching you out of that book and he was higher up on the church food chain than your dad was."

He cast her a quick, startled glance.

"And now *we* have a child to think about because your vasectomy failed," she said low. "I'm sure you just couldn't resist going to the doctor to verify that."

He shook his head as if in a daze. "I don't have to," he said. "You're the most honorable person I know. I know the baby's mine because I know you."

That surprised her, but it didn't let him off the hook. "Ten days," she muttered. "You let me go ten days without a word."

"Giselle," he said. She could hear the pleading, the uncertainty, in his voice. "I needed time to get used to the idea and I didn't know how to tell you that I'm *really* not happy about this."

"Oh, believe me, you made your opinion perfectly clear. How can I live with you knowing that? How can I bring a baby into the house knowing you resent it?"

He shrugged helplessly. "I don't know. All I know is I love you and I'll do whatever I have to do to make you happy. *Resent* isn't the right word. *Fear* is the right word. You don't know what it's like to watch your daughter burn to death right in front of you. You don't know what it's like to carry three of your children through fire, being on fire, knowing they're on fire. You don't know what it's like to be told those three children died anyway and *nowhere* in that mess did the Lord show up to help you. You don't know what it's like to lie in a bed for a year where everyone around you is dedicated to saving your life, except for you, and you're wishing—no, *hoping*—to die, too."

Giselle's anger vanished. There just wasn't much she could say to that. She looked out the window as they drove for quite a long while, through her old neighborhood, into Independence, a route she knew so well she could close her eyes and name every cross street in the three-and-a-half-mile stretch from I-70 to I-435. They were a mile from their destination before she understood his intention. She gasped.

He looked at her sharply. "I'm sorry I've never shared this with you, Giselle. I— I didn't want to mix my old life with my new one."

"I wanted to ask you at Christmas," she said softly, "because you were so . . . in pain, but I didn't know how."

"I wouldn't have brought you here then," he returned, just as softly. "That's the hardest time of the year for me, although not nearly as hard now with you and the pack, the tribe."

He didn't speak again until they stood at the massive headstone that bore the names and birth dates of his four children—and one death date, July 14, 2001. Almost a dozen bouquets of daisies in varying stages of decay lay strewn on the ground in front of the stone.

"I loved my children," he said. "I adored them utterly and completely and they *died*," he said, clearing his throat and attempting to be matter-of-fact, "in the most horrifying way imaginable. I didn't even get to bury them and say goodbye because I was in my coma and I had no one to take care of business for me. The irony is that I know Knox would've taken care of me if I hadn't been such an asshole to *him*, too." He paused. "They aren't here. I put this stone here because I needed some way to hold onto them."

Giselle bowed her head then, her soul absorbing his pain and grief like a sponge, internalizing it, making it hers. She reached for and found his hand, lacing her fingers through his, and squeezed just a bit. He squeezed back.

"I come here often. I've been here every day since you told me you were pregnant, wondering what to do, how I'm going to relive the joy and pain that children bring. I know that as soon as our baby's born, I'll fall in love again, but—"

"You think the Lord's going to punish you and take him away from you."

He said nothing for a moment, then whispered, "Yes."

She looked up at him then to find him watching her. His cheeks glistened with moisture. "Please stick with me, Giselle," he whispered. "I love you and I'm a selfish bastard, I know, but I need you. I needed you from the first moment I saw you."

Giselle nodded. How could she do otherwise? She loved him and she'd promised.

"Why did you think you had to shoulder this alone?" she whispered. "At the beginning of us, you asked me what I wanted from you and I asked you to let me help you carry it. You *promised*."

"Giselle, you assume the pain of everyone you love, everyone you protect. I watch you do it every day. You did it with Eilis and it devastated you. You did it with Justice and you worried for weeks—hell, years. You do it with the tribe. You do it with the burn victims we tend to, with random people who just need a helping hand. I see what happens to you when we come home at night. You—" He wiped his hand down his face. "You feel it in your soul and then you ache. Did you think I'd lay mine on you, too? I promised you that before I saw what you do and there was no way I was going to add to that."

She swallowed. "Bryce, of all the people in the world who might need my help, you are the only one who *deserves* it. You're the only one I've promised it to, the only one who's entitled to it. I'd ignore the whole world if you'd let me help you with your pain." She paused, tears streaming down her cheeks. "I'm sorry."

He started. "For what?"

"For—" She huffed, sniffled. "I don't know. I'm sorry I made you think everyone else's pain meant more to me than yours. I'm sorry I made you think you were less deserving."

His jaw dropped. "*Giselle!* You didn't. I swear, you didn't. I just— I've been carrying it alone so long I didn't know how to offload some of it."

"But I want to do something to help you and you won't let me."

"You don't have to *do* anything. Your presence, your love, has helped more than anything I could've ever imagined. Your family— Giselle, I don't know how I survived all these years alone without you, without the pack. Hell, without the whole tribe. I have a real family now. I belong somewhere that I'm not a black sheep. You've given me that." He pulled his hand out of hers then to pull something out of his suit coat pocket: A long, narrow red velvet box. She bit her lip. "I had this made for you. This was why it took me so long to come to you."

Giselle took it slowly, carefully. She opened it and her brow wrinkled in confusion that quickly blossomed into awe when she picked it up and studied it.

A platinum charm bracelet embellished with an emerald at the clasp, it had only two charms: The keys from *Rape of a Virgin*, one an exact replica of the phallus and one an exact replica of the baby pacifier. An oversized platinum heart hung from the clasp.

*I want to
fuck you,
Giselle*

Her hand flew to her mouth as she read the engraving. She swallowed, her soul overflowing again with the love she'd always had for him, even before she knew his name.

"I hated Michelle so much I was glad she died, that I didn't have to have her hounding me every second of every day for the rest of my life. I feel like I met you years ago, lost you somewhere along the way, then found you again. You're the only woman I have ever loved. In my mind and heart and soul, you're my first wife, my only wife. The love of my life. Please forgive me. Please come back to me."

Giselle looked up at him and bit her lip, unwilling to say it but knowing she must. "I'll come home with you for now, but you have to get help if you want me to stay. If you don't want to go to the foundation's therapists, we'll find someone else. I'll even go with you if you want, but we—I—can't live like this anymore, not with a baby coming. Something has to change."

He stared at her, aghast.

"Don't ask me to sacrifice our child on the altar of your guilt and fear. If you want to be with me, those are the terms."

He said nothing for a long time as he looked off into the distance, his expression by turns angry, wary, and hurt. "I need to think about that for a while."

She nodded. "That's fair." She leaned against him and wrapped her arms around him until he was ready to leave.

Bryce still slept when she got out of the shower and began to dress carefully in her navy-and-white polka dot linen dress. For jewelry, she wore only her wedding ring and the charm bracelet Bryce had given her. If anyone asked to look at it, they got what they deserved for being nosy.

"Where are you going?" he murmured from the bed.

She turned and looked at his naked body, the one she loved so much for what it had done to rescue three children, for the big, kind heart it held, for the brilliant mind that it sheltered, for that deep, dark, tortured soul that she adored which lived and breathed inside that broad chest.

She studied the man who had made tender love to her all weekend, giving her everything, taking nothing.

"It's Sunday." His eyebrow rose and she shrugged. "You know how much I miss going to church. Our baby needs to know his heritage. He needs to be around sweet, gentle people who aren't savages. He needs to understand that the church is full of honorable people and that honor comes in a lot of flavors, that there's honor in being a regular, everyday nice guy. He needs to know that the vast majority of the people at church are not us, not the pack, not the tribe; haven't done what we've done, seen what we've seen, think how we think. 'Justice at all costs' is not most families' motto." She stopped. "You're more than welcome to come with me."

He stared at her for a long time, his face inscrutable. Then he sighed. "You go. I'm not ready yet."

"Okay," she said, and kissed him on the forehead, but when she turned to leave, he caught her wrist and tugged her gently down onto the bed so that she lay snuggled up against his chest, her head cradled in the crook of his arm.

"I love you, Giselle," he murmured, and, his big hand cupping and caressing her cheek, he kissed her deeply, carefully. She found herself growing aroused all over again. He pulled away from her enough to speak. "I'm *so* sorry. I know you have no reason to trust me now, but that's the truth. Please don't leave me."

She swallowed. "I can't promise you that right now. I won't be able to trust you until you go to therapy and work at it. I don't want your guilt and shame—the Rule Book—to stand between us anymore."

He stared down at her for a long time and she nearly lost herself in those beautiful green eyes. Then he spoke low:

"You were wearing faded black canvas pants and a white jacket that had patches all over it. Your tee shirt said, 'Toto, I don't think we're in Kansas anymore.' You had a brown belt hanging off your neck." Giselle's eyes widened and she felt the color drain from her face. "You had a man on his knees in front of you, learning from you. I took one look at you and all I could think about was backing you up against the wall and fucking you. Hard." He paused to take a deep breath.

"You were *so* young, but you intimidated the hell out of me. I wanted some of that—whatever it was you had—for myself, to do what I needed to do to be the kind of man that *that* girl would want."

She gulped. "You?" she breathed, her chest beginning to heave, her tears beginning to fall. "That was *you*? I— You— I knew what you wanted from me and I— I never had a chance to know you. You were so— *Gorgeous*, and I was so . . . *not*."

"Stop it. I wanted *you*, Giselle. *Not my wife.*"

She was a model. Blonde. Tall and thin, fragile.

Giselle thought she would never be able to breathe again.

"Okay, so it took you a few years to grow into your beauty. It only took me an hour to become a beast." She opened her mouth in protest, but he forged on. "When I went to Knox's house to study that night, I'd been married for two months and I already knew I'd made a huge mistake. What I wanted, that I wanted it with you—a woman who wasn't my wife— It terrified me. I wanted you so badly I couldn't think of anything but you for weeks, months. Years. I thought maybe, if we— I don't know. Somewhere in the back of my mind, I thought if I could make love with that girl, just once, she would give me some of whatever she had that I needed."

He released a breath with a long whoosh. "I held onto that girl all the way through my divorce, wondering what had happened to her, trying to figure out how to find out who she was, where she went. You don't know how many times I wanted to pick up the phone to call Knox to find out if he remembered that, if he could tell me her name—and I planned to the second my divorce was final." He paused. "Giselle, I fell in love with you when I was twenty-four years old and I've carried you in my heart for the last eighteen years. You gave me strength. You gave me hope."

She choked and put a trembling hand to her mouth.

"I remembered last night after you went to sleep," he murmured, his thumb caressing her bottom lip lightly. "Even if I'd had the courage to divorce Michelle then, I couldn't have had you. In that area of my life, between sex, marriage, church, my parents, I was weak, unsure, easily led. You would've chewed me up and spit me out—and I *knew* that."

Tears spilled over and ran down her face, dropping into the pillow, disappearing as if they had never existed. She began to hiccup. "Knox said— After I left you in the park— He said you had been in love with me for a long time. I thought he just meant— He knew?"

Bryce nodded. "He saw my reaction, knew what it meant, knew me well enough to let it lie. I don't think Knox knows you saw me. I know I didn't—it would've been worse if I'd known, if I'd known you felt the same way I did."

"I waited for you," she whispered, weeping, her voice broken.

"You're the woman of my soul, Giselle, and I knew it the first time I saw you. And the second. And every time I've ever looked at you. I will do whatever I have to do to keep you." He swallowed. "I'm here. On your terms."

106: Potsdam Declaration

November 2008

THE BED DEPRESSED UNDERNEATH JUSTICE AND SHE GROANED. KNOX scootched toward her, his back against the headboard, until his hip brushed her back.

"Lunch time?" she croaked.

"Happily sucking away."

She sighed in relief. A chance at a couple more hours of sleep. Thank heavens for the breast pump.

"I have a surprise for you today. Well, a couple of them, really."

Yay. She'd rather sleep. "What?"

"I'm not *telling* you. That's why they're called surprises."

"So . . . all you really wanted was to tell me to get my ass out of bed and get dressed?"

Silence. Then, "Well. Yeah. That. What you said."

"When did you turn into such a little boy?"

He chuckled. "When I fell in love with the little girl on the front row."

Justice snorted, answered by a little baby snort, and she laughed. She opened her eyes and turned over to see Knox sitting as she had felt him, cradling their bald newborn, one end of a bottle in his hand and the other plugged into Mercy Hilliard's mouth.

"Big badass Chouteau County prosecutor Knox Hilliard: A born dad," she murmured wryly. "Who'd'a thunk it?"

"Vanessa thinks so."

"Vanessa was twelve. She didn't need to be bottle-fed and have her diapers changed. She could speak in complete sentences."

"Complete sentences help. You should be glad I already know how to raise a teenage girl."

"Please. You probably terrified the girl."

"The point was to terrify her mother and her mother's cronies. Which I did. And her boyfriends."

"Except Sebastian."

"Ah, but there's a reason I don't know about that little fling, isn't there?"

"Point taken."

"So c'mon, get ready to go."

Justice didn't answer, but looked up at him, that beautiful man who'd lost ten years off his face, who no longer looked so haunted and cold, so troubled and hopeless—and hadn't for months. Professor Hilliard sat here in their bed with her, wearing a ring that proclaimed him hers, holding the child they'd made together.

He hadn't bothered to shave this morning and his scruffy face always made her heart pound a little faster, her breath come a little shorter, her juices flow a little faster. She wrapped her hand over the top of Knox's denim-clad thigh and stroked upward, slow, measured.

"What if I had plans for today?"

Too distracted by the baby, by his delight in his new daughter, he didn't notice when her hand slid around to the inside of his thigh. "Did you?"

"I do now," she murmured and cradled Knox's cock in her hand. His nostrils flared as he looked down at her, stunned. He hardened immediately.

"Iustitia," he breathed. "Are you sure?"

"I'm so wet for you right now I can't think straight."

He looked down at the baby, who, wide awake, stared adoringly up at her daddy, intermittently sucking, taking her time. Mercy savored her meals like a sommelier savored each small sip of wine. "Shit. She's not going to be done anytime soon."

Justice sighed. "Eilis warned me it'd be like that."

"I don't believe that. Nothing gets between Sebastian and his bed, especially if Eilis is in it."

"You're misinformed, trust me. Girls talk."

His eyebrow rose. "Oh? Have you learned anything?"

"Boy, you really don't pay attention to much, do you? The blindfold should've been your first clue."

"I'm not going to let you hang out with those two anymore, especially that freak

Giselle."

She laughed and his broad smile deepened his crow's feet.

"Go find your first surprise. It's on the kitchen table."

Justice, still chuckling, sat up and swung her legs over the edge of the bed. She glanced over her shoulder at him to see him staring at her hotly, her back bare for his inspection—and he took his time about it. "So can your other surprise wait?"

"It can now," he replied gruffly. Poor man; he'd been so patient with her the last few months and without a word of complaint.

She smiled and went to the kitchen to find yesterday's *Wall Street Journal* on the table. Her brow wrinkled. She'd looked all over for that yesterday, hadn't found it, and assumed Knox had left it somewhere. She picked it up and gasped.

On the back page of section A was a full-page ad:

Loving parents
Sebastian Taight and Blackwood Securities
are proud to announce the marriage of
Iustitia "Justice" Jane McKinley, Esq.

to

Dr. Fort Knox Oliver Hilliard
July 23, 2007
and the birth of
Miss Clementia "Mercy" Lilly Dianne Hilliard
September 24, 2008.

The terms of the OKH Enterprises Proviso have been met.
Knox Hilliard will inherit the majority shares
on December 27, 2008.

Cut it a little close, didn't you, Knox?

Justice didn't hear Knox behind her until he said, "That was Sebastian's idea."

"But, Fen—"

"Look on the editorial page."

And there! Her jaw dropped. She covered her mouth with a trembling hand at what stared back at her from the page: A complete rundown of Fen's evil from start to finish—in her words. It had been signed by Sebastian Taight and Justice McKinley.

"But I— But he— I didn't give him permission to use that."

"Yeah, don't give him stuff he asks for without finding out why he wants it. He's evil like that."

Dazed, she couldn't utter a word.

"Look on the front page."

And there, featured prominently, an article detailing the investigations now swirling around Fen.

"That'll give the FBI enough information to work with, and Fen'll be arrested and indicted soon enough. I've given them the go-ahead to dig up my dad. I don't think they'll find anything, but they have a couple of brand-new tests they want to try out on him." Knox wrapped a free arm around Justice's waist and pulled her back against his chest. The baby lay in the crook of his other arm. "Wall Street exploded in ticker tape yesterday, Jack won half of Vegas even though the bookies are screaming foul, Congress had a collective heart attack, and *you* were the topic of conversation all over talk radio. What did she know and when did she know it?"

She sighed, seeing her career as a commentator crashing into a big brick wall, and she said as much.

"Oh, I doubt that, considering Sebastian, Jack, and I have been fielding phone calls and emails for the last twenty-four hours asking about radio and television appearances—not from us, mind you, but from *you*. Now, Mercy's asleep," he whispered as he nuzzled Justice behind the ear, "and I need to reward you for extraordinarily good work this semester, Miss McKinley."

"You keep going like that, I'm gonna have to get Viagra sooner than I thought," Knox muttered, disgruntled, as they pulled out of the driveway some time later. "This is why I didn't want to marry a younger woman."

Justice laughed. "How's that working out for you so far?"

He flashed her a wicked grin. "I think I'll keep her around for a while."

"Oh, hey!" Justice said, distracted when she looked into the diaper bag. "Stop by

Hy-Vee. We're almost out of diapers."

Justice liked walking around the grocery store with her baby on her shoulder; people stopped to talk to her, to coo over Mercy and ask about the baby's particulars. Justice felt . . . normal. Not a prosecutor, not a pundit, not the OKH Bride or mother of the OKH Baby. She was just a woman taking care of her family, and the grocery store was the great equalizer.

She grabbed a package of diapers and threw it in the cart, then headed to the orange juice section to find Knox. She saw him at the other end of the aisle with a bottle in each hand, his head bowed as he compared labels. He started when a woman with a sleek black ponytail and a seductive smile touched his arm.

Justice sucked in a breath and began to smile as she drew closer.

" . . . to see you again, Miss Quails," Knox said politely as if he didn't remember exactly what he'd said to her the last time he'd seen her. Sherry opened her mouth, but Knox continued, "My wife and daughter are around here somewhere, if you want to meet them."

Sherry stiffened and looked as if she would decline, but Justice said, "Right here," and handed Mercy to Knox. Justice's gaze bored into Sherry's, but Justice knew she had changed too much for Sherry to recognize her.

"Miss Quails," Knox said. "This is my wife, Justice McKinley Hilliard. Perhaps you remember her?"

Sherry's eyes widened and she sucked in a sharp breath, blood rushing to her cheeks.

"Just so you know," Justice said matter-of-factly, "he fucks *much* better than he looks."

They laughed the entire fifteen minutes it took to get out of the grocery store and to Eilis's house. To Justice's surprise, the massive gates were open. Not only that, but at least fifty or sixty cars littered her driveway, roundabout, courtyard, and lawn.

"Oh," Justice whispered when she saw two huge banners draped from one barren tree to the rooftop festooned with colorful balloons.

CONGRATULATIONS, KNOX AND JUSTICE
HAPPY BIRTHDAY, MERCY

"The Dunham tribe," he said when he turned the car off, then caught her complete incredulity.

"Wha— But your birthday—"

"Doesn't matter. It was a done deal when Sebastian and Jack placed that ad. This is for me, us, you, and it's way overdue. A welcome-home party, basically. I haven't been to one of these things since I killed Parley. I wasn't welcome, plus I don't want to be within shouting distance of my mother. So today," he said, taking a deep breath, "is the first tribe party I've been to in fifteen years and . . . "

"And you're nervous."

He released the breath he'd taken on a long whoosh. "Yeah."

"So this is surprise number two?"

"Sort of. There's one person in particular I want to introduce you to."

She looked at him, expecting him to tell her, but her attention caught on the dozen or more people who spilled out of the front door and headed for their car, the most recognizable being her two very pregnant sisters-in-war. Then she gasped and pointed at the man leading the way. She stuttered, then squealed. "That— That's Morgan Ashworth! Knox! He's *here*!"

"Control yourself, Iustitia," he drawled as he opened his door and got out. "One of your prophets, right after Walter Williams, I know. Devoted disciple. Surprise."

"You're *related* to him," she accused hotly, "and you never told me!"

"There's a reason for that," he said once he'd come around to open her door and hand her out. "Whatever you do, don't tell him he's part of your personal mythos. He'll hear 'prophet,' mistake it for 'God,' and never be able to get his head through another door ever again." His smile was warm as he opened the back door to get Mercy. "Welcome to my tribe, Iustitia."

107: Good Night Sweet Prince

3:57 A.M.

"JUSTICE, WAKE UP. JUSTICE!" THE URGENT WHISPER IN HER EAR BARELY BEGAN to register when a large hand clamped around her chin like a vise and turned her head. A mouth pressed against her ear. "Listen to me very carefully. Somebody's in the house. Get your gun and shoot to kill."

The adrenaline surged instantly and she was wide awake. She nodded, reached to her night stand, secreted her Glock under her pillow to quietly pull the slide. "Be careful," she whispered. Knox rolled out of bed and pulled on boxers, then crept out of the room, finger on the trigger of his own weapon.

She had chosen to come back to this fight and she'd see it to its end.

Justice at all costs.

She glanced over at the crib where Mercy lay sleeping, swaddled tightly. Her heart in her throat, she waitedwaitedwaited and was not disappointed when a dark figure appeared in her bedroom door . . .

The blast propelled the man back into the hall wall where he slid down it and was still, head and arms limp as if he were a rag doll. The baby screamed. Justice bounced off the bed and went to the door, all pretense of stealth gone. She heard Knox's hoarse bellow, then another gunshot. Two, three more. She turned and grabbed the phone to call the police, but the phone was dead and her cell was in the basement. Knox's cell was gone from his night stand, so he must have already called.

"Justice!" Knox roared from somewhere deep in the house. "Get Mercy and get out!"

That was when she saw the flames crawling over the walls and the ceiling, down the hall toward her. She didn't have time to put anything on over the oversized Oxford and gray boxers she already wore. Mercy's wail barely registered as she slammed the bedroom door closed and turned her gun on the beautiful mullioned window she adored. Another shot, then another. Fire began to lick under the door and she knew it wouldn't be long before it ate the door and flashed overhead.

Grabbing anything she could find for warmth and having the presence of mind to grab the diaper bag, she picked up her screaming baby and wrapped her well, then proceeded out the window into the bitter December air, her bare feet landing hard on the broken glass. Gathering everything up in her arms, she ran like she had never run before. Flames blew out what remained of the window behind her, forcing her to fight to stay upright. Fire licked at her feet before she could recover and outpace it. She was aware of the glass embedded in her soles only because it gave her traction in the frosted grass, which would also cool her burned feet. She felt no pain.

Sirens wailed in the distance, both KCPD and rescue, coming closer, and she began to breathe easy.

Then another dark figure stepped out from the shadows and planted his fist in her face.

7:00 A.M.

Giselle could always call in sick and probably should. Her boss had been dinging her to stay home until she delivered and finished maternity leave; Bryce agreed, but didn't push.

She felt that would show weakness, so of course, she didn't do that. This pregnancy had been very difficult for her; she'd spent almost nine months battling her body and she seemed to lose skirmish after skirmish.

Bryce had done his best to support her and while he *had* gotten used to the idea of another child, his nightmares grew worse as her belly grew bigger. She had shocked him when she told the therapist about them; he hadn't known. The therapist told them it might get worse before it got better—and it would be a long time before it got better. The path was rocky, but Bryce was proving his love and commitment to her by walking it and she would walk it with him.

She'd started by getting her guns out of the house.

Giselle had not asked him to go back to church with her, but occasionally he would ask if she minded his company. She thought that might be an empty gesture on his part to make her happy, but she decided it best to simply thank him for going with her. She didn't know if he would ever go regularly, but right now, for the next few years, Giselle only cared about getting him better.

Bryce had balked at using his father's name as their son's middle name. "I loved my father, Giselle, but that's the last thing I need for the rest of my life. What was your pirate grandfather's name?"

"Elliott."

"That's it."

"Bryce, do you know how many cousins I have named Elliott?"

"Four?"

"Six, not including Taight kid number two."

"One more's not going to make any difference. And if we ever have a girl—"

"Oh, hey, don't get any bright ideas. I'm done with this whole pregnant bit. I'm way too old for this bullshit."

"Are you *sure?*" he'd asked slowly with a wary expression. "Because I'm okay with it if you want more."

"Positive."

Giselle fixed her lunch, then grabbed her briefcase and drove to work. She parked and trudged into the building, into the elevator, rode up the elevator, trudged to her office, closed her office door somewhat so she could hang up her coat.

A dull pain hit her way down low in her belly. That wasn't new, but it was a different kind of pain.

Another pain struck her, sharp and swift that time, and she put her hand to her back. Then another in her belly this time. She doubled over, her eyes shut tight against it until she felt her legs become drenched. She assumed her water had broken, but it was too soon; at thirty-five weeks, she still had five more to go.

She opened her eyes and fell to the floor, twisting to protect her belly, but striking her head. She didn't know if she fell because she was so weak or because she had somehow slipped in the blood pooled around her feet. The carpet was hard and wet under her and she felt immensely icky. Who would clean up this mess?

Fighting to stay awake and lucid, she tried to remember where the phone sat so she could call an ambulance. She inched along the carpet, propelled by her feet and elbows. It took her what seemed forever to get twelve inches, and when she looked back to see how little progress she'd made, she wanted to cry, but she couldn't spare the energy. She was the only protector this child had at this moment and it was up to her to keep him safe. That was her job; that had always been her job. One way or another, she protected people.

The walls shook when her office door slammed open and she vaguely recognized a voice. It belonged to her boss, she thought, but suddenly couldn't remember his name.

He was talking to her—why couldn't she remember his name? He stroked her hair and face. "Giselle," he said urgently, "wake up for me, honey. Come on, open your eyes for me."

"Water," she whispered. Thirsty, so thirsty. Her eyes would not open no matter how hard she tried.

The lip of a bottle was pressed to her lips in a moment and she drank, then the faint sound of sirens wailing closer and closer pierced her soggy, foggy brain.

Who'll tell Bryce?

"It's okay, Giselle," said that man again whose name she couldn't remember, which embarrassed her. "We'll find him."

Please don't take me away from Bryce. He won't survive my death.

"Nobody's leaving anybody. You just put that out of your mind."

There was much commotion, metal clanging, people hollering "This way!" but it seemed farther and farther away. She was tired now, so tired. She felt a prick in the back of her hand and then she went to sleep.

8:20 A.M.

Justice awoke slowly, her head throbbing, her face aching, her feet on fire and cracking with dried blood. She waggled her jaw back and forth, grateful it wasn't broken. She tested her nose and that, too, was intact. She tried to flex her feet, but that really hurt. She remained still and listened carefully for any hint of Mercy. There was none and her chest constricted in fear and anguish.

She opened her eyes to see that she lay on a cot in a large, dimly lit room that looked like an empty storeroom. The blankets she'd managed to take from her bed cradled her. She wasn't bound, but she wouldn't be going anywhere with glass embedded in her feet and her heels and calves burnt to a crisp.

Light came from an office where a man cussed as another gave directions. "Look, the tabs go in the back and you wrap them around the front."

"Shit. You do it, then, if you're such an expert."

Just then, Mercy squalled and Justice breathed a sigh of relief. Not only was her precious baby alive and in the building, but someone at least made an attempt to take care of her, however clumsily.

Fen had done this to them. If Knox hadn't already died in the fire, he wouldn't live out the day. Fen would make sure of that.

Justice's chest ached so much she curled in on herself, tears pouring down her face as she sobbed. Four years ago, she'd fallen in love with a Knox Hilliard who didn't exist. The one who *did* exist had tricked and terrified her into his bed, seduced her with his wicked magic, and caught her by letting her go. He'd torn down a stuttering, timid little girl and built, in her place, a woman. He'd taken her and pulled her inside out, taught her grace, sensuality, and power. He'd won her love and her trust, her respect and admiration for the man he was, not the fantasy she'd concocted.

He was nothing she'd ever wanted and everything she ever needed—and she would probably never see him alive again.

Mercy wailed then and continued to wail for what seemed hours while the oafs, confounded by that small being, tried to shush her. Justice's breasts ached and she finally decided to do what was best for her baby right now because she didn't have a clue what was best for her in the long run. "Hey!" she croaked, then cleared her throat. "HEY!"

The men in the front scrambled to get through the doorway. "She's hungry," Justice said. "Hand her over."

Without a word and with great sighs of relief, they gave Mercy to her and scurried back to their office. She shifted as well as she could on the cot and hummed to Mercy as she rooted and then found Justice's nipple and latched on. She sucked to her heart's content, oblivious to the probability that she would lose her father today—the father who loved her with his whole soul—and Justice continued to cry silent tears of despair.

At least Justice would have the most precious thing Knox Hilliard had ever given her, the best part of him, and she had to protect that at all costs.

She tried to trust in Knox's brilliance and cunning, his courage and strength, his love for her and their daughter, his family's determination and unwavering loyalty. Neither he, nor they, had gotten this far to fail, but this was too devastating to overcome, too unexpected.

They should never have let their guard down. Justice wondered if the rest of the pack had been ambushed and she shuddered to think that all of them might suffer.

Justice turned the situation over in her head, looked at it, took it apart and put it back together again seventeen different ways.

Fen had lost what remained of his life the minute Sebastian and Jack had placed their ad, when the Journal had printed Sebastian's letter. The feds had pounced immediately. As Justice had suspected, they'd been waiting for Fen to make a wrong move that they could prove—for which they had waited from the moment a

Mormon bishop had gone to them with Fen's confession more than a decade before. The FBI had played Knox the same way he'd played them.

This was Fen's last gasp. His reasoning was clear: If he couldn't have OKH, neither could Knox.

Her thoughts were interrupted by her captors, who brought her the diaper bag. She requested aspirin for the pain in her feet and they brought it, with a bottle of water. Mercy continued to nurse until they both fell asleep.

IO:II A.M.

Bryce was in the middle of interrogating an expert witness and the woman, some self-proclaimed forensics expert whose credentials hadn't checked out, had made a fool of herself. He could tell the jury had grown impatient with her, so he continued to push their buttons by questioning her just a bit more, reinforcing their annoyance that she wasted their time.

Clerks very occasionally came and went from the bench, delivering messages and taking messages away. His interns sat behind him in the gallery, clicking away on laptops, and texting back and forth with the office. Bryce vaguely wondered how he'd done his job before aircards.

Bryce had just finished his questioning when the judge said, "Recess. Counsel in my chambers."

He and his adversary exchanged looks and she shrugged; her second chair stood. He glanced over his shoulder at his second and indicated that she should go with them.

The four of them filed in and saw that the judge paced. He looked up to see Bryce and said, "Kenard, your wife's been taken to St. Luke's emergency room. Geoff Hale's been trying to find you all morning."

Bryce thought his knees would give way. His head swam. He didn't think about anything. He made no assumptions, raised no scenarios in his head. But that ache— that too-familiar ache that he had had when he was told his family had perished—it was back in full force and he could barely breathe.

" . . . second chair?"

"Yes," he muttered absently, having not really heard nor understood the question. "Sarah can carry it. I gotta go."

It seemed such a long way from downtown to the Plaza, and in the middle of the day, the traffic was a nightmare. In his haste, he had forgotten the fastest way to get there. Finally he parked and ran into the building, pushing people out of the way to

677

get to the admitting desk. The clerk checked her database and then said, "Your wife is in surgery, Mr. Kenard. If you could please fill out these papers and let me see your insurance card, I'd appreciate it."

Bryce did as requested, though he resented it and yet, it gave him something to do. That done, she directed him to the surgery waiting room, where he ripped off his suit coat and tie, then paced alone for half an hour before it occurred to him to call in the pack to pace with him. Knox didn't answer.

"What happened?" Sebastian demanded once he arrived and found Bryce.

"I have no idea. Judge just told me to get here and no one seems to be able to tell me anything."

"Can't find Knox on his cell and apparently, every lawyer in Chouteau County's in court because nobody's answering phones."

"Lilly's not answering either."

"Oh, she and my mom are probably—"

"Mr. Kenard?" Both men turned to see a nurse in the doorway. "Your wife is out of surgery and in recovery."

"How is she?"

"Doing as well as can be expected," she said. "Come with me. The doctor would like to talk to you."

He followed her out and down the hallway. "My son?" His heart and soul were wrapped up in that baby and had been since he'd fallen in love with Giselle for the third time in his life. He *needed* to see that boy, talk to him, rock him. His son. Giselle's son. The life they had made together.

"He's in the nursery, doing well. I'll let the doctor talk to you."

He waited in a little anteroom with three chairs and a small table that held a phone and a little thing of fake flowers. He only noticed because there was nothing else to look at while he waited. The door opened suddenly and he jumped.

"Mr. Kenard, I'm Dr. Sanford." They shook hands and the doctor, still in scrubs, didn't waste any time. "Your wife had what's called a placental abruption. This is when the placenta separates from the wall of the uterus. We were able to deliver the baby, but she needed a lot of blood. We tried to save her uterus, but because of the bleeding, we had to perform an emergency hysterectomy. She won't be able to have any more children."

Bryce gulped. His heart ached suddenly—for her, for himself, for the children they couldn't possibly have together. That neither of them wanted more seemed irrelevant at the moment.

"The other thing is that she has a pretty severe concussion and so we're monitoring her for now."

"Concussion? How?"

"She fell and hit her head on the floor."

Bryce put the heels of his palms to his eyes and wheeled away. Could it get any worse?

"Can I see her?" he asked when he had calmed himself as much as possible.

"Not now. She's in recovery and won't be awake any time soon."

"What about my son?"

"Oh, he's healthy. He's a little older than we were told—" He saw the puzzled look on Bryce's face. "Paramedics got that information on the scene. I don't know who from. Anyway, he's maybe two or three weeks shy of full term, and that's just fine. Would you like to see him?"

"Yes. Thanks."

Once in the nursery, Bryce approached the bassinet with dread at what he might find, even though everyone had assured him that the baby was okay. The boy was tiny and more wrinkled than he remembered his other children being.

He had a mop of bright orange curls and Bryce grinned suddenly. If ever he had a shred of doubt that this was his child, it was gone. *Scot through and through* indeed.

"Would you like to hold him?" the nurse asked softly. "The doctor gave his okay."

"Yes, please," he whispered and the tiny creature was picked up and placed in his arms. She led Bryce to a rocking chair and gave him a tiny bottle of formula.

"He's probably not hungry yet, but—"

Bryce tuned her out. He'd done this four times already; he was an old hand at it.

He rocked that baby for hours as he waited for permission to see Giselle. The boy awoke, cried, and Bryce plugged his mouth with the bottle until he'd taken a few sucks. He looked into the familiar gunmetal gray eyes all newborns have and wondered if they'd lighten to Dunham ice or darken to Kenard emerald.

"I love you, kid," he whispered and held him close as he fell asleep again, "and I desperately love your mother."

"Mr. Kenard," said a nurse softly, leaning over his shoulder, "your wife's awake and asking for you. I'll take the little one so you can go see her."

Bryce gave his son back to her carefully, then dashed down the hallway and asked directions to find her. He found her room and ran in to see her in the bed, wan, listless, and her eyes half closed. He felt like he'd been kicked in the gut to see her like this, the strongest, most fearless woman he'd ever met—the woman he had to work to take, over and over and over again, the one who occasionally took him.

But. She was alive and awake, and that was all he cared about right now.

"Giselle," he breathed and she turned to see him, her face lighting up.

"Bryce! Have you seen him? Is he okay? They told me he was, but . . ."

"He's fine. He's wonderful. How are you?"

"I have a headache," she said, her face making that very plain, but her body radiated good humor and he needed it now more than he ever had.

Bryce pulled a chair up to the bedside, leaned in, and buried his face in her belly. He felt her hands in his hair, stroking him, caressing him as if he were the child. And he began to cry, long wracking sobs—for her, for the child, for the family he'd lost. For himself.

He had almost lost Giselle—again. Permanently.

It was a long while before Bryce could lift his head and he took her hands and kissed them. "Did they tell you?" he asked quietly. "You had an emergency hysterectomy."

She gasped, her eyes wide, and then she grinned. "Fabulous! I hate having periods with a passion. There's no such thing as an elective hysterectomy, you know. Saves me the trouble of begging someone to do it."

He had to laugh at that, no matter how shaky it was. So, she'd been serious when she'd said she wanted no more children. Trust her to want exactly the opposite of what most any other woman would want. He'd started to grow bitter again, to feel guilty for bringing their future childlessness down on their heads, but her reaction quelled that.

He could not afford to bring more guilt into their marriage.

"How's your head now?"

"Still pounding. I want aspirin but they're being nasty about that."

"You lost a lot of blood. They had to transfuse you."

"I don't care. Aspirin's the only thing that works." Giselle placed a hand on his arm and bit her lip, her eyes sparkling. "Bryce. We made a *baby*."

He couldn't help the slow smile that spread across his face. "Let me go get him for you."

"Beat you to it," said a nurse from the doorway as she wheeled in the acrylic bassinet. "Figured you'd be up to saying hello to him now."

Bryce lifted the little burrito out and carefully laid him in his mother's arms.

Giselle gasped and breathed, "Wow, look at that hair! It's *orange*! I *so* didn't expect that."

Bryce laughed. "My dad's hair was that color."

She looked at him sharply, wary. "Are you going to be okay with that?"

Bryce smirked with the pride of a new father and ruffled the little orange curls with his fingertips. "I'll be all right."

Soon Lilly, Dianne, Eilis, and Sebastian joined them and the five of them gathered around Giselle and Duncan Elliott Dunham Kenard to ooh and ahh, because little baby feet are the best things in the world.

When Justice was startled awake by the sound of Knox's roars echoing in the storage room, three thoughts occurred to her at the same time:

He was alive.

He'd found her and the baby.

They had a chance.

Justice and Mercy still lay on the cot and she watched as Fen and Knox circled each other, slow dancing with firearms. Her heart thundered and she could barely see through her tears, her trembling.

"You and your wolf pack have sneered at me for years for not dirtying my own hands," Fen hissed. "So here I am, Knox. I know I'm done, but I'm taking all three of you with me."

Justice knew why Fen would want to kill her: She'd done what she'd told him she'd do after he'd threatened Knox. One scathing email to four of her closest liberal friends and his name had become hazardous waste nationwide—

—but in spite of her hesitation in bringing a child into this mess, she had never really believed that anyone would actually be willing to kill a newborn baby.

With that thought, Justice carefully and painfully twisted to lay Mercy behind her and lightly pin her between the wall and her body. She absolutely couldn't turn over because it was too painful and too awkward, and because she was afraid she'd drop the baby. She slowly and carefully, with much pain, drew her knees up to her chest and folded in on herself to give any bullet that might come their way more mass to travel through. Mercy would *not* die while she could provide a shield. Justice and Knox wouldn't live out the day, but Mercy would never be without love and family.

She tried to believe that Knox could protect them, and she kept close the memory of how he had killed Lionel Jones the day she had interviewed for her job and felt no remorse—how horrified she'd been, how outraged—

—and here *Justice* was, eighteen months later, having killed a man in defense of her daughter and husband—and felt absolutely no remorse.

Justice must have moved, squishing Mercy too tightly, because she began to wail again and distracted Fen just enough that Knox was able to close the distance between them and put his gun to Fen's temple.

"So here's how it's going to be, Fen," Knox muttered. "You can walk out of here and stay alive or you can go in a pine box. Your choice."

"They're going first," Fen snarled as he pointed his gun at Justice. She closed her eyes so as not to see her own death.

The nearly simultaneous booms were deafening and Mercy screamed, held her breath as babies do, then caught another breath and screamed again. Justice had barely enough time to raise her head before the FBI broke in—

—more gunshots.

Shouting.

Pounding feet.

Justice glanced at the carnage on the floor. Fen lay on his back, nearly headless. Knox lay on his stomach close enough to Fen to touch, bloody and still, his beautiful blue eyes closed, his gun still held loosely in his hand.

Justice swallowed and closed her eyes tight, then sobbed when she heard him pronounced dead at the scene.

8:34 P.M.

"I'm so pissed at Knox," Sebastian snarled as he paced the Den of Iniquity while Eilis lounged nude in bed, nursing Alex, enjoying the lush sensuality of motherhood. His hands on his hips while he paced, he continued to rant. "He couldn't call, couldn't show up—what's that about?"

The phone rang then and Sebastian burst out of the bedroom to the studio to answer it. Chouteau County prosecutor's office. "Knox, you bastard, Giselle's—"

"Shut the fuck up, Sebastian. It's Eric."

Sebastian stopped and found his heart racing immediately, his anger turning to panic in a microsecond.

"Sit down and listen to me."

Sebastian sat only after Eric began to speak again. He fell back against the wall and slid down it helplessly, his soul dying with every painful word. He wasn't aware when he dropped the phone and drew his knees up to his chest to press his face in them to sob.

"Sebastian, what—?"

He shook his head at the sound of Eilis's voice above him, the feel of her hand in his hair, because he couldn't form words, couldn't make his vocal cords move.

"Get dressed," he whispered, hoarse, when he could finally speak. "I have to go back to St. Luke's."

"Oh, no! Giselle?"

He shook his head. "You have to go to Truman Medical Center."

She said nothing for a moment, then, warily, "Why?"

Sebastian swallowed the bitter pill of shame and guilt, of the heartbreaking loss of his brother, the pain Knox always thought he should know.

"Justice needs you," he finally said. "Take diapers, clothes for Justice, for the baby. Justice needs . . . well, everything. She's lost everything." He choked. "We have lost everything."

"Lost everything . . ." she repeated slowly. "I don't und—" Her eyes widened and she released a strangled breath. "Sebastian, no. Please don't say—"

"Fen," he whispered. "Fen did it. Three weeks before the handoff and he just—" He looked up at her then, his cheeks wet. Her eyes darkened until they looked haunted and tears spilled over. Sebastian raised his face to the ceiling, holding his head as if it were going to explode, and howled.

"KNOX!"

11:02 P.M.

Justice carried a sleeping Mercy on her shoulder as she limped barefoot into the morgue. The painkillers had somewhat dulled the pain in her feet. Her burns had been treated and the glass extracted from her soles, but though she hurt, she had work to do and Knox's daughter to love and care for.

Mercy had not come out unscathed and guilt rode Justice hard.

She dreaded this moment. She had been asked to come identify the bodies, but she stopped short when she saw the once-beautiful blonde woman already at the window. Her eyes narrowed. So. This was her mother-in-law.

Trudy Hilliard glanced at Justice but turned back to the window, its blind now closed. She wept, her face streaked with tears. Justice felt no sympathy. How could she?

"I hope you're happy now," Justice murmured as she took a place beside her, not looking at her. "You leave a trail of bitterness and hatred, death and destruction in your wake like slug tracks, don't you?"

Trudy stiffened, then gasped, whirling to face Justice. She was livid, and Justice now knew where Knox had gotten his hot and quick temper as well as who had given him and Eilis their golden beauty. "How dare you! Who are you to say such a cruel thing to me?"

"I'm the mother of your granddaughter, the baby your husband almost succeeded in killing."

The woman gasped and stepped back, her attention drawn to Mercy. "May—

may I see her? Please?"

Justice looked at her then and she felt her power emanate from her, encompassing Trudy. Trudy's eyes widened just a bit.

"If you touch her, I'll kill you," Justice said matter-of-factly, satisfied when Trudy took another step backward, clearly frightened. "Why should I think you'd treat your grandchild any better than you treated your children?"

Trudy swallowed, then took a step to escape around Justice, but Justice would have her say. She stepped in front of her. She was taller than Trudy and the fact that she was barefoot, had a baby on her left shoulder, and a limp did not in any way negate the badge she wore on the front pocket of the jeans Eilis had loaned her, nor the gun in the holster wrapped around her thigh that the FBI had not seen fit to take away from her, all things considered.

"Do you know what you have done?" Justice could see that she wanted to slap her, but was too terrified. "In case you haven't actually thought it through, let me remind you." Justice coldly, methodically ran down the list of everything that had happened from the first moment Trudy had seduced Fen.

"And that—" Justice pressed her finger to the morgue window when she finished her recitation. "—is the end result. Your husband is dead. Your son is dead, not that you care, but he despised you; your daughter hates you. You have no more family who will claim you—your sisters and brothers-in-law, nieces and nephews abandoned you a year ago.

"Your home and everything in it are *mine*. I sent the sheriff out there a little while ago to padlock it pending probate. OKH is *mine*. I'll make sure to acquire everything else you own, too. Of course, it's December and it's cold and all you have are the clothes on your back and your car and whatever's in your purse—which is far more than what you gave Knox when you kicked him out. I doubt you have a clue how to live on your own, working, earning money. And don't even *think* about getting a lawyer to fight me for any of it because I'll kick his ass from here to New York and back. Life as you know it is over. Ain't karma a bitch?"

She let Trudy pass then, and the woman ran sobbing from the morgue.

Justice limped back to the elevator without identifying anyone, since Trudy had already done it, and rode it to the ground floor. Eric sat in a chair in the emergency room lobby, his elbows on his knees and his face in his hands. Richard stood facing a wall, pretending to read a dedicatory inscription there. Occasionally his shoulders shook and then he'd take a deep breath. Patrick sat on the floor with a bottle of beer in his hand, back to the wall, and stared at something. Hicks wandered around, his hands in his pockets, his head bowed.

"Justice," Eric murmured as she walked past, "I went to your house to find your cat. I . . . didn't know what else I could do for you. I took him to the vet. He had a few scratches and his whiskers were singed, but he was fine otherwise. Just thought you'd want to know."

Dog was alive and well. She breathed a sigh of relief for that teeny bit of good news. "Thank you, Eric," she whispered.

Eilis sat on a seat across from Eric, her hand on her bulging belly, shopping bags full of emergency provisions for Justice on the floor at her feet. Justice sat down beside Eilis to nurse Mercy under a light blanket, then she went to sleep at the nipple.

The Chouteau County prosecutor's office had been the first to know what had happened. When Knox hadn't shown up or called by eight, Eric and the rest of the county jurisprudence system had known something had to be terribly wrong. At 8:07, a pair of Kansas City detectives had burst through the courthouse doors and sprinted up the stairs to the prosecutor's office.

Eilis had arrived at the emergency room before Justice had, once Eric had given her instructions, and stayed in the room where she was treated. She had left for a while to get diapers, assorted baby paraphernalia, and clothes for Justice, as she had nothing now except what she'd had on when she'd escaped with Mercy—Knox's shirt and gray boxers. She had their baby and a few blankets. She had their cat. Their house, everything in it, the two other things Knox had loved, his bed and his books—gone.

Eilis and Justice sat together and cried slow, silent tears for Knox and for Mercy, who had lost her father—and her hearing.

Lilly and Dianne swept in just then, panicked, and Justice miserably recited everything that had happened that day. They both wept with Justice and Eilis, with Eric and Richard and Patrick and Hicks.

Justice glanced at her wedding ring every so often. Her official wedding to Knox was set for New Year's Day at 12:01 A.M. It would be Knox's second wedding-that-wasn't and the reason for it made Justice begin to grow short of breath anew.

"Eilis," she whispered, stunned at a new realization, "I'm a *widow*. A twenty-six-year-old *widow*." Eilis wrapped her arm around Justice's shoulders and they put their foreheads together.

It wasn't long until the sound of a gunshot from the parking lot pierced the night. There was nothing really strange about gunshots outside Truman Medical Center, considering its location and its status as a level one trauma center, nothing strange about doctors and nurses bursting outside followed by a gurney rolling back through the emergency room doors not long after that.

It rolled right past the four women, the sheet over the body's face unable to hide the length of blood-soaked blonde hair that fell over the steel rails of the gurney.

108: Bells and Whistles

December 31, 2008

11:58 P.M.

J USTICE LOOKED AT RICHARD WHEN HE SPOKE.
"Are you ready?" he murmured under the last soft strains of Chopin's Nocturne Op. 9, which swirled around them like an aural mist.

"I think so."

Richard smiled and patted Justice's right hand where it lay nestled in the crook of his left arm. "At least you're not late."

Justice chuckled. "I think Knox would've killed me if I had been."

"It's not like he wouldn't have had a reason to." Richard glanced at his watch.

"Do I look okay?"

"Oh, Justice," Richard breathed.

She blushed at his respectful tone and adjusted her bouquet: black pansies and violets woven in long braids to the floor interlaced with long gold, silver, and white ribbons. She swept a hand down the white silk dress overlaid with shimmering iridescent organza, making sure she looked as crisp as she liked. Though Giselle and Eilis had only just checked her over ten minutes before, she worried about how securely the strands of diamonds and pearls that wove in and out of her curls were fastened.

The music faded away, perfectly timed to the clock that began to strike midnight and, except for the rustlings of hundreds of people waiting, everything was still as the last chime faded away. Then—

Oboes, violins, trumpets, and harpsichords rang out at exactly 12:01 A.M. on New Year's Day and echoed around the marbled Grand Hall of Union Station: Bach. The Brandenburg Concerto No. 2 in F Major, first movement.

Chairs scraped the marble floors as those hundreds of people stood to look back at Justice and Richard.

Down the long aisle toward the center of Union Station, under the enormous and locally famous clock that had just struck, stood Knox in black tails and white tie, looking back at her, eagerly, anxiously, flanked by Bryce and Sebastian, also in white tie. Directly across from them stood Giselle and Eilis, in black velvet under shimmering black-and-gold organza, gold, silver, and white ribbons embellishing their dresses wherever appropriate.

In front of Giselle and Eilis stood Eric and Patrick, and in between the two groups stood Judge Wilson, who seemed a lot happier about this wedding than he had about the wedding he'd performed a year and a half before.

Justice smiled.

Richard walked her down the aisle at a moderate pace so that Justice could see and silently greet with smiles the masses of people who had come to Kansas City for the very public wedding between the OKH Enterprises heir and the golden girl of conservative punditry.

From the back, the celebrity parade began: politicians and commentators on Justice's side of the aisle; the academicians and lawyers, artists and entrepreneurs on Knox's side. The cream of Kansas City society was present, with almost no consideration given as to who should be seated beside whom. They stood amongst the cadre of attorneys in the Chouteau County justice system, almost all the deputies, and most of the rest of the county employees. If there were any missing, Justice couldn't name them. Judy gave her a cute grin and a wave, which she returned.

A few Kansas City police officers and FBI agents, and half the state troopers who patrolled the section of highway that ran through Chouteau County—in dress uniform—were also sprinkled throughout the congregated. Hadley and his wife were on her side of the aisle and Justice stuck her tongue out at him. He roared a laugh, the troopers nearby whooping right along with him. Justice grinned, and she could feel Richard's chuckle.

A good portion of the population of Wright and Douglas counties had shown up, to the wedding coordinator's consternation. It had only taken one black look from Justice for her to get enough chairs set up to accommodate them.

Jack and Lydia Blackwood looked absolutely stunning together with their two striking adolescent children and their equally striking three-year-old twins.

Melinda Newman, with an adorable six-year-old girl next to her, gave her a nervous smile, too distracted, Justice was sure, by her very, very dark and handsome escort. Justice snickered into her flowers and Melinda blasted her with a dangerous scowl.

Over there was Geoff Hale and his wife, plus most of the partners and spouses of Hale and Ravenwood.

And on the other side were Mr. and Mrs. Van Horn, Christopher, and their other two children—the whole family having been assimilated into the tribe, unable to resist Sebastian when he was dead set on getting his way.

The entire executive staff of HR Prerogatives had turned out, including its new CEO Karen Cheng, whose daughter had died and whose marriage had not survived her death.

Mitch Hollander, CEO of Hollander Steelworks, also spouseless, stood with Senator and Mrs. Oakley.

More than two hundred seats toward the front flanking both sides of the aisle were Knox's tribe—*her* tribe. Morgan had insisted on sitting on Justice's side of the aisle and winked at her as she passed by. She blushed, then almost laughed out loud when she saw Knox roll his eyes. Mixed amongst them were other people special enough to the whole pack to be drawn into the family.

This wedding wasn't about Justice and Knox at all. It was about the end of a long, hard journey and the beginning of new, happy ones for all six of them and a fresh start between Knox and the Dunham tribe. The unusual day and time was, in Justice's estimation, perfect.

Aunt Dianne served as mother of the bride, Mercy enfolded in her arms and leisurely taking a meal, a wide-eyed Alex Taight in a baby carrier at her feet chewing on his toes. Richard's wife Alisha stood next to her, the seats next to her reserved for Richard and Patrick. Beyond that stood Hicks and his wife.

Aunt Lilly served as mother of the groom (as she always had), burping Duncan Kenard against her shoulder. Next to her stood Eric's fiancée, Anaïs Franklin. The empty seat next to Anaïs was for Eric. Beyond that, Dirk and Stephanie Jelarde stood.

The only person missing was Vanessa, who had begged off politely enough, claiming Whittaker House's nationally infamous New Year's Eve masquerade. Knox had known when they set the date she wouldn't be able to attend, since that masquerade brought in a full third of Whittaker House's yearly revenue. Justice didn't buy it, though; Vanessa was avoiding someone and Justice had a pretty good idea who—certainly not Sebastian, who managed Whittaker House's capital. In lieu of her attendance, though, she'd arranged for everything Knox would need to recuperate in the Hilliard suite at Whittaker House and would be waiting for them when they arrived later that day. Whittaker House would be their home for the next few months.

It was a long journey to Knox and Justice felt every step in her soul, her heart rejoicing not that she was in the middle of her fairy tale wedding, but because Knox was alive.

In those agonizing hours between the time Knox had been pronounced dead at the scene and the moment nurses and doctors had burst from an elevator racing an occupied gurney *out* of the morgue, Justice had died a thousand times with memories of each word, each kiss and caress and sigh, each laugh, each argument, each dance—knowing that she had only had her fantasy for a year and a half, wanting more, but grateful for what she had and the precious gift he'd left her.

Then her stubborn husband, barely alive, having been noted to have a pulse and resuscitated, had been rushed to an operating table to repair the extensive damage.

"Who gives this woman to be married to this man?"

Richard looked at Justice and smiled; she returned it merrily. Patrick and Eric turned to stand at Justice's left. "I, Richard Connelly," he said, loudly, clearly, so that it rang through Union Station as if it were a courtroom.

"And I, Eric Cipriani."

"And I, Patrick Davidson."

Richard spoke again. "We, the unindicted co-conspirators of the Chouteau County prosecutor's office, give this woman in marriage. For the *second* time."

Laughter exploded throughout the marbled hall and Knox would have laughed harder if he could've, but it took about all he had to chuckle and stand upright at the same time—and he'd refused a cane. Bryce and Sebastian didn't stand as groomsmen for this wedding; they were there to catch him if he fell.

Justice smiled as Eric and Patrick took their turns to kiss her on the cheek. Richard placed her hand in Knox's and kissed her on the cheek, then left her there with her husband. He took his seat between his wife and Patrick. Justice looked at Knox and smiled wide; she had never seen him so beautiful.

Exhausted

Happy

Pale

Joyful

Weak

She gave her bouquet to Giselle and wrapped her arm around Knox's waist. She laid her other hand flat on Knox's abdomen to steady him as much as possible.

It would be a long night for everyone, as there was much business to be conducted, but Knox had insisted the wedding go forward as planned. In turn,

Justice had insisted on having his medical team present.

Judge Wilson began to speak, though he could be counted on to keep his comments brief; he was a rough old backwoods judge of few words. Justice had always imagined he would've been most happy being a circuit rider.

"The first time I married these two," he said, his voice filled with warmth and cheer, "Justice *thought* she was participating at gunpoint."

Most of the congregated gasped, but those who knew Knox a little better chuckled and shook their heads.

"I wouldn't have agreed to do it at all, except I saw how she looked at Knox when she thought nobody was watching. Oh, hell, what am I saying? *Everybody* saw that."

Light laughter ran through the crowd in waves, and Justice glanced at Knox with a blush and a bite of her lip. He chuckled at her and reached up to smooth a curl out of her eye.

"Which brings us to today and the events that have transpired this month," he concluded, a wry tone in his voice. "It just couldn't be that Knox would get down on one knee and say, 'Justice, I love you. Will you marry me?' and have a nice little church wedding, because Knox Hilliard *never* does anything the easy way."

The entire place guffawed, including the wedding party, and Knox had the good grace to look sheepish.

"Say your vows, boy."

Knox turned to Justice as well as he could with her arm still around his back, to run his finger lightly along Justice's jawline, to play with a large copper curl. There was a suspicious glimmer in his eyes. He did not stop looking at her or playing with her hair as he spoke.

"My wife," he began, then cleared his throat. Justice marveled that his voice hadn't suffered from his death and resurrection—because he *had* died. Its timbre was robust, powerful, full of a kind of joy that she had never heard before. Her nose stung when she remembered what he'd told her of the time that he'd spent elsewhere while his body lay in the morgue. She didn't believe that any of what he told her had actually happened, but he had shared it with her anyway, knowing she would dismiss every detail as trauma-induced hallucination. Justice had sat silent throughout, listening, not allowing her skepticism to show because it was important to *him*. He believed—Giselle, Bryce, Sebastian believed; Eilis *wanted* to believe—and it gave them peace. That was all that mattered.

"Iustitia, my wife, sacrificed her freedom to marry me. If I could not have married her, I would have married no one; OKH would be Sebastian's and Bryce's company with my blessing. I forced her to marry me, then let her go the next day because what I had done to her was evil. I have never known such despair and pain in my life as the day I watched her drive away, knowing I would never see her again, talk to her, touch her, kiss her. Yet two days later, she came back to me, believed in me, loved me, stayed with me. I have never known such joy and hope in my life.

"Fully comprehending the risks and what would be asked of her, she chose to fight this fight with us and she has fought well. She took on the Chouteau County prosecutor and won. She took on a bully and a barbarian and won each battle. She took on Fen Hilliard—three times—" He stopped abruptly, then his lusty laugh rang out. *"Priceless!"*

Out of all those hundreds of people, only about twenty understood Knox's comment enough to laugh, but it was so genuine, so full of merriment that it sounded like many, many more and others joined in. It was good to laugh at a wedding.

Knox waited, then continued. "She took on Fen Hilliard and won. She took on an intruder in our home and won. She ran barefoot through fire on broken glass to save our daughter's life and succeeded. I would have nothing if it weren't for her. I have no words to express my love for her. She is a woman of power and strength, fire and depth, and I pledge everything I have—including my life—to her."

And because Justice was the bride and she could do what she wanted to do, she leaned forward and kissed him softly. He returned it until Judge Wilson cleared his throat. "Save it, kids," he muttered. "You're messing up my rhythm."

Then it was Justice's turn. She cleared her throat, staring into those very, very dark blue eyes she thought she would never see again.

"'Let me not to the marriage of true minds admit impediments. Love is not love which alters when it alteration finds, or bends with the remover to remove: O no! it is an ever-fixed mark that looks on tempests and is never shaken; it is the star to every wandering bark, whose worth's unknown, although his height be taken. Love's not Time's fool, though rosy lips and cheeks within his bending sickle's compass come: love alters not with his brief hours and weeks, but bears it out even to the edge of doom. If this be error and upon me proved, I never writ, nor no man ever loved.'"

By the second sentence, Knox was murmuring it with her, with her cadence, a tear rolling down his cheek, an amazed smile on his face.

They would not exchange rings this night; those were still on their rightful fingers, never to be taken off.

"Do you, Fort Knox Oliver Hilliard, take this woman as your lifelong mate?"

"I do."

"Do you, Iustitia Jane McKinley Hilliard, take this man as your lifelong mate?"

"I do."

"I now pronounce you husband and wife. Again. Okay, *now* you may kiss the boy, Justice."

Their embrace was tight, their kiss long and deep. When they finally pulled apart, Knox whispered, "I love you, Iustitia."

"I love you, Knox. Please don't do that to me again."

"Never."

They turned and Justice looked over her shoulder, up to the balcony of the Bistro. With a smile and a nod, electric guitar, synthesizer, and drums pounded through Union Station, ricocheting off the marble walls and floor. The choir of Justice's faith had consented to play the recessional: "Freewill."

Half of the guests were shocked, but the other half—those politicos on Justice's side of the aisle—laughed.

It took a long time for Knox and Justice to make their way back up the aisle, between Knox's difficulties and greeting people, shaking hands, garnering hugs. Bryce and Giselle, Sebastian and Eilis, followed closely behind them and socialized while keeping an eye on Knox. They'd only made a quarter of the distance to the end of the carpet before "New World Man" began.

Meanwhile, Back at the Ranch . . .

JANUARY I, 2009

12:50 A.M.

THE OKH PRESS LIAISON MET THE PACK AT THE END OF THE RED CARPET. The wedding coordinator made sure the guests filed in the opposite direction, toward the vast front lobby of Union Station while the chairs were rapidly cleared. Everyone but Justice, Knox, and Mercy, the rest of the pack and their pups, would dance and snack, drink and mingle all night long. Five hundred-plus people with a legitimate excuse to have a party.

After some time, an elevator ride up to the mezzanine, and quite a bit of shuffling, Justice and her family were arranged on a dais behind a podium littered with a dozen microphones. It bore the logo of OKH Enterprises, as did the navy curtain behind it. Camera flashes had already begun to pop and news camera lights and booms were everywhere.

"Are you all right?" Justice whispered to Knox when he sighed and carefully rolled his head around on his neck.

"I could use some more drugs," he murmured in return, "and I'm really tired." Her heart ached; he certainly looked worn out. She'd spend this wedding night driving to Mansfield, listening to Mercy's snortles and snuffs and Knox's pain- and narcotic-induced sleep, making sure he didn't leave her again anytime soon—and that was just fine with her.

Prepared, Justice dug in her tiny reticule for his painkillers. Knox swallowed them with a gulp from a water bottle swiped from the podium. He took a deep breath and stepped up to the microphones.

"Ladies and gentlemen, good morning." The room stilled but for the usual noises of technology. "As of five days ago, I inherited the majority shares of OKH Enterprises, the company my father, Oliver Hilliard, founded and my uncle, Fen Hilliard, built to its present success.

"As you are all aware, four weeks ago, I shot and killed Fen Hilliard in defense of my wife and daughter. Subsequently, my mother, Trudy Hilliard, committed suicide. The reasons why this happened are detailed in a letter to the editor at the *Wall Street Journal*, so I won't belabor that.

"With regard to the events of December fourth: I have been cleared of any wrongdoing in Fen's death and the shooting deaths of two intruders in our home. My wife, Justice McKinley Hilliard, has been cleared in the shooting death of a third intruder.

"As you also know, I was shot three times by a federal agent for reasons which are still unclear and under investigation. I would like to express my heartfelt gratitude to Dr. Powell, who noticed I wasn't really dead before she started to carve me up—"

A wry chuckle rolled in a wave around the room.

"—and all the members of the medical team who worked to save my life that night. They have worked tirelessly for the last four weeks and have graciously allowed me to stand here on this day with my family.

"With regard to my alleged criminal activities during my tenure as Chouteau County prosecutor: For the last four weeks, my financial advisor, Sebastian Taight, and my attorneys, Bryce Kenard and Eric Cipriani, have cooperated with the FBI fully to account for my actions, as I have been unable to do so. With their assistance and information, I have been cleared of all suspicion of bribery, extortion, blackmail, fraud, money laundering, racketeering, and murder, amongst a variety of other things I don't care to recite.

"I resigned my position as Chouteau County prosecutor as of two hours ago, December 31. Chouteau County executive assistant prosecutor Eric Cipriani will be taking over my duties in full as of right now, January 1, and will run for that position when the term ends. I want to offer him my full support in his campaign; I can think of no better man to lead Chouteau County's law enforcement in a new direction. As of this coming August, I will be teaching law at Brigham Young University.

"With regard to the official disposition of OKH Enterprises: Eilis Hilliard Logan Taight, as you all know, is my sister and the new CEO of OKH Enterprises as of December 27. She is highly qualified and in a unique position to look after the interests of OKH employees as Fen did and to continue the philanthropic tradition that Fen began. We have no interest in changing anything that Fen has done, because he did very well as steward of my father's company and for that, we thank him. Eilis shares Fen's business philosophy as well as his blood and is sensitive to the distress Fen's passing will cause.

"Morally, this company belongs to all six of us: Me, Justice, Sebastian, Eilis, Giselle, and Bryce. We were forced to purchase my inheritance in cash, in property, in time, in lost opportunities, heartache and fear, and finally, in blood. It could not have been done without all of us working as a team. So we've gathered in the remaining shares of OKH stock in order to take the company private as equal owners.

"What my father built was good. What Fen made it into was grand. We believe Eilis can commingle and internalize the spirits of her father and mine, and lead the company to an even brighter future as a family operation. Thank you."

Knox signaled to the room full of reporters to open the floor for questions and picked one of dozens screaming and gesturing to go first. Someone lifted the podium off the platform and out of the way. A microphone was passed from person to person as his or her name was called, in deference to Knox's condition.

Reporter:	Ms. Logan, will your position as CEO of OKH Enterprises be a front for Mr. Taight's leadership?
E H L Taight:	No. I don't run shadow operations.
Reporter:	Mr. Hilliard, you bear a striking resemblance to Fen Hilliard. Is it possible that you, too, are his son?
K Hilliard:	No. DNA testing has confirmed that I'm Oliver's son.
Reporter:	Ms. Logan, you are well known to be the Goddess, the Muse to Ford. Who is Ford and is he the man in the painting with you?
E H L Taight:	If Ford wants to present himself and answer your questions, he may. Today is a day for business, not art.
Reporter:	Mr. Hilliard, how do you feel now that you've been cleared of all allegations made against you through the years?
K Hilliard:	You know, right now I don't even care. I'm just happy to be alive and with my family, especially my wife and daughter.
Reporter:	Mr. Taight, you're a well-known art speculator, you have extensive training in art, and now there are whisperings in the art community and on Wall Street that you are in fact Ford himself and on the

strength of that rumor, the value of Ford paintings has skyrocketed. Would you care to comment?

S Taight: No, and no more questions about Ford will be entertained.

Reporter: This question is for Mrs. Hilliard. Mrs. Hilliard, will you continue to work in the Chouteau County prosecutor's office as an AP until your family's move to Utah?

J M Hilliard: Yes.

Reporter: Mr. Taight, congressional hearings are scheduled later this month to question you concerning your dubious acquisition of several companies that you subsequently dismantled. Mr. Kenard, Mr. Hilliard, and your respective wives are also requested to be present. Would you care to comment?

S Taight: I don't recognize Congress's right to compel me to answer for actions that aren't crimes to begin with and then to compel me to prove myself innocent of them. If someone wants to bring formal charges against me, fine. Do that, then prove me guilty. We've informed Congress in no uncertain terms that we're staying home to watch the Superbowl.

Reporter: And Senator Oth has warned you that you'll be cited for contempt and jailed if you fail to appear. Comment?

S Taight: That's a fair accusation. I do hold Congress in contempt, particularly Senator Oth. If I end up in the can, I'll consider myself a political prisoner and don't think Justice and her print and talk radio cohorts won't have a few things to say about that.

Reporter: So, Mr. Hilliard, what are you going to do next?

K Hilliard: Dude, I'm going surfing.

The End

Notes

While I've obviously taken liberties with how a "backwoods redneck" county could be run a bit independently of reality, I'd like to cross a couple of Ts and dot a couple of Is:

Knox would in no way qualify as a candidate for a position at Brigham Young University.

In the late 1990s (when Bryce would have had his vasectomy), a clip device had come into popular and regular use that eliminated the need for cutting and stitching the vas deferens. The device is used to clamp the vas deferens once it has been crimped like a garden hose. An official study in 2006 has put the failure rate of one of these devices at 25%. Many urologists with a history of successful traditional vasectomies have placed its failure rate closer to 50% in their private practices. The idea that Bryce would have been encouraged by his urologist to choose this type of vasectomy at the time he would have had it is very probable and the likelihood that it would have failed is very possible.

Please visit moriahjovan.com/talesofdunham for vignettes and outtakes, FAQs, soundtracks, libraries, a directory of the businesses and locales mentioned, and other goodies that will let you remain in The Pack's world a little bit longer.

Tales of Dunham

The Proviso
book 1

Knox Hilliard's uncle killed his father to marry his mother and gain control of the family's Fortune 100 company. Knox is set to inherit it on his 40th birthday, provided he has a wife and an heir.

Then, after his bride is murdered on their wedding day, Knox refuses to fulfill the proviso at all. When a brilliant law student catches his attention, he knows must wait until after his 40th birthday to pursue her—but he may not be able to resist her that long.

Sebastian Taight, eccentric financier, steps between Knox and his uncle by initiating a hostile takeover. When Sebastian is appointed trustee of a company in receivership, he falls hard for its beautiful CEO. She has secrets that involve his uncle, but his secret could destroy any chance he has with her.

Giselle Cox exposed the affair that set her uncle's plot in motion—twenty years ago. He's burned Giselle's bookstore and had her shot because it is she who holds his life in her hands. Then she runs into a much bigger problem: A man who takes her breath away, who can match and dominate her, whose soul is as scarred as his body.

Knox, Sebastian, and Giselle: Three cousins at war with an uncle who will stop at nothing to keep Knox's inheritance. Never do they expect to find allies—and love—on the battlefield.

moriahjovan.com/talesofdunham/the-proviso

Stay
book 2

At 12, Vanessa Whittaker defied her family to save 17-year-old bad boy Eric Cipriani from wrongful imprisonment and, possibly, death. She'd hoped for a "thank you" from him, a kiss on the cheek, but before she could grow up and grow curves, he left town.

Fourteen years later, Vanessa is a celebrity chef at the five-star Ozarks resort she built. Eric is the new Chouteau County prosecutor on his way to the White House.

Four hours apart and each tied to their own careers, their worlds have no reason to intersect until a funeral brings Vanessa back to Chouteau County, back to face the man for whom she'd risked so much, the only man she ever wanted—

—the only man she can't have.

moriahjovan.com/talesofdunham/stay

Magdalene
book 3

Kindly Mormon bishop Mitch Hollander, while reorganizing a merger between his steel company and a manufacturer that occurred under perilous circumstances, meets brash and brilliant Cassie St. James, one of Wall Street's toughest strategists and a former prostitute. Their immediate attraction is just as strong as the gulf between Cassie's ruthless attitude toward sex and Mitch's LDS morals, which include no sex outside marriage. Meanwhile, Mitch's scheming subordinate in the church hierarchy, Greg Sitkaris, whom he's trying to have arrested for embezzlement, threatens everything Mitch holds dear, including Cassie and Mitch's flock.

A Mormon bishop.
An ex-prostitute.
A man with a vendetta.
Let the games begin...

moriahjovan.com/talesofdunham/magdalene

Dunham
The Past

It's 1780.

The Americans are losing their desperate fight for independence from the most powerful nation on Earth. Britain's navy is crushing outposts up and down the eastern seaboard and the Americans' pitiful navy consists mostly of small-vessel privateers on missions of profit.

"Captain Jack" Celia Bancroft is one of those privateers, whose list of debts of honor is a nautical mile long. Sailing for the Americans is the current project on her to-do list, and once she has finished all her tasks, she will then be free to sail on a tide of whimsy.

Commander Elliott Raxham, cashiered from His Majesty's Royal Navy, is a newly made British earl who schemes for his own independence—from the title he never expected to inherit and the country that has betrayed him time and again.

They meet in a Caribbean tavern where he steals a kiss that starts a brawl she finishes. In retaliation, he steals her ship's figurehead and, if that isn't a grave enough insult, proceeds to chase her across the Atlantic to collect on the promise in her kiss.

With that, the romance is on, but the adventure is only beginning as Elliott and Celia face obstacle after obstacle in their own fight for independence—a new life together on the American frontier.

moriahjovan.com/talesofdunham/dunham

Delilah
The Future
coming July 4, 201...?

Three teenagers are caught up in a post-apocalyptic nightmare. They're forced together to navigate their altered biology, mediate the constant conflict between the males, and rise up against a government far too interested in dictating who has children with whose DNA.

moriahjovan.com/talesofdunham/delilah

"Twenty-dollar Rag"
a Dunham tale

. . . featuring Vachel Whittaker from *Stay*, many soap-opera years in the future . . .

Regina Westlake sees nothing wrong with her clubbing lifestyle until the gorgeous guy cleaning her pool refuses to play her games. When he's hired to be her arm candy for a formal event, he makes his disdain for her clear by re-dressing her in something far more appropriate than what she had worn to the party.

Shattered, she takes his contempt, his dress, the memory of his kiss—and rebuilds her life from the ground up. She never expects to see him again, but when she does...

moriahjovan.com/talesofdunham/twenty-dollar-rag

About the Author

MORIAH JOVAN writes what her imaginary friends tell her to write. Thus far, they have shown up in the novels The Proviso, Stay, and Magdalene, published by B10 Mediaworx, and will, most likely, continue to order her around until she hits on the right drug and dosage. Fortunately, her husband is very understanding of all the other people in her life and her children have no need of their own imaginary friends since they know all of mommy's. Moriah has a bachelor's in creative writing and journalism from the University of Missouri at Kansas City, and in 2011, she was a panelist at the Writer's Digest conference and the Sunstone Symposium. She is a flagrant manufacturer and dealer of the meth known as "ebooks."

You can find Moriah at:

moriah@moriahjovan.com
moriahjovan.com
twitter.com/moriahjovan
facebook.com/moriah.jovan

Printed in Great Britain
by Amazon.co.uk, Ltd.,
Marston Gate.